HOUSE
RULES

The Wild Cards Universe

The Original Triad

Wild Cards

Aces High

Jokers Wild

The Puppetman Quartet

Aces Abroad

Down and Dirty

Ace in the Hole

Dead Man's Hand

The Rox Triad

One-Eyed Jacks

Jokertown Shuffle

Dealer's Choice

The Novels

Double Solitaire

Turn of the Cards

Stand-Alones

Deuces Down

Death Draws Five

Pairing Up

The Card Sharks Triad

Card Sharks

Marked Cards

Black Trump

The Committee Triad

Inside Straight

Busted Flush

Suicide Kings

The Fort Freak Triad

Fort Freak

Lowball

High Stakes

The American Triad

Mississippi Roll

Low Chicago

Texas Hold 'Em

The British Arc

Knaves Over Queens

Three Kings

Full House

Joker's Moon

HOUSE
RULES

A WILD CARDS MOSAIC NOVEL

Edited by
George R.R. Martin

Assisted by
Melinda M. Snodgrass

And written by

Stephen Leigh | Mary Anne Mohanraj
Caroline Spector | Peter Newman
Kevin Andrew Murphy | Peadar Ó Guilín

HARPER
Voyager

Harper*Voyager*
An imprint of HarperCollins*Publishers* Ltd
1 London Bridge Street
London SE1 9GF

www.harpercollins.co.uk

HarperCollins*Publishers*
Macken House
39/40 Mayor Street Upper
Dublin 1
D01 C9W8
Ireland

First published by HarperCollins*Publishers* Ltd 2024
1

A catalogue record for this book is available from the British Library.

ISBN: 978-0-00-828361-2

This novel is entirely a work of fiction.
The names, characters and incidents portrayed in it are
the work of the author's imagination. Any resemblance to
actual persons, living or dead, events or localities is
entirely coincidental.

Typeset by Palimpsest Book Production Ltd, Falkirk, Stirlingshire

Printed and bound in the UK using 100% Renewable Electricity
by CPI Group (UK) Ltd

MIX
Paper | Supporting
responsible forestry
FSC
www.fsc.org
FSC™ C007454

This book contains FSC™ certified paper and other controlled sources
to ensure responsible forest management.
For more information visit: www.harpercollins.co.uk/green

For C. D. Doyle
treasured friend
fantasy fan

Copyright Acknowledgements

WILD CARDS

THE VIRUS WAS CREATED on Takis, hundreds of light years from Earth. The ruling mentats of the great Takisian Houses were looking for a way to enhance their formidable psionic abilities and augment them with physical powers. The retrovirus they devised showed enough promise that the psi lords decided to field-test it on Earth, whose inhabitants were genetically identical to Takisians.

Prince Tisianne of House Ilkazam opposed the experiment and raced to Earth in his own living starship to stop it. The alien ships fought high above the atmosphere. The vessel carrying the virus was torn apart, the virus itself lost. Prince Tisianne landed his own damaged ship at White Sands, where his talk of tachyon drives prompted the military to dub him Dr Tachyon.

On the other side of the continent, the virus fell into the hands of Dr Tod, a crime boss and war criminal, who resolved to use it to extort wealth and power from the cities of America. He lashed five blimps together and set out for New York City. President Harry S. Truman reached out to Robert Tomlin, Jetboy, the teenaged fighter ace of the Second World War, to stop him. Flying his experimental jet, the JB-1, Jetboy reached Tod's blimps and crashed into the gondola. The young hero and his old foe met for the last time as the bomb containing the virus fell to Earth.

'Die, Jetboy, die,' Tod shouted as he shot Tomlin again and again.

'I can't die yet – I haven't seen *The Jolson Story*,' Jetboy replied, as the bomb exploded.

Thousands of microscopic spores rained down upon Manhattan. Thousands more were dispersed into the atmosphere and swept up by the jet stream, to be spread all over the Earth. But New York City got the worst of it.

It was 15 September 1946. The first Wild Card Day.

Ten thousand died that first day in Manhattan alone. Thousands more were transformed, their DNA rewritten in terrible and unpredictable ways. Every case was unique. No two victims were affected in the same way. For that reason, the press dubbed xenovirus *Takis-A* (its scientific name) the *wild card*.

Ninety per cent of those infected died, unable to withstand the violent body changes the virus unleashed upon them. Those victims were said to have drawn the *black queen*.

Of those who survived, nine of every ten were twisted and mutated in ways great and small. They were called *jokers* (or, if they also gained powers, they were called *knaves*, or *joker-aces*). Shunned, outcast, and feared, they began to gather along the Bowery, in a neighbourhood that soon became known as Jokertown.

Only one in a hundred of those infected emerged with superhuman powers: telepathy, telekinesis, enhanced strength, superspeed, invulnerability, flight, and a thousand other strange and wondrous abilities. These were the *aces*, the celebrities of the dawning new age. Unlike the heroes of the comic book, very few of them chose to don spandex costumes and fight crime, but they would soon begin to rewrite history all the same.

These are their stories.

... excerpt from *A Wild Guide to the British Isles: Exploring Cornwall*

K EUN ISLAND IS A tidal island off the Atlantic coast of Cornwall, windswept and stony, with a long and rich history.

Three miles of mudflats and an ancient stone causeway connect the rocky island to the Cornish mainland during low tide, but when the tide comes roaring in, with frightening speed, the link is submerged and Keun becomes a true island, accessible only by boat. Almost five times as large as St Michael's Mount on Cornwall's south coast, Keun has a history that is as full as that of the better-known tidal island and even more colourful.

The island has been inhabited, off and on, for millennia. Archaeologists have found Stone Age cairns there and the remnants of standing stones larger and stranger than any of those at Stonehenge. A ringfort stood upon the island's sheer black cliffs during the Dark Ages; later, a crude castle of rough-hewn stone went up in its place.

For hundreds of years, the island was the stronghold of a clan of reavers and pirates known as the Hounds of the Sea, who raided and plundered up and down the coasts of Cornwall and into Wales and England. It was from them that the island got its name, *keun* being Cornish for 'hound'. They were finally extinguished in 1308 by Piers Gaveston, new-made First Earl of Cornwall, who put to death every member of the clan and razed their castle. Legends claim that the last surviving pirate pronounced a curse on Gaveston as he died.

Thereafter, the island remained uninhabited for two centuries, save for seabirds and an occasional fisherman. The fisherfolk did not like to stay overnight, however; it was said that the island was haunted. There were also tales of merfolk in the waters surrounding Keun Island; some stories spoke of beautiful mermaids who lured sailors to their doom, others of more grotesque creatures out of Cornish folklore or from the fevered imaginings of fantasists like William Hope Hodgson and Howard Phillips Lovecraft.

Humanity returned to the island in the 1500s. A new castle arose atop the cliffs on the seaward side of the island, and a fishing village formed on the landward side. Keun was a poor place, however, and cursed with ill luck. Over the years, half a dozen noble families came and went, many of them leaving legends of their own behind, each darker and more forbidding than the last.

The final and greatest of the lordly manors of Keun was called Loveday Castle, the seat of the family St Gerren. They held the isle for the best part of a century, but when the last of the line, the widowed Lady Morwen (known as Mad Morwen to the locals) died during the Great Storm of 1703 as the castle collapsed about her, she left no heirs, and the ruins of Loveday were abandoned and left to decay.

For most of the century that followed, the island's only inhabitants were half a dozen inbred fishing families who lived in the village below the ruins. In 1857, however, a wealthy merchant, styling himself Marcus St Gerren and claiming descent from the noble family of yore, laid claim to the island and moved in. He pulled down the overgrown ruins of the old castle and used its stones to build a large, splendid mansion on the site, which he named Loveday House.

He and his family took up residence there for several generations, but the villagers liked to say that St Gerren and his descendants found neither peace nor love in all their days at Loveday. The family fortune dwindled with the passage of the years, and madness and ill health seemed to plague many of Marcus St Gerren's children and grandchildren.

By the turn of the twentieth century, most of the money was gone, and the great house had begun to decay – a process that continued until the Great Depression, which took the remains of the family fortune. The last St Gerren attempted to sell Loveday House but found no buyers; the mansion had become a white elephant, too huge to maintain without servants, impossible to heat, its paint peeling, its foundations cracked. When old Tristan St Gerren died in 1937, Loveday was abandoned once more and left to rot. And so it did, for the better part of a century.

The new millennia brought changes to Keun, however. Rock climbers and hikers found the island's magnificent cliffs and stony trails, and the seabirds that nested there in such numbers attracted nature-lovers and bird-watchers. The decrepit fishing village had a rebirth as a holiday destination: antique shops, guesthouses, B&Bs, and quaint pubs and restaurants sprang up in its granite cottages.

And at last, a new owner purchased the mouldering corpse of Loveday House and set about restoring it to its former glory.

The 'new lord', as the villagers call him, is a mysterious billionaire who goes about in a hooded cloak, always masked . . . though he seldom wears the same mask twice. He goes by the name Jago Branok and seems to have no limit to his wealth. A dozen mutually contradictory tales are told in the village about his origins, his history, and his intentions, but on one point most of the villagers agree: 'Lord' Jago Branok is a wild card of some sort. An ace, a joker, a knave – no one is quite certain . . .

Restoration continues to this very day at Loveday House. The house and its extensive grounds remain private property, closed to tourists and casual visitors save by invitation, but tales of it are legion, and the locals will be glad to share them over a pint of ale and a plate of fish and chips in one of Keun's many pubs.

Longing for Those Lost

by Stephen Leigh

Part I

SALT SPRAY SENT DROPLETS dancing on Gary Bushorn's woollen flat cap and doused his already sodden trouser legs and trainers, though his long, rubberized weather jacket was stoutly resisting the water's assault. Still, the frigid seawater felt good on his skin, and the late October wind didn't bother him. Faint tendrils of steam rose from where clothing met skin.

He pulled out an old pocket watch, secured to his belt loop by a silver chain, from where it was nestled in the coin pocket of his jeans to shield its face from the corrosive spray. The watch was his late wife, Caitlyn's. A few decades before, Gary had repaired the then-broken timepiece – originally an anniversary gift from Caitlyn's mother to her father – as a gift for Caitlyn. She had in turn gifted it to her daughter, Moira, just before her death. Moira had returned it to Gary for safekeeping a few months before she drew the black queen and died herself.

The watch was Gary's most prized possession, representing as it did all his memories of Caitlyn and Moira. He glanced at the time – twenty-five to one – and placed the watch back in its pocket.

'You say you've fished down this way before, Cody?' Gary steadied himself on the wall of the wheelhouse cabin of Codman Cody's boat, the *Fear na Gcrúb*. The water was choppy, feathered with whitecaps. The prow of the *Fear na Gcrúb* tore a foaming path through the waves as the boat lifted and fell and lifted again.

Gary was holding tightly to the gunwale as the boat rolled heavily in the cold, grey swells; Codman Cody simply swayed easily with the motion, his hands (four fingers on the right hand, two on the left that looked more like the claws of a crab than anything human) tight on the ship's wheel. The *Fear na Gcrúb* – *Man of Hooves* in English, and the term in Irish for the Joker playing card – was a working boat, smelling of fish and brine and Cody's own unique odour, her flanks draped with nets and ropes, her planks slick with fish scales, despite continual scrubbing.

Gary had hired Cody's boat to take him, Duncan MacEnnis, and Jeremy Fingers down to Cornwall. The trio had been invited to a weekend on Keun Island. They'd left Rathlin Island in Northern Ireland the previous evening, spending an uncomfortable night on the boat.

'Aye,' Cody offered in answer to Gary's question, though his gaze didn't leave the waves. 'Though not often. Diesel fuel's too dear, and the fisherfolk here know the local shoals and banks better'n me. Besides, they ain't overly friendly towards foreign boats takin' fish from their waters. I stay further north, generally. So, are yeh gents lookin' forward to this posh party?'

'Don't know how posh it'll be, but the invitation surely was. I could show you – handmade calligraphy in gold ink on thick vellum from some Lord Jago Branok. You heard of the man?'

Cody managed a shrug. 'I know the name if not the man. Caught a few whispers when I've been down this way about how this Branok could buy and sell most'a the billionaires in Russia and the Middle East. Could just be talk, though. Y'know how people exaggerate such things. He puts on parties regularly at his mansion. Word is he's snagged several well-known people for guests, like Golden Boy or that German ace Lohengrin with the gleaming armour. All kinds a'famous folks have visited. Yeh can tell me more after yeh meet this Lord Branok. How'd he happen to invite yeh?'

'Not a clue,' Gary answered. 'I don't know the man. Never met him, never heard of him before. Maybe it was Constance Russell – y'know, the woman who comes to Rathlin every so often to recruit people for her sewing business? After all, Jeremy Fingers got an invite, too, and he used to be one of Constance's tailors. Maybe that's where this Branok got my name, though I still don't know why. "Former mayor of Rathlin" ain't anything all that special.'

Cody grinned at that and spat over the gunwale into the waves. 'I think yer wrong about that. The people of the island kept re-electing yeh, y'know. An' the way yeh cared for poor Caitlyn and Moira . . .'

Rathlin Island – long the home and refuge for the jokers of Northern Ireland – now lay well to the north and east, but it felt more distant than that. *Another place, another time.* Gary was suddenly assailed by homesickness and the sense of loss.

'Feck,' he muttered. His inflection was now somewhat more Irish than American – a testament to the decades he'd been on Rathlin. The mention of Caitlyn and Moira's names caused Gary to reach under the hem of his jacket. His fingertips circled the outline of the pocket watch snuggled there. 'That was a long time ago, Cody.'

'I remember, though, and so does Rathlin. Leastways, all of us older folk do, and hell' – Cody spat again; Gary watched the spittle hit the grey swells and vanish – 'even young Lorcan and Lucan know that story. On Rathlin, yer about as famous as they come.'

'*That* tells you more about Rathlin than it does about me, my friend.'

They both chuckled.

'Don't let Cody's blatherin' bother yeh, Gary.' That was Duncan MacEnnis, another Rathlin joker. Duncan was holding tightly to the rail of the *Fear na Gcrúb* with one hand and clutched a quad-based cane desperately with the other.

Gary's invitation from Lord Branok had said Gary could invite one guest to accompany him; he'd chosen Duncan, one of his oldest friends. Duncan was the now-retired police chief for Rathlin, as Gary was now the retired mayor. In 1974, as a young constable in the Belfast police, Duncan's own card had turned. His flesh had run like candle wax in a flame before hardening again into furrows and ripples along his body. His skull was hairless and pitted; his eyes jutted out from bony sockets: the Melted Man, they called him behind his back.

Duncan had been forcibly sent to Rathlin, as many jokers had at that time. He'd also become Gary's friend, not long after Gary had ended up on Rathlin himself in 1995. Since his retirement, Duncan's health had started to deteriorate – mainly, in Gary's view, due to the ravages the wild card virus had inflicted on the man's body. Gary worried about him. He had, in the final week before their departure, tried to dissuade Duncan from coming, or at least to see one of the doctors on the mainland beforehand. He hadn't been successful. *Nothing lasts forever, and every last one of us is going to die, me probably sooner than you,* Duncan had told him. *I've come to terms with that, Gary – no feckin' doctors for me. Not never.*

Gary reached out to grab Duncan's arm as the boat lurched; the crest of a wave sent foam cascading over the deck, and Gary felt Duncan stagger under the impact. He tightened his grip until Duncan steadied himself again.

'Rough weather out here t'day,' Gary said. 'Good thing we're nearly there.'

Lorcan and Lucan, the twin jokers who were Codman Cody's crew, poked their heads up from below deck, along with Jeremy Fingers, who towered above the other two. Lorcan and Lucan looked like they'd stepped out of Edvard Munch's painting *The Scream*, with elongated, sagging faces and mouths that drooped open. Jeremy appeared almost normal except for his height, until one noticed that his muscular arms were studded up and down with long human fingers that he could independently control – one of the reasons he was an excellent and very fast tailor.

'Got the pumps runnin', boss,' Lorcan said. The words that emerged from the long, slack and nearly un-closeable mouth were indistinct and difficult to understand for anyone who didn't know the twins. 'We're gonna get lunch ready before it becomes any rougher out here, since we're still a few hours out.' Lorcan waved to Cody. 'Poor Jeremy's looking a little green, though. We already told him that if he loses his lunch below, he gets to clean it up.' Lorcan and Lucan slapped Jeremy on the back and laughed as the trio vanished again below decks.

'There 'tis, boys,' Codman Cody said and pointed one of his fat, webbed fingers towards the southeast. 'Keun Island. We're slidin' along the southern headland of Cornwall now, and Keun's that tall, large island out where you see the bay openin' up. Too far away yet to see much, though. Branok owns a fancy mansion on top of the seaward cliffs. Some say they've seen strange things around the place, especially at night, and there are all sorts of odd stories about Keun Island in general. Some'a the folk who live there don't seem entirely natural – not jokers like us, yeh ken, but somethin' else entirely.'

Duncan cleared his throat. His fingers were white with the pressure of holding himself upright as he clutched at both rail and cane, and he was breathing heavily. 'I checked out Branok through my police connections, but honestly, I didn't get much. The man does seem as rich as feckin' Croesus. There ain't much information about Branok out there – which to me is more than a bit suspicious.'

Cody pressed a finger to one nostril and sent a stream of thick, yellow snot into the sea. 'Ah, there yeh have it. The feckin' rich can make anythin' they don't want people t'know just vanish.' Cody snapped the two fingers of his left hand with a faint fleshy thud.

'I don't believe that,' Gary answered. 'I think the truth eventually comes out. I hope so, anyway.'

'Yer just a feckin' hopeless optimist, Gary,' Cody answered with a chuckle, then stamped on the decking and shouted out loudly, 'Lorcan! Lucan! Let's be gettin' a couple lines out and see if we can catch somethin' for dinner tonight.'

Promises Redux

by Stephen Leigh

Thursday

K EUN ISLAND PROTRUDED FROM the aquamarine waters of the
Celtic Sea – a defiant middle finger of hard Cornish granite that ocean
storms had been unable to pummel into submission. The island's
high seaward cliffs defiantly faced the ocean as if daring the curling waves
to attack, though the mainland side rose more gently from the water.

As Codman Cody pointed out to Gary, the tides in the area were massive,
vicious, and dangerous. At low tide, one could walk or drive the couple miles
or so of causeway from the mainland to the village of Keun, though the
causeway vanished quickly when the waves rushed back in, cutting off the
tidal island until the next low tide. Over the years, several 'idjits' (as Cody
termed them) had waited too long to try to walk or drive back and been
swept away – occasionally to their deaths. The rusted remnants of a few
unfortunate vehicles pocked the sandy mudflats at low tide as a mute reminder.

The harbour on Keun was on the mainland side, the colourfully painted
houses and shops of the village dotting the lower slope of the island just
beyond. Gary glanced past the village and the steepening incline to the
fanciful towers and turrets of Loveday House, Lord Branok's mansion, at
the very summit of Keun Island. The Victorian-era edifice appeared to hold
the village at arm's length, staring down haughtily from the heights and
reachable only by a single torturous, switchbacked road.

'It's a good hour's walk from here, I'm told, especially being uphill all
the way. Hope he'll at least be sendin' a car for yeh tomorrow, though I
notice he didn't offer to fly yeh out here. For a rich man, he's rather a
cheapskate,' Cody told Gary and Duncan as he nosed the *Fear na Gcrúb* into
its assigned slip, with Lorcan and Lucan setting out the fenders and wrapping
lines around the dock cleats.

Gary had packed a large rucksack for the weekend; Duncan had a rolling
suitcase. Gary picked up his pack, swung it around to get one strap on his
shoulder, then fitted his arm through the other strap and settled the heavy
weight into place, before grabbing the handle of Duncan's suitcase. Their

taxi was waiting at the end of the quay. They were staying at a local B&B tonight; Jeremy intended to remain on the boat and walk up to Loveday House tomorrow morning.

'Still want us back here around seven for dinner, Cody?' Gary asked. 'Or would you rather be shut of us until Sunday when we leave?'

'And let that nice haddock we caught go t'waste? Not a chance. The twins already have it filleted and ready. See yeh both then.'

Gary had reserved a twin room at the Morgawr House, an inexpensive B&B down in the village. The online reviews had been mixed but indicated that while Morgawr House was certainly not fancy, it was at least clean. Like most independently owned B&Bs, it was cash only – no credit cards. Gary was paying for the two of them, knowing that Duncan had only a tiny pension as income; he'd offered to do the same for Jeremy, but Jeremy had insisted he'd be fine bunking with Lorcan and Lucan for the night.

While Gary was hardly rich, he at least had a modest investment thanks to Gregg Hartmann's estate. On Rathlin, with few expenses and bills, it would be enough for the rest of his life – as long as he remained frugal. He'd already paid Cody up front for estimated expenses, with a promise to settle anything overlooked, plus a bit of profit against Cody's missed fishing income on their return. There were two hundred pounds in small notes folded in his wallet (now a bit less once he paid the taxi driver) along with his debit card; that would do for the weekend. He hoped so, anyway.

Morgawr House turned out to be a dwelling painted a sad brick-red that was slowly weathering into an even more dismal salmon. The proprietress opened the door when Gary knocked. Lamorna Penhollow – he knew her name from the website – was a stout, red-faced woman who looked to be in her fifties, with eyes set a little too wide on her face, a small nose, and an equally small, pursed mouth, placed above a protruding lower jaw that gave the faint suggestion of a fishy snout. A large, cartoonish painting of what Gary assumed was the Morgawr Serpent adorned the entranceway wall, while behind the woman, a dim hallway led into the recesses of the house. A faint smell of bleach, must, and electric heaters billowed out around her. She stared at Gary a little too long and at Duncan for even longer.

'Ah, you must be Mr Bushorn and Mr MacEnnis. I'm Mrs Penhollow, though there's no Mr Penhollow any more; I've been widowed these past six years now. Come in, come in; I have your room ready. Let me show you . . .'

'Wonder where she buried Mr Penhollow's body?' Duncan muttered in a stage-whisper, though the woman didn't seem to hear him. He leaned heavily on his cane as they moved along a well-worn carpet. 'Maybe I should check out the back garden. A body would make great fertilizer.'

Gary ignored him.

The room she showed them was small but looked to be well-maintained: two single beds, a desk, two chests of drawers, as well as a tiny ensuite bathroom barely large enough for one person.

'Here are your keys, gentlemen,' she said. 'I go to bed around nine, but this key unlocks the front door; the other key is for your room. I serve breakfast between seven-thirty and nine; when you wake up, just go seat yourselves in the dining room. Ring the bell on your table, and I'll be in. There are a few other guests staying here tonight; if you don't meet them tonight, you likely will tomorrow. I believe they're also going up to Loveday for the weekend . . .'

Springs protested as Gary sat on one of the beds after Mrs Penhollow's departure. He rummaged in his pack for the fireproof bedsheets and bathrobe that Constance had sewn for him and laid them out on his bed. He raised an eyebrow at Duncan. 'Well?'

Duncan shrugged. 'It's just one night. I can manage to sleep anywhere for one night. We should check out the mantelpiece in the dining room. If she had Mr Penhollow cremated, I'll wager his ashes are there next to his picture.'

Gary grinned. 'That's better than buried in the back garden. Let's go see if we can find something interesting in this village.'

'Take a look at the sign, Gary. A bit of a chest fetish all around, don't'cha think?'

Gary glanced up to where Duncan was pointing, one hand still wrapped carefully around the handle of the quad-based cane against the relative steepness of the street. The signboard dangling above them swayed in the strong, cold breeze. It portrayed an underwater scene of a bare-chested and well-endowed mermaid perched on a treasure chest, pearls and jewellery spilling out from under the lid while the sand around her was littered with coins. THE MERMAID'S CHEST, the sign proclaimed in large Old English lettering, with ANTIQUES, ODDITIES, & OTHER TREASURES, NIGEL WALMSLEY, PROP. underneath. The glass front of the shop displayed a random selection of the items for sale. They could see an older man and a younger, very attractive woman behind the counter.

'We should go in and look around,' Duncan said with a grin.

They'd been walking – slowly, due to Duncan – along the single street winding up the hillside where most of the village shops were located, looking at the window displays and occasionally going inside, if only so that Duncan could warm up and rest. Despite the island's copious number of square miles, Keun boasted less than six hundred permanent inhabitants. The economy was largely based on tourists, but in late October, there were few of that species about. So many of the shops were closed and shuttered. Gary suspected that, for most people, walking around Keun would be far more interesting when the weather was warmer. For Gary, whose body always ran far hotter than a normal person's, the autumn chill was actually pleasant.

'If it's the woman in there who's caught your eye, she's well out of your league or mine,' Gary answered, shaking his head. He pulled the door open, a bell dancing and jingling above them in response, and motioned to Duncan to enter.

The man behind the counter – Nigel Walmsley, presumably – flashed an artificial and well-practised smile as he came towards them; the young woman just glanced up before looking away again. Walmsley was an odd-looking man: only a few inches taller than five foot, heavily balding, with bright-green eyes that were too large, a mouth that threatened to split his face in two if he yawned, and teeth the colour of dirty playground sand. The hand he extended towards Gary had lacy webs climbing up towards the knuckles. Gary remembered Cody's comments about the Keun residents and Mrs Penhollow's similar appearance.

'Welcome,' the man said. He released Gary's hand quickly, and the smile vanished. 'My, your hand is rather . . . um, *hot*.' His voice was polished and almost musical, with a strong Cornish accent. 'What might I show you gentlemen today?' he added, recovering his smile.

'We're just browsing,' Gary told him.

'I was drawn to your sign outside meself,' Duncan interjected. 'It's quite . . . striking.'

Gary gave Duncan a narrow-eyed glare; Duncan just grinned back at him.

'Yes, I think it is, too,' the shop owner responded. 'My wife, Susan, was the model for our mermaid.' He nodded towards the woman, who looked up again and gave the quick, white-toothed smile of an actress or model.

Gary could think of nothing to say to that admission.

Duncan coughed. 'Well, then, 'tis certainly a fine likeness,' Duncan remarked, with a lingering stare at Susan.

'Mr Walmsley, what can you tell me about this?' Gary asked suddenly, looking intently at a necklace in the nearest case.

'Ah, that's a fine discerning eye you have there, sir.' The man opened the back of the case, spread a rectangle of black velvet on the top of the case, and laid out the necklace: finely crafted silver in a Celtic knot pattern, set with small, blood-red rubies at the intersection points. 'This was found right here on Keun Island among the ruins of old Loveday Castle, which was once where Loveday House now sits. According to the provenance in my possession, this was discovered by Lord Marcus St Gerren when he came here to Keun in 1857 to reclaim his family's property. It was Lord St Gerren who eventually pulled down the ruins of the castle destroyed in the Great Storm of 1703 and built what we now know as Loveday House on the same site. Lord St Gerren believed this necklace originally belonged to Lady Morwen, also known as Mad Morwen – the last of the St Gerren line to live in the castle before its destruction in the Great Storm . . .'

The Walmsley man was still droning on about the St Gerren family, the

Great Storm, Mad Lady Morwen, and Keun Island history. Gary noticed that Duncan had shuffled over with his cane and was speaking with Susan, who seemed more interested in dusting the shelves than listening to Duncan. Gary sighed.

'. . . rubies are genuine, as you no doubt have noticed, making this necklace an extremely good investment, even if the provenance is somewhat inconsistent. Rubies with such stunning colour from that age were usually sourced from Macedonia, so it's quite likely that these stones travelled from there to Cornwall sometime between 1600 and 1700, to be set in this exquisite, chased silver. I can tell you that Lord Branok himself has expressed an interest in this very piece; he already has a fine collection of Keun antiques that he's purchased from me, so you might wish to buy this while you still can. If you have any questions regarding my reliability and reputation, you might enquire at Loveday House. I can assure you that you're not going to find anything approaching this in potential value, even in the best shops in London or Paris.'

Gary quickly interrupted as he saw Walmsley take a breath to gather steam for another barrage of words. 'Thank you for all this fascinating information, Mr Walmsley,' Gary told him, hoping that the lie wasn't obvious on his face. 'I'm afraid my friend and I are already late for an appointment, but I'll certainly try to stop in again later this weekend and look at this and your other tempting items. Duncan, we *really* need to go,' he said more loudly.

'We're late for *what* appointment?' Duncan asked in mock innocence when the door jingled closed behind them.

Gary didn't bother to answer. 'Duncan, you came off as some doddering, old, infirm lecher of a joker, staring at the man's wife and chatting her up. I tell you this as your friend: I was embarrassed for you.'

Duncan gave a scoffing laugh that turned into a cough. 'And I tell yeh this as *yer* friend,' he answered. 'That's pure shite, Gary. I don't have time left t'be worryin' about such trifles. An' the woman hardly seemed offended. So, yeh were embarrassed for *me* – so what? I was embarrassed for *yeh*, pretending to be interested in that feckin' trinket that was probably made in China last year. "Oh, and I'll be certain to stop in again later, Mr Walmsley . . ." Sure, and that's likely.'

This isn't worth arguing about or losing a friend over, especially given Duncan's condition . . . Gary sighed in defeat. 'Sorry, Duncan. I shouldn't have made a fuss. I'm just tired, is all – I don't think I slept more than a few hours on the boat last night, and we've had a long day already. C'mon – it's time we got back to the Codman's boat for dinner. Let me call a taxi for us so we don't have to walk all the way down to the marina.'

If Duncan realized that Gary actually meant: *so you don't have to walk all the way back*, he didn't mention it.

◆

In the *Fear na Gcrúb*'s galley, a makeshift table – a door placed over two trestles – was laden with a huge steaming platter of breaded fillets of haddock, with sides of mushy peas and fried chips. Pint cans of a local stout stood alongside the plates. With Cody, Lucan, Lorcan, Jeremy, Duncan, and Gary all in the galley, it was a tight fit for the jokers, and Jeremy had to duck his head to keep from hitting it on the roof.

There were candles in jars on the table as well, and Cody gestured to them as they sat. 'Gary, mind lighting those for us? A bit of an atmosphere, don't'cha know.'

Gary picked up the nearest jar and stuck his finger down to the wick. He closed his eyes, concentrating: a small flame rose from his index finger, setting the wick alight. He quickly did the same with the other jars, grimacing as the flame charred and blistered his fingertip.

Lorcan wordlessly handed Gary a glass of water; he plunged his dark-skinned hand into the tumbler to ease the pain and watched as the burns began to heal.

'Dig in,' Cody said to the group. 'Lucan, pass Duncan the platter to get us started. So, how was your afternoon in Keun – Gary? Duncan?'

'The B&B will be nice enough, I think,' Gary told them. 'For one night, anyway.'

'Even if the owner herself looks a bit like a fish.' Duncan laughed, holding up a fillet he'd speared with his fork. 'For that matter, so did the owner of the antique shop we checked out.'

There were chuckles around the table. 'Ahh, THE MERMAID'S CHEST, was it?' Cody asked. 'I know the place. The owner's nice enough, but he can go on, can't he? Knows a hell of a lot about Keun and Cornish history, though. Yeh gotta give him that much credit.'

'And he'll vomit out every last morsel of that history, too, won't he, Gary?' Duncan said. 'When yeh see the man's wife, you know what chest the store's named after. That's for damn certain.'

'Duncan . . .' Gary began, then stopped himself. He pulled his hand from the glass of water. The skin of his forefinger was again healed and unbroken, though the water on his hand steamed.

Gary saw Cody's eyebrows rise as he glanced from Duncan to Gary and shook his weathered head. 'Well, we chatted up some of the locals here in the harbour when we were out gatherin' supplies. Didn't we, boys?' Cody said, obviously wanting to change the subject. Lorcan, Lucan, and Jeremy all nodded in agreement. 'There's all sorts of fantastic lore that gets told to strangers to impress them, just like the shite we tell Rathlin tourists. And just like Rathlin's stories, everyone knows they're just tall tales, gossip, and outright lies – though I think it's worse here on Keun. There's lots of talk of strange things happening around Loveday House at night, and the place is reputedly haunted. Yeh'll find several of the Keun locals claim to be descended from merfolk, or have personally seen the ghost of Mad Lady Morwen, or who *know* that "little people" called *buccas* inhabit the old tin mines on the island, or who have glimpsed the midnight washerwomen who can wring their sheets to pull a person's arms right out of their sockets. And if yeh believe 'em, they'll sell yeh trinkets to take back home with yeh.' Cody's gaze went to Jeremy, accompanied by a wide grin. 'Now ain't that right, Jeremy?'

There was laughter at that from Lorcan and Lucan; Jeremy smiled sheepishly, his face turning red.

'G'wan – show Gary and Duncan what yeh bought,' Lorcan said with his slurred, moist voice.

'The twins dragged me into a souvenir shop.' From his pocket, Jeremy pulled a carved stone in the shape of a dog. The fingers along his arm moved the carving up and down from wrist to elbow to shoulder. 'This is Arthek the Hound, a famous Keun dog, and the stone for the carving came from the cairn where Arthek is buried.' He stopped. 'That's what I was told, anyway,' he added.

'G'wan,' Lucan encouraged Jeremy. 'Give Gary and Duncan the whole story.'

Jeremy sighed. 'Fine. Let me see if I can remember it all. There was a Prince Vador . . .' Jeremy's voice trailed off, and he looked at Lucan.

'*Cador*,' Lucan said. 'With a C. Cador St Gerren.'

'. . . Prince *Cador* St Gerren ruled Keun from Castle Loveday back in the 1500s, and Arthek was the prince's favourite hunting hound. One day the prince summoned his dogs for a hunt, but Arthek didn't respond, so the prince went off hunting without the dog. On his return, Arthek came bounding up, and Prince Cador noticed that the hound's jaws were dripping with blood.

'Now, Cador had a young child. Apprehensive that Arthek had done something unthinkable, Cador went to the child's nursery and found the boy's cradle overturned, his wet-nurse dead on the floor with her throat torn out, and blood splattered everywhere. There was no sign of Cador's son. Arthek was whining and whimpering all the while. Cador, furious, drew his sword and struck off poor Arthek's head. But even as Arthek's head hit the floor, Cador heard a baby's cry from underneath the overturned cradle: his son, alive and unharmed. And next to his wailing son was the body of a huge wolf, with Arthek's bite marks on its throat. Y'see, Arthek had killed the wolf to save Cador's son.'

Duncan applauded softly. 'Now, that's a fine story. Let me guess at the rest: Prince Cador built a fine resting place for the loyal and brave Arthek, which still exists up there near Loveday House.'

Lorcan, Lucan, and Cody all laughed at that, pounding the table. Pint cans rattled on the wood.

'Yeh totally nailed it, Duncan,' Cody said. 'Only, there's a few wee problems with that tale. Turns out there never was a Prince Cador or an Arthek the Hound. The truth is some fella named Angus Walker came to Keun

Island from London around 1750 and took up residence. He was the landlord of the Baying Hound Inn, which sat near the ruins of the castle before Loveday House was built. He invented the whole story to promote his inn, claiming that a nearby cairn of rocks was the resting place of Arthek. He'd escort people into the castle ruins – for a few coins, of course – to see the supposed room where Arthek killed the wolf and saved Prince Cador's child. Angus and the Baying Hound Inn are long gone, but Arthek's story still gets repeated, and the souvenir shop sells carvings of the dog to gullible tourists, as yeh can see for yerselves.'

There was more laughter, and Jeremy, fingers wriggling all along his arms, cradled his head in his hands.

'It's actually an attractive rock and a decent carving, Jeremy. I might have bought one, too,' Gary told him. 'You'll get your money's worth back telling people that story.'

Jeremy held out an arm to Gary, the carving passing down from finger to finger. 'Since you like it,' Jeremy said, 'I make you a gift of the carving, Gary. You can pass along the story. Just leave my name out of the tellin', if you would.' Jeremy set the carving down next to Gary's plate. 'Someone pass me the chips before they get cold,' he said as the others around the table sniggered.

The conversation passed to other subjects. More pints came out, and the mound of haddock fillets slowly vanished, as did the chips, though the bowl of mushy peas remained half-eaten.

'Y'know,' Cody remarked as he opened a new pint, 'everyone in town is saying that this Branok has only invited jokers and deuces to this soirée of yours – no aces, no really famous people, if yeh don't mind my saying so. Seems he's done the same once or twice before, generally in the bad weather months after the tourist season is over. Some of the locals refer to it as "Lord Branok's Charity Ball".'

Duncan snorted. His prominent eyes rolled, and sweat dripped down the channels of his face. When Duncan reached across the table for the last fillet, Gary saw the man's hand trembling. 'Duncan, you feeling OK?'

'I'm feckin' fine,' Duncan said sharply, then added, as if to soften the tone, '"Charity Ball." Don't sound like a feckin' compliment to me. But havin' no aces around sits fine with me. I don't need no one sneerin' down their ace nose at me because they got lucky with the virus and I did not.'

It's not the wild card virus that worries me with Duncan . . .

Gary shrugged, leaning back in his chair. 'Usually, jokers and deuces are totally ignored. I think it's fine that this Lord Branok is including us in his events. I'm not going to criticize him. I'm looking forward to meeting the man.'

'Same here.' Jeremy nodded to Gary. 'This should be fun. It's not every weekend I get to spend time in a mansion, haunted or not.'

'Well, I'll wait t'meet the man before I make up me mind about him.' Duncan took a long draw on his pint, then set his mug down wearily. 'I'd suggest yeh all do the same. It'll likely save yeh some disappointment.'

'Ah, yeh were a bitter old fart even before yeh retired, Duncan,' Cody interjected with a chuckle. 'An' yeh haven't changed a whit.'

Duncan grinned.

With that, the conversation drifted to other topics. Gary checked his pocket watch around ten-thirty. 'This has been grand, but we should be going, or Duncan and I won't get a taxi before the pubs close,' he commented. 'I'll call Loveday House in the morning to send a car for us. Jeremy, why don't you meet us at Morgawr House around nine-thirty in the morning? If you don't, you'll have to hoof it up there to Loveday House. It's a long walk and every bit uphill.'

'I'll be there,' Jeremy answered.

'Good. Cody, thanks for your hospitality and the fine meal. We'll see you again on Sunday for the trip back.'

Cody grinned and pointed at the table with his two-fingered hand. 'Just don't be forgettin' that,' Cody told him. The stone carving of Arthek stood there in a pool of spilled stout. 'Or I'll have Jeremy bring it with him tomorrow.'

Friday

In the overcast, dim October morning outside the windows of the limousine, the Victorian-era gables and turrets of Loveday House huddled above them, the spires looking as if they were about to rip open the low clouds scudding past.

'Looks like every haunted house movie I can remember,' Duncan grumbled. 'All we need is a thunderstorm and a Vincent Price narration.'

'You're showing your age, Duncan.' Gary glanced over at Jeremy in the facing seat. Duncan had been restless all night, and Gary had worried about the rattle of his friend's breathing. 'Hey, Jeremy, do you know who Vincent Price is?'

Jeremy gave a half-shake of his head. 'Some old actor?'

Gary turned to Duncan. 'See?'

'Yeh know who Price was, though, so yer an old bastard, too,' Duncan grumbled. 'The place looks like it's staring down at us – and not in a good way.'

'I don't agree,' Gary told him. 'I rather *like* the house. It feels – I don't know – grand and yet welcoming. Like a home, not a hotel or anything like that.'

'Yeah, like any of *us* could afford a home like that.' Duncan laughed aloud as the limousine moved smoothly through the final curve in the road. The tyres crunched on a crushed seashell driveway leading to a wide set of stone stairs ending at a huge portico and a set of massive, ornate double doors with intricate stained-glass windows.

The doors opened as the limousine came to a halt; two liveried staff members emerged, one of them walking quickly down the steps to open the doors of the limo, the other going to the boot and pulling out their luggage. Gary noticed another member of staff pushing a wheelchair from the side of the house towards their car.

'Welcome to Loveday House, gentlemen.' The servant's accent sounded vaguely French to Gary. 'My name is Étienne, and I'm one of the footmen for Loveday. Lord Branok is waiting to greet you inside. Mr MacEnnis, we have a wheelchair for you.'

'I don't need yer feckin' wheelchair,' Duncan told the man.

'Hey,' Gary told him. 'They're just trying to help.'

Duncan sniffed at that. He clutched his cane and shook it in the direction of the wheelchair. 'I'll manage those stairs with this, damn it.'

'As you wish, sir,' Étienne answered. The suave politeness in his voice didn't change, but Gary saw the man's eyes narrow slightly as he waved away the wheelchair.

Gary took Duncan's arm as the servants preceded them with the luggage. Despite Duncan's bravado, he obviously found the steps difficult, grunting and groaning with each movement. He was breathing heavily by the time they reached the top, the furrowed skin on his face pale with the effort. Gary and Jeremy waited with Duncan until his breath finally slowed. He shook off Gary's arm as they walked towards the open doors of the mansion.

'Wow,' Jeremy breathed as they entered the house. 'Would you just *look* at this place!'

Gary could only share Jeremy's awe. The entrance hall was cavernous, with walls of dark, polished wooden panelling, studded with gold-framed paintings of landscapes and portraits of what Gary assumed were former owners of Loveday. The nearest one to Gary was of a woman with thick and wild midnight-black hair and fierce eyes: LADY MORWEN, the plaque on the frame said. The ceiling was tall, rising up to arches two storeys above them. The back wall held a massive stone hearth surrounded by a marble mantel carved with intricate Victorian vines and fanciful animals; a wood fire was already crackling and dripping glowing embers there. On either side of the hearth, doors presumably led to the other ground-floor rooms of the mansion. A wide, carpeted marble staircase lifted from a polished, mirror-like sea of hardwood several strides in front of them, dividing at a landing halfway up to curve off left and right to a gallery overlooking the entrance hall, where corridors led deeper into the structure.

Everything spoke of wealth: the carved mermaids that formed the newels at the bottom of the staircase; the intricately lathed spindles supporting the oaken handrails; the tall windows sending shafts of cloud-filtered sunlight into the hall; the marble busts staring at them from niches along the walls.

'Can yeh imagine how many feckin' servants this Lord Branok must employ to keep up with all this?' Duncan commented.

'I certainly can,' a sonorous and deep male voice answered. A figure emerged from the shadow of the staircase, wearing a black cloak with its hood pulled up. 'After all,' he continued, 'I have to pay their wages.'

Under the shadow of the hood, Gary could see a black half-mask with an additional feathered wing that covered the entire left side of the man's face. He pushed back the hood, revealing longish hair as darkly sable as the mask. He untied the cape as one of the servants came forward to take it from him, but he left the mask on. The eyes behind the mask were compelling and striking, with irises a strange grey-blue at odds with the black hair. The man's gaze bored into Gary as he stared.

'Please accept my apology for not being here to greet you immediately,' he said. 'I had to see to preparations, and you're the first guests to arrive.'

'Lord Branok?' Gary stepped forward, his fingers nervously stroking Caitlyn's pocket watch. 'Forgive my friend's language. And I'm sorry if we've arrived too early; the invitation didn't give a time, and I'm afraid I didn't think to ask when I called for the car.'

Branok waved away the apology. 'It's nothing, Mr Bushorn. A trifle. I'm very glad you're here. Mr MacEnnis, it's good to meet you, and Mr Bushorn is fortunate to count you as a friend. And Jeremy Fingers, as well; I've heard good things of you from your former employer. I trust your trip from Rathlin wasn't too difficult. The sea can be unpredictable this time of year.'

'You know who we are?' Jeremy asked.

Branok gave a short chuckle. 'A good host should know all he can about his guests, don't you agree? For instance, I know that Mr Bushorn and I also have a mutual friend in Constance Russell and that she sends him annual gifts she's made.'

Gary's head went back in momentary surprise. 'Call me Gary, please, Lord Branok. And yes, Constance is a dear friend whom I'm sure we both treasure.'

The corner of the lips under the mask lifted in a quick smile. 'If I'm to call you Gary, then all of you must call me Jago. "Lord Branok" is so dreadfully formal.'

'Speaking of formal, what's with the mask?' Duncan asked. 'Is it because it's nearly All Hallows?'

Jago favoured him with a slight smile before Gary could intervene. 'Hardly. I've been reviving the old Cornwall tradition of guise dancing.' He pronounced the name not as *gize* but as *geeze*. 'Why, there are several groups about Cornwall performing now, even out of season: the Turkey Rhubarb Band in Penzance or the St Ives Guisers, for instance. The masks and costumes in guise dancing allows someone to perform anonymously in an outlandish or mischievous manner. And I personally find that masks are quite freeing. I'll arrange for a demonstration after dinner tonight, especially since we have a few musicians among the guests – as long as you're all willing to take part, of course.'

'If I may ask, Lord . . .' Gary stopped. 'That is, Jago – why *did* we receive your invitation? I mean, we're grateful and very much looking forward to our weekend here, but why *us?*'

'I invite people because I know them, know of them, have known them in other circumstances and other places, or know who they might become if given the opportunity.'

Gary frowned, puzzled by the evasive answer. 'But you and I have never met in *any* circumstance. So, what is it that you think I might "become"?'

The smile returned under Jago's mask. 'What would you *like* to become?'

Gary gave a confused laugh. 'I've no idea how to answer that.'

Jago adjusted his mask and brushed back his hair from his forehead. 'I've found that people generally bring their own answers here to Loveday House. I just ask the questions.' His gaze drifted past Gary to the front doors as they heard the sound of tyres on the gravel. 'There are a few more of our guests. If you'll excuse me, I must attend to my duties as host . . .' He gestured towards the clot of staff members, all in the same basic uniform, who had begun to gather near the staircase around a masked, portly man. He looked suspiciously familiar to Gary, though he couldn't quite place him.

'Hitchcock!' Jago called out, which made Gary shiver as he realized that the man resembled that famous director. 'Please have some of the staff show Messrs Bushorn, MacEnnis, and Fingers to their rooms and inform them of the day's schedule.'

'Certainly, sir,' Hitchcock said in a broad Cornish accent; the nasal, deep voice was also eerily familiar. Hitchcock gestured to four of the staff, then spoke to them briefly. Gary heard only the last of the instructions. 'Elbrekt, if you'll take charge, I'll go with Lord Branok to see to the new arrivals.'

The quartet came hurrying over to Gary, Duncan, and Jeremy, with three of them picking up their luggage. 'If you will follow us, gentlemen,' Elbrekt said.

As they followed behind the staff, all of them masked like Jago, Duncan leaned closer to Gary. 'This Jago guy is beyond weird. He's hiding secrets. I can feckin' *feel* it.'

Gary sighed. 'We all hide our secrets, Duncan. You and me included. That's hardly a crime. Let's give the man a chance, shall we?'

They didn't start up the massive grand staircase but instead went around the back of it to where an old-fashioned lift waited to one side of the fireplace; Duncan didn't object to the accommodation this time.

The lift brought them quickly up to the first-floor balcony; Elbrekt opened the cage door. 'This way, please . . .'

He led them to the right, then turned down a long corridor with doors as well as additional hallways leading away at erratic intervals. He stopped at one of the first doors. A staff member set down Duncan's luggage, opened the door, and placed his bags inside. He handed Duncan the key, then bowed slightly before departing towards the head of the stairs.

'Mr MacEnnis, this will be your room,' Elbrekt said. 'Mr Bushorn, you're just down the hall; Mr Fingers, you'll be a bit further along.'

The ritual was repeated at Gary's door, and as he stepped inside, holding his key ('Now then, Mr Fingers, let's get you settled . . .'), the door closed behind him.

Gary stopped, his mouth open. Another staff member was in the room, a bundle of towels in her arms: a woman who, aside from the house uniform, was wearing an emerald-green domino mask.

It was her appearance that stopped Gary. *She could almost be Caitlyn. Even with the mask, I can see the resemblance: her hair, her mouth, the way she stands . . . And those eyes, green as summer grass - that's Caitlyn as I first knew her back in '95.* He found himself wanting to touch her face, to see if it would have the same porcelain hardness of Caitlyn's, the gift and curse of the virus.

The woman nodded to him, almost as if she understood his thoughts. 'Good mornin' to you, sir,' she said. Her accent, like Caitlyn's, was distinctly Irish. 'My name's Ceallaigh. If you require anything during your stay, all you need do is ring for me.' She set the towels down on the canopied double bed, then gestured to a button on the nearest wall. 'This will sound your room's bell in the servants' quarters on the second floor. Either myself or, if I'm not available, another staff member will respond. Is this room to your liking, sir?'

For the first time, Gary's attention went to his surroundings. The room itself was huge; the double bed with its canopy seemed small in the space. There was a desk with a telephone and a table with four chairs set around it, though there was no television - which reflected Gary's home on Rathlin. The room might have been decorated by Rathlin's Island Treasure Souvenir and Gift Shop in Church Bay. On the walls were stunning photos of Rathlin Island set in gilded frames: the West Lighthouse, the South Lighthouse, the East Lighthouse, Bull Point, and Robert the Bruce's Cave - all very familiar to Gary from his long walks around Rathlin over the decades. There were photos of puffins nesting, seals on a rocky outcrop that Gary knew well, the old Rathlin ferry steaming into Church Bay, and so on.

A massive and ornate grandfather clock sat in the corner next to the windows, the brass pendulum swaying in the glass chamber underneath. A fireplace jutted out from the wall nearest the bed, with a small fire already ablaze in it behind a wire screen, surrounded by blue-glazed pottery tiles and topped with a polished stone mantel, on which sat vases of bright sea asters, dog violets, and forget-me-nots, the bouquets punctuated with the bright scarlet of poppies. Puffins and lighthouses adorned the gauzy curtains over the room's windows.

Ceallaigh, seeing his gaze, pulled back the curtains so that he could see the expansive panorama of the mansion's grounds running out to the edge of the sea cliffs, with the choppy waters of the Celtic Sea stretching out towards the horizon. She then went to a set of doors alongside the windows and opened them to reveal the balcony outside with another small table and chairs. The scent of salt air filled the room.

"Tis a lovely view you have in this room, I think,' Ceallaigh remarked, 'and the balcony's a grand place to take a meal or watch the sunset with a drink in your hand. Wouldn't you agree?'

Gary nodded wordlessly. *Did Lord Branok do this for every guest's room, decorate it so it's familiar to them?* He'd have to ask Duncan and Jeremy what their rooms were like.

He turned to examine the rest of the chamber – through an open door he could see a bathroom the size of the entire main room in his Rathlin cottage, with more island memorabilia scattered around it.

'This is . . . amazing,' he said finally. 'I'm speechless.'

Ceallaigh grinned. 'Lord Branok will be pleased to hear that.' Then her visage changed, becoming more solemn as the emerald eyes behind her mask seemed to darken. 'The staff or Lord Branok himself will be telling this to every guest, and it's important for you to know: Loveday House is larger than it might appear, and it can be easy to lose your way within it. Should you wander too far into its interior, you may become hopelessly confused. I wouldn't advise that, as it can be dangerous.'

'You haven't lost any guests forever, have you?' Gary asked.

Ceallaigh pressed her lips together in something resembling a smile. 'Some sections of the house still have no electricity,' she continued. 'Other parts, especially the upper floors and turret rooms, haven't been renovated; the floorboards there may be rotten and give way underneath a person's weight. If you feel you must go exploring, please summon me or any of the other staff and have us guide you to where you want to go. Lord Branok would be distressed if any of his guests were hurt.'

'I'm sure I'll be fine,' Gary began, but Ceallaigh lifted her hand.

'There's a bit more, sir, if I may. Please don't be tempted to leave the house after sunset. Keun Island isn't as safe as it may appear – especially at night. Some of the locals have probably already told you that Loveday House is reputedly haunted.' Under her mask, her mouth twitched in the ghost of a smile. 'Mind you, sir, I don't believe in ghosts meself, but wild creatures are another matter. Keun Island is quite large compared to, say, better known tourist locations like St Michael's Mount, and there's abundant and some-times dangerous wildlife here. There are aggressive boars wandering about Keun, especially up here, and criminals *are* real enough. We lock the doors and close the shutters every night, as you'll see. So stay inside, please. I promise, Lord Branok will keep you more than entertained.'

Then her smile was back, along with the gleam in her eyes. 'Now,' she said, 'I need to put these towels away for you. Since guests are arriving at various times this afternoon, there won't be a formal lunch. Instead, Lord Branok will host a cream tea at four in the library, where you'll meet and mingle with the other guests. There will be finger sandwiches and cakes and, of course, tea, though Lord Branok wants to stress that no one should be handling or holding books if they have drinks or food in their hands; many of the books in the library are quite valuable. Dinner will be at eight in the main dining room. For now, might I have the kitchen prepare you some lunch? Chef Daniel makes a delightful and hearty seafood chowder, if you'd fancy that.'

Gary had to smile at that. 'I *love* a good seafood chowder. There's a restaurant on Cooraghy Bay on Rathlin that makes an incredible fresh chowder every day. I have it at least once a week.'

'I'm sure ours will be its equal or perhaps even better.' That smile – the mirror of Caitlyn's smile – touched her lips again. 'Would you like me to get your friends' lunch orders as well? I could have their food brought up here to your room so that you could eat together.'

'That would be wonderful, Ceallaigh. You must have read my mind; I was going to suggest something like that myself.'

'It's my pleasure.' Ceallaigh inclined her head to Gary. 'I'll leave you to freshen up and unpack while I check with your companions. Is there anything else that you need from me, sir?'

'Now that you mention it, there's a set of sheets in my rucksack that I need to put on the bed, but I can take care of that myself.'

'Don't bother yourself,' Ceallaigh answered quickly. 'Just pull them out when you unpack and leave them on the bed – I'll put them on the mattress while you're at tea. What time does your pocket watch say 'tis?' she asked. She didn't even glance at the grandfather clock.

Gary pulled out Caitlyn's watch, checking the filigreed hands under the glass of the lid. *She must have seen the outline of the watch in my pocket . . .* 'Twenty to twelve,' he told her. The grandfather clock had the same time.

'Then I'll have kitchen send up your lunches by twelve-thirty. It was good to make your acquaintance, Mr Bushorn. I'm certain you'll enjoy your time here.'

'Thank you. I'm sure I will.'

The door closed. Gary lifted his rucksack onto the bed. He put Jeremy's stone carving of Arthek on the bedside table. He started to pull his clothing (and Constance's bedsheets and bathrobe) from the pack but stopped when he thought he heard a breathy voice call his name. He paused, listening.

'Gary . . .'

Yes, it was his name, sounding as if it were coming from just outside his room, and that voice . . .

It sounded like that of his stepdaughter, Moira, in better times, before she'd drawn the black queen. Her card had turned in their cottage on Rathlin, and Moira had died in his arms, screaming as he tried futilely to comfort her, her body twisting wildly in his grasp as bones cracked and splintered inside her. Blood had poured from wounds as the jagged, broken ends ripped and tore through her skin and clothing, coating both her and Gary in gore.

Gary felt himself sweating at the terrible memory – one that had haunted him for years afterwards.

'Gary . . .'

He went to the door, pulling it open and wondering if it might be Ceallaigh's voice he'd heard, but though he looked up and down the hallway, there was no one there. He stood listening for what seemed like minutes, his body trembling and his breathing fast, but he heard nothing further.

Taking a deep breath, he went back into the room and closed the door. 'It was nothing,' he told himself aloud, needing to hear another voice. The balcony doors were still open, the curtain rustling in the strong sea breeze. 'Nothing but the wind and my imagination.'

By the time lunch arrived, Gary had nearly forgotten about the voice. At twelve-thirty on the dot, Ceallaigh escorted a trio of waiters into Gary's room with a trolley, set the table for three, placed the lunches as Duncan and Jeremy came to his room, and vanished just as suddenly – with a masked smile – to leave them alone.

Jeremy was ecstatic about his room. 'You jus' wouldn't believe it – there's all sorts of sewing stuff in my room: yarn, thread, and fabrics samples framed on the walls, pictures of some of the designs I made or was part of. There's even a sewing machine, so if either of you need your trousers hemmed or a tear repaired, just come to me. It's like they knew exactly what I'd like to see around me.'

Duncan wasn't quite so impressed. Gary asked him if his room was full of Rathlin stuff, too. 'Feck no – it ain't like yer fancy room at all. Mine's decorated with old wanted posters, crime scene pictures, and shots of the Belfast police station I was in and the Rathlin station as well. Branok must think that an old cop wants to see more of those than he's already seen. What's really weird is that I feckin' recognize those crime scene pictures. They're all from cases I was involved in. There are copies of my commendation letters up on the walls, too – and I don't know how the hell he got hold a'those.'

'It seems Lord Branok knows a lot about all of us,' Gary said.

'And *we* know almost nothing about *him*,' Duncan responded, 'which I don't like at all.'

Gary took a spoonful of his chowder. It was glorious: the creamy, buttery stock thick with pieces of sea bass, shrimp, crabmeat, scallops, clams, and fluffy potatoes, flavoured with spices, garlic, green onions, and carrots. 'I know this much,' he said reflectively as he put his spoon down and leaned back in his chair. 'Jago's chef makes as good a chowder as I've ever tasted. Maybe the best I've had, in fact.'

Jeremy nodded in agreement, his mouth full of the massive club sandwich in front of him. 'It'll be interesting to see who the other guests are,' he said after he swallowed. 'I saw one of them from my window, walking across the lawn – a woman with long, reddish hair. She went out to the edge of the cliffs and sat down, just staring out at the sea. She could have been a nat, for all I could see.'

'Or some damned ace,' Duncan muttered. He had a plate of fish and chips in front of him, the fish plump and perfectly breaded, the chips thick and golden-brown.

'I guess we'll find out soon enough.' Gary took another spoonful of the chowder. 'My God, this is just incredible. You all should try a spoonful . . .'

The library, like the rest of Loveday House, was stunning: a vast room on the ground floor, dark-panelled with high bookcases on all sides, the highest shelves accessible only via rolling ladders. The outside wall was dominated by stained-glass windows depicting scenes from famous books – or so Jago told them. While Gary was reasonably well-read, many of the images were entirely unknown to him. For that matter, many of the book titles were also unfamiliar. Largely leather-bound and expensive volumes, some were classic literature with well-known authors, but the titles, authors, and languages of others that Gary pulled from the shelves were entirely a mystery.

Some books were obviously ancient in origin and fragile, especially those placed on the higher shelves. Jago warned his guests (as Ceallaigh had advised Gary earlier) to be careful. 'Some of these books are extremely rare and expensive,' he said. 'I don't mind anyone looking at them or even reading them, but please be extremely gentle and leave them in the same condition you found them.'

The cream tea was set out on tablecloth-draped library tables running down the centre of the room, with servants circulating around to whisk away the fine china plates as soon as they were abandoned.

Gary knew a few of the other guests. Dr Bradley Finn, the centaur-like joker who was the head physician at the Blythe van Renssaeler Memorial Clinic in New York City's Jokertown, was relatively famous even to the outside world. Cosmos, the blind, levitating juggler, had enjoyed fame as part of the juggling duo Cosmos & Chaos until their break-up. Gary could remember watching one of the duo's last performances together on *Peregrine's Perch*. And he'd at least heard of Roger Ravenstone (aka the Amazing Ravenstone) and his wife Bibi, both of whom also performed with the musical group The Jokertown Boys, though Gary had never heard or seen any of their performances.

He introduced himself briefly to the two others: Ink, an Asian joker with spiked dark hair and tattoos that seemed to crawl across her skin of their own - or Ink's - volition. She was also, Gary learned, Babel's personal assistant. As Babel was the second in command for the Committee for Extraordinary Interventions, the ace arm of the U.N., Ink must be privy to some pretty interesting secrets. There was also a woman with long red hair and a neck nearly as wide as her shoulders - Merryn Kersey, who, Gary was told, was sometimes called by the joker name of Whooper, which supposedly referred to a Cornish legend - though what Cornish legend, he had no idea.

All the guests, without exception, appeared to be either jokers or deuces like Gary.

Gary had brief, polite conversations with everyone but soon found himself wandering from one conversation to another without saying much. Jeremy and Duncan seemed to be pleasantly immersed in the social atmosphere, with Duncan chatting up both Ink and Merryn a little too obviously, though neither woman seemed particularly impressed.

Gary was standing by the windows, staring at one brightly coloured glass scene and wondering whether he could ask Dr Finn to take a look at Duncan when he felt someone at his shoulder. He turned slightly to see Jago, still masked, though this one was bone-white.

'Do you know what that window is depicting?' Jago asked.

Gary shook his head.

'Have you heard of the poet Sappho?'

'She was an early Greek poet, if memory serves. Back when I was living in New York, I once bought a book of her few surviving lines of poetry and read it. She was from the isle of Lesbos, wasn't she?'

Jago seemed to smile under his mask. 'Ah, a well-read man. She filled nine entire volumes with her poetry, but fewer than seventy complete lines were thought to still exist - the ones in the book you bought. But here in this library, I have two complete volumes of her nine, handwritten on papyrus rolls. This scene of two female lovers is from the first of those books.'

'Then those rolls are worth a fortune.'

'They are utterly beyond price.' Jago turned fully to look back into the room, where the guests were talking, their voices a quiet background. 'You're not enjoying yourself?'

Gary gave Jago a wry smile. 'Everything so far has been a delight. It's just . . . well, I'm not all that comfortable with people I don't know, especially in a crowd. I'm fine one on one - like talking with you - but in social situations like this, I confess to a tendency to stay on the sidelines and listen.'

'Yet you were a mayor. Surely you had to endure crowds and pressing hands to keep getting re-elected?'

Gary chuckled. 'There aren't a lot of people on Rathlin - only about 125 or so, far fewer than even here on Keun - and I knew everyone by name in almost every meeting. That's not the case right now. And if you don't mind my saying this, for a man known for giving large lavish parties, I've noticed that you're not circulating around yourself. Maybe we're not so different?'

It was difficult to tell how Jago reacted to that question. Nothing changed in his eyes behind the mask nor in the mouth under it. But his head lifted slightly, and he gestured towards the gathering. 'Then let's plunge in together, shall we? I will introduce you, so these people won't be strangers any longer.'

Gary took a breath and gestured towards the others in the library. 'After you,' he said.

With Jago escorting him, Gary found that he had little trouble getting to know the others and that he enjoyed the conversations he had. He even had the opportunity to ask Dr Finn to talk to Duncan and see what he thought. He also noticed that once Jago had taken him around the circle, their host excused himself and departed the library. But Gary remained, talking to the others. Dr Finn and Merryn both invited him to sit next to them at dinner that night. Duncan left early, saying he wanted to take a nap before the evening's activities began. Jeremy was still talking to Ink, Cosmos, and the Ravenstones.

Gary said his own goodbyes as the sun was starting to touch the low cloud banks clinging to the western horizon. He went outside to look at the sunset, though the servant who opened the door leading to the lawn reminded Gary that he'd need to be inside before full dark, as all the doors would be locked then as per Lord Branok's orders.

There were benches set along the sea cliffs at the end of the manicured lawn. He saw Merryn seated on one of the benches. 'May I join you?' he asked.

Merryn nodded silently, and he sat down alongside her. She was wearing a jumper against the October chill. Gary was, as usual, only in shirtsleeves. When Jago had introduced Gary to Merryn, she'd given him the outlines of her story. 'I lost my parents when our boat ran into rocks on a fog-bound night. My card turned at the same time. There's a Cornish myth about the Whooper of Sennen Cove, not far from Land's End. That myth goes that sometimes – always on a beautiful day when the skies were a lovely clear blue – a strange, thick mist would gather over the cove. From the mist would come a strange whooping sound. It was said that this mythological Whooper could predict storms and had a marvellous ability to prevent fishermen from venturing out whenever a storm might be coming in. Well, the virus gave me the similar gift. Ever since, I've had this intense desire to call out into storms, mists, and fogs to help lost ships. Hence my joker name and the ugly thickness of my throat.'

'I can feel the warmth radiating from you,' Merryn said now, after a few moments. Her Cornish accent seemed somehow stronger outdoors. 'I feel like I'm sitting next to a heater.'

'Sorry. Would you like me to move away?'

She shook her head, her long red hair swaying. 'No. I rather enjoy it.' There was another silence then, as she pointed to the cloud-wrapped western horizon. 'That's a fog bank coming in; I can feel it. I'll want to call out into it soon.'

'Then do it. Even though we're not supposed to be outside, there's nothing to stop you from opening the windows of your room. I'd love to hear this sound you make.'

She looked at him for several moments. Then she stood and leaned her head back. Gary could see muscles and sinews rippling inside that great neck. Her mouth opened as she took a deep breath.

She exhaled.

Gary would never describe the sound as a *whoop*. It was instead a long, melodic, and nearly operatic contralto – a series of notes that swelled and lifted, growing in volume until Gary nearly brought his hands to his ears. The sound might have been the ululation of some great grieving creature, hidden in the mist. The notes were laden with grief and loss, and Gary found sympathetic tears welling in his eyes at the sound.

Memories came to him, unbidden: Caitlyn's porcelain face, fixed in time by the wild card even as it slowly turned her body to stone; Moira's too-young, teenaged face showing her fear at knowing that her card must turn soon. He saw both of their deaths replay before him again, making his breath come faster, causing the wooden slats of the bench to begin to smoke under his hands.

He pulled his right hand away to touch the watch in his pocket. *Caitlyn, Moira – your deaths tore out pieces of myself that I've never been able to replace, and the wounds still ache. I don't know that I'll ever recover from losing both of you . . .*

'Gary?' Gary came out of his reverie with a start. He realized that Merryn had stopped 'singing' into the dusk and the approaching fog.

'Sorry,' he said, lifting his left hand from the bench and glancing down at the scorch marks burned into the wood. 'Merryn, the sound you make . . .'

'I know,' she said with a wan smile. 'I know.' She looked out to sea once more. The sun had vanished behind the fog bank, and the sky was darkening overhead. 'We should go in before they lock us outside.'

Gary reluctantly let his fingers release Caitlyn's watch. 'Yes, we should.'

Gary went upstairs to get ready for dinner; the door to his room was open, and Ceallaigh was inside. She had made his bed with Constance's sheets

and was also laying out a costume for him: red-and-yellow flame-like ribbons
– long enough to flow down to the floor – trailed from the top of a black
mask and were also attached to a black shirt and trousers. Ceallaigh was
still wearing her own mask.

'I didn't realize that a costume was required for dinner,' Gary said.

Ceallaigh shrugged. ''Tis more for the guise dancing afterwards. Lord
Branok has a costume for each of the guests, and the staff will be in costume
as well. You're to be the Burning Man, I'm afraid, Mr Bushorn.'

Gary remembered the scorched handprint on the bench by the sea cliff.
'That's appropriate.' He held up a hand, concentrated, and set his index
finger aflame for a moment.

Ceallaigh laughed at the brief light, and again Gary was struck at how
that laugh reminded him of Caitlyn's. He quickly looked away, letting the
pain in his finger distract him.

'The Burning Man in truth,' Ceallaigh said. She picked up the stone
carving of Arthek from the bedside table and turned it around, shaking her
head slightly. 'I see you've picked up a Keun souvenir, Mr Bushorn. Not
exactly anything unusual, but that'll be something to take back with you, I
suppose.'

'Why don't you call me Gary? Mr Bushorn sounds so formal.'

Ceallaigh shook her head. 'I canna do that with a guest,' she said.

'Why not? After all, you told me to call you Ceallaigh.'

'It just wouldn't be proper here. I'm sorry, sir.' She set the carving down
again. 'I must get ready to serve at dinner, so I'll leave you to dress yourself.
Can you find the dining room on your own?'

Gary nodded, and Ceallaigh went to the door. 'I'll see you downstairs
then, Mr Bushorn,' she said, and left.

Gary felt rather silly entering the formal dining room in the costume, but
as promised, everyone else was also in costume and masked. Duncan, in a
simple grey domino mask, was dressed as a noir detective in a 1930s-style
grey striped suit, grey felt fedora, and highly polished black-and-white patent
leather shoes, with a round magnifying glass protruding prominently from
the jacket pocket. To Gary, his face and hands seemed skeletal and pale
against the clothing. Jeremy was a lanky pincushion, seemingly punctured
with large sewing pins and random lengths of various fabrics.

Bradley Finn was wearing a glittering gold mask with horns and glass
jewels, with a tuxedo shirt, vest and jacket over his human torso, his hooves
covered in cloth booties with grippy soles to give him better purchase on
the highly polished floors of Loveday House. Merryn was masked with loose,
gauzy white cloth that wrapped her head like a cloud, matched with a lacy
top and boots with miniature fog machines attached so that she appeared

to walk within her own mist. Ink's costume took its cue from her tattooed skin: she was wrapped in a soft canvas gown and mask marked with vivid swirls of colour on a deep black background.

Roger Ravenstone and Bibi were dressed in utter black, Roger with a one-eyed, raven-headed mask from which his horns protruded, and Bibi in a stunning floor-length gown, the tufts of grey feathers sprouting from her throat like a soft collar, while an actual raven – Roger's pet Lenore – was perched on her shoulder. Cosmos wore an ornate East Indian headdress with an attached bejewelled wrapping that entirely covered his blind eyes; he entered the dining room with a half dozen juggling clubs orbiting him like obedient satellites.

Lord Branok wore an elegantly tailored tuxedo, and his mask appeared to be made of beaten gold, the peaks of it lifting high above his hair and echoing the lines of Loveday House itself, so that he seemed to wear his own house as a crown.

The staff was also elaborately costumed, but Gary's breath caught when he saw Ceallaigh. In his small cottage on Rathlin Island, which had originally been Caitlyn's, there was a painting above the mantelpiece that had been there since before Gary came to the island: a woman holding a mask under her arm as if she'd just removed it from her head – that of a black-crested puffin with a white face and a prominent red and blue beak.

Ceallaigh was wearing that same mask, her jade irises peering out from the eyeholes, the rest of her body clothed in black-and-white feathers. Gary found himself staring at her appearance, wondering how this was possible.

Jago was standing behind the chair at the table's head. Hitchcock, at the entrance to dining room, was holding a bell and struck it once. A silvery note silenced everyone.

'If you will all kindly take your seats,' Jago said. 'There are placards on the table for the seating arrangements, and the waiting staff will take your order from the menu before you.' Jago took his own seat at the table's head.

Gary was placed between Dr Finn (at Jago's right hand) and Merryn, with Duncan in the final seat on that side. On the other side was Cosmos, Roger Ravenstone, Bibi, and Jeremy, with Ink (looking somewhat uncomfortable at her prominence) at the table's foot. As soon as they were all in position, the staff moved in with the wine selections while Gary scanned the menu on his plate, lettered in golden ink.

'I'd recommend the crab sandwich appetizer and then the roast turbot, Mr Bushorn,' Ceallaigh whispered quietly in Gary's ear. He hadn't realized she was standing behind his chair. 'And then there's saffron cake, the local speciality. But if you prefer something else . . .'

'No, that's absolutely perfect.' *And exactly what I might have chosen myself.*

Ceallaigh smiled at Gary, then moved on to Merryn.

Thanks to his equine body, Bradley Finn was forced to stand at the table and thus loomed over Gary, meaning he had to incline his head awkwardly any time he wanted to speak. His order had been taken by Hitchcock, who had a fake cast on one leg and a camera with a telephoto lens around his neck, like the one James Stewart had in *Rear Window*. Gary found himself tempted to ask Hitchcock for his first name, though he resisted the temptation.

'Lord Branok has expensive tastes. I haven't had this fancy a dinner in ages,' Finn said to Gary, then glanced down the table to Duncan. 'If I can ask, how old is Duncan, and has his doctor given him a diagnosis?'

Gary shook his head. 'Duncan's older than me – in his mid-to-late seventies. And as far as I know, Duncan hasn't seen a doctor in a couple of decades. I tried to get him to do that before we came here, and he absolutely refused. He's a stubborn old fool. Why, Bradley?'

Finn shrugged. 'You understand that I can't make an informed diagnosis without examining him, and frankly, the hardened condition of his skin would make that difficult, but even at the tea I noticed that he's short of breath after any exertion and unsteady on his feet. I wouldn't be surprised if he's suffering from late-stage congestive heart failure. You should see if you can convince him to be checked out by a specialist in Belfast. If I'm right and it *is* heart failure, there are medications that can slow the progression: ACE inhibitors and beta blockers, for instance. But he *needs* to see a specialist – and ideally someone who also knows the wild card, as there could well be other underlying issues caused by the virus.' Finn sighed then, picking up his fork as a salad was slid before him. Jago seemed to be watching their conversation, though he gave no indication that he could hear them. 'Sorry, Gary,' Finn said. 'I know that's not what you wanted to hear.'

'What's not what Gary wanted to hear?' Duncan said loudly, speaking across Merryn.

'That I think you'll need to keep using that walking stick of yours indefinitely,' Finn answered smoothly before Gary could respond. 'And maybe you should start seriously considering a wheelchair if you're not willing to do some strenuous physical therapy.'

'No feckin' way,' Duncan retorted. 'I ain't no damn invalid. I'm just *old*.'

With that, the conversation drifted, the table talk rising as wine and food were served. Gary spoke with the Ravenstones, with Cosmos, with Merryn, with Ink, and with Jago until the dessert plates were empty and the teapots mostly empty.

It was then that Jago pushed back his chair and stood. 'Let's take twenty minutes to let the staff clear the table,' he said. 'Then I'll meet everyone in the music room for the dancing.'

◆

The music room, with its tall oak-panelled walls and gleaming wooden dance floor, had been largely cleared but for chairs set around the room's perimeter and a small platform with a grand piano at the rear for the band. Roger Ravenstone, on guitar, joined the band – all musically inclined staff members, Ceallaigh informed Gary. They were playing a Cornish folk ballad as the guests wandered in, with Bibi singing the melody in her lovely nightingale voice. 'That's "De-Sul Vyttyn",' Ceallaigh added, *sotto voce*. 'Or, in English, "On Sunday Morning". One of my favourites.'

As the song faded, Jago took the stage, stepping up to the mic and speaking into it like someone comfortable doing so. He wore a new costume: dressed in a suit that was in tatters, his face covered with a sequined mask, and atop his head, a large wolf's skull sat like a hideous crown, the mouth opening and closing in unison with Jago's speech, as if the skull itself were talking.

'Welcome to the guise dance,' he said. 'Guise dancing has long been a tradition in Cornwall over the twelve days of Christmastide, but it's now frequently performed outside the holiday season. The dancers are clothed in elaborate costumes to both disguise their identity and to give them the freedom to perform in a mischievous or outlandish manner. There are some specific moves to certain guise dances, such as the Turkey Rhubarb Dance, which is traditionally the final dance. But let's start with a simple freestyle promenade around the room in our costumes. Feel free to indulge your own impulses and just move however you wish to the music. There's no "wrong" way to do guise dancing, in that sense. Musicians, if you will . . .'

With that, Jago leaped off the stage in a tornado of ebon tatters, gesturing to his staff members to join in as the band started to play an energetic reel.

'Come, Burning Man – time for us to dance,' Gary heard Ceallaigh say as she took his hand and, swaying in time to the music, led him onto the dance floor. Gary felt rather self-conscious as the circle slowly gyrated around the room. Ceallaigh pressed close to him. 'No one knows you, and no one here will judge you, sir,' she whispered. If he felt too warm to her, she said nothing. 'Just feel the music and let it move you.'

Gary took a long breath, trying to forget his unease and do as Ceallaigh suggested, allowing the music to push him forward. He glanced behind to see Duncan in the circle, doing his best with his cane while Ink urged him on. It appeared that Dr Finn was performing a solo dressage routine, with Merryn laughing alongside him. They circled the room three times before Jago called a halt and the music stopped.

'Now that everyone has the basic idea,' he said, 'I'll have two staff members demonstrate a simple guise dancing routine, and we'll add onto those as we go.'

Ceallaigh and another female staff member came forward. The band started a new song: the steps were simple enough: hop, hop, hop, pause, stamp left-right-left, pause, turn to the left and repeat the sequence, turn to the right and repeat, turn to the front again and start anew. Duncan sat in a chair against the wall, evidently already winded, but Ceallaigh and Merryn pulled Gary into the dance as Ink and Bibi did the same with Jeremy, and other staff members joined in with Finn and Cosmos.

As Jago had promised, other steps were added as the dance floor filled. There were soon far more people dancing than Gary remembered being at the dinner, and others kept entering the room until there was nearly no free space. The music was pounding through the loudspeakers, louder than before. The lights had dimmed also so it was becoming difficult to see as well as hear. Gary found himself confused and disoriented, as if he'd been drinking far more than he actually had.

Cosmos is juggling hatchets *now? Those look heavy and real, and where did his clubs go? The blades are coming so close to Jeremy* . . . Before he could shout a warning, Ceallaigh tugged him away towards the stage, and Gary boggled at what he saw there.

Next to the stage, a man-sized cockroach was dancing, its carapace rattling like castanets. *That can't possibly be a costume - those legs are too thin, the head too small, and all its limbs are moving independently* . . .

Gary blinked. Ceallaigh's hand on his was no longer Ceallaigh's; it was Merryn who was dancing with him . . . no, he realized, *not* Merryn but an older version of her, her hair streaked with grey around her mask. 'I'm Merryn's mother,' the woman stage-whispered to Gary. 'I loved her so much.' Then the not-Merryn released Gary's hand and vanished into the chaotic swirl of dancers.

A rat-like creature danced past him, playing its own nose, which was shaped like a clarinet, as its tail flicked around Gary's legs. Then came a duck the size of Big Bird, its shell still around its body, with its head protruding from a hole in the top and its feet from the bottom. The duck's eyes found Gary, and the bill opened to reveal rows of daggered teeth like those of a tyrannosaurus, with grey strips of flesh caught in between. Its breath smelled of rotting meat, and it spat thick blood-red strands of saliva as it quacked at Gary before pirouetting away.

Gary found himself now momentarily alone in the midst of the dance, his mouth open as he spun around, looking for anyone familiar. A long-haired woman near the door danced her way towards him; she was the very image of the painting of Mad Morwen in the main hall, down to the dress she was wearing in the portrait. As the woman passed him, she spoke in English but with a strange, archaic accent. ''Tis in your mind lock'd, I am, and yourself holds the key. We know what we are but know not what we may be. We meet later tonight.'

'Wait!' Gary shouted at the woman, but she was already past him and lost among the dancers.

Duncan was no longer in a chair against the panelled walls but back on the dance floor. *My God - that's my Moira dancing with Duncan. She's looking at me and smiling. Waving. That's her, I swear* . . . He wasn't sure how he knew, but he *knew*: that was his beloved stepdaughter, unmasked and impossibly alive.

Seeing Moira, Gary's breath left him. He pushed through the others on the floor in pursuit of her, some of whom shouted at him in protest. Hitchcock glared at him with insane eyes, holding a long knife dripping blood onto the parquet as if he were Anthony Perkins in the shower scene of *Psycho*. The volume of the music continued to rise. Finn's stallion body was between Gary and Moira, with the rat clarinettist dancing underneath Finn's belly.

When the dance swept Finn past him, Moira was gone, and Duncan was now partnered with Ink, her tattoos forming words: *This is the dream in which we live* . . .

Gary was disoriented, the room spinning around him. He could feel the house releasing this altered, surrealistic world, as if the very doorways were breathing out the atmosphere – not with malice but snatching random images from his mind and the minds of everyone here and dangling the images before them, the house not caring whether they were benign or dangerous. Gary could feel his forehead getting hotter; smoke began to curl across his vision. He tried to pull the mask from his face, but it refused to budge, as if it had been mysteriously glued to his skin. While yellow flames flickered around his vision, he heard a cry and saw Duncan collapse onto the parquet floor, his cane spinning away.

With Duncan's cry and his collapse, the surreality of the guise dance also vanished, and the music stuttered to a halt, leaving Gary's ears ringing. He tore off his mask, which was scorched but came away easily. There were only the other guests present now. Gone were the strange, almost malevolent creatures that had joined the dance: the gigantic cockroach; Mad Morwen; the rat playing its clarinet, the tyrannosaur-toothed duck encased in its shell. Moira.

There were only Jago, Ceallaigh, Hitchcock and the other staff members on the dance floor with their guests.

Dr Finn and Gary both rushed towards Duncan.

'I'm jus' feckin' fine, so yeh all can get the hell outta my room.'

Duncan glared at the quartet around his bed: Gary, Jeremy, Dr Finn and Jago. Gary looked to Finn, who had a stethoscope in his ears, bending at the waist as he listened to Duncan's chest. He'd discarded his mask, though Gary, Jeremy, and Jago remained attired in their costumes.

'You're sounding better now, but I'd like to get you to the hospital on the mainland so they can give you a proper check-up,' Finn said as he straightened up. 'You may have had a small coronary incident. If that's the case, there's medicine you should be starting on.'

'The tide's out, and the causeway's clear,' Jago said to Duncan. 'I can have Horace drive you in.'

'No,' Duncan said firmly. 'None of that's happening. I'm fine.'

'Duncan, you don't *know* that,' Gary said. 'Why not have the hospital run a few tests? I'll go with you.'

'I don't *want* 'em poking and prodding me,' Duncan answered. 'It's my body and my choice, and that's the end of it. No hospital. No doctors. No medicine. Now – just clear out and let me get some sleep. I'll be fit as a fiddle in the morning.'

Gary looked at Finn. 'I'll at least stay with him tonight.'

'No, yeh won't,' Duncan answered. 'Lord Branok can have someone from his staff look in on me a couple of times. Right?'

'As you said,' Jago responded, 'it's your body and your choice, and yes, I can have staff members check on you periodically.'

'Good,' Duncan said. 'We're agreed, then. So the lot of yeh get yerselves back downstairs. Have a pint or three in the drawing room with the others.'

'Duncan . . .' Gary began, but Duncan lifted his hand.

'No. Shut yer gob and save yer breath, friend. Do as I said, and I'll see yeh on the morrow. Go before I throw yeh out meself.'

Gary spent a while in the drawing room with the others. He found himself checking Caitlyn's pocket watch incessantly, and by eleven-thirty, he'd excused himself to Jago and the guests and departed, taking the grand staircase to the first floor. He found one of Jago's staff emerging from Duncan's room as he passed. 'How is he?' he asked the maid, whose nametag proclaimed her to be Colette.

'Mr MacEnnis is sleeping peacefully, sir,' was the answer in a strong French accent, and Gary moved on to his own room. There, he undressed and slid between Constance's sheets. However, his mind wouldn't shut off, and sleep eluded him; after half an hour of staring at the ceiling, he pulled the sheets aside and put on Constance's bathrobe. He went to the balcony doors, opened them, and stepped out into the night air. The lawn was illuminated only by a crescent moon and starlight, though he could hear waves smashing against the rocks below. He thought he saw something – an animal? a hunched-over person? – moving across the lawn out by the cliffs.

The fine hairs on his neck lifted as he heard Merryn's call sounding in the darkness, mournful and sad. And mingled with Merryn's wordless call, he also heard his own name – 'Gary . . .' – and shivered.

That was his stepdaughter's voice again. Moira's voice.

Gary stepped back inside and shut the balcony doors. He put the key to his room and Caitlyn's watch in the pocket of the robe and slipped out into the hallway, which was illuminated by Victorian-style wall sconces every few paces. Merryn's voice was muffled now, but Moira's was clear. 'Gary . . . I'm here, Gary, and so is *Máthair* . . . We're here . . .'

Barefoot, Gary padded down the carpeted hallway, pursuing the voice, but it receded from him as he walked. It seemed he'd walked into a maze; the hallway twisted and turned, and the elusive voice led him down hallways leading off both right and left. The carpet under his feet changed colour and texture, then vanished entirely until he was treading on bare polished wood, then rougher, wider planks. The electric lights in the wall sconces vanished and became gas-fed flames.

Moira's voice still called from the darkness ahead, insistent. 'Gary . . . we're here . . .'

As he approached another intersection, he saw a woman standing there, gazing at him. Under ringlets of bright red hair, her skin was flawless and milky, and the wide and round eyes held irises the stunning green of Irish grass. '*Caitlyn!*' he breathed. 'My God, is that really you?'

A faint smile appeared on her face, gleaming like that of a porcelain doll. 'Oh, Gary. I've missed you so much, and so has Moira.'

'I'm here now,' he told her. If this was an apparition, he didn't care. She was real; he could see her breath lifting the blouse she wore, and she was so close he could almost touch her. 'My God, let me hold you again, Caitlyn.' He heard his voice shudder with emotion. He pulled the watch and its chain from his robe's pocket. 'Look, I have your watch. You should take it.'

But she shook her head. 'I'm so sorry, Gary, but it's not possible to go back. Not this way.' With that, Caitlyn stepped quickly to the left and down the intersecting hall.

Gary ran after her. 'Wait! Caitlyn!'

When he reached the turning, she was nowhere to be seen. Down that hall, the gaslight sconces gave way to guttering torches belching dark smoke that gathered like storm clouds below the ceiling, while the floor underneath his bare feet was stone.

Gary coughed as he walked down the smoky hallway for a bit, but it was obvious that Caitlyn was gone, perhaps into one of the rooms whose doors studded the corridor. Gary had no way of knowing which.

He started to turn to retrace his steps. Stopped.

One of the doors opened, hinges creaking, and someone in a hooded, fur-trimmed purple cloak emerged to stand before him, only a few paces away. In the torchlight, Gary could see eyes beneath the hood, a sharp nose, and glossy strands of long, midnight-black hair. *The portrait* . . . 'Lady Morwen,' he breathed.

She answered him, but now she seemed to be speaking an odd patois of Cornish, Early Modern English, and archaic French that Gary couldn't easily understand. Her voice was sibilant with anger. He heard the name 'Morwen' in her reply. She pointed to the floor imperiously, as if she expected him to drop to his knees before her. 'Kneel to me, you blackamoor,' he heard. Then, first in what sounded like French, *'S'agenouiller!'* – then in what Gary suspected was Cornish, *'Mos war benn-glin!'*

When he didn't move, she gave a shriek of fury and lunged at him, grabbing the hands Gary lifted in defence as her fingernails raked his arms. He felt his body respond to the attack, heat rising from within him. Morwen's eyes widened, and she shrieked again, this time in pain. She released his hands, backing away from him and staring at her own hands; he could see blisters already forming on her palms and fingers. She gestured at him, screaming words he couldn't understand, then plucked a knife from a scabbard on her belt and flung it at him. Something on the wooden pommel glittered as it spun.

The knife hit his bathrobe but didn't penetrate; instead, the weapon dropped, clattering on the stone flags of the corridor. As Gary bent to pick it up, Morwen leaped on his back, her hands pulling at his hair and tearing at his robe. He grabbed the knife and brandished it in her face. Morwen then turned and fled back into her room, pulling the door shut behind her.

Gary didn't wait to see if there would be another attack. He retreated back the way he'd come, back to the gaslit halls. He half-ran, half-walked, turning more than once down another corridor to one side or the other, casting glances back over his shoulder constantly until he was out of breath and could run no more.

He halted, panting. He had no idea where he was or which way would lead him back to his own familiar corridor. Moira's voice had vanished; the corridors were silent, and he was alone and lost. He remembered Ceallaigh's warning earlier in the day: *Loveday House is larger than it might appear, and it can be easy to lose your way within it. Should you wander too far into its interior, you may become hopelessly confused. I wouldn't advise that, as it can be dangerous.*

'Well, I'm definitely lost, Ceallaigh,' he said aloud, mostly to hear his own voice. He looked at the knife in his hand. The handle was smooth, polished hardwood nearly as dark as his own skin with a large ruby inset in silver on the pommel. The faceted jewel appeared genuine to Gary's untrained eye; the blade was certainly solid and real and the edge keen – there was nothing ethereal about it at all. 'And this place is certainly dangerous.'

His breathing was returning to normal, though he could feel his heart thudding loudly in his chest. He had little choice but to continue to walk and hope that he'd find himself somewhere familiar or that he'd stumble upon a staff member who could give him directions or escort him.

He began walking. The knife in his hand gave him some comfort; if something leaped from the shadows to attack him, he wouldn't be entirely helpless. He kept thinking about the dance earlier: the man-sized cockroach, the duck with incisors in its beak, Mad Morwen, the horror-film-like costumes that could have been the actual skin of awful creatures, the way the house seemed to contain far more space than it possibly could.

Gary wasn't sure what else Loveday House could conjure up. He heard doors closing ahead and behind him, and he had the sense that the house was shifting, changing around him even as he moved through it. The maze of corridors was alive, as if the house itself were closing off paths and leading him where it wanted him to go.

He'd been walking for what seemed like hours, but the soles of his feet were feeling carpet again, and the wall sconces had gone from gaslight to electric. He kept walking – the corridor dead-ended on yet another hall, leaving him only one way to turn. He did so and found himself looking ahead to the distant but familiar sight of the gallery overlooking the main entrance. He recognized the door to his own room and reached into the robe's pocket to take out his key.

His breath left him then. *The pocket watch . . .* He plunged his hand back into the pocket, hoping it was somehow lost in a corner. Nothing. He wanted to scream his frustration. *She took it, or I lost it during our struggle.* But he had no idea how to get back, or if he even could, with the way the house had seemed to shift and change around him.

Feeling simultaneously furious and depressed, he unlocked the door to his room and went in. He closed the door and leaned back against its solidity. He realized he was still holding Morwen's knife; he placed it on the night-stand next to the carving of Arthek. He looked at the hands underneath the glass of the grandfather clock: one-fifteen, it said.

That seemed impossible. He thought he'd been wandering lost for half the night, not just a little over an hour.

Saturday

He hadn't thought he'd ever get to sleep, yet he woke the next morning to see daylight between the folds of the room's window curtains.

The previous night now had the aura of a dream – enough that Gary wondered whether any of the experiences had been real. He blinked to clear his vision as he looked at the bedside table and saw a knife with a ruby-studded hilt there. The sculpture of Arthek was alongside it, but not Caitlyn's watch. Gary reached out – he could see blood clotted in the scratches on his arms from Morwen's fingernails – and picked up the weapon; it was heavy and solid enough. He put down the knife again, an empty hollow bored in his chest.

Not a dream, then. It was all real.

Gary took a quick shower, dressed, and started to leave his room to go downstairs – then stopped. A silver watch chain was wrapped around the faceted glass of the Victorian doorknob, with Caitlyn's watch dangling at the end. He picked up the watch, turning it over to look at the familiar engraving:

To Patrick, Love Shannon – Caitlyn's parents, the watch that her mother had given her father on their first anniversary and that had come to Caitlyn after their deaths. Gary found his vision shimmering behind tears, holding it again.

'Thank you,' he whispered to the air, not knowing whom he might be addressing.

He unwrapped the chain carefully from the doorknob and put the watch back in his pocket, fastening the chain to the closest belt loop. He took a long breath and opened the door.

Down the hall, Duncan's door was propped open, with a maid straightening up inside. 'Sir, if you're looking for Mr MacEnnis,' the maid said, 'he's gone down to breakfast. It's being served in the drawing room.'

Gary felt a new surge of relief at that news. 'Thank you,' he said, and made for the Grand Staircase. Even before he entered the drawing room, Gary could hear people talking. 'Gary!' Jeremy called out as he entered. 'How was your night?'

'It was . . . very strange,' Gary answered shortly. Several of the other guests were already in the room, including Duncan, with everyone seated at a large round table. Gary took the seat next to Duncan and leaned close to him. 'How are you feeling this morning?'

Duncan shrugged. 'I told yeh last night: yeh needn't be worryin' about me,' he answered, just as quietly. 'But yeh preferred to listen to that quack horse doctor.' Gary sighed, and Duncan shrugged again. 'Yeh asked,' he said, 'and Doc Finn ain't here, so he can't take feckin' offence, can he?'

'I take it you had a strange night also, then?' Jeremy said from the other side of Duncan. 'Everyone's talking about seeing or hearing odd things. Ink, show Gary what you showed me.'

'Sure,' the woman said. She ran tattooed fingers through her spiked hair. 'When I came up last night – well, early this morning, actually – I kept hearing something or someone tapping at my window and hooting like an owl. I opened the curtains, and this is what I saw.' Ink slid a sheet of paper across the table. The drawing, in pencil, was of a large, winged man with an owl-like face and beak. 'It was flying and hovering right at my window, staring at me. When it saw me, though, it flew off towards the cliffs.'

'That's the Cowanden,' Merryn commented, glancing at Ink's drawing. 'The Owlman of Cornish legend. There were two young girls, back in 1976, who said they were camping near the church down in the village when they were confronted by this Cowanden, with pointed ears and as big as a man. His eyes were glowing red, they said, and he had claws like pincers.'

Ink was nodding. Her fingernails, painted bright purple, tapped the drawing. 'That's what I saw. Absolutely.'

'Ah, yeh drank too much of Branok's whiskey, and it gave you nightmares,' Duncan commented. 'Yeh didn't see nothin' at all.'

'I did,' Ink insisted.

'Yeh were drunk and seeing t'ings. Me, I slept like a baby.'

'You know what,' Ink said, snatching up the drawing, 'I was feeling really bad all night since I was the one who pulled you out on the dance floor before you collapsed. But now I don't feel quite so guilty. You're a fucking asshole, Duncan MacEnnis.' With that, she pushed away from the table and left the dining room.

'Hey, I'm sorry. I didn't mean—' Duncan called after her, but the closing of the door cut off the apology.

The Ravenstones, directly across the table, stirred. Bibi didn't speak, but Roger did. 'Honestly, we had a strange experience last night, too,' he said, scratching with his right hand at the base of one of the two small horns on his head. He adjusted his eye patch. 'I'd left my guitar and fiddle in the music room after all the dancing had ended, and Bibi and I went back to grab them. We could hear a band playing a wild, frantic folk dance as we came down the hall towards the music room – great stuff, actually – and there was a woman singing in Cornish along with the band, with a voice as lovely as Bibi's own. Well, *almost* as lovely.' He smiled at Bibi, and she put her hand over his, smiling back. The raven on Bibi's shoulder watched their hands with its beady black eyes, its head tilted. 'I thought, great, we'll go in and listen. But when I pushed open the doors, the music stopped, and there was no one at all in the room, though someone had taken both of my instruments from their cases. My guitar was leaning against one of the chairs and had been put in an alternate tuning I never use. I don't mind telling you that the experience gave me the shivers.'

The raven fluttered its wings. 'Dreams,' it croaked – just that single word – and Roger chuckled uneasily.

No one seemed to want to talk after that. Roger and Bibi left, saying that they'd see everyone at lunch. Merryn rose, going to the side table and pouring herself a cup of tea.

Gary followed her, getting tea and a scone for himself. 'I heard you calling into the fog last night around midnight,' he said to her. 'You must have been restless, too.'

'It was more than that,' she said. 'I was out on the lawn – I know that's against all the rules – and looking down at the ocean from the top of the cliff, I felt like I *had* to call, had to protect any boats out there with the heavy mist coming in and huge waves smashing themselves against the cliffs. Then—' She caught her upper lip in her teeth for a moment. 'I saw a boat, my *parents'* boat, drifting towards the rocks below. So I called and called and called, trying to warn them away, but for some reason they couldn't hear me. As I watched . . .' She stopped. Her teacup rattled in the saucer as her hands shook. 'I saw the boat picked up by the waves and hurled against the rocks at the base of the cliffs. I saw it breaking up; I saw my parents tossed out into the waves. Then the mist closed in and became so heavy I couldn't see anything below. I just sat there for hours, calling.'

Gary put a hand on her shoulder for a moment, then pulled it away, afraid it would be too warm for her.

'At some point, I must have gone back to my room, because I woke up there. I went back to the cliff edge this morning and looked, but there wasn't any wreckage I could see.'

'Merryn, I'm so sorry.'

Likely she had dreamed the whole thing, since he had heard her voice calling from inside the house last night. She looked at him, her head turning on her too-wide neck. 'What about you?' she asked. 'What happened to you last night?'

He hesitated, then started to tell her the tale: how he'd heard her calling, how he'd also heard Moira's voice out in the corridor and had tried to find her, how everything had shifted around him, how Mad Morwen had attacked him, and how the house had led him back to safety and his room. He left out the bit about Caitlyn's watch, however; it felt better to do that.

'When I got back, Merryn, I still had Morwen's knife. The knife's up in my room right now. It wasn't a dream. It couldn't have been. That's what frightens me.'

◆

Gary sat in the library, surrounded by the quiet and the silence, staring out at the lawn and the ocean beyond the cliff edge without really seeing it. A book in a blue cloth-bound case sat unopened on his lap.

'I hope you're not planning to set that book on fire,' he heard Jago say. He looked to his left to find the man standing alongside his chair, wearing a mask as usual – this one with prominent ridges above the eyes so that they stayed half in shadow. 'That would be a tragic loss. You're holding an 1898 first edition of *The Two Magics*, which includes the first publication of Henry James's *The Turn of the Screw*. That book would sell for around £3,000 or more today, given its excellent condition. An interesting choice you've made, considering – don't you think?'

'I've been very careful with it,' Gary told him, but he lifted the book from his lap and set it on the table next to his chair.

Jago's gaze followed his movements. 'You seemed rather contemplative when I came in. Were you meditating?'

'In a sense, I suppose I was,' Gary answered. 'I was listening to your house. I think she's confused, sad, and a little afraid, and doesn't know how she should respond.'

Jago gave a small chuckle at that. He pulled one of the library chairs around to face Gary and sat, crossing his legs easily as he leaned back against the cushions. 'You're an interesting man with a unique way of seeing things, Gary, but I'm afraid you're making a mistake. My house might be unusual, but it *isn't* sentient. Loveday can't talk to you, and it can't feel. It just *is*, and people bring their own dreams and issues with them. I take it you went wandering last night, despite the warnings that I know Ceallaigh gave you. Did you experience anything interesting?'

Gary hesitated, not knowing how much of what had happened last night he wanted to admit. But then he'd already told Merryn. He now gave the same account of his night to Jago.

'Mad Morwen's knife with the ruby in the pommel . . . you still have it, you say?' Jago asked.

'In my room. I'd have brought it down to give it to you, but I wasn't sure you'd be here. It came from your house, and thus it belongs to you - and besides, if that ruby's genuine, it's worth a small fortune.'

Jago lifted his chin at that. 'I'd rather you kept it,' he said. 'It may be more valuable to you than to me.'

'So, was that *real*, Mad Morwen and all?'

'Did it feel real to you?' Jago asked.

'The knife's genuine enough. Does that mean Mad Morwen haunts this place?'

'I don't believe in ghosts,' Jago said quickly. 'Some people come here, and the house seems to react to their presence. I suspect you're one of those.' Jago took in a long breath, letting it escape slowly from his mouth. He leaned forward and tapped the case of *The Two Magics* gently with a forefinger. 'But despite the rumours and the gossip, I assure you there are no ghosts here. You don't believe in ghosts, do you, Gary?'

'Right now, I'm not quite sure what I should believe.'

'Then you're a wise man.' Jago tilted his head, looking at Gary. 'Still, one has to be careful when wandering around. You don't know what precious possession you might lose or if it will ever be returned.'

Gary took in a breath. 'What are you saying? Did *you*—'

Jago spoke before Gary could finish the question. 'I know this house. You don't. Not yet, in any event. I'm merely telling you how dangerous Loveday House can be for those who aren't careful. But I'm curious: earlier you said the house is a "she" - why do you think that?'

'Loveday just *feels* like a woman to me.' It was the only honest answer that Gary could give, and Jago's eyes behind the mask demanded honesty from him. 'Everything about this place makes me think of Loveday House as female. Don't you feel the same?'

They both heard the chime of a bell then; at the sound, Jago uncrossed his legs languidly and stood. 'That will be the call for lunch. Would you accompany me to the dining room? We might continue our conversation there.'

But they didn't. Hitchcock intercepted Jago as they arrived, taking him aside and speaking to him with some urgency; Jago made bland apologies and went off with Hitchcock, leaving Gary to dine with the other guests.

After lunch, Gary asked Duncan if he wanted to explore Loveday's greenhouse, but Duncan said he'd rather take a nap before dinner. Jeremy, Ink, Cosmos, and Merryn accompanied him instead. Gary found the greenhouse startling in its own way, with plants that he – who kept an extensive garden on Rathlin – couldn't identify at all. There were a few of Jago's staff in the greenhouse, tending to the plants, and when Gary pointed to some of the unfamiliar species, a gardener, who said her name was Ysella, laughed. 'Lord Branok travels extensively,' Ysella said, 'and sometimes he brings back plants we've never seen ourselves. That one over there, with the eight-lobed wide leaves, is *Fatsia japonica.*'

'I remember touching one of these plants during a trip to Japan,' Cosmos said. He was floating a foot above the ground in a lotus position as if sitting on a pillow, his eyes closed, an index finger and thumb around a leaf as he rubbed it. 'It's also called the paperplant, isn't it? Too bad it's not flowering at the moment; the flowers are very strange-feeling, with tentacle-like fringes.'

'Very good, sir,' Ysella responded, nodding. 'It's also known as Japanese aralia. But some of the plants here I've honestly never heard of, seen before, or read about. Anywhere. Even Lord Branok doesn't seem to know what they are. We do our best with those, though with occasional failures, I have to admit.'

After the tour of the greenhouse, Gary went out onto the lawn, where some of the others were playing croquet in the mild sunlight. He spent most of his time talking with Jeremy, Ink, and Merryn. When the light began to fail, he looked at Caitlyn's watch: *six-thirty.* 'I need to go up to my room to freshen up and dress for dinner,' he said. 'I'll see you all later.'

He knocked on Duncan's door as he passed; there wasn't an answer, so he went on to his own room. Ceallaigh had laid out a tuxedo for him on the bed. There was also an envelope placed on top of the tuxedo. The note inside had been written in an elegant hand using a fountain pen:

> *Please bring Morwen's knife to dinner. As I've told you, it's yours to keep, but I'd like to see it. — Jago.*

Gary finished dressing early and decided he'd go down anyway. Jago had said drinks would be available in the drawing room; he could get a nice dram of Redbreast, his favourite Irish whiskey. Perhaps Jago would be there, and Gary could show him Morwen's knife. He wrapped the blade in tissues, slid the knife into the inside breast pocket of the jacket, and headed down.

Jago wasn't there, but the Redbreast tasted fine as he sipped it. Cosmos and Finn came in to sit with him. 'I checked on Duncan a little after five,' Bradley told him as they watched Cosmos juggle three glass ashtrays without touching them. 'I worry about his lack of strength and his colour. I thought his pulse was a little slow, but otherwise he seemed fine, and his heart sounded normal enough. I don't feel he's in any immediate danger. I reported all that to Jago. Duncan still insists he's not seeing the specialist in Belfast that I recommended to him. I hope you can convince him to change his mind.'

'I'll certainly try,' Gary told Finn, 'but Duncan's been dodging doctors for decades now. He's become an expert in that specific martial art. No offence.'

'None taken.' Finn chuckled. 'I have several patients at the clinic who have black belts in the same art.'

One of the staff stuck his head into the room. 'Dinner will be served directly, and Lord Branok is ready to join you. If you gentlemen wouldn't mind moving to the dining room . . .'

Jago, masked as usual, intercepted Gary at the door to the dining room and took him aside. 'You have Lady Morwen's weapon?' he asked. 'May I see it?'

Gary handed him the knife, watching as Jago turned it in his hands. The man's lips pressed together in a tight line as he examined the blade before handing it back to Gary. 'Thank you. As I said, it's yours now. Rubies were reputedly Lady Morwen's favourite jewel. That particular ruby is quite spectacular. I'd keep the knife with you, were I you.' His head tilted slightly as he spoke, his eyes behind the mask holding Gary's gaze.

'I'll do that.' Gary slipped the knife back in the jacket pocket.

Jago nodded to that. 'Let me take the knife's dimensions later; I'll have one of our staff make you a proper leather sheath to carry it.'

'That's very generous of you,' Gary said, as he followed Jago into the dining room.

Fifteen minutes later, the starters had been served (with Ceallaigh, as before, attending to Gary), but Duncan's chair remained empty. Gary started to say something, but Jago spoke up. 'Hitchcock,' he said to the butler, watching attentively as the staff served, 'would you mind going upstairs to inform Mr MacEnnis that dinner is being served? He might still be taking a nap. If he wishes, have someone bring his dinner to him in his room.'

'Certainly, sir.' With a quick bow of his head, Hitchcock turned and left.

It was another fifteen minutes until he returned, at which point Hitchcock went to Jago and spoke into his ear. Gary leaned towards the conversation; he couldn't hear what was being said, but he could read

Jago's eyes and the slight shake of his head as Hitchcock stepped back from his chair.

'The rest of dinner will be delayed, I'm afraid,' Jago said, standing and looking more at Gary than any of the others. 'Hitchcock informs me that Mr MacEnnis isn't in his room and that his cane is also gone. There's no indication that anyone else has been in the room, and he's left no note telling us where he might have intended to go. The maid was last in there around a quarter to five, and Dr Finn checked on him around a quarter past and actually talked with Duncan, which was the last time we're aware that anyone saw him. Hitchcock, please coordinate the search within the house, since the staff know the layout best. I won't insist that guests be part of the searching, but if you wish to help, it would be appreciated. If you don't wish to assist, please remain in the drawing room for the time being. We'll provide everyone else with torches, and you'll assist me in searching the grounds. Duncan can't have gone far on his own, after all.'

None of the guests wanted to remain in the house. Torches ('Flashlights, for you Americans,' Jago added) were brought and handed out to the guests, and they went outside onto the lawn. Another fog was drifting in off the sea, heavy wisps crawling the grass like ghostly slugs; the wind was picking up and blowing the fog along. Above, the sky was clear, with the Milky Way arching up from the southern horizon while a half-moon straddled the zenith. Jago carried a shotgun, broken open with two shells visible in the barrels, cradled in the crook of his elbow. 'There are wild boars on the island,' he reminded everyone. 'There's another shotgun available if someone feels comfortable handling it.'

Roger Ravenstone lifted his hand. 'I hunt occasionally, and I'm halfway decent at skeet shooting.'

'Fine.' Jago gestured to a nearby servant. 'Enyon, please bring Mr Ravenstone the other shotgun and several shells. Let's all stay in groups of three or more. Everyone should remain well back from the cliff edge, especially with the way the wind is picking up,' Jago warned. 'I don't want to lose anyone. Roger, Bibi, Dr Finn, please search the grounds to the front of the house. Cosmos, Jeremy, Ink, I'd like you three to scour the lawn towards the village side. Gary and Merryn, you're with me . . .'

Jago led Gary and Merryn to the seaward side of the lawn. Clouds were streaking across the sky and a strong breeze off the Celtic Sea tugged at their clothes, carrying salt spray with it. Their torches – large, bright LED models – made searing blue circles as they swept the beams over the befogged grass. Gary saw nothing untoward as his stomach knotted in worry with every minute. They separated, walking a few paces apart and moving from the house towards the cliffs and the sea.

They hadn't been searching for long when Gary heard Merryn's characteristic *whoop*. Gary's heart sank, thinking that Merryn must have found

Duncan and fearing the worst. When Gary and Jago finally located Merryn by following the sound of her calls, she was already halfway down the cliff's sea stairs towards where angry waves lashed a rocky small beach. The fog had vanished, blown away entirely. Gary looked over the side, clutching at the rail. Their torch beams played over the wet rocks below, but they saw no one.

'Merryn!' Gary called into the wind. 'Is Duncan down there? Have you found him?'

Merryn pointed out to the surf. 'Not Duncan,' she shouted back. 'It's my mother! My father! Look!' She pointed her torch towards the ocean; they glimpsed, faintly, a small boat with two figures in it. Then it was gone again as Merryn half-ran, half-slid down the concrete stairs to the shingle and started wading out into the waves, her mournful *whoop* louder than the wind and the sea.

'*Merryn!*' Jago bellowed. '*Don't!*'

Gary started down the long stairway after her, but Jago grabbed his arm, holding him back. Merryn was swimming now, out towards the boat.

'It's too late for us to do anything,' Jago said. 'She's made her decision, and it's all up to her.'

Gary pointed his flashlight towards Merryn and the boat; he thought he saw the couple turn their faces to Merryn and reach for her. Then they were out of the range of the torch's light, lost in a sea of grey gloom. Gary continued to stare down, hoping to see Merryn again, but he did not.

'Lord Branok!' The shout emanated from Hitchcock, panting as he lumbered from the house. He glanced from Jago to Gary, then back again. 'Duncan is almost certainly wandering inside the house. We have found his cane.' He paused. 'It was in one of the older sections, sir, if you take my meaning.'

Jago gathered the guests in the drawing room, where he told them that he'd prefer they remain in their rooms or in the rooms on the ground floor nearest the front of the house, while he and a few trusted members of his staff searched for Duncan, citing again that sections of the mansion had yet to be renovated and could be dangerous.

'In the older parts of the house, it's unfortunately easy to become lost at night or to have an accident. Roger and Bibi have promised to give a private concert in the music room for those who might be interested, and I've instructed the kitchen staff to serve food and drinks for everyone. Also, Merryn has decided to take a boat to return to her own family, so she won't be joining you; she sends her apologies. So, please – enjoy yourselves. I'm certain we'll find Duncan directly.'

With that, Jago bowed and started to leave the room with Hitchcock. 'I'm going with you,' Gary said quietly, pulling Jago aside at the door. 'I've already wandered those "older parts" you're talking about, remember? If Duncan's there, I want – I *need* - to help find him.'

Jago nodded. 'Go get dressed in something you don't mind getting soiled, and I'll meet you at your room in a few minutes,' he said. He and Hitchcock departed.

With a glance back at the other guests, Gary followed. He made for the grand staircase. Before he could reach it, Ceallaigh intercepted him. 'Here,' she said, handing him a crystal decanter filled with a golden-brown liquid and a tumbler that matched the decanter. 'Redbreast,' she said in response to his enquiring look. 'I thought you might want a dram before or after – as long as you promise to go easy with it.'

'Thanks,' he said.

'I'm sorry about your friend bein' lost, Mr Bushorn,' she said. 'I know how much he means to you.'

Gary lifted the decanter and tumbler. 'Thanks again,' he told her. 'That means a lot.'

In his room, Gary placed the decanter and tumbler on his nightstand and put Morwen's knife on the bed. He dressed in jeans and a T-shirt, then put on the bathrobe Constance had given him for protection. He slid Caitlyn's watch into his trouser pocket and attached the chain, then picked up Morwen's knife and put it in the right-hand pocket of the bathrobe. He poured a finger of whiskey from the decanter and went to the balcony. The wind had remained strong, and clouds were still moving swiftly overhead. He wondered where Merryn might be, and if it had really been her parents in the boat. He lifted his glass in salute towards the whitecaps visible on the ocean and took a sip.

He wasn't sure how long he stood there: waiting for Jago to knock on the door; watching the slow dance of the clouds; listening to the ocean tearing at the rocks of Keun Island; smelling the brine of the sea; feeling the chill of the wind dying as it met his warmth; sipping the alcohol-fuelled fire of the Redbreast. His thoughts were restless and unfocused. Everything was all muddled in his head – Duncan's disfigured face, Jago's masked one, the strangeness of the guise dancing, the surreality of wandering the house afterwards; Mad Morwen's attack . . .

He couldn't make sense of anything that had happened here. It was as if he'd stepped into a fevered, impossible alternate dimension in the last few days.

Jago still hadn't arrived. Gary lifted the tumbler and drained what was left of the whiskey, grimacing as he did so, then went back inside and closed the balcony doors.

As Gary sat there, he heard footsteps in the hallway outside, as if someone were walking towards his room, but it wasn't Jago. The sound was odd: a heavy footfall, then a strange double sound: *clomp, tap-clomp*. The footfalls started from somewhere around Duncan's room, continuing down towards his own room. *Clomp, tap-clomp; clomp, tap-clomp* . . . The sound stopped outside his door. Gary listened for a knock, but then the sound continued past his door, as if the person outside had grown tired of waiting. *Clomp, tap-clomp; clomp, tap-clomp* . . .

Gary rose and went to his door. *Clomp, tap-clomp; clomp, tap-clomp* . . .

He opened the door, looking to his right to where the sound was heading. The wall sconces flickered, and the hallway was dim, so it was difficult to see clearly. There was a figure several feet away, leaning on a quad-footed cane and looking back over his shoulder at Gary. That skull-like face couldn't be mistaken.

'Duncan?' Gary said.

Duncan – if it *was* Duncan – didn't answer. He just turned away and continued pacing deeper into the house. *Clomp, tap-clomp; clomp, tap-clomp* . . .

'Duncan!' Gary started after him.

All the lights went out at once.

As Gary called out in alarm, the lights snapped back on – but he was no longer in the same place. There were none of Loveday's ornate doors set in the walls of the hallway now. A step or two in front of him, the corridor ended abruptly: at a door he knew all too well. It was if someone had taken the front facade of his cottage on Rathlin Island and inserted it into Loveday House's corridor. The thatch of the roof hung down from the ceiling like an unruly, grassy curtain, as it once had when Gary first arrived on Rathlin; he'd long since replaced the original thatch with slates. The rough stone walls that he meticulously kept whitewashed were smashed against the faux-Victorian wallpaper covering the plaster-and-lath of Loveday. The old granite stone threshold, worn lower in the middle by decades of shoes crossing over it, was the same as he remembered, as was the thick, rough piece of oaken timber (that Caitlyn had always claimed came from a wrecked ship) that served as the framing above the door.

Neither Caitlyn nor Gary had ever locked their door on Rathlin; Gary pressed the latch, pushed, and the door opened. Before him was the interior of his cottage on Rathlin, with Caitlyn and Moira seated by the peat fire and Duncan sitting at the rough wooden table. Gary could smell the burning peat, so familiar an odour on Rathlin. All of them were looking at him.

Gary started to enter, but even though none of the trio inside moved, the door slammed in his face. When he tried the door again, it was locked. He heard Caitlyn's voice from behind the wood: 'There's nothing for you on Rathlin, Gary. Not any more. Don't try to go back there. I wish you could, my love, but it's not what you should do.'

Gary pounded on the door with a fist. 'Caitlyn! Please!'

'This isn't for you yet, Gary,' she answered, but her voice sounded distant and faint. 'It may be, one day, but not yet . . .'

Gary took two steps back and rushed at the door, turning his shoulder to hit the wooden planks, but he encountered no resistance.

He stumbled into darkness, falling onto what felt like damp stone. When he lifted his head, he found himself again in the area where he'd encountered Mad Morwen the previous night, unless it was some equally strange place within Loveday House. He pushed himself up as his eyes slowly grew accustomed to the guttering, smoke-wrapped light of torches.

'What is it that you want from me?' he cried out to the darkness, to the empty corridor, to Loveday House itself. 'Why show me the people I love if you're only going to steal them away again?'

But there was no answer to his query, just the echo of his own voice rebounding from cold stone. Gary pushed himself back to his feet, breathing hard.

It was then that he heard the creaking of a door behind him – a sound he remembered from last night. Gary felt in the pocket of the bathrobe for Morwen's knife as he turned.

He was too slow.

He heard the blade slicing through air at the same time that something struck his forearm, still encased in Constance's bathrobe. The impact momentarily made his hand go numb and his fingers open, and the knife he had been holding went skittering across the stone floor. Morwen was there, glaring at him as he grabbed his injured arm. She held a small sword in her hand and was staring at Gary's right arm, which throbbed from her strike. But the sleeve of Constance's bathrobe was untouched, and there was no blood, though Gary was certain he'd find a nasty bruise below later.

Morwen snarled wordlessly and slashed at Gary's midsection. He tried to retreat from the blow, too late, but again the blade couldn't penetrate the cloth.

Morwen threw away the sword with a cry, her face a rictus of anger and rage. She screamed at him; he could understand little of what she was saying in the patois of Cornish and archaic English, though the hostility in her speech didn't need words. She lunged at Gary, her hands clawing at his neck and face. He could feel her long nails digging into his skin, hot blood flowing from the furrows.

Gary grabbed her shoulders, his own anger rising. Smoke curled away from where his fingers were bunched in the thick cloth of her robe. She spat at him, still trying to reach his face. Gary shoved her away. She staggered back a few steps. 'We hate thee, *vil du euthvil! Dyowl!* Satan!'

Someone pushed past Gary from behind. *Duncan . . .* Duncan was between them, unsteady on his feet as he stooped with a groan to pick up the knife that Gary had dropped. Morwen confronted him, still spitting curses, and Duncan cursed back at her. 'Feck off, bitch! That's me friend, and yeh canna have him!'

Morwen screamed again. She rushed at Duncan, shoving him hard. His legs buckled, and he went down on the stone flags, the knife in his hand clattering away once more. Morwen ignored Duncan, snarling as she leaped once more at Gary, her hands grasping for him. But Duncan's intervention had given him time.

Flames erupted from between Gary's fingers, and Morwen screamed at the touch of them, desperation giving her strength. Her fingernails raked just under Gary's left eye, dangerously close, and Gary felt strips of flesh tearing away from his face.

But with the pain and his anger, the flames around his own hands strengthened. The sleeves of Morwen's robe caught fire, the flames spreading quickly along the cloth. Morwen screamed again, this time in genuine pain and terror. Gary felt that pain as well; his fingers released her, unable to hold the woman any longer as huge blisters rose from his scorched hands. Morwen scrambled back and away from him, striking at the flames and tearing the robe from her body, fixing him with a glare of pure loathing and revulsion as she tossed the flaming rags to the stones.

Then her gaze fixed on something behind Gary. 'This castle is mine, Lord Branok,' she said, scorn in her voice as she spoke his title. 'Mine. Not yours.' She spat on the ground in front of her before fleeing into darkness.

'Gary!'

Gary looked over his shoulder to see Jago and Hitchcock there, both armed with shotguns. Gary ran to Duncan, who was sprawled on the flagstones. He sank to his knees alongside the joker. Duncan's eyes were open, staring blindly at the ceiling above him. Gary touched Duncan's face with blistered and bloodied hands. There was no reaction from his friend. Droplets of red fell from Gary's wounded face onto the flagstones next to Duncan and stained the front of his bathrobe.

'Let me, sir, if you will,' Hitchcock said, kneeling next to Gary. He touched pudgy fingers to the side of Duncan's neck, then felt for the pulse at the man's wrist. He shook his head at Gary, at Jago, and closed Duncan's eyes with his hand. 'I'm sorry, sirs. We're too late.'

Gary sagged, all the air leaving his lungs, almost falling to the ground himself. He took in a deep, sobbing breath. 'No,' he moaned, and again, 'No . . .'

'Can you stand, Gary?' he heard Jago say. 'Let me help you up.'

Gary felt hands under his arms as Jago and Hitchcock lifted him to his feet. He wobbled unsteadily in their grasp. He fought to stay standing.

'I believe you need to see Dr Finn,' Hitchcock managed to say.

'You absolutely do, and you will,' Jago told him. He looked at the blackened remnants of Morwen's robe, still smouldering on the stones. 'Do you think you can walk?'

Gary nodded.

'Good. We'll start back then. Hitchcock, I'll take care of Gary. I need you to send people to bring Duncan's body back.'

'Indeed, sir,' Hitchcock answered. 'Consider it done. You and Mr Bushorn should go on.'

Jago stooped to pick up Morwen's knife from the stone flags and handed it back to Gary. 'Here. If you decide to stay, you might need this again sometime – though you should practise holding onto it. And if you won't stay, consider the knife a far better souvenir of Keun than a bad carving of a dog that never actually existed.'

Gary blinked. Everything was confused, uncertain. He was exhausted, and his hands throbbed, though the blisters were already beginning to heal. He managed to tear his gaze away from the image of Duncan's unmoving body. 'Stay?' Gary asked. 'At Loveday?'

Jago shrugged, as if dismissing the offer. 'For now, let's just get you to your room and Dr Finn.'

When Finn came into Gary's room, Gary was sitting at the table, with Ceallaigh dabbing gently at his wounds and the dried blood that streaked his face. His burns, as usual, were already largely healed.

Finn's eyebrow rose at the sight of Gary's face as he set down his medical bag. 'I'm not even going to ask,' he said. 'I'll try to numb things before I start stitching you up, Gary, but this is still going to hurt, and I can't promise that there won't be scarring afterward.'

'Do the best you can, Bradley,' Gary told him. 'That's all I ask. I trust you – no one's done more for those afflicted with the wild card virus.'

Finn sighed and clopped into the bathroom, which was barely large enough for him. They heard water running in the sink. 'Let me wash my hands,' he called back into the other room, 'then we'll clean up these injuries properly so I can see what we're dealing with. Ceallaigh, I need you to have someone bring us several new flannels and towels. We're going to go through what Gary has in the bathroom pretty quickly, I'm afraid. And if there are more medical supplies somewhere in the house, I could do with additional antiseptic and bandages.'

'I'll do that immediately, sir,' Ceallaigh answered.

'Thank you.' Finn turned off the water, shook his hands dry, and backed carefully out of the bathroom. 'Gary, you ready to get cleaned up and stitched? I won't lie, this will likely be somewhere between uncomfortable and rather painful.'

Gary sighed, closing his eyes. 'Go on.'

Jago came into Gary's room as Dr Finn was beginning to stitch up Gary's face. He watched the progress with a studied, noncommittal expression. When Finn finished and moved on to examining the deep scratches on Gary's hands and the bruise left by Morwen's sword strike, now swollen and rapidly purpling, Jago cleared his throat.

'By the way, Doctor,' Jago said, 'we've recovered Duncan's body. Hitchcock has brought it to the scullery. If you don't mind, once you've finished here with Gary, I'd like you to examine it. I'll call the local coroner and let him know that you'll be giving him your findings in due course. Given your reputation and experience, the coroner has agreed to sign off on that, since he couldn't be here until tomorrow morning at the earliest. The tide is in, the causeway's under water, and both the coroner's office and the police station are on the mainland.'

'Of course,' Dr Finn said. 'We've almost finished, which I'm sure Gary is very glad to hear.'

Dr Finn emerged from the scullery a few hours later, towelling off his hands as he looked to Gary, Jago, and Jeremy. 'Nothing I see indicates anything but sudden cardiac death, especially given what we know of Duncan's medical state – unless any of you have something to add?'

Jeremy shook his head; both Gary and Jago remained silent.

'That's what I thought,' Finn continued. 'I've spoken to the local coroner by phone; as you said, Lord Branok, the coroner's willing to accept my findings and issue the death certificate unless someone in Duncan's family insists that there should an autopsy.'

'Duncan didn't have any close family.' Gary shook his head. 'All his immediate relatives are dead, and he never talked about anyone else. I honestly wouldn't know who to contact.'

'What about yourself, Gary?' Finn asked. 'You were as close to Duncan as anyone, I expect. If you say you need a full autopsy for your own closure, then I'll call the coroner back and arrange to do that tomorrow. I could stay on a little longer to help if he's amenable, and if it would make you feel more comfortable.'

Gary sighed. 'No. I don't think Duncan would want that. Not if you don't see any signs that it was anything else.'

'I don't. I examined the body closely – there were no wounds, no needle marks or punctures – with the scarring of his flesh from the wild card virus, it'd be difficult to puncture in any case – no obvious broken boncs, and no signs of poisoning. What little bruising there was is consistent with a fall onto a stone floor, which is where you both said he was found.' Finn's shoulders rose and fell. 'He was old; he had a dodgy heart. In my opinion, that's what took him.'

'Don't worry about the authorities,' Jago told Gary and Finn. 'I'll handle the bureaucracy; I've already made a call to Genn Truscott, who's the DS at the police station and a good friend. I'll make a call to the local Member of Parliament; she's also a friend of mine. There won't be any trouble getting Duncan's body released; Gary can take him back to Rathlin for interment tomorrow. I'll also have the local funeral home deliver a casket for the boat ride home – unless you'd rather I had the body flown back?'

'No,' Gary told him. 'We'll escort him back. That's what he'd want.'

Jago nodded. 'I understand. I'll have Hitchcock clear out one of the freezers downstairs in the kitchen so we can place the body there overnight. The funeral home will come over tomorrow morning.'

'I'll sew a shroud to cover him before you do that,' Jeremy said. 'There's a bolt of fabric in my room that would serve nicely, if you don't mind, Lord Branok. I can have it done in an hour. Less if need be.'

'Excellent. I'll have someone send up a few other suitable bolts to your room, just in case. Was Duncan religious at all? I can have the vicar come from the village to give a blessing.'

'Thank you, though Duncan never attended any church in all the time I've known him,' Gary said. 'But I'd like to go in and sit with Duncan for a while.'

'Absolutely. If you don't mind, I'll also sit with you for a bit.'

Dr Finn had covered the body with a sheet. Gary pulled it down until he could see Duncan's virus-savaged face. Gary stared at his friend, feeling hot tears welling in his eyes. He blinked them away until he could see the face clearly again.

'Damn it, Duncan,' he said. 'This wasn't supposed to happen. Maybe this *wouldn't* have happened if you'd taken better care of yourself. I should have made you do that. This was largely my fault for bringing you here when in my gut, I knew better.'

Gary felt Jago's hand on his shoulder, though it fell away quickly. 'You're not responsible for this,' Jago said. 'Duncan made the choice to ignore his condition. His body, his choice, remember? Morwen's attack is what sent him into cardiac arrest, not you.'

Gary stared down at Duncan's face. It blurred once more in his vision. 'I was his friend. I should have pushed him harder to get help, to take medicine that might have prevented this. I should have insisted.'

'Yes, you were his friend,' Jago repeated. 'Don't you think that if you *had* pushed him harder, you might have also pushed him away and lost that friendship?'

Gary put his hand under the sheet and found Duncan's hand. His flesh was cold, like touching a piece of marble, while his own hand was so warm. *If I could give you some of my warmth, would that bring you back?* Gary squeezed Duncan's hand; there was, of course, no response. 'Have you lost family, Jago? Lost friends?'

'Everyone who lives long enough ends up losing people they love,' Jago answered. 'Just look at yourself and your fellow house guests if you want examples. Your wife died because of what the virus did to her, while your stepdaughter drew the black queen. Dr Finn has lost several friends, family members, and patients over the years. Cosmos lost his partner Chaos before they could reconcile. Roger Ravenstone's parents, like your Moira, drew the black queen. You're surrounded by loss here.'

Gary released Duncan's hand and turned to Jago. 'What about Merryn? She could still be alive, couldn't she?'

Jago shrugged. 'She might be,' he admitted. 'Somewhere. But if she is, it's not in the world we inhabit.'

'I don't understand.'

'No, you don't. But you might one day.'

'What about *you*, Jago?' Gary asked. 'Who have you lost?'

There was a long hesitation, and Gary thought Jago wasn't going to answer, that he'd say something typically cryptic and leave the room. But instead, Jago only cleared his throat. Behind his mask, his eyes glistened. 'Like you, Gary, I lost my wife and my daughter. Long ago, in a bombing. It's something I try not to remember, but I saw their bodies in the rubble . . .' His lips pressed together, and it was several seconds before he spoke again. 'Those are terrible images that will never leave me. I also know that there's nothing anyone can say or do that will ease the pain or make those memories go away, no matter how good their intentions.'

Gary could only nod at that. 'I remember, too: Caitlyn's final breaths, the horror of watching Moira die in my arms and being helpless to save her. I sometimes wish I *were* a believer, so that I might imagine that they're now in a better place.' He gave a bitter laugh. 'But I don't believe that. I can't.'

'I don't believe that either,' Jago replied. 'Perhaps for different reasons. All any of us can do is make what compromises we can with what remains of our lives. I have. I believe you will also.'

Sunday

Ceallaigh knocked on his door, then entered, holding a breakfast tray. Gary was on the balcony in his bathrobe, looking out on the lawn and the broken clouds scudding across the sky; he glanced at Caitlyn's watch as he heard the knock: ten o'clock. Jago had said that the funeral directors would come to transport Duncan down to Cody's boat around eleven.

Ceallaigh came onto the balcony, still wearing her mask, and set the breakfast tray down on the table there. She looked at Gary's stitched face, her eyes widening slightly. 'That must hurt terribly,' she said.

'It's worse than it looks, but the painkillers Bradley – Dr Finn – gave me are working,' he told her. 'Dr Finn said the facial swelling would go down in a few days, and that I should have a local doctor take out the stitches in a week or so. He said there might be some mild scarring, but . . .' Gary shrugged. 'Do I look a horror?'

'No,' Ceallaigh answered softly. 'You look very lucky, sir. You could have easily lost an eye.' She lifted the silver cover from the breakfast tray. 'Black tea, a scone with clotted cream, one egg over-easy, buttered toast, and fruit. So . . . I understand there's a possibility you might be staying on here at Loveday House?' Her eyebrows lifted in question above the mask.

'Jago asked me if I might want to do that.'

'And do you?'

Gary hesitated. 'I don't know,' he said. 'I'm . . . Well, I don't know quite *what* I'm feeling. Confused, I suppose. Conflicted.'

'Do you have family or close friends back on Rathlin? Or somewhere else?'

Once I did: on Rathlin, in New York City. Now . . . 'No. Not really.'

'Then maybe here's as good a place as any. Why not at least talk to Lord Branok? Some of our guests have taken their breakfast and already left. I'll ask him to come up.'

'I don't want to bother him.'

'I'm sure he won't mind.' With that, Ceallaigh went inside. He heard her lift the telephone and speak to someone. 'I'll tell him,' he heard Ceallaigh say, and a moment later, the woman poked her head out from the room. 'Lord Jago will be up directly,' she told Gary, then went back inside. He heard the door to the room open and close again.

A few minutes later, there was another knock.

'The food isn't to your liking?' Jago asked, glancing at the breakfast tray as he stepped out onto the balcony.

'It's fine. I'm just not particularly hungry.'

Jago pulled up the remaining wrought iron chair on the balcony and sat next to Gary. 'My offer still stands,' he said. When Gary glanced over at the man, he wasn't looking at Gary but out towards the lawn and the landscape beyond.

'I appreciate that.'

'But?'

'What really happened last night?' Gary asked him. 'Did I actually see Caitlyn, Moira, and Duncan? Did I *really* encounter Lady Morwen the Mad, who supposedly died centuries ago?'

There was a soft, reserved chuckle from Jago. 'Your face answers the last question for you. As to the former, do you *believe* you actually saw your wife and daughter?'

Gary shook his head. 'I . . . I don't *know*.'

'I've told you that there are no ghosts here in Loveday House,' Jago said. 'But whether you believe that or not, the decision to go or stay is still yours to make. For now, you should dress, pack if you think that's necessary, and come downstairs. Hitchcock's having some of the staff bring Duncan up in his casket, and the hearse should be here soon to take you, Jeremy, and Duncan down to the harbour. I've cleared everything with the Cornish authorities as well as those in Northern Ireland. There shouldn't be any issues with you escorting Duncan back home.'

He rose from his chair and nodded down to Gary. 'Whatever you choose to do, I consider it an honour to have met you.'

Gary had called Codman Cody earlier to let him know what had happened, but he could see Cody, Lorcan, and Lucan staring with shocked disbelief as the funeral director and his assistant slid the bronze casket from the hearse and placed it on the wheeled casket carrier. They rolled the casket solemnly down the gangway and onto the boat. Jeremy and Gary walked slowly behind it. Cody's eyes widened further as he looked at Gary's bruised and stitched face, though he said nothing.

'Lorcan, Lucan, secure poor Duncan in the back of the wheelhouse,' Cody said. 'We'd never get that casket down the stairs. Then get one of the tarpaulins to put over it, though I doubt that at this point if Duncan will care one way or t'other if it gets a little wet.'

Afterwards, the funeral director and his assistants turned to go, leaving the casket carrier on the boat. 'Lord Branok said you'll likely need it when you get to Rathlin,' the funeral director added before he left. 'He's paid for everything, so it's no worry.'

As Lorcan and Lucan escorted Jeremy below, Cody put his hand on Gary's shoulder. 'This ain't how any of us expected to be going back when we came here. I'm so sorry, Gary. We've all lost a good friend.'

'I know.' Gary looked up to where Loveday House loomed above Keun Island. He set his rucksack down on the deck at his feet. He'd come to the harbour with the full intention of accompanying Duncan back to Rathlin. *It's the right thing to do – my last trip with a good friend. And I could stay on Rathlin for the rest of my life in the old cottage, surrounded by memories.*

Yet as he gazed up at Loveday, he remembered seeing Duncan with Caitlyn and Moira in Loveday House, in the main room of his cottage back home – in a room that couldn't possibly have existed in the halls of Loveday. He also remembered Caitlyn's remonstration to him when he tried to go to them: *This isn't for you yet, Gary. It may be, one day, but not yet . . .*

'I suppose we should be startin' back,' he heard Cody say now. 'The weather report's good this afternoon; we should be back on Rathlin soon enough, an' then we can put Duncan to his final rest and have a bloody grand wake for him afterwards. The whole island will come, don't'cha think?'

Gary nodded. He heard Cody moving towards the wheelhouse. 'Lorcan, Lucan, get your arses back up here. Ship the gangway, an' loose the lines. We're leavin'.' The diesel engine of the boat grumbled into life, water gurgling at the rear of the boat as Lorcan and Lucan started to pull in the aluminium gangway.

'Cody,' Gary called out. 'Wait.'

The engine died, and Cody poked his head out from the wheelhouse. 'Gary?'

'I'm . . . I'm not finished here,' Gary told him. 'You and Jeremy take Duncan back. I'll get back to Rathlin on my own, but it might be a day or two yet.'

'Yeh sure about this?' Cody asked.

'I am. Sorry.' With that, Gary picked up his pack, swung it onto his back, and stepped off the boat and onto the dock. Lorcan, Lucan, and Jeremy nodded to him silently, and pulled up the fenders protecting the side of the boat as Cody restarted the engine. Gary watched as the *Fear na Gcrúb* slowly left its slip and puttered towards the end of the pier. Gary waved at Cody, who waved back.

When the boat left the mouth of the harbour for the open sea, Gary turned away. He shrugged his rucksack into a more comfortable position and started walking up the slope towards Loveday House.

The house seemed to pull him towards itself more strongly with every step. It also didn't quite look the same to him as it had the first time he'd seen it on Friday – there seemed to be more turrets, and the supporting side towers appeared taller than he remembered. As the crushed seashells of Loveday House's driveway ground together beneath his shoes, he wondered if he'd been seeing it wrong all along.

There are no ghosts in Loveday House, Jago had insisted, but there were mysteries within Loveday, and those mysteries had wrapped their enigmas around Gary, binding him in their tendrils. *People bring their own answers here to Loveday House,* Jago had also said. Gary wondered if that were true, and if so, what answers he was holding within himself.

He strode up the steps, but before he reached the doors, Jago himself pushed them open. His eyes glittered behind his mask. 'Pleased to see you again, Gary,' he said.

Ceallaigh was also just inside, standing at the foot of the grand staircase. She was unmasked, her brilliant eyes the deep colour of Irish grass watching him.

'Go on,' Gary heard Jago say behind him.

Gary walked slowly towards Ceallaigh, not daring to reach out for her but only examining her face with his gaze. He had thought he'd find Caitlyn's face gazing back at him, but while there was some resemblance, he saw now that there were far more differences. *The deep lines around her eyes, around the corners of her mouth, on her forehead; the way expressions move so easily across her face. She looks much older than Caitlyn ever looked . . .*

'You're not her,' he managed to say.

'No, I'm not,' she answered. 'I understand what you wanted, but I'm not her. I'm just me. Ceallaigh. I'm sorry, Mr Bushorn.'

'Gary. Please. And there's no reason to apologize.' Gary managed a huff of amusement and self-deprecation. He pulled out Caitlyn's pocket watch and held it in his hand. They both looked down at it in his palm. 'I still have her and Moira. Duncan, too. They're here—' He slipped the watch back into his pocket '—and here.' He tapped his forehead. 'They're wherever I am as long as I remember them.'

Ceallaigh smiled at that. She cupped Gary's face gently in her hands, her eyes holding him. 'And you're here now,' she said. Her hands fell away again. 'Gary.'

With a nod, Ceallaigh turned and began climbing up the staircase.

Gary felt Jago's arm on his shoulder. 'I'm sure you must be hungry after the walk back here. Let's have some lunch, you and I.' His hand still on Gary's shoulder, Jago began walking the two of them towards the drawing room. 'We can celebrate your decision while we talk about what you might wish to do here at Loveday House. Welcome home, Gary.'

Longing for Those Lost

by Stephen Leigh

Part II

LUNCH FOR GARY WAS another bowl of Chef Daniel's splendid seafood chowder, as well as some crusty fresh-baked bread slathered with local butter, though thinking of Duncan diminished the taste of the chowder. Jago's own lunch was light: a salad and a clear soup with thin-sliced mushrooms bathing placidly in the broth like lily pads in a pond. Neither Gary nor Jago paid much attention to their food. Gary took a few spoonfuls of the chowder and set the spoon on the plate under his bowl; Jago, masked as usual, picked at his salad as he gazed at Gary across the table. Behind Jago, through the room's windows, Gary could see the grounds' crew busily at work trimming the grass and bushes around Loveday.

Gary lifted a hand to point at the stitches on his face. 'Ghosts shouldn't be able do this,' he said.

Jago nodded in agreement. 'They shouldn't, and they can't.'

'Then what is Mad Lady Morwen, if not a ghost?'

Jago took a long, slow spoonful of his broth. 'For you to know that, I'll need to tell you more about Loveday House and me.'

Gary waited, silent, as Jago savoured another spoonful, and Gary wondered if the man was going to answer.

Then Jago dabbed at his mouth with his napkin, setting down the spoon. His gaze found Gary's. 'There are no ghosts here,' he repeated. 'Loveday House, despite its reputation, is not haunted.' Another pause, then, 'Loveday House also isn't sentient. The house can sense your dreams and desires, yes, but it has no conscious thoughts, at least not in the way we think of them. You saw your wife and daughter last night, did you not?'

Gary nodded.

'That was Loveday responding to your thoughts and emotions,' Jago continued. 'The stronger those are, the more tangible the images Loveday sends you.'

'But I certainly didn't think about Mad Morwen or wish she'd attack me.

Yet she was also extremely tangible.' Gary touched the stitches once more for emphasis.

Jago gave Gary a small smile. 'That's the second part of what I need to explain to you. There are infinite worlds we can't see: other dimensions, alternate worlds where every possible version of this one exists – all the paths history never took in our world. Even time isn't necessarily the same there: it might run far slower, or faster, even run backwards. Go to one of those worlds, and you could be back in the 1300s or thrust forward into an alternate 2300. One of those worlds could have resulted when you chose to go left instead of right – and your life inevitably changed as a result.' Jago tapped a finger on the tablecloth. 'For instance, in one of those worlds, at some point Duncan chose, or was persuaded – maybe even by you – to see his doctor. He received medication, treatment, or surgery, and is still alive.'

'The butterfly effect,' Gary said. 'Like in Bradbury's story "A Sound of Thunder". I read that long ago: step on a butterfly back in the Cretaceous and you change the entire future of your world. But assuming I even believe what you say about these alternate dimensions, what does all of this have to do with Loveday?'

'There are places in our world where the walls between those alternate dimensions are very thin. If you find one of those places, it's sometimes possible to move from one world to the next . . . and the next and the next and the next.' Jago had picked up his fork, spearing a leaf of lettuce with every *next*. His gaze searched Gary's. 'Loveday House is one of those places,' Jago said. He lifted the fork, then put it down once more. 'I was infected with the wild card virus on the *Queen Mary*. Eventually, I discovered my ace. I can sense those other dimensions, those alternate realities. I can open doors into them, though I don't always know what's behind them. And Loveday House has many, many doors, as you know.'

Gary's eyes widened, the movement pulling at his stitches. He put a hand to his face. 'Ouch,' he muttered.

'You're healing quickly, Gary. The swelling's gone down visibly since last night, and your cuts are starting to close and fade.'

'I'm lucky that way,' Gary said. 'So, you're claiming Mad Morwen's still alive behind one of Loveday's doors, in one of those other dimensions? And she can leave that dimension for ours?'

'Not completely. And Morwen's not just behind one door. There is some . . . well, let's call it "leakage". Doors and even entire rooms do move around within Loveday House. Not only that, but there are more Lady Morwens inhabiting Loveday than the one you encountered: different versions of the same woman from other realities. I've met a dozen Mad Morwens here in Loveday, none of them particularly friendly. They all believe Loveday belongs to them and them alone.'

Gary touched his face once more, a finger tracing the stitched cuts Morwen

– his Morwen, anyway – had inflicted. 'That sounds dangerous. No wonder you tell your guests not to go wandering through Loveday.'

'I also seal off any doors behind which I find her lurking,' Jago answered. 'But there are many doors in Loveday and sometimes more than one way in or out of them, and there are often things behind them that are a danger. I'm certain there are other Morwens I have yet to find . . . and worse things as well.'

'Then why stay here in Loveday if it's so potentially dangerous?'

'Because those portals also hold potential gifts and treasures. Gary, you found your family here, didn't you? I found Ceallaigh by entering one of Loveday's portals, as I found nearly all of my staff.' Jago smiled under his mask. 'Loveday House often does give more than it takes. My guests are generally quite safe and comfortable as long as they stay in the "finished" areas of the house. Ask Ceallaigh or Hitchcock if you don't believe that.'

Jago took a few bites of his salad. When he finished, Gary could see that his attention had now shifted to another topic. 'Gary, have you thought about what you might want to do here at Loveday House? I wonder if Hitchcock might not have room for another under-butler, or perhaps someone to keep the library in order, or . . .' Jago gave the flash of a smile. 'Maybe you could be the dance master and teach our guests guise dancing. That seemed to go down well.'

Gary's eyebrows lifted higher, and the stitches pulled again. 'These are going to need to come out soon.' He sighed. 'Dance master? I'm not qualified. At all.'

'You move well enough, better than some people much younger than you, and you'll have sufficient time to learn several of the dances before our next set of guests arrive. Ceallaigh and quite a few of the rest of the staff also know the basic dances and can partner you; you'd enjoy that, wouldn't you? Yes, dance master sounds perfect. I'll telephone Richard Darke; he's the leader of the Turkey Rhubarb Band in Penzance. He's close enough, and Horace – the young man who chauffeured you up here on Friday – can drive you to and from their studio. Richard can give you lessons and teach you the steps for several of the dances. You needn't worry; our guests aren't likely to know guise dancing at all, so you'll seem an expert to them. You'd also be in charge of the music room and ballroom, though you can have staff members help you there. "Dance Master Bushorn" has a nice ring to it, don't you think? It's a role that will serve Loveday House well. You can continue to stay in the room you already have without charge, meals included, and we will negotiate a salary to your satisfaction. I think that would be perfect. Are you willing to give it a go?'

Gary didn't know what it was that made him answer. The taste of the chowder . . . the sunlight on Loveday's lawn . . . the memories of the weekend . . . seeing Caitlyn and Moira . . . Ceallaigh's touch on his arm . . .

'Yes.' The affirmation slipped out before he could stop it. 'But Duncan's funeral . . .'

'Not an issue. I've used an excellent helicopter pilot down here; I'll arrange for him to fly you over there and back. Your friend's boat won't get back to Rathlin for another day or so – call him when it does, find out when the burial will be, and I'll set things up with the pilot. So . . . does Loveday House have a new dance master?'

'All right,' Gary said. 'I'll do my best.'

'That's all I ever expect from my staff.' Jago extended his hand across the table. Gary took it; Jago's grip was firm and solid.

They shook hands.

The next day, Jago sent for Keun's doctor to take out Gary's stitches. 'Dr Thomas Quiller, sir,' Hitchcock announced as the doctor was shown into the front drawing room. The doctor was a short and elderly man. Like Nigel Walmsley and Mrs Penhollow, Dr Quiller also had the odd 'fishy' look of a native Keun inhabitant.

The doctor wasted little time. He set his battered leather bag down on the nearest side table with a brief, silent nod to Jago. He examined Gary's face and arms from behind a pair of round eyeglasses that made his already bulbous eyes appear even larger, giving the occasional 'hmm' or 'ahh'. From the bag, he produced a pair of scissors and tweezers. 'Looks like decent enough work, and your cuts are nicely healed already,' he said. 'Frankly, these stitches could have been removed days ago. How long have they been in?'

'It's been a day and a half now,' Gary answered, to which the doctor gave an audible huff of disbelief.

'My dance master is a very fast healer,' Jago commented.

The doctor gave them both sceptical glances, but set to work, snipping and pulling out the threads. 'Just send your bill to me as usual, Doctor,' Jago told Quiller as the man was packing away his instruments.

The doctor nodded to Jago as he tightened the leather strap around the bag and gave a final glance at Gary.

'Fast healer,' he muttered as Hitchcock arrived to show him to the door. 'Bollocks.'

Jago rose from his chair with a faint smile prowling his lips. 'That's one task done,' he said, opening the door of the room. 'Now, it's time I formally introduce you to the staff of Loveday. You're one of them now, after all. Hitchcock's already gathered the house staff.'

There were at least twenty-five people crowded on and around the grand staircase in the hall, all of them in the uniforms of the maids or the liveried footmen. Ceallaigh was among them; she was the only one whose name Gary knew, though he recognized some faces from having seen them over the weekend. Gary smiled at Ceallaigh as Jago continued to speak.

'You already know Hitchcock. The young man to his right is Elbrekt, our under-butler; the woman to Hitchcock's left is Madame Amélie, our house-keeper. These other gentlemen and ladies are our illustrious footmen and maids, without whom this house wouldn't long survive.'

'Please don't give me all their names now,' Gary said. 'I'll never remember them, though I'm sure I'll come to know them all in time.'

There was polite laughter at that from the group. Jago gave a sweeping gesture towards Gary. 'Everyone,' he said, 'this is our new dance master, Gary Bushorn. He's joining our staff as of today, so please make him feel welcome.'

A barrage of applause echoed in the hall, and Gary, embarrassed, lifted his hands. 'Thank you all,' he said, 'but the ovation's hardly necessary. I'll need the help of each of you getting to know Loveday House, so all I'll ask is that you be patient with me.'

Jago nodded in agreement. 'Well said. Now that you know Dance Master Bushorn, I trust all of you will help him to feel comfortable here over the coming weeks. Now, you may all return to your rooms or to whatever duties Hitchcock and Madame Amélie have given you for today,' Jago told them.

With that and a loud rustling of clothing, the house staff dispersed.

For the rest of the day, Gary toured the house with Jago. He met the kitchen staff, which included Chef Daniel Ott ('Chef, I have to tell you that your seafood chowder is by far the best I've ever tasted . . .'), the sous-chefs, station chefs, prep help, and dishwashers. Then there was the grounds staff, also in charge of the orangery and greenhouse, with Annie as the head groundskeeper and her several assistants; the garage staff headed by Horace, the regular chauffeur, along with a few assistant drivers and mechanics. They visited the stables so Jago could introduce Gary to Tobias Müller, the stablemaster, and his staff.

By mid-afternoon, Gary's head was whirling with half-remembered names and faces, and he was glad when Jago pleaded that he had duties to which he had to attend and suggested Gary should return to his room and rest before dinner.

When Gary opened the door to his room, he noticed that his rucksack lay empty on his bed; his clothes had been taken out and placed, neatly folded, into his dresser drawers, which were still open. Ceallaigh was in his bathroom, restocking it with new towels and flannels. His bathrobe, freshly laundered, was hanging on a hook there. 'Ceallaigh,' he called out. 'You're not my maid any more. I can get my own towels and all; you just have to show me where.'

'So, you're intendin' to sack me, then?' Ceallaigh asked. 'Have I done somethin' to offend the new dance master?'

'No, of course not,' Gary answered in a rush, then saw the smile, so much like Caitlyn's, on her face. 'Ah. You're pulling my leg.'

'Guilty as charged. But Madame Amélie has given me the responsibility for this room, so I remain the dance master's maid.' The smile vanished, to be replaced by a frown. 'Unless you'd prefer another maid to fill that duty for you. If you're not happy with me, I could suggest Madame Amélie assign you to Isolde or Colette or Zoe . . .'

'No. Not at all. Not necessary,' Gary said, cutting off her litany of names.

Ceallaigh laughed, a gentle chuckle. 'That's good. There is one thing, though.'

'What's that?'

'Now that you're considered staff, you'll be takin' meals at the tables below stairs, with Hitchcock and the rest of the house staff. You wouldn't mind sitting next to me tonight, would you, especially since you're new to everything right now? I know the routines and everyone's name and what they do here at Loveday House.'

'Only if you'll also tell me how *you* came to be here.'

A nod. 'Aye. I can do that.'

'Then I'll look forward to it.'

Ceallaigh's face went serious. 'I'll come up at seven to take you down for dinner, then.' A pause. He heard her take a breath. 'Gary.'

When Ceallaigh returned at seven, her maid's uniform was gone, replaced by jeans and a jumper over a white T-shirt. Dinner was a pleasant hour or more, if a bit on the loud side with everyone talking in the servants' hall, their voices echoing from the high ceiling and plaster-and-lathwork walls. Gary was surprised at the number of languages and accents he heard from the diverse staff. With everyone seated at tables in one large hall, there was no sense of privacy – though the food was wonderful. Gary kept his conversational questions light, though he was always aware of Ceallaigh's presence near his side.

After dinner, Ceallaigh walked Gary back up to the grand staircase that led to his room. Once there, she paused. 'You know where you're going now, do you not?' she said.

'I do. Thanks – I think I would've been a little lost trying finding my own way back to here from below stairs, but I'll remember from now on.'

'That's grand. Thanks for sitting with me tonight and letting me introduce you to some of our tablemates. I trust you'll remember their names?'

'I enjoyed it, and I'll remember *some* of their names,' Gary told her with a rueful smile. 'Though . . .'

Ceallaigh cocked her head at that. 'Though?'

'Earlier, I mentioned that I'd like to know how you came to be here at Loveday, and you said you'd tell me. I'd still like to hear that tale. And I have that Redbreast you brought me up in my room, and I hate to drink alone.' He looked at his pocket watch. 'It's not that late.'

Ceallaigh took a step back from him, her mouth slightly open as if she were trying to decide how to respond.

'Oh . . .' Gary exclaimed quickly. He could feel his skin growing hot. 'It's not . . . It's been far too many years since I've ever . . .' Gary released all the air in his lungs in one loud exhalation. 'Ceallaigh, I'm just a stupid old man. I honestly meant nothing more than I'd like to hear your story if you're willing share it with me.' He saw her watching as a tendril of smoke emerged from the left cuff of his shirt. He pressed his right hand against it, snuffing out the flame. 'I'm sorry, Ceallaigh. When I get embarrassed, I can run too warm, and I'm well beyond embarrassed at the moment. I wasn't trying to suggest anything more than a chat between two friends. I didn't mean to imply that I expected anything more than that.' He shook his head and ran agitated fingers over his grey and thinning hair. 'Just forget I said anything.'

'Gary.' She pressed her fingers against his forearm, then pulled them back quickly with a grimace. She cradled the hand to her waist. 'I'm sorry, too, if I misinterpreted what you were sayin'. I do enjoy your company, and you're not stupid or too old. In fact . . .' She stopped, her face flushed, her arms tightening around herself. 'Let's just leave it at that. Tonight, you'll have t'drink your Redbreast alone or not at all. I'll tell you my story sometime, too. Just not tonight. We broke the mood, I'm afraid.'

Gary managed to smile at that. 'We did indeed. But if you ever need a dram of Redbreast, you know where to find one.'

She returned the smile, and Gary felt his body cool. 'That I do. I'll see you tomorrow. After all, I'm still your maid.'

The next few weeks were the busiest of Gary's life in many years. There was little time for anything but his quick trip over to Rathlin to attend Duncan's funeral and the glorious, loud wake the island held for him, trips into the town for dance lessons, memorizing steps, practising them with Ceallaigh and the musicians among the staff, and learning the main rooms, corridors, and vital places of Loveday (at least where they could *usually* be found).

Just when Gary thought he might be able to take a breath, Jago announced that there would be another party with several guests in two weeks. Gary, like the rest of the staff, was swept up in the preparations in his role as dance master and MC for the guise dancing and other musical entertainments (a role, Gary learned, that Jago was pleased to give up): organizing practices; learning to set up and use the sound system in the ballroom; testing the equipment to make certain it was all in working order with backup systems for the inevitable breakdowns; consulting with the servants to determine where best to place chairs and tables for the guests in the ballroom; doing the same for the music room, where more intimate concerts would take place throughout the party days; working with the graphic designers and printers on the staff to create pamphlets for each performance; consulting with Jago, Hitchcock, Madame Amélie, and Elbrekt to coordinate between the five of them what the House staff needed to accomplish, which staff members needed to be flexible to cover all the activities, the timetable and scheduling necessary to do all that; and so on.

Gary went to bed exhausted at the end of every day, yet overall satisfied at what had been accomplished and pleased with the way everyone in Loveday House cooperated to bring it all together. Working with Hitchcock was a special pleasure; the man was a consummate genius at creating order out of chaos and seemed to know more about the workings of Loveday than anyone – with the possible exception of Jago himself.

Lying in his bed on Constance's fireproof sheets, Gary wondered what tomorrow would bring as the guests finally arrived. Jago had told Gary who would be coming. Gary had heard some of the names before, but not all of them, though he didn't know any of them personally. From what he could tell, the guest list Jago had rattled off to the staff consisted of mostly aces. They differed from Gary's party companions, who all uniformly had been jokers, even if Dr Finn was more widely known.

Gary remembered Duncan's comment about aces: . . . *havin' no aces around sits fine with me. I don't need no one sneerin' down their ace nose at me . . .* – Thinking of poor Duncan caused a few tears to trickle down Gary's cheeks, steaming and evaporating before they reached his chin.

Gary sniffed and wiped at his face with the back of his hand.

Aces aren't so different from jokers, he thought to Duncan's memory. *Some of the aces I've met were more screwed up than any joker.*

Gary checked to make sure his alarm was set, then turned off the light on his bedside table. It wasn't long before sleep claimed Gary, and images of his years on Rathlin Island filled his dreams.

Lady Sri Extricates Herself, Emerging Not Entirely Unscathed

by Mary Anne Mohanraj

THE WEEKEND'S ADVENTURE STARTED so well – sun shining, birds chirping, everything blissful in the way it only is when you're young, reasonably good-looking, and quite comfortable in the financial arena. Who could have predicted that it would all fall apart so quickly? Not me, certainly.

We'd stopped in a rather charming antique shop on our way to Loveday House; Reggie and I had been invited to a mysterious house party. He'd been inclined to decline the invitation, perfectly content to continue rusticating with his horse and hounds. But after three months, I'd had rather enough of English country life and was clamouring for a morsel of entertainment. Since Reggie had flat out refused to take me to London again anytime soon – I had to admit, my misadventures on our last visit had got a trifle out of hand, and it would likely take some time for that poor policeman to forget my face – I begged him to accept this invitation instead. Eventually, I wore the man down.

'Oh, look at this tiara,' Reggie said admiringly, holding it up to glint in the light. 'This is rather fine. Would look quite smashing with that aquamarine sari, don't you think, the one with the silver trim?'

Reggie has impeccable taste, which is some compensation for a host of more irritating traits. The sparkling blue and silver creation he held in one long-fingered hand would set off my black hair rather well. 'I'd have to wear my hair up for the proper effect,' I noted.

'Even better,' Reggie said, smiling. 'Then everyone can admire your horn as we dance.'

When my card turned, a few years ago, it had left me with two gifts. The first had taken some getting used to: a curving horn that rose from the back of my neck, gleaming ivory. It reminded me of a jackal's horn, from the ancient legend of the *nari comboo*; such horns were supposed to bring good luck in a variety of forms, though it certainly hadn't seemed like luck at first.

In Mumbai, I'd mainly kept the horn hidden under my hair, as the sight of it greatly distressed my parents, but since coming to the UK, I'd taken to revealing it on occasion. It was rather fun, shocking natives with the horn as I walked down High Street on Lord Reginald's arm. They didn't know what to make of me.

With the horn came my second gift, my power, which had led me to this little shop, and to the tiara that Reginald was now settling on my head. It landed with a click of rightness, and the sense of relief that I felt with a good finding. A little wave of tiredness, too; it always took something out of me. The shopkeeper obligingly held up a mirror, and I nodded in satisfaction.

I hadn't been searching for anything in particular this time, but occasionally, I 'found' lost items anyway, and they often proved useful. I didn't know who had lost this, but perhaps its owner would turn up.

In the meantime, the piece would be of more use decorating my head than sitting in the shop. 'Wrap it up, please.' And, seeing that a pair of cuff links had caught Reggie's eye, glinting with star sapphires that matched the gems in the tiara, 'And those as well, please.'

Reggie's eyes brightened; it took so little to make him happy. If only we could have stayed that way, blissful in our ignorance!

Now, I don't really think I can be blamed for all this *fol-de-rol*, no matter what Reggie says. It all started back home in Mumbai, and if pressed, I must point the finger at Aunty Anu for landing us in this mess.

I was gliding along quite gracefully, dividing my time between studies at university and a rather entertaining sampling of all Mumbai's nightlife has to offer a young lady of means – which is quite a bit more than her parents or aunties might suspect. Trying to keep my love affairs untangled and out of the gossip rags was honestly so time-consuming that I hardly had a moment to keep up with my studies. That, I'm afraid, was my fatal error. My failing grades attracted the attention of my otherwise fairly absent father, and when it became known that I was in danger of flunking out of university altogether, there was much righteous thundering in our uptown flat.

Matters devolved from there. My dearest mother was normally the most indulgent and kind-hearted of creatures, who could deny nothing to her only child. Well, she became convinced that, without a solid degree, I would never find a mate on the feverish Mumbai marriage market. There was much weeping and wailing, enough to set a daughter's teeth on edge and make her contemplate packing a suitcase and fleeing to the States, hoping a kindly cousin might take her in.

Still, I'm confident that, with a little time and assiduous application of energies, I could have recovered the situation. My mother has always been susceptible to my various persuasions, and as for my father – he'd forgotten the entire affair by the time his lunchtime biryani was served.

Unfortunately, that was when Aunty Anu stepped in. She has always had far too much influence on my mother, her youngest sister – the youngest of nine, so as you can see, I have a plethora of aunts overly involved in my daily business – and she said, I quote, 'Your daughter, Srilatha, is on the path to ruin! If you don't find her a husband ASAP, the girl is undoubtedly bound for a life of degradation and despair!'

They started parading the most appalling lot of ineligible bachelors in front of me that you can imagine, and in order not to break my poor mother's heart, I was forced to swathe myself in yards of sari, bedeck myself with the contents of her jewellery box, and bite my tongue, so as to give the appearance of a properly brought up young lady. You can imagine how long that was likely to last!

I made it three weeks, which I have to say is a testament to my character and strength of will, the legacy of the Chelliahs for generations untold. Finally, though, I broke. When faced with the last in a string of unimpressive young men, I made my excuses and fled to my friend Rupa, who has always been able to extricate me from my worst scrapes.

Now, how does all that lead to me standing on the steps of Loveday House in jolly old England, with a handsome lord on my arm? I can only plead temporary insanity.

I arrived at Rupa's flat in rather a desperate state and laid the whole thing out for her. Rupa listened with the gravest attention, while simultaneously sewing at frantic speed on her machine, undoubtedly creating one of those marvellous constructions for which she was famous throughout the city. You can see just from that what a brilliant mind she must have, and you will understand why I put myself entirely in Rupa's hands.

'The solution is obvious, my dear,' she said, as she bent over an intricate bit of embroidery.

'Oh yes?' I had downed three cups of chai and at least a dozen biscuits by that point and was feeling somewhat fortified, ready to hear what the clever girl had come up with.

She spooled more golden thread onto the machine, her brow furrowed in glorious thought. 'The simplest solution to your dilemma is to get married.'

I became quite alarmed. 'No, you must be unwell.' Rupa couldn't be herself, to be so confused. Even though I felt quite panicked at the thought, I kept my tone moderate and gentle, so as not to distress the poor creature. 'The goal here is to *not* get married.'

Rupa shook her head and started the machine going again, fingers flying. 'But don't you see? Once you're married, you'll be free to do as you please.'

Her words landed on me like a thunderclap. She was right, of course! It was only my unwed state that had landed me in this predicament. Once married, I'd no longer need to concern myself with weeping mothers, thundering fathers, or nosy aunts. For a moment, I felt I had risen to the heights of glory – but a moment later, I came crashing down to the depths of despair. There was a flaw in dear Rupa's plan – a rather nasty fly in the proverbial ointment, as they say.

I asked, 'But husbands can be rather controlling as well, can't they?'

She shrugged and with that shrug managed to convey utter confidence, such that I was already reassured. 'You need the right kind of husband, of course.' Rupa smiled, looking up from her silken fabric with a bright countenance. 'And by the greatest of coincidences – it must the fates themselves intervening, the stars aligning in your favour – I think I know just the chap. Have you met Lord Reginald?'

I had, in fact. He was visiting Mumbai for the season and had been attending all the best parties, but I hadn't exchanged two words with him. I admit, I mostly went to those parties only long enough to make a visible impression on the aunts in attendance, and then retreated to more congenial entertainment with my own crowd in the bars and nightclubs of the city.

Rupa continued, as her machine whirred on, 'Well, he is also under a great deal of pressure to marry and, presumably, secure the family line of succession.'

I knew his pain; my heart stirred in sympathy. Lately, my mother would *not* stop going on about all the grandchildren she thought I should hurry up and start producing; I confess, I found myself rather despising the creatures before they even arrived.

Rupa's voice dropped a register lower, and I leaned in towards her. 'Unfortunately, Reginald has absolutely no interest in settling down just yet, and – if you can keep a secret?'

I assured her that, of course, I was the soul of discretion. A Chelliah is wholeheartedly reliable.

'From what I've heard, Lord Reggie isn't positive he wants to settle down with a member of the female sex when the time finally does come. He says there's so much more that the world has to offer . . .'

'I would have to agree wholeheartedly,' I replied. My heart swelled in sympathy once more; clearly, this Reginald was a kindred soul. Indeed, the thought of being confined forever to the pleasures of one sex (not to mention, one person!) had weighed heavily on my own mind in the midst of all this marriage foofaraw.

Rupa continued, 'I'm afraid he hasn't had the courage to share that revelation with his own mother yet . . .'

'Say no more,' I put in excitedly. 'I see what you're getting at. If I were to marry Reggie . . .'

'It would solve both your problems; exactly,' Rupa replied. 'Your families would be delighted, and you could continue on your own merry ways.' She paused, then added discreetly, 'I gather that Lord Reggie's family, while rich in titles, is also slightly embarrassed of funds, and since your own family has done so well in the pickle business, and your mother would undoubtedly be thrilled at your acquiring a title . . .'

I was overcome with enthusiasm and gratitude. 'This is a brilliant plan and takes care of everything to perfection – providing Lord Reggie doesn't desire to secure the line of succession imminently? There's no need for any bothersome pregnancies and the like?'

'Oh, not for years,' Rupa said. 'Once you're married, take the appropriate precautions – that's between you and your doctor. After that, you can simply sigh and complain that you have not yet been blessed with such a happy event. The aunties will be forced to subside.'

'Smashing,' I said. I was on the verge of demanding she take me to him right that moment, but a sudden thought caused my heart to skip a beat. 'But stop. What if he – or even I – were to fall in love with someone else? You must admit, it could happen.' I couldn't deny that, in the past, after sportive play in the bedsheets, I had on occasion been overcome with fondness for my partner therein and had even fancied myself in love. All such passions had faded with the rising of the sun so far, but if one were to prove more steadfast . . .

'Oh, that is the simplest of things,' Rupa said airily. 'Should any difficulty arise, vis-à-vis one of you falling madly in love and being obliged to marry someone else for fear of a shattered heart – well, you and Reggie would simply get a divorce, spit-spot. Nothing could be easier.'

I had to admit, she'd addressed my every concern to the letter, and I could see no flaw in her plan. 'Let us go to him at once.'

Rupa smiled and whipped the fabric out of the machine. 'As soon as you change into this salwar blouse. Your own is tragically out of fashion, my dear; you should never try to dress yourself, you know. How many times have I told you?'

'I'm more than happy to put myself entirely in your hands.'

If only Rupa could have accompanied me to England, I would never have got into such a pickle. She had been my bosom companion throughout my childhood, the differences in our backgrounds never coming between us, but although I begged her to come with me, she demurred. 'I really can't leave the textile business now, when it's finally getting a little headway . . .'

Of course, I couldn't ask her to give up the chance at financial stability for my own selfish needs, so I nobly left for England on my own – or rather, accompanied by Reggie.

We'd had a glorious wedding in epic Mumbai style, but soon afterwards, he'd been summoned home by the pater ('You must learn how to manage the family affairs, now that you're finally settled down.'), so we'd packed up and headed off to the airport, where Rupa came to see me off.

'You'll have a husband to take care of you now, the gods grant him luck.

He'll need it!' Which seemed entirely unfair, as surely I was at least as likely to be taking care of Reggie?

Regardless, that brings us to our current adventures, or near enough. Married life had gone swimmingly at the start, and I was particularly pleased to discover that Lord Reginald was quite gifted in the bedchamber. That kept us occupied for quite some time. To cover everything else that happened in those first months would take far too long, given the urgency of our present circumstances, and besides, you might get the wrong impression of me. I often find that events are easily misinterpreted.

In truth, Reggie rather put a damper on my more interesting ideas. I thought it would be amusing to use my power to 'find' his mother's favourite pearls swimming in the cock-a-leekie soup, but Reginald was quite short with me about the idea. I'd thought he was more sporting than that! Marriage is not for the faint of heart, as Aunty Aarti always said. Aunty Aarti was one of the most terrifying of the aunts, not least because she had the annoying habit of generally being right.

The next challenge to my marriage arrived in an entirely unexpected form.

We were greeted by the impressive Hitchcock on our arrival at Loveday House. 'The master is occupied at present but will be down to greet you shortly; in the meantime, please join the other guests on the veranda for luncheon.'

Servants took away our luggage, and Hitchcock gestured us onwards.

We proceeded there apace, as we hadn't eaten since breakfast at the B&B at least two hours ago, and after all our walking up and down the narrow streets of the town, my poor stomach was feeling the need for some serious sustenance. I fell upon the buffet and quickly began loading up my plate with a rather glorious array of cold luncheon meats, cheese, baked pasties, pickled onions, and more – when a startled voice cut through the sea air like a knife: 'Reggie? Is that really you?'

A tall woman stood across the veranda, shading her eyes against the autumn sun. Ash-blonde hair, beautifully proportioned; I was struck by the thought that she would look *stunning* in a sari. My mother had always despaired of my figure, saying that I had too much at the front and too little at the back, and one reason why it was clear that Rupa was brilliant was that she somehow managed to create clothes for me that eliminated all such concerns.

'Steph?' Reggie said, incredulous. 'What are you doing here? Shouldn't you be off somewhere, being a world-class ace surgeon?'

She was hurrying over, practically throwing herself into my husband's embrace, and Reggie seemed happy enough to catch her. She was talking in a low voice now, and the wind from the sea caught her words and carried them away before they could make it to my ears. I couldn't help noticing that, plastered to his body, her form looked even better . . .

'Steph, I'm sorry.' Reginald was finally pulling back, looking flustered. 'I should introduce you – this is Srilatha, my wife.'

The woman looked flushed, perhaps embarrassed to be quite so close to Reginald. She took a step away, inclining her head. 'Pleased to meet you. I'd heard Reggie had got married in India.'

Reggie went on, 'Sri, this is Dr Stephanie Smithson, an old, dear friend.'

I smiled at the woman, showing my teeth. They were good teeth; my parents had made sure of that, though it had cost rather a small fortune. 'Any friend of Reggie's, Dr Smithson, is a friend of mine. I'm sure we shall grow to be great friends,' I said, though the truth was that a little coal seemed to have lodged itself in my chest, burning merrily away.

I was determined to ignore it, though. So what if Reginald had an old friend who was the cat's whiskers? At this close distance, the clear blue of her eyes and perfection of her features could not be missed or denied. We'd always said we would both be free in this marriage; that was the whole point of getting married, after all. I determined to give the two of them the privacy they so clearly were in need of.

'I think I'm not actually as hungry as I thought. And this food looks lovely, but perhaps a trifle bland for my tastes.' I put my plate down on a nearby table. 'I'm sure you'd both like to catch up, old friends and all that. I might just nip down to the kitchen, see if they have some chilli sauce on hand – the hotter the better. I'll be back in a trice!'

The doctor looked distressed. 'Lady Srilatha, I don't mean to drive you away!'

On closer examination, she seemed almost as if she was on the verge of tears. Maybe that was just the wind, irritating her eyes, but clearly, I would be right to give them some time alone. 'Not at all, not at all!'

She hesitated, then said, 'There is something I'd like to speak with Reggie about, and it's a rather personal matter . . .'

Personal, indeed! 'Say no more! Discretion above all is the code of the Chelliahs, and even though I did marry Reginald, I will be a Chelliah until I die.' That was something of a point of irritation with Reggie's mother, in fact, that I didn't use his name. Lady Srilatha Chelliah was apparently not quite correct, but she – and the rest of England – would just have to get used to it. 'I will away to the kitchens and return imminently!'

A brisk walk was a tonic against all ills, my father always said. I hurried away, boots clipping across the veranda tiles, careful not to turn and look back.

Hitchcock intercepted me as I left the veranda. 'Lady Srilatha, is there something I can do for you? You haven't eaten a bite.'

'I was just going to nip down to the kitchens and ask them for some chilli sauce—'

'I will send a servant . . .'

'No – please, Hitchcock.' I put a hand on his black-coated arm, and I cannot say what he saw in my eyes, but he seemed to understand the absolute necessity that I be the one to visit the kitchens.

'The house is very large and quite confusing to navigate; Lord Branok
would prefer guests not wander unaccompanied. Perhaps Tamsin might escort
you down?' He clicked his fingers, and a servant appeared quite suddenly at
his shoulder, a young woman with curly red hair, green eyes, and a sombre
mien – too sombre for one so young and fair, I thought, but perhaps she
carried a secret sorrow, as so many do.

'That would be lovely, thank you,' I said. It was a little bit of an obstacle
to my plans, I quickly realized, that I didn't actually know the way to the
kitchens, but luckily, Hitchcock was here to take care of the matter before
it emerged. He seemed almost as skilled as Rupa in that way – a sort of
preternatural instinct – and I was quite pleased to learn that Lord Branok
had such a masterful aid. Everyone should have a Rupa or a Hitchcock to
hand. Indeed, sometimes I wondered how anyone survived this world without
one.

Tamsin led the way down long passageways, twisting and turning; it wasn't
long before I was completely lost. I had trouble with maps at the best of
times, but this house was something else entirely; I couldn't have hoped to
find my way back to Hitchcock and the veranda. The girl led me unerringly
to the kitchens, though, where it was the work of a moment to secure the
required chilli sauce and tuck it into a pocket of my coat.

'Shall I take you back now, miss?' Tamsin asked.

I hesitated. The problem was: I didn't know if I had given Reginald and
the doctor enough time. The last thing I wanted was to walk in on them
still deep in confabulation; that would be impossibly awkward. Much better
to give them a little more time, just in case.

'Actually, Tamsin, I would love to see the gardens. Do you think we could
take the long way back? Unless you have to be somewhere?'

The girl's eyes widened, and she sniffed a little, as if holding back tears.
'No, no. I have nowhere else I need to be.' She guided me to a door that
led outside. 'The gardens are just this way, actually – the cook's herb garden
first, and the potager, close to the kitchens. After that, I could take you to
the rose garden, which is lovely this time of year; the roses are entering their
second flush . . .' Tamsin seemed quite knowledgeable about the gardens
and went nattering on – I admit, I rather tuned the sense of the words out,
as what I know about flowers you could fit onto the head of a thimble. But
it was clear the girl was unhappy. Her voice had that little tremble in it, the
kind that says, *I'm not going to cry, but I really want to . . .*

By the time we'd finished the rose garden and gone onto the Japanese
garden, with its little teahouse and koi pond, her voice had gone from
trembling to full on warbling, with a dash of operatic shuddering thrown
in, and I couldn't ignore the situation any longer. 'I say – not to pry, but
you seem troubled. Is something the matter? Can I help?'

She stopped in the middle of the raked gravel walk and burst into tears.

I never know quite what to do when someone is crying, but I had some tissues in my coat pocket – Rupa always says one should carry tissues, in case of emergency – and I was delighted to be able to pull them out and press them on her, patting her shoulder gingerly in a way I hoped was comforting. 'There, there. I'm sure it's not so bad, whatever it is. Things will look brighter in the morning. Every cloud has a silver lining . . .'

I probably would have kept mouthing platitudes for some time – Rupa said I could be a bit of an idiot that way – but when I said 'silver', the girl's sobs grew even wilder.

'I say – you'll do yourself an injury if you keep on like that.' Maybe sympathy wasn't the right approach, and she needed a bit of the old martial tone. 'Now, pull yourself together, young lady, and tell me exactly what the matter is.'

That seemed to be the ticket, because with one last, gasping sob, Tamsin stopped her waterworks, like turning off a tap. She rubbed away the tears with a cotton sleeve and blew her nose with my tissues, stuffing them in a pocket afterwards – thankfully, she didn't try to give them back to me; that was the problem with the fabric handkerchiefs of yore, so thank goodness we live in more modern times – blinking up at me through dew-lashed eyes. 'I can't find it! That's the problem.'

Oho! Lost something, had she? This might be a problem I could actually solve, which would take my mind off the whole Reginald and Stephanie situation. There was nothing I liked better than solving other people's problems. If you could only study *that* at university, perhaps I might have actually passed a class or two. 'What have you lost?'

She frowned. 'I haven't lost it exactly. I never had it. But I have to find it. I have to find the tiara!'

Now, that was rather strange. For one, I had just bought a tiara less than two hours before. For another, unless England was far more different to India than I'd realized, servants didn't usually go around with tiaras. If they had tiaras, they'd likely have servants of their own and wouldn't *be* servants, if you get my meaning.

I asked, agog with curiosity, 'What does this tiara look like?'

She said immediately, 'It's made of the finest silver, intricately worked, set with three star sapphires, surrounded by clusters of small diamonds.'

By all the gods, it *was* the self-same tiara I had purchased not two hours ago. This would have shocked me more, if it weren't for my power; the wretched thing did play tricks like this on occasion. The girl must have been aching for her lost item, wanting it badly. Usually, a person had to actually be near me, ideally touching me, before I could find the thing they'd lost, but the owner of the B&B last night had said there was something strange about Loveday House. Perhaps it had amplified the girl's desperate desire somehow?

No matter. The thing was to get the full story. 'And you lost this tiara, even though you never actually had it?'

'It was my great-great-great-grandmother's! The treasure of our family, from the olden times, until my great-great-great-grandfather lost it in a poker game. He wanted to bet his wife away as the wager, but she wouldn't have any of that. So he bet every single one of her family jewels and lost them all – and the house and lands, too.'

'This house?'

She shook her head. 'Oh no. The manor house, up on the hill in the centre of town. It's a grand place; they've made it into a museum now. But that doesn't matter; all that matters is the tiara.'

'But why? If it's been gone for this long . . .'

'Because without it, I'll never get married!' And then she was off, crying again, and I was out of tissues. So I just stood there helplessly, while the girl sobbed and wiped her nose with already snotty tissues, and in bits and spurts coughed up the whole story.

There was a boy, of course, and he was wealthy, and his mother wouldn't stand for him marrying a simple shopgirl. Tamsin had been perfectly happy working in the local bookshop, but the boy was going to be a lawyer or maybe work in finance. He was still in university, so it wasn't all decided yet, but either way, he was going to be someone important, and his mother didn't want him throwing himself away on the bookshop girl, so Tamsin had decided it was time to reclaim the lost inheritance, and the best part of it had always been the tiara, or so the family stories went, but it had been lost generations ago, and no one knew what had become of it – but everyone said that if there was anywhere something might be hidden, it was Loveday House, so Tamsin had taken all her courage in her hands and quit her bookshop job and taken a position as a servant here, and for three solid months, she had been searching this house in every free moment, but she couldn't find it – she couldn't find it anywhere – and the boy in question, he was going back to university tomorrow, and she was never going to see him again!

It all came out like that, in one fell swoop with barely any punctuation. Tamsin had started walking again, leading me through the gardens while she spoke, and we were almost at the veranda again by the time she finished her story. 'If I can just find it again and turn up at his mother's house wearing it, then she'll have to see that I'm just as important as her son is, or I could be.'

While I wasn't sure that a lad who didn't have the guts to stand up to his mother deserved a girl as determined as this, I could see that she had quite completely got it fixed in her head that the solution to all her troubles was the tiara, and I was glad that I could be of some help.

'You know, I think I may have seen a tiara just like that one.'

Tamsin stopped still, her face brightening with hope, like sunrise over the grassy knolls of Ireland. Yes, the cad definitely didn't deserve a girl like this, fair as the scintillating sunlight, dancing on the waves at Girgaon Chowpatty! Still, the heart wants what it wants, and the wee lass wanted him, so . . .

'I actually bought one just like it in an antiques store in town this morning. It'll be in my luggage. Perhaps we should go to my room and take a look?'

Before the girl could answer, Reginald strode up to us, Dr Smithson at his side. 'Sri, darling, I have to speak to you *immediately*. It's a matter of life or death!'

'But—' I protested.

Tamsin shook her head, her light dimming. 'It's probably not the one, miss. And I have no right to any other . . .'

'Look,' I said urgently, 'let me deal with this, but then we *will* go through my luggage and take a look, all right? It'll just take a moment.'

Tamsin looked across the veranda – Hitchcock was there, fingers in the air, as if he'd just snapped them again. 'I can't right now; I have to go, miss. I'm supposed to be working, and I can't afford to lose this job. They gave away the bookshop job months ago. But I could come by your room later, a little before dinner?'

I hated to put the girl off, with her heart's desire hanging in the balance, but I didn't want her to get sacked either. 'Yes, yes. Please do. I'll be waiting.'

'Thank you, miss. Very kind.'

Tamsin hurried off, leaving me alone with Reggie and the doctor.

Reginald frowned. 'What was all that?'

It would take too long to explain. 'Never mind, dear. You said it was important – a matter of life and death?'

'Yes, that's right.'

The doctor frowned. 'I wouldn't call it life and death myself.'

'Well, maybe not life and death, exactly . . .' Reggie opened his mouth, hesitated, closed it again, looking confused, which admittedly, was a pretty frequent expression on my dear husband's face. 'Look, it's a complicated story; maybe we should sit down somewhere, so Steph can tell it to you properly.'

Hitchcock shimmied up, appearing as if out of nowhere. 'We've set aside the plate you made earlier. If you've found the chilli sauce you required?'

I nodded, pulling the bottle out of my pocket as evidence.

'Excellent. Then might I suggest the small drawing room for your meal? It's quiet there, and if you close the door, you're unlikely to be disturbed by the other guests.'

'That sounds perfect, Hitchcock. Thank you.' My stomach rumbled loudly, and I flushed in embarrassment. Not exactly the kind of impression you want to make on your husband's *old friend*. 'Please lead the way.'

We made a strange procession, I'm sure – Hitchcock with my plate in hand, me with my chilli sauce, and my husband and the doctor bringing up the rear. But I didn't much care. Right now, all I needed was a few bites to fill my stomach. After that, I wanted to hear *everything* Dr Smithson had to say.

We were well ensconced in the small drawing room (which wasn't as small
as all that, making me wonder just how large the large drawing room might
be), with a cosy fire in the fireplace, and three well-upholstered armchairs
pulled up to it. The pair of them had insisted that I finish my meal before
they started, so I'd rather gulped it down, and since Hitchcock had kindly
indicated that we were to make ourselves free of the sideboard, I'd followed
it up with a few swigs of a rather fine sherry, which was a bit of all right
and settled my senses considerably. Once that business was taken care of,
the good doctor, who insisted I should call her Steph from now on, launched
into her story.

She'd arrived the night before and had brought with her a very valuable
object: an ancient medical text that she had promised to sell to our host,
the mysterious Lord Branok, for a rather significant sum. But on that first
night, she'd got lost on her way to meet with him and entered a room that
she was sure wasn't there before.

'There was something quite terrible in that room.'

'What?' I asked, leaning forward eagerly.

'I – I can't speak of it. Not yet.' She cast a speaking glance at Reginald,
which he seemed to catch quite clearly, though neither appeared to think it
worth explicating to me. 'But the important thing is that it shocked me so
much that I dropped the book, and then *something* snatched it and stole it
away.'

Reginald stepped in to pick up telling the tale. 'The poor woman has been
searching and searching ever since, avoiding our host at every turn, because
she really doesn't know what he will do if she doesn't hand over the book.'

'Is he such a monster as that? I mean, a sale is one thing, but if she
doesn't want to sell it any more, then she doesn't have to, does she? A man
with a place like this must be rolling in the stuff, so surely he understands
how buying and selling work.'

Stephanie flushed red, a flush that climbed all the way to the roots of her
blonde hair. It was a little alarming; I still hadn't got used to how transparent
these British faces were, how every little emotion showed so evidently on
them. It must be rather embarrassing.

She admitted, 'I have, in fact, already spent the money.'

'But aren't you a brilliant ace surgeon? That's what Reginald said, after
all, and I think I've even heard of you, in the news. Aren't you rolling in
it, too?'

'I had a debt of honour to pay,' she said soberly. 'That's all I can say of
the matter.'

Well, I understood that, of course. Debts of honour – nothing to be done
about them – simply had to be paid, and they could be deuced inconvenient.
My heart went out to the poor woman. 'I see, I see.'

'I can raise the funds, of course, but it would take quite some time –
several months of work at least. And I just don't know how Lord Branok

will take the need to wait. Ever since I arrived in town a few days ago, I've been hearing the strangest rumours about him and this place . . . Oh, if I could just find the book!'

'Yes, I see. Find the book, and all of these difficulties will just evaporate, like snow on the mountaintops.' Wait, that wasn't quite right, was it? Did snow on the mountaintops actually evaporate? Didn't it stay there forever? Maybe it was the opposite of what I'd meant to say . . . Oh, language was a bother sometimes. Best to just forge on, though, tally-ho and all that! 'I'd be delighted to help in any way I can, of course. My power should be quite useful here, and I'm sure it will be the work of a moment to set it all to rights. We'll find the bally book, you can hand it to our host, and pip-pop, all's well.'

No sooner was word spoken than it was turned to deed, and we were up and out the door, leaving the discarded remnants of my meal behind. I paused only long enough to take Steph's hand – oh, it was warm and soft, with long, fine fingers, of the sort that might caress you gently – or, given her profession, slice you open with consummate skill, which was attractive in its own way, and maybe it was better not to examine *that* thought too closely – to gather the imprint of the lost item.

My parents had found my power quite useful when it emerged, often setting me to finding my father's chappals, which he was forever mislaying, and my mother's glasses (which she wouldn't lose so often if vanity didn't lead to her taking them off frequently). They didn't even mind my displaying the talent at parties; the Mumbai elite found it reasonably entertaining, often demanding I perform for them like a trained monkey. *Srilatha, darling, see if you can find my gold bangles! You can't imagine where I've hidden them!* Their locations were never as clever as they imagined. I'd always thought there must be some better use for a finding power, and now, here I was, rescuing a damsel in distress. Two today, if the tiara turned out to be the right one! That would be a good day's work, and I could rest easy for a solid month after that.

Her fingers were steady in mine – no trembling maiden here!

I caught the scent of it – not an actual scent, you understand, but that was how it felt to me, and my nostrils flared in response. 'That way!' I said, pointing up the central staircase, and we galloped away.

Such a triumphant beginning, yet it came to such a disconsolate end! I regret to report that although we covered rather a lot of ground, we were entirely unsuccessful. At first, it seemed like the object was merely out of our reach. In the large drawing room (which was, as it turned out, immense), my power drew me to the lintel over the doorway, and behind it, what appeared to be a nook or perhaps a ledge; it was darkly shadowed, beyond our sight.

Unfortunately, it was also quite out of reach for any of our trio – until the good doctor sighed, glanced warily at us both, and then *grew*. I'd known

Dr Smithson could shrink; that had been in the papers and was much of the secret to her surgical success. But apparently, she could expand as well, at least up to six feet five or so – tall enough to reach the top of the lintel, put her hand into the nook, and discover . . . nothing. The space was empty; apparently, my power had led me astray.

I honestly couldn't think of a time that had happened before, and I worried that I might be getting ill. The Chelliahs are a stalwart bunch, all in all, but we do have a tendency to catarrh and similar pulmonary distempers, which can lay us out in an instant. I coughed, experimentally, but as I did not dissolve into a fit of racking coughs, I determined I was, in fact, perfectly healthy. The power had simply misfired, somehow.

No matter; we would try again – and once more, I took Stephanie's hand in mine. I admit, I did not mind the excuse!

But the next location proved no more fruitful, nor did the one after that. It was as if the house itself stymied our every attempt. I would feel the presence of the book, with absolute certainty, yet by the time we reached it, which often required quite a lot of stairs and passageways, the sense of it had often dissolved into an airy nothingness.

By the fourth location, which required Stephanie to shrink to under two feet tall and climb up into a chimney, emerging rather filthy and empty-handed, she was looking quite dubious as to the weight of my abilities. As for myself, I was plunged rather deeply into the depths, as I was completely failing to impress the good doctor, either on my own account or as a rival for my husband's affections. I was making a mess of it, and in the process, had made a rather a mess of *her*.

Reggie said, 'Maybe we should give it up for a bit? I think it must be teatime; a spot of tea might give you more strength for the finding.'

As if summoned, Hitchcock appeared in the doorway of the room we were in (I couldn't tell you what room it was, except that it was quite crowded with paintings of frightening old biddies, all of which seemed to glare at me with the same expression as Aunt Anu – it was as if my worst nightmares had been washed clean of all melanin and then captured in oil and canvas), and he solemnly announced, 'I am glad you have not got too lost. You do remember that you are meant to have a servant guide you in this house, rather than wandering about on your own? At any rate, it is time for tea, and Lord Branok has finished his work and will be able to join you.'

I was reluctant to give up the hunt, but Stephanie interjected, 'Oh! Please tell his lordship that I won't be able to join him for tea. As you can see, my clothes have got in a bit of a state, and I must take some time to refresh myself.'

That was rather cheeky of her, to refer to the liberal coating of black soot across her hair, face, and body in that manner, but Hitchcock merely nodded, appearing to take it at face value. Well, without her, any search would be much less effective – not that it had *been* effective thus far. Maybe Reggie was right, and a few cups of the old Ceylon would set me to rights. I was curious to meet our mysterious host as well.

We followed Hitchcock obediently away.

'I see you're enjoying the selection?'

'Rather!' Lord Branok's people had set out a proper afternoon tea – none of the scone plus cuppa minimalism you might find in less generous homes. They understood that a person wanted something solid and sustaining when three o'clock rolled around, something that might carry them through to the evening's entertainments, suitably fortified. The table was laden heavily with assortments of savouries – all delicate and dainty in appearance, but I can tell you that if you consume a dozen asparagus rolls, watercress and cucumber sandwiches, ham and chutney and cheese biscuits, creamy mushroom tartlets, crispy fried prawns, and a nice spot of egg salad – well, you won't be feeling any lack of substance there.

Then you move on to the scones themselves, spread liberally with lashings of jam and clotted cream (I had got a trifle upset with Reggie once because he insisted on putting the jam on top, when any fool could tell you that the jam needed to be right up against the scone, creating a layer that adhered, so that the clotted cream might land delicately above, like a cloud descending onto the mountaintop; it had made me seriously question the wisdom of our marriage, when I could not sway him in that regard), accompanied by strong Ceylon tea (two sugars, plenty of milk). Oh, I might have a Darjeeling or a Lady Grey on occasion, but for getting the job done, a good Ceylon is what I want, and if it's a sturdy builder's tea, made more of dust than leaves, that's fine with me. It will cure whatever ails you.

To top it all off, they had stuffed a host of autumn blackberries in a three-tiered cake, layered with cream, and accompanied by one of the fruitiest champagnes I'd tasted in quite some time. Lord Branok certainly didn't stint his guests, and I was delighted to be able to tell him so.

In fact, I said exactly that, to his face – or rather, to his mask, because the lord had arrived wearing a rather dramatic grey silk cloak with a hood, and a mask to match it. Rather odd, but one doesn't question one's host on such matters, of course.

'I'm glad you're enjoying it so,' he said. 'And please, no need for such formality – you must call me Jago.'

And wasn't that splendid of him? Ever since I'd arrived in Reggie's circles, he'd been forever introducing me to his old school friends, and they were all Lord This and Lady That, and even if I was a lady now myself, the appellation still felt rather odd, like a hat that had been designed for someone else and that you'd managed to jam onto your head, but you knew neither the cut nor colour suited you. 'So nice! I'm Srilatha, or Sri, if you like. I've been enjoying myself immensely.'

'Lovely, my dear. Though enjoyment isn't all there is to life, is it?'

That was an awkward question, wasn't it? Not quite the thing to shove on a guest you'd only just met, asking them to question their entire mode of being. The bewilderment I was feeling must have beamed forth from my face, because Jago smiled and went on before I could muster any kind of decent response.

'I must greet my other guests, and then I'm afraid I have some pressing business to attend to. But once you're finished with tea, perhaps you and your husband might care to join some of the guests in the library? They thought they might play a parlour game or two.'

Where *was* my husband? Ah, there, talking to another guest – a rather striking young man, tall and lanky, with a mop of dark hair and skin just a few shades lighter than my own. Reggie was leaning in close, so their shadows intertwined.

'We'd be delighted,' I said firmly. I was feeling quite discombobulated, and Reggie was so eminently predictable and soothing. It might be time to assert a few of my wifely rights, and surely nothing is more wifely than agreeing to engagements for your husband without asking him first.

'Excellent – and after that, I'll see you at dinner. Afterwards, I hope you'll both join us for guise dancing. I've had masks laid out in your room, should you care to participate; I hope I may look forward to seeing you there.'

'We wouldn't miss it,' I declared.

Jago smiled, tipping his head, and strolled away into the crowd, leaving me to my cake and champagne.

I don't mind confessing that I was feeling a touch melancholic in that moment. My finding attempts had repeatedly come to nothing, and my husband was off, talking to someone else – an ace, by the look of the flames that the young man was conjuring in his hand, flaring yellow, red, blue, green. *His* power hadn't failed him.

'Why so sad, child? You have a face meant for laughter, I think, not tears.'

The woman who'd addressed me was older, though it was hard to place her age. Masses of silver dreadlocks fell to her waist, but her skin was smooth, a rich brown, almost the same shade as my own, with hints of red underneath. Her eyes were slightly unnerving – dark irises floating in pools of scarlet. For a moment, I was reminded of my ayah's demon tales, of *rakshasas* that haunted the jungle, but this woman's smile promised pleasure, not fear. She was somewhere in her fifties, if I'd had to guess, but she carried herself like a Bollywood star, clearly knowing just how stunning she was. Beside her, I felt like a child.

'I'm fine, ma'am.' I straightened my spine; it wouldn't do to let down the Chelliah side now.

'Oh, don't *ma'am* me, please. You're young enough to be my granddaughter, but I don't need the reminder!'

'Surely not,' I said. Neither of my grandmothers looked like her - nor had they when they were forty years younger. 'I'm sorry - I'm forgetting my manners. I'm Srilatha Chelliah.' Properly, I should have included the *Lady*, but the truth of the matter was that I was getting rather fed up with the whole nobility thing.

'And I'm Ezili-je-Rouge, but my friends call me Ezili. Would you like to be one of my friends, child?' She swayed towards me, and the scent she wore wrapped around me, intoxicating, sweet citrus and vanilla. I felt quite dizzy for a moment, and then a man's laughter cut through her spell.

'Stop playing with the child, Ezili.' Now *this* man looked like someone I could be related to - one of my great-uncles, perhaps, with strong South Indian features. 'I'm Jayewardene, and Ezili is an old acquaintance of mine.'

'Acquaintance? Such a paltry word you give to me?'

'*Friend* wouldn't be quite right now, would it? And though I'm retired, you wouldn't want me to call you my enemy.' His eyes sparked, and the woman subsided.

'Jayewardene - Indian?' I asked.

'Sri Lankan, actually. I hope you chose the Ceylon tea; my family owns a tea plantation in the hill country near Nuwara Eliya.'

I smiled. 'I did, actually; it's my favourite.' There was something poking around in my brain, trying to find its way out - a bit of knowledge that might be helpful, yet I couldn't pin it down. That was so often the way, wasn't it? 'Jayewardene - I swear I know that name.' Something political, I thought. A minister or some such? I was never able to keep all those government people straight.

The man shrugged. 'I had a little notoriety, once upon a time, but I'm just an old retiree now, a regular visitor to this house. I do enjoy conversations with our host; he's a man of most penetrating insights, with deep knowledge, when he cares to reveal it. It's a shame he's too busy with his affairs to join us now - I think he'd rather enjoy the game Ezili has planned for us.'

My interest was piqued. I'd always been rather good at parlour games - give me a good round of 'Animal, Vegetable, Mineral' or 'Name the Bollywood Star', and I'm likely to run away with the crown.

'It's called "Shame",' Ezili said breathily. 'I do hope you'll be playing?' Her eyes seemed to glow scarlet in the late afternoon light.

I felt a touch of uneasiness then; I'd never heard of such a game, and my knowledge of games was quite extensive. In the midday heat of Mumbai, there was little else to do with one's time. Yet there was no sign of Dr Smithson, so I couldn't effectively begin that search again, and there was no sign of Tamsin either. I might as well play, at least until it was time to dress for dinner.

I poured myself another glass of the champagne and poured it quickly down my throat. Something told me I'd need fortification to get through what was coming next. 'Let me just collect my husband, Reggie, and we'd be delighted to accompany you. It sounds fascinating.'

I made my way across the room, noting as I went that Reggie's companion was just departing, leaving him standing all alone. Perfect. I touched my husband on the arm, saying, 'Reginald, we've been invited to play a delightful game with those charming people over there. Shall we join them?'

Reggie frowned. 'Oh, my dear, I'm afraid I've made a prior engagement. The young man I was speaking to – he's just gone off to change – is a serious tennis player, and I gather Lord Branok has some very fine courts. You must allow me the chance at a match. I've promised him.' His voice was rich with yearning, as if his heart's desire rode on the bouncing of a yellow ball on a green field.

I could just imagine the pair of them, athletically rushing about in their tennis whites, in that rather exhausting English sportsman way. Why Reggie insisted on exerting himself so, I could never understand, but he would undoubtedly sulk for hours if I denied him this pleasure.

I determined to be gracious. 'Oh, of course, of course.' I'm afraid a rather plaintive tone may have crept into my next words. 'You'll meet me in our room, to dress for dinner?'

'Certainly. Six o'clock?' He was already looking away, towards the door the young man had exited from.

'Six o'clock,' I agreed. Reggie was smiling as he abandoned me, and there was nothing for it but to gather myself and cross the room to Ezili and Jayewardene. 'I'm afraid my husband is otherwise engaged, but I'd be delighted to join you.'

'Excellent, excellent,' Ezili said. 'We'll do our best to make sure you're not bored.'

I found myself trapped in the library, pulled up to a low table with Ezili, Jayewardene, Jayewardene's grandson – a rather fetching young man of 20 or so – and two other guests: a married couple who had the unprepossessing names of John and Jane Smith, with features to match. The library was a rather cramped room filled altogether too thoroughly with books and armchairs and tables and what not. I suppose it was well enough for those who liked such things, but to be honest, books had always rather given me a headache. It was sort of astonishing, in retrospect, that I'd made it to university at all.

'Here's the game,' Ezili said, leaning forward so that her generous breasts were on quite dramatic display. 'We must take turns offering literary quotations. The first to identify the work of literature gets to offer a quote next, and everyone must drink if they haven't read the book in question. Oh, I do hope our host manages to finish up his work and join us; I'm sure he would excel.'

I could feel a fine dew breaking out on my forehead. This was likely to be a disaster. Maybe I should make my excuses and retire to my bedroom, though I was so wedged in that I'd be obliged to have half the party out of their chairs in order to escape. I had determined to do it – hang the inconvenience – but before I could, Jayewardene's grandson spoke up. He had a strong accent, and while his English was excellent, it was also just a touch slow on delivery; it did not seem to be his native tongue.

'Oh, I will be terrible at this. I've spent the last several years immersed in ancient Tamil texts; I can't remember the last time I read a book in any other language! You are trying to humiliate me!' His face held a flush of pink under the brown, and his eyes were wide and pleading.

Ezili laughed throatily and said, 'Well, it is called "Shame", as I said. But nonsense – it is just a game. Surely you are not such a coward as to run away?'

Jayewardene's grandson subsided, grumbling, into his chair, and after that – well, obviously I couldn't possibly leave. I didn't have nearly the excuse he did, and besides, if I abandoned him, then he'd be the butt of their jokes. If I stayed, I could at least divert the humiliation somewhat, so the worst of the sewage might splash on me instead of him. A Chelliah is noble! A Chelliah defends the weak! A Chelliah never runs from a fight!

'Here's the first quotation,' Ezili said. 'Don't worry, I'll make this an easy one: "I have loved the stars too fondly to be fearful of the night."'

Jane Smith spoke up immediately. 'Oh, I know that one. It's Galileo, of course.'

Her husband shook his head, 'Dear, it can't be. Remember, these are supposed to be literary quotations. It must be from a book or a play or a poem . . .'

'I'm *sure* it's Galileo.'

Jayewardene was shaking his head, smiling slightly, and after a moment, volunteered a response. 'People often think that, you know. But it's actually Sarah Williams, from her poem, "The Old Astronomer to His Pupil". Let's see – how does it go? "Though my soul may set in darkness, it will rise in perfect light / I have loved the stars too fondly to be fearful of the night."'

'Correct!' Ezili declared. 'Now, all the rest of you, drink!'

There was a well-supplied drinks trolley at the ready, and my sole consolation was that it appeared to stock a Macallan, my favourite Scotch. That would keep me company in my despair. I gulped down my first shot, feeling the fire warm my throat and belly. Ah. Consolation indeed.

His grandson groaned. 'Oh, I should have known that. I'm quite sure we studied it in school.'

Jayewardene lifted a finger. 'All right! My turn. Let me just think a moment . . .'

Thinking would do me no good at all. I turned to the consideration of the amber beauty of the liquor, gleaming in the motes of sunlight that poured like liquid gold through the high library windows. It was going to be a long time until six o'clock.

I cannot say at what point I lost my scarf, my shoes, my socks, my sweater, and the last remnants of my sang-froid. I cannot even pinpoint the moment when the rules of the game changed, and rather than simply drinking, stripping *and* drinking became the rule of the day.

I was not entirely unhappy at first, as I was wearing quite a few more layers than, say, Ezili. And when she did lose a round, she chose to remove her blouse, rather than any of her less revealing options, baring two generous breasts cradled in a lacy red confection that made me wonder if I had made a grave error by dating primarily in the realm of people roughly my own age.

But the fact of the matter was, I was far worse at the game than anyone at the table, and as the level of Macallan in the bottle dropped, so, too, did my capacity to make reasonable guesses. My dress went next, and only the warmth of the liquor kept me from expiring of sheer embarrassment. Thank goodness Rupa had always instilled in me the need to wear quality underthings. Still, I couldn't survive much more of this.

I'm afraid I was on the verge of completely disgracing Lord Branok's library and scandalizing his sober books, when the clock finally chimed six, releasing me from honour's cage.

'Oh, I'm so sorry,' I said, hastily gathering up my various elements of clothing and layering them on as best as I could in my inebriated state. 'This has been just delightful, a real treat, but I promised my husband that I would meet him and dress for dinner . . .'

'Of course,' Ezili said. 'Go, go, child. You mustn't keep him waiting. Husbands are not always very understanding.'

As I exited the room, a voice came after me, unfortunately attenuated, so I could not quite determine who had spoken. 'Just remember to keep your promise tonight! I'll be waiting . . .'

Promise? I would have cudgelled my addled brain if I could, because I had absolutely no recollection of a promise. Well, perhaps the faintest recollection. Now that it came to it, I could perhaps hear my own voice saying, 'After the dancing, I hope you will allow me to visit you in your bedchamber.'

That might be a problem for Reginald. Or it might not. The real question, though, was: whom had I said it to?

'Dear, are you wearing your dress backwards?'

Reginald looked startled when I slipped in the door. It had taken me some time to find my way; I'd had to ask directions of three different French maids before I finally made it to the refuge of our bedroom. Rather a nice room, reminiscent of my childhood home: a dark four-poster rosewood bed, hung with mosquito netting (a bit odd, since this region was not prone to mosquitoes, as far as I knew); spare but elegant furnishings; snowy white bedding; double doors that opened out onto a Juliet balcony with a view of the sea.

But my husband had asked me a question, and I mustn't let myself be distracted by mere decoration. He deserved a prompt response.

'No, of course not.'

The denial was reflexive, the way one performs when your schoolteacher asks if you've been glancing over at your classmate's paper during the exam. Even if you *have* done such a thing and might consciously consider it the honourable thing to fess up and take your medicine, it is almost impossible to do so, I've found. The back of the brain rises up and denies culpability as reliably as one's leg will fly up into the air when the doctor's little hammer goes bang upon one's knee. That is just the way of it, as I'm sure all would agree – a common trial of the human condition. But it did put me in a bit of a jelly, or as you say, a jam, or even a pickle, if you want to invoke my own family spirit – pickles being essential to the livelihood of myself, my mother and father, all of the assorted aunts and uncles and grandparents, and of course, Reginald and his extended kin as well.

I have lost track of things, rather. That often happens when one is caught in a pickle, I find. Let me start again.

The problem was that I had never lied to Reginald, nor he to me; our arrangement had been founded on an agreement of complete honesty, and up until this point, it had sufficed very nicely. To be sure, it had not in actuality been much tested, as of yet – we'd only known each other six months and only been married for three, so there had scarcely been time for the bloom to leave the rose, so to speak. And though we were, in theory, free as birds to find pleasure and entertainment with anyone else we chose, the fact of the matter was that we had been first so busy with arranging all the wedding business and then with the wedding itself and then with the abrupt relocation to jolly old England, there had been no *time* to take advantage of our little arrangement.

Once we'd made it onto his family's hereditary estate, that vast and draughty house with its astonishing number of bills, there'd been nothing but time, but the house turned out to be set inconveniently far from anyone else. Oh, there were servants, but one cannot disport oneself with one's own servants, of course. It would be entirely not the done thing. And since Reginald didn't want to go to London – or anywhere much – and seemed perfectly content with me in his bed at night and his horse and hounds during the day, there had simply been no opportunity to explore other options, until I'd finally persuaded him to accept this invitation.

Now, though, there were opportunities aplenty, and really, I was being a complete fool, not simply confessing all. It would be much the simpler.

With me, deed generally follows hard on the heels of thought, and as soon as I'd parsed all that out in my head and realized that the sharp pain in my middle came from lying to Reginald – Chelliahs are unfailingly honest, not least because it can be so confusing keeping track of a lie – I realized that the solution was plain.

'Oh, actually, I was mistaken. You are absolutely right, my dear – I *have* managed to put my dress on backwards.'

It would be honestly difficult to deny, given that my generous endowment meant that the fabric was stretched quite uncomfortably tightly across the front, and gaped most unbecomingly at the back.

'Can you help me remove it, please? I am not entirely steady on my feet at the moment, and a touch of assistance would be most welcome.'

I held up my arms, which was as much as I could manage, because the room was swaying as dramatically as if we were on a ship at sea. Perhaps the Macallan had not been the wisest choice.

'But how in the world did that happen?' Reginald deftly came forward and relieved me of my dress, and of course that was the moment when a knock came upon the door. It was as if this house was determined that everyone present should enjoy the sight of my underthings.

But Lord Branok had graciously provided plush white robes, hanging just behind the door, so it was the work of a moment to swathe myself in something more appropriate, before Reggie opened the door.

One of the maids waited there, presenting a note on a silver platter, which Reginald dutifully received before closing the door again. 'It's for you, my dear.'

I knew that I would still need to explain the matter of the backwards dress, but reading the note would give me a few more moments to organize my thoughts. 'Oh, it's from Tamsin.'

'Who?'

'Tamsin, you know – oh no, well, I suppose you don't – you were occupied with Dr Smithson at the time – well, in any case, she says that she cannot come now, but if I will only wear the tiara to the guise dancing tonight, she will meet me there, and we can determine the truth of the matter.'

'The truth of what matter?' Reginald demanded. 'Really, Sri, you are making no sense at all, and I must insist that you explain to me what is going on.'

'Of course. Just help me with my sari, and I'll explain everything. And you can tell me how the tennis match went . . .'

Reggie was still in his whites, but with hair neatly combed and no signs of perspiration, he didn't appear overly exercised.

'As for that, it didn't.' He frowned, furrows deep on his broad forehead. 'I could have sworn the servant I spoke to gave me very clear instructions, but I couldn't find the ruddy tennis courts.'

I had tucked the sari end in by then and wound it around, handing the far end to Reggie to hold taut. He took a few steps away and held it precisely; he was really quite good at that sort of physical task.

'I spent two solid hours hunting for them and ended up almost falling off the edge of the cliff for my troubles.'

'My dear!' I was rather engaged in managing my pleats – such a bother to get them right! – and it was hard to feel any actual concern, given that he was standing right in front of me, so had clearly escaped unscathed, but a wifely expression seemed called for in that moment.

'No, no, I'm fine. But the wind can certainly be a bit stiff-ish out there.'

I assured him, as we finished the pleating, and he helped pin the fall to my shoulder, 'I shall take the utmost care should I venture onto the cliffs.'

'See that you do.' He stepped back, frowning again. 'Now, you were saying? What's this about the tiara? The one we purchased this morning?'

I told him the whole story, starting with weeping Tamsin in the Japanese garden on the gravel path, and her frustrated quest for the great-great-great-grandmother's tiara (though I saw no need to go into detail about *why* we'd taken the long way back; there is such a thing as too much honesty). Reginald is as much a sentimentalist as I am and certainly agreed that if I had the opportunity to smooth the path of true love, it was my clear duty to grab a rake and get smoothing.

Especially as the task was so simple in this case. Reggie unpacked my smaller bag, and there were the purchases from this morning, sparkling in the light of the setting sun that streamed over our west-facing window. (A west-facing window is so much kinder to guests, don't you think, so they have every opportunity for a leisurely waking? Lord Branok really was the perfect host.) The tiara did set off my aquamarine sari just as well as Reginald had suggested, and the coordinated cuff links, though of a different pattern and style, looked quite handsome stuck through the little openings in his cuffs.

But pulling out the tiara had reminded me, even in my still rather topped-up state, of our other quest. 'Oh, have you had a chance to speak to Stephanie again?'

'No,' Reginald said, frowning. 'She's been avoiding Jago so assiduously, it's meant avoiding us as well. She'll be at dinner, though, so perhaps we can grab a word. Perhaps we can skip out on the guise dancing and help her search again . . .'

'I don't know,' I said dubiously. 'Lord Branok seemed quite particular that we participate; I think it must be rather important to him. And if Stephanie is dancing, he can't be expecting her to simultaneously be conducting some sort of business exchange. I'm sure at this point, he's given up on any thought of the book for the night, and we should have plenty of time after the dancing to search.'

'I suppose that makes sense,' Reginald agreed. 'Now, about that dress . . .'

I knew I wouldn't be able to avoid it forever, and the time had clearly come for the axe to fall. I bent my neck for the blade and launched into the tale of 'Shame'.

I suppose I should have been grateful that rather than being shocked or appalled, Reginald seemed inclined to laughter at the image of my being stripped of one article of clothing after another due to my admitted weaknesses in the literary arena. By the time I'd got to the *Hamlet* debacle (which had cost me my second sock), he was laughing out loud – guffawing, you might even say – which showed a certain want of fine feeling in him that I found quite distressing. Sometimes I thought I had been too hasty in agreeing to this marriage, even if it had been Rupa's idea, and even if Rupa's ideas were almost never wrong.

Almost is such a troubling word, don't you think? Rather a wolf in sheep's clothing. So often, one is inclined to put faith in it, to assume the best outcome possible, when it might be wiser to plan for the worst, so that when the wolf shows up with blood around its mouth, you know exactly whom to blame for the missing lambs.

Still, a husband was undeniably convenient at times. 'Can you help me put my hair up, dear?' In the absence of Rupa to assist me, Reginald made an adequate substitution.

Once he'd finished, I considered myself in the glass. The horn curved smoothly up from the top of my spine, rather elegant in its way. I'd thought about having it tipped in gold, but even in its pure ivory state, it had a certain *je ne sais quoi* about it. And when Reggie settled the tiara on my head and passed along the silver-sequined mask that our host had provided (what a perfect addition – however had he known?), the final effect was quite stunning. I'd be a little sad to give the tiara up, in fact, but true love and all that, what? Needs must.

Dinner was a formal affair, quite the menagerie of masked creatures. It might've taken a lesser soul some time to sort out who was who, but it was immediately clear to the bright Chelliah brain that the flame-red feathered mask seated across from me belonged to the young man who had so interested my husband: John Montaño by name, I'd learned, although he went by the rather charming sobriquet, the Candle, when he was exerting his ace abilities. He was demonstrating them now, to the wide-eyed attention of John Smith, seated to his right in a domino mask, and his wife, Jane, seated to my right in a matching mask. To my left, at the head of the table, was our host, resplendent in a far more elaborate grey silk mask that rose in a feathered sweep above his forehead and dipped down past his chin.

I saw, to my slight displeasure, that Reginald in his simple gold mask had been paired with Dr Smithson (who wore a rather unnerving mask in the form of a white skull, perhaps as a nod to her medical ability), and they were sitting, heads together, speaking most animatedly. But perhaps that was better than having him with Ezili, who wore a glittering crimson mask dripping baubles that pointed the way to her cleavage? Ezili sat opposite a man I hadn't yet met, an older Black gentleman, from what I could see around his simple white mask. And the party was finished with Jayewardene and his grandson at the bottom of the table, both in rather colourful masks of red, green, orange, and gold, which I believed to be the colours of the Sri Lankan flag. I'd always rather enjoyed flags and maps and all that kind of thing in school – anything that didn't have to do with words, actually. A picture is the business for me, anytime, and the more colourful, the better!

As I said, it was easy enough for me to identify everyone in the party, and when our host asked us all to introduce ourselves, I learned the name of the final member: one Gary Bushorn, who was apparently a long-term guest of the house and would be instructing us in guise dancing after dinner.

'Have you been enjoying your stay thus far?' Lord Branok asked – Jago, he had said to call him, though that seemed a touch familiar for someone so imposing.

I answered honestly, 'Yes, though for a country house, there does seem to be rather a lot going on.'

'That is often the way of it at Loveday House. When people arrive here, their lives often unfold differently from how they might have before. Secrets are revealed; different choices are made . . .'

'And your guests enjoy that? Having their secrets revealed and all? I mean to say, if they have secrets, maybe they want them to *stay* secret. That's the whole nature of a secret, what?'

'Do you have secrets, my dear?'

I noted that Jago hadn't actually answered my question, but I was a good sport, happy to follow the conversational ball where he tossed it, especially since I was an open book. 'Oh no. Everything about my life is completely clear.'

'Even to yourself? It is a rare soul who knows herself that well.'

I did feel a little uneasy flutter at his words, though I couldn't have said why. But before we could pursue the matter further, a servant burst into the room most officiously, right between the soup (a delicate fennel consommé) and salad courses.

Lord Branok half-rose from his chair. 'Sarah? Is something the matter?'

'Oh, my lord! It's the goose!'

He frowned. 'What has happened to the goose?'

'It's been stolen, my lord! Disappeared right from the yard, just as Old Timothy was about to slit its throat. And he's the one what took it!' She pointed to the Candle, who shoved his chair back from the table, looking outraged.

'Hey, that's not OK,' John Montaño said. 'Do I look like the kind of man who would steal a goose?'

Lord Branok said placatingly, 'Please don't concern yourself, John. Now, Sarah, you really can't come in and accuse my guests like this. This goose isn't for dinner tonight, is it? You'd scarce have time to cook it.'

'No, my lord – I was going to start preparing it to roast for tomorrow's dinner.'

Branok nodded. 'Fine, fine. I'm sure your eyes were only playing tricks on you, and the goose will turn up in due course. You know how things are in this house. Why don't you go back to the kitchen and make sure Stephens isn't messing up the salad. You know he always puts on too much dressing, and it's a great trial to your tender chef's heart.'

With a squeal of dismay (not unlike that of a stuck goose), and a cry of 'The salad!', Sarah whirled around and disappeared from the room, leaving the rest of us trying very hard not to look at John Montaño, who was blushing red as a flame. It was really too odd; what would the man want with a goose?

The rest of dinner passed without incident, though a simmering tension seemed to lie upon the entire party. Dr Smithson, of course, was undoubtedly anxious about her book, and I did rather wish we could rush through both dinner and dancing, so we might get on with helping her look for it again. Surely we would have better luck this time! And of course, Tamsin would come to claim her tiara at the dancing, so that would be one less item to worry about. Perhaps I could turn my talents to finding the goose as well and relieve John of any suspicion of goose-napping? Really, it was astonishing how often things went missing around here. At Reginald's home, I could go a month without having any need of my power at all.

Lord Branok regaled us all with tales of his prior life, which most of the table seemed to find fascinating, though it was all a little taken up with books for my taste. The man had worked in libraries and bookshops throughout the land, it seemed – Sheffield, Birmingham, York, Edinburgh, Plymouth. That was all well and good for those who liked the things, but for those of us less enthralled by the written word, yet another account of how he'd stumbled across a rather nice little edition of Marlowe's plays in a dusty corner of some forgotten bookshop rather failed to captivate.

Perhaps he noticed my distraction, because eventually Branok turned the topic to games of chance instead, and there, my interest was wholly captured. I never could resist a good game – or better, a good bet! Sadly, though I asked the table if anyone would care to flutter a wager on the outcome of the night's guise dancing, perhaps betting on how many would trip over their own feet or lose their masks in the process of flinging themselves about, none took me up on my wager – not even my own Reginald. I really began to wonder how well suited we were!

♥

Mr Bushorn stood in the centre of the parquetry floor, looking quite relaxed. Almost everyone from dinner had come along for the dancing; only Jayewardene and Lord Branok had begged off, saying they were both looking forward to some quiet time in the library. I wondered uneasily whether anyone had passed along to Branok exactly what had been taking place in his quiet library earlier in the day – hopefully not!

'Now, I assume that many of you haven't tried guise dancing, but I promise you, it's quite easy to learn. I'll talk you through the sequence, and we'll walk the steps a few times, until everyone is comfortable – then we'll have the musicians start up, and we'll do it for real. And once you're all up to speed, I encourage you to have fun with it. Guise dancing has historically been an excuse for all sorts of mischievous behaviour, as people can hide behind their masks. All right? Everybody, choose a partner, please!'

'I think *you* need a partner,' Ezili said loudly.

'I'd be happy to demonstrate with you, Miss je-Rouge.'

'Oh, I *insist* you call me Ezili . . .' She swept into his arms, but before she could get too close, he took a firm grasp of her hand and shoulder, repositioning her with some space between them.

I was happy to start off with Reginald, but as the dance progressed, we switched partners over and over again. The Candle was a little tall for my taste, but he bent over quite readily, which showed a graciousness that I appreciated. The second time we spun around, he added the flourish of a ripple of red flame, and I barely stifled a shriek – but then I saw the mischief in his eyes behind the mask and realized that I felt no heat from the flames.

'You are entirely safe, I promise!' he said. 'And if I did manage to burn you, rest assured that I could heal you just as readily.'

Well, that was rather dazzling, wasn't it? No wonder Reggie was so taken with the man. And indeed, a few turns later, they were in each other's arms, swaying to the vibrant beat of the music, getting closer and closer . . .

'Miss!' a voice called out to me from the shadows, as the music crescendoed to its final flourish. The dancers laughed and broke up to refresh themselves at the sideboard, and I was able to slip away from the crowd to have a few words with Tamsin. She'd found me at last!

'Oh, there it is!' Tamsin stretched a hand up to my head, and then pulled back, as if unsure of her welcome.

'Please don't hesitate, my dear. I'm only too happy to hand the trinket over to you. What matter a few sparkly baubles, should they stand in the way of two hearts beating as one?'

I reached up and disentangled the tiara from my hair, which turned out to be a little more difficult than I'd hoped, as my hair had got slightly tousled with all the whirling about and was now quite intricately wound up in the tiara's band. But finally, I was able to work it free and pulled it down, ready to hand to the girl – when the lights suddenly went out!

A horrible sound echoed through the room, a sort of ghastly *HONK*, and I felt a stiff breeze and the rustling of great wings – and then I am embarrassed to admit that I cried out! Not out of fear, of course, but overcome by pain, because *something* had taken a bite out of my palm, snatching away the tiara in the process.

When the lights finally came up again, they found me standing bereft, blood dripping off my hand and making artistic patterns on the parquet floor.

'Srilatha!' Reginald hurried over, with all the husbandly devotion a woman could ask for, though I noticed that the Candle stayed close by his side.

Dr Smithson rushed up and extended her hand, clearly asking to be allowed to examine the gushing wound. 'This is bad, but I can take care of it. Someone run to my room and get my bag, and I'll sew this up for you.'

I almost collapsed right then. No one on this Earth will dare say a Chelliah is not bold, but even though I'm perfectly capable of facing ghostly honking creatures in the night, the thought of a needle deliberating poking its way in and out of my tender skin did induce a decided faintness in the old noggin.

'That won't be necessary,' the Candle said, holding up a hand that suddenly rippled with green flame. He reached out and gently took my hand in his, and a warmth slid over my hand and arm, rushing through my whole body, making my knees go weak.

And then it was over, and he was releasing my hand, which showed nothing but a bit of dried blood to indicate anything had ever been amiss.

'Well,' Dr Smithson said. 'That's handy. People like you are going to put me out of business.' There was a tinge of resentment to her tone, and I couldn't blame her – she'd studied for many long years, probably banging her head on medical tomes into the early hours of the night, and along comes this one, and just, *whoosh!* takes care of it.

'I'm happy to leave most healing to you, Doc; medicine is not my calling,' he said, smiling.

'What in the world was that?' one of the Smiths said. Jane, presumably, by the gown she wore, though honestly, with the domino masks and their rather similar build, it would be easy to confuse them.

I had the answer, of course. 'It was . . . the goose.'

Tamsin burst into tears, and then everyone was comforting her, and the whole story came out – there was no real reason to keep it a secret, after all. Soon, the entire company had decided that we would abandon dancing for the evening and hunt for the goose and the tiara instead. My power rarely worked on living creatures, but if it had kept hold of the tiara, perhaps I could search for that and find them both together.

'Let us divide into pairs,' Reginald boldly proclaimed. 'We can cover more ground that way.'

'Yes, excellent idea,' the good doctor said. She took my arm firmly. 'I will go with Srilatha. Just in case that healing doesn't stick and the wound reopens – it'll be safer to have her with me.'

My hand felt absolutely fine, but before I could say so, Stephanie stepped on my foot, quite deliberately. Oh! Of course, this was the perfect opportunity to seek for the missing book!

John Montaño was mumbling something about how his healing was absolutely going to stick, what was she talking about, but Reginald was already leading him away, and the rest of the party had broken up into pairs as well – Ezili and Gary, the Smiths, then the young Jayewardene grandson saying he was going to find his grandfather and Lord Branok in the library and apprise them of events.

Tamsin was tasked with remaining in the room, in case the goose returned to the scene of his crime, and though her eyes welled with tears once more, she agreed. Within moments, we were off!

You wouldn't think it would be a difficult thing, finding a goose with a tiara, even in a house of that size. After all, a goose is rather a large, dramatic sort of bird, and even if one were to run across a goose and be inclined to pass it by – assuming, perhaps that it was merely out for a final saunter before it met its fate as the centrepiece of the evening repast – the fact that said goose had a tiara in its beak or claw, or perched on its foolish head, would surely be enough to help you twig the fact that this goose was not behaving in a goose-like way.

I fully expected that, as Stephanie and I wandered the halls of Loveday, we would quickly hear about the direction of the goose from more than a few servants – *oh yes, the sparkle of the tiara, you can't miss it, it's thataway!* – but instead, nothing of the sort! There was no sign of the creature.

But no matter, because before long, Stephanie had lain her hand upon my arm, leaning into me in the flickering light of a hallway bulb that wanted changing, saying, 'Dear Srilatha, we can leave the goose to the others, can't we? Please, can we try once more to find my book?'

She had swayed so close, I was surrounded by her scent, of meadow grass and wildflowers, and I was quite intoxicated. And her face, so pleading, her voice, so soft and full of gentle anxiety. I didn't understand why Reginald had said as we were heading down to dinner: *I hope Steph doesn't get too frustrated by this whole book business – she has a fearsome temper when she's riled.* He must have been mistaken, thinking of some other woman altogether, because the woman beside me showed no indication of temper at all. But then, Reginald had a terrible memory; he was forever insisting that he had said or done something that I was absolutely positive he hadn't.

I said yes, of course, and took her hand in mine, closed my eyes – oh, her scent hit even harder then – and I caught the scent of the book as well. Old books smell like chocolate and coffee – a sweet, musky smell – and this

must have been a very old book, as it was quite intoxicating. I didn't know
how I'd missed it before!

The scent led us straight to the library, and would you believe it – the
book was right there! Sitting out on a table, innocent as you please, as if it
had never as much as heard a scandalous word, much less spoken one.
Stephanie fell upon it with a glad cry, pressing it to her bosom, as they say,
and I was a little jealous, I admit, wishing I might be that book.

'Oh – how can I ever thank you?'

'Not at all, not at all. Happy to be of service, of course.'

She took a step closer, tilting her head down towards me. 'I did have one
idea of something you might like . . .'

And then she was kissing me, soft lips against my own, the book pressed
between our bosoms, and that was much better than before, although in actuality, it would be better to have no book at all. The corners were rather pokey.

'Lady Srilatha!' It was Jago Branok, walking into the room. 'I am so sorry
to hear that apparently my goose has made off with your tiara! I am shocked
– shocked! – and deeply regretful.'

I shrugged. 'Oh no, not to worry; it's not my tiara.'

He frowned. 'It's not? Everyone else seems to think it is – it's the one
you were wearing at dinner tonight, is it not? I noted it particularly; it seemed
quite fine, with those star sapphires . . .'

I suppose that would be a bit confusing, and I attempted to clarify. 'Oh,
yes, I mean, it *was* mine, but I was in the process of giving it away to its
rightful owner when the goose made off with it.'

'This is most confusing,' Branok said, frowning. 'Maybe we should sit
down, and you can tell me all about it. And oh – Dr Smithson! I see you
have my book. Speaking of treasures . . .'

'Yes,' Stephanie said, handing the massive tome over with a relieved smile.

There – that was one problem taken care of, at least. I felt a swell of pride
that threatened to wash over me, like a heaving winter tide. Pride and tide
– that was rather nice. I could make something of that, perhaps a poem
dedicated to Dr Smithson, Stephanie, my Steph – oh, I was getting ahead of
myself. It was only a kiss. Perhaps she was just caught up in the moment;
surely that was it. The relief of finding the book . . .

But as we obediently followed Jago to seats by the fire, so we might
unburden ourselves of all the relevant stories, Stephanie leaned over and
whispered in my ear, 'I'm in the Blue Suite.'

Did that mean what I thought it meant? I think it did!

It was some time before we finished our conversation with Jago, bringing
our host up to speed on the tiara situation, then spent some time hunting
for the tiara and goose ourselves, to no avail.

At ten p.m., Jago gathered his guests in the large drawing room and said, 'While I applaud your willingness to lend yourselves to my housemaid's romantic cause, I would prefer you not wander the house at night, as it can be dangerous for the unwary. Please do stay in your bedrooms, or if you feel the need to visit the library or the kitchens, call for a servant to escort you. One will be happy to oblige. We can continue the search in the morning, but I am sure the bird will become tired at some point, and it will become much easier to find. Assuming it hasn't flown away entirely . . .'

We dispersed obediently, but when I found myself back in my bedroom with Reginald, I was disinclined to stay there. I was burning to discover what Stephanie had intended with her intimation that she would be in the Blue Suite and rather felt that I deserved a triumphant heroine's reward for finally finding that blasted book. But what of Reginald? I couldn't simply abandon my husband. Could I?

'Dearest,' Reginald said, once we were in the privacy of our bedchamber. 'You remember the agreement we made in Mumbai? That this marriage would be convenient for us both, but it was not meant to trammel us?'

'Oh yes, I remember exactly.'

'Good, good. Now, I wouldn't want to do anything to upset you, of course, but assuming you are still of the same heart and mind, I *have* received an invitation to visit John Montaño in the Green Suite this evening, and I think I would like to accept.'

'Well, that's quite the coincidence!' I said. 'For I have received an invitation to visit Stephanie in the Blue Suite this evening, and I would definitely like to accept!'

'Splendid, splendid!' Reginald did look a little startled and added, 'I rather thought that Steph had always harboured a bit of a *tendre* for me, but I must have been mistaken, all these years. Just as well, really.'

He shrugged and ran fingers through his hair, artfully disarranging it. Reggie looked the very picture of the young British lord, mask and all, and I felt a pang of fondness for him. He was a sweet chap – maybe this would all work out, just as Rupa had intended.

He bent down and kissed me on the cheek. 'Have a wonderful evening, my dear.'

With his long legs, it only took a few strides before he was at the door. I did want to see to my own hair, which had been rather tousled by the removal of the tiara, so I took a moment to step to the dressing table, picking up a comb.

Meaning I was turned away, gazing at myself in the mirror, rather than at him, when I heard him carol merrily as he left the room, 'Oh, by the way, I mean to tell you that I received a letter from your aunt, Anu. I've invited her to come for a visit. Won't that be fun?'

What? I spun around, but the door had already closed firmly behind him. What an arse! Had he really invited my aunt to our home? Chills ran down my spine at the very thought. She had been sending me weekly letters since the wedding, demanding news of the blessed arrival on the instant it was indicated, asking why there was no word of one as yet, wondering if Reginald and I should see a doctor, or perhaps an astrologer, learn if there was something in the stars preventing us from conceiving the next generation.

I thought I'd successfully put her off and managed to avoid any discussion of our assiduous contraceptive practices in the process, but apparently, when her efforts failed with me, she'd turned to my unwitting spouse. And I use the word 'unwitting' advisedly, as Reggie was surely far more lacking in wits than I'd thought him, if he could mention an aunt's visit with such blissful approval. I was plunged into the very depths of dudgeon, and only the knowledge that we were booked to stay at Loveday House for two more days gave me any consolation. At least she couldn't get at me here!

I finished arranging my hair and departed for the blue room. Perhaps a pleasant interlude with Stephanie would suffice to distract me from my despair. I could but try.

I had asked a servant previously for the location of the blue bedroom and had been informed it was one floor above, three doors down from the stair-well, on the east side. That seemed simple enough, and despite's our host's rather dramatic warning about the house being dangerous at night, I thought a Chelliah could navigate two hallways and a stairwell without much diffi-culty. We'd tromped all over the place earlier in our searches for the book and the tiara, and though the house was vast and we'd been mostly unlucky, nothing untoward had occurred.

I did encounter a few difficulties on the way up, however. As I opened my own door, I saw another open at the far end of the hallway and saw Reginald slipping inside – I hesitated, wanting to make sure all was clear before continuing. It was one thing to give your husband your blessing for a dalliance, but somehow it seemed a little much to actually watch it going on.

Once the door had closed safely behind him, I started down the hall, only to see the same door opening again a moment later. Had John changed his mind? Was Reginald about to be given the boot? What would that mean for my own evening plans?

But I was startled to see Ezili emerge instead; despite the mask she still wore, there was no mistaking her lush figure. She said not a word, only winked at me, and then ducked across the hall and through another door. Music sounded forth as she opened it, a jovial jazzy beat, and her hips swayed as she sashayed inside. It closed behind her, and silence fell once more – an oddly complete silence, given how loud the music had been a moment ago. Lord Branok must have truly excellent soundproofing in his walls. Given his guests' late-night predilections, that was probably for the best.

It was tempting to try to conjure up a reason why Ezili had been in the

Candle's room, but really, that was no business of mine. Perhaps she had injured herself while searching and had requested a bit of healing? Maybe she had been searching with him and merely accompanied him back to his room, chatting? It mattered not.

I headed up the stairs, determined to stay focused on my own affairs. Only to be almost bowled over by Tamsin, turning the corner on the stairwell, rushing down.

'Tamsin!' I cried.

Seeing her did rather put a damper on my already somewhat doused spirits, as I felt keenly that I had failed her. But she gave no response, simply continuing most hastily down the stairs, as if she didn't see me at all. The mask she was wearing seemed to have changed as well. The servants had all worn simple black masks before, but now hers was adorned with grey goose feathers, which seemed to be cunningly woven into a veil of some sort; this fell loosely over her head, cloaking that glorious red hair until it was almost invisible among the grey feathers.

Then she was gone, leaving me standing, blinking on the stairs, wondering if I had imagined her entirely. She must have ducked into a room without my noticing. Very strange.

I continued up the stairs, then oriented myself – east would be on my left. I counted doors. One, two . . . The second door burst open, and Jayewardene's grandson practically fell out of it, half-dressed with trousers unbuttoned and shirt discarded, only a tie on his upper half – a tie that a woman's hand reached out and grabbed. She laughed, and I thought I could recognize the voice as Jane Smith's, though I couldn't imagine John Smith would be amenable to—

But before I could take that thought to its natural conclusion, I heard him call out from within the room, 'You're not getting away that easily, I'm afraid.'

And then the grandson was pulled back inside the room most decidedly, presumably to join them both, and the door slammed shut behind them.

Well. I like to think that I'm a student of human nature and that nothing is likely to surprise me, but I must admit, I hadn't seen that one coming. I gathered myself together, and then the door opposite, the second door on the west wall, flung itself open, and this really wasn't possible – it was Ezili again, this time speaking quite intently to Gary Bushorn, the guise dancing instructor. She appeared to be pleading with him, but he firmly pushed her out and shut the door in her face.

I didn't know where to place my eyes; I also didn't know how she had made it upstairs to his room, while I had been on the only set of stairs. But she gave me no chance to ask her any questions, as with a determined look on her face, she opened his door again and stepped boldly inside, slamming it behind her.

Well. I would be relieved, after all this, for a little bit of calm from

Stephanie. She, at least, seemed a relatively sensible sort of person. I proceeded to her door and knocked three times, not too loud.

The door opened before me, but the room within was oddly dim. And the scent of it – oh, the scent was like a blow to my heart: cinnamon and cardamom and cloves, coriander and curry leaves. It smelled just like Rupa's cooking – I may not have mentioned this before, but Rupa is a sensational cook; she does everything so well, it's quite hard to believe sometimes – which was impossible, as my dear Rupa was on the other side of the world.

I stepped into the dimness, pulled forward as if a rope had swung out, wrapped itself around me, and dragged me inside. For the life of me, I could not have turned away from that door. It closed behind me.

Oh, this was impossible.

'Rupa?'

Because there she was, in front of me, standing at her window, looking out at the lights of the city below. She turned at the sound of my voice, and there was a sight I never thought I'd see: a trembling lip and eyes that welled with tears. Could this be the same woman who had so confidently given me advice and guidance from my toddling days?

'What is it?' I asked. 'What's wrong?'

'I love you.'

'What?' The sentence was simple enough, declarative and clear, but the sense of it was completely lost on me.

'I love you, *kunju*. And I know you don't love me, and so I sent you away to marry that idiot—'

'He's not an idiot,' I protested, although I had been thinking exactly that not long ago, but she had kept talking, so I fell silent, not wanting to miss a word of this.

'—so you'd be safely on the other side of the planet, and I could get over all this, get over you, get on with my life . . .'

'Oh, my *rasathi*!' My princess! The scales had fallen from my eyes; all was clear. I loved Rupa with every fibre of my being!

And I had never loved Reginald – well, I hadn't ever thought I had, actually. I'd certainly never said so, and neither had he; we had just rubbed on reasonably well together, and it was a convenient arrangement, one that would allow me to go on quite easily with my life the way it was, which was all I'd ever asked out of life, but now here I was, wondering if perhaps there was more to life than just getting along easily—

I stepped forward and pulled Rupa into my arms, my lips bending down to touch hers. When they finally touched, I knew that something that had been terribly wrong for years would be put right.

Only a few last moments to endure. Then, lips touched, the light brightened, Mumbai fell away – and there I was, in Loveday House, with Dr Stephanie Smithson in my arms and my heart a wretched puddle on the floor.

'I'm so sorry,' I said, letting go of her and stepping back. 'I – I don't think I can do this.'

She looked a little disappointed, but said, 'It's all right, I understand. It's Reginald.'

'It was never Reginald,' I said, a piercing truth that stabbed my soul, though I didn't know how to explain it to her further.

'It's probably for the best,' Stephanie said, shrugging a little. 'The truth is, I've never actually been with – well, it was probably just the heat of the moment, the excitement of finding the book finally.' She blushed. 'I got carried away. I think – I think I'll just go to bed now, if it's all right with you.'

'Yes, yes, of course.' I had troubled the poor woman enough already. I managed to give her a polite smile, and then I left the room, feeling as if all my wits had been jumbled and jangled. It was a miracle that I managed to make it back to the stairwell and down the stairs without taking a nasty tumble; I was practically sleepwalking the last steps back to my door. It would be a cold and lonely room, but that was all right. Even if Reginald had been there, it would have been just as cold and lonely. I knew that now.

I opened the door, stepped inside, ready to finally strip off my sari and my mask and fling myself onto my bed to ponder how I had got myself into this mess and whether it would be in any way possible to get myself out of it. But all such plans were driven out of my head, by what awaited me in that room – Aunty Anu!

She stood there, ramrod straight in the light of the moon, hand firmly on her cane, although I'd never seen her seem to actually need it. Her sari was pressed to within an inch of its life, making me conscious just how dishevelled mine had become in the course of the night's adventures; the safety pins Reginald had applied hours ago were now barely sufficient to keep it on my body. Aunty Anu had a slim figure but was no less commanding for all that; if I tell you that you must imagine a rod of iron with just enough flesh on it to appear vaguely human, that will start to give you a sense of the woman. Maybe it was her decades as a schoolteacher that gave her voice that crack of the whip to it – I'm sure she regretted that the days had passed when she could beat her students into obedient submission. Or maybe it was just natural talent – regardless, I'd always withered under her onslaught, and in Mumbai, I spent a good portion of my time assiduously attempting to never be alone in a room with her. Yet here we were.

This damned house! It seemed determined to throw up phantasms to bewilder and bedevil its guests. What business did it have, borrowing my dreams and nightmares for its mischief? The only consolation was that they seemed to dissolve upon being pressed, which was tragic in the case of Rupa but would be a tremendous relief with Aunt Anu. I strode boldly forward, determined to walk right through the figure and dissolve the shade, banishing it back from whence it came - only to collide quite violently with Aunt Anu's form.

'What on Earth is wrong with you?' my aunt demanded.

I staggered back, feeling as if I'd walked into a rather sharp and pointy wall. 'You're really here!'

'Well, of course I'm here, where else would I be?'

'Mumbai?'

'Don't be ridiculous. I came as soon as I realized what a disastrous state you were in. I wrote to Reginald and told him I was coming; he must have told you . . .'

'He did say something, but I thought you'd go to his house. What are you doing *here*?'

'Well, when I arrived there, his parents - lovely people - told me where you had both flitted off to, and I did try to call, but there seems to be something wrong with the phones here, as every attempt to reach either of you or the house itself simply failed to go through, so there was nothing for it but for me to get on a boat and come here myself.'

'But you get so horribly seasick.'

'I know.'

'But why are you here, Aunt?'

'I have a terrible revelation.'

I almost didn't want to ask, because the last terrible revelation - that Aunty Anu was actually here - had practically stopped my heart, and I wasn't sure I'd survive another one.

'Your marriage—'

'Yes?'

'—is invalid!'

'What?'

Before she could go on, the door opened, and there was Reginald, returning to our bed like a good husband should, though perhaps I might send him off to take a bath first, as he did look quite thoroughly mussed . . . oh, wait.

'Reginald, do you know what Aunty Anu's talking about? She seems to think there's something wrong about our marriage.'

'Ah. Well, I did mean to tell you about that.' He was blushing furiously, his fair skin turning a fearsome red. He came further into the room, closing the door quietly behind him.

I frowned. 'So you knew? Did you know she was coming to visit so soon?'

He bit his lip. 'Her letter might have mentioned something about arriving on the weekend. That was why the invitation to this party seemed so fortu-itous, don't you know? Just the thing to take our minds off the problem—'

'What problem?'

Aunty Anu threw in, 'He's already married!'

'What?' It made no sense.

Reginald started talking quickly, his words tumbling over one another. 'I did mean to tell you. You see, John and I had the most terrific tiff four months ago, right before we were supposed to go to India together on our honeymoon, and so I went alone, and he stayed home, and then Mumbai was a wonderful distraction, and then I met you, darling, and it somehow seemed like just the thing to heal a broken heart, as we were over anyway.'

I shook my head. 'But we got married! There were elephants!' Not that elephants proved anything, I supposed, but they were so very large and so very solid.

'Yes, I thought he'd filed the divorce paperwork already – it was such a terrible row we had. Although I suppose I should have realized that there'd be something for me to sign, too. I honestly did think we were over completely. I never meant to deceive you, Sri.'

'And now?'

He had the look of a man caught between the Devil and the deep blue sea, as they say, and I was jolly well tempted to push him into that sea. But he somehow summoned up the courage to declare, 'The truth is, I love John. We've made it all up; it was really all just a big misunderstanding. I took something he said in entirely the wrong way, and he's explained the situation clearly now, and I see how mistaken I was.'

'So, you don't want to be married to me?' An ember of hope kindled in my chest. Could it be so simple?

'Not so fast, young man!' Aunty Anu's voice was loud and got louder as she went on. 'There were promises made to my niece! There were wedding gifts given, dowries procured—'

I tried to head her off. 'Aunty! My parents promised me they weren't engaging in any of that dowry nonsense. It's so horribly sexist . . .'

'Be quiet, child!' She started thumping her cane on the floor for emphasis, and the thumps grew louder with every sentence that followed. 'You see what happens when you let men take advantage like this? They walk all over you. But this *lord* has made promises to you, and he is going to live up to them! I came here to make sure it all gets taken care of. He can divorce this man and marry you again – no elephants this time, just a bit of paperwork to file.' By now she was practically bellowing, and it would be a wonder if her cane didn't knock all the plaster off the ceiling below. 'And *then* you can get on with making babies, which is what you *should've* been doing all along, and don't even *try* to lie to me – I *know* you've been using contraception.'

A knock on the door, but I couldn't answer it in that moment; I felt transfixed, frozen in place.

'Hello? Is everyone all right in there?'

Oh, Lord. It was Branok.

Reginald rushed to open the door for our host. Jago came in, with Tamsin close behind. The tiara shone on Tamsin's head, though not as brightly as her eyes.

'We were just coming to tell you that all was well. Tamsin insisted you'd want to know that we've found the tiara *and* that dratted goose – in the greenhouse, if you'd believe it – and how we're going to recover the espaliered pear trees – well, never mind all that. We heard the most disturbing thumping from downstairs – and the shouting? Ah, this must be your aunt, yes? Reginald told me that she might be joining us.'

I glared at my – I was about to say my husband, but he wasn't really. He wasn't my anything any more. He had lied to me and deceived me and really behaved in the most shocking way, and maybe it had been easier for him like that. A part of me could understand that, taking the easy road. Another part of me was disgusted. The code of the Chelliahs would never allow for such chicanery.

'Well, Srilatha,' my aunt said, 'what do you have to say for yourself?'

'For myself?' I had done nothing wrong that I could think of. Throughout this entire escapade, I had only tried to help people. Jago's eyes were fixed on mine, and his expression was calm but somehow encouraging. 'I think, Aunty Anu, that what I have to say, right now, is that I cannot go back to Reginald's house.'

Lord Branok said, 'You are welcome to stay here longer, Lady Srilatha. We certainly have enough room.'

'That is very kind, Lord Branok. But I'm not actually Lady Srilatha, it turns out – just Srilatha Chelliah. And I think I prefer it that way.'

'As I said, I would prefer you call me Jago. And I will call you Srilatha.'

Reggie stood there, looking confused, like a dog caught between a treat and a walk, with no idea which to pant after first.

'Oh, go to him, Reggie. Go, be happy. I'll try to do the same.'

Reginald hesitated for one last moment, then, with a grateful speaking glance, he fled. Just four of us here now.

I turned to Tamsin. 'I'm so happy for you! Now you can get married.'

'Actually, miss, I wanted to tell you. My sweetheart, he called me up and said that it didn't matter what his mother said; he wanted to marry me regardless, tiara or no tiara. We've already called the minister and will be wed in two weeks. I hope you'll be able to come.'

'Even better,' I said, smiling. 'I'm glad you found a man who deserves you.'

Tamsin smiled, dipped a little curtsey, and left the room. And then there were three.

'SriLATHa,' my aunt said rather loudly – but at a stern look from Jago, she moderated her tone. Even Jago's fearsome masked visage wasn't enough to quell her completely, though. 'Your parents will be very disappointed in you for abandoning this marriage.'

I could shout right back at her, but it seemed unnecessary. A calm, sensible tone, an analytical approach – I now understood that this was the key to managing Aunty Anu. The schoolteacher in her wouldn't be able to resist a logical explanation. 'This was never a marriage to begin with, Aunty. It was a charade, which I knew; I just didn't understand the extent of it. I should never have gone through with it in the first place. When I explain to *Amma* and *Appa*, they'll understand, I promise.' I might not explain *everything* to them, of course. The details of 'Shame', for example, could be allowed to fade into the mists of time.

My aunt looked bewildered but asked in a quite reasonable tone, 'So you're staying here? You're not coming back to Mumbai?'

I shrugged. 'For a little while. I need to – figure some things out. Write some messages, see what kind of reply I get.' It was possible, of course, that Rupa felt nothing for me at all. But somehow, I didn't think so. Loveday House wouldn't treat me so poorly. 'If my host will allow, I will remain here; his house is a good place to think . . .'

Lord Branok nodded acquiescence, his eyes bright with amusement.

'. . . And if it's not too much trouble, perhaps I might invite my servant Rupa to join me? You remember wonderful Rupa, Aunty – the soul of discretion. So you need have no concern, my dear Aunt, I will be most properly chaperoned.' A pleasant bubbling fizz was rising through my chest, much like the bubbles rising in the best fruity champagne – very soon, I felt, I might well go pop! I murmured a few last words, frothy hope effervescent in my aerated heart: 'Rupa will take very good care of me, and I intend to take excellent care of her.'

An Indian blue robin swooped in through the open window and began carolling a merry tune – it had travelled far from home, but had settled in with delight. Clearly, Loveday House approved.

Longing for Those Lost

by Stephen Leigh

Part III

LADY SRI STAYED ON at Loveday House for an additional two weeks, much to the staff's consternation, as Gary learned from Ceallaigh. 'The Horned Lady has made advances to several of the House staff, both male and female,' she said to Gary. 'Colette, who's her room servant, says she knows for certain that Lady Sri has consummated at least a few of those flirtations. She's seen the evidence, if you take my drift. Yesterday, I served Lady Sri lunch in the drawing room, and all of a sudden, she's tellin' me how she can sense you have feelings for me that go beyond just friend-ship, and she had the bloody cheek to ask me if I'd already shared your bed or if I was planning to. Just like that.' Ceallaigh snapped her fingers. 'Like she was asking if the weather was to my liking. The woman has no difficulty speaking whatever she's thinking, I'll give her that.'

They were in Gary's room in the morning, sitting on the balcony and looking out over Loveday's grounds. They'd made tea, and Ceallaigh had brought along some still-warm scones from the kitchen. She had come to see if Gary's room needed anything, and Gary had convinced her to join him as they broke their fast.

He sipped the tea, letting the mug hide his face as he pondered how to respond to what Ceallaigh had just told him. 'And how did you answer her?' he asked finally.

'How d'you think? She's still Lord Branok's guest, after all, and I wasn't about to tell her to keep her bleedin' nose out of my business, though I tell you, it was tempting.'

For a minute that seemed far longer, neither of them said anything, paying too much attention to their breakfast and the scenery in front of them.

Ceallaigh was the first to break the stasis. 'We should probably talk, you and me. But not right now. I have to do some thinking.'

Gary wondered exactly what 'thinking' Ceallaigh needed to do and on what subject. He could imagine what she might want to say after her 'thinking'. *Gary, I enjoy talking with you well enough, but that's all. I know you've said I remind you of your wife, Caitlyn, and I know how lonely it must be for you as a widower, but I do not find you attractive in that way. You're too old for me, anyway, no matter what Lady Sri might think . . .*

He didn't press her. 'Whenever you're ready to talk, just find me. No matter what you have to say.'

Ceallaigh smiled. 'I'll do that. I promise.'

A few days later, Lady Sri came into the library as Gary was talking to Jago about a new guise dance he'd learned from Richard Darke in Penzance. Jago, and belatedly Gary, rose from their chairs as Lady Sri entered. Her hair was up, leaving the ivory horn at the back of her neck clearly visible.

'Lord Branok,' Lady Sri said to Jago, 'I can't tell you how much I appreciate you allowing me to stay here at Loveday House for so long. It's been a very restful and wonderful visit, and I feel entirely rejuvenated. Thank you.'

'I'm delighted to hear that,' Jago responded. 'Though it sounds as if you're now planning to leave us.'

'I'm afraid so. I've just received a wonderful call from my oldest and dearest friend Rupa. I will be departing for London this very evening so that I might join her in Mumbai. I've already set Colette to pack for me. I'll call for a taxi as soon as I know she's finished.' Lady Sri's smile threatened to overwhelm the sunshine streaming through the library's window.

'There's no need for that,' Jago told her. 'I'll have Horace drive you to Heathrow when you're ready. Just tell me when your flight is leaving.'

Lady Sri's smile widened even further. 'That's so perfect and gracious of you, Lord Branok. I can't possibly thank you enough.' She turned to Gary, then. 'Your own maid Ceallaigh's such a delight, Dance Master. Don't you agree?'

Gary started, not expecting to be addressed and wondering at the change of subject. 'I certainly do,' he said reflexively.

'Then you must take very good care of her,' Lady Sri said. She nodded to both of them and left the room, still smiling, her aquamarine sari seeming to glide above the oriental carpet that graced the room.

Behind his domino mask, Jago's eyes were gazing, unreadable, at Gary. 'I would agree. Ceallaigh is indeed a delight.' He cleared his throat. 'Now then, about that new guise dance . . .'

Two days later, after dinner in the staff room, Ceallaigh walked out with Gary but didn't escort him to his room. Instead, she guided him along the downstairs hallways, stopping at a purple door along one of the corridors.

'My room,' she told Gary, opening the door, 'but don't you be getting any ideas. 'Tis only because I promised to tell you how I came to be here.'

Ceallaigh's apartment was hardly as grand and fancy as his own; hers had only high and narrow windows to let in outside light bounded by the stone foundations of Loveday House. Still, it was clean, the furniture solid, the floorboards gleaming and polished, the walls freshly painted, with a small sitting room for receiving visitors, a bedroom, and an ensuite bathroom.

Gary looked around, examining the framed pictures she had out on the sitting room's table and on the walls, wondering who these people might be in the black-and-white photos. He thought he could recognize Ceallaigh in a few of the shots, but while the scenery appeared to be Ireland, it was not an Ireland that Gary recognized. There were no cars in the streets; all the carts and carriages were horse- or mule-drawn, and many of the houses were one storey and thatched. All the pictures seemed to evoke a long-vanished past.

'These photos look old, and that one rather looks like Dublin Castle,' Gary said, pointing. 'I've visited there and seen pictures of old Dublin, but I don't recognize those towers or that dry-stone wall that's all pocked and broken or that huge wooden gate set in the wall with one side shattered. And the flag flying over the gate – I can't tell the colours in black and white, but that's neither the Irish Republic's flag nor the British Union Jack.'

Ceallaigh handed Gary a glass with two fingers of amber liquid in it; she held an identical glass in her hand and took a sip. Her eyes closed as she swallowed. 'Redbreast, with a splash of water to bring out the flavours. You are right, Gary. Those photos *are* old, and that one *is* Dublin Castle, though not one you ever visited. As for the flag, that's the *Clan na Gael*, adopted as the official flag of the new Irish Republic when Daniel O'Connell and his Repeal Association managed to get the Acts of Union taken down after the 1831 Rising – an emerald banner with thirty-two gold stars, each representing one of the Irish counties.'

Gary, familiar with Ireland's troubled history after decades in Northern Ireland, shook his head. 'Um, *what* 1831 Rising?'

'Take a sip of your whiskey, Gary. You asked me to tell you my story, and I'm goin' to oblige. You might want to take a seat . . .'

'You already know,' Ceallaigh told Gary, 'that some . . . well, actually *many* of us here in Loveday House ain't from your world or your world's history. That's my tale also. I'm from *that* Ireland, the one in the photos you were so fascinated by, not from the Ireland that you know yourself. It was Lord Branok himself who brought me here and likely saved my life in doing that.

'Y'know that 1831 Rising I mentioned? I was caught up in it. Aye, me. Rebellions are generally dirty, chaotic, and violent affairs; ours was little different. The English weren't about to give up our part of their empire easily, especially having lost the Americas. Ireland was a lot closer to them, and they had far more capacity for waging war than we did. But we were fighting for our home and for our freedom.

'There were some Loyalists who didn't want us leaving the United Kingdom, of course, but my family and friends weren't among those. Daniel O'Connell gave us fiery words that made our very blood boil, and 'twas certain the Irish would not fail this time to throw off the chains England had wrapped around us. England, for their part, sent over squadrons in their red coats to walk our streets and protect the Loyalists; we painted those coats even more red with their own blood. We refused to fight them the way they wanted to fight: in battle lines stupidly facing each other. No, we fought them however we could and did not easily get shot ourselves: picking them off one by one, firing from rooftops and around corners or behind rocks, using explosives when we could.

'Look at the picture of Dublin Castle again. You see the gate all broken? That was *my* doing, Gary, my last effort. I went to that gate dressed like a poor fishmonger pushing her wheelbarrow, but underneath the stinking fish, which was all the guards stationed at the gates noticed, the barrow was stuffed with black powder. I set the cart down in front of the gates as if exhausted and shook me hair out from under me cap. They jeered at me and called me a "disease-ridden harlot", a "dollymop", a "threepenny upright". I shouted similar abuse back to them, called them "vile lobsters" and "ballockless meaters". I then lit the fuse and ran, after a final obscene gesture at the soldiers. I heard shouts from the guards, heard the loud reports of their muskets and the shrill whistling of the balls as they passed close to me or bounced off the lane's cobbles. The cart exploded in thunder; a rain of wooden and iron shrapnel showered them, and the guards cried out in terror and pain. At the same time, I felt a terrible agony in my back, and the impact knocked me down.

'I don't remember much after that. I felt someone lifting me and carrying me away as my awareness went slowly to black – Lord Branok, it was, though I didn't know that at the time. I don't know how long I was unconscious, but when I opened my eyes again, I was *here*, in Loveday House, and being tended to by Dr Quiller, who showed me the long splinter of wood he'd taken from my back, sharp-pointed and dark with my blood for the length of my forefinger and more.

'"If it had hit you an inch or so higher and closer to your spine, you'd have been dead with this buried in your heart," he told me. "Even so, you're lucky Lord Branok found you before you bled out entirely."

'I didn't see Lord Branok again for three days. When he came to see me, he handed me that picture. "I thought you might want to know that Dublin Castle was taken by your people, who came pouring in after you took out the gate. That's your flag flying over it now."

'He told me that, back in my old home, it was already a year and more later, even though only a few days had passed here, and that the new Republic had elected O'Connell as president. I didn't understand then how that could possibly be, but I understand it now . . .

'Anyway, that's the story of how I came to be here. When I'd healed up fully again, a few months later, Lord Branok took me back to see "my" Ireland. He asked me if I wanted to stay there, but I hardly recognized the place. It was already 1863 there, not 1831, and the people I knew back then were either dead – my parents among them – or much older. O'Connell himself had passed away in 1847, and the people who'd been my age when I was last there were more than three decades older and elderly.

'People there were still complaining about the *An Drochshaol,* the "Hard Times" in the 1840s, when a potato blight destroyed the crop that many depended upon, especially in the interior landlocked counties. President O'Connell decreed that all Ireland's ports should be thrown open to bring in food as necessary and that crops raised in Ireland would be kept for the people, so the Great Famine in your Ireland never happened in mine, saving over a million lives and keeping many Irish from emigrating to America.

'But the current papers there were full of talk about some Ulster Riots, led by Loyalists in Armagh, Derry, and Belfast, who were still unhappy about the separation from England and wanted repatriation. Over five hundred people were killed in the rioting in just the last few weeks, the papers were saying. It seemed to me that Eire would never be entirely free of unrest.

'So, I told Lord Branok nay, I dinna want to stay there, where I knew no one any more,' Ceallaigh continued. 'He brought me back to Loveday. Gave me a job and me own rooms. I've been here fifteen years now, and even if I wanted to go back to "my" Ireland, I have no idea what year it would be there or if I'd recognize the place at all. I like your world, and I like Cornwall and Keun Island. It's clean and safe, there's good food for all, electricity for anyone who wants it, and I've made good friends here. I do read the papers and watch the telly now and then, and I know that's not the case everywhere. There's trouble enough in your world, too. But here on Keun . . .' She lifted her hands and let them fall again. 'I feel safe,' she repeated.

They sat in contemplative silence for some time, just sipping their whiskey and looking at the pictures of this Ireland that never existed in Gary's world.

Finally, his whiskey gone to a faint trace of amber, Gary set down his glass. He slipped Caitlyn's pocket watch out of his pocket and glanced at the hands there. 'I should probably go. Hitchcock and I are planning to start looking over at the stored holiday decorations tomorrow to decide which ones to put up for the party Jago has planned over Christmas.'

'Gary,' Ceallaigh began. Stopped. She put her own glass alongside Gary's on the table; they chimed as the rims came in contact with each other. 'I once told you I don't think of you as stupid or foolish or too old, but I never finished that statement. So I will now. Would you want to stay here with me tonight? We can talk about you or more about me, or just be here together, if that's all you want. There's no pressure for it to be more. But if you want more, well, I'm open to us knowing each other more intimately. If you truly need to go, though, then do that, and we can pretend I never said any of this.'

Gary felt his breath catch in his throat. *Caitlyn, it's been so long. Would you forgive me? Would Moira have understood?*

'I can't stay here,' Gary said, and saw Ceallaigh blink hard and catch her upper lip in her teeth before nodding. He thought he could see disappointment in her face. 'But if you'd like to spend the night, we could go up to my room, where I have sheets that won't smoulder or catch fire underneath me.'

Gary rose from his chair and held out his hand to her.

After a breath, Ceallaigh took it. Rising up on her toes, she cupped her hands around his face, pulled him down towards her. The kiss was longer and far more urgent than Gary had expected.

Gary and Hitchcock were in a corridor below stairs near the lift, pulling out and opening cardboard boxes stored in a large room there. The one before Gary had *Lights for Ballroom Greenery* written on it. Gary sighed, looking at the piles of neatly tied loops of green wires and electrical lights packed inside. 'At least it's not just one big, snarled mess,' he said to Hitchcock, who was looking into a similar box with *Entrance Hall Christmas Decorations* written on it.

'We keep an excellent staff here. They all know I'm fastidious and stuffy and do my best to avoid difficulties as well as any kind of complications,' Hitchcock answered drily and slowly, as usual. 'Hence, everything is nicely bound up. That way, nothing can escape before the next time it's needed.'

Gary couldn't decide if that was a joke or not. He was saved by the lift cage coming down, bearing a masked Jago and Annie. Annie was dressed in her usual stained overalls, with various gardening tools stuffed in the pockets or carabinered from loops.

'Hitchcock,' said Jago, 'I told Annie we'd find you here. She believes she's found the perfect tree among the pines on our lower land to place in the Blue Room.'

'I believe it will do perfectly, Hitchcock,' Annie said. 'It's the right height and well-shaped. But I want your imprimatur on it before I send out a group to cut it down and haul it in here. Four eyes are better than two, eh?'

'Very well.' Hitchcock gave a long sniff through his nose. 'Gary, if you'd carry on in my absence? I'll send Elbrekt down to assist you.'

'Thanks. I appreciate that.'

'Very good, then. Annie, if you'll lead the way . . .' The trio started to head for the lift, but Gary called out before they reached it.

'Jago, do you mind staying a few minutes? There's something I need to talk to you about privately.'

Jago glanced at Gary curiously through the eyeholes of the mask but said nothing until the lift started to ascend.

'Jago,' Gary began.

Jago lifted his hand to stop him. 'You wish to tell me about you and Ceallaigh, do you not?'

That statement left Gary with his mouth open, unable to say the speech he'd rehearsed in his mind.

Amusement lifted the corners of Jago's lips. 'Gary, there isn't much that happens in Loveday that I don't know about. I really don't care about the sleeping arrangements that you and Ceallaigh may have made, though I'm pleased that you were intending to inform me about it. I presume you're both consenting adults, and I also assume the two of you can continue to handle your staff duties. If I'm wrong about either of those things, then we have a problem, but I don't think that's the case. Am I correct?'

Gary had to chuckle. 'You are.'

'Then fine. Just carry on.' Jago clapped Gary on the shoulder. 'You and everyone here have a lot to do to make the house ready for our Christmas guests to arrive. So see to it. Ah, here comes Elbrekt to help you now . . .'

Bah, Humbug, Murder

by Caroline Spector

'WOULD YOU LIKE ME to take your luggage to Loveday now?' the chauffeur asked, gesturing to Constance and Temperance's suitcases.

'Those two are going up with you,' Constance said, nodding at the hard-cased bags. 'But not this one.' She held the handle of her knitting bag tight and then gave it a quick shake. It carried all manner of sewing and knitting effluvia: skeins of yarn, knitting needles, scissors, scraps of fabric, and so on. Snuggled at the bottom of it all was her trusty Walther PPK. Though she'd had to use her shears to kill a man in 1967 – he'd more than deserved it – it comforted her that she wouldn't have to be near a target to protect herself should a situation arise.

A soft breeze picked up a strand of hair from her neat chignon. Though it was a silvery-white now, she was still quite proud of it. Aside from her hair, she was remarkably well-preserved and spry, and looked much younger than her years.

'Good God,' she said, turning around, looking at the Christmas decorations with sharp, hazel eyes. 'This place is the very definition of twee.'

'And I know what a fan of twee you are,' Temperance said with a laugh. It caused the paintbrushes she had instead of hair to rattle and clack. They hung down her back, varying from short to long. Their tips were sable soft. 'And I know you love saying "twee", too.'

The village was indeed twee – almost treacly. In addition to THE MERMAID'S CHEST, there were various darling little shops along the main thoroughfare.

Garlands of greenery hung everywhere. Instead of the traditional Christmas touches, there were seashells and fancifully carved fish tucked among the boughs. Blue rather than white fairy lights wrapped the swag. Some of the fish looked as if they were jumping out of water. There were some with articulated tails moving in the wind. Ornaments of scale-like iridescence dotted the greenery. Draped across the boughs were shockingly bright pink blooms with almost obscene dark, fleshy fuchsia inside. She'd never seen blooms so disturbingly sexual, and they were most definitely inappropriate for Christmas.

Constance noticed two peculiar-looking people walking by. They had oddly elongated heads, huge eyes, and pale, faintly bluish skin.

'Do you want to go in here?' Temperance said, gesturing to THE MERMAID'S CHEST.

Constance stepped closer to the shop and peered through the window. 'Not my usual thing, antiques. Unless you count me as one; I am terribly fond of me.'

Temperance rolled her eyes. 'When I became your ward, I didn't realize that I'd have to put up with such a conceited granny.'

'I'll have you know, I am no one's granny,' Constance *harrumphed*. 'I'm still quite fetching for a woman my age.' She gave a self-deprecating smile.

Temperance looked down and frowned at her battered Doc Martens boots – a classic style Constance could get behind wholeheartedly. Fashion, in addition to her work for Silver Helix, had been her life for five decades.

Constance touched Temperance's arm, saying, 'But I'm very glad you're my ward. I hate how we came to this situation, but I'm so very happy I could be the one to help.'

The bell over the door jangled as they entered the shop. It was no bigger than a moderate-sized front room and crowded with furniture and knick-knacks. The mustiness of old books and beeswax polish in the air was comforting.

Behind the counter was a short, balding gent who had all the hallmarks of a fellow just past his prime – though that likely wouldn't have been too robust either.

'Good afternoon,' he said. 'Welcome to THE MERMAID'S CHEST. I'm the proprietor, Nigel Walmsley. Do ask if you need anything.'

Constance had just spied a pair of bejewelled knitting needles in one of the glass cases when the bell over the door jangled again.

One after another, three people entered. The first was a strikingly beautiful blonde woman. Constance knew who she was; most people would. Not only was she breathtaking, but she was also a famous actor.

'You!' she said, pointing at Constance, clearing the space between them in three steps. Her accent was French. 'I'm furious with you!'

Constance knew why she was angry. 'Margot . . .' she began.

'I don't want to hear your excuses!' Margot said in high dudgeon. Constance thought she was overacting just a bit. 'You *promised* me that dress! I *didn't* ask any of the other designers, because I *trusted* you. And it was for the Academy Awards! No wonder I didn't win.'

This was nonsense, of course. But there was no talking to Margot when she was overset.

By now, the two other people – one of them a joker – had crammed themselves into the shop. Constance was acquainted with one, and the other she felt as if she should know.

'Constance!' the joker said, clearly surprised. He was tall and looked like Krampus, Santa's dark rival. Constance knew him from his work as a surgeon on the *Queen Mary*. Because of his visage, he'd lost his entire general practice. Patients found him altogether too frightening, and parents refused to take their children for even one visit. Even other jokers were known to shy away from him. 'What are you doing here?' he asked.

'Archie,' she replied, using his given name. 'What a lovely surprise! This is my ward, Temperance. Temperance, this is Archibald Clegg.' Though she knew people called him Krampus rather more often than not.

'Constance,' Krampus said with a terrifying smile. 'Allow me to introduce Candice Kane. Goes by Kandy Kane. She was on the second season of *American Hero*.'

'Pleased to meet you,' Kandy Kane said, extending her hand.

Constance gave it a quick shake. By accent and manners, there was no doubt Kandy Kane was a Yank. She was a pretty thing, but Constance got the distinct impression that Kandy Kane had dismissed her as if she wasn't important the minute they shook hands. *Silly twit*, Constance decided.

'Miss Kane,' she said, trying not to be annoyed. 'My ward, Temperance Walker.'

'It's very nice to meet you,' Kandy Kane said. She lacked sincerity.

'What brings you to Keun, Constance?' Krampus asked. 'I'm guessing the same reason we're here. Christmas party at Loveday House? Kandy, Margot, and I walked down to see the village.'

Constance nodded as she pointed to the knitting needles in the case. Nigel promptly retrieved them and offered them for her inspection.

'We are here for Christmas,' she replied. 'Neither Temperance nor I wanted to spend it in London this year.'

'What about my dress?' Margot interrupted.

Constance sighed. She ignored Margot and examined the knitting needles more closely. They were for show, not use. Ill-balanced, heavy from gems and silver at the head, they weren't at all practical. But she liked finding pretty objects that had to do with her skill and power. She put the pair at 1920s or '30s vintage.

'Oh my God!' Temperance exclaimed, looking at her phone. 'Someone murdered Black Dog! The bastards!'

The adults, save Kandy, glanced at one another with dismay. Constance was filled with ambivalence. She believed in joker's rights, but Black Dog's methods were too extreme.

'I don't see that it's a big deal,' Kandy said. 'Wasn't he in prison? Like, wasn't he a criminal?'

'He wasn't a criminal,' Temperance said hotly. 'He started the Fists so there would be consequences for killing jokers. And it doesn't matter if you have dosh or not to get off. Killing jokers isn't taken seriously as a crime. That's why Black Dog mattered.'

'You teenagers are so melodramatic,' Kandy replied. 'I read somewhere that he was a terrorist.'

'I'm not being melodramatic,' Temperance snapped. Her paintbrushes rattled as she struggled to control her shaking. 'I'm a joker,' she continued. 'Do you know how many times I've been bullied because I look like this?' she said, gesturing to her brushes. 'I've lost count. And *nothing* was ever done about it. My mum and da were murdered because they were in a social centre for jokers waiting for me when it was bombed. If I could only find the shites who did it . . .'

'Hey, people with the virus are either unlucky like jokers or lucky like me,' Kandy said, with the conviction of someone who obviously didn't know what they were talking about.

'You're an absolute quim,' Temperance said.

'Be that as it may,' Constance interrupted, putting a gentle hand on Temperance's arm, 'it isn't polite to say so . . . And unfortunately, there will be repercussions from his murder, and it'll be bad for nats *and* jokers.'

'What's that?' Kandy Kane asked, pointing at a ring in the case on the counter, obviously finished with talking about Black Dog's murder.

Nigel pulled it out and placed it in her hand. Constance recognized it immediately. A ring consisting of a series of five closed hands was distinctive to one group only: the Twisted Fists. She closed her eyes. Terrible timing finding that ring here now.

'Oh, it's pretty enough. You know, if you were dressing down,' Kandy Kane said as she slipped it on her finger. It was a loose fit.

'That's not a good choice,' Krampus said. 'Not at all.'

Kandy held her hand out as if looking at an engagement ring. 'I don't see why not. Isn't this just like those Cladd . . . what do you call it? The ones with the hands holding up a heart?'

'*Claddagh*,' Krampus said and held out his hand.

Kandy Kane glowered at him, then took off the ring and dropped it into his palm. His fingers closed around it, and he squeezed it tight.

'What's this doing here?' Krampus asked, holding out the ring. There was a thread of anger in his tone.

Nigel took the ring and gave it a quick polish with a cloth before putting it back in the case. 'Oh, it's one of those estate things,' Nigel replied. 'There was a large collection of jewellery, and this was in it. I thought someone might like it as a curiosity – nothing more.'

'Well, I don't understand all the fuss,' Kandy said. 'It's just a ring. And a cheap-looking one at that.'

'It's the symbol of the Twisted Fists,' Constance said softly. 'Black Dog's group. I've only seen one other person with a ring like this. And they're dead now.'

'The Twisted Fists?' Margot asked. 'You knew someone with them?'

'Yes. He helped save the country. But Black Dog's methods – killing five nats for every joker murdered – isn't something *I'd* do,' she replied. 'But my friend and I had a mutual respect for each other. He liked my work for joker's rights. And I liked the direction he was trying to take the Fists in.'

'Great,' Kandy said flatly. 'They have their own jewellery line. Is this like an engagement ring? "Here honey, would you marry me? And by the way, I'm in an organization that kills people."'

'What an unpleasant conversation for Christmas Eve,' Nigel said, interrupting them.

'A ring with the symbol of the Twisted Fists? Why would you even keep such a thing in your shop?' Krampus asked. He frowned, and his face twisted into something frightening. The other people in the shop drew back. He was the very embodiment of Krampus at that moment. When he stamped his hoof, sparks flew.

'Who cares?' Temperance said. 'Better the Fists than the nats who killed my parents. At least I understand *why* the Fists do it. Blood will flow. Make no mistake about that.'

There was silence as the adults, aside from Constance, tried to look anywhere except at Temperance. Temperance began swiping angrily on her phone, ignoring the adults.

'My apologies,' Krampus said. Even apparently contrite, his face still looked like a terrible mask of rage. 'It's just . . .'

'No need,' Constance said. 'You're a surgeon. You save lives. Killing people isn't what you're trained to do. I can see why the ring upset you.'

'No more talk of terrorists!' Margot exclaimed. 'I'm certain even they take the holidays off.'

There was another uncomfortable silence, then Kandy said, in a bored voice, 'Well, if no one is going to buy anything, we should go back to Loveday.'

'I'd like these,' Constance said, holding out the knitting needles.

'An excellent choice,' Nigel said, smiling. 'They're from the '30s. Shall I wrap them up?'

'Yes, please do,' she replied.

Kandy Kane tapped her foot impatiently. Krampus and Temperance glowered at Kandy. And Margot remained oblivious to everyone around her, having discovered a mercury glass mirror. Kandy gave her a baleful look.

Constance dreaded the walk to Loveday.

Large and imposing, Loveday loomed on a rise overlooking the sea. It was festooned with every manner of winter and Christmas holiday finery one could imagine. Garlands of greenery entwined with ribbon and white fairy lights roped the columns and porch railings. Large wreaths, decorated with nuts and small ornaments, hung on the elaborately carved double doors. Smaller versions of the wreaths hung in every window. The only part of the house spared the enthusiastic bedecking was the belvedere that stood dark against the grey and rapidly dimming twilight. Constance noted that the strange fuchsia flower she'd seen in the village hung from some of the wreaths here, too. These were a more appropriate dark crimson.

Constance stopped and stared. She hadn't halted just because it was rather a lot to take in – so much Victorian froufrou *was* difficult to absorb all at once – but for the most part, she'd stopped because she was tired. The rest of the group stopped as well. She appreciated their patience with her slow progression. The temperature had already dropped by the time they'd left The Mermaid's Chest and had continued to do so as they made their way to Loveday.

Foolish, she thought. *Walking all this way from the village.*

Fat snowflakes started falling. Constance had a collapsible umbrella in her bag and was glad of it. Standing behind her was Krampus, who took it from her and held it over her head. He smelled like burning straw and ash, and his breath was hot against her neck.

The driveway and path were made of crushed shells, and there was a pleasant, crunching sound as she walked. It wasn't treacherous in the least. The path curved up to three deep steps leading to the porch.

'Impressive, isn't it?' Kandy said, her eyes gleaming. 'And it's *huge* inside. You should see the entrance hall.'

'It's more of a foyer,' Margot said, giving Kandy Kane a narrow-eyed look. 'An entrance hall sounds small.'

'Well, I don't care what you call it,' Kandy replied, giving Margot an annoyed glance. 'It's cool, and I like it. I'd like to live in a place like this, as long as I didn't have to clean it.'

'If you had a house like this,' Constance said, 'you could afford maids.'

Kandy gave Constance a sharp look, then shrugged her shoulders. 'Me or someone else paying. Whatever works.'

They arrived at the porch, but before anyone could lift one of the brass rappers, the doors opened, and they were enveloped by the smells of ginger biscuits, puddings, peppermint, and woody evergreens. Cocoa was definitely being made somewhere inside. Standing before them, holding one of the doors open, was a squat man wearing an impeccable black suit, dark tie, and a bright white shirt.

'Good evening,' he said, drawing out *evening*. 'Won't you come in? Welcome back, Ms Kane, Madame Bellarose, Dr Clegg. Ms Russell and Ms Walker, now that you are here, the party is complete. Lord Branok will be happy you've all arrived. I'm Hitchcock, Lord Branok's butler.'

'After you,' Krampus said to Constance. He bowed and gestured for her to enter.

'Isn't this strange weather for this time of year?' Kandy asked, stepping across the threshold. 'I thought it didn't snow in Keun. At least, that was what they told me before I left London.'

'Stranger things have happened, I suppose,' Krampus replied with a shrug, whipping his tail around his waist. It very nearly hit Kandy, and she glared at him.

'Is Kandy right?' Constance asked Hitchcock. 'It does seem peculiar.' She looked closer at Hitchcock, tilting her head to one side. 'I have the oddest feeling I've seen you somewhere before.'

'I think not,' Hitchcock replied. 'I am certain I would remember such a pleasant encounter. Yes, Ms Kane, the snow is most unusual. But these things do happen every century or so. It keeps us on our toes.' He took Constance's umbrella from Krampus.

Another servant – a handsome, dark-haired fellow – appeared and whisked it away. A willowy young maid took their coats, hats, and scarves before vanishing down one of the corridors. It was disconcerting. But all that was quite overshadowed by the entrance hall.

The crystals making up a massive chandelier cast little rainbows on the Persian rug. The carpet was woven of silk with a delicate pattern, and it had a subtle sheen. It almost filled the enormous entryway. Facing the door was an elegant split staircase rising up to the first level. At the landing, a stained-glass window depicted all manner of fantastic creatures in a roiling sea. It was so startling and skilfully done that, for a troubling moment, Constance felt as if the waves were moving.

On the walls – those not punctuated with doorways to other rooms – hung a collection of art, as fine as Constance had ever seen. Through the double doorway to her left was a large drawing room. Like the hall, paintings adorned every wall. In the centre of the room was a Christmas tree about three and a half metres tall.

'This is all . . .' Constance said, looking around the room, '. . . a lot to take in.'

'Most of our visitors express the same sentiment,' Hitchcock replied, giving them a slow, rather creepy, smile. 'Tea is being served in the blue drawing room. Unless you'd prefer to go straight to your rooms. Your luggage has already arrived and been put away.'

'Tea sounds lovely.' Constance was very much ready for tea.

'A cuppa sounds good,' Temperance agreed, looking up from her phone. 'Is there Wi-Fi here? Can't get a signal on my phone.'

'Maybe you could go without your phone, just for one night,' Constance said. If Temperance kept looking for news about Black Dog, things could get ugly. Her ward was passionate about all things to do with violence against jokers. It troubled Constance, despite her own work for joker rights, for Temperance was more extreme in her views.

'Very well,' Hitchcock replied. His voice was deep and languid. 'Do follow me.' His walk was like his voice, slow and deliberate. Constance had a flash of Grace Kelly wielding scissors in self-defence.

Hitchcock led them to the blue drawing room, which was not at all awash in the expected colour.

'You're just in time!' Gary Bushorn exclaimed as he rose from one of the three delicate tables clustered together.

They knew each other from her visits to Rathlin Island. She often recruited joker tailors from there to work at her atelier. His hair was close-cropped with grey sprinkled through it, but his face was remarkably unlined for his age.

Constance smiled, happy to see him again. It had been almost a year, and she'd brought her annual gift for him and had included an extra present she hoped he would enjoy.

'I was wondering what was taking so long. I expected you earlier.' He gave her a quick hug, kissed her on each cheek, then took her hands in his. 'Where have you been?'

'We stopped at the village,' she replied. It was good to see him. 'It was terribly . . . twee.'

Gary laughed. 'I know how you feel about twee things. Come, I'll introduce you. I see you've already met up with Margot, Kandy, and Archie.'

'Yes,' she replied. 'We ran into them at THE MERMAID'S CHEST. I had no idea they were going to be here. A very pleasant surprise.' She decided it was better just to leave the incident between Temperance and Kandy out of the mix. For now. 'This is my ward, Temperance. I told you about her in my letters.'

'You did!' Gary said, taking Constance's elbow as he ushered her forward. 'Good to finally meet you, Temperance. This is our host, Lord Jago Branok.'

Lord Branok stood and stepped forward, extending his hand first to Constance and then to Temperance. Constance noted the thick, crisscrossing scars on his warm palm.

A gold mask covered the top half of his face. He was striking despite the oddness of the mask and his choice in apparel.

'Thank you for the invitation,' Temperance said.

Lord Branok gave her a crooked smile.

'Never been to a place this posh before.'

'I'm honoured you came,' Lord Branok replied.

He wore a navy-coloured tweed suit with a vintage feel to it. The lapels were a shade too wide to be considered fashionable, at least not in this century. The trousers were high-waisted with a full break. The ox-blood red tie was Windsor-knotted. His attire was completed by a waistcoat and a white shirt.

'I'm delighted to meet you both,' he said. 'Let me introduce you to the rest of your Christmas companions.'

Tea was delightful. At least, it started out that way.

There were introductions all around. Constance secured a seat opposite

Barbara Baden, second in command of the United Nations Committee for Extraordinary Interventions, known commonly as the Committee. Barbara's ace name was Babel, and she could translate any language – or change the speech of those around her into incomprehensible gibberish.

Gary and Bastet shared the table with them. Bastet was a joker, but that didn't bother Constance one bit. Only the most extreme afflictions made her uncomfortable – and even then, Constance was adept at hiding her reaction. Bastet, she found charming. With her black cat's head and human body, she resembled the Egyptian goddess she was named after. Once, at a party they'd both attended, a tipsy Bastet had revealed to Constance that she could also turn into a house cat. Constance, a wee bit totted herself, had vowed to keep Bastet's secret safe.

Babel tucked a strand of dark-brown hair behind one ear and then bit into a tart. The expression on her face was bliss.

'Try one of these,' she said, taking a sip of tea. There was a trace of an Israeli accent in her voice. 'They're amazing. You should have the scones, too. Heavenly. I've been all over the world and have never eaten ones this good.'

Babel finished the tart then went back to work on her scone.

'You're far from home, Ms Baden,' Constance said. She helped herself to one of the little sandwiches. 'What brings you here?'

'Please, call me Barbara. This was going to be an unhappy time of the year for me,' she said. There was a moment when her eyes became shiny with tears, but they vanished just as quickly. Years of learning to control her emotions during diplomatic assignments served her well. 'Klaus wasn't in the mood to celebrate.'

Constance fiddled with her sandwich, embarrassed that she'd brought up the painful subject of Klaus and Barbara's rift. They were famous enough that news of their falling-out had spread far and wide. It might have been selfish, but Constance was glad for another heart-lonely soul in the house.

She missed Arthur, her own love of forty years. A love she'd only just realized despite the decades they'd spent working together. They would be separated for yet another four years due to his obligations to the country. In a series of blood-soaked events the previous year, he'd been placed on the throne to help heal a divided nation. Those obligations chafed at her now that their lives were so close to the end, and each year together was precious.

'Miss Russell,' Bastet began, inclining her cat's head towards Constance. The white hairs on her black muzzle were the only indication of her age. 'I have admired your work for years. The clothing you've made to accommodate jokers' bodies is remarkable.'

There were few things that pleased Constance as much as her work being appreciated. Whether creating something for jokers or nats, it didn't matter to Constance; what she made was going to be beautiful. She'd built her business on it.

'That's terribly nice of you,' Constance replied. 'It brings me joy. Is it difficult being a Living God?'

'For the most part nowadays, no. After the war for New Egypt, I left and went back to Las Vegas. But there aren't as many of us jokers left here since the migration to the moon. I don't suppose you could recommend someone who could make a gown for me?' Bastet straightened her jumper nervously. It had a cat on it wearing a Santa hat and was aggressively ugly. 'I know you've retired for the most part, but if it's not too much of an imposition . . .'

'Just don't *expect* her to make you anything,' Margot said from the other table. 'She'll disappoint you.'

'Oh, do leave off, Margot. I apologized,' Constance said, biting into her cucumber sandwich. It was made with butter and a small squirt of lemon, just the way she liked it.

'Not enough,' Margot said darkly.

Temperance rolled her eyes at Margot with the contempt only a 16-year-old girl could serve.

'I thought the Cadbury people were sending me down here to get me out of their hair over Christmas, but this isn't what I expected,' Kandy said.

'You're most welcome, Ms Kane,' Jago said.

'Call me Kandy, everyone does.'

Constance couldn't quite place her accent. The States had a remarkable number of them, but still far fewer than London.

'I expected them to fob me off into some crummy B&B, but this is top notch. And the decorations are different, too. Never seen some of these styles before. And there isn't any of that *Jesus is the Reason for the Season* stuff.'

Constance blanched. She wasn't terribly fond of Christmas herself. It brought up bad memories from when she worked for the Krays in the '60s. And how she'd ended Ronnie Kray so that he couldn't hurt any woman again.

However, Kandy Kane was just dreadfully rude. If she were to be less kind, Constance might call her a naff hag. But that wouldn't be polite.

Jago cleared his throat and said, 'Loveday House isn't really one thing or another this time of year. There are traditions from Europe, but you can find other holiday decorations from other places scattered around, too. It's a large house, and many of the staff aren't from Keun.'

The sun was almost completely down, but the snow was still falling, harder now. There was a strange quality to the light, almost a jade colour. Constance had never seen the sky that shade before and certainly not when it was snowing. Every so often, a window frame creaked as the wind hit it.

'Lord Branok, how did you come by Loveday House?' Bastet asked. 'It's . . . unique.' She shivered a little, rubbing her hands together.

Gary reached across the table and took her hands in his. Bastet's golden eyes widened as his power became evident. His hands started to warm her almost instantly. Bastet gave a little purr and shut her eyes.

For the most part, Gary was able to control how hot his body became – though there were a few times when he couldn't be mindful about it. That was why Constance brought him sheets and a robe made with her wild card ability every Christmas. He had the misfortune of often setting his bedding on fire while asleep, but it wasn't a problem when she gifted him with garments and bedding made with her power. Those never caught fire. At least not for a year, after which her power began to fade on the items she made.

'Thank you,' Bastet said, smiling at him. 'You're very kind. Please, Jago, do go on.'

'I'm interested, too.' The voice belonged to a man close to Constance's age who was being escorted into the room by Hitchcock. His trousers and jumper looked as if they were from the bottom of his dirty-laundry basket. He was nondescript with muddy grey hair and watery brown eyes.

'Mr Thomas Downs,' Hitchcock said slowly, drawing out the *owwwns*. 'Again.'

'Hello, everyone,' the newcomer said. 'Did I miss anything? Thanks for getting me here, Hitchcock. I got lost coming from my suite. Funny that. But a little maid I met along the way turned me in the right direction, and there was Hitchcock, just in time. She had a most interesting accent. Don't think I've ever heard one like that.'

'Digger Downs,' hissed Babel under her breath. Constance thought she heard her say, 'Bastard.' But she couldn't be sure.

'Barbara Baden, as I live and breathe!' he said mischievously. 'Or shall I call you Babel? Never sure about that. Anyway, it's a pleasure to see you again. How's Lohengrin?'

With a look that could melt glass, Babel turned back to her scone and tea. Only Constance noticed that her hands shook as she put her teacup to her mouth.

'Kandy Kane, aren't you looking festive?' he said, turning his attention to her. 'We should talk later.'

A sweet smile, which didn't hide the hostility in her eyes, came over Kandy's face. 'I'm on vacation, Digger. You know that. Why don't you just go away? Forever.'

He shrugged his shoulders, clasped his hand to his heart and then said, 'Force of habit, my dear. I'll do my best.'

'I must be cursed,' Margot sniffed. 'First Constance and now him.' Malice dripped from her lips as she glowered at Downs. 'You're a vile little man who writes lies in your stupid magazine. The world would be a better place without you and your kind.'

'Stop flattering me,' Digger said, smiling at her. 'I write about you only because I love you, Margot. That, and you really do boost readership.'

'Lord Branok, please tell us more about Loveday House,' Bastet said, trying to change the subject.

Downs smirked and took a seat at Krampus and Kandy's table. Kandy pointedly ignored him. He smiled as a servant poured him a cup of coffee instead of tea. He lifted his cup to Kandy, who returned the favour with narrowed eyes and a vicious smile.

'Philistine,' Barbara muttered.

Jago nodded at Bastet, then adjusted his mask. Constance noticed he hadn't touched the little cakes on his plate, nor had she seen him drinking the tea in front of him.

'Many years ago, I discovered Loveday and was immediately drawn in,' he began. 'At the time, it was in a dreadful state of disrepair. Indeed, I'm still working on restoration and improvements, so it's best to be careful when you're moving about the house – you never know what you might find. I suspect I'll be working on the house forever. Old houses require so much attention.'

'The villa I rent every summer is like that,' Margot said. Her plate was empty, and Constance knew why. Perpetually on a diet, Margot had a terror of becoming fat, convinced it would ruin her career. 'There's always something going wrong. Of course, it is a more rustic way to live, so I don't mind the inconvenience. It's only for a month or so.'

'It sounds as if you've had a rough time of it,' Devlin Pear said, shooting Constance a grin. He was the biggest surprise of the guests thus far. She knew him from Silver Helix. He could shrink to a tiny size, but sadly his clothes didn't shrink with him. Constance had been called upon to make him apparel using her power to protect him when he was using his. He was retired now, however – as much as anyone ever retired from the Silver Helix.

'It is a burden,' Margot said solemnly, an expression of eternal suffering accentuating the beautiful lines of her face.

It took everything in Constance not to roll her eyes just like Temperance was wont to do. Constance thought she would knock herself unconscious if Margot continued being . . . well, Margot. She did notice Temperance looking at Margot and shaking her head. Then Temperance looked down at her phone, and a frown crossed her face.

'I've heard about your house parties,' Babel said, turning her chair to face Jago. 'But little about you.'

Jago tugged at the bottom of his waistcoat, then shifted in his seat. 'I'm not interested in fame, Ms Baden. I retired quite comfortably several years ago.' His attention turned towards the window, where the muffled sound of snow had been replaced by hard-hitting fine grains of frozen rain. It sounded as if sand were being blown against the windows.

Temperance was frowning at her phone, tapping on it with growing annoyance. Finally, she looked up at Jago. 'Do you have Wi-Fi?' she asked him, anxiety in her voice. 'I asked Hitchcock earlier. My phone isn't working. I'm trying to find out more about what's happening with Black Dog.'

'Apologies,' Jago said. 'Your mobile phones won't be working properly in this storm. And our landline is spotty at best. I'm terribly sorry.'

'What happened to Black Dog?' Bastet asked.

'Someone murdered him,' Krampus said. 'Temperance read about it on her phone while we were in the village. They don't know how he died. Bloody peculiar business.'

'But I thought he was in the Hague,' Bastet said, with a shaking voice. 'How did this happen? And why now?'

'That's what I'm trying to find out,' Temperance replied. 'Someone got to him. And now all hell is going to break loose. The Fists will want revenge. And a lot of jokers will be terrified, because if it can happen to Black Dog, none of us are safe. Whoever did this should've known there would be retribution.'

'This isn't good,' Devlin said, shooting Constance a concerned look. 'The joker enclaves will be a nightmare.'

'If we can't get a line out,' Babel said, 'I do have a satellite phone. But for emergencies. I'm not sure this qualifies.' She sighed. 'I don't ever really get away from the Committee.'

'It might work,' Jago allowed. 'But the storm is . . . unusual. One might even say extreme. I should mention that you shouldn't wander outside after dark.'

Constance didn't particularly mind not having phones going off willy-nilly all the time, even if it was to get updates on the Black Dog situation. All three jokers appeared affected by the news, and Constance couldn't blame them. She'd seen enough brutality against jokers to last a lifetime.

But having no mobile signal would make things quieter. Fortunately, Temperance wasn't completely glued to her phone, but she did look extremely upset. And the notion that anyone would be daft enough to go for a stroll on a night like this was a puzzlement to Constance.

'Maybe we can hear more of Jago's story,' Digger Downs said. 'After all, there's nothing we can do about any of that right now.'

Constance didn't like the gleam in his eye. Margot, Kandy, and Babel all seemed to dislike him intensely. She wasn't familiar with his work, but if it was anything like the British tabloids, there wasn't much there to like at all.

'If you insist,' Jago said. 'I was born in Cornwall, though not on Keun. As a young man, I attended Oxford, where I studied under Professor Tolkien and met C.S. Lewis. During the war, I was part of the British Expeditionary Force – one of the lucky ones evacuated from Dunkirk. I returned to France for D-day, but my luck ran out not long after, and I lost my leg. While I was recovering back in London and being fitted for a prosthetic, I lost my wife and daughter to a V-2 rocket. There did not seem much to live for after that.

'Like many of you, I have been touched by the wild card. I suppose you could call me an ace, though I am a far cry from the heroes of the Committee and the Silver Helix. I was on the *Queen Mary* on 15 September 1946, on the way to New York . . . not as a passenger but as part of the crew. I had taken a post as the ship's librarian. I have always loved books.

'When the *Queen Mary* returned to England . . . Well, I suspected the wild card had done something to me, but I did not know what, and when I saw how the jokers were being treated, I felt it was safer to remain inconspicuous. It was quite a while before my . . . symptoms . . . began to make themselves apparent. I began to heal. My hair had gone white; now it turned dark again. I became stronger, more limber; my aches and pains vanished. And my stump grew a new leg.' A brief smile touched his lips, beneath his mask. 'I had no family left, no close friends. I spent the next few years travelling, working in libraries and bookshops in Sheffield, Birmingham, York, Edinburgh, Plymouth. As I grew more vigorous, I took on more strenuous work, too. Construction, shipbuilding, mining. Hard labour. I sailed to New York again, this time on the *United States*. A far more pleasant crossing. I visited Barcelona, Rome, Morocco, Singapore, and Hong Kong, and spent a year in France. In those days, I was far from wealthy. What money I had, I spent on books.

'No matter where I wandered, though, I could feel Cornwall calling me back, so finally I returned. I remembered all the tales I had heard of Keun as a child. So, one day, I walked across the causeway to see the island for myself . . . and I found Loveday House.

'It was perfect. Ruined, to be sure . . . but like no other place on Earth. And so large. I needed a place to keep my books.' Suddenly, there was a delighted smile on his face.

'How much room do you *need* for books?' Kandy asked. 'There are e-readers. Books clutter up a house. Just how many *do* you have?'

'I have no idea,' Jago said, leaning forward eagerly. 'We'll visit the library after tea.'

'Would you like more tea, ma'am?' a pretty servant girl asked Constance softly. Her eyes and hair were dark brown. Her complexion a few shades lighter. There was a lilting quality to her voice, but Constance couldn't place her accent. 'I have a fresh pot here.'

Constance shook her head. 'No more for me.'

Her table companions declined as well. The other tables were being taken care of by their own servants. It seemed a bit much for just their small group, but she supposed Jago liked entertaining in style. Heaven only knew how many servants were needed just to keep a place the size of Loveday running smoothly.

'I don't know about anyone else,' Krampus said with a growl. There was a collective gasp at his voice, though there was nothing to be done about the way he sounded any more. 'But I'm full as a tick, and I would like to see Jago's library. If it's half as impressive as what I've seen of Loveday thus far, it will be a bibliophile's dream. And I count myself as one.'

'If everyone has finished,' Jago said, 'I'll be happy to oblige.'

Fortunately, the public hallways at Loveday were wide. Like some *Phantom of the Opera* Pied Piper, Jago led them through a twisty route. Constance was glad that her sense of direction helped her keep track of their way. Though breadcrumbs might have helped, those wouldn't lie on the carpet for long. She'd seen glimpses of staff, but it was clear they'd been instructed to be as unobtrusive, yet efficient, as possible.

They passed a room with wide doors draped with greenery. Inside, a servant was methodically brushing the felt on a billiard table. There was a fire in the fireplace, and the leather chairs flanking it were being attended to by yet another servant. A cart with crystal decanters of liquor was situated under one of two tall, jade-coloured, moiré silk-draped windows.

Next to the other window was a games table inlaid with a chess set of fantastically carved sea creatures. A game appeared to be in progress. Constance wondered who was playing and where they'd gone off to. The servant sweeping the billiard table nodded at Constance, and she nodded in return.

They passed a formal dining room with more servants inside. One was fussing with a floral arrangement, another smoothing the tablecloth. Yet others were setting out silver and plates. A thin woman wearing all black was directing the work.

Jago led them to yet another turn. Constance saw the glass door to the conservatory down a hallway branching off from the main corridor.

At last, Jago stopped at a double doorway and gestured for them to enter. She heard Devlin and Barbara gasp as they stepped through. She and Temperance were the last to arrive, and Constance understood why the library was Jago's pride.

From Loveday's exterior, Constance would never have imagined a room this spacious. Her curiosity was quickly overwhelmed by the breathtaking scope of Jago's collection of books. There were floor-to-ceiling bookcases. They were beautiful wooden cases that looked like oak but were ever so slightly different. The room smelled of leather, books, and the tang of ambergris. Under one of the stained-glass windows was a reading nook appointed with deep cushions. Spiral steps went to a narrow balcony circling the room. There were ladders on tracks on each lower wall. Overhead, a row of three Edwardian brass and amber-coloured glass chandeliers cast a rich glow. There was a large Persian carpet in the middle of the room. Situated on it were deep divans upholstered in brocade. Comfy chairs, perfect for having a read, dotted the room.

The group spread out, drawn to the books. Behind one of the divans was a shelf of beautifully matched copies of the entire works of Dickens. Constance noted that they were in order of publication. At the end of the shelf were three books, one a thick copy of *The Mystery of Edwin Drood*. She put down her knitting bag and carefully slid it out. The publication date was 1871. Paging through it, she saw it was a completed text. *Edwin Drood* hadn't been finished when Dickens died in 1870. Next to it were two other books: Dickens novels that had never existed. She returned *Edwin Drood* to its spot and pulled out the adjacent volumes: *Phineas Rose*, published in 1872, and *The Plight of Maise Stubbs*, published in 1874. She opened a page at random in *The Plight of Maise Stubbs* and began reading. It read as if Dickens had penned it himself, not a pastiche.

She turned to face Krampus when she heard his hooves on the wooden floor. As he came around the divan, they were silenced by the rug.

'What has you so intrigued?' he asked, stepping beside her. His dark-brown fur was slightly ruffled, as if he was irritated.

'Something quite impossible,' she replied, pointing at the last three books.

He read the spines, then looked at her with wide eyes. 'What is this?'

'I wish I could explain it.' Loveday was something peculiar, and she wasn't sure how she felt about that, gorgeous library or not.

A cry from Temperance came from across the room. Constance turned and saw her pulling a large art book from one of the bottom shelves. She sat down cross-legged, the book cradled in her lap.

There were excited murmurs from each guest as they found volumes to delight them. There were beautifully bound copies of everything from Shakespeare to Kafka to more recent popular fiction publications. Constance saw Jago whispering with Babel, who was shaking a book at him.

'It's amazing, isn't it?' Gary asked, slipping beside her. She could feel warmth pouring off him.

'It's remarkable. But also very odd.'

'It is,' he agreed. 'I'll show you to your suites, and then I thought you and Temperance might like a private tour. It's been ages since we caught up. Would you like to go as well, Archie?'

'Might I beg off?' Krampus asked. 'I'm not near enough done here in the library. Jago suggested some medical tomes on the second floor he thought I might enjoy. Though I confess, one of these odd editions of Dickens has me intrigued.'

'Look here!' Margot exclaimed. 'It's a biography of Golden Boy. I didn't think this was out yet.' She immediately flipped to the back and checked the index. 'Of course, I'm in it!'

'So, you and Golden Boy . . .' Kandy said.

'Oh yes, it started a while ago. We're *mad* about each other.'

'They've been canoodling for quite some time now,' Digger Downs said. 'I did an article about the three of you. Seems both of you have dated him.'

Margot looked at Kandy Kane with surprise. 'I didn't know,' Margot said. 'He's never mentioned you. I suppose it wasn't that serious. Digger, you are nothing more than a parasite.'

'Well, it wasn't anything except a one-night stand,' Digger said.

Kandy turned pale, then flushed red. 'It was much more than that, Digger. And you know it.'

He shrugged. 'I only know what my sources tell me. And they're usually pretty accurate about this sort of thing.'

'You're an asshole. Margot was right: you are a parasite.'

'It's a living. Doesn't matter any more. I'm retired.'

'All very well for you now that the damage is done.'

Constance and Gary looked at each other, weary expressions on their faces. Now that the bad behaviour of their own youth was well past them, they found the drama unfolding a bit silly.

'Let's pry Temperance away from whatever she's so intently looking at,' Gary said. 'I'll show you the house.'

'That would suit me fine,' she replied. 'Do you think I'll have a chance to see the library again?'

Gary slipped her hand into the crook of his arm. 'After the guise dancing, we'll spend some time here. Jago is always happy to have people enjoy his library.'

'It's a curious place.'

'Curiouser and curiouser?'

'How adorable of you,' she said with a chuckle. Then she looked at him with concern. 'You really enjoy living here?'

Gary nodded, and for the first time in many a year, she thought he looked genuinely happy. 'It's a strange and wonderful place to live,' he said. 'I also get to be the guise dancing master. We have guise dancing all year long here.'

'I thought guise dancing was a seasonal thing.'

'Normally, yes. Now, let's see what Temperance has unearthed.'

Temperance was hunched over an art book of paintings by Magritte. It was filled with images of jokers in the strange, surrealistic style for which he was known.

'He doesn't usually do portraits, you know,' Temperance said. 'All those images of faceless people. People say he must be a joker and those are commentary, but does it matter? He did these, and they're beautiful . . .' She hugged the book to her chest. 'I want to paint like this someday. Gary, do you suppose Jago would let me borrow this? Just while we're here?'

'Let's ask him,' Gary replied. 'Jago, a moment, please?'

Jago walked across the room and glanced down at Temperance. 'That's one of my favourite books of his collected work.'

'It's beautiful,' Temperance sighed. 'May I borrow it? Just for tonight?'

Jago gave her his peculiar smile. 'Of course. I'm so very glad you found something that speaks to you. My library is to be enjoyed.'

'Oh, thank you so much,' Temperance said, climbing to her feet.

'No bother at all, my dear. I'll have it sent up to your suite.'

Constance walked around the bedroom of her large suite. It overlooked the snow-frosted roofs of the orangery and greenhouse. The conservatory – as far as she could tell, given Loveday's twisty makeup – was on the other side of the house.

She trailed her finger across the top of the rosewood dresser. She opened a drawer and noted that the jointing was perfect, just as it should be. *Most likely a Finn Juhl,* she thought. *Or an extremely good copy.*

The bed was Art Nouveau, with swooping organic lines. A hand-knitted stocking hung from a pretty silver hook on the footboard. A delicate Empire chair sat in one corner of the room. Constance turned around. From the ridiculously expensive and eclectic furniture to the silky Persian rug on the floor, it was the perfect room for her. That is, if she had unlimited money and exquisite taste.

Flower arrangements dotted the room as well. Most of the blooms were out of season, and there were even a few of the strange blood-red and fuchsia blossoms like the ones decorating the garlands in Keun.

In the sitting room – as cosy a place as one could wish for on a snowy Christmas Eve – a garland of white roses and evergreens was draped across the mantelpiece. There was a pleasant, but not too hot, fire going.

Clearly, someone knew exactly what would make her comfortable. No doubt, Gary had had a hand in that.

Her suitcase was nowhere to be seen. An armoire matching the bed took up most of one wall. She opened it to see what was inside and discovered her case neatly stowed and her clothes put away. A sachet of lavender hung from a pink ribbon on the rack.

The dove-grey dress with hyacinth-coloured silk embroidery she'd brought for tonight's formal dinner was already laid out on the bed. Next to the dress was a lorgnette-style black domino mask and a note written in a fine, old-fashioned longhand. It read:

Dinner at eight p.m. Masks optional.

There was a knock on the door. Gary was waiting in the hall for her to join him. A door next to her room opened, and Temperance stepped out.

'How's your suite, Constance?' Gary asked her.

She nodded. 'It's brilliant,' she said. 'I'm not certain I've ever been to a house or hotel this beautiful. And the attention to detail in the suite is quite amazing.' She turned to Temperance. 'What about your suite, Temperance?'

'It's incredible. Just incredible. Jago must be a mind-reader. In my suite, there are the most beautiful paintings. And I think they're originals! Oh, and the furniture! It's so posh. It's like your flat, Constance, only better!' She slapped a hand over her mouth. 'I didn't mean it like that! I love your flat. It's just . . .'

Gary nodded. 'He does a thorough job of making sure his guests have everything they desire.'

'Exactly!' Temperance said with a sigh of relief. 'It's just like he read my mind.'

'Thus far, it's been a . . . remarkable visit,' Constance said. 'Loveday is . . . interesting.'

Gary took them on a circuitous route, down hallways, through connecting rooms, and finally down to the wine cellar.

He clicked on the fluorescents, and at the end of the rows of wine, there was a Stygian darkness. The room had a ripe, briny odour.

Temperance whistled. 'That's a massive amount of wine.'

'Jago entertains a lot, so he keeps it well supplied.'

Constance began walking down the second row of bottles. Barrels were set on their sides, the interiors divided into quarters. Tags dangled off various bottles. She read one, and it didn't say *Drink Me*. That disappointed her a wee bit. The wine bottles got dustier as she went down the row. The dates on the tags changed as well: *Drink in 1946. Drink in 1921. Drink in 1897.*

She rounded the aisle, and standing at the end was a woman. Her hair was wild, her clothes peculiar in design, and she had a feral gleam in her eyes. 'There will be only one mistress here,' she said with a growl. 'I won't permit it. None of the women he invites deserve Loveday. None but me. She's mine.'

With that, she spun and disappeared around the corner. Constance trotted to the end of the aisle, but there was no evidence the wild woman had ever been in the cellar – just the lingering smell of rotting leaves and pungent earth.

Suddenly, from the darkness behind her, she heard steps coming towards her. How anyone could be in there without a light or a torch baffled her. Perhaps it was where the woman had come from.

'Don't worry, luv,' came a whisper from the blackness. There was the faint scent of Brut Pour Homme. The accent was East End and the voice all too familiar. 'We're comin' for you.'

She stepped back, stumbling as she did so, and grabbed hold of the edge of a wooden cask. *That voice,* she thought. *It can't be.* The owner of that terrible voice haunted her dreams even now, decades after she'd killed him.

'Did ya miss me, Constance?' It was an angry hiss.

She turned and fled to the door, her sensible boots rapping against the stone floor. There were hallways spinning off the entrance. Normally, her sense of direction was flawless, but this didn't look like the way they had come in. Wet-sounding footsteps behind her were coming closer and closer. Her breath hitched in her chest, and her heart was rabbiting. There was a stitch in her side, and she held a hand to it. She chose one of the hallways and ran down it.

She rounded a corner, and Temperance and Gary stood in front of a row of four stone prison cells. 'These are left from when Loveday was a fortress,' Gary was saying, as he opened the door of a remarkably sturdy-looking cell. The bars were a bit rusty but still thick and intact.

Constance tried to catch her breath.

Temperance touched her arm. 'Are you OK?' she asked. 'You need a doctor?'

'I was running . . .'

'Did you fall behind? I'm so sorry,' Gary said. 'I thought you were with us.'

The whispers and wet steps suddenly seemed ridiculous. Perhaps it had been a waking dream. That had happened before. Some things she could never truly leave in her past. This last incident proved that. The Krays and the events surrounding her involvement with them would always haunt her. You didn't kill a man and come out the other side unscathed. Unless you were a sociopath.

'Oh, it's nothing,' she said lightly. 'I was turned around, and then I couldn't find you. It's terribly embarrassing to admit I panicked.'

'It's easy to get lost here,' Gary said. 'Just . . . be careful. Loveday can be confusing.'

Temperance stepped into a cell and rattled shackles attached to the wall. 'Someone was serious about keeping people in here.'

Gary laughed. 'Jago hasn't touched some parts of the house yet. But he might want to keep this as is. You never know when you'll need a dungeon.'

With a look askance at Gary, Temperance moved to the next cell. There was a happiness to Gary now that surprised Constance. The last few times she'd seen him, there had been a lingering, low-grade sadness about Gary. It seemed Loveday agreed with him.

Constance slipped into the cell with Temperance. It was a tight fit with the two of them inside. There was a rough stone bench mortared to the wall. It was worn smooth on top. She sat down, looking at Gary through the bars. As she did so, Temperance left the cell and wandered out of sight.

'Would you like me to shut the door so you can see how it feels?' Gary offered.

'No.' Even with the door open, she felt claustrophobic, as if the room were closing in and swallowing her up. 'You look well,' she said to distract herself.

'The only difficult thing right now is dealing with losing Duncan,' Gary said sadly. She could feel his temperature beginning to rise, heat radiating from him. The dank room became warm, almost toasty, and her old bones appreciated it. 'The virus hadn't been kind to Duncan, to say the least. I guess I knew – and so did he – that he wasn't going to be around for very long.'

'None of us will be,' Constance said, stepping out of the cell. She began walking down the hall towards Temperance. 'Gary, do you know anything about a wild woman running around Loveday? Is she a guest? Does she live here like you do?'

An uncomfortable look crossed Gary's face. His lips twisted for a moment; then he said, 'That would be Mad Morwen. She appears sometimes, claiming Loveday is hers. She's not right in the head.'

Yes, plainly. But other than the creepy words, Constance had to admit that nothing untoward had happened. The sounds from the darkness were far worse. And she wasn't going to talk about that with anyone – not even Gary. Her attention returned to him, and she saw his clothes smouldering.

'Gary, you're going to catch your clothes on fire.' She pointed at his hand. The skin was charred and curling off.

He looked down and flexed his fingers. She could still feel his warmth, but the air around him returned to normal – at least, normal for Gary's lingering heat.

'Where to next?' Constance asked. Temperance was at the end of the hall, where steps led up to the ground floor.

'The turrets are wonderful,' Gary replied. 'This is the first time I've been able to show people around and not get totally lost.'

'Lead on, Macduff,' Constance said. 'Or lay on, if we've decided to go after those turrets.'

'I think I'll just lead,' Gary said. 'We should be done in time for you to dress for dinner.'

Constance had been to many a fine Christmas dinner, but none so proud as the one set at Jago's table.

A parade of servants brought in covered dishes revealing duck, goose, stuffing, roast potatoes with tarragon, parsnips, Yorkshire puddings, sauces, jellies, and a green vegetable that Constance didn't recognize but that smelled divine.

As with the sitting room of her suite, it was everything one could want in a Christmas dinner, and they all tucked into it with happy abandon – except Margot, who wouldn't give herself a night off from dieting, not even on Christmas Eve. She only nibbled at small portions of the veg and duck.

'I was a little surprised that you're having a party over the holidays,' Devlin said politely. 'Most people want to be with family this time of year.

My own lads are with their in-laws this year. We alternate. This is my year off.'

'Many people don't have family,' Jago replied, tucking into the goose on his plate. 'And there are people like Miss Kane—'

'Really, call me Kandy. Miss Kane sounds so stuffy.'

'Kandy,' he continued, 'is quite alone here in the UK.'

'You have no family, Kandy? None at all?' Bastet asked. She wore a gold mask over her head with cut-outs for her ears so it would sit properly. 'That's so sad.'

'Oh, I have family,' Kandy replied haughtily. 'They're a bunch of classless idiots. My card turning was the best thing that ever happened to me. Got me the hell away from them.'

'That's a bit harsh, Kandy,' Digger said with a slight smile. 'I didn't know you weren't on good terms with your family.'

'That's none of your concern. It isn't like you trade in the truth, anyway.'

Digger buttered a dinner roll, popping a bit of it into his mouth. Smiling at Kandy, he said, 'I'm retired now. You could tell me the colour of the panties you're wearing, and I wouldn't publish it. All that snooping about was before I hung up my hat.'

A brief laugh came from Margot. 'No one cares what her panties look like.'

Kandy glared at Margot. Then her features smoothed just as suddenly. 'When I get back to America, I'm going to be in a movie, and it's not some D-list one. Between that and the Cadbury's money, I'm going to be a household name. I'll be set financially. Just like Margot.'

Krampus set his silverware down loudly. 'I'm certainly not a fan of gossip rags, and Mr Downs isn't exactly as well known over here as it appears he is across the pond, but sniping at one another is hardly a pleasant way to spend Christmas Eve.'

'Hear, hear,' Devlin said, raising his wineglass. He was small enough that he had a booster cushion on his chair so that his head and torso would clear the tabletop. 'Let's toast Jago: a finer host I can't imagine. Thank you for having us as your guests.'

The rest of the party stood and raised their glasses towards Jago, who nodded to them with a crooked smile. 'It's my distinct pleasure to have such an interesting group for the holidays,' their host replied as they sat down and went back to their dinner.

'Jago, you must know a lot about all of us,' Babel said. She cut a piece of her goose and then gave him a speculative look. 'Otherwise, how could you make everything so perfect for each of us? But we know nothing about you.'

Jago rested his silverware on his plate, then dabbed his mouth with his napkin. 'I was on the *Queen Mary* on my way to New York when the virus hit in 1946,' he began.

Perhaps he's a joker after all, Constance thought.

'All of you know what happened there. I was lucky to escape alive.'

'But . . .' Kandy began, looking perplexed. 'Are you a joker?'

Jago laughed, then started eating again. Between bites, he said, 'No, my dear, not a joker at all. Though I was changed by the virus, I was far more fortunate than most.'

'Then what's with the mask?' Kandy asked, staring at him.

Bastet gave a low growl. 'I think it's impolite to ask.' She turned towards Digger Downs. 'I've lived long enough in the States to know who you are, Mr Downs, and I'm not a fan. It's a good thing you've retired. A good thing, indeed.'

'But Jago, you have the voice of a young man,' Babel said, trying to bring the conversation back to safer grounds. 'You have the carriage of one, too. Unless you were a child when the virus hit the Queen Mary, you would be an old man by now.'

'You have the right of it, Ms Baden,' Jago said, taking a sip of wine, then smiling broadly at Babel. 'My body regenerates. Slowly, but it does. I realized I was changing when I was still a young man. I spent my time after I was infected travelling the world.'

'You could have gone anywhere,' Margot said. Using the elegant silverware, she was pushing the food around on her plate, though not eating. However, she didn't neglect her wine. 'Why here? Loveday is nice, but it's not Paris. You could have gone somewhere sunny. It's so dreary here.'

'Margot!' Constance said. 'What a dreadful thing to say.'

'It's true,' Margot replied, finishing the last of her dinner wine. Constance was pretty sure Margot was sloshed. 'England is a grey place. And America is too bright, noisy, and uncouth.'

'America is just fine,' Kandy said, glaring at Margot. 'We're not uncouth, and we're not too loud. If you like it so much in France, you should stay there, you over-the-hill hag.'

Margot shrugged. 'Better to have had a career than none at all,' she said with a slight smile.

There was a long, uncomfortable silence.

'I think Christmas at Loveday has been top notch thus far,' Krampus said, wiping his mouth. He gave a toothy smile, and even Constance recoiled. It was all razor-sharp teeth and lolling tongue. His smile dropped. 'I'm so sorry. Sometimes I forget what I look like now. You know it ruined my practice. Can you imagine bringing your children to see me?'

Just then, servants brought in desserts, sweet wines, and champagne, interrupting him. Everyone had a fresh glass of some new libation.

'I'd like to give everyone some chocolates,' Kandy said, pulling out a pretty box from an even prettier purse. The box and purse matched her dress, which was done up in a festive berry red and evergreen. Constance was surprised you couldn't see the outline of Kandy's dinner given the amount she'd eaten and the tightness of that garment. Margot had watched every bite Kandy ate with envy.

'Are these the same confections you used on *American Hero?*' Babel asked, eyeing the box dubiously.

'Not exactly,' Kandy replied. 'Different candies do different things. Chocolates are different than the hard candies I used on the show.'

'Margot,' Kandy said, plucking one of the chocolates from the box. She held it out to Margot. 'A peace offering. This one is low-calorie. I know you're watching your weight. The camera is so unforgiving.'

Margot frowned at Kandy but took the chocolate anyway. Then Kandy offered the box to Temperance, who was sitting to her left. Temperance took a chocolate and passed the box to Digger Downs, who plucked a purple choccy out and then handed the box to Babel. As each guest in turn took a proffered sweet, Kandy watched and smiled.

'They can be fun,' she said, grinning toothily. 'I promise. Just wait until everyone has theirs before you eat.'

The box came around to Constance, and she eyed the confectionery with suspicion. Four chocolates were left, each wrapped in a different colour. She took a red-and-silver striped one.

'What do we do now?' Bastet asked. She held her chocolate between her index finger and thumb as if it might need to be dropped at a moment's notice.

'You eat them, of course,' Kandy said, as if talking to someone rather slow. 'All together now.'

'Very well,' Devlin said, popping the chocolate into his mouth. He closed his eyes, savouring it. The rest of the table did likewise.

It was simply the very best chocolate Constance had ever tasted. Like Edmund eating Turkish delight in *The Lion, the Witch and the Wardrobe,* Constance thought she could be happy eating these chocolates forever. But when she opened her mouth to say so, 'God Rest Ye Merry, Gentlemen' came out in a perfect velvety soprano. Constance couldn't carry a tune. She'd been asked more times than she could remember to *stop* singing.

That was when she noticed that all the other guests were singing various Christmas songs as well. None were out of tune, and together, it was as if they were a great choral group. The more Constance tried to express herself, the louder her singing became. She even pulled a pen and pad out of her pocket and started writing, but all that came out was the musical notation for 'Rockin' Around the Christmas Tree'.

The other guests were looking at her as if she was barking mad. Then peculiar things started happening to them. A golden nimbus appeared over Temperance's head. A moment later, one hovered over Babel's.

Constance yelled, but it didn't sound like yelling at all. She belted out 'Do They Know It's Christmas?' Then Margot, Jago, and Bastet turned into the Three Wise Men.

On either side of Constance, Gary and Devlin sang to her. Then they each touched their water cups, and the water turned a deep ruby colour, as did Digger Downs's. She could see them giggling with delight as they raised the glasses to their lips.

Despite liking her voice, Constance pounded on the table. *This isn't good!* she yelled. *She's controlling us!* Except it came out as 'Santa Baby'.

Barbara sang 'Last Christmas'.

Constance glowered, trying to say, *I can't understand you.*

Then there was something that felt like a push in her mind, and abruptly she could understand everyone. It was as if she'd been tuning a tube radio to a distant station, and it suddenly came in clear.

'I have a beard!' she heard Margot exclaim, stroking her new, long, golden, braided beard. 'Give me a mirror! I want to see how pretty I am as a man!'

'Here,' Kandy said, pulling one out of her handbag. She handed it to Margot with a peculiar expression that Constance thought was a horrific amount of jealousy. She didn't just want what Margot had; she wanted Margot not to have it.

'Oh, I *am* beautiful,' Margot said, passing it to Jago. 'You've changed, too. You look mysterious. And Bastet is a Wise Man as well.'

Jago took the mirror. 'I do look rather splendid, don't I?' He held the mirror in front of Bastet, who giggled when she saw a bright nimbus around her head.

Everyone else at the table appeared delighted by what was happening to them. Gary and Devlin held up their glasses, grins spreading across their faces. 'As a party trick, this isn't bad at all, Kandy,' Digger said, grinning. 'Much better than the candies you used on *American Hero*.'

'Those had a different purpose,' she said with a bright, artificial expression. 'I wouldn't expect you to understand. You're rather antiquated, after all.'

'Oh, I understand well enough,' he replied, chuckling. It appeared as if he enjoyed needling her. 'But your goal was never to win, was it? It was just a stepping-stone for you.'

She gave him a knowing smile. 'Other people have done the same. Look at Tiffany. White trash through and through, but she has an endorsement deal with a national jewellery chain, despite getting kicked off early.'

'Don't be bitter,' Margot said, stroking her silky beard. 'You've got the Cadbury deal. Promoting Easter eggs suits you.'

'It's Christmas,' Krampus growled. Everyone fell silent. 'My apologies; I often can't help the way my voice sounds. I know it can be disturbing. But we're having a lovely dinner, and it would be a shame to spoil it. Those chocolates were perfection.'

'I couldn't talk, just sing Christmas songs,' Constance said, looking at Kandy balefully. Constance didn't like being out of control.

'That was my condition as well,' Krampus added. 'But no harm to it.'

'And I took care of that,' Babel said. 'My power, you know. Once you both started breaking out into song, I realized what was happening. It was easy enough to rectify, though I think the two of you have had the worst of it from the chocolate changes.'

'I'm just glad you were here to do something about it,' Constance said. The light from the halo around Barbara was bright enough that Constance had to squint at her.

'Kandy,' Gary said. 'What's this all about?'

Kandy smiled, but her eyes weren't filled with Christmas joy. 'I wasn't sure who would get what. It's all harmless. Everyone will go back to normal in a few minutes. If Ms Baden hadn't been here, the singing would have faded away. I like the singing, and I love the beards. The water into wine is my favourite. Of course, some things are easier to do than others, though these Christmas chocolates are relatively trivial. Other candies are more difficult.'

'You *experimented* on us?' Constance said, appalled at the cheek of Kandy. And she was no small amount disconcerted.

'It's meant to be funny,' Kandy said. 'Not some big drama. I guess when you get older, it's harder to take some things.'

'I find this to be very troubling. Am I the only one put off by it?' Constance asked.

'I think you are, Constance,' Krampus said, giving her one of his obsidian-knife smiles. 'Even I thought singing Christmas songs was amusing. And I can only imagine how it looked with my face singing "Do They Know It's Christmas?"'

'I just wanted everyone to have some fun,' Kandy said contritely. Constance didn't believe she was the least bit sorry. 'It's a party trick. There wasn't anything malicious intended. I'm still working on making the right things happen at the right time. Plus, it all wears off.'

'That's all right, my dear,' Jago said. 'We all make mistakes.'

'I felt so happy,' Bastet said. 'Is that part of it, too?'

'Oh, I can do that anytime,' Kandy said. 'Any time at all.'

'I'm going back to my suite now,' Constance said tersely. 'Would you mind escorting me, Temperance? Jago, thank you for the lovely dinner. I'll see the rest of you at the guise dancing.'

'I'll walk you up, too,' Gary said, rising.

'Don't mind at all,' Temperance replied, standing up. 'Not at all. And it doesn't matter how old someone is, Kandy. What you did was dodgy.'

'A merry Christmas to you, too,' Kandy said with a smirk.

'Thank you for escorting us back to our suites, Gary,' Constance said. 'Dinner ended rather . . . suddenly. My apologies for taking you away.'

Gary shrugged. 'I can see why you might want to leave early. And dinner would be breaking up soon anyway. But Kandy is something, all right. I'm just not sure what exactly.'

'She's an arsehole,' Temperance said.

'Temperance!' Constance exclaimed. 'Language.'

'Well, she's still a minger,' Temperance replied. 'How did she even get invited?'

'I think Jago was asked to invite her by someone at Cadbury,' Gary replied. 'I guess even . . . unpleasant people deserve a decent Christmas.'

'She seems determined to make Christmas a misery for the rest of us, tasty chocolates notwithstanding,' Constance said, pulling the key to her suite out of her skirt pocket, then inserting it into the lock. 'How long do we have before the guise dancing starts? I want to change into something more comfortable. Though I'm not sure if I'll be dancing.'

'But you must!' Gary said. 'It'll take your mind off other things for a little while.'

'Loveday has changed you, Gary,' she said, turning the key. Temperance did the same, then slipped into her suite. 'Are you truly happy here?'

'I am,' he replied. 'Jago has been very good to me.'

'Then I am happy for you,' she said, taking his hand and giving it a pat. 'And I'll try to give you a dance tonight. No matter what, you'll have something to laugh at.'

When Constance and Temperance rejoined the party an hour later, the guise dancing was well underway.

Constance looked around. Some of the other guests had yet to arrive. Bastet, Devlin, Kandy, Krampus, and Digger Downs were noticeable in their absence.

Guests and servants were holding hands, making a circuit of the music room. Some servants were singing in a strange language Constance didn't recognize. In the centre of the circle, Margot spun about madly. Her hair was a wild, golden-white nimbus. Babel was dancing with her, dark-haired yin to Margot's yang. They pirouetted around each other, graceful and at the same time filled with an earthy power.

The music made Constance sway and clap her hands. She felt how easily it could take her over. It sounded like a Regency-period Scottish reel by way of Takis. Not that she knew what an alien Takis dancing song might be, but she suspected it would sound this peculiar.

The singing grew louder, and then, as had happened at dinner, there was clarity about what she was hearing.

Babel's power, Constance thought, remembering how she'd translated Constance's singing into regular speech during dinner. As she listened, she realized that this was some strange variant of English. She understood the lyrics now. And she wished she hadn't.

We take the new cut silver tree
And deck it in such finery
We light the branches one by one
And crush the flames when she is done
Roast her to a crisp sensation
Serve her for our delectation
All take hands and sing with me
Underneath the silver tree

'Would you like to join in?' Jago asked. 'Most people find the dancing liberating.'

There was enough liberation going around, Constance thought. Through force of will, she managed to stop clapping along with the music, though it was so compelling. She shook her head; the song lyrics were unsettling to say the least.

'It's a bit fast for me. I'll wait for a slower song.' She found the guise dancing unnerving. Jago escorted her to a small table near the dance floor. 'Don't let me keep you from your guests,' she said.

'Constance, you *are* one of the guests.'

'You do have the right of that,' she acknowledged.

'How did you come by your teenage ward?' he asked, sitting next to her. He was dressed in mid-twentieth century garb and seemed quite the image of a man at play during that period. His mask was black now and matched his long-sleeved rayon shirt and pleated trousers.

'We met at an outreach centre for jokers I've been funding,' she replied. 'Her card turned, and she became the target of bullying at her school. It happens all the time. I wanted a safe place for people whose card turned them into jokers. A place where they could have something of a normal life. Unfortunately, we've been the target of vandalism more than once.'

'I hope no one was hurt.'

'Sadly, Temperance's parents were killed during an attack on the outreach centre. She had no other relatives willing to take on a teenage joker, so I thought it best if she came and stayed with me.'

'That's a lot of responsibility.'

'You mean for an old bird like me?' She laughed. 'Be that as it may, there was no one else. She's sweet but a bit of a radical in that way teenagers often are. Of course, it doesn't help that her mum and da were killed in that bombing. We've rebuilt the centre, but it'll never feel like a completely safe place again.'

The music swelled as they sat in silence.

'I suppose that's why she seems so sympathetic to the Twisted Fists?' Jago asked.

'Probably,' she replied.

Bastet and Devlin were coming into the room together. Devlin was a foot shorter than Bastet, who wasn't that tall herself. His ace power allowed him to shrink down to the size of a penny.

Bastet and Devlin together baffled Constance. There had been no indication they knew each other at all. Constance could tell Bastet was upset. Devlin was talking to her and patting her arm.

The song changed, and Temperance came and threw herself down on the chair next to Constance.

'That was amazing,' she said, smiling at Constance and Jago. It took a moment for her to regain her breath. 'Did you see Margot and Babel? It was brilliant madness.' She looked around the room. 'I don't see either of them now.'

Glancing around the room, Constance noted that Margot and Babel were indeed missing. Kandy and Krampus made appearances at last, coming in separately. The pace of the new song, which had started slowly at first, began to pick up. Kandy spun with the rest of the dancers, a delighted expression on her face.

Archie made his way over to Constance and Jago. There was a slight hitch in his step that hadn't been there before. 'I miss dancing,' he said as he sat down awkwardly. His tail kept getting in his way, and he finally gave up and sat on the edge of his chair. 'But when I dance now, I either scare everyone off the floor or sparks fly from my hooves and singe people's clothes.'

'You wish you could still enjoy a dance now and again,' Jago said sympathetically. 'Is there any way I might help? We could clear the floor for one song . . .'

'Oh no!' Krampus exclaimed, waving his tail frantically, knocking a chair next to the table over as he did so. 'That's completely unnecessary. I've really made my peace with it. This is the hand I've been dealt. I came to terms with it long ago.'

'But it must be so difficult,' Temperance said. 'My joker is bad, but yours is so much worse. I don't know how you're not angry all the time. I know I am.'

Krampus gave Temperance a smile, and she recoiled. She might have been sympathetic to Krampus, but it didn't make him any less frightening to look at. 'It does me no good to be angry, does it?' he asked. 'This is my lot in life. What else could I do?'

'There's always *something*.'

'Sometimes, there's nothing to be done,' Constance weighed in. 'It's the way of the world.'

'Constance is right,' Jago said, taking a sip of his drink. 'I've seen much in my years, and the futility of finding a remedy for some situations could drive you mad.'

Temperance jumped out of her chair. 'That you expect jokers to accept their fate quietly is rubbish. I won't do it, and Krampus shouldn't either.' She strode out of the room with her shoulders tense and her hands clenched into fists.

'Shouldn't you go after her?' Jago asked. 'I don't know a lot about teenagers, but she doesn't look like she should be alone.'

'I'll give her a few minutes to calm down. She gets this way when serious issues surrounding jokers come up.'

'I could ask Gary to play a slow song, and the three of us old people could dance. Give the children a chance to catch their breath?'

A laugh barked out of Constance. It wasn't a ladylike sound at all. Krampus's tongue lolled out of the side of his mouth.

'We're a bunch of codgers, that we are,' Constance said. 'Nowadays I cackle like a crazy old bag.' Shaking her head, she stood. 'I suppose I should check on Temperance. Your Loveday is an interesting place, isn't it, Jago?' she said. 'I'd almost say it was haunted if I believed in such things.'

'You might be right,' Jago said. He leaned close and whispered in her ear. 'Even I don't know all its secrets.'

As she started towards the staircase to the suites, Constance realized that she didn't remember if she'd taken her knitting satchel with her when she'd left the library. Accompanied by the music from the guise dancing, it took her a few more twists and turns than she'd thought it should before she located the library, only to discover Temperance running from the room.

'Constance!' Temperance exclaimed, and an expression of relief crossed her face. Her paintbrushes clattered, and she was shaking. 'I'm so happy you're here! I just . . . Come see.' Grabbing Constance's hand, she pulled her into the library.

Lying on the floor was the former Digger Downs.

'I don't suppose he's just having a rest?' Constance sighed.

'No! No, no, no. This is how I found him. I've never seen a dead body before.'

'Let's not assume,' Constance said, crouching beside the body, then putting her fingertips to Digger Downs's neck. There was no discernible pulse, so she grabbed his wrist and tried there. But it was clear he was quite dead. 'Well, this would explain why he wasn't at the guise dancing,' Constance said gently, placing his hand back on the floor.

'We should get Jago,' Temperance said. 'He'll know what to do.'

Constance inspected the body.

'What are you doing?' Temperance asked, voice trembling.

'Checking to be certain,' Constance replied.

'Of what?'

'He might have met with foul play.'

'He was old. Sometimes old men . . . just die of natural causes.'

'And sometimes,' Constance said, pulling her hand from behind Digger Downs's head, fingertips bloody, 'they don't.'

While Temperance went to find Jago, Constance pushed herself to her feet, knees cracking. She wasn't graceful doing so. She could hear what sounded like a faint conversation – or at least half of one. She poked her head out the door and then followed the sound. As she peered around the corner, she saw Babel speaking in German on her satellite phone. Constance could only understand *mein liebe* – my love. Then she heard Babel crying.

At that, Constance turned, hurried back to the library, and slipped back inside.

Jago and Gary looked down at the body.

'Mr Downs is indeed dead,' Jago said.

Constance held up her bloody fingers as she studied the room. Nothing seemed out of place, until she saw a bit of gleaming metal under the divan. Crouching down again, her knees protesting, she used the end of her scarf to retrieve a candlestick. It had a smear of blood on the base. Holding it up for inspection, she held Jago's eyes.

'Murder, then?' Jago said.

'It seems so.'

As she put the candlestick back where she found it, a piece a paper caught her eye. It read: *The First*.

The wind outside was intensifying, and the snow sounded more like sand being blown against the house. 'We don't know who could have done such a thing. Would you vouch for your staff?' She considered the piece of paper in her hand, then she held it up to him.

Jago nodded, taking the paper from her, then helped her stand. 'Of course. None of them knew Mr Downs except as a guest. And most wouldn't be acquainted with a Yank muckraker at all.'

'Then that leaves the other guests . . .' Temperance said slowly.

'I'm very troubled by that piece of paper I found under the couch,' Constance said, walking to one of the leather upholstered Queen Anne armchairs. As she sat, she spied her knitting bag beside the couch where the candlestick had been found. She got up and retrieved it, then went back to the chair and sat again.

'That's a sign of the Twisted Fists,' Temperance said softly. 'They always number their victims.'

'There *aren't* any Fists in our party,' Jago replied. 'Everyone is vetted. I know more about them than they do about themselves.'

'Be that as it may,' Constance said, 'you can't possibly know *everything*. Everyone has secrets.'

'Even you?' Jago asked.

'Even me,' she replied. The gun in the bottom of her knitting bag was testament to that. She doubted he knew about it. Few enough in the Silver Helix knew she'd insisted on the same training (though less rigorous) as the field agents. She still practised with her Walther and was a more than decent shot – especially after her cataract surgery.

'So, this is where everyone has gone,' Margot said from the doorway. She took one look at the scene and said, 'Is he dead?'

Jago nodded. 'Unfortunately.'

Margot nodded. 'Good. He was a vicious little man.'

'You're just saying that because he printed some not-so-nice things about you,' Kandy said, trying to squeeze past Margot into the room. It was starting to get crowded with everyone bunched up at the doorway. Kandy stared coldly down at the body.

'He wrote worse about you,' Margot snapped.

'This isn't a competition to see who had it worse from that gossipmonger,' Babel said. 'And this certainly looks as if some kind of foul play was involved. Maybe we should get Krampus in here? He's a doctor, after all.'

The stained-glass window made a cracking noise, as if something large had slammed into it. The guests started, heads swinging towards the window.

'Good idea,' Jago said, ignoring what had just happened outside.

Another slam, as if something – or someone – were trying to break the glass. Then there was picking at the lead. How anyone could be picking at it, much less in the raging storm, baffled her. But again, no one else reacted, so Constance kept quiet.

'Gary, would you please find Krampus and bring him here?' Jago asked.

'On it,' Gary said, slipping out of the room.

'Being happy that a person is dead when it appears as if foul play was involved doesn't look good for you,' Constance said, glancing from Kandy to Margot.

Margot shrugged. 'Why should I pretend to be sorry he's dead? I'm not. And what slammed against the window?'

'It's common decency,' Temperance said. 'Don't speak ill of the murdered.'

'In this case,' Kandy interjected, 'whoever did it was doing the world a favour.'

Jago tapped a staccato pattern on his leg. 'Digger had retired. He wasn't hurting the two of you or anyone else.'

Gary returned with Krampus. Devlin and Bastet were in tow.

'Let us through,' Gary said with exasperation.

'Do as he says, please,' Jago said. His tone brooked no nonsense. 'Krampus, would you be so kind as to examine the body?'

The other guests shuffled further into the room, each taking a place around or near to the body. Krampus squatted on his haunches and began examining the remains of Digger Downs.

'He hasn't been dead long,' Krampus said, laying a dark hairy hand on Digger's neck. 'Body's still warm.' Turning over Digger's hands, he said,

'There are deep defensive scratches on his palms and the back of his hands.'

Constance noticed that Bastet stepped back, looking uncomfortable. Even more peculiar was Devlin holding her hand and patting it, almost as if he were trying to calm her.

'But I don't think the candlestick killed him,' Krampus continued. His voice was a deep angry growl. His long red tongue slid out of his mouth and caressed his razor-sharp teeth. 'Though it was a good blow to the head, there appears to be only superficial damage from the candlestick.'

'What about the blood?' Temperance asked. 'Seems like there's more than would be there for a minor knock to the noggin.'

'Scalp wounds tend to bleed,' Constance said. The rest of the party looked at her, a variety of expressions on their faces. 'I read, and I watch crime shows on the telly. You learn a lot.' Mentioning her more extreme experiences didn't seem prudent.

'Not to stir up trouble,' Babel said, 'but I saw Devlin and Bastet leaving the library when I was looking for the bathroom. They both seemed rather upset.'

Bastet bristled, and then Devlin put his hand on her arm, shaking his head. 'There wasn't anything sinister happening,' he said. 'We just ran into each other on our way to the guise dancing and decided to take another look at the library one more time – in case we didn't have an opportunity to see it again before we left.'

Bastet nodded in agreement. Krampus pointed to Downs's hand and the angry scratch marks there. 'These certainly seem like the kind of scratch marks a cat might make.'

The only sign Bastet gave that she was upset was her eyes narrowing into golden slits. 'Very well,' she said. Her voice trembled. 'I did see him, and I did scratch him. I decided to take a nap in the library. There are some excellent places to curl up in here. I was startled awake by someone.' She pointed at Digger Downs. '*That* someone. He was petting me without permission. It was disgusting. So I scratched him. Then I turned back into my Living God form and started dressing. That's when Devlin came in.'

Devlin nodded. 'She was upset.'

'I was half naked!' Bastet said. 'Digger kept trying to apologize, but I'd had enough. Devlin took me back to my suite so I could calm down. And later we came to the guise dancing. Digger Downs was alive when we left him.'

'At the time, you certainly seemed distracted,' Babel said.

'What about you, Babel?' Kandy asked. 'You were near the library. Why were you there?'

Babel rolled her eyes. 'Because I was looking for a bathroom – I mean the loo. After Bastet and Devlin rushed off, I was also curious about where they were going.'

'Didn't he write all sorts of awful things about you and Lohengrin?' Kandy asked. 'During tea, we all saw how much you hated him.'

Babel huffed. 'You and Margot had the same reaction.'

'Stop it this instant!' Jago adjusted his mask with a jerk. 'We have a corpse and at least three people who had grudges against him.'

'There's another possibility,' Temperance said sadly. 'Black Dog's murder might have provoked someone. There is this piece of paper with *The First* written on it.' She held it gingerly.

'But that would make all the jokers suspects,' Babel said. 'Bastet, Krampus, and even you, Temperance.'

'Maybe Jago, as well,' Devlin added. 'After all, who would suspect him? And we don't *know* if he's a joker or not. Only that he said he's not.'

'Are you kidding?' Gary asked angrily. 'Jago barely knows Digger Downs! You might as well say *I* killed him!'

'You *are* a Yank,' Temperance said. 'You Yanks seem not to like him very much.'

'And what does that have to do with the price of kumquats?' Gary snapped. 'There's no telling *what* happened here!'

'Well, there's also her,' Margot said, pointing at Constance. 'Who knows what horrible things she's capable of? She's a jokers' rights advocate. And she's unreliable. Also, I'm French. Do not lump me in with the Americans. Or the British.'

'Are you on about that stupid gown again?' Constance asked, pulling out her knitting. 'Really, keep up with what's happening.'

'And what's that?' Margot asked.

Constance worked the end of a row of stitches, then started on the next row of the sweater. 'We have several possibilities, don't we?' she began. 'Digger Downs was hated by Margot, Kandy, and Babel.'

'Hate is a strong term,' Babel said. 'A better word for what I felt was . . . frustration. You can't fight rumours and innuendo.'

'Nevertheless, you were on the receiving end of hurtful stories about your personal relationship.'

'Yes, but I certainly wouldn't kill someone over it,' Babel said. 'I'm on the Committee, for pity's sake. For me to murder someone . . . even if I were so inclined – which I'm not, despite how awful he was – I wouldn't be stupid enough to do it here. And I have far better tools, were I so inclined.'

'Well, *that's* certainly a point in your favour,' Kandy said sarcastically. '"I can kill more efficiently than what's happened here." Wow. I mean just: wow.'

'Then there's Margot and Kandy,' Constance continued. 'Both also had unpleasant tales told about them by the deceased.'

'Speaking of the deceased,' Gary said, 'should we do something about the body? We can't just leave it here.'

Jago nodded. 'You're right. We should get some of the staff to put Mr Downs in a place where his body can be kept until the authorities are told. We'll inform them as soon as we can get a phone line out.'

'Any suggestions on where to store him?' Gary asked, rubbing his temple. He left a small char mark there.

'Perhaps one of the refrigerated storerooms. We can keep him there for now.'

'Another moment before he's moved,' Constance said. 'We should take photos and a video of the scene for the police. But before we all go, I must say: it is quite remarkable how everyone here has an alibi. Well, almost everyone. Babel, of course, has no one to vouch for her. But Margot and Kandy haven't told us theirs.'

'We were together,' Margot said, glaring at Kandy. 'Having it out about Golden Boy. We couldn't have done it. And why would either of us? I'm not ruining my life for some has-been gossipmonger. There are better places to get gossip now, anyway. And they're far nastier than anything he's ever written about me. And what about the jokers?'

Constance shrugged and pulled out a second ball of yarn, then began working it into the pattern of the sweater she was knitting. 'If we're still entertaining the notion that a joker is killing to avenge the death of Black Dog, then yes, I suppose the jokers are suspects, too.'

'What about Temperance?' Kandy asked. 'She's talked a lot about how she understood how the Twisted Fists could be so radical. And Krampus seemed pretty upset about the Twisted Fist ring I found at THE MERMAID'S CHEST.'

'Except for changing after dinner, Constance and I have been together,' Temperance said, looking as if she would happily tear Kandy's head off. 'Neither of us could have done it.'

'I saw you leave the music room before Constance did,' Gary said.

'The dancing,' Temperance said, 'made me feel so peculiar that I had to get away for a little while. I thought I'd go up to my suite, but I got turned around. And that's how I ended up in the library.'

'That's plenty of time to murder someone,' Margot said.

'Enough,' Jago said imperiously. 'We won't solve this by pointing fingers at one another.'

'Indeed,' Constance said, putting her knitting away. 'No one is going anywhere in this storm. Whoever did the deed is still here and can't leave. We wait until the storm passes and sort things out from there. Easy-peasy.'

'Except for Mr Downs, who won't be easy nor peasy any more,' Temperance said.

Constance gave Temperance's hand a pat. 'Let's go to my suite and put up my knitting bag. I'm feeling a little tired.'

'You can't just leave,' Krampus said. 'You're both suspects!'

'As are you, my dear,' Constance replied, gesturing to the group. 'As are all of you.'

'Tea or sherry, Temperance? Gary?' Constance asked.

Gary shook his head and grimaced.

'Or . . . eggnog. I can smell the brandy in it. That would be quite the thing if we weren't trying to sort out this Digger Downs situation.'

'Sherry . . .' Temperance made a retching sound.

Constance laughed. 'Well, I'm not going to give you a pint, nor any of this nog.'

'You should,' Temperance replied, shaking her Medusa-like, paintbrush hair. 'My first corpse. Is that like My Little Pony? Only with more blood.'

'What do you make of all this, Gary?' Constance asked, plopping her knitting bag onto the bed. 'Who do you think is most likely to have done away with Mr Downs?'

He shrugged. 'I don't see anyone in this group hating him enough to kill him.'

'Babel seemed more heartbroken than murderous at tea,' Constance said. 'But Kandy and Margot . . .'

'Of the two of them, Kandy gets my vote as Most Likely To Do Away With A Bloke,' Temperance said as she went and stood in front of the fireplace, reaching out to warm her hands. 'She's as mean as they come.'

'I hate to speak ill of one of the guests.' Gary went across the room, took Temperance's hands in his own, and began to warm them. 'But she *is* truly awful. I don't think Jago would have invited her were it not as a favour to a friend.'

'We're such an odd collection of misfit toys, aren't we?' Constance said, pulling out skeins of yarn and organizing them on her bed. 'What is the reason for this peculiar collection of guests?'

Gary looked uncomfortable. 'You're all orphans of a sort, and these were favours done for previous guests. In your case, Constance, your old friend Mick told us about your circumstances, and Jago agreed you needed something special this year.

'Kandy is here because of the Cadbury people. Her work for them left her alone for the holidays. Hearing that she's estranged from her family doesn't come as a shock.'

'Yeah, that's no stunner,' Temperance said. 'What about the rest?'

'Jago invited Bastet. He said she was alone because so many of the Living Gods have gone to the moon. She asked that Devlin be invited.'

'Babel?' Constance asked, untangling her yarn. She gestured for Temperance to come and help with balling the skeins.

'Her lover is Lohengrin,' Gary replied, toying with the edge of a pillow, which began to smoulder under his touch. He yanked his hand away. 'He's not celebrating anything this year due to . . . personal matters. Again, her invitation was solely Jago's doing.

'Margot's invitation came at the behest of her publicist. Margot was in the States. Something happened to her at a high-stakes poker game. She won't discuss it. They want her functional for a film she's supposed to be shooting after the holidays.'

'She doesn't seem at all bothered by anything,' muttered Temperance.

'Krampus is here because he's been alienated from his family. They shunned him when he became a joker. Jago heard about it and was furious. He made certain Krampus had a safe place to go for the holidays. Krampus specializes in jokers' special medical needs.'

'And Digger Downs?' Constance asked.

'Again, a favour for someone else. Much to Jago's amazement, Digger Downs's publisher contacted him about an invitation for Digger. Apparently, being the nosy guy he is, Digger was curious about Loveday. After much consideration and many promises of no publicity or stories, Digger was invited. And he was keeping his word. He might have been poking everyone, but that was what he did. There was no indication he was up to any mischief. And as he said, he was retired.'

Constance pulled out the remaining items in her knitting bag, except for her Walther. Gary didn't need to know she had it. Even Temperance didn't know. It was for the best.

'What do you make of the Twisted Fists possibility?' Gary asked. 'Maybe someone does want revenge for Black Dog's murder.'

'Temperance was with me!' Constance exclaimed.

Temperance shook her head. 'Not all the time. We were apart for an hour after dinner. And then I got so turned around on my way to my suite. Well, you know the rest of that. I suppose I could look very guilty, to the right person.'

'That leaves Bastet and Krampus,' Constance said. 'I don't pick either of them as a murderer. But you never know what someone is capable of, given the right set of circumstances.'

'I think it's best if you and Temperance stay in your suites,' Gary said. 'Wandering around Loveday is tricky under normal circumstances, much more when there's a murderer about. I'm going to find Jago and see if we can contact anyone on the outside. Will the two of you be OK on your own until I get back?'

'Of course, we will,' Constance replied. 'We'll be safe as houses.'

Constance hadn't wanted to go back down into Loveday's cellars again. But when she opened the door to her suite after hearing a noise in the hall, she'd glimpsed Bastet's tail through the handrail spindles heading down the stairs.

Constance came to the top of the staircase and saw the tail vanish around another turn. She followed it down the staircase and down a couple of corridors until she was at the landing to the stairs leading into the cellar.

The air was cooler than in the main house, and the dank mustiness triggered memories from her earlier visit. Loveday was peculiar and a mystery in its own right – one she wasn't certain she wanted to solve. First, there had been the nightmarish storm that had seemed to spring from Loveday itself, and then there had been the strange sounds from both without and within. And now a murder. Christmas was taking an altogether unpleasant turn.

She slipped down the stairs and stopped abruptly as she saw Bastet's cat form fully now. Riding naked on Bastet's back was Devlin Pear, shrunk down to the size of a Ken doll – not as tiny as she knew he could go, but small enough to be riding Bastet as if she were a pony. Then Bastet turned left at the bottom of the stairs, heading in the direction of the dungeon cells.

What the two of them could be up to, Constance couldn't fathom. Then she saw Devlin dismount and grow to his normal size. Bastet changed from her cat to her joker form. Both were naked now. They fell into each other's arms. Devlin stroked Bastet's fur-covered belly, then his hand slid up, cupping her breast. Bastet purred and slid her hand down his chest, teasing his nipples and then lower . . . and that was when Constance decided to turn back.

She had no problem with sex between consenting adults. She just didn't need a front-row seat.

Creeping away, she passed the entrance to the wine cellar – that cavernous place she never wanted to enter again. No lights bloomed from the darkness. What sounded like a whisper sent a chill down her spine, but she couldn't scurry up the stairs for fear of revealing herself. And as she softly slipped upwards, she could swear there was a cold breath at her back.

As Constance hurried up to the ground floor, she decided to look around the library and see if she could find anything that might indicate who murdered Digger Downs. The door to the library was shut but not locked. She slipped into the darkened room, but before she'd taken even three steps inside, one of the reading lamps snapped on.

With a little yelp, she brought a hand to her chest. Sitting in one of the leather Queen Anne armchairs was Krampus. He stared at her with a terrible gaze.

'You startled me half to death,' she said, heart pounding. 'What on Earth are you doing in here?'

'I could ask the same of you,' he replied. 'I thought the killer might come back to the scene of the crime. And here you are.'

'If that's the case, we both look guilty.'

Next to him was a glass of some kind of amber liquor. Whiskey, she supposed. 'Is there any more of that?' she asked.

'There's some over there,' he said, gesturing towards a cart loaded with bottles and glasses, much like the one in the billiard room. 'And I checked them. None of them seemed to have been tampered with. No odd smells.'

The rug was plush, and her boots sank into it a little as she made her way across the room. 'And why would you suspect poisoning?'

'Bitter almonds,' he replied. 'A tell-tale odour of . . .'

'Cyanide poisoning,' she finished for him. 'I suspected poisoning, but I didn't smell anything peculiar.'

'I have an extremely good sense of smell since my card turned. I suppose it's one of the few benefits of this . . .' he said, gesturing to himself. He sounded bitter.

'I can't imagine how terrible it must have been to be changed in the way you were,' she said with a sympathetic voice. She poured a whiskey, then took it over to the chair opposite his and sat down. 'It ruined your life.'

Krampus's long red tongue rolled out and lapped at his drink. It was horrible and fascinating at the same time. 'It did, and it didn't,' he said with a soft growl. 'I never would have worked with jokers before it happened, never would have treated their ailments. And now, in some cases, I help them say goodbye to loved ones and end their suffering.'

'You perform assisted suicide?' She wasn't appalled, though she knew she should be. The suffering of jokers and humans in extremis had been something she'd been party to more than she would have liked. What the wild card virus could do to a body was unspeakable. 'And was Mr Downs in that sort of situation?' she asked calmly.

He smiled, and she struggled not to shy away. No matter how softly spoken he was, his smile never failed to make her profoundly uneasy. His teeth and claws could do who knew what kind of damage. It was easy enough to imagine him gutting her without a thought.

'No,' he said. 'Though sometimes I do help people do something terrible, I would never take a life – except to end suffering. It goes against everything I hold dear.'

Constance considered him. It was difficult to tell exactly what he was thinking. At that moment, his face wore a rictus smile.

'And revenge? Where do you fall along the line with that?' she asked.

'You mean Black Dog and the Twisted Fists?' he replied.

'I do,' she said, nodding. In for a penny, in for a pound and all that, she figured. 'You have the skills. Why not?'

Grinding rusted gears would have sounded better than his laugh. 'For one, because I'm not a sociopath. And secondly, I'm too smart to kill a person under these circumstances.'

'So, you admit you have considered it?'

'Who hasn't thought about killing someone?' he asked, draining his glass and standing. 'Haven't you?'

Constance had no answer for that. After all, she'd done more than think about it.

After leaving the library, Constance got turned around once again. Loveday seemed almost like a living entity – or at least, it felt that way to her. It was constantly confusing, and she wasn't used to getting lost.

She was halfway up the stairs to the suites when she heard someone talking. It sounded like Babel, but before she reached the landing, doors slammed shut and then the hallway was silent.

A young servant came down the hallway with a tray of serviettes and cellophane-wrapped treats. They were in little paper cups inside small open baskets. Both the serviettes and treats were neatly tied with silver ribbon.

'Evening, ma'am,' the girl said. Her accent was unrecognizable to Constance. She sounded Irish, but without the lovely lilting quality to her voice. 'Would you like your bed turned down and a treat?'

'Do you do this for all the guests?' Constance asked.

'Yes, ma'am. It's a Christmas Eve tradition here, to end the evening with tea and a treat of some kind. There should be a nice pot of tea in your sitting room already.'

The maid made her way to Constance's suite and used a housekeeping key to open the door. She then stepped aside so that Constance could enter.

There was still a cheerful fire in the fireplace. On a low table between the chairs and settee was a carafe of hot water and a teapot. Arranged neatly on the table were small bowls with a selection of loose teas, a tea strainer, milk, sugar, lemon, and two cups. And there was Temperance, looking very vexed indeed.

'Where have you been?' she snapped. 'I came out of the loo, and you'd gone.'

'I'll tell you in a moment,' Constance replied. The maid set the treats down on one end of the table, rearranging it so that they fitted. 'Thank you,' Constance said, following her to the doorway.

Margot's suite was next to Constance's. The maid went there and knocked but was met with silence.

Before Constance's door was fully shut, there was a shriek, and the maid dashed out of Margot's suite. Constance stepped into the hallway and caught the maid by the arm. Temperance was right behind her.

'Hush, my dear, hush,' Constance said to the maid, trying to calm her. 'What has happened?'

'In th-th-there,' the maid stuttered, pointing at the open door to Margot's suite.

Constance stepped inside. On the floor, eyes staring glassily upwards, lay Margot. The maid's forgotten basket lay beside her, treats scattered. With a few steps, Constance was next to Margot's body. She crouched down and gently touched Margot's neck. There wasn't a pulse, but she was still warm.

'Go and get Jago,' Constance said briskly. 'I'll stay here.'

'Y-y-y-yes, ma'am.'

As the maid scurried off, Constance considered Margot's body. Unlike Digger Downs, Margot showed no signs of wounds at all.

A moment later, Temperance ran into the room. 'Oh, not again,' she said, eyes big with surprise.

'It appears that Mr Downs isn't the only one to meet up with the killer tonight,' Constance replied.

Temperance crouched down next to Constance, touched Margot's hand, and pulled back. 'She's still warm,' she said. 'Oh, no!'

'What is it?' Constance asked.

Temperance pulled out a piece of paper from under Margot's other hand. *The Second* was written on it. Before Constance could ponder this any further, Babel hurried into the room.

'I heard a commotion in the hallway,' she said. 'And now I see we have yet another body. They're starting to pile up like firewood.'

'Perhaps not quite that deep,' Constance said. 'But this isn't the Yuletide I was expecting.'

'It's certainly making me glad I'm Jewish,' Babel said. 'Have you sent for Jago?'

'Yes,' Constance replied, rising to her feet and walking into the hall. 'I sent for him, and I hope he'll bring Gary along. I'd feel better if he were here and I knew he was safe.'

'What's all this racket?' Kandy snarled, throwing open her door on the opposite side of the landing. There was a pink satin sleeping mask perched on her head, and she wore pyjamas with a print of chocolates on them. 'Sleeping is the most interesting thing to do here, and now that's been screwed up.'

At that moment, Jago and Gary came running up the stairs, taking them two at a time. They came to an abrupt stop at the doorway to Margot's suite. Jago went utterly still. Gary looked at Constance, who shrugged.

'Everyone should go back to their suites and lock their doors,' Jago said.

'Do you suppose that will help?' Constance asked. 'Margot was found in her suite with the door locked. There's no sign of a struggle. No obvious injury. Only this.' She held up the paper with *The Second* written on it.

'You seem to know rather a lot about this sort of thing,' Kandy said. She pointed at the paper in Constance's hand. 'It has to be one of the jokers! Why else are the deceased being numbered?'

'That could mean anything,' Babel said briskly.

'Well, it doesn't take a wizard detective to see what's before you,' Constance said.

'Then everyone gets a partner,' Gary said.

'I don't think so,' Kandy scoffed. 'One of you is a murderer. I have no intention of being next.' She turned and flounced into her suite, slammed the door shut, and threw the deadbolt in place.

'I don't think she's going to be helpful,' Babel remarked.

'She's a cu—' Temperance started.

Constance interrupted her. 'She is indeed, but it's almost Christmas morning and we have two dead bodies. Miss Kane's disposition – for good or bad – is irrelevant right now.'

'Kandy can stay in her suite alone if she wants to,' Babel said. 'I suggest the rest of us gather together. Safety in numbers and all that.'

Jago nodded. 'We can use the drawing room. And Krampus should inspect the body.'

'I saw him in the library a little while ago,' Constance said.

'I'll have someone fetch him,' Jago said. There was a bellpull in a small alcove in the wall. A few minutes later, Hitchcock appeared. Jago sent him to get Krampus.

Hitchcock returned promptly. 'Unfortunately, Mr Krampus wasn't in the library. I have members of the staff looking for him. No doubt, he'll be up shortly.'

'Come, Constance,' Babel said, holding out her hand. 'Let's head on down.'

'I'd prefer to stay and see what Krampus has to say about this murder,' Constance replied. 'I have a morbid curiosity.'

'Then I'll gather the rest of the guests and get everyone to the front drawing room,' Babel said. 'I assume all the rooms on this level are suites?'

Jago nodded. 'Yes, they're all clustered together here. Temperance, Constance, and Margot's suites are along this wall.' He gestured at three doorways in a row. Constance and Margot's doors stood open. 'And the rest of the guests are on the opposite side.'

Constance looked around and noticed that Hitchcock had vanished once again. *Like the Cheshire Cat,* she thought. But then, just as suddenly, he reappeared, leading Krampus up the stairs.

'Not another one,' Krampus growled, shaking his head. He clumped into Margot's suite and squatted next to her body. He examined it carefully, saying, 'This is a lot like Digger Downs's demise. Without the head wound, of course. But until I see a toxicology report, I'd be hard-pressed to determine exactly what killed her. I could speculate, but that would be all it was.'

'No smell of bitter almonds this time?' Constance asked.

'I didn't say that. Just that I couldn't be sure what killed her.'

'Hitchcock, will you have Margot's body taken to the cooler? Then lock the door behind you. Use the master key,' Jago said.

'Very well,' Hitchcock replied, nodding. 'I shall see that it happens with alacrity.' He used the same bellpull Jago had, though he gave it more tugs.

'Let's go down,' Gary said.

'I need a moment in the loo,' Constance said, turning towards her door. 'Temperance can stay with me, and we'll be down shortly.'

'Why didn't we go with the others?' Temperance asked, fiddling with her paintbrush hair. 'I don't feel safe up here alone.'

'We'll be fine. I need to do something first.'

'Well, you're not using the loo like you said you were going to.'

'That's because I stayed for a different reason.'

Constance went to the French doors leading to the small balcony off the sitting room. Her breath fogged the glass, and she noted that the snow had abated a little. But there was still a breeze. The sky was all abalone, lit by something in the distance. She opened the doors to the balcony. 'What are you doing?' Temperance asked, coming to stand next to her.

'I need to get into Margot's suite,' Constance replied.

'Are you completely mad?' Temperance exclaimed, grabbing Constance's wrist. 'Why would you want to go in there?'

'I need another look around the suite without anyone being the wiser. I imagine by the time I get to Margot's suite, her body will have been moved. And Hitchcock will have the door secured. He's terribly efficient.'

'You're a loon, you know that?'

'No, my dear, just determined.'

She gently pulled her hand from Temperance's grasp. As she opened the doors fully, she had to push against the snow accumulated there. Some snow chunks fell into the room. Swirling flakes blew in as well.

She leaned forward on the balcony. The railing seemed firm, no crumbling mortar at all. Below, something near the greenhouse moved erratically. Constance chose to ignore it. 'Both our suites and Margot's have the same balcony,' she continued. 'Though this one is made from stone and wrought iron and hers just wrought iron. This is a good jumping off point. All I have to do is go from one to the other. Thank God, Loveday has all the bits and pieces from one time or another all jumbled together. There's a gargoyle head there.' She pointed at the stone head jutting from the wall between the two balconies.

'I'm not going out there in this weather,' Temperance said.

'Of course not,' Constance replied. 'I'm going.'

Constance started unwinding her scarf, ignoring the fact that Temperance looked gobsmacked. Constance set about retrieving her gloves, coat, and hat. After she had those in place, she began winding the scarf around her waist. It was exceptionally long and made of a gossamer weight cashmere. Having made it with her power, it was indestructible while retaining all the softness of the yarn.

'What the bloody hell?' Temperance said. Her voice was rising. 'You're seriously going to climb from this balcony to the next?'

'Oh, it's not that far,' Constance replied. 'And I'm not climbing, I'm hopping.'

'If it has to be done, let me do it,' Temperance pleaded. 'I'm smaller than you are. And . . . well, young.'

Constance started tying one end of her scarf to the metal railing. After a few tugs, she had it tightened to her satisfaction. 'You don't know what to look for. And I'm well aware of my age.'

'And you know what to look for?'

'Yes, I believe I do.' Constance gave her a smile and gently cupped Temperance's face.

'Then tell me, and I'll look for you.'

'I'll know it when I see it,' Constance said. 'If you get caught in there, it will look especially damning, seeing as how you're a joker.'

'And it'll look better for you?'

'No, I'm an old woman. Even should I fall, I've had a long and good life.'

'And what about me if something happens to you?' Her eyes were shiny with unshed tears. 'What happens to me then?'

'I need you here in case something goes awry.'

'Like you falling to your death, I presume.'

'Let's cross that bridge when we come to it.' Constance snugged her hat on tighter and tugged at her gloves one more time. 'And now, dear, I'm off.'

It occurred to her, as she steadied herself against the exterior wall while standing on the slippery railing, that this was one of the more foolish things she'd done in her life.

A gust of wind took her breath away for a moment. Then she shrugged with all the bravado she could muster. She was glad for the rubber soles of her low-cut boots. They would help a bit. It wasn't too far to the other balcony.

She wiped some snow out of her eyes and saw something dark move against the ground. It came to a stop under her. *Don't think about it, just go.*

And so she did.

The small gargoyle head, with its obscenely lolling tongue and bulging eyes, had a flat skull. She landed on it easily. It was the staying on it that was scarier. She let out her breath for just a moment, then immediately had to slam her hand against the wall for balance.

'Constance,' she heard Temperance say, voice trembling, 'be careful.'

Normally, she would have said something witty or cantankerous, but even the slightest movement might send her tumbling down before she could make the other leap.

Then there was a growl from below.

'Constance,' it snarled. Despite the cold, she began sweating. 'Did you come out here to play?'

She glanced down for a moment. The black thing below was a figure now. She could smell cigarettes and cologne. Her hands were sweating inside her gloves, but she forced herself to gather her strength to jump from the gargoyle to Margot's balcony. She *didn't* need the distraction of her past right now.

Below her, she heard skittering, like the sound of razors against stone. Stone covered the walls of the ground floor, and it was as if something were trying to gain purchase there.

She couldn't think about anything but getting to the other little balcony before whatever was down below managed to climb up to her.

Her hair tore loose from its braid and blew in the air, wild and witchy. Her scarf flew, whipped about, and momentarily obscured her vision. She jumped, then slammed belly first into the railing with an *oomph*. There was a moment of teetering, and then she fell forward onto the balcony, landing awkwardly on her side.

Gasping, she got to her knees and grabbed the door handles to Margot's suite, but they didn't budge.

Oh, bloody hell, she thought. She rattled them again, trying to keep the sound as quiet as possible.

'Constance,' the thing that now sounded like Ronnie Kray said. 'You done both of us wrong. Killing me. Letting Reggie go to prison for what you did. Nothing right about that, was there?'

'Shut up,' she said, panting now. There was an experimental tug on her scarf from below. She began fumbling with the scarf's knot. It was tight, and her hands were clumsy in the gloves. She yanked them off to get a better grip.

'Leave me alone, you bastard. Some people need killin'. And you were one of 'em, Ronnie. And it were self-defence. It were.'

There was another tug, this one harder. Her hands shook; she knew what was coming for her. Ronnie's ace had been razored fingertips. Despite her attire made with her power, he still terrified her.

The knot came free, and the scarf vanished over the railing. Frantically, she rattled the doorknobs, and abruptly, they turned. She spilled into Margot's suite. Rolling onto her back, she shoved the doors closed with her boots. With a grunt, she sat up, then flipped the lock shut. A hand with a gold ring grasped the top railing of the balcony, then released it abruptly, and vanished.

Constance yanked the heavy curtains shut, as if that would protect her against whatever was outside.

She leaned back on her elbows, then sank to the floor and stared at the ceiling. The warmth in the room slid into her old bones, and she wished Gary and Temperance were with her. She shut her eyes for just a moment, letting all the weariness she felt wrap around her.

Then her eyes snapped open.

Enough of that shite, my girl, she thought, rolling over onto her tum. She pushed to her knees and then got to her feet. She fumbled for the penlight in her pocket and swept it around the suite.

A metre and a half away from her was where Margot's body had been found between the fireplace and settee. Her suite was the mirror image of Constance's. Nothing seemed amiss. No signs of a scuffle. Margot's body had been found without a mark on her, unlike Digger Downs's.

Constance moved to the bedroom. She opened the armoire and found Margot's clothes neatly arranged. Classic pre-wild card glamour shots of movie stars adorned the bedroom walls. But when Constance looked at them more closely, they were all of Margot recreating those classic images. On the opposite wall were framed posters from two of Margot's best-known films.

Her first film, *Le Petite Chat*, was a moody black-and-white piece about a girl discovering her sexuality. The other one, *Firecracker!*, was Margot's most successful film. It was about a woman finding her sexuality. Margot had a certain range.

The Art Deco-style bed was still made up. Cosmetics were arrayed on a vanity matching the bed. Its mirror was ringed by large bright bulbs. Constance studied the items arrayed there but determined nothing was amiss. Foundation, powder, concealer, blusher, bronzer, and brushes were all neatly organized. It would have been obvious had anything been moved.

Still, she sniffed each item to see if they smelled peculiar. The only thing she noted was that the face powder made her sneeze.

Meticulously, she made her way through Margot's bedroom, searching under the bed and around the nightstands. Finding nothing useful, she returned to the sitting room and began exploring it. She glanced at the scripts Margot had stacked on a small table next to the fireplace. A tea set with gold lightning handles was laid out on the coffee table residing between two Halabala armchairs.

The settee completed the cosy arrangement of furniture. Constance kneeled and felt around the base of it. Her hand closed over something crinkly, and she pulled it out. It was a small square of silver paper. Constance tucked it into the pocket of her cardigan and buttoned the pocket closed.

She gave the sitting room one last careful turn, then decided she had found all she was going to find. She tried to open the door to the hallway, but it was locked from the outside. She'd assumed the lock would open from the inside. For a moment, she contemplated yelling for help. At this point, she'd almost rather risk being caught than climbing between the balconies again.

'Bloody hell,' she whispered. She felt like crying; she was so vexed and afraid. 'Bloody goddam hell.'

◆

Constance cracked open the French doors onto the balcony and peered outside. Her gloves lay there, no more than a half metre away. There was no dark figure on the balcony, and she breathed a sigh of relief. She couldn't leave her gloves for anyone to find, but she also didn't want to take the time to put them back on. It would be simple enough. Grab her gloves, jam them into her empty pocket, then jump back. *Easy-peasy.*

She eased open the right-hand door. A sudden gust of wind yanked it out of her hand, sending it slamming against the wall. It was loud enough that she thought it would wake the dead. She grabbed the door again, stepped onto the balcony and closed the door firmly behind her.

Snow had already started covering her gloves. She grabbed them, the snow slid off, and she jammed them into her pocket. From below, the sound of scratching started again.

'You're back,' Ronnie said gleefully. 'You shouldn't have come outside.'

'Oh, bugger off,' Constance whispered. 'Just piss off. You're dead. And I've had a perfectly lovely long life while you've been in the cold, hard ground. You've been nothing for decades.'

She saw Temperance waiting for her at the other balcony, shivering from the cold. Constance threw her right leg over the railing, straddling it. Then she brought the left alongside the right. There was more snow on the gargoyle head now, making it even more treacherous than before. She longed for Gary's heat. It would melt the snow off in a trice. *If wishes were horses,* she thought, *beggars would have had that damn gargoyle head cleared.*

She leaned out over the gap between the railing and gargoyle head and hopped. There was a sickening moment when she thought she'd plummet to certain death – if not from the fall, then from whatever lurked below.

There was the familiar crunch of boots on snow as she landed. But this time, she didn't even try to slow down. She hit the snow, felt the flat stone head, and before she could slip, pushed off.

She hung in the air for a moment, her heart feeling as if it were climbing out of her throat. Then, much to her surprise, she felt Gary's warm hand catch her left forearm and Temperance's cooler hand catch her right.

But something had caught the heel of her right boot. As they lifted her over the railing, the boot was already slipping off. She kicked herself free, losing the boot as she did so.

'Hang on, Constance,' Gary said. 'We've got you.'

Her foot was quickly becoming numb from the cold. For the first time in many a year, her socks weren't something she'd made but a present one of her tailors had knitted. The socks were beautiful and perfectly done, but unlike her own work, utterly useless in this situation.

Hands wrapped around her ankles. She could feel her other boot slipping off. In addition to Constance's light frame, Gary and Temperance struggled with the weight of the thing holding Constance in its grip. She groaned, feeling as if she were being torn in two. There was a moment's relief when the hand on her left leg released, but then it grabbed her just above the knee. The other hand joined it on the right side.

'Constance,' Ronnie said, 'who are your friends?'

'What the hell is that?' Temperance exclaimed, every bit as frightened as Constance.

'We've got to get her up now,' Gary said. 'Before it's too late.'

'Now would be lovely,' Constance said, gasping. 'An absolute delight. This thing is going to kill me. Or try to, at any rate.'

Together, Temperance and Gary took purchase against the stone railing and yanked her up and over. As she cleared the railing, the Ronnie thing released its grip. Its razored fingertips slid uselessly along her trousers, until it caught on her socks. She screamed as it sliced into her right heel.

And then it was gone.

They carried her inside, blood dripping from her foot. Gary stacked pillows from the divan atop the footstool, then propped Constance's foot on it. Temperance appeared from the loo with fluffy white towels. 'I'll call Krampus to sew up your foot,' Gary said. 'You're bleeding so much.'

'It's a little razor slice.' The pain was making her queasy and light-headed. 'No need to call anyone. I've sewn up wounds before.'

'What are you planning on doing?' Temperance asked, reaching gingerly towards Constance's foot with a towel.

Constance held her hand out. She reached for the towel, and Temperance reluctantly handed it over. Gently, she began dabbing at her foot. It was bleeding enthusiastically, but the cut itself was smaller than it felt.

'Temperance,' she said, 'be a love and bring me my knitting bag. I need to cut this sock off. It'll make it easier to sew the wound.'

Temperance stood rooted to the ground for a moment, then went into Constance's bedroom. She returned with the bag and held out a tin of plasters. 'I found these in the loo.'

'Sensible girl,' Constance said with a smile. 'Can you thread a needle for me? And please find my scissors.'

Temperance dug about in Constance's bag. Then she gasped. Constance and Gary exchanged worried glances.

'Is everything OK?' Gary asked.

Temperance didn't reply, but a moment later, she held out Constance's scissors . . . and her Walther. Mutely, she gave both to Constance.

'Could you thread a needle for me, Temperance?' Constance said as she placed the Walther on the table next to her. She began cutting her sock off. Temperance tried to thread the needle, but her hands were shaking too much. Gary took it from her and expertly threaded it. He handed it to Constance with a baffled expression.

'You brought a gun to Loveday?' Gary asked. His voice was like a piano wire about to break. 'You're here as a *guest*. Constance, you need to explain this to me!'

'Gary, don't shout at a bleeding woman,' Constance said, wincing as she slid the needle into her heel and began sewing. 'Temperance, can you retrieve a sock from my armoire? There's a good girl. Gary, I bring a gun with me everywhere I go now. Generally, more than one. I know it's not terribly British, but I'm not well-loved in the anti-joker community. I've had my atelier firebombed. My life has been threatened more than once. We had to make the drive here from London. Two women all alone, even with a driver, need protection.' Constance held her now-sewn foot in the air. 'Now that I've sewn this heel up using my power, it'll stay repaired and will be protected. Pass me a plaster or two, if you'd be so kind.'

Silently, Gary handed them over. She put a couple of plasters on the wound and then pulled on the sock. 'I'll limp, but I won't bleed all over everything.' She stood, wincing just for an instant. 'I believe I know who killed Margot and Digger Downs. More importantly, I think I know why. I presume everyone except Kandy is already in the drawing room. Let's gather her and meet up with them. It's time to get this all sorted.'

The Christmas tree in the drawing room was cheerful with ornaments gleaming in the fairy lights. The bright colours clashed with the events of the evening. Constance was ensconced in a wingback chair next to the fire. Her injured foot was propped up on a footstool. Opposite her, in a matching chair, sat Kandy.

Ringed around the room were the rest of the guests. Devlin Pear and Bastet sat on a loveseat, glancing nervously at each other. Krampus leaned against the wall, his barbed tail wrapped around his waist. Jago stood next to the fireplace, one arm draped on the mantelpiece. Babel sat in a spindly chair. She wore a hideous Christmas jumper, red and green plaid trousers, and black velvet flats. She eyed Constance warily.

Temperance had taken up residence on the floor next to the Christmas tree, and Gary had settled against the doorway. None of them looked happy.

'What's all this about?' Jago asked. 'What special knowledge do you have about what's been happening?'

'She's just a crazy old woman,' Kandy said contemptuously. 'I'm not sure why you're indulging her.'

'It certainly couldn't hurt,' Gary said. 'It isn't as if we're going anywhere.'

'The snow's let up,' Krampus remarked. He glanced at the clock on the mantel. 'It's getting on for daybreak. I imagine we'll be able to dig out sometime soon.'

Jago nodded. 'I have snowploughs here. They'll make quick work of what's piled up.'

'Out with it, Constance,' Devlin said. 'You've got our attention.'

'Don't talk to her like that,' Babel snapped.

'That's quite all right,' Constance said cheerfully. 'We're all on edge. I suppose I should explain what I've discovered.'

'That would be nice,' Bastet said, purring. It didn't sound as if she was pleased.

'I found everyone's alibis to be a little too pat,' Constance began. 'Most of you told part of the truth, but all of you omitted certain details. From the beginning, Ms Baden's alibi seemed weak.'

All eyes turned towards Babel, who appeared confused and a little angry. 'Why on earth would you suspect me?'

'Just what I said – you didn't have much of an alibi,' Constance replied. 'Only that you'd gone to the loo, and the last time you'd seen Digger Downs, he was alive. However, as I was waiting for Temperance to arrive with Jago, I heard you talking to someone in German. I followed the sound, nosy creature that I am, and found you on your satellite phone. You were clearly upset. You were supposed to be in the loo, but you'd gone off to talk with your lover, Lohengrin. You didn't want anyone to know you were using the satellite phone to call him. That doesn't look good for the head of the Committee. I suspect if we check the timestamp, we'll discover you were talking with Lohengrin when Digger Downs was murdered.'

Babel stared at Constance but didn't dispute what she'd said.

Constance politely cleared her throat. 'I heard you again as I was returning from following Bastet and Devlin.'

'Wait!' Devlin said loudly. 'You were following Bastet and me?'

'Yes.' Constance smiled, looking altogether too pleased. 'You were riding Bastet down to the cellars, where the two of you shagged.'

'You're accusing Bastet and me of having a tryst?'

Constance adjusted her foot. 'It's not accusation. It's a fact. Before Downs was murdered, you discovered Bastet arguing with him about the scratching incident. The reason you both were late to the guise dancing was because you were comforting Bastet. You're still married, Devlin. I imagine you'd prefer your wife not to get wind of this.'

'She divorced me,' Devlin said sadly. 'After I went to The Hague. I don't care what she would think about this, but Bastet is a joker, and there are people who wouldn't understand.' He took Bastet's hand and gave it a squeeze. Then he gently kissed her cheek.

'I asked Devlin to keep our relationship quiet,' Bastet said. 'We don't see each other often. When I received the invitation, I asked Jago if he would invite Devlin. I imagine he divined why.'

Jago nodded. 'It wasn't an imposition. And who am I to stand in the way of true love?'

'Or true lust,' Kandy snarked.

'Then there is Krampus,' Constance said, ignoring Kandy. 'If the theory that the murders were due to the slaying of Black Dog were true, then all three jokers would be suspects, including our good doctor here. Given the collapse of his practice and how he was ostracized by everyone he knew from before his card turned, that would make him a likely candidate. But the Twisted Fists revenge theory started breaking down as soon as I realized neither Krampus nor Bastet could have done it. The timing was off. And Temperance certainly didn't, despite her professed understanding of the desire for revenge against nats. She has been with me this whole time.'

'That's not exactly true,' Temperance said, unravelling the cuff of her jumper. Unlike Babel's, it was positively demure, with tiny white skulls on a field of black. 'We were separated for an hour after dinner. Plenty of time for me to do the deed.'

'Yes, but there were other guests who saw him alive during that period,' Constance said. 'Now, the cause of death for both Digger and Margot is peculiar. It could be possible that Krampus had a hand in that, but he takes his responsibilities as a surgeon as seriously, if not more so, than most do. And a short conversation with him made me realize he was as intent on figuring out what happened to Digger Downs as I was.

'The Twisted Fist revenge theory was a clever distraction,' Constance continued. She adjusted the knitting on her lap to better conceal her Walther. 'I, however, thought Margot had killed Digger. Her temperament was hot-headed, and she carried a grudge – believe me, I am well aware of this – but then she turned up dead, and that led me to one conclusion.'

Constance pulled her Walther from below her knitting and pointed it at Kandy. 'You, my dear.'

'You told me you used that only for self-defence!' Gary exclaimed.

'And you knew about this weapon and didn't tell me, Gary?' Jago asked quietly.

Gary looked at Jago, then nodded. 'She does have a lot of enemies, and she promised to behave herself.'

'I'm terribly sorry, Gary,' Constance said. 'And to you, Jago. But this did seem a rather necessary time to use it.'

Kandy stared at Constance, then her eyes narrowed. 'Why would I kill them?'

'You had two very good reasons. The first, you hated Digger Downs for the unflattering things he said about you and Golden Boy. And you hated Margot even more because she'd had the relationship with Golden Boy you wanted. You saw yourself as quite the catch, yet Mr Braun threw you over as if you were nothing more than a quick shag.'

'That's not what happened at all,' Kandy hissed. '*She* was the temporary infatuation. I was going to be the one he was serious about.'

'But that didn't happen, did it?'

Kandy schooled her features and relaxed back into her chair. 'And how exactly did I commit these murders? You and Krampus both said there was no evidence as to the cause of death.'

'I wondered about that myself,' Constance admitted. 'But I got to thinking about it. And then I found this in Margot's suite.' She unbuttoned her cardigan pocket and retrieved a small piece of silver paper. It was cheerfully striped in green and red. 'I'm certain we all remember the chocolates from dinner. And their festive wrappers.'

'Those were harmless!' Kandy said.

'Yes,' Constance said grimly. '*Those* were, but the ones you gave Margot and Digger weren't. Those were quite lethal.'

'Don't be ridiculous,' Kandy said, rubbing her palm against her slacks. 'Margot doesn't touch chocolates.'

'But you made her low-calorie ones for dinner.' Constance adjusted herself slightly. Sitting in one position too long was hard on her old joints. 'And there's nothing that she liked more than sweets – something she couldn't indulge in because of her endless diets. So, you had the perfect method to kill her: convince her that her chocolate was low-calorie, and she was happy to consume it.'

'You're full of it,' Kandy said, twisting her mouth in a most unattractive way. Kandy glared at Constance. Then she lunged forward as if to snatch the sweet wrapper but instead plucked the gun out of Constance's other hand.

Everyone drew in a sharp breath as Kandy leaped to her feet. 'Crazy old women shouldn't be allowed to own firearms.' She swung the gun around. 'You don't really believe this crap, do you?'

'Let me have the gun,' Gary said softly.

'That wrapper proves nothing,' Kandy said.

'Give it up,' Temperance said. 'You don't go swinging guns around if you're innocent.'

Kandy trained the Walther on Temperance. 'You're a child. You know nothing. This proves *nothing*.'

'Temperance is right,' Babel said. 'You look very guilty right now. Holding a gun on a room full of people isn't generally the act of an innocent person.'

'Stop saying that!' Kandy snapped.

'You really have spent a lot of time pointing a finger at the jokers,' Krampus remarked.

'Well, what about her?' Kandy waved the pistol at Constance, then turned to her. Kandy turned to Constance. There was a desperate gleam in her eyes. 'It looks like you've got it all figured out. Then there's no reason not to do this.'

She pulled the trigger, but the Walther just clicked. She pulled it again, and still nothing happened. 'What the fuck is this?'

Constance stood up, letting her knitting fall to the floor, then plucked the Walther from Kandy's hand.

'My dear,' she said, tucking the gun into her knitting bag, 'I took the magazine out before our little party. I'm not foolish enough to have a loaded pistol about unless I'm going to use it.'

'Then why have it in the first place?' Kandy shrieked.

'Misdirection, my dear.'

Gary took Kandy by the arm. She tried to jerk away, but he held her fast. 'Jago,' he said, 'where would you like her kept?'

'It won't be long until we dig out and the police can be called,' Jago said. 'Let's keep her down in the dungeon.'

'No!' Kandy cried, pulling against Gary's grip. 'You're not putting me down there!'

Constance knew exactly how Kandy felt but lacked sympathy for her. After all, she was quite murderous. And badly behaved in general.

Constance looked outside and saw that it had stopped snowing. The sun was coming up. Hitchcock opened the door to the entrance hall as Gary was taking a sobbing Kandy away. 'Ah,' he said in his bizarrely calm voice. 'Breakfast is being served in the dining room. I'll get the keys for the cells and meet you down below, Gary.'

Temperance stretched and got up off the floor. 'I don't know about the rest of you blokes, but I'm famished.'

'If anyone still has an appetite, please come with me,' Jago said.

Constance gathered her belongings and smiled at Jago. 'I do think I could eat something as well.'

The rest of the room nodded. Solving murders was a hungry business.

And finally, of this Constance was certain: Loveday House was a dreadful place to spend Christmas.

Longing for Those Lost

by Stephen Leigh

Part IV

AS SOON AS THE roads were cleared of the snow, Loveday House was besieged by the authorities and the press. Digger Downs's and Margot Bellarose's deaths, as well as the detention and arrest of Kandy Kane as the accused murderer, were the subject of blaring headlines and media memes. Hitchcock and Elbrekt wrangled the influx of reporters and kept them outside, while Gary was recruited into helping Jago with the local constabulary, in the form of DS Genn Truscott, the detective superintendent of the local police, her officers, and the coroner, as well as shuttling the remaining party guests to and from the library, which served as the interview room.

With Hitchcock and Elbrekt on duty outside, it was Gary who answered the bell to greet DS Truscott and her entourage, including the coroner, and escort them into the house, their yellow, white, and blue cars parked on the drive along with a hearse, while fellow officers moved the reporters back outside the wrought iron gates of the driveway, yellow crime tape secured across the drive flapping in the sea breeze. Reporters snapped pictures and spoke into their video camera lenses.

Truscott had a pleasant, round face with prominent smile lines around the mouth, though her expression was solemn. She and the others stamped off the snow on their boots on the thick doormats Hitchcock and Gary had placed there earlier in anticipation. 'Boots stay in the entrance hall,' Truscott told her team. 'Get your shoe covers on; I don't want anyone tracking snow and dirt on Lord Branok's expensive rugs.' She winked sidewise at Gary as she said it.

Jago appeared as the police officers were still removing their boots. He gave Truscott a quick, familiar embrace; she didn't seem put off or startled by the white domino mask Jago was wearing.

'Genn,' Jago said in a whisper close to her ear that only she and Gary could hear. 'Glad it was you who came.' Jago then moved back and spoke more loudly for her subordinates. 'DS Truscott, I apologize for dragging your people out into this weather over Christmas, but I had no choice. I've two bodies for Dr Sheets to take back to her lab - I believe she'll find they were poisoned. I also have the person who killed them for you to take into custody.'

'Nice of you to have wrapped everything up in a bow, Lord Branok,' Truscott answered, her voice flat and her face still serious. 'A fine Christmas gift.' She smiled then, the lines around her mouth deepening. 'I wish everyone involved in our cases would be so diligent.'

'I wasn't the person who solved the crime,' Jago responded. 'That honour belongs to Ms Constance Russell, who put all the pieces together.'

'Then I'll want to speak to Ms Russell at length. We'll also need to take statements from your staff and guests, of course.'

Jago nodded. 'Gary, would you be kind enough to find Constance and accompany her down to the library? Then gather the other guests and any staff who had significant contact with our guests. You can seat them in the dining room until they're called and have Chef Daniel send up some food and refreshments for them while they're waiting their turn. DS Truscott, if you'll follow me, you can take my own statement there.'

Gary found Constance in her room, as expected. 'The police are here,' he told her. 'They want to hear your story.'

'And I'll give it to them - at least the parts I want them to hear. I believe I might gloss over my Walther, for instance, and the Krays.' Constance gave a wry shrug. 'I'll make sure that next year you get a new bathrobe and sheets and maybe a few shirts as well. Loveday doesn't seem to be entirely safe, after all.' She gave a breathy sigh. 'Well, I might as well get it over with. Hope this DS Truscott likes strange stories.'

'I think she might be used to them around here. And she and Jago seem to be friendly with each other.'

Constance patted Gary's cheek at that. 'Lead on, then.'

Dr Sheets had the bodies placed in the truck and departed - with the press eagerly filming the removal of the two covered stretchers from the house - before Gary returned to the library with Constance. Kandy Kane was whisked away in the back of a cruiser a few hours later, similarly covered by the press. DS Truscott and her team remained at Loveday for much of the day, taking statements from everyone, including Gary.

By evening, the reporters had left their cold and snowy Loveday vigil, retreating back down to the village to be out of the weather. The guests were finally released by Truscott, with the admonition from the detective superintendent that they might be needed to answer follow-up questions later on. The yellow crime tape was taken down.

Babel had a Committee helicopter flown in; she took Krampus, Bastet, and Devlin with her to make their own connections in London.

Constance and Temperance emerged from their room not long after; their luggage was brought down by Elbrekt and the footmen Cadan and Raymond. Gary was waiting for them in the entrance hall, while Hitchcock lingered at the front doors.

'Are you sure you don't want to stay a while longer?' Gary asked. 'It wasn't much of a holiday.'

'I believe I'm quite ready to go.' Constance gave Gary a quick peck on the cheek. 'I'm glad you've found somewhere you fit, dear,' she added. 'And found someone to share it with, too.'

Temperance remained silent, the paintbrushes in her hair swinging as she lifted a single eyebrow. Gary wasn't sure she shared her companion's enthusiasm.

Gary gave Constance a kiss on the cheek in return, then glanced outside. 'Your car's here.'

The crushed shells of the driveway crunched beneath tyres as the Rolls-Royce that had brought them to Loveday pulled up to the front doors. The driver opened his door, then came around to open the rear doors for Constance and Temperance.

'Thank you for a truly memorable and interesting party, Lord Branok. Make sure you keep Gary safe, will you?' Constance said as Jago belatedly joined them. Hitchcock opened the front doors, allowing Temperance and Constance to walk out into the cold, bright Christmas Day. Gary watched as they slipped into the back of the car, waving as it pulled away from Loveday.

Jago came to stand alongside Gary as the car made its way down to the lights of the village and the causeway. 'I think I may be having fewer parties in the future if they continue to cause this much of an upset.' Jago laughed at his own comment, but Gary could hear no amusement in his voice at all. 'I hope you don't mind, Gary.'

Gary shrugged. 'It's your house, your parties, and your guests, Jago,' he said. 'I'm just your dance master. But at least Constance managed to catch the murderer. Maybe you should hire her as your in-house detective, though I'm not sure DS Truscott would appreciate that.'

Ceallaigh moved fully into Gary's room two weeks later. They'd spent most of the last few weeks sharing Gary's bed, since it had fireproof sheets. Gary had worried that Ceallaigh might find sleeping overnight with him too hot and uncomfortable, but Ceallaigh had quickly made the discovery that if

Gary slept under Constance's sheet and she slept on top of it with another sheet and blanket over her, she didn't feel Gary's heat much at all – in fact, in winter, it was quite nice to snuggle up to him.

To Gary, they seemed to fit together easily, quickly, and well. Being with Ceallaigh felt like how it had been with Caitlyn and Moira, though without the terrible worry of how soon the wild card virus might rear up and snatch away both his lover and his stepdaughter. They fell into their own routines, their own habits. Gary found that he could talk with Ceallaigh for hours when they were together and off duty, and he missed her presence when they were apart.

Over the next few months, his apartment became *their* home within Loveday House.

Which was not to say that Gary was entirely comfortable here. He still remembered the room somewhere in the depths of Loveday that had opened to reveal the interior of the small house back on Rathlin, with Caitlyn, Moira, and even Duncan seated inside around the hearth. He couldn't bring himself to ask Ceallaigh how to find it again.

Yet one night, when he could hear her sleeping deeply alongside him, he slipped out of bed, put on Constance's bathrobe and placed Morwen's knife (in its new leather sheath) into one pocket, and went searching the corridors of Loveday once more.

Once he was well away from the room and walking deeper into the house, he called out softly into the darkness. 'Caitlyn? Can you hear me? Moira? Where are you? Please! I want to see you again!'

'I'm here,' he heard a woman's voice answer, but so faintly that he couldn't tell whose voice it was. 'Come to me.'

The sconces along the hallway went out all at once. Gary gasped, startled, as light returned an instant later, but this time the sconces held guttering torches alight with flame, filling the hall with the scent of smoke and a faint haze. Under his feet, he could see plain, roughly cut wooden boards. Gary heard the creak of door hinges behind him; he clutched Morwen's knife in his hand as he turned.

Morwen was standing behind him, midnight hair frothing around her neck and shoulders. She grinned, as if amused at his fright and the way he brandished the blade, exposing teeth the colour of old ivory with gaps where some were missing. 'You're no warrior, are you, Dance Master? Your hand trembles with an old man's palsy. Why, with just a step, I could snatch away that dagger of mine you hold. You could not stop me. You are weak, like the others of your time who come here. Weak and pitiful. You are no better than a mange-ridden dog fighting for scraps under the table.'

'I'm not afraid of you, Lady Morwen.'

'You should be, dancing fool,' she answered.

'I don't need your dagger, Lady Morwen.' Gary placed the weapon back into the pocket of his bathrobe. He held up his hands, fingers spread. 'Do you remember my flames? Do you remember what they felt like?'

She hissed at that, backing away from Gary. 'I hold skills and spells also, you *vil du euthvil*. You Satan. *Le démon*,' she said. 'Flame? Pah!' She spat on the floor between them. She began to mutter words in a language that Gary didn't recognize, her hands weaving intricate patterns.

Gary started to feel a constriction in his chest, as if something heavy was sitting on it. Then the pain began, radiating from his chest into his arms. Gary cried out involuntarily as Morwen continued chanting and moving her hands. The pain worsened, making him gasp. He backed away from her, but she followed, grinning as the strange words continued to hammer at him. He could feel the impact of each syllable, like fists hitting him. He staggered. Part of him wondered distantly if this was the same agony Duncan had felt when his own heart failed.

To the left side of the hallway, Gary heard a door open. He looked and saw Caitlyn there with her porcelain and perfect face, Moira behind her. Caitlyn stepped out. Gary could see the interior of their Rathlin house behind her as she placed herself between Gary and Morwen.

'Get away from him,' Caitlyn said. 'Get yourself back to your own place, Morwen, and stop bothering my man.'

Morwen hissed at Caitlyn, but her hands stopped moving and the pressure on Gary's chest and the pain receded.

Caitlyn gestured at her door. 'You should step through, Gary. This ain't Morwen's time. Not yet.'

Morwen was cursing loudly in her strange archaic tongues as Gary slipped past Caitlyn and into that impossible Rathlin interior, feeling the welcoming warmth of the fire and smelling the familiar odour of burning peat. Caitlyn followed, moving as stiffly as Gary remembered. Moira ran to him, and soon her arms were around his waist. She seemed to be eleven or twelve at the most, well before the virus inside her expressed and killed her. His own arms went around her, hugging her. He saw Caitlyn smiling at the sight. It was if he had stepped back decades in time.

'Gary,' Caitlyn said, 'you're safe here.'

'Caitlyn,' he began, but words failed him as he choked back a sob.

Still holding Moira to him, he went to Caitlyn and embraced her. She lifted her face to him, and he kissed her lips. Under his, they felt already stiff and unyielding as the virus slowly transformed her into a ceramic-hard image of herself – a process that would eventually kill her. He could still remember the day that had happened, as he could also remember the day that Moira had drawn the black queen and died.

'It's so good to see both of you. I can't tell you how much I've missed being with you.'

Moira gave a cry-laugh at that. 'I love you so much, Gary.'

He smiled. 'And I feel the same about you and your *máthair*.' He glanced at Caitlyn as he said it. *I should tell her about Ceallaigh . . .* He knew that, but it didn't seem right. Not at this moment. Maybe never.

After all, Caitlyn and Moira had died years ago. Their being in Loveday was simply the house plucking them from his memory and creating them for him.

Not real. It's not actually them at all.

Or was that true? Jago had said that the house was a nexus for alternate dimensions. That was certainly the case with Mad Morwen. She was 'real' enough, and Caitlyn and Moira seemed the same. Maybe these *were* Caitlyn and Moira, just from a slightly different timeline. If he told Caitlyn about Ceallaigh, she would be hurt, confused. She might feel betrayed.

So he said nothing about her at all.

He opened the door to their room and glanced up and down the hallway. Morwen was nowhere to be seen. 'I need to go now, Caitlyn.'

Caitlyn didn't protest or try to convince him to stay. She simply nodded stiffly.

'I'll come back,' he told her, wondering if that was true or if he could even find his way back here. Then he walked out into the corridor.

The door shut firmly behind him. He walked back down the hallways until the electric lights lit his way, the familiar carpet was under his feet again, and he recognized where he was.

Inside his room, Ceallaigh was still asleep. He didn't wake her.

He didn't say anything about the night's experience the next morning. It wasn't until he and Ceallaigh were sitting on the room's balcony around the small wrought iron table there, Gary in shirtsleeves and Ceallaigh dressed but also wearing a jacket against the morning chill, that he finally decided to say something. They drank black tea with Chef Daniel's scones steaming on a plate between them, along with a small dish of clotted cream. They could hear the calls of gulls and the waves of the Celtic Sea lashing the rocks below the cliffs.

Gary lifted his head. 'Last night, after you were asleep,' he said slowly, 'I went wandering. I . . . I found Caitlyn and Moira again – or at least what Loveday could give me of them.'

Ceallaigh said nothing, taking a long sip of her tea. Gary saw the tea shivering in the cup and heard it rattle on the saucer as Ceallaigh set it down again. She looked at Gary, as if waiting.

'I wanted to tell them about you and me,' he continued.

'So, did you?' There was no accusation in her voice but also no sympathy. Her tone was devoid of emotion, as if she were afraid to even ask the question. Her voice trembled like the tea in her cup.

He shook his head mutely.

'Why not?'

'I just couldn't find the right words somehow.'

Ceallaigh sniffed. She pulled her jacket more tightly around her shoulders. 'And what would the right words have been, Gary?'

He lifted his shoulders and let them fall again. He sighed.

'I've already told you, Gary. I'm not your Caitlyn or a Caitlyn substitute, and I don't ever want to be or intend to be that. I'm just *me*. The person here in front of you. If that's not what *you* want . . .'

'You *are* what I want,' he said. 'You're *all* that I want.'

'If you expect me to believe that, then don't go wandering around Loveday at night,' she answered. Her eyebrows lifted as she looked at him. 'Irish lasses, no matter what yeh might have heard, don't care for straying men. Especially for one who might also be pining for a lost love.'

There didn't seem to be a safe answer to that. Gary reached for one of the scones and spread clotted cream on it. He bit into it; Ceallaigh's gaze was on him as he chewed and swallowed.

'These are delicious,' he said. 'You really should try one.'

'I think it's time we had another party,' Jago said to Gary, Hitchcock, Elbrekt, and Madame Amélie. He'd called the quartet into his office for a meeting. 'I've sent out invitations for four weeks from today. This will be a very different set of guests from our past affairs: some of the most powerful aces in Britain and their guests will be attending. I don't believe we'll have the same' – he hesitated, evidently choosing the next word carefully – '*trouble* with this set of guests. At least, we can hope not.'

It would *be nice if no one died this time.* Gary thought it but didn't say it, though he noticed Jago's eyes fixed on him behind the mask.

'Gary,' Jago continued, 'we'll have a guise dance again with this crew, so make sure you have the staff brush up on their steps, and you might confer with Richard Darke about any spring seasonal dances we could adapt. Hitchcock, you and Elbrekt will coordinate with Madame Amélie as to the room decor for when the acceptances to my invitations come in; Madame Amélie, I'm sure you'll make the right choice of maid for each. I'll give you the guest list and some details. Elbrekt, I'd like you to speak with Alan Turing; I'll also give you his contact information. He intends to have a contest of sorts with some of our guests, so see what he might need and how to set up the grounds, if you would. Beyond that, I think you all know how to proceed at this point. I know I can trust everyone to make this a truly memorable event.' Jago stood up behind his desk. 'That's all I have at the moment. Let's get the preparations underway.'

Two Lovedays

by Peter Newman

Stuart

THE AIR WAS FRESH as I got out of the cab. It was early, and birdsong mingled with the sound of my family arguing. My mum and sister to be precise.

I sighed. The sooner Kelly was old enough to move out, the better it would be for all of them.

I asked the driver to wait and walked towards the house. They were all standing at the front door, cheeks pink as the dawning sky above them. It was immediately clear that Kelly wasn't happy. My sister and I aren't that good at hiding our feelings. It's hard to pretend when you turn tomato red at the drop of a hat. She was wrapped in a padded jacket and scarf, her bags all packed and ready. Dad looked even more ill than usual. He had his old dressing gown on – the one with a hole in one elbow. I tried to remember a time before he had it and failed.

Mum was already dressed, but Dad was the first to spot me. 'There he is.' He smiled, and I felt it lift me. 'Our hero.'

Mum and Kelly turned my way, and as they did so, their warm regard washed over me, too. I'm an ace, and my power is drawn from the belief of others. The more people I have around me who are on my side, the stronger I am. Kelly had been the first to activate it, when we were kids, but these days, Mum and Dad did, too. In the presence of my family, I'm faster and tougher than a normal man.

I'm just . . . more me.

My suddenly sharpened hearing caught Mum whispering in Kelly's ear as clearly as if it was mine. 'Stop making a fuss; your brother's here.'

'I know that,' Kelly hissed back. 'I'm not blind.' I saw the lines in Kelly's face shift from annoyance to genuine pleasure as her eyes settled on me.

I walked up the short, cracked garden path and greeted them all with a hug – a gentle one for my dad and a firm one for the others. The muscles in Dad's body trembled under my hands. It had cost him to get out of his chair to see us off.

I squeezed my eyes shut when they started to water, then went to my mum. I could feel her ribs beneath her shirt. The familiar smell of her perfume was sharp to my enhanced sense of smell, and beneath it, I detected the tell-tale scent of cigarettes. She'd started smoking again. Not a good sign.

When it was Kelly's turn for a hug, she clung to me like a life raft on a stormy sea.

Sometimes, it's not great having superpowers. As I hugged them all, I saw the house over their shoulders in too much detail: every crack in the walls and paintwork; the mould settling in the corners where the gutters had broken; nettles choking the life out of the little garden. The last few years had been hard on my family. It made me sad to see how it was grinding them down. I promised myself I'd sort it out when I got back.

Mum passed me an envelope. 'That's for you, in case you need to buy Kelly anything while you're in Cornwall.'

I felt the thin wedge of notes inside, weighing the envelope for a moment before passing it back. 'It's OK, Mum. This is all expenses paid, remember?'

She wasn't convinced, and the envelope danced back and forth between us as we spoke. 'Best to be on the safe side. What if something unexpected comes up?'

'Then I'll cover it. I'm working now.'

'But you need that money for *you*. What about putting aside a deposit for your own place? And getting your own car? And flights to Nashville aren't cheap!'

One of the downsides of having a public romance on the go was that Mum knew far too much about Stella for my liking. 'It's fine, Mum. Really. Anyway, I've got to go; the meter's running on the cab.'

She didn't look happy about it, but she gave me a kiss and stepped back, the envelope pinched tight in her hand. 'Bye, love.' She turned to say goodbye to Kelly, but my sister was already off down the path, like a bird taking flight.

I gave my parents an apologetic smile on her behalf, scooped up all of Kelly's bags in one hand as if they weighed nothing – yes, I was showing off – and headed after her.

Kelly

I hate my mum. She hates me, too. She pretends she doesn't, but she does. It's, like, my first holiday in forever, and she made me wear that stupid jacket, even though she knew I hated it. What a bitch!

I don't hate my dad. But I don't love him either. I feel sad about him, you know? He's like a ghost. Or one of those paintings with the creepy eyes that follow you about. Even when he was around, he'd be half asleep. I knew he was ill. I knew I should feel something about that, but I didn't. It's hard to get upset about someone who isn't there.

I was already in the cab when Stu got in. He had to give directions to the driver, so we didn't pull out straight away. Mum and Dad just stood there, waving like idiots. Lame. I didn't wave back. Why couldn't they just go back in the house like normal people?

As soon as we pulled out, I took off that stupid jacket. It's puffy and ugly, and I stuffed it into the footwell and stamped it down with my feet.

'You OK?' asked Stu, twisting round to face me.

'Yeah. I'm a bit hungry.'

'Didn't you have breakfast?'

'Mum did me an egg with some burned toast.' I made a vomit face. 'I didn't eat it.'

'I thought you liked eggs.'

'I like *your* eggs. Hers are made of plastic. And we've run out of sauce.'

'We'll get something at the station, OK?'

I smiled at him. 'Yeah.'

Stu is, like, a proper big brother. He's kind, and he actually talks *to* me instead of *at* me. And he's a real superhero with powers and everything. He's big into all of the aces and keeps press clippings and things in a scrapbook, but he's going to be bigger than all of them one day. It's sometimes weird to think that he's my brother. Our family are all so . . . boring. And then there's him. I don't know what I'd do without him, to be honest. Kill myself, probably. It's been really shit since he moved out.

I'd been looking forward to this holiday for ages. It was this posh do on an island with all these famous guests. And me! Stu got to take a plus one. I thought he'd ask his girlfriend, Stella. She's famous, too, so she'd fit right in. But he didn't; he picked me instead. I don't know why. I'm nothing special.

'What do they do at posh parties?' I asked.

He shrugged and looked worried. 'Guess we'll find out when we get there. The invitation wasn't very clear.'

'Can I see it?'

'Sure.'

The envelope was a cream colour, and it felt soft and spongy. Inside was this thick piece of card with fancy swirls around the edges and the nicest writing I'd ever seen. It looked like a letter from a Disney princess but with less glitter.

Jago Branok invites you and a guest for a weekend of relaxation, good food, stimulating company, and entertainment at Loveday House.

'Do you know him?' I asked.

'Jago? No.'

'Have you looked him up?'

'Er, no.'

I shook my head. Stu was weird sometimes. 'Give me your phone then.'

'I thought you had a phone?'

'Got no data left.'

He unlocked his and passed it over. There was an image of Stella on his home screen. It gave me a funny feeling in my stomach to look at her. Stella's got really good hair and no spots. I poked her in the eye with my finger to open up a search. It didn't make me feel any better.

I tapped in Jago's name. Images of a man came up. In the first one, he wore a mask that looked like a smiling wolf's face. The second was more like a sombre emoji. I scrolled through some more pictures, trying to find one of his actual face. There weren't any. There weren't many pictures at all, actually, and he was masked in all of them. I hunched forward and tried another search, then blinked at the results.

This was getting interesting.

Stuart

We talked on the way down to the coast. An hour by cab, followed by another four by train to Cornwall. Kelly was keen to know all the details of my latest trip, but she was also annoyed with my constant travelling. I thought I'd been gone only a couple of weeks, but she reminded me it'd been more like a month. She was tight-lipped about school and her friends – single word answers mostly. If she was to be believed, everything was 'fine'.

And I wanted to believe her – I really did – but Mum had told me a very different story. Apparently, Kelly had been getting into trouble with her teachers, and her grades had moved from average to bad.

I didn't see it, though. The person Mum described didn't bear any resemblance to the bright-eyed girl sitting next to me. Hopefully, this weekend would give Kelly the distraction she needed and the time to open up to me more.

'Do you think he's ugly?' she asked.

'Jago? I've never thought about it.'

'Nobody's ever got a picture of his face. Some people think he's a joker. Like, a really gross one. I don't, though.'

'Why's that?'

'He doesn't look like he'd be ugly.'

I raised my eyebrows. 'I think he's a bit old for you.'

'*Stu!*' she retorted, her face immediately going flame red. She punched me on the arm. I barely felt it. My ace wasn't as powerful with just Kelly fuelling it, but I was still significantly tougher. 'Don't be a dick.'

'Sorry. Do you know how old he is?'

'It says he was born in 1917. No way! That would make him . . .' She paused, the tip of her tongue appearing as she worked through the numbers. 'Like, 104! That's *ancient*! He doesn't look ancient.'

'Some people age better than others,' I agreed. 'Enigma is still an active member of the Silver Helix, and he's even older than Jago.' I'd heard that Enigma might be at the party, and I could hardly believe it. I've been following the Helix since I was little, and Enigma is in my top ten favourite heroes. He isn't flashy like some of the others, but he's probably saved more lives and had a bigger impact on history.

Kelly looked up from the phone and gave me a worried look. 'Is this an old people's party?'

I laughed. 'That's what's bothering you?'

She gave me a shrug. 'Be a bit boring if it's just us and a load of smelly pensioners.'

The concern on her face was so genuine that I laughed a second time. 'I don't have the full guest list, but Colin told me that Jason McCracken is going to be there.' When she didn't react, I added, 'The latest Redcoat!'

Kelly's fingers tapped on my phone screen a few times and a picture of the man appeared. He was standing in front of Buckingham Palace like a sentinel. He looked every inch the hero, like he'd stepped out of a comic book. There was an easy smile on his face, the kind that tells you that everything is going to be OK, no matter how bad things are. I'd practised that smile in the mirror many times over the years.

We both looked at the image for a while. 'He's fit,' she said.

'He's a keen swimmer, and he plays rugby, and there's a video of him lifting weights somewhere.'

Kelly immediately started tapping on the phone again.

'And he used to be in the army, so yes, he's very fit.'

Kelly rolled her eyes. 'All right, Stu.'

I'd loved all of the Redcoats since I was a kid and had collected everything I could over the years. Redcoat was more than just one ace; it was a title passed from one hero to the next since the 1950s. I had King Arthur's commemorative plate, because Jason was on it, and the Redcoat miniature with removable jacket. But my most prized possession was the official guide. It was limited edition, tracing the history of the first five to take on the mantle. To me, Jason seemed like the best one yet – a man worthy of the uniform.

It was nice to see that Kelly recognized that, too.

Kelly

Jason was ripped! I watched videos of him until Stu's phone ran out of battery. The swimming ones were the best. Everyone looks like a twat in Speedos, but he almost got away with it. He had those lines that really fit men have on the sides of their stomach. Like arrows pointing the way to their dicks.

Actually, the weekend was looking all right. I was going to get to hang out with my brother and his hero mates. I was curious about Jago, too. He was old, but he seemed cool as well. I was full of egg sandwich from the station, which was pretty nice – like, maybe a seven out of ten? Way better than Mum's but not as nice as Stu's.

I stood at the top of some old stone steps that went down into the sea, waiting as the waters receded enough to reveal the causeway, which looked old and bumpy like the surface of the moon. The wind was fierce, and the spray stung my face. Pretty soon, I couldn't feel my nose. I didn't care. I liked it. It felt real, you know? Not like school or being at home.

Stuart came and stood next to me. 'You OK out here?'

'Yeah.'

'It's really cold. Where's your jacket?'

I shrugged.

'Have you lost it?'

I didn't look at him. 'Maybe.'

If it was Mum, she would have gone off her nut. Dad would have given me a boring talk about how I should be more responsible, but Stu didn't. After a moment, I felt him putting his jacket over my shoulders. It was warm and a little big for me, but, like, in a way that was cute instead of shit.

'Here,' he said. 'You can borrow this until I get you a new one.'

Best. Brother. Ever.

'To be honest,' he added, 'the other one didn't suit you.'

'Right? Made me look like a yellow balloon.'

'Who bought it?'

'Dad.'

We exchanged a look as a lone car made its way towards us along the causeway.

I started to make out the island as it slowly emerged from the fog. It looked miserable. Lots of seagulls flying about and not much else. Everything was grey. Grey cliffs. Grey sky. Even the sea looked a bit grey.

Then the sun came out from behind a cloud, which made the island a bit prettier, but it was still . . . I dunno, hard? The little tufts of green I could see didn't do much to cover the stony ground, and the cliffs reminded me of broken knuckles, all sharp and messed up. Like if you didn't respect them, they'd turf you into the sea without a second thought. I fancied walking those cliffs.

A couple of locals wearing old man clothes came and helped us carry our luggage down the steps to the causeway. They looked rough – and not in a good way. One of them took my arm to steady me, even though I didn't ask him to. His fingers were like sandpaper on my wrist.

Stu thanked them, and they kind of grunted at us. I think one of them said something, but his accent was so thick I couldn't make out the words, so I just smiled at him and kept going. He smiled back though. Ugh. His teeth were grim! All wonky and yellow. Like he was an extra in some history film. His eyes were funny, too, but I didn't look long enough to figure out why. Probably a perv.

I pulled Stu's coat tighter about me and hurried on. The man turned his head and watched me go. I could feel his gaze on my back. And my arse probably. I glanced back. Yep. He was still staring, not even pretending to do otherwise. His mate was doing exactly the same. Both were smiling these weird little smiles. I shivered. Definitely pervs.

'You all right?' asked Stu.

I moved a bit closer to him. 'Yeah.' We kept going until we reached the causeway. 'If someone ever tried to hurt me, you'd sort them out, wouldn't you?'

'I'd never let anyone hurt you.'

'I know, but what would you do to them? Would you use your powers to beat them up?'

He stopped walking and turned to look at me. 'I'd use them to keep you safe.'

'I know that! What about them?'

'I'd make sure they couldn't do it again. You sure you're all right?'

I nodded and looked back the way we'd come. I was hoping to see those men so I could flip them the finger, but they'd gone. I imagined Stu punching their stupid teeth out of their stupid faces and felt much better.

Stuart

A sleek car came to pick us up. It was a limousine. I didn't recognize the make, but it was clearly vintage and in perfect condition. The gleaming paintwork was racing green, polished and without scratches, and the hubcaps could double as mirrors if you needed them. A man in a smart suit stepped out and loaded our bags into the boot – completely ordinary, except that the man wore an oval mask made of silver scales. In a moment of peak Britishness, I pretended everything was normal. I also offered to help with the bags, but he simply waved the idea away as if it were the silliest thing he'd ever heard. He didn't say much, just opened the door and waited for us to get in. I had the feeling I'd insulted him somehow.

As the limo set off, I thought about what Kelly had said. Would I use my powers to beat up someone? The idea made me uncomfortable. All of my training is in first response and disaster management. Closer to a fireman than a soldier. I like it that way. Of course, I'd be furious if someone threatened Kelly, but even when my power is at its weakest, I'm freakishly strong. If I hit someone – *really* hit them – it'd likely do lasting damage. And if I was amped up? Well, I'd put my hand through a concrete wall before, so I could easily do the same to a person . . .

I looked out the window to distract my brain from that image. The sea stretched on either side of us, lapping menacingly against the sides of the causeway. In a few hours' time, it would vanish again, cutting us off from the mainland.

The causeway eventually became a road and wound its way towards the back of the island, and the limo slowly climbed it until our destination rose before us, like something out of a dream. Loveday House sat at the top of the cliffs, overlooking the sea. It was a Victorian mansion that Jago had famously been restoring. I say famously, but I only knew because Kelly had been reading up on it. I really don't know anything about architecture.

There was something timeless about the house, though. It looked like the kind of place King Arthur would keep as a summer home or where you'd send a wizard to go to school. Even from a distance, it loomed over us. High roofs and elegant towers came first, and then the long walls, sprawling outwards. It was too big to see all in one go, and I had to turn my head from side to side, trying to digest the view in chunks, and then put them together in my head afterwards.

As we pulled into the long drive, I saw stables set apart from the main house and, next to them, another building, only one storey but big enough to fit my flat into it at least four times over. Was it a second house? I wondered. Maybe Jago had elderly relatives who couldn't handle stairs.

'What's that?' asked Kelly. 'Is it a car park?'

I leaned over and looked out of her window, surprised by what I saw. 'It's a helicopter pad.'

'That's awesome.'

The limo came to a stop, and we stepped out onto the driveway.

'Even the gravel's posh here,' said Kelly.

I crouched down for a closer look and found the white and grey stones were actually crushed seashells. Everything about this place screamed money. I worried about how my sister and I would fit in here.

The 'second house' turned out to be an extended garage to hold Jago's fleet of cars. The driver opened it up, and I caught a glimpse of what might have been a Jaguar, alongside something that looked like a space-age car from the 1960s. It had to be bespoke. Perhaps he'd got it from a film set.

I spoke to the driver as he got back behind the wheel. 'What about our bags?' He pointed us towards the main doors. 'Yes, but what about our . . .' The rest of my sentence was drowned out by the limo's engine as it drove into the garage, leaving us on the driveway.

I shrugged at Kelly, and she laughed.

The two of us headed towards the front doors. Loveday seemed even bigger up close. The main doors were heavy-looking. Someone had painstakingly carved flowering vines into the wood along with a number of strange-looking creatures. A lot of them had tentacles. One was a kraken, I think.

'What's that?' asked Kelly. She was pointing at a man with a fish's head. A mantle of scales sat on his shoulders. 'There's something in his mouth.'

She was right. The carver had made a tiny shape visible behind the two fans of spiny teeth. With Kelly around, I have perfect twenty-twenty vision, so I could make out the details. 'It's a face. A young girl's, I think.'

'That's so cool!'

I raised an eyebrow and didn't comment further. Two brass door-knockers shaped like snarling hounds were set into the wood at the level of my chest. I took the rings held in their jaws and knocked three times.

Boom.

Boom.

Boom.

Too quickly, someone was at the other side. The door swung open to reveal a masked face. A third hound, snarling just like the others.

'Welcome to Loveday House,' it said.

Kelly

It was him! Jago Branok. I recognized him immediately. He was taller than Stu and had this dark suit on that looked proper vampire. The mask was hot, too. It didn't look silly on him or like a piece of costume. He wore it like most people wear watches. No big deal, you know?

'Hello,' said Stu. 'I'm Stuart Hill, and this is my sister, Kelly.' He fished around in his pocket and produced the invitation. 'We're here for the weekend.'

The eyes behind the mask regarded us for a moment. I think Jago was smiling – maybe amused. 'Yes, I know who you are.' He turned to look at me straight on, and my knees went a bit wobbly. 'Please, come inside and be welcome.'

'Are you Lord Branok?' asked Stu.

'Indeed I am.' He extended a hand. 'Delighted to meet you both.'

I blinked. He was answering Stu, but he'd offered his hand to me first. To me! Nobody ever did that. Most adults didn't even notice me. It took me a moment to get over myself, and then I took his hand. Jago was wearing gloves. They were leather but really soft.

'A pleasure,' he said. His voice was like that leather. I reckon if I'd died then, I would have been all right with it. He shook Stu's hand and added, 'And do call me Jago.'

We were in the mother of all hallways. It was massive. The floor was super shiny polished wood with a strip of red carpet running down the middle to a staircase. I'd never seen anything like it. The stairs were wide enough that I could stick my arms out and not touch both sides. They split at the top and curved off to the left and right. And there were doors everywhere! Off to the sides, a couple past the stairs on the ground floor and what looked like more upstairs as well. It wasn't like our house, where all the doors were the same. Each of these was a little bit different, and they all looked interesting. Maybe all posh houses were like this.

Before I could think about it, I said, 'Can we see the house?'

'Would you like me to give you the tour?' asked Jago.

I meant to say yes, but this funny little squeak came out of my mouth instead, and my cheeks and chest went bright red. I wished I had a cool dog mask to wear; then people wouldn't be able to see my dumb face.

'If you don't mind,' said Stu.

'I would be delighted. It will just be a taste, mind you, and then I'll show you to your rooms. I imagine you'll want time to settle in before dinner. It should be quite the event.'

I followed along after them as Stu struck up a conversation. 'Can I ask you about the other guests?' he said. 'I'm dying to know who else will be here.'

'This weekend, I am hosting a distinguished company of aces and a select few others of special significance.' He glanced at me again, and I blushed again. 'There are two members of the Silver Helix: Alan Turing, whom you likely know as Enigma, and Jason McCracken, our dashing young Redcoat. He has brought his partner with him, the Reverend Gladys Turney. We also have representatives of the Committee, Stone Rockford and . . .'

While they talked, I looked around. We'd come into what Jago called his parlour. I'd never been in a parlour before. It was like a living room without a telly. There were lots of wooden chairs with fancy cushions and swanky oil paintings. One of them was of Jago standing on the cliffs, looking out over the sea. He was wearing a different mask, but it was definitely him. It was night-time and the sky had these purple streaks all over it and loads of stars. He had a gun in his hands. The tip was smoking.

I wanted to ask him about the gun, but I didn't, because I was distracted by another painting. It was this woman in a fancy dress standing in a posh study. She had her chin up and was looking out from the canvas like those rough girls in the playground who want to have a go. But she wasn't rough. Her hair was done in curls, and she had a necklace with big fat rubies in it that her hand was resting on.

'Who's that?' I asked.

Jago looked from me to the painting and then back to me again. 'Oh, just a bit of old history. If you follow me, I'll show you the music room. Do either of you play piano, by any chance? Or the harp?'

Stu started apologizing. The only instruments we'd ever played were recorders. I could make a sound on one like a dying mouse, but that was about it.

I didn't say anything. I'd seen the look in Jago's eye when he first saw that painting. He'd covered it up fast but not fast enough. It was like Mum's face when she got a call from the bank.

He was scared.

Stuart

My suitcase was waiting for me in my room. It looked scuffed and sorry for itself in such sumptuous surroundings. There was a tall oak wardrobe in one corner – the kind that looked like it led children to Narnia – and a grand bed with a hand-carved headboard. The desk by the window looked out towards the open sea. It struck me how quiet the place was: no traffic, no neighbours putting on the washing machine at two in the morning. It would have been nice to bring Stella here, get some time together in private, but I stood by my decision. Kelly needed this more.

Now that I was alone, the power of my ace faded, leaving me ordinary. For me, being normal is a bit like what it's like for everyone else when they have the flu. I can still function, but it's much, much harder. Suddenly, I can't run as fast or as far. I can't see or hear as clearly. I get cut as easily as everyone else, my strength shackled once more within the limits of a human body.

The shifts are jarring. One minute, I'm just Stuart Hill; the next, I'm a superhuman. As a result, I don't like being alone for too long, although I prefer that to being around people who don't have faith in me. That's the worst thing of all: being weak in a crowd. My ace doesn't let me know what others are thinking or feeling, but I can tell when someone is fuelling it. Whenever I see Kelly, I get an instant rush for as long as she's nearby. She was the first to fuel my ace, and maybe it's just me playing favourites, but I'd say she gives me the strongest boost of any individual.

She isn't the only one, though. Mum and Dad also activate it, and Stella, and people who I've proved myself to, one way or another. I now added Jago to that list.

It had been such a surprise when he'd opened the door – like a sudden shot of adrenalin. I knew Jago had made a generous donation to Reachers, and I also knew that he'd requested me by name; I just didn't know why. Perhaps he was a fan.

There was a mask on my bed, alongside a note that read:

To be worn at dinner

The mask covered the top half of the face and had been carved from wood and then painted in layers to give it a three-dimensional look. It was an old man's face, Caucasian, with deep lines around the eyes. There were several scars: one that got very close to the right eye, and another, paler one, that ran jagged across the right cheek. There was something familiar about the mask, but I couldn't place where I'd seen it. I wondered if it was a historical reference, maybe a famous statesman or person from Keun's past.

A brilliant thought struck me: I could ask Enigma about it! He'd know for sure, and it would give me something to talk about over dinner.

I remembered that when I'd started dating Stella, my confidence would always drop when I was getting ready to see her. Clothes that were normally fine suddenly seemed ill-fitting or a bit tired, or I'd notice a hole in them for the first time. Turns out that getting ready to meet your idol and some of the greatest heroes of the age has the same effect. I had only three shirts with me and as many ties. I tried them all in combination and was still fussing over what to wear when I heard a knock at my door.

It was Kelly. As always, her presence brought my ace to life again. She'd put on a black dress and was wearing it with an odd mixture of awkwardness and defiance. It made her look older, because it was much less girly than the things she'd normally have to wear at family dos. Less frills. Less fabric in general. There was no way Mum knew anything about it. She'd been given a mask, too; hers was of a cat. It was highly detailed and made her look quite impish.

'What do you think?' she asked.

'Suits you.'

'Yeah?'

'Really.'

She tugged her dress down at the back self-consciously. 'I like my mask. How did he know cats are my favourite?'

'Probably a coincidence. It's not like I love old men.'

'Just old women.'

Kelly was making a joke about the fact that Stella is ten years older than me. I glared at her. 'Not funny.'

'Sorry. Your mask is gnarly, though.'

'I think it might be someone famous.' I turned my head from side to side. 'Does it remind you of anyone?'

'Like Grandad but more badass.'

'Huh. It does look a bit like him. Ready to go down?'

She shrugged. 'I guess.'

I stood up as straight as I could and offered her my arm. It was time to meet Redcoat.

Kelly

I felt braver with my mask on. Nobody would see me blush now. Me and Stu walked down the stairs together like we were a lord and lady. It was the first time I'd worn my secret dress. I'd seen it months ago but couldn't afford it, and I knew Mum and Dad would never buy it for me. They always want to put me in white things and pink things, with flowers and shit on, like I'm still eight years old. I went in the shop anyway and tried it on. It was proper classy. As soon as I saw myself in the changing room mirror, I knew I had to have it. I folded it up and tucked it away in my bag and then walked out of the changing room. My face was so hot as I made my way towards the door, I reckon you could've seen it from space.

Nobody stopped me, though. When I got onto the street, I felt amazing. Like, for once I was in control. Course, I had to hide it from my parents. It was way too cool for them. But that just made it even better. It was my secret dress. Wearing it made me feel powerful. Not just 'cos of the dress itself, but because I'd taken it.

We went into this big dining room that was super polished so the light from the chandeliers glimmered off everything. Other people were coming in, all wearing masks as well. Stu was looking at them, and each time he saw one, he got this goofy grin on his face. I went and sat down next to him. Even though the table was huge, it didn't look big because it was packed with stuff. I had, like, three plates, a bowl, and all the cutlery in the world. How many forks do posh people need? They were all different sizes and shapes. The handles had these little curving seashells etched into them.

I was just going to say something to Stu when I realized someone was staring at me. I turned round, and there's this old man there. Not cool old like Jago – just, you know, old. He was wearing a mask painted up like the night sky, which, to be fair, looked pretty good. He had really dark skin, and there were a few bits of white hair left on his head which reminded me of our street after most of the snow's melted. Pretty sad.

'Hello. I'm Gary.' He held out his hand, and I shook it. Gary cleared his throat and said, 'I think you're in my seat.'

'What?'

He gave me this patient look and pointed at the table. There was a folded bit of card that said: *Gary Bushorn*. 'They like to do things a certain way here. It takes some getting used to.'

But I wanted to sit next to Stu! I got the urge to take that stupid bit of card and throw it on the floor. Before I got the chance though, Jago arrived. He walked straight over to us. No. To me.

'Good evening, Ms Hill. I see that you've met our dancing instructor.'

Gary gave me a look and rolled his eyes, like he thought Jago was being silly. I didn't think Jago was silly at all. He was still looking at me, holding out his hand, which I took, obviously. 'Allow me to escort you to your seat.'

He walked me round the table to sit next to him. The other spaces filled up pretty quick after that. Everyone was wearing masks, even the people pouring wine into our glasses. I waited to see if they were going to swap mine out for apple juice or some other bullshit, but they didn't. I picked up the glass and sipped it. It was wine, but not like anything I'd had before. This was smooth and a bit fruity. I liked it. I drank some more. Then this man came up and reached for my glass.

'I haven't finished!' I said.

Jago chuckled to himself, and then I realized the man wasn't stealing my drink; he was topping it up. Was this place for real? The booze definitely tasted real. I grinned at Stu across the table. This was going to be a great night.

Stuart

I was seated between someone called Gary Bushorn and Enigma. Alan Turing himself. Close enough that I could reach out and touch him! He'd been given this long-nosed mask to wear that made him appear villainous. I knew his skin was metal, but he was wearing makeup to cover it. It was expertly done. I tried not to stare – the operative word being 'tried'. Enigma noticed me out of the corner of his eye, and I froze, unsure what to do. If I kept staring at him, it would be rude, but if I looked away, it would be suspicious.

As my internal panic rose, Jago saved me by tapping his glass with a spoon. 'Allow me to formally welcome you all to Loveday House. We have been graced with many remarkable guests over the years, and this weekend will set the bar even higher. I'm aware that many of you already know one another, but, for those who don't, a round of introductions are in order.

'Let me begin with Ms Kelly Hill.'

Kelly was caught mid-sip and coughed over her glass of wine.

'A young woman destined for great things, I'm sure. Then, we have Stone Rockford of the United Nations Committee for Extraordinary Interventions.'

I saw a huge white man wearing an eagle's mask. He appeared to be in his late thirties with the build of a professional wrestler, bald, and with the kind of jawline 12-year-old me wished I'd had. The man exuded confidence. I didn't know much about the Committee, but Rockford was obviously important.

'Next to him,' continued Jago, 'is the Reverend Gladys Turney.'

He was gesturing to a dark-haired woman, probably around Stella's age, with a dove's mask and a gentle smile. I'd never heard of her, which meant she was either very new on the scene or I didn't know quite as much as I'd thought about Redcoat. Jago had said she was his partner but hadn't been clear what kind. Were they an item or did they work together? I began to hope that they were dating and that Redcoat was in the market for a hero partner, by which I meant me. Hell, in his case, I'd settle for sidekick.

'And next to her is Hal Anderson, better known as Tinker. He is also a member of the Committee.'

A Caucasian man in his thirties with messy sun-bleached hair and a tan gave a casual wave. He'd taken off his mask and left it hanging from the back of his chair. 'Nice to meet you all,' he said, his accent strong, Australian. He was wearing an expensive shirt, but he'd left several of the top buttons undone, exposing a muscular upper body. The guy obviously spent a lot of time in the gym and knew he looked good. Was I jealous? Maybe a little bit.

Jago didn't have to introduce the next guest. I already knew everything there was to know about Redcoat. Jason McCracken was even more impressive in real life than he was on the posters, photos and miniatures I'd collected. Six foot six inches tall, light-brown hair, green eyes, square jaw – it was like he was made to be a hero. He looked a little uncomfortable at the attention, but there was no doubting the sincerity in the smile he gave us. There was something inherently good about him. A sense of integrity.

I barely heard Jago introducing Captain Donatien Racine, but something about the name was familiar. It wasn't enough to take my attention from Redcoat, though. I recognized the mask he'd been given immediately. It was a composite made of the faces of all the previous people to wear the hero's mantle. Everyone was there, from Henry Astor, the first Redcoat, to Annie Kemp, Jason's predecessor. All dead in the line of duty, most of them at an early age. I was beginning to suspect that Jago had an interesting sense of humour.

Redcoat gave me a nod. Me. He noticed me! I nodded back slowly.

Jago's voice continued on in the background. '. . . Gary Bushorn, who has become something of a permanent resident here at Loveday, and a welcome one. He is also our guise dancing instructor, should any of you wish to . . .'

I tuned out and tried to decide what I should say to Redcoat when we got the chance to speak. I wondered if he'd brought the coat with him and if he'd let me see it.

Redcoat caught my eye and gave another nod, but this time he looked away from me and towards Jago, who I realized was watching us with a little amusement in his eye. Everyone was.

'Maybe you two should get a room,' said Tinker, and everyone laughed.

I think – yes, I think that was the moment I died.

Jago cleared his throat. 'As I was saying, this is Stuart Hill, a new ace who works for the Reachers charity, though you most likely know him as Hero McHeroface.'

My hero name had come from a charity auction. Needless to say, I'd hated it at first, but as time went on, I'd begun to make peace with it. People tended to shorten it to Hero, which I quite liked, and when I thought about the lives changed by the money raised, it put things into perspective.

All of that went out of the window when I saw the reaction it got from the assembled group. I saw Redcoat smirk and turn his head as he tried not to laugh. I heard Tinker make no such effort as he beat the table and cackled. Rockford's laugh was higher than I expected from such a big man. Even Gladys hid her face behind her hand. I felt a little betrayed that Kelly had joined them and a little alarmed at how loud she was being. Then it hit me: she was drunk. She was also sitting on the opposite side of the table, well beyond my reach. This was going to be a problem.

'And last,' said Jago, 'but by no means least, we have a man who needs little introduction from me: the Silver Helix's Alan Turing, also known as Enigma. Now, with those formalities out of the way, let us eat.'

Dinner was incredible. Five courses, all with names I'd not heard before. There was crabmeat soup to start with, then some other kind of shellfish that tasted oddly sweet, followed by a rich stew with an endless supply of fresh bread. I'd be hard pressed to tell you what kind of stew it was or what was in it. There were definitely vegetables lurking within the thick sauce and . . . lentils? Dessert was a fruity pie with cream. I saw Kelly look confused and knew she was trying to find the custard. I'd done my best to help her navigate the cutlery for each course, though to be honest, I was just working in from the outside and hoping for the best.

Enigma asked me questions every so often, things like: how much can you lift? How fast are you? Does your ace manifest in other ways? My answers were vague, and I'm sure it was irritating him, though he didn't give any outward sign. Thing is, how strong or fast I am varies a lot. I've held up support beams to stop buildings from collapsing, leaped directly onto rooftops from street level, carried four children on my back at once while running from a burning building, but I've never tried to measure my ace precisely.

Tinker leaned across the table. 'We got a lot of strong blokes in this room, McHeroface. Think you got what it takes to stand out?'

Rockford, Redcoat, and Tinker all looked like supermen compared to me.

'I don't know.'

'That's a pussy answer,' Tinker said.

Redcoat gave him a look, and Gladys politely attended to her dessert.

'No offence, ladies,' Tinker added. 'But how about we put the new boy through his paces? See what he's got.'

Enigma raised an eyebrow. 'What do you have in mind?'

'A little dick-measuring contest for us aces.' Tinker smiled. 'You'd be up for that, right, Stone?'

Rockford thought about it for a moment, then grinned and nodded. 'What about you, Captain?'

Captain Racine . . . I knew that name. Although the Silver Helix were my favourites, I'd followed all the famous aces as a child, and Racine was definitely one of those. I looked at the man. He was bearded, tough-looking, well into his fifties, maybe older, but still lean and fit. Despite the plain white mask he'd been given, I recognized the face.

'*Tricolor!*' I exclaimed. 'You're Tricolor.'

He winced when I said it and replied with a soft French accent, 'True, but if you call me Captain, I will call you Stuart. Much more agreeable, no?'

'No.' I nodded, then caught myself. 'I mean yes! Sorry. I mean yes.'

Tinker laughed. 'You're a fucking riot, McHeroface! Is that a yes, Captain?'

'It is.'

'Right, that just leaves the Helix boys. You game?'

'This isn't really my forte,' said Enigma, 'but I would be very interested to see how you all do.'

'You like to watch, eh? Thought so.'

Tinker's attitude was clearly annoying Redcoat, who leaned forward with quiet authority. 'That's not appropriate.'

'Sorry, mate.'

'You don't need to apologize to me.' He gestured in Turing's direction.

There was a brief staring contest, and then Tinker put up his hands. 'Sorry if I spoke out of turn, Mr Turing.'

'That's all right,' Enigma replied. 'I developed a thick skin against thoughtlessness long before my card turned.'

'All right!' Tinker continued. 'You in, McCracken?'

Redcoat glanced at Gladys, almost as if asking permission. She gave a very slight nod. 'I'm in,' he said. Watching the two of them made me miss Stella. It also made me wonder how he and Gladys had managed to keep their relationship so private.

I sat back as the servants began to clear the dessert. That wasn't it, though: a cheeseboard and several bottles of port were brought out.

While I was wondering if I could possibly fit in any more food, Gary put a friendly hand on my arm. I felt the heat of it through my sleeve, like leaning on a radiator. 'How are you doing, Stuart?'

Maybe it was the wine or the genuine look in his eye, but all of a sudden, I was talking, and it was hard to stop. 'I'm OK. Do you think I'm struggling – is that why you asked? This is my first time meeting everyone, and I've looked up to so many of them for so long, and I really wanted to make a good first impression, but I think I've messed it up. You think I've messed up, don't you? Oh God, I've messed up.'

He squeezed my arm. 'Take a breath, man. You gotta relax. At the end of the day, they're just people, same as you and me.' I found that hard to believe. He must have read it on my face, because he added, 'I'm serious. You don't need to be perfect. From what I understand, you're doing just fine being you. Keep doing that.'

'Thank you. It's Gary, isn't it?'

'That's right.'

We shook hands. His was warm, unnaturally so. Maybe he was an ace, too. We chatted for a while. Gary made it easy, and I started to feel better. The port was sweet and smooth. That helped, too. It occurred to me that Kelly would probably like it a bit too much. I looked over to see how she was doing, bracing myself for the state my sister was likely in by now, but all I saw was an empty chair.

She was gone.

Kelly

Sometimes you just need to piss. I hadn't realized how drunk I was until I tried to stand up, but when I did, I knew I was well gone. If Stu saw me, I'd be in big trouble. Luckily, he was too busy grinning at fit Jason. Couldn't blame him. I felt the same. Shame Jason was obviously with Gladys. I didn't think priests were allowed to bang people, but maybe she was making an exception in his case. Couldn't blame her either.

I did my best not to stumble as I left the dining room. One of the masked staff said something and tried to steady me. I shook free and kept going. Maybe I told him to get off. Maybe I told him to eff off. I'm not sure. The only thing I was sure of was needing to find the toilet, fast.

Took me a while. Almost too long for my bladder. Loveday House was huge! When I did find it, it was smaller than I'd expected, kind of tucked away under the stairs. The bog roll was lush though. Afterwards, I found myself lingering in the hall. It wasn't that I didn't want to go back to the others; it was just that, if I did, they'd figure out I was off my face, and that would be embarrassing. I didn't want Jago to think I was trashy.

So I went for a wander instead.

It was fun for a bit. Then I got cold and decided I'd probably sobered up enough to go to the dining room again. Except, I wasn't sure where I was any more. Normally, I've got a good head for directions, but the more I looked about for a familiar landmark, the more lost I got.

Just as I was starting to really shit it, I found myself in this corridor on the first floor. It seemed a bit different – like, not as well looked after. There was this little wooden table with curly feet and a vase on it with dead flowers inside – not preserved or anything, just dead. And it was even more dusty than my house. Mum always has a go at me about cleaning my room, but she lets the kitchen get in a right state sometimes. I saw a door that looked interesting. The doorknob was an octopus head. I tried turning it, and it stuck, like it was locked. But then there was a loud crack and the handle turned. I opened the door.

It was pretty dark inside, but I could see a little girl's bed and a wardrobe. Was weird though, because apart from the bed, it didn't look like a kid's room. I was going to leave, but then I saw some peeling wallpaper in the corner. That was it. I can't resist pulling on peeling wallpaper. Same with loose threads and scabs.

Nobody was about, so I went inside. There were flower patterns on the wallpaper but with tentacles instead of leaves. By standing on tiptoes, I could reach the flap of hanging paper with my finger and thumb. I gave it a good tug, and it peeled away without tearing. The exposed wall was cold with damp and had cracks running through it. I heard something move on the other side. Probably a rat.

I went a bit closer. I do that sometimes: go the opposite way to the one I'm supposed to. Don't know why. It happens only when I'm on my own or drunk with mates. It's not like I don't get scared, because I do. I get proper scared sometimes. But, like, I get scared, and then something in me says 'fuck it', and then instead of running away from stuff, I go at it.

I couldn't hear the rat, but I was sure it was still there. It was funny to think of rats being in a big posh house. A little bit of dust puffed out of the crack and tickled my nose. I sneezed. It sounded too loud.

'Bless you, child,' said a woman's voice. It was coming from the other side of the wall, and it was creepy as all hell.

Needless to say, I screamed my fucking lungs out.

When I was done, she spoke again. 'This is no place for you.'

'Yes, it is. I'm a guest.'

'You mistake my meaning. I am speaking your English, am I not?'

'Sort of.'

She made an angry tut and muttered something about 'insensible peasants'. I scratched an itch on my leg, not really sure what to say.

'Here,' she said slowly, like one of my teachers when they're trying really hard to be patient, 'where one world becomes another, no one is welcome.'

I just stared at the wall. What was she talking about?

'Do you understand? The usurper's wrath will fall on us equally if we are discovered.'

'Well, I won't say anything if you don't.'

'Let me make your silence still sweeter. Keep my secret, and I will share with you another.'

This sounded super shady, but I do really like secrets, and I was going to keep quiet anyway, so if she wanted to give stuff away for free, that was her loss. 'OK. I promise I won't tell anyone. What's your secret?'

'Step close, so we might reach across the divide.'

'Do you think I'm thick? Just tell me the secret from there.'

'No. This secret is substantial; it cannot be spoken. It must be passed from hand to hand. To claim it, you must find your courage and approach.'

'I'm not scared of you.'

'Come then.' The dust puffed from the crack, blown outwards by her breath. I reckoned her mouth was pressed right up to the wall.

Every horror film and serial killer documentary I'd ever seen told me this was a bad idea. But she was on the other side of the wall. It wasn't like she could do anything from there, was it? I had this feeling she was watching through the crack, daring me.

I edged forward until I was right by the wall.

'Yes. I see you, child. I see you.'

Something was being pushed through the crack towards me. It was a bit too thick for the space, so it was dislodging old plaster and brick as she worked it forward. I could see it was small and metal. I leaned closer, squinting into the dark.

'Take it.'

'I'm not putting my hand in there!'

'You must,' she urged.

I should have walked away, but I didn't. *Fuck it,* I thought, and stuck my fingers into the crack. I had to force them in. The wall was old and crumbly and damp. As it gave way, this rank smell went right up my nose – like all the worst bits of the sea. But then I got it, just by the tip of my middle and index fingers. I began to wiggle it free. It was slow going, and I slipped a few times, but it got easier as I went.

When I was done, I was holding a tiny key. The last time I'd seen a key this small was when I'd got a secret diary for my birthday. It had a shitty plastic lock that was too easy to break, so I never used it. The key wasn't even as long as my palm and was thin as a pencil. Even the head wasn't that big. There was something etched into it that I couldn't make out. It was cool in my hand, and heavy for how small it was. 'What's this for?'

'A lock.'

'To what?'

'Every lock in Loveday is unique. Only one will fit this key. Find it, and the treasure within will be yours to take.'

'What's in it for you? Why are you giving stuff to me? I don't even know who you are.'

'Lady Morwen is my name. In my youth, many sought to order my time and say where I might go and where I might not, and say what I might do and what I might not. Now, their tongues lie still and silent.' There was another puff of dust as she added, 'I see my maiden self reflected in you.'

'How'd you make that happen, people letting you do what you like?'

'You ask for another secret?'

'Yeah.'

'Such things cannot be given here. You must seek me out, and for that . . .'

It went suddenly quiet. 'What did you say?'

No reply. There was nothing. Suddenly, all I could hear was my own breathing and then . . . footsteps coming from back down the corridor. I went to hide the key but then I realized the one problem with my special dress was a lack of pockets. I popped it down my front and had to stifle a squeal. It was really cold!

I tried to peek out of the door so I could spy on who was coming, but I'd forgotten about my mask – it stuck out further than my nose and gave me away. A light swung round, shining right in my face, and then I found myself looking at a metal hound with Jago's eyes.

He was carrying a torch in one hand and a pistol in the other. I'd never seen someone with a gun in real life. He carried it like it was no big deal, but it felt like a big deal to me. Mum would have shit a house if she'd seen it.

'There you are,' he said. 'We were beginning to worry you'd miss the guise dancing.'

'Sorry. I got lost on the way back from the toilet.'

'I am surprised you got this far.'

I just shrugged, and he added, 'Though I admit the house can be confusing, especially at night. Even I get lost here sometimes.'

'Yeah?'

He gave me this long look that was hard to read, and I got a shiver that ran down my back all the way to my legs. 'Once or twice, yes.'

'Hard to imagine you being lost.'

'Between you and me, I quite enjoy it. Now, shall we get back to the others, Ms Hill? Your brother looked quite concerned when I left him.'

Stuart

I blinked awake. It was still dark, and I was sluggish and half-asleep. Something wasn't right. The curtains were open, and an erratic light flickered at the window, as if there were a storm outside. In the staccato flashes, I saw a woman. A woman standing at the window. Inside my room! She was wearing a long shawl and a dark dress that pooled at her feet. The glimpse of her face showed an exultant expression.

Slowly, I sat up. It struck me that I was afraid of this woman. She was, at best, strange and in my room without permission. Confronting her without my ace while in my underwear seemed less than appealing. Nevertheless, I got up, wrapping my sheet around me for modesty.

'Excuse me,' I said.

The woman ignored me. I could only just make her out in the dark.

'Excuse me,' I repeated, a little louder.

There was another flash of lightning, followed almost immediately by a boom that shook the windows. I got a better look at her, and the hairs on the back of my neck prickled with alarm. She looked familiar. I couldn't place where I'd seen her before, exactly, but I was sure it was since I'd arrived at Loveday. Trouble was: all of the guests and staff had been masked during dinner.

I was halfway across the room when a loud knock at the door made me jump, distracting me. When I looked back, the woman was gone. So was the storm. Outside, the sea was black as a starless sky.

Fully awake now, I checked for confirmation she'd been anything other than my imagination. There was nothing except for the curtains themselves. I was sure I'd closed them before going to bed.

With some reluctance, I went to the door to find a miserable-looking Kelly standing there, smothered in a baggy hoodie and several blankets.

'Can I come in?' she said. 'I can't sleep.'

'Sure,' I replied. She was probably hungover. I pulled the curtains closed. The woman had gone, but my sense of unease remained.

Everyone looked a little tired the next morning, but it was nice to see them without masks. I watched Gladys as she ate breakfast with Redcoat. Her hair was shorter than the woman I'd seen in my room. Thought I'd seen. The whole thing had the sense of a half-remembered dream now.

Tinker came and sat down next to Kelly and me. He nodded towards Gladys. 'She's pretty tasty, eh?'

I glared at him.

'Yeah, right. You probably haven't even noticed her next to that prime bit of Scottish beef!'

I gripped my cutlery tight and ground my teeth to stop me from saying something I'd regret. Kelly was taking a breath to reply in my place, and from the way she was looking at Tinker, I knew that I couldn't allow that to happen. 'Did you have any odd dreams?' I blurted.

'Reckon I did, actually.'

'What were they like?'

'I was in bed, right, but I couldn't move. Stark naked in the dark with everything on show, and someone was standing at the end of the bed, looking at me and nodding, like I was a dog for sale.'

'Was it a woman at the end of the bed?'

'Yeah, mate.' He punched me on the arm and grinned. 'But it wasn't that kind of dream. Now, you ready to show us what you've got?'

'I think so.'

'Great, I'll round up the others, and we can get started.'

Kelly leaned over to me as soon as Tinker left. 'You have *got* to trash that twat.'

By mid-morning, we were assembled out on the lawn. The air was cold and fresh, the kind that cut straight through to the bone. I was looking forward to getting moving, but I was also nervous. This was a chance to prove myself to my heroes. I wanted to show them my best side. And I had to trash Tinker; Kelly was right about that.

The competitors were me, Redcoat, Tricolor – no, I mentally corrected myself: *the Captain* – Tinker and Rockford. Jago, Kelly, Gladys and Gary were all watching from a safe distance, while Enigma addressed us all.

'Jago has asked me to oversee today's sport. A contest between aces is a fascinating idea, but one that comes with a number of inherent problems. Given the variety of your powers, there are always questions of fairness and of not setting tasks that unduly favour one of you over the others. With this in mind, I have prepared a series of tests that, overall, should balance out the final result.

'Let us begin with something simple: the shot put.' He indicated a marked area on the grass, where a heavy metal ball sat in a white circle. 'Stuart, would you please start us off?'

I walked over to the circle. The ball was heavy but no great challenge to me. I could feel my ace being charged by more than one person – Kelly and Jago, I guessed, because I'd yet to impress the others. With their support, I was stronger and faster than a normal person. Probably not as strong as Redcoat, though. I realized I'd find out very soon.

Enigma explained that the ball could not drop below the shoulder, and that it had to travel within a thirty-five-degree angle. Any deviation would mean the shot wouldn't count. I'd be given four attempts to achieve the greatest distance. He asked me if I understood, and I nodded.

I'd not done the shot put before, but I watched the Olympics with Mum and Dad whenever it came on. I tucked the ball behind my ear, wound up, and threw. The ball flew a satisfying distance, which Enigma measured at a glance as 30 metres and 84 centimetres. Nobody questioned it. My third throw was the best one: 31.5 metres. Kelly cheered me on from the back, and the others politely applauded, but I got no sign if I'd impressed them or not.

The Captain took the ball and flew up into the air, directly above the circle. This seemed like cheating to me, but nobody else complained, so I kept my mouth shut. He then spun in the air and threw. Even so, he didn't beat me. The relief at not being last was palpable.

Redcoat was next. Watching him, I realized that the Captain and I hadn't used the proper form. Redcoat spun several times, using the momentum to slingshot the ball out over the lawn. His first shot beat my best. His second shot beat that. His third beat that, coming in at 39.5 metres. He didn't take a fourth.

'That was incredible!' I said as he walked back to us.

'Aye, well, the shot put came from the Highland Games, you know, so I had to put on a good show.'

'You definitely did that.'

He gave me a slightly awkward smile and then turned to watch Rockford as he approached the circle. It felt like the conversation had been closed. Gary was right: I was trying too hard, but I didn't know how else to be.

Rockford was changing as he walked. The man was already big, but he seemed to be acquiring an additional heaviness. Greyish stone was slowly creeping over his flesh, forming itself like a rough second skin all over his body. He picked up the ball, spun round once and practically sent the thing into orbit.

'Yes!' he roared.

'Nice one, mate,' said Tinker.

Enigma cleared his throat. 'Foul.'

Rockford scowled, the expression exaggerated by his thickened brows. 'What?'

'Your arm was too low. By definition, the sport demands a put rather than a throw. You threw the ball a great distance, but I have not measured it, because you did not put it.'

Rockford tried again.

'Foul,' said Enigma.

'It was not!'

'Foul.'

'Arrgh, fine!'

His third and fourth tries were much more careful. I suspected with practice, he'd beat us all easily, but, when he was done, Redcoat remained in the lead, though I'd moved to third place. That meant there was just Tinker to go.

He sat down in the circle with his back to us, hunched over the ball in his lap. A couple of minutes passed.

'Tinker?' asked Enigma.

'One minute, mate.'

Another couple of minutes passed. The Captain started to look irritated.

'There we go,' said Tinker. 'No, hang on, just got to tweak the fin a little . . .' He carried on talking but in a murmur.

Just as we were all starting to lose patience, he stood up and put the ball behind his ear. It looked different somehow. Bulkier. He didn't spin or even lunge, just made a lazy extension of his arm. The ball flew from his fingertips.

Literally. I saw some kind of wings and what looked like a number of cheap cigarette lighters strapped to it, spitting fire. To my amazement, the ball drifted off over the lawn under its own power.

'Surely that's cheating,' said Redcoat.

Enigma turned to him. 'Many would call your advantages unfair, Jason.'

Fifty metres. The damn thing flew for fifty metres before it ran out of fuel. Tinker had won the first contest.

I swore to myself that I wouldn't let him win the second. The others clapped politely, except Kelly, who had folded her arms.

'Next,' said Enigma, 'is clay pigeon shooting.'

Rifles were handed round. Tinker immediately started fiddling with his. Redcoat checked the weapon like a professional soldier, which of course, he had been. Rockford and I seemed equally ill at ease, and the Captain refused his entirely.

I sighed. This was going to be tough.

Kelly

Stu was doing all right. Kind of. Even I could see he wasn't really standing out. It was making me depressed. And it was unfair. Like, the French bloke in the leather jacket could shoot laser rainbows from his hands and the little discs were blowing up as fast as they arrived. How was Stu supposed to compete with that?

Tinker was going next. The twat had tricked out his rifle, and I was worried he was going to beat Stu's score as well and then boast about it for the rest of the day. Because he would. He was that kind of bloke.

It was getting cold out here, even with Stu's jacket. My toes were going numb, and I had the feeling Enigma would keep them doing these games all afternoon.

'We can go inside if you'd prefer,' said Jago.

I jumped. Didn't realize he'd been watching me. 'I ought to stay out here.'

He followed my gaze. 'Your brother is going to have to learn how to manage on his own at some point.'

'Yeah, but not now.'

'Especially now. It's up to you, of course, but there's something I'd like us to discuss.'

'What's that?'

'Your potential.'

'You sound like my career adviser.'

He chuckled, and I felt this little flush of pleasure. 'This is not the kind of opportunity you'll get at school, I promise you.'

'What is it?'

'Not here. Inside. It's not a matter for public consumption.'

I lowered my voice. 'Do you mean you don't want Gladys to know?'

'Precisely. This offer is for you. No one else.'

'All right, I'll come.'

Jago Branok was one of the richest, weirdest people in the world. I had to hear him out. I had to. Still felt like shit leaving Stu, though.

If Jago was a perv, this would have been the perfect time for him to try it on, because it was just me and him. There weren't even any staff in this part of the house. As we walked down the corridors, we talked. Mostly, I talked. Jago was interested in me. Not *interested*. He wasn't flirting or anything. It was weird but nice. I told him about school and Mum being a nightmare, even a bit about my friends. Sometimes, I had the feeling that he already knew the answers before I said them. But then sometimes he seemed surprised and would ask lots more questions.

Stuff like: 'How old were you when you noticed your brother was different?'

'I was seven.'

'Are there other aces in your family?'

'Nah, just Stu. He's the special one.'

He gave me a funny look. 'Was it tough when your father died?'

'What are you talking about? Dad's sick, but he's not dead.'

'Forgive me; I must have mixed him up with someone else.'

For the first time, I wasn't sure I believed him.

We came to a room with a posh-looking door. Jago took out a set of fairy-tale keys. There were loads of them, all different sizes and shapes. He found the one he needed really quickly, and we went inside.

'Are all your doors different?'

'Yes. Each one is unique. Do you find that strange?'

'Well, yeah. But, like, not in a bad way.'

His brows rose behind the mask. 'I'm glad you approve, Ms Hill. What do you think of my study?'

I looked about. It smelled like a library. Lots of books and wood. There was this big fancy desk, bookcases, and what looked like a picture of a hedge maze on one of the walls. Without thinking it through, I said, 'There's no window.'

'That is deliberate. I come here to think, and the outside world can be distracting.' He was about to say something else when there was a knock at the door. One of his staff was there, and they whispered something to Jago.

'I see,' he replied, then turned to me. 'Apologies, Ms Hill; something has cropped up that requires my attention. I'll be back shortly. Please make yourself comfortable until my return.'

I nodded. Just as he was closing the study door behind him, I saw the other man pass him a pistol. I thought about following them, but when I peeked out the door, they'd already gone.

A couple of minutes passed. I got bored and a bit guilty. I shouldn't have left Stu. He was going to be really upset when I saw him again. A good sister would have stayed.

The books weren't proper books at all. They didn't have titles on them, just numbers. I pulled one out and opened it. The spine cracked like it'd busted. All the pages were handwritten, and I realized this was someone's diary. Of course, I started reading it.

All appears remarkably similar except in the matter of these things: the prevalence of three-fingered women, the interminable rain, and the lack of a North Star. While there may be subtleties that elude me at this point, I feel no need to extend my visit. New horizons beckon, my appetite merely whetted by this diversion.

Weird. I was going to read some more when I noticed the desk had a face. Someone had carved one of the corners into a dog's head. It reminded me of the mask Jago wore, except that this had proper dog's eyes. They looked at me accusingly.

'What?' I asked the desk. But it didn't reply, *because it was a desk,* and I felt pretty stupid.

Then I noticed there was a drawer in the desk with a little keyhole above the handle. I had a tingly feeling in my stomach. It looked just the right size. I pulled out my key, and it fitted. *Yes!* I opened it up.

The drawer was deep and stuffed full of random things that were obviously thrown in in a hurry. You know, like when you're told you can't go out until your room is tidy, so you chuck it all under the bed or in your drawers so your mum can't see it.

There were ornaments inside, but nothing I liked. They were all squat and ugly, like things old tribes had made hundreds of years ago. I saw some pictures of Morwen, too: four old photographs taken outside Loveday and a small painting. Underneath them, right near the bottom, was a ring and another key. The ring was thick and black, with these dark green veins that you could see if you held it up to the light. I tried it on, but it was too big for my fingers. Sat pretty well on my thumb, though. I wanted to keep it. Felt bad to steal from Jago. Except, in a way, I wasn't stealing. Morwen's deal said that whatever was in the drawer was mine. Anyway, Jago was loaded. He wasn't going to miss one ring. And, if he really liked it, he wouldn't have dumped it in here.

After thinking this through, the guilt went away. The key was mine, too. I picked it up. It was bigger than the one Morwen had given me but had that same weight. The head of the key looked like a trident. Somewhere in the house would be a door to match, and I had the feeling I'd seen it already on the first floor. I put the key in my pocket and locked up the desk.

A few minutes later, the man that had come to get Jago knocked on the door and came in. 'The master regrets that he has been delayed and suggests that you return to the other guests.'

'OK.'

'Would you like me to escort you outside?'

'No thanks,' I said, squeezing the keys in my pocket. 'I think I know the way.'

Turned out I didn't know the way exactly, but I got there in the end. The door was in the run-down bit of the house. It was thicker than the others, more like my front door than an internal one. There was a musty smell to it, like really old, wet clothes. That nearly put me off, but I'd got this key now, and I wanted to see what was on the other side. If Jago knew what I was doing, he'd probably be pissed off. But Jago didn't know. Nobody did. It was my secret.

I had to twist the key with both hands to get it to turn. The three-pronged head dug into my palms sharp enough to mark the skin. When it finally moved, it went hard, and I heard the heavy bolts slam back into the door. A bit of my blood was smeared on the key. Stupid thing. I put it back in my pocket, had one last check nobody was about, and then went through.

For a moment, it felt like I was falling. My heart lurched as if I'd missed the top step, and then I was standing in a room made with mismatched stone bricks. There was a tapestry on one wall with flowers and vines on it and, when I peered at it, I could see little naked people tangled up in them. There were no lights in the room, but I could see OK, thanks to the daylight streaming through the window. Except, this light looked purple.

I went over to the window to see if it had coloured glass like in the church Gran used to go to. When I got there, I just stood there like a twat, my mouth hanging open. There wasn't any coloured glass. There wasn't any glass at all, just an opening that looked out onto the beach. The clouds looked shimmery, like petrol splashed in puddles. They were swirling against one another in this weird way. Watching them made me feel sick. The sea was weird, too, so dark and green it was nearly black.

How long did I stare at it? Felt like ages. Then I noticed there was a woman down on the beach. Her long dress and shawl were rippling in the wind. So was her hair, which was blacker than the water. She turned and lifted her head so that she was staring straight at me.

I ducked away from the window. Had she seen me? Did it even matter? It's not like I cared what some strange woman thought. I shook my head, annoyed at myself, and stood back up, putting on my best *whatever* face. But the woman was gone. I looked up and down the beach, but there was no sign of her. She'd vanished.

Floorboards creaked nearby, and I heard this other noise – somewhere between a sick person breathing and water going down a plughole. I don't know what makes a noise like that, but when I heard it a second time, louder, like it was getting closer, I decided I didn't want to find out. I ran from the window and back out of the door, slamming it shut behind me while I fumbled for the key.

Why do things always take longer when you're in a rush? A cold breeze blew out through the cracks in the door, and I shivered, but I had the key in my hand now. The lock was still stiff, and my hand started to bleed as I wrestled with it.

'Come on, you stupid piece of shit,' I muttered.

Finally, the key turned, and the bolt started to move.

But it stopped halfway, then fell back again. I blinked at it, then looked at the door, and my heart really sank.

The door didn't fit the frame properly any more. The top beam bowed in the middle. Not a lot, but enough. I slammed the door again as hard as I could, and it jammed in the frame. I couldn't close it fully though, and even worse, I couldn't lock it.

Fuck it. That would have to do. My hand was stinging like a bastard, and I was feeling really sorry for myself.

Suddenly, I didn't want to explore any more. I wanted to go and find Stu and talk about stupid things and get him to make me an egg sandwich. Yeah, that would sort me out. Don't know why, but I started to run back instead of walk. Just really needed to see him, I guess.

The further I got from the door, the angrier I felt: angry at myself for leaving Stu in the first place and angry at Jago for tempting me away with a promise of something amazing and then abandoning me with shit all. Yeah, this was all Jago's fault. What a prick.

Stuart

My powers started to fade after the clay pigeon shooting. I glanced back towards our audience to find a Jago-and-Kelly-shaped hole where they'd been moments before. I told myself it was nothing to worry about; maybe she'd needed the toilet or a glass of water. They'd return shortly, and my powers would come back with them.

Time seemed to pass extremely quickly after that. Before I knew it, the next test had begun. When my turn came to retrieve an object Enigma had thrown into the water, I was completely ordinary. Luckily, I'm a strong swimmer so didn't utterly disgrace myself. Saving dignity is a long way from being spectacular, though.

Walking back up the stony beach, the wind bit at my soft skin. I looked for Kelly again. She still wasn't there.

Enigma asked us to follow him to the next challenge. I wondered what it was but then realized it didn't matter. Whatever the task, I was destined to lose.

The day passed in a series of humiliations. Enigma had applied his keen intellect to the problem of how to fairly test us, using a barrage of activities to measure our speed, strength, adaptability, and endurance. Shot put, clay pigeon shooting, swimming, weights, running races, climbing, a balance beam, and a version of dodgeball.

For me, it was loss after loss after loss.

As soon as I was able, I left the gathering, doing my best to ignore Tinker's comments. Though I tried not to show it, each one stung – but none of them cut as deep as Redcoat's reaction. He hadn't said anything critical; the man was too decent for that. I'd seen the pity in his eyes, though, and the way the others dismissed me with their bodies. It was clear that, to them, I hadn't just lost: I'd turned up to the wrong league.

It was all I could do not to run as I headed back to my room. Once there, I took out my phone and messaged Stella.

I miss you. Today has been terrible. Have you got time to talk?

Maybe I should have brought Stella here instead of Kelly. Stella wouldn't have abandoned me on the most important afternoon of my life. I wished she were here with me, holding me. On Keun Island, America seemed even further away than normal.

My phone dinged and not in a good way: the message had bounced. Poor signal, apparently. Great. I went to the window and tried again . . . *Ding*. Another bounce. Clearly good internet was not on Jago's priority list.

I shivered. It was cold in my room, and the curtains billowed in the breeze. Had someone opened my window while I was out? Annoyed, I went to close it and stopped at the sight of the gloomy sky. It matched my mood perfectly. Clouds rolled in from the horizon, the kind that promised lots of rain.

I tried texting a few more times before dinner and got the same results.

Nobody had said what the theme for dinner was. Was I supposed to wear my mask again or was that just for the first night? I picked it up anyway, just to be safe, and made my way downstairs. To say I wasn't looking forward to seeing Tinker again was a huge understatement.

When I arrived, the other guests were already gathering in the dining room. Everyone but Kelly, Tinker, Gladys, and the Captain. I began to worry about Kelly's absence. What if something bad had happened to her?

Although the table was laid, the room seemed oddly quiet. No staff were in evidence, and Jago had not yet appeared. Redcoat and Enigma were talking quietly with Rockford. I thought about joining them but couldn't find the courage. It was almost like being at school again. They were the cool kids, and I didn't have the status to stand next to them any more.

Just as I was starting to feel awkward standing by the door, Gary came over and put a sympathetic hand on my arm. 'How are you holding up?'

I marshalled a smile from somewhere. 'I'll survive. Where is everyone? Seems quiet compared to last night.'

'I saw Hitchcock locking up earlier. They always seal the house after dark.'

'Do they always air the house in the day?'

Gary frowned. 'Only in the summer, why?'

'I keep finding my window left open.'

'Ah.'

'You don't sound surprised.'

'Stay here long enough, and nothing surprises you any more.' His focus seemed faraway. 'This house . . .'

'What?' I prompted.

'It's got a lot of history.'

'I don't know what you mean.'

He patted me on the arm. 'You will.'

I gave him a polite smile. Maybe Gary wasn't as together as I'd first thought.

While Gary and I were talking, I was aware of the others continuing their separate conversation. Gradually, the rumble of Rockford's voice was becoming understandable to me. He wasn't talking any louder, but my hearing was improving by the moment. Something was triggering my ace.

'. . . wasn't in his room when I called on him for dinner. It's bugging me that he's not here. That man never misses a meal.'

'There is no meal to miss as yet,' replied Enigma. 'Perhaps he knows something we don't.'

As the aces continued to chat, I looked about to find Kelly standing in the hall. She seemed guilty. My first thought was relief. Thank goodness she was OK! Reassured that she was safe, I allowed myself to feel angry with her again. 'Where have you been?'

Gary cleared his throat. 'I'll catch up with you both later.'

She didn't answer until Gary had moved well out of earshot. 'I . . . went exploring for a bit and got lost in the house.'

'For the whole day?'

She looked even more guilty. 'Yeah. How did the competition go?'

'How do you think?' I snapped.

'Sorry.'

'I don't understand, Kelly. Why would you leave me to fail? You know what this means to me.'

'I'm *sorry*, OK!' Her face began to crumple.

Normally, that's enough to quell my temper. I can't bear to see her upset. This time, though, it just made me more annoyed. If anyone should be crying, it was me. It didn't help that I was fairly sure she was lying. 'No. It isn't OK. Saying sorry doesn't change what you did.'

A look of horror crossed her face, and she turned to run from the room, tears pricking the corners of her eyes. Immediately, I regretted being so hard with her. Before I could follow, the lights above us flickered twice and went out. Though I couldn't see her, Kelly's footsteps rang out clearly, and I followed them to the main hall.

A second later, I heard the sound of multiple thuds, the unmistakable crack of breaking bone, and a woman's scream.

'Kelly?' I called out. 'Kelly!'

'I'm OK.'

A little of my panic eased, but while the screaming had stopped, I could still catch the sound of laboured breathing nearby, accompanied by a soft whimper. Kelly might be unharmed, but somebody still needed my help.

I put my worries to one side and assumed a calm expression. Even though whoever was injured wouldn't be able to see it, I found it helped me to find the right tone. 'Help is coming. Can you talk?'

'Yes.'

I knew that voice. 'Gladys?'

'Yes.'

'It's me, Stuart. I'm on my way. Keep talking so I can find you.' As I passed Kelly, I took her arm. 'Stay close.'

There was a pause. Then Gladys exclaimed, 'I don't know what to say!'

'Tell me where you first met Jason.'

'Oh, I was at a New Year's party, one of those last-minute things. It hadn't been the best year for me, and I'd been planning on having a quiet night in. I was looking forward to it, actually. Just me, a bottle of wine, and Edward – that's my cat. Are you sure you want to hear about this?'

'Absolutely. Keep going.'

'I had a call from a friend . . .' She paused, sucking in a painful breath. 'Sorry, I had a call from a friend who insisted I come out and have fun instead. Luckily for them, I hadn't started on the wine, and Edward is very understanding, so I forced myself to dress up and call a cab. When I arrived, Jason was—'

'That's brilliant, Gladys. I'm here now.' I let go of Kelly and kneeled down alongside Gladys. 'Where does it hurt?'

'All over. Sorry, that isn't very helpful, is it?'

'Are you bleeding?'

'I don't think so.'

'I'm going to start an examination of your injuries. We don't have any light, so you're going to have to be my eyes. Can you do that?'

'Yes.'

'Good. Talk me through the places that hurt starting from your head and working down.'

Gladys remained coherent as she talked, which I took as a good sign. She'd struck her head, back and shoulders multiple times. The bone I'd heard snapping had been in her left ankle. I kept talking to her as the others began to arrive, thankfully bringing a light source with them.

'Do you have any allergies?'

'No.'

'Are you taking any medication?'

'Just antihistamines. I feel light-headed. Is that normal?'

'You're going into shock. It's quite normal after a fall.'

Redcoat came and crouched down next to me. He took Gladys's hand, and she immediately tried to sit up, despite both of us telling her to stay where she was.

There was a determined look in her eye as she said, 'I didn't fall. I was pushed.'

'Are you sure?' asked Redcoat.

'Yes. The lights went out when I was at the top of the stairs. I stopped and tried to get my bearings, and then I felt hands on my back. Someone did this on purpose, Jason.'

Redcoat's nostrils flared. 'Don't worry – you're safe now. I'll deal with whoever did this.'

Rockford, who had also joined us, shone his torch up towards the stairs. If anybody had been there, they were long gone now. 'We need to find Tinker,' said Rockford. 'And Captain Racine.'

'And our host,' added Redcoat. 'Ask him what kind of game he's playing.'

'Jago wouldn't do this,' said Gary.

Redcoat turned angrily. 'Can you explain to me where he is or what he's doing?'

'No, but I'd wager he's trying to fix the lights.'

'Where are his staff then? Why hasn't anyone come to let us know what's going on?'

'I'm sure they will soon.'

Redcoat scowled. 'You'll forgive me if I don't take your word for it.'

I could feel the tension rising to dangerous levels. 'Our priority should be safety,' I said. 'We need to get Gladys medical attention, and we need to locate everyone in the house. From the guests, it's Tinker and the Captain who are missing. Gary, do you know the staff by name?'

'Yes.'

'I'll need a list to work through.'

There were limited supplies on hand, but we were able to get Gladys some painkillers. I set the others to work finding a better light source and bringing blankets to keep her warm until we could safely move her somewhere more suitable.

I felt a tugging at my wrist: Kelly.

'I'm going to get Gladys a blanket from my room. Back in a bit.'

'I don't think you should be wandering about in the dark on your own. We don't want any more accidents.'

'Your brother is right,' said Enigma. 'As he's busy, I will escort you.'

Kelly made a frustrated noise too quiet for Turing to hear. 'Be careful,' I told her.

'Stop worrying,' she replied. 'You're worse than Mum sometimes.'

'Ouch.'

I watched their shadowy forms ascend the stairs and attended to the sound of their receding footsteps when they rounded the corner. As soon as I could no longer see or hear my sister, I started worrying anyway.

For the first time in a while, I felt sorry for Mum.

Kelly

'Are you sure this is the way to your room?' Enigma asked for, like, the third time.

'I think so,' I lied. 'It all looks strange in the dark.'

He shone the torch on the nearest doors to see if I recognized any of them. I know he was trying to help, but I was still pissed off that he got to hold the torch and I didn't. Despite what I'd said, I did recognize some of the doors. Truth was: the house didn't look any weirder to me in the dark than it did in the day. I liked Loveday House. It was cool and a bit fucked up, just like me.

'Between you and me,' said Enigma, 'I find people difficult.'

'Yeah?'

'Yes. I excel at solving puzzles and cracking codes. Anything with numbers, really. You see, no matter how difficult a problem is, there is an underlying logic, a pattern that can be understood and interpreted given enough time.'

He sounded like a teacher. One of the boring ones. Why Stu thought he was so great was beyond me.

'People,' Enigma continued, 'rarely conform to a pattern. More than once, I've been caught out by that. Take you, for example. I don't understand your behaviour at all.'

I turned to him and had to squint, as he was shining the torch at me.

'I know this isn't the way to your room and am confident that you know this also. You are clearly deceiving me, but the reasons for this remain elusive. What possible cause would you have to lead me the wrong way through Loveday when another person is suffering and needs our help?'

Oh shit. He was on to me. The truth was: I wanted to check on that funny door, the one I'd opened with the key and couldn't shut. But I couldn't tell him that, so I made up a lie instead. 'I, um, got lost earlier, and I left my jacket in one of the rooms. It's Stu's, actually. He lent it to me when I lost my jacket on the way here.'

'You've lost two jackets in as many days?'

'Yeah.'

He looked at me for a moment. 'Then we had best find it quickly, along with a blanket for the Reverend Turney.'

It didn't take me long to find the door. It was open. A cold wind blew through it, through me. I shivered. Actually, this bit of the house did look different in the dark. Really different. I could dimly see into the room, and through it, the window, and through the window, stars. Way too many stars.

'Remarkable,' said Enigma.

I heard footsteps crossing the room, and then Morwen came into the torchlight. I ducked out of sight. I don't know why. I just . . . didn't want her to see me.

She walked right up to Enigma like he'd come into her bedroom without knocking. 'Name yourself.'

'I am Alan Turing; you may have heard me called Enigma. Are you part of Mr Branok's staff?'

She pulled a face like a slapped arse. 'I am no man's servant. I am Morwen.'

'Were you named after Lady Morwen? A descendant perhaps? The resemblance is striking.'

Instead of answering his question, she put a hand on his face. 'Ah, there is no softness to your skin, man of metal, just clever artifice. Now, answer: will you be my champion? Will you love and serve and put an end to the usurper of Loveday?'

There was this weird pause. I thought, at first, he was trying to think of the best way to tell her to fuck off. But she was staring at him really fiercely and still cupping his cheek with one hand, and he was just staring back. I wondered if they were going to kiss or something.

Then he said, 'Yes. I will do whatever you wish, Morwen.'

'*Lady* Morwen.'

He nodded. 'Lady Morwen.'

She smiled, and I shivered again. 'I hear tell that many guests dwell with the usurper, each as remarkable as you. Weigh them and speak to their worthiness.'

'There are representatives of the Committee and the Silver Helix here. They are all well trained aces with an array of superhuman powers. I tested their limits only this afternoon.'

'Tell me each detail, man of metal, so we may sift champions from chaff.'

Oh shit. This was really, really, really bad, and it was all my fault. My stomach was clenching so tight I was glad we'd missed dinner. I had to tell Stu and Jago. Luckily, I knew how to be quiet when I had to be, and I had to be a fucking ninja if I was going to get away without being seen.

One step. They kept talking. Two steps. I was holding my breath and gritting my teeth. They still hadn't noticed me.

I risked the third step a little quicker, and by the tenth I was practically running. Only problem was, Enigma still had the torch. I stumbled on into the dark, while he told Morwen all about Redcoat.

Stuart

Gladys was as comfortable as we could make her, and now that the pain-killers were taking effect, she'd started to fall asleep. Rather than move her, we'd set up camp around her at the bottom of the main stairs. I was still worried about Kelly.

'What do you think?' asked Redcoat.

'She's stable for the moment, but I'm worried about a possible concussion and getting her ankle set properly. She needs to be taken to hospital for scans and treatment. I want to call an air ambulance. Do any of you have signal here?'

They all shook their heads.

'Tinker would be able to get a call through,' said Rockford.

'Then we need to find him,' I suggested. 'Otherwise, the best thing would be to wait until morning. If we can find Captain Racine, he could fly to the village to place a call, or even the mainland if necessary.'

Redcoat began to pace. 'We can't leave Gladys like this, and we don't know when or if Tinker and the Captain are coming back. I'm going to head out tonight for higher ground and make a call.'

'It won't work,' said Gary.

'Why?' Redcoat stopped pacing. 'What aren't you telling us?'

Gary held up his hands. 'I'm just saying: Stuart is right. It's better if we wait this out. Besides, the house is locked down until tomorrow.

'A lock isn't going to stop me. Rockford, can you look after Gladys?'

The big man jerked a stone thumb to his stone chest. 'She'll be safe with me.'

We all turned at the sound of rapid footsteps on the stairs. Kelly had come back, with Enigma following, nearly running to keep up. She was going so fast she tripped and had to hold onto the banister to stop herself from falling.

'Careful,' I warned. 'One injury is enough to deal with.'

She didn't slow though, just kept powering towards me.

'Do you have the blanket?'

This did make her stop. 'I . . . no, I forgot.'

'Oh, Kelly, you had one job.'

Kelly jumped as Enigma spoke from close behind her. A little of his makeup had been smudged on his left cheek, and the torchlight glinted from it. 'Your sister got lost. Easy to do in the dark.'

Even in the poor light, I could see the rosy sheen of her cheeks and familiar pout of her lips. I couldn't tell if she was angry or upset. Probably both.

'I'm afraid all of the excitement has got to her,' Enigma continued. 'There is some good news. Though we didn't encounter any of Mr Branok's staff on our travels, it seems they have not locked all of the exits.'

'Excellent,' said Redcoat. 'Can you show me?'

'I can.'

Redcoat took a torch from Gary, leaving the other one with Rockford. 'Lead on then. You coming, Stuart?'

A little flutter of joy took my heart. 'Me?'

'You examined Gladys. The doctors will need to question you.'

'Yes,' I said, feeling like an idiot. Of course they would. I jumped up.

As we made our way towards the stairs again, Kelly tugged at my sleeve. 'I have to talk to you.'

I watched the two torches rapidly ascending the steps without me. 'We can talk when I get back.'

'It's really important, Stu.'

'So is this.'

'Keep up!' called Redcoat as he rounded the corner.

I leaped after them, taking the stairs two at a time.

Kelly called after me, 'Stu, we have to talk *now!*'

'When I get back,' I said firmly. 'Stay safe!'

We moved through the house quickly. Enigma and Redcoat talked as they went, evaluating the situation without my input. I felt like a child overhearing the grown-ups talk. They were worried, and so was I. Gladys was hurt, Kelly seemed to be all over the place, the Captain was missing, and given how strange the evening was becoming, I was even starting to worry about Tinker.

'Go on,' said Redcoat. He was wearing the coat now: a military style jacket that hung down to the backs of his knees. Despite the circumstances, I couldn't help but be excited every time I saw it.

Enigma looked across at us with a quizzical expression.

'You know how I feel,' Redcoat continued. 'I don't like Lord Branok. Imposing all these bizarre rules on us and not explaining himself. Hiding behind a mask. Vanishing just before the power went out. If he were poor, we'd call him a looney. But he's rich, so we call him eccentric. There's more to this, Alan, and if I've worked that out, then you must be way ahead.' Redcoat flicked his torch at the other man. 'So, go on. What are you thinking?'

'I have theories. There is certainly more going on at Loveday than we're being told, and there is a high probability that we are in danger. The best-case scenario is that Jago Branok has exposed us to risk via neglect. The worst case is that he has done so through malice. We should be on our guard.' Enigma came to a stop and shone his torch at an open door; I could feel a breeze coming through. 'Here we are. You'll have to climb out, but I'm sure that won't be a problem for two people with your training and fitness.'

Redcoat frowned. 'You're not coming with us?'

'I'd only slow you down.'

Redcoat nodded, then put a hand on Enigma's shoulder. 'Keep an eye on Gladys for me? She trusts you.'

'Of course,' he replied, then turned to me. 'I'll take care of your sister, too.'

'Thank you.' Although I was annoyed with Kelly, I'd hated leaving her when she was scared. Knowing that Enigma and Rockford were there helped a lot.

Enigma waited as we stepped through the door. I was waving goodbye to him, looking over my shoulder, so I didn't see the step. I had this horrible feeling in my gut, like I was falling too far, and then I was stumbling in behind Redcoat. He steadied me one-handed.

'Easy there.'

'Sorry.'

Someone had left the window open in this room, and the night air was vicious. I briefly wished I'd asked Kelly for my jacket. There was a damp smell that had leached into the walls of the room, which seemed to have been made in the style of a medieval castle. Perhaps this had been part of the original structure before Jago's restoration? I had the distinct feeling the walls would be wet to the touch, but I didn't have time to test the theory as Redcoat was already at the windowsill.

'The climb doesn't look too bad, but there's a jump at the bottom. Think you can handle it?'

'Yes,' I said. Of course I did. What else do you say when your hero asks you to step up?

'Good man.'

My heart swelled. My powers, however, did not. I still had a long way to go to get Redcoat's respect. He swung out of the window with ease and made short work of the climb. By the time I was easing myself out into the night, he was already halfway down the wall. Luckily for me, there were lots of holds in the rough stone walls, and I'm a practised climber.

Redcoat's torch guided me down, and he called instructions and encouragement as I followed him. In the dark, it was hard to estimate the jump at the end. I didn't like the look of it, though. A bad fall would see me needing the air ambulance more than Gladys. Suddenly, this seemed like a terrible idea.

'Come on,' Redcoat called. 'I'll catch you.'

I believed him and kicked off from the wall, doing my best to aim myself at his waiting arms. For a long second, I fell – then he caught me, taking the momentum with a bend of his knees before placing me upright on the rocks.

Before I could thank him, he was leading the way towards the cliffs, and I hurried to keep up with the only light source.

The path was treacherous and made more difficult by the pace Redcoat set. Even so, I knew he was slowing down for me. That stung. And it was so unfair! If he had believed in me, even a little, I wouldn't be such a burden.

We were both keeping our eyes on the little strip of path illuminated by the torch, focusing on the next step in front of us. I'd thought the wind was bitter before, but as we crested the top, I realized how much shelter the rocks had been giving us.

Shivering, I took out my phone and checked for signal. Nothing. 'No luck for me – shall we keep going?'

'Where in God's name are we?'

When I looked over at him, I saw his face turned up towards the sky in disbelief. The clouds were thick, heavy, their shapes seeming to slide over one another with a strange liquidity. In the gaps between them, I saw clusters of stars, vivid purples and greens. Dad always said that you'd never seen the night sky until you'd got out of the city, and he was right. Reachers had taken me to some pretty remote places over the last year: Kilimanjaro, La Silla Observatory in the Atacama Desert, and several oil rigs in the North Sea. I'd stolen glances at the sky in all of those places and been rewarded with beautiful views. None of them were remotely like this. The feeling in my gut was different, too. Instead of wonder, I felt strangeness.

I don't know how long we stood there – probably no more than a minute or so, but it seemed longer.

Eventually, Redcoat looked down but not at me. 'Are those people on the beach?'

He pointed with his torch. The few stars peeping through cast an eerie light that didn't reach the sea, leaving it black. But Redcoat was right. Something was moving on the beach, moving in great gravity-defying bounds: a strange misshapen object that seemed to writhe against itself in the dark. Reluctantly, we both moved further along the cliffs, until we stood on the edge, overlooking the water, with the beach to our right.

I strained to see, feeling the loss of my enhanced senses keenly, but as my eyes adjusted, I began to realize that it was not one thing on the beach but two, struggling against each other. One was a person, upright, their legs kicking sometimes against the sands, then cycling wildly in the air. The other was horizontal, but in flight, so that the two people formed a lower case 'r' shape. The airborne figure was driving the other one towards the water.

A horrible feeling settled in my stomach. 'They're fighting,' I said aloud. 'We have to help.'

Redcoat stood for a moment, making the sign of the cross. 'This isn't an earthly sky. We've stumbled into some kind of hell. I knew Lord Branok was twisted, but I never expected this.'

'We have to help them,' I repeated, and started looking for a way down. Without the torch, it was impossible. 'Redcoat!'

At the sound of his name, my hero snapped to his senses. 'Stay here. I'll handle this.'

'What about me?'

He turned and fixed me with a look. 'You're not ready.'

The words were like a punch in the gut.

He turned to go, but both of us were stopped in our tracks by a flash of light. It came from below. A rainbow glimmer, gone as fast as it had come. I'd seen that kind of light before, just hours ago, when we'd been carrying out Enigma's tests: Captain Racine! The flying ace down there had to be the Captain, and he was dragging someone to their death. But why?

The two figures launched from the beach in a much larger bound, taking them out above the black water. I lost sight of them for a few moments, until there was another flash of light from the Captain's hands, which were locked on his victim's shoulders. The afterimage repeated across my dazzled vision: a body falling, his kicking legs gone limp. I did not see or hear it, but I knew they would be swallowed up by the icy sea.

If the Captain's attack hadn't killed them, the temperature would just as surely, assuming they didn't drown first. To rescue that man I'd need lights, a helicopter, a team. I needed my powers. Panic began to rise, but I took a breath. Always better to focus on what you do have than what you don't. Redcoat was still here. He'd find a way.

'You need to help,' I urged him.

'No. We need to leave here before we lose more than just our lives, and we need to wring answers out of Lord Branok.'

'That man is dying. We can't leave.'

'He's already dead, Stuart.'

'We don't know that!' I protested.

His look was uncompromising. 'Yes, we do.'

Was that true? The odds were bad, but you never give up on someone until you know for certain. I set my jaw. 'Please. I can't save them, but you can.'

I realized I was shouting to be heard over the wind. That same wind masked the woman's footsteps until she was right on us. I saw a flowing silhouette glide towards me, fabric rippling behind her like a set of wings.

'You are the child,' she said. 'The one with the fool's name.'

I gaped at her, too surprised to speak.

'And you,' she continued, dismissing me as she walked past, 'are the one named Redcoat. Such a weak name. Jason is stronger, a better fit for a champion.'

Redcoat took an involuntary step backwards, bringing him close to the cliff's edge, and pointed the torch at her. 'Who are you?'

'I am Lady Morwen,' she said, reaching out to him. 'And I bind you to service.'

A deep unease stirred within me, followed by growing fear. Redcoat did not reply to her. He just stood there as she closed the last of the distance between them and cupped his face, smothering the torchlight with her body. She'd approached him like some long-lost lover, but I was certain there was nothing loving about her.

'You are mine,' she repeated in the dark.

He sounded far too natural as he replied, 'I am yours, Lady Morwen.'

'*Redcoat!*' I shouted. 'Wake up! We need you.'

He didn't reply, didn't even look at me.

Morwen did, however. 'I have no use for this one. Let us be rid of him.' She stepped back, and I could see the torch again. Redcoat immediately strode towards me, closing off my angles of escape. I looked for some sign that this was a trick or a terrible joke. If he had winked in that moment and Tinker had appeared from behind a rock, laughing, I would have rejoiced. Anything would have been better than this.

Was I dreaming? It had the logic of a dream. There was no way I could hope to beat him, no way I could escape him on the treacherous paths with no light. I knew just how good he was.

'Please,' I begged. 'Don't do this.'

He grabbed me one-handed and lifted me off the ground. I continued to plead as he turned and carried me to the cliff's edge. Beneath us were bleak rocks and a void of water. Around us, the screaming wind. I made one last try.

'Remember who you are! You're Redcoat of the Silver Helix. You swore an oath to your King and country. You're Redcoat!'

The only reply I got was Morwen's bitter hiss. 'He is Redcoat no more.'

The memory of our shot-put trial came to mind as Redcoat gathered himself to throw. I began to flail, trying to get a grip on him as I shouted, but he was relentless. I saw that strange sky one more time, and then I was launched into the air, into the cold. The starless dark grew beneath me until it was all I could see.

Helpless, I fell into it.

Kelly

Stu was gone, and I didn't know whether to wait and confess when he got back or to talk to Gary or Rockford now. Gary was nicer, but he seemed a bit useless. Rockford was probably better; he was some kind of big deal. Thing is, I hate getting into trouble. If I told Rockford what I'd done, it'd all become official, and I'd get into big shit. Maybe Mum and Dad would find out and my life would be over.

There was this weird humming sound, and then the lights all blinked back on. 'Shit,' I said, covering my eyes.

Rockford gave me a disapproving look.

'Sorry.'

A voice behind me made me jump. 'It is I who should apologize, Ms Hill.'

We turned round to see Jago standing at the door to the dining room. He was still carrying that pistol from earlier.

'Damn right,' agreed Rockford. 'Tinker's missing. Captain's missing. The lights stopped working, and all your people vanished, and then Gladys got pushed down the stairs and broke her ankle! What the hell's going on?'

'I am afraid I've gravely failed in my duties as host. There will be time for recriminations later, but for now, let me lay out the situation, and then we can discuss what must be done.'

Rockford gave a nod of assent, but he didn't look happy about it.

Jago glanced at Gary. 'As some of you are already aware, Loveday is an unusual house. To understand it, there are certain things you must accept. Firstly, that this world is not the only one in existence. There are many versions of our world – as many as you can imagine and more. In this one, the wild card turned you, Mr Rockford, into an ace. In others, it killed you. In still others, you never contracted it in the first place, were never born, or died in a car accident ten years earlier.

'I have a gift – my own ace – that allows me to find safe pathways between these worlds, and I've made it my life's work to explore them. Loveday House is unique in my experience, in that it sits on a nexus point where many of these worlds brush against one another. Through the reconstruction of the property, I've been able to control the flow of things moving between the worlds, travelling when it suits me while keeping other, less desirable travellers out.'

Rockford grunted. 'Other travellers?'

'Yes. In some worlds, I am not the inheritor of Loveday House. In one particular world, Lady Morwen did not die in a storm, but she did experience a storm and it took her sanity. In her world, there is no wild card virus – no aces, jokers, or deuces. But, like me, she became aware of other places beyond her own, and, like me, she sought to use Loveday – her version of Loveday – to explore them. The two Lovedays can blur into each other, our actions carrying over from this house to hers and back again. Sometimes, I would find a door left open that I'd been sure to close, or a picture I'd put up would also appear on her wall. We soon became aware of the connection. After that, it was only a matter of time before we met.'

As Jago talked, I started to feel more and more sick.

'At first, things were amicable enough. It is a singular pleasure to find one is not the only world-wanderer, and that allowed us both to overlook certain differences of opinion. By the time it became clear that our intentions were incompatible, we had already shared a great deal of knowledge, and that sharing deepened the connection between the Lovedays.'

'You coming to a point soon?' asked Rockford.

'Forgive me; there is too much to say now, too many gaps to fill in the time we have. Suffice to say that there was a great falling-out. Morwen is dangerous, and I did not want her having access to the many doors of Loveday, in either her house or mine. To curtail her, I sealed her house completely and separated it from my own. Over the years, she has attempted to force her way out. Things from Morwen's world still manifest here some-times, and I am quick to remove them, lest they re-establish the connection too strongly.'

'That's why you freaked out over her picture!' I said.

'Yes, that was the cause of my alarm. If Morwen's presence takes hold here, I could lose control of the house entirely.' His gaze fell on me with intensity. 'You are surprisingly perceptive, Ms Hill.'

It made sense now: why I'd found those things of hers locked up in his desk. They'd been like – I dunno – things from an ex that you get rid of so you don't have to think about them any more. Only, Jago's ex was a mad invader from another world, and I'd let her out. Or back in. Whatever.

'The reason I locked the house down tonight was for your protection. Morwen is trying to force her way into Loveday and, from there, to any world that pleases her. It seems that she's got a lot further than I'd thought.'

Rockford folded his arms. 'Not saying I'm buying what you're selling, but if it's true, and there's no virus in her world, why are you so scared of one nat?'

'In other worlds, there are different routes to the extraordinary. Morwen has a way to sway others to her cause. She can turn an allegiance with a few words, force you to abandon your dreams, or set friend against friend. For a time, she even held sway over me.' Jago shook his head, like he was remembering something bad.

Gary cleared his throat. 'She's handy with a knife, too.' His hand came to rest on a knife on his belt. It had a ruby set in the handle, and Gary squeezed it so hard his knuckles went white.

Everyone shut up for a bit. In the quiet, we became aware of this odd whirring sound. It reminded me of this wind-up spider that I got for Halloween when I was six. Gradually, we all noticed it and started looking for the source.

'It's coming from the dining room,' said Gary.

He was right. I could hear it clearly now: this whirring noise that came with regular taps. Jago began to back rapidly away. I peered around him and saw this weird robot caterpillar thing. Imagine someone had got a car battery and a load of magnets, and then stuck cutlery to it to make the legs, and then animated it. It looked like that.

'That's Tinker's work,' said Rockford. 'And I've seen something like it before. Get back!'

Everything happened really fast after that. Rockford grabbed me and swung me behind him as he put himself between the robot and Gladys. The robot started to accelerate into the entrance hall. Jago ran backwards, raising his pistol and firing.

There was a sound like thunder but too close and indoors. Then there was another big bang. This one came with a flash of light and heat. I felt a sting on my arm, really sharp. And when I looked, I saw my sleeve was torn, and there was this red line of blood there. My blood. The room went a bit wobbly for a moment.

Gladys must have woken up again, because I heard her screaming.

'Everyone all right?' asked Rockford.

'I got a cut, but I'm OK,' I said.

'Same,' added Gary.

Gladys collected herself. 'I wasn't hit. I - it just pulled my ankle when I flinched. Thank you for protecting me, Stone.'

Jago staggered over to the wall and leaned on it, his back still to us. 'We'll need to take a trip to the medicine cabinet. I've got bandages there.' Something about the way he moved scared me. He was still holding the pistol, but he was letting it dangle at his side. Blood ran down his arm and onto the grip.

'This is Tinker's fault,' said Rockford. He sounded angry. I was really glad he wasn't angry with me and that I hadn't had time to tell him what I'd done wrong.

'No,' said Jago. 'This is Morwen. She's found a way in, and she's started turning our friends against us.'

'So—' began Rockford.

But he didn't get a chance to finish. The big front doors blew open, and I saw the French bloke – Captain whatever-his-name-was – come flying in really fast. He was going straight for Jago with his hands out. They started to glow. Rockford caught one of the doors out of the air and threw it at the Captain, who blew it into splinters as he crashed into it. I watched as the Captain flew overhead and started righting himself in the air.

'Come,' said Jago. 'It's me they're after. We have to move this fight away from the Reverend Turney.' He started to limp towards the dining room, then fell. Gary and I rushed forward to catch him. 'Apologies,' he added. 'I seem to have lost quite a lot of blood.'

I glanced at his front and immediately wished I hadn't. He'd been cut up pretty bad, and there were four dinner knives sticking out of him, three in his belly and one in his thigh. 'Oh shit.'

As we helped Jago towards the dining room, Rockford moved to cover our escape. 'Get out of here. I'll handle Tricolor.'

A blast of rainbow light fired across the room at Jago, but Rockford caught it in his hands with a grunt. 'Go!' he ordered.

We staggered through the dining room and into another hallway. There were crashes and shouts behind us. It sounded like a proper riot going on. I hoped Rockford would be OK. He was all right.

We were about halfway along the hall when Redcoat appeared at the other end. I did not like the way he was looking at Jago.

'What now?' asked Gary.

'Ms Hill, take the keys from my belt and open the door to our left.'

There was a ring of keys attached with a long chain. I unhooked the chain, snatched it up and gasped. It was more like picking up a weight, and I was already supporting Jago with one arm. Also, there wasn't any door. 'What door? I can't see a fucking door!'

'Look again.'

He said it so matter-of-factly that I shut up and did it. And the door was right there. It was creamy, same as the walls. Not as grand as the other doors I'd seen, with little butterflies etched into the metal around the handle. I tried to find a butterfly key.

Redcoat began marching down the corridor towards us, his hands curled into fists. 'I know the truth about you, Branok.'

'I highly doubt that,' Jago replied.

Just as I was about to shit myself, I found the key and opened the door. Redcoat broke into a run.

We practically dived through, and I let go of Jago to slam the door behind us, locking it tight. As the mechanism clicked, the sound of Redcoat's footsteps cut off. I pressed my hands against the door, expecting Redcoat to smash it from the frame, but it was silent on the other side.

'Well done,' Jago wheezed. 'But we must keep moving. It won't take them long to find us again.'

'Where are we going?' asked Gary.

'Medicine cabinet first, I think, and then the armoury. It's time for us to strike back.'

Stuart

Everywhere I looked was blackness. There was no sense of up or down, just cold and dark. I'd managed to take a breath and keep it when I'd struck the water, but I could already feel the itch in my lungs. Rather than swim straight away, I waited, holding myself still. Gradually the momentum of my fall was checked by the water, and I began to float. Once I was confident which way to go, I swam hard for the surface. No light penetrated the water and so, when I finally lifted my head to take a breath, it was as if I was emerging into another world. Again, I was struck by the strangeness and brightness of the stars.

I gasped down two more lungfuls of air and twisted to take in my surroundings. The beach and the house were in sight, and something else was in the water nearby: a pale oval glittering in the starlight. A face – no, a mirror-ball mask! I recognized that mask. The man dropped by the Captain was Hitchcock, one of Jago's staff. He was still alive and trying to keep his head above water. Training kicked in, and I started swimming towards him. Hitchcock's head vanished for a moment, then reappeared, spluttering.

'Hey!' I called. 'Help is on the way. Keep swimming.'

His masked face snapped towards me, and though I couldn't make him out, I recognized the desperation in the movement. He was bobbing strangely as well, dipping deep, then scrabbling back to the surface.

'Are you hurt?' I asked.

'My arms,' he gasped. 'I can't move them.' His voice took on a new tone of desperation. 'I can't swim!'

'Don't worry – I can swim for both of us. You're going to be fine. Just hold on a little longer.'

It was when I clamped my hands onto him that Hitchcock started to believe. Swimming suddenly became easier, each kick and stroke lifting me a little higher in the water. The night sharpened into focus.

'Breathe through your nose,' I told him, cupping my hand under his chin and swimming us both back to shore. He'd need urgent medical attention by the sound of it – most likely for burns and a score of minor injuries, and we'd both be at risk of hypothermia.

There were rocks hidden in the water, and I realized that only by sheer luck had I not been broken on them when Redcoat tossed me into the sea. If he'd wanted me dead, he could easily have dropped me directly onto the rocks. Had he deliberately thrown me clear of them? I wanted to believe with all my heart that my hero had not fallen completely under Morwen's power.

The thought of her made me falter. Going back to land meant going back to her. It meant facing Redcoat again. Panic threatened to suffocate me, but I pushed it down. *Focus on what you can do. Take one step at a time.* I'd get Hitchcock to safety first. I could do that. Worry about the rest later.

We crawled out of the sea onto the beach, picked ourselves up and staggered back towards the house. Its roof against the night sky bore little resemblance to the lines and angles of Loveday House as I remembered them.

The man barely spoke, but I did my best to keep him talking as we walked. There was no way I could get him up to the window Redcoat and I had come through, but we found a servants' entrance. The silhouette of the house looked strange and old as it loomed over us.

'K-k-keys,' Hitchcock said through chattering teeth. 'In my p-pocket.'

I moved his dangling arm aside and pulled them out. It took a few tries for my numb fingers to get the key into the lock, and at first it didn't want to turn, as if the key was badly cut. When it finally clicked, we both breathed a sigh of relief and fled the lash of the wind.

Together, we groped our way through the house. Hitchcock was a hesitant guide, and more than once, we got lost in the dark. The corridors were damp, with unlit torches lining the walls. I wasn't sure which way we'd come in, but I'd not seen any areas of Loveday in such disrepair until now.

It was with great relief that we finally stepped back into an area of the house we knew. I felt a strange lurching sensation, as if I'd been in a fast-moving lift, but I barely paid it any mind, for there was light and the promise of warmth in the corridor. Hitchcock directed me to some blankets and the laundry basket. The clothes there were an odd mix, but I didn't care. They were dry.

I changed quickly and then helped him to do the same, using the opportunity to examine the man's injuries. He had multiple bumps and bruises, but what I feared most were the burns on his shoulders. They were deep and would leave permanent damage. However, there was little I could do for them at the moment. For now, keeping him warm and safe was all I could offer.

I helped him back towards the entrance hall. At the sight of it, we both stopped to gasp. It looked as if a war had been fought here. One of the front doors was hanging from its hinges, while the other was absent entirely. I saw scorch marks on the walls and ceiling, and smashed furniture scattered across the floor.

Gladys still lay at the bottom of the stairs, a little space of calm amid the carnage. I settled Hitchcock next to her, making him lean forward to keep his burns from touching the wall, and swaddled us all in blankets. 'Where are the others?' I asked.

Gladys wiped her bloodshot eyes and began to speak. 'It was awful. After you left, Tinker tried to blow us up, and then Captain Racine attacked us. If it wasn't for Stone Rockford, I dread to think what would have happened.'

'Where is he?' I looked round for any sign of Kelly. 'Did the others abandon you here?'

With a shaking voice, she told me about the other guests attacking them. If I hadn't just been thrown into the sea by Redcoat, I would have assumed her delusional. '. . . They fought for a long time, but in the end, Stone managed to grab Racine and hold him down. We were trying to reason with him when a woman arrived with Alan. She said something to Stone, and he let Racine go – just let him go, just like that. And they left as if nothing had happened.'

Morwen. It had to be. 'Did they do anything to you?'

'No. I stayed as still and quiet as I could, but she'd seen me, I know she had. It was strange. I felt as if I was a piece of furniture to her, or something less than a person. Does that make sense?'

'Yes,' I replied. 'I know exactly what that feels like.'

'Oh! Where's Jason? Did the two of you get through to an ambulance?'

'There was no signal.'

'What about Jason?'

I locked down the feelings rising in my stomach. 'He's still trying to find a way to deal with the situation. I'll stay with you until he comes back, I promise.'

'Thank you.'

The sound of footsteps broke the moment. Enigma came into the hallway and started to approach us. Gladys had just told me he'd been with Morwen, but even if she hadn't, there was something in his manner that was uncharacteristically threatening.

I shrugged off the blanket and stood up. 'I'll handle this, OK?'

'What are you going to do?'

'Keep you both safe.' I held her gaze for a moment with a confidence I didn't feel.

She nodded at me. 'I know you will.'

Hitchcock blinked up at us, seeming to realize that something was wrong. But both of them trusted me to deal with this. The colours in the room became a little brighter, the smells sharper, the sounds clearer.

I turned to face Enigma, who was crossing the room towards us. To me, he seemed slow. Though his metal body gave him an ageless appearance, he moved like an older man.

'You are supposed to be dead,' he said.

'Please stop,' I replied. 'I don't want to fight you.'

'Surrender then. It is your only real option.'

'What?'

'Yesterday was most informative. Your ace performs at mediocre levels and is unreliable. This fight is already over.'

He was getting close. I moved to meet him so that there would be space between us and the two injured people in my care.

'Your strength is not enough to stop me,' he continued, 'and you cannot employ your speed effectively and protect your charges. This means that—'

Before he could finish, I stepped close to him, and we locked hands, pushing one against the other. I was stronger, but he was too heavy for me to move. He grunted with the strain. 'As expected, you take a child's approach.'

'This isn't the fight,' I replied. 'The question isn't whether you can beat me; the question is *why?*'

Enigma attempted to push me aside, but even using all of his body weight, I barely moved.

I kept talking. 'Redcoat was supposed to kill me, but he didn't. I believe he's fighting her, and if that's true, you can, too. Think about who you are. Think about what you're doing. Explain your reasoning!'

'I serve Lady Morwen.'

'Why aren't you serving your King and country?'

'I serve King – no, I serve . . .'

'Why are you trying to hurt innocent people?'

'I . . .'

'You hate violence! You're famous for it, so why are you fighting me?'

The anger in his face faded. He didn't stop immediately, but his eyes began to flicker, as if he were reading something very, very quickly. Then he went rigid.

He bowed his head, unlaced his hands from mine, and stepped back. 'My apologies, Stuart.'

I didn't let down my guard straight away. 'Are you OK?'

'Ashamed of myself, but it's hardly the first time. Though you may not believe me, I am free of her control.'

'How did you do it?'

'Her power speaks to a deep part of the mind. It implants a conviction that overwrites normal thought, making rationalization virtually impossible. But when you forced me to weigh my current actions against those of a lifetime in service and my own values, the truth became undeniable.' Enigma frowned. 'There is much here that we do not understand, but one thing is clear: Jago Branok is the key to unravelling our mystery and, I hypothesize, to solving it. We must find him before Morwen does.'

'Jago's hurt,' said Gladys. 'Kelly and Gary were helping him.'

'Then,' Enigma replied, 'they are both in grave danger.'

Kelly

We took another random turn through a door with an angry face carved into the handle. We'd picked up bandages for Jago, but there hadn't been time to put them on, because the guests controlled by Morwen were hunting us down. Every time we stopped for a breather, Redcoat found us, and we had to run again. It was hard work carrying Jago, too. My pits were sweating pretty bad, and Gary was like some old furnace. He was so hot, I kept expecting him to glow.

Even scared out of our minds, we were slowing down. It wouldn't be long before they caught us.

Jago glanced at me through his mask. 'Keep at it. We're nearly at the armoury.'

I looked at him, covered in blood and dragging one leg as we carried him on. 'What are we going to do when we get there?'

'Fight back. Retake Loveday from Morwen.'

'No offence, but you and Gary can't even fight me right now.'

'It's not that kind of fight, Ms Hill. We don't need to defeat our guests; we just need to restore Loveday House. The power Morwen has over the other guests works only in her world . . .' He paused to cough violently; I saw blood specks on his glove when he took his hand away. 'Do you understand?'

'No.'

'As she takes Loveday House from me, Morwen's reach extends. If we can seal her power again, the others will be free of her control.'

'How do we do that?'

'There are many ways: lock her back in her version of the house, remove all traces of her presence from Loveday, or subdue Morwen herself.'

I looked at the pistol in his hand. 'You mean kill her?'

'If it comes to it.'

He said it so gangsta-like, you know? I think that scared me more than anything. I could tell Gary didn't like it either.

We came to a tough-looking door with green leather panels. Jago let me find the key. His hands were shaky. I didn't know much about treating wounds, but even I knew we needed to disinfect his injuries and patch him up. If we kept running around, he'd probably die.

The key wouldn't turn. I checked with Jago that it was the right one and then tried again. Nothing.

Jago led us towards another door. On the way, we passed a picture of a withered flower. There were tiny faces on the petals. It didn't look like it belonged here.

The second door was also locked, and the key didn't work.

Jago slumped like his injuries were catching up with him. 'She's locking me in. Of course she is. It's her revenge.'

Gary and I did our best to keep him moving, but it was only a matter of time before they got us. We tried three more doors, all locked. By the third one, Jago wasn't speaking, and his head flopped about all loose, but I was getting pretty good at matching keys to doors now.

Problem was: none of them were working.

Me and Gary both gasped when we came into the dining room. We were back where we'd started! I had this feeling that was exactly what Morwen wanted. Rockford and the Captain's fight must have finished, 'cos I couldn't hear any smashing from the main hall, only quiet chatting. One of the voices almost made me cry for joy: Stu!

'Come on!' I said to Gary, and we put in one last bit of effort.

My smile dropped off my face pretty fast when I saw Enigma was there, too. 'Watch out,' I said. 'He's not on our side.'

Stu smiled at me, like everything was going to be OK. 'He wasn't, but he is now. Let me take Jago.'

And he did. As if the man weighed nothing. Quick as you like, Stu checked him over, peeled the bloody clothes off the wounds and started sorting them out. Me and Gary just sat down next to Gladys and some bloke in a disco mask.

When Stu was finished, I reached over and put a hand on his arm. 'Morwen's done something to the others, and they're all gonna come after Jago.'

'I know. Enigma and I have a plan.'

'You'll keep him safe, yeah? You won't let him die?'

'I'll keep you all safe, I promise.' He hugged me and gave me that smile again. It's a really good smile. Only thing is: it doesn't work on me as well, because I remember him practising it in the mirror at home.

I sat there while he and Enigma talked about what was coming next. Stu looked so brave that I felt this funny feeling in my belly. I had to help him.

I had to make this right. The keys were still in my hand, still way too heavy for what they were. All useless now that Morwen had done her thing.

'Someone's coming,' said Stu. 'But they're not on foot, they're . . . on wheels. It must be Tinker.'

Enigma got up. 'He remains under Morwen's control. We will handle him together. The rest of you, stay back.'

They took up positions by the door to the dining room. I stood up, too. Jago was the only one who saw me move. His eyes widened for a moment, like he knew what I was going to do, but he didn't say anything.

I gave him a nod and started to creep up the stairs. There was one door in the house that would definitely still be open, and it was up to me to close it.

Stuart

My power was fluctuating, making it hard to track Tinker's approach. People's hope was fragile, flickering in and out, and at least two of those who believed in me were hovering on the edge of consciousness. I took a deep breath. To keep their belief in me alive and be able to actually help them, I'd have to continually earn it.

'Are you ready?' asked Enigma. He stood by the door as we'd planned.

The recent memory of Redcoat telling me I wasn't came to mind. I pushed it away. 'Yes.'

Despite the powerful aces coming, the biggest threat by far was Morwen herself. We were going to make her our priority. I'm not used to fighting people – it doesn't sit right with me – but I could see there was no other option. One word from her, and we'd become her slaves. Was this a power of her voice? Her eyes? Pheromones? Or some magic we didn't understand? I wondered if my enhanced senses were a disadvantage against her.

While we stood there, the whirring got louder: a high-pitched engine noise reminiscent of an angry insect. Tinker rode into the hall on a mechanized serving trolley. Crockery had been broken into long, knife-like shards and loaded onto a makeshift launcher on one hand, and in the other, he held a bulky-looking sphere with cutlery taped around it. As far as I could tell, he was steering the trolley with his hips in a vaguely obscene manner.

As per the plan, Enigma pretended to still be on Morwen's side. 'You deal with Jago and the others, while I hold off Stuart.'

'You got the easy job there, mate,' Tinker replied, his eyes seeking and finding Jago quickly. He hefted the cutlery grenade, but before he could throw it, Enigma grabbed his arm.

I crossed the room to them in a couple of bounds and wrapped my arms around Tinker, before bodily wrenching the man out of his contraption. It didn't matter that I was smaller than him; it was as easy as lifting a baby. He tried to fight me, but there was no real contest. His strength was limited by his body, whereas mine was limited only by my ace.

Enigma checked Tinker from head to toe, stripping away a number of suspicious-looking objects as he did so. Tinker took the opportunity to headbutt me. I barely felt it when his nose broke on my forehead.

'Listen,' I said. 'Morwen is controlling you. You need to think about what you're doing and remember who you are.'

He struggled against me for a moment, then stopped when he realized it was useless. 'How about you fuck off instead?'

I tried reasoning with him. I told him that his actions made no sense, that he was part of the Committee, and we needed him. I even tried playing to his ego.

His reply to all of this was: 'Did you miss the part where I told you to fuck off?'

'Can you try to get through to him?' I asked Enigma.

'Oh yeah, that'll work,' sneered Tinker. 'If you want to bore me to death.'

Enigma was silent as he thought this over. I could see him considering multiple options at high speed. Quickly, he nodded to himself, having come to a conclusion. He lifted a hand and struck Tinker a heavy blow to the back of the head.

'Enigma!'

'Apologies, but the situation is desperate and the probability of reason working on Tinker is extremely low. It will also give us a chance to see if Morwen's control is broken by a lapse in consciousness.'

I put Tinker on the floor near to the others, and Enigma bound his hands and feet. I had little love for the man, but it felt wrong to have knocked him out. Enigma's hands were like hammers, and I couldn't help but worry about the potential for a skull fracture or internal bleeding or brain damage. We both crouched over him anxiously. At least, I was anxious. Enigma gave little away.

After a couple of minutes, Tinker's eyelids flicked open. 'Ahh, shit. It's still you.'

I gritted my teeth. 'How are you feeling?'

'Like I just face-checked a train.'

'Do you feel like yourself?'

'Yeah, yeah. I'm OK now. You mind untying me?'

Enigma shook his head. 'It could be a bluff.'

'I'm not bluffing, you great metal fairy! I'm me again. Straight up. Sorry about trying to blow you all to bits, but I wasn't in my right mind. It was Morwen. She did something to my brain, told me to kill Lord Branok, and I was all, "Cool, want me to kill anyone else while I'm there?" like she'd just asked me to pick up some beer. I know I can be a dick sometimes, but this was something else.' He looked down for a moment and then straight into my eyes. 'Thanks for stopping me, Hero. If you hadn't, I'd be living with Jago's blood on me hands.'

'That's OK.'

'You better untie me quick. You're gonna need my help.'

'Explain,' said Enigma.

'I'm just the advance party. Morwen's coming, and she's bringing the others with her. No offence, mate, but without me, you haven't got a chance.'

Enigma frowned. 'It could still be a bluff.'

'I don't think so,' I replied. 'And even if it is, we can handle him.'

I hoped we wouldn't regret our decision.

While Enigma freed Tinker, I glanced back to check on the injured. They all appeared stable, but someone was missing.

My heart raced faster, and I gave them all a hard look. 'Where is Kelly?'

Kelly

I got nearly all the way to the room before I walked into the Captain and Rockford escorting Morwen. They weren't fighting each other any more, just trotting along behind her like two really obedient dogs. Morwen halted and raised her hand. The two men stopped immediately. 'Ah, the little mouse appears once more.'

'You tricked me!'

'No tricks, only choices fairly offered, woman to woman. Now you must make another: will you serve? In return, I will teach you to be strong.'

I pretended to look interested. 'Strong like how?'

She made a gesture to the others. 'Go, bring me Lord Branok's head.'

The Captain leaped into the air and shot off like a bloody rocket. Rockford jogged after him.

Then Morwen turned back to me. 'Strong enough to make champions jump to your words. Are you not tired of doing what others demand?'

'Yeah.' That wasn't a lie either.

'Then join my side. I see you have done me great service already.'

'What?'

'You have stolen his keys.'

I tried to put them behind my back like some twat in a cartoon, even though she'd already seen them.

'Give them to me.'

'I thought you'd locked all the doors already.'

'You are sharp; that is to be much admired. Yes, my Loveday was sealed, but now my Loveday is dominant, that seal extends to Branok's also. With his keys, I would break that seal and open any door I pleased. Place them in my hand, and any reward you can name will be yours.'

It's weird. I really think she could have given me anything, but I wasn't tempted, not even a little bit. 'No thanks.'

Her expression went really hard, and she looked me straight in the eye. 'Give them to me, now.'

I started to walk towards her. It was the right thing to do, you know? I don't know why I'd been so difficult about it. I'd give her the keys, and then she'd give me loads of cool stuff. No problem.

'Better,' Morwen muttered.

That annoyed me. She was right and everything but, like, she didn't need to be a dick about it. Jago wouldn't have done that. I felt this little lurch in my stomach, as if I had moved without taking a step, and then I noticed a painting of Jago hanging on the wall. He was holding up a map and pointing to something on it. Behind him was a big rocky entrance to some kind of old temple. It looked cool. Jago was cool, I thought. Much better than Morwen.

'What are you staring at, child?' she snapped. When she saw the picture of Jago, she flipped her nut and screamed, like, really loud. Then she ripped it off the wall and threw it on the floor, face down. 'Banish Lord Branok from your thoughts and give me the keys.'

My head snapped round to her, and I found my feet hurrying to her side. I knew that doing what she said was right. There was this familiar feeling I had building, though, the kind that says: *fuck it.*

Morwen gave me a shitty smile and held out her hand.

All right, I thought. *If you want the keys, I'll give you the fucking keys.* They felt heavy as I scrunched them together in a bundle.

'Here you go,' I said, and stabbed them down as hard as I could, right into the old bitch's palm.

Stuart

I had to steady myself. My little sister had vanished again. She'd been acting strangely when I'd last seen her. Why hadn't I paid more attention? I'd just assumed she was in shock. I shook my head. Who knew what Kelly was thinking these days? But this wasn't her fault; it was mine. I'd brought her into this nightmare, and it was my job to keep her safe. It was also my job to look after Gladys and Hitchcock and Gary and Jago. By leaving, Kelly had made those things incompatible, putting me in an impossible position.

From upstairs, I heard running footsteps. Heavy, like an elephant's. And closer, but harder to make out, a sound like the wind. 'Rockford's coming,' I warned. 'And he's not alone.'

Enigma had moved over to protect Jago, while Tinker sat on the floor with the spare bandages, a battery salvaged from his serving trolley contraption, and a cluster of wires. 'I've got an idea. Keep them busy for a bit.'

'How long do you need?' I asked.

Tinker just shrugged and kept working.

'Don't worry,' I said to the civilians, 'we'll protect you.'

And, to my relief, they seemed reassured. Enigma and Tinker nodded, too. I felt stronger, faster. We could do this.

A moment later, the Captain flew out over the stairs. One of his eyes was swollen shut, and he looked battered but far from beaten. It was strange to think about someone in pain and visually impaired, and not use that information to help them. Instead, I worked out how best to approach from his blind side. As I did this, he came to a hovering stop in the air above us and threw his hands out in Jago's direction.

I started to run, kicking off the lower steps and then off the handrail, sending me shooting towards a higher section of wall.

Enigma dived forward as rainbow light exploded from the Captain's hands. The shot was intended for Jago, but Enigma blocked it with his body, the blast knocking him to his knees.

My feet met the wall, and I bent my legs, aiming myself at the flying ace, and kicked off hard. He tried to spin away, so fast, but not as fast as me any more. I managed to catch his ankle as I passed him, dragging him back down to earth. Blasts of laser light shot wildly around us. A part of me despaired at the risk to the others, and I considered slamming the Captain into the floor with my momentum. But I was strong now, perhaps too strong. What if I killed him? I hesitated, and the Captain kicked me in the side, turning my landing into a stumble. He tried to kick free and fly away, but I grabbed the banister, anchoring us.

'Over here, Hero!' shouted Tinker.

I snatched the Captain's other leg as he tried to kick me again and began to swing him round. I'd need a lot of momentum, and the man to be dizzy, if this was to work. Faster and faster I spun, whirling the Captain around like a child, until I started to feel sick. Then I let go.

It was probably the most graceless flight the Captain had ever taken and also the shortest. At the last second before impact, Tinker pressed a button, and the bandages leaped into life. They wrapped around the Captain like a fabric octopus snapping up prey. The next second, he was trussed up tight at Tinker's feet.

'Quickly,' Enigma gasped. 'We need to find a way to restore his mind before Rockford gets here.'

'Does that mean I can smack him?' asked Tinker.

'No!' the two of us replied in unison.

'I'll reason with him,' said Enigma.

'I don't remember you using pretty words with me.'

Enigma dragged himself over to where the Captain lay. 'Perhaps when this is over, you will reflect on why that was.'

I didn't pay any more attention to the banter or to the approach Enigma was taking. Rockford was already rounding the main stairs. He took one look at us all and jumped, a stone bomb falling fast towards Jago.

Kelly

Morwen screamed like I'd just cut her hand off. I was running before she stopped, running about as fast as I've ever run in my life. The house wasn't right; I could feel it. It was cold before, but this was a different kind of cold. I didn't like it as much. It was easy to find the door, though. Loveday was getting smaller as I got to know it, and this was the third time I'd come here. The door hung open, and the frame was so warped I could see from here that it wouldn't close.

I didn't stop running.

The funny feeling when I crossed through was there again, but much less. The gap between the houses was smaller. Because of me. I had to do something about that. Morwen's house looked older than Jago's, but the layout was similar or close enough for me to find my way. Somewhere behind me, I could hear Morwen shouting. She was coming after me, but she was old, so I was faster.

I got to the place in Morwen's house that corresponded to Jago's office and went inside, closing the door behind me and jamming a chair under the handle. That should buy me enough time to mess things up. Hopefully. The room had a different feel to Jago's – like a draughty, pompous version. But it did have paintings in similar places, and a big old desk, which was what I'd been hoping. I took out the little key and tried to unlock the drawer. The click as it turned was such a sweet sound. Inside were pictures of Jago, books that Jago had written, and ornaments of his. She'd been trying to forget about him the same way he'd been trying to forget about her.

I smiled this little smile, the one that sends my mum up the wall when I do it. Then I grabbed the stuff out of the drawer and put things where I thought they'd match in Jago's office. As I put up each one, there was this feeling in my belly, like if you fall down a step or go over a hill too fast in a car.

Morwen came to the door. She was nearly out of breath, but that didn't stop her from shouting through it. I didn't want to hear anything that old witch had to say, so I started singing as loud as I could. First thing that came into mind was 'Happy Fucking Birthday'! I don't know why, 'cos it wasn't my birthday. I sang it anyway, loud as I could, and stuffed all of Morwen's things in that drawer. There were too many to fit easily, so I stamped it in with my foot.

Morwen was pounding on the door so hard it opened a crack.

I slammed the drawer shut and locked it. How could I hide the key?

'Attend to me, little mouse!' Morwen shouted.

Oh shit! I stuffed the key into my mouth.

'Attend, I say! Come forth and unbar the door.'

I swallowed. Urgh, it was horrible. I was worried it wasn't going to go down at first, and then I was worried that it *was* going down. As I thought about this, I realized that what I should do was go and unbar the door. So I did.

Morwen stepped inside and put a steely hand on my shoulder. Then she took in the room. 'What treachery has Branok wrought?' A look of panic crossed her face. 'His cursed eyes adorn the walls, watching me from all sides. His painted smirk cuts at my courage. No, not Branok. You!' Her grip grew so tight it hurt. 'You dare conjure his foul image here! You will bleed for this! You will bleed!'

Stuart

I jumped to meet him. There was nothing else to do, no time to think. If Rockford landed on Jago, Jago would die. It was as simple as that. I slammed into the huge man, sending him back against the stairs and me sailing across the room. I felt pain in my shoulder from the impact, then my back as I landed. After that, I was too stunned to think or feel anything.

Rockford's landing came a moment later and shook the ground beneath me. He'd hit the stairs like a wrecking ball and gone straight through them. I could already see him getting up, though. When I did the same, I felt weaker than I had before. They might all believe I could protect them from Tinker and the Captain, but Stone Rockford was clearly another matter. And right now, they were too close to the fight. Gary was doing his best to move Jago away from the stairs, and Tinker and I moved Gladys between us, while Enigma got Hitchcock clear.

'What's the plan?' I asked.

'He's too strong to fight,' replied Enigma. 'We must talk him down.'

'Hate to break it to you, mate,' said Tinker, 'but he don't look like he's interested in chatting right now.'

Rockford seemed to be in agreement. He broke his way out of the staircase, sending dust and wooden splinters in all directions. As before, he set his sights on Jago. Enigma bravely stood between them. He was holding his side, where the clothing had been burned away to reveal a set of gleaming metal ribs. As Enigma talked, Rockford marched. I couldn't tell if the words weren't getting through or if Rockford simply wasn't swayed. It wasn't going to work. We would have to fight. Somehow.

'Take him together!' I shouted and jumped onto Rockford's back. I wasn't able to exert any real pressure on his stone neck, but I tried to tilt his head away, hoping to slow him down at least.

Tinker picked up his launcher and fired a barrage of shards at Rockford's knees.

Little puffs of dust and porcelain blew outwards, but Rockford kept going. I pulled with all my strength, trying to twist him off course. It did nothing. Enigma reasoned, ordered, and pleaded, switching tack with remarkable skill. Rockford swept him aside like a doll with one sweep of his arm.

Tinker ran forward. He had that strange-looking bomb in his hand and it seemed like he was going to stick it to Rockford's chest. However, with surprising speed, Rockford lunged for him. I was taken along for the ride, more like a rucksack than a real opponent. My senses registered the cracking bone as Rockford's fist shattered at least two of Tinker's ribs, sending him spinning backwards.

With everyone else out of action, Rockford stood over Jago, one fist raised. I looped my arm around his, trying to gain leverage. He paused only to shake me off, throwing me across the room. I landed in a crouch, the wind knocked out of me. My power was even weaker. Nobody here thought I could save them from this, not even me. I tried to cross the room again, but I was so slow now - too slow.

Rockford raised his fist again.

Kelly

Morwen shook me hard enough to make my teeth clack together. 'What have you done to my house?'

'I made it Jago's again, so you'd be sealed up.' I hadn't meant to tell her that. There was this feeling that answering her was the right thing to do, but I found I didn't care as much.

'Undo your foul work.'

'I can't.'

'You dare defy me?'

'No. I mean, I can't help even if I wanted to. I locked your stuff in the desk, and I've swallowed the key.'

'Regurgitate that key, or I'll cut open your belly and pluck it from your innards.'

I didn't want to be sick, and suddenly her words were just words. I could do what I wanted again. Morwen didn't seem to have noticed though.

'OK,' I lied, and reached a finger towards my mouth. She took a step back, giving me a clear run to the door. Didn't want her grabbing me, so I kicked her in the shins, hard as I could. Hurt my toes but hurt her more! She screamed again, and I ran out into the corridor.

The hallways looked more familiar now: same wonky stone walls and shitty lights, but there were more Jago things about. Felt like the pictures of him were giving me approving looks as I ran, urging me on.

Morwen was coming, too. I could hear her running. Reckon it was the fastest she'd gone in a while. We raced each other through Loveday's rooms. Sometimes, the walls seemed a bit damp and crumbly, and sometimes they seemed normal. Sometimes, I'd see weird things I didn't recognize, and sometimes, I'd see weird things I did, but I always felt like I knew where I was going, like Loveday had my back. Finally, I came to that cold room with no glass in the window that had the view of the funny sky. I made myself not look at it, then I stepped into the corridor, panting. The frame wasn't warped any more, and the door closed easily. I caught a glimpse of Morwen on the other side just before it shut.

'I will strip the bones from your skin!' she screeched.

The handle tried to turn in my hand. I gripped it tightly and fished out the door key.

'I will curse your loins and every child that issues from them.'

I got the key in the lock and started to turn it. Like last time, it didn't want to rotate all the way. The metal cut into the skin of my hand.

'I will spit on your—'

Click.

Morwen's voice cut off, and I fell against the door in relief, cradling my hand to my belly. I'd fixed it. I didn't have to feel like shit any more.

There was nobody about to witness my success. I checked again, and when I was sure it was just me, I had a little cry.

Stuart

For what seemed like an age, Rockford held his fist in the air, poised to bring it down on a defenceless Jago. By the time I'd closed the gap between us, he'd started looking from his hand to Jago and back again. The man's demeanour had changed. Confusion had replaced aggression.

'Please don't hurt him,' I said.

Rockford turned to me in shock, then lowered his hand. Gradually, the stone covering his body began to recede, leaving him with a very troubled expression. 'I'm sorry,' he said to the room.

'It wasn't your fault,' I replied. 'It was Morwen. She did something to you.'

He shook his head, staring at his hands. They had started to shake. 'I should have been stronger.'

I got Gary to make a round of tea while I checked injuries. Tinker had broken two ribs and was in a lot of pain. Enigma was impossible to diagnose, but he claimed to just need some rest. Captain Racine was awfully battered from head to toe but was himself again at least. The others were either in shock but stable. Gladys, Hitchcock, and Jago needed urgent attention, though Jago was refusing any suggestion of going to hospital.

As soon as I was satisfied that everyone was safe, I addressed the room. 'I need to find my sister and the rest of the staff, and we need to send someone to bring a medical team here.'

'My people are safe,' said Jago softly. 'You will find a phone in my computer room. Ms Hill has the key.'

'Is that where she's gone?'

'She went to restore order, and by my reckoning has met with great success. You should be proud of her.'

I crouched down by Jago and tried to keep my voice calm. 'Where is she?'

He didn't answer straight away. Over the sounds of laboured breathing and Gary passing out cups of tea to the injured, I heard marching footsteps. Redcoat had returned. He came through the ruins of the main doors. My usual elation at the sight of him was tempered by the hatred in his eyes.

'Gladys,' he called, 'are you all right?'

'Yes, Jason.'

He continued to cross the room, his attention firmly on Jago. 'Close your eyes for me, love. You won't want to see this.'

I stood up. 'It's not Jago's fault. It was Morwen. Everyone's back to normal now.'

'Normal?' He gestured around at the broken room and the injured people. 'There is nothing normal about this place. We are in a house of lies and depravity, run by a masked demon. While he lives, there'll no end to this.'

'Steady on there, mate,' wheezed Tinker. 'Did you get hit in the head, too?'

'Stop, Jason,' said Enigma. 'What we need are answers, not more violence. The immediate threat is over.'

Redcoat was only a few feet away when Rockford put his huge body between us. I could see the stone slowly creeping back up his neck. 'I've already hit too many good people today,' he said, putting a steadying hand against Redcoat's chest. 'Don't make me add you to the list.'

The answering punch was so fast it took us all by surprise. A super-powered strike delivered directly to Rockford's jaw. The stone protection hadn't reached his face, and he went down like a felled tree.

'Jason, no!' screamed Gladys.

Redcoat wasn't listening to her, though. Most of the other aces were in no state to fight, but the Captain managed to raise a hand. Rainbow light flashed out, and Redcoat spun, catching the blast on the back of his coat, scattering it harmlessly before continuing forward, a murderous expression on his face.

I stepped over Jago and struck Redcoat square in the chest with open hands. He gave a grunt of surprise as he flew backwards, losing his footing.

The man used his momentum to roll as he fell, tumbling once before coming up on his feet.

'You're stronger than you let on yesterday, Stuart.' His eyes narrowed. 'Are you in league with Branok?'

I kept my hands spread and my voice calm. 'There's no need for us to fight. Jago isn't the enemy. Morwen is.'

'Don't you see? They're the same. Two demons presiding over a doorway to hell! I'll give you one chance to step aside.'

'You're Redcoat. The best of us all. I won't let you soil your name with innocent blood.'

'Trust me, there's nothing innocent about that man. Now stand aside. Last chance.'

My throat was suddenly too tight to speak, so I just shook my head. Perhaps Morwen still had him. I wanted to believe that. Whatever the truth, I could not let Redcoat become a murderer. The room was with me; I could feel it: Enigma, Gladys, Tinker, Hitchcock, Gary, Captain Racine, and Jago himself. They all trusted me to handle this, and I could not let them down.

He came forward, more wary of me this time. I tried to push him back again, but he knocked my hands aside with a circular motion of his arms and tried to grab me. Only my enhanced reflexes allowed me to get out of the way. Faster than he could follow, I stepped away from his swing and wrapped my arms around him. With this much support, I hoped to match him in strength. We struggled against each other for a few seconds, and then he twisted his arms, breaking my hold.

The next thing I knew, his elbow was in my stomach and then my face, and then his booted foot was sweeping my legs. I hit the floor hard, but his follow-up kicks hit even harder. My toughened body absorbed the blows as I curled into a ball, but they still hurt. When they stopped, I lowered my hands to stare up at him.

'Stay down,' he warned. 'You're not a fighter.'

A sudden surge of strength flooded through me, and I heard Kelly's voice. 'He's not like you. He's a proper hero!'

I looked back to find her panting in the doorway. Her face was puffy and red. She'd been crying recently, and she was holding her hand as if it was hurt. Her chin was raised defiantly, though. I gave her my best smile.

'Don't worry, Kelly. I've got this.'

'I know. Go fuck him up.'

Redcoat swung another kick at me. I caught his foot in both hands and flung his leg upwards. He stumbled and fell as I leaped to my feet.

'Stay down, please,' I said. 'I don't want to fight you.'

Redcoat dived between my legs to get at Jago, grabbing at him, but I caught him by the collar and dragged him back before he could land a blow. As I swung him clear, I realized he had something new in his hand: Jago's pistol.

He rolled sideways to get a clear shot, his fingers already squeezing the trigger. I didn't have time to stop him firing, but I had time to take a single sidestep to move between them, to hold out a hand and hope that he wouldn't cross that line.

The air was alive with shouts and cries. They seemed drawn out to me, slow. I picked out the sound of the hammer of the pistol slamming down and the boom of the bullet being launched. I saw Redcoat's eyes widen with horror as he realized I had moved into his firing line.

The bullet slammed into my palm, making my fingers naturally curl around it. I felt the sting of impact, but that was all it was. A sting. The bullet did not burst through the other side or even break the skin. I opened my hand in wonder, to find the bullet still there, squashed flat.

The horror in Redcoat's eyes changed to amazement, and my powers grew still further. Finally, he believed in me as well, but I took no pleasure in it.

'It's over,' I said.

He stared at me for a moment. I couldn't read the emotions playing on his face, but he dropped the gun. The sound of it clattering on the floor was awfully loud.

'I didn't mean to hurt you, Stuart; you have to believe that.'

'I do.'

'It's this place. It's all wrong. Lord Branok is wrong. It's messing with my mind.'

'It's OK. You can rest now.'

Eyes still on me, he sank to his knees and covered his face with his hands.

Not wanting to think about him, I turned to Kelly. 'We need a medical team here. Jago says there's a phone in the computer room. Can you handle the call?'

She jangled a big set of keys at me. 'Course I can.'

Kelly

For once, I was glad that I wasn't an adult. After I'd called for an air ambulance, things got pretty real. Everyone was knackered and angry and full of questions, but luckily, they were all for Jago, not me, because I reckon Enigma would have figured out it was my fault in about ten seconds flat if he'd thought to ask me. I played up being tired and went to bed. Turned out that was truer than I thought, because I slept for hours.

The next day, I went to Jago's office and knocked on the door.

'Come in, Ms Hill.'

I went in. He was wearing bandages under his suit, but he looked way better than I'd expected him to.

'How did you know it was me?'

'All of my other visitors have used a much more officious knock.'

I put his keys on the table. 'Thought you'd want these back.'

'Thank you, and not just for the keys. Your actions saved us all.'

'I thought you'd be angry with me . . .'

'In my opinion, an adventurous spirit is something to be cultivated, not punished.'

'That's not what my mum says.'

'Between us, I suspect your mother and I would disagree on a great many things, Ms Hill.'

'Yeah. She's not big into masks and tentacles. Anyway, we're going soon, so I wanted to say goodbye and . . .' I took out the little key Morwen had given me and the key to her door. 'You should probably have these, too. You might want to wash the little one again, just in case.' I didn't meet his gaze. 'I . . . um . . . I liked it here. I won't forget Loveday, and I'm sorry you're in the shit with everyone.'

He looked at the keys for a while and then back at me. I still didn't meet his gaze.

'In a few years' time, when you have completed your studies, I'd like to offer you a job.'

'What?' Now I did look at him.

His eyes had gone crinkly behind the mask, like he was grinning. 'A job. As my assistant. You'll have to live here, of course.'

'For real?'

'Yes.'

'What would I do?'

'Assist me in my duties.'

'That could mean anything.'

He was still smiling. 'Indeed. It is an unusual post that is uniquely challenging, but you've already displayed the required resourcefulness and have adapted to the house with remarkable speed.'

'It's really nice of you, but I don't think my parents will let me.'

He laughed then, out loud. 'In a few years, they won't be able to stop you. It's time for you to consider your future, Ms Hill. There are many pathways you could take.' He held up a finger. 'Don't give me an answer right now. Think on it. I will be in touch when you're of age.' He stood up and offered me his hand. 'You can keep the ring as a memento.'

I went bright red. I'd forgotten all about the ring I'd stolen from his drawer. 'Oh. Um. Thanks.'

'Take care, Ms Hill.'

'Bye,' I said, and we shook hands.

He was still smiling as I left. I think he already knew my answer.

Stuart

It was time to go home. A lot of the guests had already left, either by air ambulance the previous night or as soon as a taxi could take them. I was standing on the steps, waiting for Kelly, when Enigma came to find me.

'Good morning, Stuart.'

'Good morning, Enigma.'

'Please, call me Alan. On behalf of the Silver Helix, I wanted to express our thanks for your intervention.'

I felt my chest puff out at the praise. 'I was just doing my job.'

'True, and you were doing ours when we were unable to. Without you, a truly terrible threat would have been unleashed on the world. Though the public will never be aware of what transpired here, they are in your debt.'

If I were a dog, I'd have been rolling around on the floor with joy. I did my best to stay professional. 'Have you had any news about Redcoat?'

He sighed. 'I understand that you and Jason travelled beyond this world and that it had a profoundly traumatic effect on him. His behaviour since then has been regrettable, to say the least. Moreover, it seems to me that his final attack on Jago Branok and yourself occurred when he was no longer under the effects of Morwen's compulsion, and as such he is entirely responsible for them.'

'What's going to happen to him?'

'He will be given a break from active duty and support to come to terms with what happened. He is very upset over his recent conduct, especially regarding his actions against you.'

The memory of our fight made my bruises twinge. 'I hope he finds a way past this.'

'He asked me to make a request on his behalf.'

'Oh?'

'One moment.'

Enigma went back into Loveday and returned shortly afterwards with a suit bag. 'He asked if you would look after this for him, until such time as he has earned the right to wear it again.'

I didn't need to look to know what was inside, but I looked anyway, pulling the zip a little way down to expose the iconic red fabric beneath. 'I . . . thank you. I hardly know what to say. Please tell him I'll keep it safe.'

'Excellent. I hope you have a pleasant journey home.'

'It was a genuine honour to meet you, sir. Alan.'

'Keep up the good work, Hero. I'll be taking a keen interest in your future endeavours.'

And with that, he shook my hand and left. I just stood there, unsure of how to feel. I think I was stunned, mostly.

Kelly turned up shortly afterwards with her bags. She looked surprisingly upbeat.

'I'm sorry I dragged you into all this,' I said.

'That's OK. I like shitshows.'

'I'm proud of you, Kelly.'

She stopped and smiled at me. 'Thanks, Stu. You were awesome yesterday. Told you that you were the best.'

We walked towards the waiting car together. 'Remember,' I added. 'We can't tell Mum and Dad about any of this.'

She nodded very seriously. 'I know. That's why we had to sign those papers.' We got into the car, and it started to pull out of the drive. 'It's been really scary and all, but it's been good, too, you know?'

I looked at the suit bag sitting on my lap, felt the weight of it, and thought about how the other aces had said goodbye and how it was so different to when we first met. I was one of them now. An equal.

'Yes,' I agreed. 'I know. But let's never do this again, OK?'

'Mmm,' said Kelly. She'd turned to look out of the window at Loveday House.

I decided to do the same. Even as it faded from view, I had the strangest feeling I'd see it again one day.

Longing for Those Lost

by Stephen Leigh

Part V

THE LADY MORWEN THAT Kelly had dealt with wasn't Gary's Lady Morwen. He realized that as soon as Kelly described her; her speech patterns were too 'modern', and the area in Loveday from where she'd emerged wasn't at all near where Gary had encountered 'his' Lady Morwen. No – these were two different Mad Morwens from divergent alternate time-lines, each with her own abilities but both harbouring the same hatred of Jago and of the people he brought into the house. The same megalomania.

It hadn't seemed worth explaining all that to Kelly and the others, nor did he know if Jago wanted him to reveal that much of Loveday's inner workings. So, Gary said nothing except to Jago. All that mattered was that Jago knew that this was yet another Lady Morwen and that Kelly seemed to have dealt with her.

Gary was pleased with that. It was enough. At least, it was for now, anyway, though it started him wondering about how Jago might handle the next occurrence and how Gary should react to it if and when it happened.

The tabloids like the *Daily Mail*, *The Sun*, and the *Mirror*, as well the general social media had a field day with Lord Branok's party, or the 'Aces Badly Dealt Fold' gathering, as the *Daily News* headline proclaimed. The erratic behaviour of the aces and the injuries they had sustained even reached across the Atlantic to the *National Enquirer*, *Aces!*, *TMZ*, and *E!*, though the articles generally didn't rise to front-page-headline status, given that the aces involved were mainly Brits.

A whirlwind storm of reporters and TV cameras once again besieged Keun Island and Loveday House, though not quite with the hurricane ferocity and breadth that had accompanied the deaths of Digger Downs and Margot Bellarose and the stunning arrest of *American Hero*'s Kandy Kane. This time, it was mainly the London tabloids, television, and social media commentators that arrived, clamouring for more salacious information. Gary and Ceallaigh watched through the windows of the ground floor as Jago held a single press conference before the main doors of Loveday House, with Hitchcock and Elbrekt solemnly flanking him, ready to intercept anyone who might attempt to storm the podium placed before the steps.

'Lord Branok's not happy,' Ceallaigh said, her arm entwined with Gary's as she leaned against him. 'Look, his cheeks are red below his mask, and it's not the weather causin' that.'

'I wouldn't be happy either if I had to talk to that crowd.' Gary shook his head. 'The British reporters are more aggressive than those in the States. Still, if it hadn't been for Kelly and Stuart Hill, this would have been a lot worse, with a much higher body count. There'd be an entire *sea* of reporters out there now from all over the world, with politicians and other authorities calling for the head of the person they thought responsible – which would very likely have been Lord Branok. No one died this time. There were just bruised egos and bodies. Jago can explain it away as a group of aces whose pissing contest got rather out of hand.'

Ceallaigh's head tilted towards him. 'Pissing contest?'

'Never mind. I'll explain later. But Jago's confident he can handle them.'

The press briefing didn't last long, and Jago didn't linger to take questions. They saw him leave the podium after a brisk ten minutes, striding back towards the main doors as reporters shouted unanswered questions and cameras flashed. Madame Amélie opened the door just wide enough to let Lord Branok slip inside; Hitchcock and Elbrekt remained outside to prevent anyone from approaching, with liveried footmen Étienne, Niall, Raymond, and Enyon joining Hitchcock as further backup, just in case. Gary released Ceallaigh's arm, backing away from the window as Jago beckoned Madame Amélie and Gary over. He ushered them into a side room before addressing them. His eyes glittered in his mask's eyeholes, his demeanour serious.

'Madame Amélie, Gary, I'm going to also say this to Hitchcock as soon as he's free, as well as to Chef Daniel and any others who understand what Loveday is. You must caution your charges not to go wandering in some sections of the house – I trust you both know what areas I mean – and to avoid opening any unfamiliar doors. Our young Ms Hill has hopefully prevented this particular Mad Morwen from interfering with anyone at Loveday for the nonce, but we can't be certain how long that may be the case or when someone might unearth yet another Morwen. Everyone must be vigilant going forward. If there are problems or concerns, I expect to be notified immediately so I can deal with them. Is that understood?'

'I will inform the house staff immediately,' Madame Amélie said.

Jago waved a hand towards her; the woman nodded, closing the door behind her.

Gary waited until he heard the latch click into its slot in the escutcheon.

'The house feels restless to me,' he told Jago, 'despite this new Lady Morwen being locked away.'

Jago frowned. 'As I've told you before, Gary, the house *isn't sentient*. It's not a person, and it doesn't *feel* anything. Nor do any of the Morwens control it. None of them.'

'I understand that. But you've told me that Loveday House *can* pick up on strong feelings – fears or affections or what have you – and reflect those back, as it has with my Caitlyn and Moira. Well, Loveday House, for whatever reason, has connected with me. I felt that when I first came here, and it's much of the reason I stayed on when you asked. And now I'm feeling Loveday roiling underneath the surface. Morwen's various iterations have infected it, and none of the Morwens are your friend.'

Jago gave an audible sigh. 'I've had to deal with her many times over the years that I've owned Loveday House. I can handle Lady Morwen. Any of them. Believe me.'

'I believe that was true in the past, Jago. I just hope that continues to be true.'

'I don't know if I should tell you this,' Ceallaigh said a week later as she and Gary lay together in their bed. The windows were open to the night breezes and were billowing inwards. Ceallaigh snuggled close to Gary's heat.

There was no moon that night, and the room was nearly pitch black, so Gary could see only vague images of the furniture. His arm was around Ceallaigh, a greater darkness against her pale Irish skin.

'If you don't know, then maybe you shouldn't say anything. But I suspect you will.'

Ceallaigh slapped Gary's chest.

'Ouch,' he said. 'That stung.'

'You deserve it, you cheeky bastard.' She turned away from him, sheets rustling. She was silent long enough that Gary began to wonder if she was genuinely annoyed with him. Then, her voice came from the darkness. 'I've heard from other maids on staff that they've had to call Lord Branok to deal with strange occurrences recently.'

'Strange occurrences?'

'Usually at night. Nothing terrible or dangerous, just . . . *unusual* and somewhat disturbing. There was a strange pig-like creature snorting and bellowing and roaming the corridors on the servants' floor last Sunday. They could all hear its hooves clacking away on the tiles. Jago and Elbrekt came down with their shotguns. They didn't manage to kill the beastie, but they did chase it from the house. Me friends Colette, Maire, Solène, and Isolde reported someone banging on doors another night, but when they opened their doors to look, no one could be seen in the hallway. Lord Branok came down to investigate, and though there were scratches and dents a'plenty on the girls' doors, they never found anyone or anything who might be responsible. And just last night . . .' Ceallaigh went silent.

Gary wondered if she'd decided not to say more. 'Last night?' he prompted.

'Last night . . .' Ceallaigh's voice again drifted through the room's darkness. 'Madame Amélie woke from a terrible dream to find a man in her room . . . or what appeared to be a man. He was standing in front of the banked fire in her fireplace, naked and backlit, and what was hanging down between his legs didn't seem to be a human appendage at all. There was also a foul smell in the room, making Madame Amélie nauseated. When she screamed, the coals flashed as if lit from the very fires of hell, and when she could see again, the apparition was gone.'

'It could have been just the remnant of a nightmare.'

'Maybe, but the creature's foul smell remained. Those who came in response to her scream all smelled it – "like that of a carcass left to moulder and rot for a month," Chef Daniel described it. The odour was still lingering in the air when Lord Branok came. They moved Madame Amélie to another room for the rest of the night. Isolde stayed with her, with a revolver that Lord Branok gave them in case the fiend returned.'

Gary felt Ceallaigh shudder, and he rolled over to embrace her. He decided not to tell her the similar stories he'd heard from Hitchcock, from Elbrekt, from Annie the groundskeeper. He also didn't tell her that he could *feel* the turmoil inside Loveday House, its sleep as uneasy as his own. He kept all that to himself but resolved to speak with Jago again tomorrow.

'Morwen's door is locked, Gary,' Jago insisted. He was wearing a red mask that covered half of his face. 'None of what's happened of late is her doing, and there's been no injury to anyone. They're just troubling images and sounds. Nightmares, if you will. That's all.'

'Then what's causing them?' Gary asked.

'Loveday has many doors, and one or more of those may have opened, creating this leakage. If so, I'll find them and seal them again. But I'm telling you that Kelly locked her Morwen's door, and we've done the same for your Lady Morwen. Her claws have been clipped.'

'Doors can be locked and unlocked from either side,' Gary persisted. 'Maybe Kelly's key wasn't the only one. Maybe Morwen has kept her own. If I could find her door again, I'd check myself.'

'Doors are not always found in the same place here, especially in the deeper reaches of Loveday.'

Gary laughed shortly and bitterly. *If they did stay in the same place, I might*

find Caitlyn, Moira, and Duncan whenever I wished, and avoid Morwen's attacks.
'I know that all too well, I'm afraid. But you're *certain* that Morwen's door
is locked? Both of them?'

'Tonight, after dinner, we can go there and find out.'

'I'll wear Constance's bathrobe and bring Morwen's knife.'

A trace of a smile touched Jago's lips. 'After dinner, then. I'll come to
your room.'

After dinner, as promised, there was a knock on Gary's door. He opened it.
'Jago, please come in.'

Gary was wearing Constance's bathrobe over his clothes, and Morwen's
dagger lay heavily in the right pocket. Jago wore a bedroom jacket over a
white shirt, black trousers, and a new mask with a flowing wing. He had
two large LED torches, one of which he handed to Gary, but if he carried
any weapon, it wasn't visible.

Ceallaigh stood leaning against the balcony doors, looking concerned.
She'd not been happy when Gary had told her what he and Jago intended.

'Lord Branok,' she said, 'I trust you'll take care of Gary and keep him
safe.'

'I intend to,' Jago answered. 'But I don't believe there's anything to worry
about. No one's been harmed by any of the apparitions we've seen of late,
just frightened.'

Gary hugged and kissed Ceallaigh, then followed Jago out into the hallway.
They followed the corridor until they reached the end, then followed its
continuation to the left. That hallway was dim, the wall sconces flickering,
old wallpaper that looked to be from the 1930s or '40s peeling from the
walls. They flicked on their torches, which made dual circles of bright, bluish-
white light, revealing ragged carpeting with the nap worn down nearly to
the backing over the floorboards. Further down, the electric wall sconces
gave way to gas ones, and there were passageways leading into new hallways,
sometimes at strange angles.

Gary felt the familiar sense of being lost as the carpeting gave way to a
floor of broken tiles, then to just bare wood. The halls were now lit by iron
sconces from which hung metal baskets with coals glowing inside, and the
smell of smoke was strong. Their torch beams stabbed through a visible haze.

'Here,' Jago said at last, stopping before an iron-barred wooden door with
ornate scrollwork. The door was slightly warped, so that it sat faintly askew
in its frame. 'This is your Lady Morwen's chamber.'

Jago reached down to the door handle: ancient bronze, burnished with
the touch of innumerable hands. Jago's fingers tightened around it. He
twisted and pulled; the door moved only slightly.

'You see, it's still locked.' Jago sounded relieved, but when he pulled harder, now rattling the door in its frame, a familiar mocking laugh came from behind the scarred boards, causing Gary to shiver and put his hand on the pommel of Morwen's dagger.

'Aye, I know who ye are, standing before my door: the great Lord Branok, so blindly certain of himself, and his puppet, the Burning Man. Lord Branok is but a *bobba* – an idiot and fool. *Aller se faire mettre!*' she howled in archaic French: *Fuck off.*

'Such foul language, Lady Morwen, but your words can do me no harm. This is *my* domain, not yours, and I will keep it that way – no matter what you try!' Jago called back.

'You will fail. The false Lord Branok's time is ending.' Morwen's curse was a screech, a wail carried on a dark wind. 'I've rested and recovered. I've cast the bones and glimpsed the future. This is *my* castle. You will see. The Great Storm is rising, as it did once before in my own time, and it will sweep all of you away. Can you not feel it? Can you not sense the storm's power?'

Gary felt a cold wind moving in the hallway, snaking around them with the salt smell of the sea.

Jago shook his head and gave a mocking huff. 'More empty illusions, Lady Morwen? We'll leave you to them. Enjoy the prison of your chambers.' Jago grinned at Gary. 'Now, let's check the door that Kelly locked.'

They did so, Jago leading the way through the maze of corridors. 'This one,' Jago said finally, pointing at a door that looked eerily similar to Jago's office door in the more normal parts of the house. He tried to turn the handle. He pushed hard so that the door rattled in the frame. If Lady Morwen was inside, she remained silent.

'Locked,' Jago grunted. 'You see, Gary? Everything's as it should be. Let's get back. Tomorrow, we have guests to invite. Bonfire Night is coming, after all.'

As they walked away from Morwen's chamber, Gary glanced over to Jago. 'You can't be serious. New guests again? After what happened the last few times?'

'Ah, but I am serious, Dance Master,' came the answer. 'I won't have empty threats disrupting my plans.'

The Nautilus Pattern

by Kevin Andrew Murphy

I T WAS A LOVELY, if slightly blustery, late afternoon in early November when Nigel Walmsley wove his way up the winding road to Loveday House, as he had so many times before. But rather than carrying a pair of eighteenth-century Blue John cassolette urns to burn incense at the ends of a mantelpiece or a marble Euripides to ornament Lord Branok's library, this time he was bringing a treasure far more precious and beautiful: Susan, his wife.

Susan Strathmore sat beside him, pert in antique hunting pinks – but mostly for fun, since Loveday's fox-hunting days were long past, and this weekend, the promised shooting would be for pigeon and pheasant. Susan had kept her last name from her modelling days, along with her looks and her figure. Her cloud of carefully coiffed golden ringlets looked artless, and her blue eyes sparkled.

Once again, he found himself wondering – as he always did – why she was with him. What had she seen in him that day in his antique shop that made her tie her life to his? Especially given her former taste in men?

Perhaps it had just been stability she was seeking, but whatever it was, he was grateful. She added a spice to his life that he had never envisioned having, even in his wildest dreams.

'Pay attention to the road, Nigel!'

'Sorry, dear.' Nigel turned his gaze back to the treacherous turns. It wouldn't do to go off a cliff – especially now, having finally received an invitation to one of Lord Branok's legendary parties . . . and what's more, for Bonfire Night. Nigel knew that Jago Branok was a wild card of some sort – probably a joker, since they were most common and he always kept his face covered – but he'd poured enough money into Keun (and Nigel's own pocket) to have earned the right to be called Lord Branok, regardless of whether he was in fact heir to any piece of paper from the Crown. As for his guests, usually they were famous folk – aces and royalty, captains of industry and the like, not local nat antique dealers and their wives, no matter how pretty.

Susan, that is, not Nigel. Nigel knew he had the Keun Island look – and a bad case at that: small, watery-eyed, and balding, with a weak chin. That came of being descended from inbred fisherfolk; even a nice singing voice didn't make up for it.

Susan's former beau, Dylan Hardesty, on the other hand, had been huge even before the wild card. Then the virus had taken that frame and enhanced it, turning him into an antlered sex god, the spitting image of Cernunnos off the Gundestrup Cauldron – or Herne the Hunter, as he had liked to style himself. Compared to that? It was enough to make any man feel inadequate.

But Dylan had been gone for thirty years now – dead, most said, in the Rox War, in New York, where he had last been sighted riding a horse naked across the Brooklyn Bridge. Though with the Rox War, what was truth and what was fantasy was hard to say, given the psychic projections of the Rox's ruler, the knave Bloat, which ranged from lance-wielding Boschian fish knights to the Statue of Liberty turned into a pornographic pin-up, to say nothing of Bloat transforming Ellis Island into the Rox: a fairy-tale fortress composed in equal parts from childish dreams and psychic dread, with a mental compulsion forbidding all but jokers from entering its demesne. So pulling Dylan's likeness from his celebrated stag films and sending it rampaging through town like Lady Godiva's randy knave brother, was very much within the realm of probability. Susan had prayed that that was all it was: a figment from Bloat's perverted imagination, and that her first love would return to her. But days and weeks had turned to months and years, and she had come to accept Dylan was well and truly gone.

In the years since, Nigel knew, Susan had found contentment with him. Nigel hoped it was true contentment. But he also knew she had never forgotten her loss. He could see it in her eyes sometimes: those moments she remembered.

'I wonder who cancelled,' mused Susan, gazing out the window.

'Likewise,' he agreed. 'But I'm just glad they did. Wish that courier of yours had turned up in time for us to bring a gift for our host.'

'He still may,' Susan said. 'I texted him the address.'

Nigel smiled. Susan had her sources and her secrets, which was one of the many things he loved about her. A man did well to marry a woman with a little history and mystery, for surprises were what made life exciting – and seeing that Jago had given Nigel a long list of historic oddments and curios he wanted hunted down, it was pleasant when Susan used her wiles to scare one up, like the medieval French garnet choker she had once posed in for photographs as Morgan le Fay, though it had actually, or at least more recently, belonged to Lady Morwen, the madwoman of Keun. Tracking it down together had been an adventure – and a sexual one at that.

Jago had been pleased with this purchase, his first of many, and Susan allowed Nigel to take all the credit. But it would have been better for her latest find to be more timely. Nigel liked surprises but hated being late.

They'd delayed as long as they could at THE MERMAID'S CHEST, their shop, before setting out, so he did his best to make up for lost time, speeding up the switchbacks.

'Careful, Nigel!'

Nigel was being careful, but the hairpin turn at the cliff was impressive, nonetheless. Then two more twists of the road and they'd arrived at Loveday.

Susan hopped out of the car, riding boots crunching on the crushed seashells that paved the drive. Nigel followed, gazing up at the house as always.

Loveday House held a great fascination to an antiquities dealer such as himself and not the least for its history: a grand Victorian manor, built on the ruins of the much older Loveday Castle, which had collapsed in the Great Storm of 1703, taking its owner, Mad Morwen, with it. Several storeys towered up, with turrets spiring higher, up to a shining, faceted, domed skylight at the top, undoubtedly providing illumination to Jago's famous library, made of the same gleaming panes that had once bedizened the belvedere that adorned the seaward side in days past. Jago was continually adding something new he'd dreamed up or replacing something old that had tumbled down in the years in which Loveday had fallen into disrepair, home only to looters, squatters, and the occasional young birder like Nigel, who used to come up the cliffs to see the fowl, then take shelter when the weather changed.

The wide stone steps up were still much the same as in his youth – ancient granite, likely dating back to Morwen's castle, or possibly even made up of the standing stones that had once stood upon the windswept hill in the time of the druids.

The weathered old double doors were carved with floral motifs and curious sea monsters frolicking in a spiral dance, like the whorled chambers of a nautilus or ammonite, around twin bronze knockers in the shape of fierce hounds holding huge rings in their mouths. The rings were bronze as well, with the strikers in the shape of monkey's paw bight knots – a conscious attempt by Marcus St Gerren to draw on the history of the Hounds of the Sea. But placed in the hounds' mouths, as they were, they also gave the impression of pups holding enormous chew toys. The left knocker was more worn than the right, and Nigel reached up and knocked thrice.

That door was opened almost instantly by an older, bald gentleman: Hitchcock, Jago's butler. Hitchcock had a bit of the Keun Island look himself (not that Nigel had ever met him before Jago's arrival) and the demeanour of a butler from an old film – which, Nigel suspected, was probably why Jago had hired him.

'Good afternoon, Mr Walmsley, Ms Strathmore,' Hitchcock greeted them.

'Are we in time for the shooting?' Susan asked brightly.

'More than an hour past, I'm afraid, ma'am,' Hitchcock told her with a doleful tone. 'Lord Branok is still out riding with Ms Blackwood. But there'll be shooting on the morrow. Let me show you to your rooms now so that you can get freshened up, then you may join the other guests in the ballroom when you're ready.'

'Oh, all right, then.' Susan sounded slightly disappointed, until Hitchcock opened the door wider, ushering them into Loveday House's entrance hall. It never failed to impress: stunning chandeliers, black-and-white-checked chessboard tiles, and a grand staircase at the far end, leading up to a landing and then forking right and left to the gallery above and a magnificent stained-glass window.

Nigel had been at the house many times before, of course, as part of his dealings with Lord Branok, but it was Susan's first visit, and to be staying here as actual guests was another thing entirely.

Nigel met Susan's eyes and knew her excitement matched his own.

'Might I have your car keys?'

'Oh, yes, of course,' Nigel apologized, handing them to Hitchcock, who just as swiftly passed them to the first of a bevy of liveried footmen. They stepped out the front doors, then reappeared almost as quickly, lugging Nigel and Susan's suitcases, spiriting them up the grand staircase and off to the left.

Hitchcock gestured for them to follow at a more sedate pace and led them up the stairs and down the hall. Nigel was much more familiar with Loveday in its ruined state, not as it was now, extensively restored and redecorated, but he believed they were on the first floor, in the corner where the west hall met the south hall – a part of the current Loveday he had never visited before.

Hitchcock produced a key ring. From it hung a gilded key, on a brass ring with a fob depicting a mermaid. 'The key to the Mermaid Room, formerly known as the Green Room. There's a dumbwaiter between the bedroom and sitting room if you wish to take meals in your rooms, or you may come downstairs to the morning room or dining room, depending on the time of day.'

'Is the ballroom still where I remember it?' Nigel asked.

'Usually,' Hitchcock joked. He indicated a staircase behind them, with a newel-post lamp in the shape of a mermaid holding up an emerald globe, then disappeared down the stairs himself.

Nigel said, somewhat impishly, 'Shall we?' and Susan nodded with enthusiasm.

The key turned with a barely audible click, and Nigel revealed the room. It was furnished in Art Nouveau style, full of pieces with which Nigel was intimately familiar: a fireplace carved with mermaids, which he'd sourced from a Parisian townhouse; a coffee table carved to resemble a lily pad, which he'd acquired at the Bruges Zandfeesten, the renowned Belgian antiques fair; and an elegant rosewood sofa carved in the shape of a swan with a sinuous neck. A disembodied maiden's head floated above the swan as a backrest, her tresses tracing the French curves. This one was from an auction in Lyon, bought for a song but sold to Jago for the price of a whole opera, for while it was unsigned, Nigel suspected it was an early piece designed by Hector Guimard, the master of Art Nouveau.

But the room boasted other pieces with which Nigel was completely unfamiliar, notably the stained-glass panels fashioned with mermaids and the fanciful wind-borne shells of paper nautili topping the curved bay windows of the window seat.

Susan rushed forward, looking out, then exclaimed, 'Oh, look, Nigel, you can see all the way to the beach! We've got our own private stairway down, too.'

'Well, maybe not completely private,' Nigel allowed, pointing to a door to the right. 'If this is the old Green Suite, then that door should lead to the Peacock Suite. But Jago has been making so many renovations, who knows where it leads now?'

Susan flounced down onto the window seat. 'You're no fun.' She grinned then. 'Let's see our bedroom.'

'Of course, my dear,' Nigel said. 'Should I carry you over the threshold?'

'You can try . . .' Susan came towards him, towering over him, model tall, but Nigel didn't mind. It gave him a nice view.

Nigel opened the connecting door to the bedroom, then did his best to hoist Susan up over the threshold.

Once, he could have done it. Once, he'd been an avid birder, climbing cliffs at will. But he'd grown older, and Susan had gained a few curves, so Nigel didn't so much carry her over the threshold as tumble through it with her on top of him.

Thankfully, the carpet was soft. 'Nigel, are you all right?'

'Never better,' Nigel mumbled from beneath her breasts.

'Naughty man.' Susan laughed and lifted herself up. 'That's what I like best about you.' She kissed him, then rolled off to lie beside him. 'Oh, my goodness!'

Nigel looked up, seeing what Susan was seeing now, and gazed in wonder. Jago's decorators, in high Victorian fashion, had wallpapered the ceiling in poison green – specifically William Morris's 'Seaweed' pattern – though hopefully a reproduction without the arsenic. Yet hanging high in the vault, suspended by almost invisible wires, were fanciful Black Forest lamps, the front halves carved in the shapes of Germanic mermaids and mermen, bearing Edison bulbs in their outstretched hands. Their back halves were the natural branches of antlers.

'Looks as if Jago decorated for both of us,' Susan remarked. 'You're fond of mermaids, and I've always liked antlers . . .'

Susan's ex, thirty years past, had had antlers as part of his joker deformity. Nigel didn't appreciate the reminder.

'Well, we'd best get freshened up quickly. Jago will be expecting us.'

The ballroom boasted an inglenook at one end that was almost a room within a room, with cosy benches to each side, padded hearth fenders before the cavernous fireplace providing even more seating, and high pilasters holding up the elaborate marble mantelpiece. Over that hung a painting with which Nigel was intimately familiar: a hunting scene of the St Gerren fox hunt, with Marcus St Gerren leading the hunt out over the strand of Keun to the mainland of Cornwall, the tide rushing in around the feet of the foxhounds, making it look almost like they were running upon the surface of the water. Loveday House was perched like a crown on top of the bluffs in the background.

Nigel had seen the painting once when he was a teenager – a battered thing, stained with the smoke of a thousand cigars, despite being an original George Wright. When Nigel had come back to Loveday in his early twenties, it had been gone, torn out of its frame. But Nigel was learning the family trade and eventually located the rolled-up canvas at a disreputable antique dealer in London.

'How did you get it restored so well?' Nigel breathed in wonder. 'It looks almost new.'

'The Italians are experts in these matters,' Jago said simply, then admitted, 'but I also had the artist retouch it in spots.'

The Lord of Loveday House was tall, wearing well-cut riding clothes. It being Bonfire Night, he'd got into the spirit and was masked not as the usual vaingloriously black-goateed and moustachioed Guy Fawkes, but as a local Cornish character, with a cap depicting moons and stars, and a brilliantly white beard and moustache: the wise visage of Merlin the magician, who had his cave at Tintagel.

Nigel took this choice of masks to signify that Jago favoured Arthur, the new joker king, much as Merlin had favoured the original Arthur. But Nigel preferred to avoid politics.

'Well, not the original artist,' said Nigel. 'Wright died in the Forties.'

'No, not the original,' Jago agreed, inscrutable behind his Merlin mask. 'But very, very close, don't you think?'

'He certainly captured the horses well,' said a petite, ginger-haired woman in a black-velvet riding jacket, masked as Nimue, Merlin's apprentice – assuming Nimue had an American accent. She was also carrying an impressive and equally American pump-action double-barrelled shotgun, which Nigel stared at until she reached up and doffed her black silk top hat, like a magician doing a trick, then dropped her shotgun down the hat, causing it to disappear like a conjurer's rabbit.

'Ms Melissa Blackwood,' Jago said, 'may I present Mr Nigel Walmsley, our local historian and folklorist? And his wife, Susan Strathmore.'

'You can call me Topper,' said the ace.

Guy Fawkes was in attendance as well – or, at least, a man wearing a Fawkes mask and a sugarloaf hat along with the livery of a Regency dancing master, his white-gloved hands bearing a tray laden with masks. Two more guests stood beyond, masked as Punch and Judy but dressed as a pearly queen and king, with names emblazoned in pearl buttons on the backs of their jackets. Punch's declared her to be *MASH*, while Judy's declared him *BANGER*.

'Mr Gary Bushorn,' Lord Branok said, gesturing to Guy Fawkes, then to Judy and Punch, 'and Alfred and Petula Spragg, of the Silver Helix.'

Nigel recognized Mash as the former Miss Punch, an ace brawler often on the wrong side of the law, who'd changed her name and ways when she'd married Banger and joined MI7 years back.

Jago turned to Fawkes's tray and its assortment of witches', dragons', saints', and kings' masks. 'Let's see,' he said, shuffling through a panoply of Arthurian characters, pulling out a haggard old grey-moustached king and a curious joker, whose face looked like the head of a leopard-spotted snake with little giraffe horns. 'Perhaps King Pellinore and the Questing Beast? But no, I think something a bit more Cornish is in order . . .' He dug down in the pile. 'Ms Strathmore?' He held up the mask of a wide-eyed ingenue with yellow yarn hair and her mouth open in an 'O' of amazement. 'Perhaps Duffy?'

'Oh, I do like Duffy.' Susan accepted the mask eagerly. 'I've played her before.' Duffy was the star of 'Duffy and the Devil', a popular local guise dance, the Cornish variant of Rumpelstiltskin.

'And if we have a Duffy, then we must have the Devil,' Jago declared, offering the matching mask to Nigel.

Nigel paused. Duffy was a lazy servant girl who got a clever little devil to spin and sew in her place. Nigel glanced to the rest of the cast's masks, recognizing Squire Lovell, Duffy's master and later husband; Huey Lenine, Duffy's lover, both before and after her elevation to Lady Lovell; and Old Joan, Lovell's housekeeper and, secretly, a witch.

In Nigel's mind, Susan's rakish young lover would always be Dylan. And while Nigel might be Susan's husband, he had never felt like her master. Besides, the middle-aged, podgy squire felt a bit too close to home, and Susan had always liked horns.

Nigel accepted Jago's selection and put on the Devil mask.

'This being Bonfire Night, I thought I might show you something a bit special,' Jago mentioned to the assembled company, then turned to Hitchcock. 'Could you lead the way, Taliesin?'

Hitchcock, dressed in his usual butler's attire, was already masked as a fair-faced young man, with hair and a Celtic circlet, whom Nigel hadn't recognized until Jago named him: Taliesin, Arthur's bard.

'Of course, Lord . . . Merlin,' Hitchcock corrected himself. 'Please, follow me. We're going down to the oldest part of Loveday House, so follow closely, for I shouldn't want anyone to get lost.'

The ersatz Taliesin led the way across the ballroom – past a grand ebony clock with the sun and moon chasing each other in the enamelled dials upon it; past a painting with a huntsman on horseback, holding a spear and menacing some holy hermit armed with nothing more than a crucifix to defend the sacred white hart cowering behind him; and onto a plainer section of wall, where the rich rosewood panelling lay bare, save for over a dozen ornate ormolu coat hooks cast in the shape of heraldic sea dogs: fierce canids from the waist up, forming the top hooks, for hats and the like, then spike-backed sturgeons from the waist down, tails forming the bottom hooks, for coats.

'The Hounds of the Sea!' exclaimed Topper in delight.

'Indeed, the very same,' Hitchcock agreed. 'The fierce pirates who prowled these waters before being extinguished by Piers Gaveston, the new Earl of Cornwall, at the beginning of the fourteenth century. If you count, you'll note that there are fourteen hooks here. *Hounds* in Cornish is, of course, *Keun* – which is why this is Keun Island. The last Hound of the Sea pronounced a curse on Gaveston, they say, but that didn't prevent the earl from putting him to the sword and pulling their castle down. Two centuries later, the family St Gerren erected a new one in its place, the first called Loveday.' Hitchcock shrugged. 'I'm sure Mr Walmsley, our local historian, has the dates engraved in his memory, for the Devil knows the details.'

Everyone laughed at Nigel's expense, but it was good-natured – for the most part. He knew the dates, of course, but Susan was far more than his plus-one. She was his partner in all things. He cocked his head at her, and she grinned back.

'Well, I might not be the local historian,' she said, 'but one does not survive marriage to said historian without picking up a few things along the way.' Susan admitted nothing of her past – especially her misguided dalliance with joker porn – but displayed her RADA training as an actress now, holding up one hand dramatically and declaiming the dates as if she were Medea reciting a spell: '1308 . . . 1703 . . . 1857 . . .'

'Very good, Ms Strathmore,' Hitchcock said. 'And those numbers are more significant than they might seem. Count the Hounds of the Sea as you would centuries, starting with the Devil's number, thirteen, for the 1300s are the fourteenth century, which corresponds to the last hook.' Hitchcock as Taliesin glanced significantly to Nigel, then reached up and pulled on the fourteenth hook. 'It's easiest to picture the number sequence of nought to thirteen superimposed over one to fourteen, so you add one to every digit. Thusly: nought.' He pulled the first hook. 'Eight.' He pulled the ninth hook. 'One, seven, nought, three.' He pulled four more in order, adding one to each number to find the corresponding hook. 'One, eight, five, seven.' He pulled four more hooks. 'Then back to the Devil's own accursed thirteen . . .'

Hitchcock pulled on the fourteenth hook again. There was a click, and then the panel with the painting swung inwards, revealing a staircase spiralling down into darkness. 'The Devil shows us the way,' explained Hitchcock.

For a moment, Nigel thought Hitchcock meant him, since he was masked as the Devil, but Jago's butler was instead indicating the painting, where on the left, in the shadows of the secret passage and almost cut out of the frame, a swarthy rider rode a dark horse, while to the huntsman's right, a fair-haired angelic figure rode a shining white steed.

'*The Wild Huntsman*, by Richard Westall,' Hitchcock explained, 'drawing master to Victoria before she was Queen, after Sir Walter Scott's poem of the same name. The Sable Huntsman there is the Devil at the huntsman's shoulder, tempting him to become the wild huntsman.'

Nigel frowned. Herne the Huntsman, or Hunter, better known as the leader of the Wild Hunt. Just like Susan's . . .

'I always liked wild huntsmen . . .' Susan remarked.

'Blow me . . .' swore Banger. 'I knew I recognized you! Y'were in *those* films, weren't ya, with that knave, Herne?'

Susan admitted nothing, but Duffy's mask of wide-eyed girlish wonder more than a little resembled her expression thirty years ago in the film, when she beheld Dylan Hardesty's ridiculously wild-card-enhanced member.

Perhaps to defuse the tension, or perhaps simply from honest curiosity, Topper turned her Nimue mask to Jago's Merlin and asked loudly, 'Isn't *The Wild Huntsman* in the Royal Trust?'

'She's right,' declared Mash, masked as Mr Punch. 'I've seen it at Windsor Castle. How'd it end up 'ere?'

'Westall painted other copies,' Jago explained smoothly. 'I obtained it in my travels.'

'From 'om?' asked Banger, behind the mask of Judy. 'Victoria 'erself?'

There was a bit more laughter, but Jago only replied, 'Well, she was only a princess then . . .'

'Fuck a duck,' swore Banger, and either it was coincidence, or it was a singular choice of *open sesame* to control the lights, but all at once, torch sconces fitted with Arts and Crafts hammered-iron lanterns flared alight, their mica panes illuminating the path down.

'Follow me, if you please,' said Hitchcock, leading the way.

Nigel inserted himself between Susan and Banger. He felt an urge to elbow *The Wild Huntsman* as he passed, but copy or not, it was a masterpiece and one of Jago's treasures, so he contented himself with glaring at it.

The staircase spiralled down, widdershins, like Childe Rowland had once chased his sister round the church, deep into the depths beneath the manor, past passageways that had likely once hid Catholic priests and on past dungeons that had undoubtedly once held medieval prisoners. Then Hitchcock diverted them into a side corridor, leading them, if not into the Dark Tower of the King of Elfland that Merlin had once warned Childe Rowland about, at least through a storage room for unneeded garden statuary.

It reminded Nigel unpleasantly of the secret statue chamber in the local fairy tale 'Cherry of Zennor', in which Cherry discovers that the master she's gone to work for is in fact an elf lord. But unlike Childe Rowland's tale, which included multiple beheadings and a climactic sword fight, Cherry's adventure ended with nothing worse than her getting sacked. Nigel rather liked his work for Jago, so unlike Cherry, he held his tongue.

Hitchcock unlocked a round door at the end of the passage, like the door of a hobbit hole, and ushered them in, with Jago bringing up the rear. The great oak door, once closed behind them, appeared from this side to be the front of an immense wine-barrel, complete with bung. Nigel gazed around at the rest of the chamber: the wine racks with their bottles festooned with cobwebs and dust, and the faint but unmistakable perfume of well-aged alcohol.

Topper guessed it before anyone else could. 'Is this where Lady Morwen stashed her booze?'

'It is,' admitted Jago. 'I don't believe Marcus St Gerren ever discovered this place – or if he did, he kept it under careful lock and key – but it is, in fact, older than Lady Morwen.'

'Goes back t'the Hounds,' Banger guessed. 'Piracy gets ya a lot of alcohol.'

'A gold star for you, Mr Spragg,' complimented Jago. 'Indeed, the Hounds were here. But this chamber is, in fact, even older. I believe only Mr Walmsley might actually know how old, but he is certainly dressed for the occasion.'

Nigel gazed around in wonder, mentally stripping out the racks filled with priceless but comparatively recent vintages, at the Arts-and-Crafts lanterns, at the walls themselves, made from ancient stones, the ceiling itself, which comprised an enormous flat slab.

'It's a fuggy hole,' he said at last, 'a Neolithic fogou, but here in Cornwall we call them fuggy holes, like the one in "Duffy and the Devil".' Everyone looked at him, so he continued. 'The witches used to gather at them for their Sabbath, where they'd meet with the Devil, dance, and get drunk. Squire Lovell followed a hare there, but she turned into his old housekeeper, Joan. The witches chased Lovell home, but not before he learned the Devil's name, which saved his wife, Duffy, from her Devil's bargain.'

'Interesting,' said Jago. 'So, what was the Devil's name?'

'Well,' Nigel admitted, 'some versions of the tale say it's Bucka-boo. Others say it's Terrytop. But in the oldest version of the tale that I know, the Devil sings this:

> 'I have knit and spun for her
> Three years to the day,
> To-morrow she shall ride with me,
> Over land and over sea,
> Far away! Far away!
> For she can never know
> That my name is Tarraway!'

As he pronounced the last word, a huge stone slab at the far side of the room shifted, lifting like the door of the lair of the Forty Thieves in an *Ali Baba* Christmas panto.

'Ah,' said Jago, 'I had been wondering what the word was . . . Take a note of that, Mr Bushorn,' he told the Fawkes-masked dancing master, who nodded. 'Well done, Mr Walmsley. Feel free to select any bottle here you like.' He paused then, regarding the group with wizardly contemplation. 'You too, Mr Spragg, and likewise you, Ms Blackwood.'

Nigel could scarcely believe the enormity of the gift. 'But . . . these are priceless!'

'Marcus St Gerren never got to enjoy them.' Jago shrugged. 'I shan't make the same mistake. But choose quickly.'

Nigel didn't have to be told twice. He spied one bottle, covered with dust, but obviously set aside for a special occasion. Good enough for Mad Morwen was good enough for him. He brushed off the dust and saw an illustration of a swallow along with a date – 1674 – and some words. 'I think it's in Dutch . . .'

Jago glanced at it, telling him, 'Dutch bottling, but it's French Armagnac.'

'This say what I think it does?' asked Spragg, holding forth a bottle with a label in Gaelic and Latin.

Jago took it, regarding it with his Merlin mask, then translated: '"The Water of Life, bottled by Friar John Cor, for James IV, in 1510."' It might have been labelled *Water of Life*, but it looked like whiskey. Jago handed the priceless bottle back.

'I'll have what he's having,' Topper remarked, then reached into her hat and pulled out an identical bottle.

Jago ushered everyone into the dark passage beyond, then turned to Topper's Nimue. 'Madam, would you by any chance have any candles in your hat?'

'Of course. Please hold this.' She handed Jago the priceless duplicate bottle of James IV's whiskey, then reached into her top hat and pulled out a dozen pairs of pale green tapers, handing them to Jago. 'I hope you like bayberry.' She reached back into her hat. 'Let me get a lighter.'

'Allow me,' said Bushorn, who stripped off one white glove and reached for the wicks, making Nigel realize simultaneously that Bushorn was both an ace, since the wicks spontaneously caught fire, and a black man – and what's more, one Nigel had met before, because he remembered an older black gentleman coming into THE MERMAID'S CHEST before one of Jago's previous parties.

Bushorn's fingertips caught fire for a second; then he sucked them to put them out, his skin blistering almost immediately as he slipped the glove back on, and Jago passed out the tapers, one for everyone. Jago, not Hitchcock, now led the way, as Hitchcock was seemingly as unfamiliar with this section of Loveday House as the rest of them. But Jago strode confidently down corridors, listening occasionally. The candles gave off a bittersweet scent, that also, unsurprisingly, smelled a bit like bay leaves, covering up the stink of burned flesh.

As they went deeper, worked stone and brick gave way to natural stone, and Nigel realized they were descending into the sea caves beneath Loveday House. The caves were well known to be treacherous, meaning that before Jago had taken possession of the manor, every few years some brave young fool had gone missing in them. But it was low tide, and the Lord of Loveday House presumably knew what he was doing.

Occasionally, they came to a junction, and Jago paused before selecting a passage, sternly gesturing for no one to take the unselected path. Once, he held a finger to his mask's white whiskered lips for silence, taking them down through a large cave where they could hear the sea and, in the distance, the tuneless whistling of the wind.

But as they made their way across the cavern, Nigel realized that the whistling was not tuneless, for there was a melody – and moreover, a very old one that he knew quite well: '*A-roving, a-roving, since roving's been my ru-i-in, I'll go no more a-roving with you, fair maid . . .*'

Jago clapped his hand over Nigel's masked mouth, almost causing him to drop the bottle of precious brandy. Then the whistling stopped, and Nigel heard a word: '*Goslowes!*' He knew that to be Cornish for *listen*, but the speaker had a peculiar accent – or at least a peculiar accent for the accepted modern reconstructed Cornish; the last native speaker of Cornish had died in the 1700s, three-quarters of a century after Lady Morwen. But he allowed himself to be hustled along with the rest of the group, who'd gone on ahead with Hitchcock.

They emerged from the sea caves to the beach in the hard slanting light of late afternoon, the sun shining brightly, reflecting off the western sea.

'My pardon, Mr Walmsley,' Jago said, releasing Nigel, 'but the caves were less safe than I thought they would be. An unusual tide, perhaps. I had expected them to be unoccupied.'

'But they were speaking Cornish,' Nigel pointed out.

'Still, they were no Cornishmen you would want to meet.' Jago made it clear the matter was at an end, turning Nigel around. 'We're at the beach, and what better spot for Bonfire Night?'

It was true; they had emerged at the beach at the base of the cliffs – the same beach Nigel had glimpsed from the Mermaid Suite. Jago's servants were already there and had piled up wood for an enormous bonfire. It was a bit early to light it, of course, but not to get Guy and any other effigies ready. Nigel then realized that a pair of effigies was already in place, missing only their masks.

'A penny for the old guy?' begged Bushorn, masked as Fawkes. 'I'm still new to this, but I understand it's traditional to burn the Pope or the Devil with Fawkes, and you've brought the second.'

Nigel surrendered his Tarraway mask, which seemed a shame, since it was a nice bit of artistry. But given the priceless bottle of brandy Nigel had just received as a party favour, Jago seemed richer that Croesus, so he could just buy a new mask or ask Topper for a duplicate.

Bushorn did a few steps of some jig Nigel couldn't recognize without music, placed the Devil mask on the left-hand effigy, then called out, 'Remember, remember, the fifth of November, gunpowder treason and plot! I know of no reason why gunpowder treason should ever be forgot!'

With that, he stripped his gloves off both hands, placed them on the shoulders of the Devil and the unmasked effigy, and set them alight just as his mask and hat caught fire, too. He snatched them off, slamming them on the head of the right-hand dummy, and clambered down the woodpile. The wood caught fire everywhere he touched it as well, lighting the bonfire with a series of blazing handprints that the sea wind quickly whipped into an inferno. Bushorn staggered down the beach to the sea, extinguishing his hands in the surf and his face in a crashing wave, then stumbled back, dripping seawater and incinerated skin.

Nigel was too polite to inform the American that it was customary to light up Fawkes *after* sunset – it was Bonfire *Night*, after all – but the method of ignition had been singular, and Bushorn looked a horror, his hands and face terribly burned. But then Nigel watched the burned skin flake away, to be replaced by terrible blisters as Bushorn redonned the gloves, which were as inexplicably untouched as the rest of his clothing, except by seawater and soot.

'I'm fine,' Bushorn told Topper as he went over to her, 'but if you could spare something for the pain, that would be great.' Bushorn's ace appeared to be more of a deuce.

'Whiskey worked in the Old West,' she remarked, which didn't quite fit with her guise as Nimue, but taking a cowboy-era hobnail glass out of her hat was certainly magical enough, if somewhat of a let-down compared to the Lady of the Lake producing Excalibur. 'Should work now, too.' She then reached back into her hat and pulled out, if not Excalibur, a bejewelled Masonic cavalry sabre.

Topper sabred the neck of James IV's whiskey, as if it were a common bottle of champagne, then handed the open bottle to Banger to pour and returned the sabre to her hat. She then started conjuring random glassware, like a boot sale from the whole of British history – everything from an ancient Roman wine goblet to a Peppa Pig sippy cup.

Nigel received a nice bit of Waterford crystal, which Banger proceeded to fill, pouring with his left hand, as his right hand was still clutching the unopened bottle of James IV's whiskey.

'To James IV and me!' Nigel said, raising the glass. 'Can't think of a better reason to drink his great-grandfather's whiskey.'

''ow is it?' Banger asked.

'Not bad.' Nigel savoured it. 'Could do with some ice.'

Topper used her hat as an ice bucket, removing a chunk of ice from heaven knew where or when and placing it in his glass. It did help.

The glassware distributed, Banger proceeded to drink from the bottle, while Topper handed out fireworks that looked to be from the Song dynasty, Mexico City, and Queen Victoria's Golden Jubilee. Nigel received a Roman candle emblazoned with *VOTE FOR TAFT!* Bushorn lit it with a pinch of his fingertips, then lit Susan's, which proceeded to shoot purple, green, and white fireballs over the ocean, matching the paper wrapper, apparently made to celebrate women's suffrage. While not even sunset yet, enough clouds had blown in across the sun that the fireworks still made a good show.

Then the show became even more spectacular as a pterodactyl swooped into view. At least, it looked like a pterodactyl, if a pterodactyl were making passionate love to a large rectangular kite.

'Do you have any binoculars in there?' Nigel asked Topper.

Rather than binoculars, she reached into her hat and produced an eighteenth-century nautical spyglass that looked as if it could have belonged to Bobby Shafto or Admiral Nelson. Nigel used it anyway, bringing the pterodactyl into focus, revealing it to be a gargoyle wearing a cable-knit sweater and tartan kilt, bearing a large flat parcel tied with string – like a particularly outré delivery from the Narnian post.

Nigel lowered the spyglass and turned to Susan. 'Is your special courier perhaps a knave who looks like a gargoyle?'

'That would be Arran Beattie, yes,' Susan said brightly, 'but he likes to be called Wyvern.'

A moment later, Wyvern landed, revealing as he did so that, like all true Scotsmen, he went *au naturale* beneath his kilt – or perhaps unnatural, in the brief glimpse Nigel had before the kilt once more cloaked things. He also had four arms – two regular ones, and two little tyrannosaur claws coming out of the neck of his sweater, tangled with the parcel string.

'Bloody hell,' he swore in perhaps the thickest Scots brogue Nigel had ever heard. 'Special delivery for Susan Strathmore.'

Susan stepped forward, and Nigel battled an irrational surge of jealousy. Susan had always had a thing for giant knaves, and Wyvern stood at least seven feet tall – or at least the tips of his wings did.

How could a local historian compete?

Susan reached out and patted one wing leather affectionately. 'The parcel is actually for Lord Branok.' She turned to the masked Merlin. 'Happy Bonfire Night!'

Jago, unperturbed, regarded the parcel, then asked Topper, 'Scissors?'

She provided a pair from her hat. A few snips and a slash parted the paper, revealing a glass frame holding an etching – the frontispiece from an antique book – alongside the original copper plate that had made it.

Nigel recognized it immediately as one of Jago's asks: artist John Martin's original copper engraving plate for the frontispiece of *The Book of the Great Sea-dragons*, by Thomas Hawkins, circa 1840.

The etching clearly displayed a lurid black-and-white vision of ichthyosaurs and plesiosaurs battling to the death in the waves, while on the beach, beneath the pallid glow of a cloud-shrouded moon, four horrid saw-toothed pterodactyls pecked the eyes from a dead ichthyosaur.

'Remarkable,' Jago said, touching the glass. 'Anning mentioned it, but I never thought I'd track it down.'

'Anning?' asked Mash.

'Mary Anning,' Nigel explained. 'The famous palaeontologist, of "She Sells Seashells" nursery rhyme fame. Anning was from Dorset, but Hawkins was one of her best customers. And she once made it down to Keun.' Nigel gestured to the cliffs behind them. 'Our cliffs are famous for their belemnites and ammonites.'

'Amon-who?' asked Banger.

'Ammonite,' Nigel repeated. 'A prehistoric ancestor of the modern nautilus, another cephalopod, cousin to squid and octopi. Named for the spiralled horns of Amon-Ra, ram-headed god of the Egyptians. Also known as snakestones in the Middle Ages, because of their serpentine form.'

''oo cares?' said Banger, pointing a finger at the knave holding the framed etching. 'All I know is that Wyvern there runs with the Twisted Fists and ran a lorry into a Christmas fair. Last I knew, he was in the nick.'

'Y'need to keep up, Alf,' Mash told him. 'Some posh barrister sprung him last year. 'E's on probation. Lost 'is lorry licence.'

'It's legit,' pleaded Wyvern, holding the etching. ''Tweren't stolen.'

'I can get you the provenance,' Susan said. 'Anyway, it's just an etching and an engraving plate – not as if it's Martin's lost painting.'

'What I wouldn't give for that . . .' Jago stroked his mask's long white beard sagaciously.

Topper tipped her Nimue mask up to admire the etching and plate, sipping her scotch in the light of the bonfire, then slowly and ceremonially reached into her hat, withdrawing a rolled canvas bound with a red silk ribbon. 'This should be it.' She handed it to Jago, and as she did, the wind picked up, ruffling the edge of the canvas as if trying to tear it free, showing John Martin's signature.

'A most interesting wild card ability you have, Ms Blackwood.' Jago accepted the canvas reverently as the wind tugged his Merlin beard as well. 'I'd like to ask you about it later, but for now, my deepest thanks, to both of you ladies.' He nodded to Topper and Susan, then glanced to Hitchcock. 'Have these taken to the Kraken room.'

Hitchcock bobbed his Taliesin mask, signalling to a couple of footmen masked as lesser knights of the Round Table – Sir Fortnum and Sir Mason, to judge by the picnic hampers they bore – and Susan's etching and the rolled canvas were spirited away up the stairs to Loveday House.

Jago glanced at Wyvern. 'You've obviously flown a long way, and we've more than ample food, so you're welcome to some rest and refreshments before you go. It is Bonfire Night, after all.'

Nigel glanced at Banger and Mash, but they didn't seem ready to make an arrest – more the pity – so he did his best to ignore Wyvern as well, though it was hard with the way Susan kept glancing in his direction with her damned Duffy mask.

But there was also vintage whiskey flowing freely, so Nigel chose to get plastered, and it was soon quite the nicest and certainly the most unusual Bonfire Night that he had ever attended – at least until Jago announced, 'Everyone, quickly, we must get back to the house. Immediately!'

'Why?' asked Beattie. Rather than leaving after a couple of sandwiches, he'd meandered over from the servants' hampers and now stood hunched beside Susan, using one wyvern wing, like a great fleshy blanket, to shield her from stray sparks from the bonfire.

'There's a storm brewing,' the Lord of Loveday explained, indicating the dark clouds. 'A bad one. Think 1703.'

'But the forecast—' said Susan.

'The forecast has changed,' said Jago. 'Don't go anywhere near the sea caves.' He pointed imperiously to the long line of switchback stairs going up the cliffs, twisting with mad shadows from the bonfire. 'Up the stairs, immediately; get inside the house.'

'Bugger the stairs,' swore Beattie. Gathering Susan into all four arms, he took three massive strides towards the cliffs, unfurled his great wings, and launched into the air, blasting everyone with sand.

'Follow Wyvern,' Jago ordered as the knave flew off with Nigel's wife.

Nigel, whatever his feelings, did not need to be told twice. By the time they'd crossed the beach to the cliffs, the wind had started up in earnest, and once they'd gained the bottom-most landing, it was battering at them like fists.

Wyvern returned and landed on the railing next to them – without Susan. 'C'mere, lass!' He reached for Topper, who clung to the railing with one hand while with the other kept a death-grip on her antique top hat, which the wind was trying to tear from her. It ripped the Nimue mask from her face and sent it scudding down the beach.

'Wait!' Nigel cried. 'Trade you!'

'What?' she yelled back.

'Put my brandy in your hat! Give me a climbing rope, then play it out as Wyvern flies you up! It may not look like it, but I used to go birding on these cliffs!'

Topper did not have to be told twice. She disappeared the priceless bottle into her hat, then took out a climbing rope, which Nigel secured to the railing as Wyvern grabbed her.

Then they were up and off, Wyvern flapping like a weird bat. His wings were stronger than the wind, and they zigzagged up the stairs, getting the rope to others further up so that they had a lifeline in case the stairs gave way. Wyvern disappeared over the top of the cliff as Nigel made his way up.

The stairs were treacherous, dating back to the days of Marcus St Gerren. They'd been a death-trap of dry rot all the days of Nigel's youth, and even Jago's repairs and replacements did nothing to inspire confidence, but Nigel continued doggedly. Thirty years of running an antique shop had done him few favours, but the rope helped as a second handhold along with the railing. The sand from the beach whipped up and blasted him along with the spray of the ocean. Then all at once, he felt someone grab him.

'There's a duck,' said Mash, and Nigel was unsure whether it was Cockney rhyming slang for him being in luck or some reference to how wet he was, but then the former Miss Punch was dragging him up the stairs with super-human strength. Next, Banger gave his wife a hand up at the top, and then they were all three staggering across the lawn in the driving rain, following Topper's line through what looked like a herb garden. Eventually, Mash and Banger dragged him through the door into the grand kitchen of Loveday House, dripping water onto the tiled floor. A chef making a pie paused to watch in wonder.

'Is that everyone?' asked Jago.

'Yes, sir,' said Hitchcock, his sodden Taliesin mask pushed up like a welder's face-shield, 'thanks to Topper and Wyvern's quick work with the climbing rope.' He pointed to where it snaked across the kitchen, from the corner of the closed door to the countertop, where Topper was perched beside a coil of dry line, the other end of it disappearing down her hat.

'Credit to Mr Walmsley,' said Topper. 'He's the one who suggested the rope and tied it off.' She pulled out the end and smiled. Tied to it was Nigel's antique bottle of brandy.

'Well then,' said Jago, 'fair play to you, Nigel.' He glanced to the chef, who was busy stuffing meat into an elaborate Victorian copper pie mould. 'Daniel, are all your staff present and accounted for?' The chef nodded, so Jago turned to Hitchcock. 'Close the shutters. This storm is going to be . . . very bad.'

'Of course, Lord Branok,' Hitchcock told him, then went to the end of the kitchen that looked to serve as the butler's pantry. Within it was a bell board with more bells and labels than it seemed Loveday House could have rooms, and below that was an indicator panel with speaking tubes, assorted Bakelite knobs, buzzers, faceted jewel-like lights, and an unmistakable bright red panic button, which he pressed decisively.

At once, steel storm shutters closed over the kitchen windows, cutting off the pounding rain and with it what little light was coming from outside. The kitchen lights, though set in period fixtures for a mostly Edwardian-era kitchen, adjusted a few lumens brighter to compensate, automatic sensors mixing new technology with old. Nigel was exceedingly impressed – until there came a horrific thunderclap, and the kitchen was plunged into darkness, all except for the flame of a single burner, where a saucier was simmering.

'Oh, bother,' said Hitchcock, like Winnie-the-Pooh, glancing at the lights on the control board, all of which had gone dark. 'Lord Branok, I'm not certain that every shutter got closed in time. We'll have to check manually.'

'I shall see to it myself,' said Jago. 'Ms Blackwood?'

'On it,' said Topper, lighting a white taper held in an extraordinarily costly, albeit kitsch, nineteenth-century porcelain candlestick, ornamented with exquisite flowers and two monkeys wearing wigs and baroque clothes playing with a doll's house. To Nigel, it looked like Meissen's famous, if horrifying, 'Monkey Orchestra'.

She handed the candlestick to Jago, then took its mate out of her hat, different only in that the monkeys had lost the doll's house and were now threatening to sing and play a mandolin. It was clearly part of the 'Monkey Orchestra', but Nigel hadn't been aware of a candlestick in the pattern.

'I had hoped to host a fancier dinner, but I'm certain we can make do.' Jago paused, then added, 'Please, everyone, do not leave the house once night falls. We've had troubles in the past with . . . break-ins. I must leave you all in Hitchcock's capable hands while I go to make sure your bedrooms and the rest of Loveday House are secure.' He glanced then at Wyvern. 'I won't turn anyone out in a storm, especially *this* storm, so I'll have Hitchcock put you in the Lilac Suite.'

'Oh, won't that be nice,' said Mash. 'We're next door, in the Daisy Suite . . .'

Jago made his exit, while Topper continued to produce an extraordinary collection of candlesticks, which Bushorn proceeded to light.

Nigel was disturbed. Not by supper, which was lovely: they had all proceeded to have a high tea of sorts, picnicking before the inglenook in the ballroom, warmed and dried by a roaring blaze, with the best seats given to the three wettest: Banger, Mash, and Nigel himself.

Above the fire, a grotesque bronze cockatrice statuette held an ornate copper kettle on its forked tongue, boiling water for tea. Nigel tended to it with the help of Hitchcock, who'd wheeled in a tea trolley containing Jago's exquisite china and a tea chest. Banger and Mash used antique brass toasting forks to roast bangers and toast bread, while chestnuts were making delightful popping noises at the hearth.

Chef Daniel brought out the pigeon pie, which was luscious, made with Queen Victoria's favourite recipe and fit for the Queen herself – except for having been made in a pie mould ornamented with the face of a leering satyr, which reminded Nigel unpleasantly of Herne, Susan's ex. Wyvern was looking at Susan appreciatively as she served him a slice, and she smiled in return, and while Nigel couldn't fault the knave for that – for his wife was indeed a beautiful woman, and Wyvern had saved her from the storm, so being appreciative was no more than polite – Nigel felt the stab of jealousy and turned away. Instead, he focused on the hevva cake, a traditional Cornish delicacy, rich with butter and a mix of dried fruit worthy of Rossetti's *Goblin Market*.

It also didn't hurt that Topper produced not only another bottle of James IV's whiskey but a duplicate of Lady Morwen's private reserve Armagnac, which was glorious, especially soaked into the cake. Nigel got to have his brandy and eat it, too.

No, what was most disturbing was his candlestick, in a subtle way that only Nigel would notice. It was in the quintessential high baroque Germanic fashion, and it was Meissen, as he'd guessed, but when he'd checked the bottom, the porcelain mark was *wrong*. Meissen used two crossed swords in cobalt blue on white glaze – something a porcelain painter could add with just four brushstrokes. Sometimes, an extra dot was added here or there, depending on the decade. Once, they'd decided to add an asterisk or possibly *hægl*, the Old English hail rune, at the bottom. Meissen, however, had never added *beorc*, the Old English birch rune, which looked like a pointy B. By itself, it simply might have been odd, but to Nigel, who was just drunk enough, it seemed outright uncanny.

Of course, he was dealing with an ace here, one who could conjure duplicates of formerly one-of-a-kind antiques. But what if her duplicates were ever so subtly wrong?

Nigel noticed that Susan's teacup was in the 'Blue Onion' pattern, which meant it was probably Meissen as well. 'Darling, could I see your cup? I'd like to check the mark.'

Susan wordlessly and unquestioningly drained her cup and handed it to him. Nigel looked. No *beorc* rune there with the crossed swords, but a valknut in its place – a symbol made from three interlocking triangles.

Nigel turned to Topper. 'Madam, did this cup come from your hat as well?'

Topper shook her head, then Hitchcock put in helpfully, 'I believe Lord Branok brought that particular cup back as a souvenir from one of his trips.'

'To where?'

'Germany, I believe,' said Hitchcock. 'The same trip where he engaged Herr Ott, our chef, who made the pigeon pie. More tea?'

Nigel handed Susan back her cup, then checked his own before filling it. It was Wedgwood, in the 'Nautilus' pattern in pink, with the customary porcelain mark, though dated to 1811. The idea that he was drinking tea from a teacup Jane Austen could have owned was only slightly comforting, though, as the condition was so perfect that Jane could never have used it.

Jane had also probably not alternated tea with Lady Morwen's brandy or

James IV's scotch. Nigel was very tiddly, but drunk as he was, something began to click in the back of his mind: Herr Ott. *Chef Daniel Ott.* Hadn't there been some scandal, back in Queen Victoria's day, when Victoria, still mourning the recent death of Prince Albert, had decided to hire her German cousin's personal chef, Daniel Ott, only to have him murdered by hooligans? It had been an international incident – not that anyone remembered it now . . .

Of course, that was easily explained: Daniel Ott had undoubtedly had children, or at least nieces and nephews, and some great-grandson or great-nephew had inherited his name along with the pigeon pie recipe Victoria had liked so well. Family businesses, names, and secret recipes were perfectly ordinary; unknown porcelain marks were much less so.

Nigel needed another drink.

Susan was having another, too, as was Wyvern, and while the big knave's little tyrannosaur chest arms couldn't hold scotch tumblers, they could hold teacups, and he was taking two-fisted drinking to the next level. One held scotch, the other brandy, with both clasped in two claws with the third claw sticking out like Elizabeth I's little finger. 'So,' he slurred to Susan, 'what was it like . . . ?'

'You saw the film. What do you think?' Susan had Duffy's mask of girlish innocence turned to the back of her head, with the strap now looking like a flapper's headband. 'You ever been with a man?' She sipped her scotch as the thunder rumbled, loud enough to shake the walls. Wyvern dodged the question by drinking simultaneously from both cups, only to have Susan point and say, 'Yes, yes, that's pretty much how I did it, too.'

'*Susan*,' said Nigel.

'Oh, come off it, Nigel,' said Susan. 'It's not as if I have to *pretend* to be respectable. Everyone *knows*. They have the internet. How do you think I sell so much at the shop every time a hen party comes through?' Her eyes narrowed. 'And I still get fan letters and emails – mainly from lonely jokers in prison who fantasize about a nat woman who's turned on rather than repulsed by them. How else do you think I got to know Arran?' She turned to Mash. 'By the by, in case you're wondering, I recommended the barrister who got Arran out – not that you don't have a history yourself. I lived in London in the '90s, too.'

Mash did not respond. Nigel wondered how much Susan had known Petula Spragg back in their more colourful youth. He glanced to Hitchcock. 'Are our rooms ready? I think I'd like to turn in.'

Banger elbowed him hard. 'Capital idea, mate. I think Pet and I might do the same.' Banger leaned over to his wife and whispered, a little too loudly, 'Fancy a bit of rumpy-pumpy, Miss Punch?'

Nigel ignored him, looking to Hitchcock, who said, 'I shall check. The buzzers are out because of the storm, but Lord Branok had Loveday House's original bells and whistles restored, so this is an excellent occasion to make use of them.'

'Bells and whistles?' asked Mash.

'Servant bells and speaking tubes,' Nigel explained, pointing to where Hitchcock had gone to a brass and porcelain mouthpiece discreetly set into the wall at the corner of the inglenook and was blowing into it before lifting the valve. 'There's a whistle at the other end.'

Hitchcock chatted with the tube, then came back a few moments later. 'I'm happy to report that all your rooms are shuttered and secured, and the servants have prepared fires in everyone's grates.' He glanced then to Bushorn. 'If I may make an imposition, Mr Bushorn, the Spraggs are in the Daisy Suite, and Mr Beattie will be in the Lilac Suite adjacent. Those are near your quarters in the North Hall, if you could show them the way. I'll be taking the South Hall and escorting the Walmsleys to the Mermaid Suite and Ms Blackwood to the Peacock Suite.'

Bushorn nodded, his face completely healed from setting his head on fire a few hours ago, now merely begrimed with soot and sea salt.

Topper said, 'I thought I was in the Cherry Suite?'

'You were, but there was a problem with the shutters and the branches of the orchard outside.' Hitchcock smiled apologetically. 'In an abundance of caution, your things were moved to the Peacock Suite. There's a connecting door, so you'll be sharing the Mermaid sitting room with the Walmsleys, if that's all right.'

'That should be fine.'

'The Peacock Suite has the best view of the ocean, or at least, it will once the storm has passed.' Hitchcock looked around the group. 'Once you're in your chambers, please don't leave them until tomorrow. It is very easy to get lost in Loveday House, especially with the power off. With luck, we should be able to unshutter the house at dawn, and servants will come to rouse you for breakfast and Mr Beattie for his departure.'

The storm, from the rumbling that followed, seemed to have no intention of passing, but nonetheless, Hitchcock led the way out to the entrance hall and the grand staircase, with Bushorn, Banger, Mash, and Wyvern going left, while Hitchcock and everyone else went right, all bearing their assorted candlesticks refreshed with new tapers from Topper's hat.

All the paintings and ornaments Nigel had seen that afternoon looked different and odd by candlelight. Eventually, they came to the corner with the mermaid newel-post lamp, now dark, opposite the Mermaid Suite.

'Well, we might as well enjoy our proximity,' Nigel said, unlocking the door while Hitchcock handed Topper the keys to her new suite. 'Care to come in for one last drink?'

Topper agreed, marvelling at the room when she entered. Green silk draperies had been drawn to cover the windows, matching the watered silk on the wall, everything shimmering in the light of their candles and the fire dancing in the fireplace, also tinted a witchy green – by specially treated wood, Nigel supposed.

'Jago really goes all out.' Topper set her candlestick on the coffee table and went to the mantelpiece, where a pair of mermaid bookends held a selection of books seemingly chosen for the colour of their bindings. 'I've heard stories about his library. I really want to see it but can content myself with these for now.'

'Anything good?' asked Susan as Topper perused the selections.

'Lots of Cornish folklore, pirate legends, and thrilling romantic adventure stories.'

'Jago knows Nigel too well.' Susan laughed. 'And my husband has apparently been telling him about my literary tastes, too.' She made a face at Nigel, who merely smiled.

'Don't worry about me. If I don't like any of these' – Topper doffed her hat – 'it's not like I'm short of other options.'

After Topper had departed to her own suite, Susan took Nigel by the hand and pulled him into their bedroom, which was much as they'd left it, except that the green velvet curtains had been drawn and there was another peculiar green fire burning in the old French fireplace, making the chamber look even more like an undersea garden and casting dancing shadows across the ceiling from antler chandeliers.

Nigel sighed. He despised the antlers. But at least they weren't bat wings.

'So, what's up with you and Wyvern?' he asked.

'Nothing, as you know perfectly well,' Susan said, looking down at him. 'We corresponded, as I said, and in return for getting him sprung, I got us someone able to procure that mad etching Lord Branok wanted so much.' She grimaced then, rolling her eyes. 'Fuck that tart Topper for upstaging us and pulling the wretched painting out of her hat, but aces . . . what can you do?'

'So, you don't want to fuck Wyvern?'

'Oh, I've had my thoughts, but I came back here with you, didn't I? You're a lot more enthusiastic when you're jealous, Nigel . . .' She smiled wickedly. 'Let me get you out of those clothes.' She put both their candlesticks on the mantelpiece, then set to unbuttoning his shirt. 'And put down that silly brandy bottle. You've been clutching it like Pooh with the "hunny" pot.'

'You're drunk,' accused Nigel.

'And you're not?' Susan laughed. 'Now, get your arse into bed, Squire Lovell, and shag me proper, so I don't start thinking about young Huey Lenine.' She twisted her Duffy mask back around to cover her face.

Susan liked roleplaying, and Nigel missed the Tarraway mask. Susan would have enjoyed playing with the horns especially. Hunky young Huey was also fun – particularly the 'Hide, my husband's coming!' routine. But podgy middle-aged Squire Lovell was definitely too close to the truth, especially without a mask.

Sometimes, Nigel suspected that Susan still fantasized about her ex while they were making love, even though the two men couldn't have been more dissimilar. Nigel was small – every part of him, sadly – and while he had once been fit enough, thirty years of running an antique shop had done their damage.

But Nigel was here, now, with Susan, his wife, and Dylan was over thirty years gone.

Nigel pranced a few exaggerated steps of Squire Lovell's minuet from the guise dance and offered a hand to Susan. 'Milady, your dreamboat awaits.'

Susan grinned, and Nigel took a moment to appreciate that. The dream-boat was real – or as real as Hollywood and the antique business could make it: a bed in the shape of the boat from the Grotto of Venus from *Tannhäuser*. It was originally crafted for Gaby Deslys, the famous French singer and dancer, but after Deslys's death – from complications of the Spanish flu – the boat had passed into the hands of the movie industry, becoming prop for countless films: notably *The Phantom of the Opera* and *Sunset Boulevard*, where it was used for the death of Norma Desmond.

Susan got up and went to the prow of the boat bed, caressing the cupid figurehead. 'Is this really . . . ?'

'Yes, it is,' Nigel told her. 'It recently came up for sale, and while I couldn't afford it, Jago could. Now it's ours, at least for the weekend.'

Susan tossed aside Duffy's mask, struck a pose, and looked at Nigel with a mad gleam in her eyes. 'Mr DeMille, I'm ready for my close up.'

Nigel held one hand over his face, miming a half-mask. 'Sing for me!'

Susan paused, doing a double-take, then her face lit up with dawning realization, and she began to sing Christine's wordless aria.

'Sing!' Nigel cried, and Susan sang louder, and as she did, Nigel began to unbutton his shirt. Susan took his cue and began to do the same with her blouse . . .

Nigel lay in bed, staring up at the ceiling with the damned antlers dangling from it, not even minding. That had been marvellous.

The room had helped, of course. On one side lay the green velvet draperies, subtly embroidered with gold thread and beadwork, winking in the firelight with a spiralled design of the chambers of a nautilus, the storm shaking the shutters and whistling softly beyond them. Opposite, framing the door to the hall outside, were half a dozen tapestries, three on each side. 'Look, Susan,' he said, pointing them out proudly.

Susan stared. 'Is that . . .'

'*The History of Melusine*,' Nigel told her. 'Yes, really. I located them at a chateau in France. They'd been locked up since the war. It's the first time they've been back to Keun since Lady Morwen's day.'

'You said they were lost when the castle collapsed . . .'

'That's what most reputable sources said, but cloth is tough, or Morwen might have had them cellared down in the fuggy hole when the storm hit. All I know is that I followed a legend saying they got looted shortly thereafter as a secret treasure and bounced around from one noble house to another – anyone who wanted to claim descent from Melusine, Merovech, and the Merovingian dynasty.'

'Like you?' Susan asked, giggling. 'I thought you Keuners were all descended from pirates.'

'Both?' said Nigel. 'Noble families are complicated, and those tapestries are the closest anyone has to a genealogy.' Nigel pointed to the second one, which showed a beautiful woman carrying girl triplets, flying through the air towards an island whose topography resembled that of Keun, though the castle on the peak was early medieval, the right era for the Hounds of the Sea. 'Melusine's mother, the fay Pressine, scarpered off with her children to her sister, who ruled the lost island of Avalon, which no one was supposed to be able to find. But doesn't that isle look familiar?'

'So, does this mean you're related to Arthur, our new king, too?'

The less said about the new joker king, the better, as far as Nigel was concerned, but he just shrugged. 'Maybe through the original King Arthur? Melusine's aunt had to have a name, so if she was Morgan le Fay, it would make sense.'

A delicate bell began to chime and chime again from an ormolu clock on the mantelpiece, which Nigel hadn't sourced. It depicted Amphitrite flanked by baroque nautilus shell chalices in the shape of a dragon and a mermaid admiring herself in a mirror and was flanked by a pair of five-branched candelabra with yet more mermaids in green bronze.

Amphitrite's clock chimed a tenth time, echoed by the deeper bell of some clock downstairs, and the gilded dials clearly read ten o'clock. 'It's beautiful, really,' Susan told him, reclining on the swansdown pillows beside him. 'But less antiques and more sex, eh, Nigel?'

She reached down beneath the coverlet and grabbed his cock, and while Nigel was tired, it didn't take much for her to have him aroused again. 'All right then, Susan.'

When she spread her legs wide, Nigel needed no more invitation than that, entering her and thrusting until he spent what little seed he had left, then collapsed beside her, exhausted but happy.

It would have been fine if Susan, as she drifted off to sleep, had muttered 'Oh, Tarraway' or 'Oh, Huey' instead of 'Oh, Dylan . . .'

Nigel slept fitfully, waking up sometime later to a thunderclap so loud it sounded like a gunshot, like something from Bulwer-Lytton's proverbial dark and stormy night, followed by the Amphitrite mantel clock delicately chiming midnight, echoed by the distant sound of the deep booming bell of the ebony grandfather clock in the ballroom downstairs. The tapers in both candlesticks, including the kitsch Meissen with the disturbing maker's mark, had burned to half their height, but there were five tapers ready in each of the candelabras that had come with the room. The fireplace still held the weird green glow, but the fire had burned much lower. Nigel was considering putting more firewood on when he heard a scream.

A woman's voice – but not Susan's. Susan lay there, lightly snoring, her golden locks trailing across the pillow.

The scream came again then again, nearer. Piercing. Plaintive. Frightened. Also, from the sound, coming from the corridor outside.

Nigel slipped out of bed, but rather than put on his rumpled clothes from the floor, he grabbed a plush white robe laid out on the dressing valet, then lit one of the mermaid candelabras on the mantel. As he was lighting it, he heard a whistling, close enough that he could identify the source: not the wind outside the house, but the brass cover of a speaking tube set beside the dumbwaiter to the left of the fireplace, like the one Hitchcock had used downstairs, presumably there to call down to the kitchen below.

Nigel had never used a speaking tube before but knew the procedure: when someone whistled, you lifted the valve cover and spoke. Nigel lifted the cover, hesitating, then heard more whistling. A very familiar tune echoed up, his memory adding the words: *I'll go no more a-roving with you, fair maid . . .*

The maid in question was not one of Jago's French maids, but 'The Maid of Amsterdam', a sea shanty with increasingly bawdy verses that went back to at least the Jacobean era, popular with sailors as well as pirates – not that there was much of a difference, judging by some of the lads on the Keun pier.

Nigel lowered the cover of the speaking tube, then lifted the candelabra and took it with him, along with the fireplace poker, just in case, and slipped out the doorway to the sitting room, then out to the hall, where he immediately saw the green glitter of the mermaid's globe on the newel post.

The electricity was still not back, but the way upstairs was clear, for footprints showed in the recently vacuumed carpet: prints the size of a woman's foot – or a very small man's, for Nigel's bare feet were scarcely bigger. As he proceeded upwards, the wainscoting gleamed in the candlelight, as did the little brass bars that held the rug down.

Nigel went up to the landing to the third floor, glancing down the hallways and seeing no one and nothing out of the ordinary. He was about to go up the stairs to check the fourth floor when he noticed a narrow stairway across the hall, with tiebacks to each side so that a tasselled cord could be looped across for privacy. The cord instead dangled to the left, and the tieback to the right was bent, as if the cord had been yanked aside rather than casually un-looped. Someone had come this way in a hurry.

Nigel mounted the narrow stairs carefully; the carpet beneath his bare feet here was far less plush. The higher reaches of Loveday House were where

Jago was doing the most construction, and it would not do to step into a spot missing its floorboards. The staircase went up, bent right, then doubled back and continued up. The thunder sounded louder here, and the wood of both the walls and the floorboards creaked, but it was secure. Then the staircase emerged in a narrow servants' hallway, with bare boards but a light halfway down. It was good to see power had been restored.

But soon, Nigel found that the lamp was not an old gas bracket converted to electricity: it was an actual gaslight, still working. Beside it were three short steps leading up to a glass door frosted with the arms of Marcus St Gerren – a shield with a heart over a sun, for Loveday, supported by seadogs – but Nigel could see another light on the other side.

Nigel turned the handle and went through. 'Hello?'

He heard a soft sound, a mechanical *click* like someone turning another door handle, followed by, 'Mr Walmsley? Oh, thank goodness it's you!'

Topper stood there, wearing a lacy peacock-blue nightdress and nothing else except her hat. In her left hand, she held a brass candlestick that looked heavy enough to double as a club. In her right, she held a sleek silver handgun, pointed straight at his heart.

Nigel froze. What was she doing two floors up from her room when she was supposed to have been in the suite next door? Had he and Susan made so much noise as to drive her out? 'Who did you expect it would be?'

'Ghost pirates?'

Nigel paused. Topper hardly seemed the excitable type to read a volume of ghost stories before going to sleep and then have bad dreams, but she had reported the right sort books on the mantelpiece of the Mermaid sitting room. 'Was there by any chance a copy of William Hope—' Nigel broke off, the thought unfinished, roughly jarred out of his head as he realized what he was looking at, where he was standing. 'Dear God, we're in the belvedere!'

'The *what?*' said Topper, lowering and uncocking her gun.

'The belvedere,' said Nigel, waving his candelabra towards it, the light sparkling off the myriad glass panes, glittering like an insect's eyes as the rain pounded the glass in sheets, not a storm shutter in sight. 'The lookout room at the top of Loveday House. It was ruined when I was young, the floor so rotted you'd fall through if you so much as glanced at it, and some lads did. But Jago's restored everything!'

The room was both as he'd remembered and as he'd imagined it to be. The last time he'd been here, he was fourteen, a skinny thing, ascending a ladder on a dare, looking out through the ruined wall to the sea beyond, only fragments of vintage glass panes left around the edges. But now the wall of glass was restored, with smaller panes framing a wide, oval picture window with stained-glass jewels at the corners – something he'd only glimpsed in grainy vintage photos of Loveday House from the 1920s. The wide window framed the storm-tossed sea, roiling like a witch's brew as the lightning crashed and crackled.

For a second – a very split second – Nigel imagined he saw a ship out in the storm. A sailing boat: not a modern vessel, or even a classic tall ship like the *Cutty Sark*, but a square-sailed medieval cog, like one he had in an illustration hanging back at the shop, its white sail emblazoned with the black head of a hound. Then the lightning flash disappeared, and it was gone. Instead, a giant bat appeared flapping outside the wide window.

Topper screamed, and Nigel did, too. Then he realized that the bat was not a bat or even a winged vampire but a knave: Wyvern, his huge bat wings flapping wider than the window as he yelled something indiscernible. He had a pair of binoculars around his neck, held by his little chest arms, and was thankfully wearing his kilt.

Nigel raised the fireplace poker, using it as a hook to open the ornamented transom window above.

'Is Susan with you? I heard her scream!'

'No,' Nigel told him coldly. 'My wife is asleep, in bed. It wasn't her.'

'I screamed, once, but not here,' Topper said.

Nigel then saw she had dark bruises on her arm.

'Let me in!' the knave shouted over the wind. 'I'll come to the balcony door!'

He flapped out and around, to the far end of the belvedere, where a few steps led up to a glassed-in cupola dome and the balustrade outside. Nigel ran to open the French doors, but they weren't locked – or at least weren't by the time Wyvern was through with them. The left handle dangled down at an odd angle after he shut it behind himself, shaking the water from his wings like a dog.

'You heard me all the way up here?' asked Topper.

'Bat wings come wi' bat ears.' He reached one little chest claw up to cup an overlarge pointed ear. 'I heard a woman scream out in the storm, so I decided, bugger what his lordship said, that I was going out t'look for her. Forced open the shutters outside my window, flew around, then saw the light and you lot up here.' He glanced around the room, with its palm trees in a hammered-brass planters, faded couches, and sprawling wicker chairs all facing outwards to watch the sea. 'What're ya doing here?'

'You won't believe it,' Topper told him, 'but I went into the Peacock bathroom, then when I went back to my bedroom, I somehow ended up in some room all done in Tiffany turquoise, with a fortune in Tiffany trinkets and knick-knacks. Then when I tried to return to the bathroom, I was suddenly back in the Cherry bedroom and got ambushed by ghost pirates.'

'That's impossible,' said Nigel, 'the Cherry Suite is on the other side of the house from the Peacock Suite. Or, at least, it was . . . But ghost pirates? What are you talking about?'

'Aces,' Topper explained. 'Three guys, dressed like extras from a bad production of *The Pirates of Penzance*. I assume Keun has some pirate festival for Bonfire Night? They kept turning invisible or teleporting or something, and they were speaking some weird language – I'm guessing Cornish? I shot one of them point blank, but he phased out as the bullet went through him.'

'How'd you escape?' asked Wyvern.

'He phased back in and grabbed me, so I kicked him in the balls. That worked, so I ran.' Topper showed her bruises. 'I expect one's the ace and the other two are buddies he's able to use his power on.' She looked straight at Nigel. 'You're the local. Know any aces like that?'

Nigel knew a lot of locals he might suspect, but the only local ace of note was Whooper, who was more of a knave. Plus, she was a nice girl, and her power was nothing like that – not that he'd seen her in the shop in the past year, which was strange, small as Keun was. Still, anyone could turn a wild card at any time, especially with the emotions and antics around something like Bonfire Night.

Then the lightning crashed, and Nigel saw it again. 'Dear God,' he cried, pointing, 'did your ghost pirates come with a ghost cog?'

The lightning clearly illuminated the ship – there one second, gone the next – but then it hove closer, stuttering in and out of reality like frames from an old film reel, the hound's-head sail rippling in the wind. Then, in the distance, there came the mournful call of a foghorn, long and low, but rising in pitch as it came closer, modulating until it sounded like a hunting horn, echoing in through the open transom over the wide, oval picture window in the heights of the belvedere – the eye at the top of Loveday House.

The lightning crashed again, and the image shifted back and forth like the warring prisms of a seaside souvenir lenticular postcard – one second showing the ghostly cog, the next with the cog gone but an even more impossible image, a mermaid porpoising across the surface of the waves, like a dolphin or flying fish but with a woman's head and trailing tresses as beautiful and odd as the one carved on the sofa in the Mermaid Suite. And as she swam, she sang a wild and beautiful song, snatches of it carried by the wind – a song such as the sirens once sang, of longing and loneliness, but pitched high and plaintive. A cry not just to come to her but to protect her and save her – until the thunder drowned it out.

Lightning flashed again, limning the pirate cog in white and the sea in blue. Then the image flashed away, and in the afterimage, the sea glowed as witch-fire green as the wood in the fireplaces of the Mermaid bedroom and sitting room. But riding upon the waves was a horse as dark as the Sable Hunter's from *The Wild Huntsman* painting, except that its eyes were glowing green, and mounted upon its back, instead of some Germanic huntsman using his spear to menace a hermit and a stag, was Herne the Hunter himself, with the stag's antlers crowning his head, his wild mane flowing with the storm, and the white atop the waves revealing itself to not be whitecaps but froth-white hounds with glowing green eyes and scarlet ears: the Gabriel Hounds of legend.

Nigel, without asking, reached out and grabbed Beattie's binoculars, despite the knave standing a foot taller than him. He snapped the strap with a hysterical strength, readjusting the focus until he could see Dylan Hardesty, Susan's ex, his eyes glowing as green as those of the Gabriel Hounds as he raised a great golden horn in the shape of a dragon to his lips. He winded it again, sending a call across the waves and a shiver through Nigel's soul.

The message of the Wild Huntsman's horn was clear and primeval, needing no translation: *Join the hunt or be the hunted. Predator or prey.*

The thunder pealed, and another sound echoed over the crash of the waves and the howl of the storm – the tolling of a bell, deep and low in the great ebony clock downstairs in the ballroom, the heart of Loveday House, reverberating through its timbers and sounding one o'clock, the witching hour. With a shudder that shook the timbers of the house itself, the two images snapped together into one reality, like frames of a stereoscope: the pirate ship of the Hounds of the Sea together with the Wild Huntsman and his hounds, hunting the mermaid.

The Huntsman's horn sounded again, imperative, with its forked compulsions, but Nigel's soul rebelled, for he knew where his loyalties lay, and there was a third option he'd much rather choose: he was going to kill the fucking Huntsman himself.

Herne sounded his horn again, calling to the Gabriel Hounds and raising his spear. The mermaid was a slippery bitch, but she would not get away. He hurled his spear, the bronze head honed to a razor's edge, and it hurtled through the air, slicing the edge of the sea-witch's tail and leaving a bloody trail through the froth of the waves.

She screamed in pain, and the hounds bayed in ecstasy, catching the scent as they ran across the surface of the waves, then belling louder, giving tongue to their joy as Herne winded the horn again. More hounds rose from the surface of the water, the white froth forming their shaggy bodies, the green flames in Herne's eyes sparking the glow in their own.

The lightning flashed, and Herne raised his hand to catch it, the bolt transmuting into a new spear as he spurred his horse to leap high off a cresting wave beneath them, pointing the spear to strike true at the mermaid's black heart. Then a bell tolled, resounding across the waves – a ship's bell, a harbour buoy, a tolling like a grandfather clock striking one: hickory, dickory, and then *DOCK!*

The sound resounded as the horse's hooves suddenly landed on wooden planks – the deck of a ship that had appeared out of nowhere. A pirate ship with its sail ruffling over him, displaying a giant hound's head as black as Herne's Gabriel Hounds were white.

'Ah-*aaaaaaah!*' the siren cried, singing a tritone, the Devil's interval, but

Herne would not heed her spell, not with the song of the hunt resounding in his ears. The pirates, however, were another matter, unsheathing swords and daggers or withdrawing the belaying pins from the rack ringing the ship's mast.

Herne laughed, deep and loud. The siren made for worthy sport, unlike some others. He laughed again as a pirate launched himself from the rigging, a knife clenched in his teeth, only to encounter the tip of the Huntsman's spear slicing through his throat. The Wild Huntsman was showered with blood and sea spray as he caught the corpse on his antlers and swept it overboard with a dismissive toss of his head.

The wheeling of his steed continued the motion, and with a sweep of his spear, he cut through three more pirates under the siren's spell. The sea dogs clutched their spilling guts, falling to their knees as they died. Herne granted them mercy as he swept the spear back through their necks. Others stepped to the fore, and Herne dispatched four more, laughing as he did so.

But as fine as this skirmish was, it was a distraction from his true prey. Herne sounded his horn again. 'With me, men!' he cried, stamping the butt of his spear on the deck. With a thunderclap, a dozen stallions appeared, one for each new rider – steeds cut from storm clouds, dark as night except for the blazing green in their eyes. Eleven pirates leaped for their horses, but the twelfth stayed at the ship's wheel, bringing the ship to bear on their prey.

Herne sliced through two men whose unlit eyes bespoke either their resistance to the Hunt or the strength of the mermaid's call, then rode to the bow. The figurehead was in the shape of a fierce snarling hound, which Herne took as a good omen. He signalled to his new riders to hold, for they would make more speed this way, catching the wind of the storm. The mermaid was swift, able to swim as well as fly, and only Herne's power to hurl his spear to the depths of the sea or send it hurtling to the heights of the sky kept her skipping along the horizon, dodging behind the crests of the burgeoning waves. But with the hound-headed pirate ship now part of the Hunt, they were gaining on her.

Then came a lurch and a sickening roar, the sound of oak timbers rending on stone, and Herne the Hunter clutched the mane of his horse as they were launched into the air, the ship run aground on the treacherous rocks that the mermaid had lured them towards. Herne's horse corrected as they landed upon the wave-tops, and the mermaid ceased her song for a moment, giving a delighted peal of girlish laughter as she surfaced and turned to watch her handiwork.

Half of the riders were not as fortunate as Herne and were dashed to death on the jagged stones, their steeds dissolving into smoke. The mermaid rolled and dived through a wave with a flirtatious flick of her tail, leaving a trail of blood through the sea.

Herne still had half a dozen riders with him alongside his hounds, which bayed as they gave chase. The mermaid dodged through the waves, making towards the shore of an island where, high on a hilltop, a great house stood, flanked by rows of dark cypresses swaying with the storm like shifting shadows, like an old painting of the Isle of the Dead, the building's shape indistinct except for a light shining from the window at the top.

Then something launched itself from the heights of the house – a great, batlike shape, like Varney the Vampire swooping in on wires in a Victorian play. Herne wondered, briefly, where that thought had come from, then tossed it aside. The bat could join the Hunt, for the sea-witch was leaping from the waves, her fins folding out like the veils of a diaphanous gown to catch the updraught above the sea surge, bearing her aloft to the tops of the cliffs.

The Wild Huntsman sounded his horn, calling to the bat, but it did not heed the call, winging along the waves and unhorsing three riders in one fell swoop, crashing through them like a rugby flanker.

Again, Herne wondered where the thought had come from. *Rugby?* Some dim memory. But no matter. He spurred the flanks of his steed with his own cloven hooves, riding the horse as it cantered back, climbing a rogue wave that towered then curled onto itself and over him like a spiralled seashell. His mount raced out of the tube and back up onto the crest, heading for the island.

Memory flickered again, like a nightmare, with a twinge of fear. *An island. A wave. A castle of dreams.* A vast wave driven before a giant flying steel beetle, which swept the castle away, as if it were composed of nothing more than sand. Herne glanced down, into the gulf below, recalling the drowning terror, the crush of the primordial sea . . .

But that wave was not this wave, the accursed beetle was nowhere to be seen, and now Herne himself controlled the storm and with it the swell of the sea. He clapped his cloven hooves to his steed's sides, spurring his horse to sail through the air as it leaped to the top of the cliffs, the sea splashing and crashing behind him. The Gabriel Hounds were lost in the tumult, but more were recreated from the spray as he sounded his horn, chasing the sea-witch. She alighted upon the long lawn lined by the swaying cypress trees, her veiled fins becoming a trailing gown, green stained with the red of blood, and she stumbled as she ran. Land was where her swiftness failed her, so Herne had the advantage.

Three individuals ran out from the manor house then – one making his way to the mermaid, the other two heading for Herne. The first was a burly man wearing nothing except the mask of a hook-nosed woman, and he ran straight for the Wild Huntsman, punching his horse square on the nose with such terrific force that it dissolved into smoke. Herne's hooves suddenly impacted the ground, cutting deep into the sod. His satyr-like haunches were strong, bending with the impact but not buckling – yet that motion brought his head low, within range of a middle-aged woman in a babydoll nightdress and the mask of a red-capped hook-nosed man, who punched him in the jaw with even more incredible force, crying, *'That's the way to do it!'*

Herne flew backwards off the cliff, enveloped in a cloud of salty spray that obscured his vision as he began to lose consciousness, his spear dissolving in his hand, his horn dwindling as he clutched it in desperation.

Then he crashed into the water and felt the drowning terror that was more ancient and primordial even than the Hunt, the terror that had swallowed him twice before . . .

♦

Nigel watched through Beattie's binoculars as Mash smashed Dylan Hardesty right on the chin, knocking him off the cliff, antlers and all – including his outlandish wild-card-enhanced manhood, which Nigel always felt had to have been a camera trick . . . but wasn't. Then he was gone, swallowed up by the sea spray and waves.

Nigel looked the other way, seeing Bushorn helping the mermaid to the house . . . but she was a mermaid no longer, for she'd somehow acquired legs or at least a trailing dress in place of a mermaid's tail. Banger and Mash followed, high fiving each other, then going into a spontaneous victory dance, like football hooligans after an epic win.

After that the only thing that could be glimpsed outside the belvedere's cupola was the roiling sea and the sheets of rain, limned by lightning flashes, pounding the windows and cascading across the lawn as the cypresses thrashed in the wind. The pirate ship had disappeared, and the Wild Huntsman as well, and Nigel didn't know what he felt.

He'd wanted to kill Dylan, for everything he'd done – to Susan, to Nigel himself. Thirty years of feeling inadequate with the woman he loved. Thirty years of contemplating murder while excusing it as a fantasy he would never act upon because the object of his hatred was over thirty years dead and gone.

Then he wasn't – though now he must be once more. No one could have survived that fall. No one except an ace or a knave.

Nigel saw Wyvern then, flapping like a bat out of hell, with other bats following him, Stygian silhouettes cut from the cloth of night itself. Wyvern's twisted shadows multiplied behind him, and as he flew, he screamed like a bat, if bats yelled, *'Fack! Fack! Fack! Fack! Fack! Fack!'*

A moment later, he came in through the cupola's French doors, just as Dracula might at Lucy Westenra's window – if Dracula wore a kilt. Wyvern slammed the doors behind himself, but the handle dangled, broken. Then one of the shadows was there on the other side of the glass, its wings behind it, its face pressed against the diamond panes . . . except it had no face, just a smooth expanse of black skin. Above its brow curved two delicate horns, as black and lightless as the rest of it.

Wyvern stepped away, his mouth open, his little tyrannosaur claws going to his cheeks as more and more bat-winged and faceless shadows massed behind the first, their bodies greyhound-gaunt, their devilish barbed tails curling behind them in elegant Fibonacci curves. The first reached out a long claw and gently opened the door, poking its faceless, horned head into the belvedere's cupola.

'Freeze!' ordered Topper, but the joker, the knave, the devilish winged shadow – whatever it was – seemed either to not understand or not care, and advanced.

Bang! Suddenly, the faceless shadow had a mouth where no mouth had been before. It paused, as if curious at the sensation; then the whorled hole formed black lamprey teeth before sphinctering closed as the creature advanced. Its fellows followed as Topper shot three more holes in its tenebrous torso. *Bang! Bang! Bang!*

Nigel stumbled back, tripping down the three short steps to the cupola, only to catch himself on the newel-post knob, twisting it with the same hand that held the poker. He heard a click, and one of the potted palms swung aside along with the panel behind it, revealing a cobweb-festooned staircase spiralling down.

Anything was preferable to the monstrous shadow jokers, so Nigel plunged down the narrow stairs, calling, 'Topper! Wyvern! Follow me!'

He tore through the curtain of cobwebs with the poker, his candles setting stray strands alight as he descended. He tried not to set any more afire, not wanting to risk burning the place down – especially since this stair must have lain undiscovered since Marcus St Gerren's day. The bronze mermaid on the candelabra's stem looked uncannily like the one he'd seen Herne pursuing through the waves.

Nigel pressed onwards and downwards, the curtains of cobwebs hanging like the chambers of a nautilus. He wondered where the secret spiral staircase led, where its symmetry aligned with the old plan of the house and the rooms Jago had redone. Then he stopped at a slightly wider stair, almost a landing, and glimpsed something glittering in the cobwebs to his right: a small porcelain knob, painted with a delicate sprig of lilacs.

Of course. Nigel grasped it and twisted. While he didn't have Wyvern's wild card strength, he did have desperation and his shoulder. The panel popped open, and Nigel stumbled through into what could only be the sitting room of the Lilac Suite – another round tower chamber, papered and curtained with lilac silk instead of green. Topper followed quickly; a moment later came Wyvern, eyes mad, his giant wings scraping through behind him. But mad or not, he had the sanity to grab the secret panel and slam it shut, in the process severing several black fingers that twitched and writhed like nightcrawlers as they fell to the floor, until they dissolved into smoke and shadow, like evil dreams.

Wyvern shoved the panel hard, giggling hysterically. As he did, the leftmost of a pair of guardian foo dogs on the mantelpiece twisted slightly off-centre. Its mate on the right remained undisturbed, paw balanced on its ball, evidently not part of the secret door's mechanism. 'I think it's shut,' Nigel told him. 'At least until they find the knob . . .'

Wyvern glanced around frantically, then lunged away from the secret panel, using all four arms to grab an enormous Chinese apothecary cabinet from the nearest round wall and slam it into place, just as the leftmost foo dog began to vibrate. Nigel took his cobweb-shrouded poker and wedged it between the dog's violet-jade paws and the back of the mantel so that the mechanism couldn't turn.

'What are those things?' asked Topper. 'And where are we?'

'Pervy wankers,' Wyvern answered the first question. 'They was tickling me . . .'

Nigel was almost certain that *pervy wankers* was not the preferred nomenclature, but since he was at a loss for a better name for the creatures, it would have to serve. As for Topper's second question, while he couldn't recall the original decor of Marcus St Gerren – he thought it might have once been the smoking room – Jago had redone it with a mix of Victorian chinoiserie and authentic Asian artefacts. Under other circumstances, it would have been quite pleasant. 'I think this is the Lilac Suite.'

Wyvern nodded and pointed his right chest arm and a single claw at a stained-glass door ornamented with daisies opposite the fireplace. 'That's the Daisy Suite. Jago put Banger and Mash there so they could keep an eye on me.'

Topper rapped on the glass, but there was no answer.

They looked at one another in silence for a moment, the air empty except for the echoing scream of the storm, audible even behind the Lilac Suite's thick draperies and the storm shutters beyond.

Then one scream separated itself from the others – higher, reedier, but more melodious – a keening cry of anguish and pain.

Wyvern cupped one batlike ear with one little tyrannosaur claw, then told them, 'It's the joker lass.' He grabbed a cloisonné candelabra shaped as a particularly gaudy lilac chinoiserie vulture, lit its candles from Topper's taper, and led the way out into the dark hallway.

Passages led right and left, but in front of them, in place of the staircase and whatever newel-post lamp Jago had decided to change this week, there lay a third passage, unfamiliar save for a heart above a sun carved into the keystone of the arch: the Loveday crest of the St Gerrens before Marcus.

As they stepped through the archway, Nigel would have sworn he was in Loveday Castle as it might have been in Mad Morwen's day. Or at the very least, it looked like something from a sixteenth-century castle, with a colonnade that reminded him of the deer shelter at Auckland Castle in County Durham . . . not that he wanted to shelter any deer at the moment.

Nigel flashed back to Dylan Hardesty flying backwards off the cliff, and he shuddered, feeling as if he'd murdered the knave himself. But it was Mash who'd done that, recalling her glory days as Miss Punch, back before she'd changed her name and become a duo with Banger.

The scream came again, echoing through the arches of the colonnade, and Wyvern turned around, cupping his bat ears with his chest arms, confusion furrowing his heavy brows. Topper stood beside him, gun and candlestick at the ready, her far more dangerous hat perched upon her head.

Then a familiar bell chimed loudly, the ebony clock in the ballroom downstairs, and down one dark stone passage, a series of lanterns sprang alight with actual flames; it seemed Jago had the gas piped here, too. But as the clock struck a second time and the door at the end of the passage opened, making the cries of the mermaid clearer, Nigel passed the lanterns, he smelled the distinct odour of mutton fat and through the pierced iron saw what looked like an old-fashioned tallow candle.

The scream drew him on, so Nigel went through the open door, where the smell of mutton fat was replaced by the sweet smell of lignin and the perfumes of bookbinding: Russian birch tar, French lavender, musk, civet, ambergris, and the underlying scent of old vellum. Around them, glistening in the candlelight, lay shelves piled with volumes bound in white vellum, as was reserved for the most precious church manuscripts, with gilded titles in Latin. Nigel translated the nearest, though his school Latin was rusty: *The Grimoire of Pope Honorius: Annotated & Revised by Pope Joan III.*

'Jago's library.' His eyes went wide. 'We shouldn't have candles here.'

'Then Jago should've given us electric torches before he pissed off!' snapped Wyvern.

Topper blew her candle out and doffed her hat, disappearing the candle and clublike candlestick down the hole. She retrieved one, then another, then a third vintage French Ray-O-Lite electric torch, the chrome and copper in mint condition despite being over a hundred years old. The batteries worked, too. Nigel and Wyvern both blew their candelabras out, leaving the mermaid and the vulture on a research table, and continued with the electric torches, advancing towards the keening sound.

Nigel shone his torch around, gasping in awe. They were in the uppermost gallery of the grandest library he had ever seen, like the great library at Trinity College Dublin put together with the Clementinum of Prague and the Old Main Library of Cincinnati, the second two of which Nigel had seen only in pictures. He also could not think how Jago had fitted it into Loveday House, unless he'd tunnelled down into the hill. But all of that was no matter, for down on the ground floor on the other side of the library from them were a few more forbidden candles, and by their light, Nigel could spy Banger, Mash, Gary Bushorn, and one of Jago's maids gathered around the mermaid.

Wyvern loomed over Nigel and Topper. 'Fastest way down,' he said, unfolding his wings and offering them his large human arms. Topper accepted, so Nigel did, too; then Wyvern gathered them into a bear hug against his bare chest with his little joker arms around their necks. He leaped from the balcony and winged down to the group gathered in front of a grand, albeit unlit, fireplace.

The flight down was terrifying, exhilarating, and mortifying all at once, for Nigel was wearing nothing under his new robe and it was flying up like Marilyn Monroe's skirts. Banger, for sake of modesty, borrowed the French maid's apron as his fig leaf, but that was almost more obscene, especially with the Judy mask pushed up on top of his head. Wyvern had his kilt.

The mermaid was no more a mermaid than Dylan Hardesty was Herne the Hunter, no matter what the wild card had done to her. Her beautiful, waist-length tresses suddenly writhed like tentacles, revealing themselves as long, fringed gills like an axolotl salamander's, then a second later relaxed and transfigured, becoming golden ringlets worthy of Proud Maisie herself. Her dress, by candlelight, appeared to be an attractive medieval kirtle, except for the right side, where it was slashed just below her knees, revealing a fish-like tail, mottled and thick with slime and blood.

'Phlegeth-nyth, tharanak mnahn' grah'n geb hai-og!' she told everyone emphatically, clutching her appendage, trying to staunch the bleeding.

What language was she speaking? Basque? Swahili? Takisian? Nigel didn't know – not that it mattered. Blood flowed the same for jokers as for nats.

'Does anyone here know first aid?' he asked.

Banger and Mash seemed more adept at inflicting wounds than tending them. Bushorn would probably burn her if he tried.

A pair of scissors had been stuck into a mugful of pens on a librarian's desk. Nigel grabbed them and cut the flap of his new robe just above his knee, tearing the cloth in a circle until he had a wide strip of terrycloth to wrap around her tail as a bandage. The first layer soaked through quickly, and the second began to seep as well, but the third was clean as he tucked in the edges then started to use his robe's belt to tie the makeshift bandage in place, until Topper offered him a roll of pink, rubberized bandage from her hat.

That worked much better and would serve until they could summon an ambulance.

'Uln,' the mermaid told Nigel, 'mnahn' grah'n . . .' She then seemed to grasp that he couldn't understand her, so gestured to her mouth.

Nigel had dealt with enough foreign tourists that he quickly guessed. 'I think she's hungry or thirsty . . .'

'I can fetch refreshments,' the maid said with a strong French accent. She went up to the mermaid, leaning close to say, 'I'm Colette. What would you like?'

The mermaid smiled, revealing beautiful, white, and almost entirely human teeth, then seized the maid by both arms. Nigel then watched as the mermaid's lovely face lost all semblance of human shape, her curls changing to fringed gills. As she unhinged her jaws, her human teeth revealed rows and rows and rows of sharp, pointed teeth beyond them, ringed like a lamprey's, and poor Colette barely had a chance to scream before the mermaid bit off her head, then sucked on the maid's headless corpse like a human-sized juice box. She dropped the body, licked the blood from her lips with a long, pink salamander tongue, and smiled as her head and tentacular gills were replaced by the appearance of a golden-haired maiden. Opening her perfect human mouth, she began to sing, and it was the most beautiful sound that Nigel had ever heard, wordless but rooting him to the spot.

'*Bugger that!*' cried Mash, lashing out with one fist, and catching the mermaid on the jaw.

The monster flew back, losing any semblance of womanhood as it crashed through the screen and into the back of the library fireplace. It opened its bloodied mouth again and hissed, then went squirming up the chimney, just before Topper shot several holes into the fireplace.

Finding Jago or even Hitchcock had seemed like a brilliant idea, but brilliant ideas were easier had than realized. They did encounter a couple more maids and a footman, who proceeded to try to reassure everyone with some waffle about how Jago had installed futuristic holographic technology that could realize dreams from a guest's subconscious, but those were mostly harmless phantasms, though they could sometimes exert enough force to cause mild trauma, like the bruises on Topper's arms. When they were shown Colette's headless corpse, they proceeded to freak out and ran off to find Jago themselves.

The group did, however, find the door of the Mermaid Suite, the gilded mermaid on the newel post opposite far less charming and beautiful than before, having skipped from fairy tale to horror without even stopping at dark fantasy between. But Susan was still inside – untouched, unharmed, still asleep and snoring – and Nigel was just a nat. He would leave it to the aces to work out what to do about a carnivorous mermaid and a flock of faceless shadow devils.

As for Herne the Hunter? Dylan Hardesty had been missing, presumed dead, for over thirty years, and he could remain the same for one more night. So, rather than wake Susan up and tell her the whole horrific and convoluted story, Nigel just threw some more wood on the fire in case the mermaid, the pirates, or the perverted shadows tried to come down the chimney, then crawled into bed beside his wife and fell asleep.

He awoke to the sound of her screaming his name: 'Nigel! Nigel!'

He opened his eyes, then blinked and closed them again at the bright sunlight streaming in through the windows. Sometime during the night, the storm shutters had opened, and the curtains had been drawn back. The door to the sitting room was also open. Nigel could see Susan there, kneeling on the window seat, looking out of the window.

'Nigel, come quickly! It's Dylan!'

Nigel came and looked, then looked closer, since he still had Wyvern's binoculars. There, on the sand, amid the wreckage of a scattered bonfire, lay an antlered figure, looking not so much like the Celtic god Cernunnos as that giant wanker Dylan Hardesty, seeming scarcely older than when he and Susan had shot that porn film over thirty years ago.

The staircase down to the beach now lay on the beach, and the boathouse had been damaged as well – mainly because there was a wrecked pirate ship lying on it. A cog, to be specific, sporting a tattered sail bearing the snarling head of a black hound.

'I'll go and fetch Wyvern,' Nigel said, wondering what he hoped might happen but too tired even to finish the thought.

Dylan Hardesty awoke to the smell of something burning. He thought it was his nose. 'Wha—' he said, then gasped, coughing up sea water.

'*Sal volatile*,' said a voice – male but high, a pleasant tenor. 'Smelling salts. Be careful – you've had a nasty crack on the head. Who's Prime Minister?'

'That cunt,' said Dylan automatically. He opened his eyes and found himself focusing on a small man – a nat, by the look of him – who was standing taller than him, but only because Dylan was lying on his back. Standing, Dylan was about eight feet tall, not counting his antlers; this man looked barely over five. He was middle-aged, blond, badly balding, with a weak chin and an over-wide mouth.

The man gave a dry British chuckle. 'You need to be more specific.'

'Margaret Thatcher. No, wait – John Major . . .'

'Sorry, no.' The man sighed. 'It's been decades since we've had either, so we've got a different cunt now.'

Dylan realized he was lying on a beach, and it was morning. He turned his head slightly, wincing in pain, then focused on the sail of a wrecked pirate ship, emblazoned with a giant black dog's head. 'The Black Dog?'

'Killed in prison,' the man told him, 'and the Green Man is dead, too. The Twisted Fists are being run by Wayfarer now, if that's what you're wondering. Also, Queen Margaret's dead, but Elizabeth's lost son Arthur is on the throne. What's more, he's a joker, so Wayfarer has turned respectable and is standing as an MP.'

'*What?*' roared Dylan, shock quickly turning to anger as his eyes went wider. He struggled to sit up but got woozy and sank back into the sand.

'I'd say you have a concussion,' said the little man. 'Your eyes are dilated.'

'They're usually that way. They're owl eyes.'

'I told you, Nigel!' said a woman's voice. 'Back at RADA, everyone always thought he was stoned!'

The voice was familiar, and the face was too as the woman pushed what must have been Nigel out of the way. 'Susan?' Dylan asked incredulously. She had the same golden hair and lovely face as the last time he'd seen her, only now she was decades older.

'Yes, and you've got a nasty head wound. Can you sit up so we can bandage it?'

'I – I'll try . . .' Dylan did, letting Susan hold his hand to support him while Nigel took a look.

'Not too deep,' Nigel reported. 'Will need a few stitches, but for now, just some antiseptic, some gauze, and a bandage. Topper?'

A middle-aged, red-haired woman wearing a peacock-blue dressing gown doffed her incongruous antique black top hat and reached into it, pulling out a handful of surgical dressings. The man began to apply them as the woman said, with an American accent, 'You were chasing a mermaid last night. Who is she?'

A flash of Herne's memories filtered back to Dylan – a clear image of the sea siren, but no name. 'Bugger if I know.'

'Have you ever been to New York?' the woman asked.

Dylan had a flash of memory of Herne leading the Wild Hunt across the Brooklyn Bridge. 'Sorry, never set hoof there.' He wiggled his cloven hooves, glad they still worked, then realized, with some embarrassment, that he was stark naked. Herne had never liked clothes.

'Old joke of his.' Susan looked at him again – all of him – her expression half wistful, half incredulous. 'Goodness, you've scarcely aged a day. Where have you been these thirty years?'

'I–' Dylan paused, his mind completely blank. 'I'm sorry, I don't know.' He winced as the man pulled the bandage tight.

'I patched you up as best I can, but you're lucky to be alive.' Something in that voice conveyed a hint of threat underneath the tone of false cheer.

'Do I know you?' Dylan asked.

'He's my husband, Nigel,' Susan explained.

Then a second later, a fellow knave, this one with huge bat wings on his back and a small secondary set of three-clawed arms sticking out of his chest, swooped down, carrying a man wearing the mask of a wizard, whom he deposited gently on the sand.

'Thank you, Wyvern,' said the wizard, who then turned to regard Dylan. 'Mr Hardesty? Or is it Herne?'

'Have we met?' asked Dylan.

'Perhaps,' the wizard allowed, 'and perhaps not.'

Dylan had never seen the man in his life . . . not that he could remember much of his life. Thirty years? How badly had his brains been rattled? All he could remember was drowning, the water rolling over his head. Being rescued by an android?

'He has a concussion, Lord Branok,' Susan said.

Dylan suddenly looked around, searching the beach. 'Where the hell is my horn?' He struggled to his hooves, rising to his full eight feet, plus antlers, then felt his satyr haunches buckle as he passed out.

Dylan woke up in the most comfortable bed he'd ever lain in, considering that it fitted all eight feet of him, with room even for his antlers. It had red-and-yellow striped draperies, elaborately carved pilasters with centuries of lovers' initials scratched into them, carvings of naked men and women, and even a lion with a red blob of sealing wax on its nose.

Dylan recognized it immediately, given that his card had turned during auditions for a double production of *Twelfth Night* and *The Merry Wives of Windsor*, where he'd been aiming to play Falstaff. But it was from the soliloquy of another of Shakespeare's characters, Sir Toby Belch, from the first play, which Dylan had practised for auditions as understudy. The words sprang to mind as clearly as the day he'd memorized them:

'"Go, write it in a martial hand, be curst and brief; it is no matter how witty, so it be eloquent, and full of invention. Taunt him with the licence of ink: if thou 'thou'st' him some thrice, it shall not be amiss, and as many lies as will lie in thy sheet of paper, although the sheet were big enough for the bed of Ware in England, set 'em down . . ."'

'Very good, Mr Hardesty,' said the wizard, the one they'd called Lord Branok. 'It would appear your memory is returning.'

Dylan struggled to sit up, then struggled more as he realized he was restrained beneath the coverlet, his arms cuffed with heavy, if silk-lined, shackles. His hooves were, too. Even his knave strength couldn't break him free.

'Don't exert yourself too much,' Lord Branok advised. 'The treatment I gave your head wound is not instantaneous, and those restraints are stronger than they look. You're a very dangerous man, and I need to assure the safety of my guests . . . which you are not, even though I am offering you shelter. The storm is not over yet, and it's one even you might not withstand – certainly not injured and without your horn.'

Dylan raised his head and looked at the wizard standing at the foot of the Great Bed of Ware, scene of a hundred thousand seductions, debaucheries, and orgies since the Elizabethan age. But rather than the bed being set up in a tourist trap inn in Ware or the exhibit at the *Victoria & Albert* that had made such an impression on Dylan as a lad, they were in a medieval dungeon cell.

'Where the hell is my horn?'

'Safely elsewhere,' said Lord Branok. 'You may not have met me, Mr Hardesty, but I have met you – and more than once. I enjoy the actor, and I appreciate the athlete, but the terrorist knave?' He stroked his mask's beard. 'No matter which one you are, you can tell enough lies to fit this bed, so if you say we haven't met or you don't remember, I won't believe you.'

'I don't know what you're talking about,' Dylan told him honestly. For the life of him, he had no recollection of ever meeting the man – not that he had much recollection of anything at the moment.

'Or perhaps your memory is blocked,' Lord Branok guessed. 'That's also possible, given the places you might have been.'

'If you think I'm so dangerous, why would you want me as an enemy?' Dylan growled, pulling his bonds with enough strength to snap ordinary chains; but still, the silk-lined shackles held, stronger than anything he'd ever encountered.

'Ah, there it is,' said Lord Branok smugly. 'I'm dealing with Herne the Hunter, not Hardesty the athlete or Dylan the actor. I don't want you as an enemy. But if you ever did choose to hunt me, I'd lead you on the merriest chase you ever had – and the most dangerous one, too, for trust me, my lad, you don't want *me* as an enemy either.'

He looked at Dylan from behind the mask of the wise old wizard, but the eyes behind the holes looked older still, and Dylan realized that this man was no stranger to war, and while he might not relish killing, he'd killed before and would do so again if he felt he had no other option.

Dylan sank back into the pillows and stopped straining against his bonds. 'Then what do you want?'

Lord Branok paused for a long moment. 'What can you tell me of your quarry? The mermaid?'

Dylan thought back, recalling Herne's pursuit from the night before, though very little of it. 'All I can tell you is that, if Herne was after her, there must have been a bloody good reason.'

The wizard nodded. 'That's what I was afraid of . . .'

The storm had started up once more outside the windows, now shuttered again, but at least the electricity was working – including the damned Black Forest antler lamps.

Nigel felt more than vaguely useless.

He had contemplated murder, but when it came right down to it, he'd saved Dylan Hardesty's life instead. Violent revenge fantasies about a man you thought safely dead were one thing; the cold-blooded murder of an injured man was quite another.

But at least it looked as if Hardesty would be going to prison. Banger and

Mash were from the Silver Helix, and while they were mainly muscle, Gary Bushorn – who'd previously been a mayor in Ireland, despite being an American from New York – had spent all night and half of breakfast telling them about someone named Duncan, who had been investigating Hardesty decades ago for crimes here in the UK, before Hardesty turned up as Herne in New York, leading packs of slavering hounds across the Brooklyn Bridge. Suffice it to say that Susan's ex was wanted on two continents. Nigel could take some comfort in that. Looking like a Celtic god wouldn't do Hardesty much good in prison.

Susan came out of the bathroom, drying her hair with a plush green towel, and glanced up at the electric antler chandeliers and the fireplace still burning with green flames. 'What do you want to wear for dinner?' she asked.

It was a desperate attempt to avoid the elephant in the room, but Nigel was grateful for it. 'It hardly matters. I think Jago's stalling, and we're the token nats at his gala, so what are we going to do?' He pecked Susan briefly on the cheek, then went into the bathroom himself.

Couples had their habits, and one of Nigel's, which annoyed Susan, was singing in the bath, but if they weren't going to enjoy it together, he might as well enjoy it himself. The bathroom was decorated all in green, as was to be expected, tiled with exquisite soapstone mosaics depicting an Atlantean fantasy: mermaids and tritons frolicking with sea horses, sea lions, sea wolves, and even sea cows.

A lovely bath had been drawn in a huge, steaming tub in the corner, with a spa's worth of luxury soaps, scrubs, and shampoos, and a window that opened, not to the outside, but to the orangery, with a fragrant tropical frangipani blooming right there. Nigel could just climb into the tub, lather up, then close his eyes and forget about the unfortunate choice of decor.

The warm bath also loosened up his pipes nicely, and Nigel sang, 'On Keun Island there dwells a maid – mark well what I do say! On Keun Island, there dwells a maid, and she is mistress of her trade. I'll go no more a-roving with you, fair maid . . .'

'*Ooboshu, ooboshu, ooboshu mnahn' n'gh-a-og, ya bug naflog ooboshu nw'fhalma!*'

Nigel opened his eyes. He didn't know whether he was more surprised to find the mermaid in the bath with him or by the fact that 'The Maid of Amsterdam' was not only known by ghostly Cornish pirates but also by carnivorous mermaids. But he was also hypnotized by her siren song, and while her salamander body from the waist up shifted to give the appearance of a beautiful golden-haired maiden, from the waist down, there was still the slimy tail and fins of a salamander-betta.

She coiled around him, reminding him painfully of the depiction of Melusine in her bath in the next chamber; the story was that every seven days, she went to bathe alone so that her husband wouldn't discover her turning into a dragon.

The mermaid smiled, showing her teeth as she sang, the alien lyrics to 'The Maid of Amsterdam' giving way to a wordless aria. Then she reached into the water, her pretty hands becoming horrific webbed claws, as she dug into her flesh and removed . . . what was it? A poppet? A dolly? It was inky black, with axolotl gill fringes ringing its head like loops of black yarn, the blank button eyes of a shark, and the wide mouth and tail of a just-hatched amphibian.

Then she was prying open Nigel's jaws and shoving it down his throat.

Nigel didn't know if this was some hideous cultural exchange, a tit-for-tat repayment for her having eaten the maid or for him having saved her life – for there, beside the bath, he saw the bloodstained bandage he'd torn off his robe, and beneath the surface of the bath, the mermaid's wound had healed as neatly as if it were never there.

All Nigel knew for certain was that the mermaid's spawn slid down his throat like an overlarge gulp of gelatine.

Then the mermaid slid out the window, down the frangipani tree, and disappeared into the orangery.

Dylan awoke to someone frantically patting his cheek. 'Dylan! Dylan, wake up!'

He opened his eyes groggily. 'Susan?' His head hurt, and he was worn out from the strain of trying to break the restraints. Whatever they were, they were made from something stronger than steel, likely with some wild card power involved.

'Yes,' she said quickly.

Dylan looked around. He was still in the dungeon, still shackled in the Great Bed of Ware, like the set dressing for some Shakespearean BDSM. *The Kinky Wives of Windsor*. 'How'd you get in?'

'I guessed that Hitchcock would keep a spare set of keys stashed in the butler's pantry. Went to chat up the cook and nicked them.'

'Hitchcock?' Dylan asked.

'Jago's butler,' Susan explained. 'Dead ringer for the great man. But never mind; we need to get you out of here! I heard the aces talking. You're wanted for murder on both sides of the pond.'

She left a good bit unsaid – chiefly the fact that at the first of those murders, she'd been an enthusiastic participant: a Maying rite that had got completely out of hand, with Dylan as Herne the Hunter, Susan as Maid Marian, and the ancient tune and choreography of the Abbots Bromley Horn Dance. All had gone to plan until a Georgian silver hunting horn had somehow transformed into Herne's Celtic dragon horn the moment Dylan sounded it.

It had also transformed him into Herne, enabling him to summon the

Gabriel Hounds and the Wild Hunt and call forth Herne's spear from nothingness.

Dylan had awoken the next morning, back in his right mind, to find Susan gone. He'd frantically called the Twisted Fists, who sent the Green Man and his crew to cover up their accidental murder and cannibalism of a French art film director who'd started out as Dylan and Susan's friend. They hadn't meant to do it, but getting drunk on the rage and bloodlust of someone's heretofore hidden wild card power was not much of a defence.

'Has it really been thirty years?'

The lines on Susan face told the truth – guilt and grief mixed with worry. Dylan couldn't remember anything between New York and now.

'I'm sorry, I can't recollect . . .' He looked at the shackles. They were lined with blue silk bearing a decorative chainstitch embroidery in gold. It looked as if Lord Branok liked a bit of kink. 'If I had Herne's spear, I could cut through them,' Dylan offered. 'It's just bronze, but somehow sharper than anything. But I can't call the spear unless I'm Herne, and I can't call Herne without his horn, the one you gave me . . .'

It's all in your mind, Dylan, said a voice in his head, a memory. *If you believed, you could blow a kazoo and it would become Herne's horn just the same.* Then the voice was gone, and he couldn't remember who said it, only that they'd said it in his mind.

'I know it's my ace crutch,' Dylan told Susan, 'something that makes my joker into a knave beyond just my strength. But it's my crutch because *you* gave it to me. I think, when I fall too deep into character, Herne still thinks of you as his May Queen.'

'I haven't seen that horn in over thirty years, and I ended up marrying the son of the man who sold it to me.' Susan laughed, but her voice sounded strained. 'All Nigel knew was that, after his dad died, a pretty girl trying to make sense of her life was mooning over his shop window. He thought she was looking at him, not at the shop that had sold her the old hunting horn she'd given her boyfriend. And now you bring your horn back to Keun and lose it, and if it's anywhere, it's out in the storm.' Susan paused. 'What if I were to give you something else? Could you summon the spear then?'

'Maybe. It's the wild card. Anything's possible. But I think it would have to be as special as that was.'

'No pressure, then. You're asking for a love token from a silly young girl who fancied herself an actress, not a woman who's lived some life since.' Susan grimaced. 'But youth lost is experience gained, and I've had years to fantasize about what I would do with you if I ever found you again . . . More's the pity.'

'Well, it looks like you've found me again. So' – he grinned – 'why not do them?'

Susan gave him a sad look. 'Because you were dead, and I'm married . . .'

'So, you love him?'

'Yes, but – it's complicated! It's been thirty years, Dylan. After you disappeared, I had a string of boyfriends. But Nigel was the only one I ever fit with.' She sighed, her eyes going unfocused like they always did when she was struggling to recall a line. 'We had adventures, mostly silly ordinary ones – nat adventures – and disappointments, and arguments. And when it got too much, I sometimes dreamed of what my life would have been like with you instead . . . But I also never thought I'd see you again. I'd thought you were dead or at best locked away in some hellhole on the other side of the pond while the Yanks lied and said you were dead.'

He could see the conflict in her face, wished he could reach up and touch her. He'd always loved her, and it hurt to see her so torn. 'Once, then, for old time's sake?' he suggested. 'Before the Silver Helix tosses me in whatever oubliette they keep for naughty knaves?'

He could see her resolve crumbling. 'You always were the naughtiest knave . . .' Susan stroked the coverlet, and Dylan beneath it. 'What was it Mercutio said? "It must be noon, for lo, the pricks are up"?' She reached under the quilt, grasped the thickness of his shaft and stroked its length. 'Or it could be midnight, for the pricks are up then, too, and that is when Herne rides . . . or is ridden.'

To his delight, Susan slipped off her knickers, letting them fall to the floor, then flipped back the covers and paused as she saw Dylan all but fully erect.

'Goodness. Either I'd forgotten how big you were, or you've grown since the last time we were together. I think it's a little of both.' She touched him then, making his member grow even more rigid, and groaned. 'I'd forgotten how much I missed this. You already had the body of a god . . .'

Susan leaned over to kiss then lick the shaft, tracing upwards with her tongue as she swung one leg up and over him with a dancer's motion. She got astride him as if mounting her own horse for the hunt. Her labia, already wet, touched the base of his shaft and sent a thrill of anticipation through him as she stripped off her sweater, tossing it aside, then torturing him as he reached up to let loose her magnificent breasts from her bra . . . only to find that his hands were still caught in the silk-lined shackles.

He growled, and she laughed.

'Patience!' she said – half teasing, half earnest. 'I've waited over thirty years for this! You can wait thirty seconds.' She smiled. 'Or longer . . .'

She leaned back and down, until the tips of her long hair tickled his flesh and, for just a second, she looked exactly as she once had, her curtain of glorious golden curls swaying, teasing, tantalizing, until she touched the shaft with the tip of her tongue to give him the tiniest teasing lick, then let the trailing end of her hair trace the length of his shaft, pausing to kiss him once, twice, thrice, at intervals. She came down to kiss the apple of the head, slid out of its furred foreskin, and her lace-clad breasts pressed upon its centre and the hair of his belly and lower chest teased its top . . .

Dylan closed his eyes, letting memory carry him back to the last time they'd lain together, in a hayfield on an old bedspread tossed over the piled straw, making love as the sun set and night overtook them. Dylan had slipped into persona as Herne as he had imagined him, a Shakespearian *dramatis persona* writ as large as the wild card had refashioned Dylan's body, a dark twin to rule his mind as night fell.

But was it night or day? They were deep in the dungeons of Lord Branok's castle, a wizard on his island, Prospero for all intents and purposes. But there was no way of knowing whether the moon or sun ruled the sky. *It is all in your mind,* said the unknown voice in his head again. *Dylan by day, Herne by night. Sun and moon. You can play Petruchio and say the sun is the moon if you choose . . .*

Dylan felt Susan grab his antlers, using them as a handhold as she lowered herself onto him. He wanted to reach out and grab her, but the silken shackles bound his wrists, so he relaxed and let her do the work, sliding up and down with a rhythm that was soon matched by the reverberation of a bell, a clock striking the hour somewhere in Jago's mansion. Again and again, it sounded, in rhythm with their lovemaking, and Dylan counted a dozen chimes, a dozen thrusts. Was it midnight or noon? Dylan or Herne?

He came, and he chose, remembering what it was to be Herne, remembering just a pinch of his power, imagining the weight of it in his right hand. *Enter Herne, stage left, holding his spear . . .*

Herne opened his eyes, blazing with witch-fire, dyeing the vision above him as green as emeralds. 'My Marian,' Herne breathed, seeing his May Queen again after so many years, 'it hath been too long.'

Marian – Susan – paused, then touched his face. 'The fire in your eyes is back.'

'Because *I* am now back,' Herne told her. His right hand flexed, and he felt the comfortable girth of his spear's shaft; then he turned his head to reassure himself that it was there. The wood gleamed in the emerald radiance from his eyes, and even more so did the spear's head, wicked bronze honed to a razor's edge.

With a masterful pass, Herne slashed the head of the spear through the chain holding the rightmost shackle. The metal sliced like butter, but the silk ribbon laced through the links still stubbornly resisted.

'What witchcraft is this?' Herne roared.

Susan pulled herself off him, her face contorted with both pleasure and pain, and slipped off the bed. 'Bugger,' she said, inspecting the broken shackle and the silken bond, 'I think the ribbon's the work of the Seamstress, one of the Silver Helix aces. Whatever she sews is invulnerable . . .'

'The witch must die,' Herne spat. 'Will her death break the bonds?'

'Hell if I know,' Susan said, 'but I think she stitches her work with ordinary needle and thread or knits it with ordinary knitting needles. She came in the shop a few months back, one of Jago's guests for another party, and Nigel sold her some knitting needles. Maybe there's a weakness.'

'A careless stitch to unravel the sleeve of care,' Herne chuckled. 'This Seamstress will make worthy prey. Can you spy one?'

Susan examined the silken bond. 'Here,' she pronounced, pointing to one end of the embroidered chain. 'I can't see a single loose stitch, but I found the knot where she tied them off.'

'To solve like Alexander solved the Gordian one.' Herne chuckled. 'Guide my spear, my Marian . . .'

Susan did so, positioning the point of the spear at a single scintilla of silken thread. The knot caught on the tip, and Herne pressed, straining, channelling his rage and his power into the single point, but still the knot held.

'*Witch!*' Herne cried in rage, swinging the spear around to slice the shackle on his other wrist then both hooves. The alien alloy fell away, but still the blue ribbon and its gold chain embroidery held, soft as silk but stronger than iron – witchcraft worthy of the Weird Sisters and Hecate herself.

But the Great Bed of Ware was made of ordinary wood, and once he had enough slack to stand, Herne strained against the ribbons like Samson against his pillars. Then, with a resounding *CRACK!*, the bedposts broke. The stones of the dungeon were ancient but not impervious granite. Rings of the alien alloy were sunk into it, but the unbreakable ribbon was fettered to them with common clove-hitch knots that fell back into unblemished loops once the rings were cut.

The other knots were more complicated but no more impossible – especially the large blue bow knotted beneath the Great Bed of Ware, exposed when Herne tossed the mattress aside and cut the webbing of the bed's ropes.

'At last, the witch's ligature comes undone!'

Herne pulled the bow, the loops sliding free at once, giving him space and time to work on the more elaborate knots binding the ribbons to his wrists. But this was a task for patience, not rage, so Herne released his spear, letting it dissolve into mist as the Hunter's persona faded, the witch-light dying in his eyes.

'Let the moon be the sun,' he pronounced, making his exit, leaving him plain Dylan Hardesty once again, sitting there in the broken wreckage of the Great Bed of Ware.

Nigel sat in the bath until it started to grow cold, and his feet and fingertips were wrinkled and pruney. The force of long habit made him get out and grab a towel, though the cavorting merthings depicted in the bathroom's mosaics had taken on a decidedly sinister cast.

'Susan?' he called querulously. 'Susan?'

There was no answer from the next room, so Nigel went in. Susan was nowhere to be seen, but the green velvet curtains with their nautilus pattern were still drawn, and the storm rumbled outside with renewed vigour. Nigel's gut clenched as if he'd swallowed a toad, which was in fact a fairly accurate description of what had transpired. He supposed it was better than getting his head bitten off like Colette, but it didn't bode well.

Nigel hoped Jago would know what to do. To say that something odd was going on in Loveday House was the understatement of the year, but Nigel had a feeling this was odder than usual for the Lord of Loveday, so he wasn't about to go running down the halls starkers, screaming for help. He'd need to put some clothes on first.

He sighed, opening the wardrobe. Susan had taken such care packing, but it seemed easiest to dress for comfort. He put on his usual shirt and trousers, with his new favourite tweed jacket with suede patches on the elbows, then heard a noise from across the room and realized with a sick lurch that it was the dumbwaiter door, the panel carved with a portrait of Melusine.

She no longer seemed as charming as she was in the old fairy tales, dark as they were – which did not seem anywhere near dark enough – but the panel was still just the dumbwaiter door. That meant that the kitchen was sending something up, probably something Susan had ordered. Nigel realized he was hungry . . . or actually, the thing in his stomach was hungry. It roiled inside him, making him salivate, and his horror at this was matched only by the dumbwaiter door opening to reveal not a tiered tray containing cakes and sandwiches for a nice tea, but a pirate with a dagger clenched in his teeth.

The pirate leaped out, brandishing the knife at Nigel, while saying something incomprehensible. The dumbwaiter shaft then disgorged not one but two more pirates – young lads dressed like extras from *The Pirates of Penzance*, only reset in the Dark Ages and costumed too realistically. Nigel realized he could understand what they were saying, despite the barbaric accent, for they were speaking Cornish, and he recognized one of the words: *dasprena*, which meant *ransom*.

'Dasprena?' Nigel echoed, making the pirates nod enthusiastically.

One held his dagger to Nigel's throat; another grabbed him by the arm, and the third cried in delight as he ran to the mantelpiece where Susan had put the bottle of Lady Morwen's Armagnac. The Cornish he spoke was too fast for Nigel to understand, but the meaning was clear as he unholstered a sabre and struck off the neck of the bottle before Nigel could protest. '*Hwiski!*' the pirate cried in delight.

'That's not whiskey, you cretin!' Nigel protested. 'That's priceless French Armagnac!'

The pirate didn't care. He took a long pull regardless, then shared it with his fellows in celebration as they bound Nigel's wrists and forced him into the dumbwaiter, then began to send him down into the darkness and the depths of Loveday House.

◆

Susan opened another door, and Dylan ducked through and followed. Most of the hallways in the upper section of Loveday House had raised Victorian ceilings, so he didn't have to stoop for more than a few chandeliers and, once, a swag of forgotten bunting emblazoned with GLADSTONE WINS!

Dylan came to the conclusion that Lord Jago Branok had been following his career for some time, for how else could you explain the wardrobe holding all the outfits Dylan had worn for a Givenchy runway show in Paris in 1988?

He'd been slighter then, but a green kilt with Celtic knotwork that matched the shade of Herne's witch-fire could still be adjusted to fit, so he grabbed it, along with a loose jersey he'd been sorry to see go, even if it was now skin-tight. Dylan donned them, glad they appeared to have been recently dry-cleaned. But you didn't do porn, let alone joker porn, without expecting fans.

Loveday House was insane. There were doors that opened into walls, staircases that led up to ceilings with no trapdoors in sight, chutes in the floor that dropped down two storeys. Then Susan opened a grand door, and they were suddenly in a trophy room with stags' heads on the wall, as well as stranger beasts, including the head of a unicorn – either that had been put together by a talented taxidermist with the head of a goat, the mane of a horse, and the tusk of a narwhal, or Jago Branok had murdered and mounted a unicorn-headed joker while playing and hunting 'The Most Dangerous Game'.

There were weapons here, too, from ray guns sized for dwarves to an elephant gun for a joker larger than Dylan.

Then Susan pointed across the room. 'Look, Dylan!'

Dylan looked. There on the wall hung a collection of hunting horns, at least fifty of them. He hurried over and crouched on his haunches, bringing the collection to his eye level. 'Do you see it, Susan? Is it here?'

'Is it this one?' Susan pointed to a battered but brightly polished horn decorated with hounds and riders.

Dylan's heart leaped then sank. 'Close, but no. The fox is wrong, and this one has different dents.'

He looked further, then heard the sound of a throat clearing. Dylan spun and rose, seeing Lord Branok, still wearing his wizard mask, step out from behind a stuffed grizzly bear with one cyclopean eye and the horns of a bighorn sheep. 'If you're looking for your hunting horn, Mr Hardesty, you won't find it here in my collection.' The old eyes behind the wizard mask flicked to Dylan's kilt, 'Though admittedly, I sometimes lose track of everything I have. Including, it appears, you.' He glanced to Susan. 'I assume you had a hand in this, Ms Strathmore?'

Susan admitted nothing.

Lord Branok sighed. 'I often come to the Hunter's Hall when I need to compose myself before dinner. I know my guests are expecting me, and while you are not my guests, merely a guest's "plus one" and a random stray, my hospitality is not so poor as to turn you out into the storm. But please, do not test me. I came here to arm myself as well.' He did not brandish a gun but did not need to; Dylan saw enough bulges beneath his suit to hold a considerable number of weapons. Lord Branok opened a secret door in the wall. 'Come along, both of you. You will need to duck, I expect, Mr Hardesty.'

Dylan did indeed need to duck, and as he hunched through the passageway, following Susan, almost having to take the posture of an actual stag himself, he heard the loud melodious chiming of a clock striking the hour, reverberating through the walls, and counted the chimes: One, two, three, four, five, six, seven.

Dylan had no idea whether it was night or morn, but the mantel clock in the dining room read seven as well after they emerged from the doorway beside it. He straightened up. The Loveday House dining room was grand, with a long table suitable for banquets, but for now, only a few places had been set at one end near the fireplace. Seated at it, already nibbling hors d'oeuvres and sipping wine, was the winged knave named Wyvern, a middle-aged white couple dressed like Cockney pearlies, and a Black man dressed in Regency garb, like an extra from a BBC drama.

'Ah,' said Lord Branok, surveying his guests, 'I expect the others are still getting dressed?'

'No,' said the woman, the buttons on the back of her coat identifying her as *MASH* and her voice identifying her as the Punch-masked woman who'd punched Herne off the cliff last night. 'I expect they had pirates climbin' outta their dumbwaiters to kidnap them, but they weren't strong enough to bop them one in the noggin and toss them back down the shaft.'

'Or tentacles,' said the Black man. 'One came out of my toilet. And there were eyes looking at me through the bathroom mirror before I smashed it.'

'Tentacles, Mr Bushorn?' said Lord Branok, sounding for a moment as old as the aged wizard on his mask. 'And eyes? Then it is worse than I feared.'

'How did you escape?' asked Dylan. The man did not look as if he'd be much good in a fight.

'I'm too hot to handle,' Bushorn said smugly, then jerked a thumb at Dylan while looking at Branok. 'What's *he* doing here? I thought you had him safely locked up.'

'Loveday House sometimes has her own ideas as to which doors should be locked or unlocked.' Lord Branok sighed. 'And I suspect he may have had help.' He eyed Susan. 'But it is no matter, Mr Bushorn. We have bigger tentacles to fry.'

Dylan then noticed that Bushorn had sucker-shaped marks around his face and neck, which stood out pink and angry against his darker skin, but they looked to be fading already. Likely a regenerative ace, in addition to pyrokinesis or something similar. Bushorn had Dylan's respect.

Bushorn continued, 'I've heard voices, too. Voices of people I loved, people I lost.'

Branok shrugged, whether out of callousness or weariness, Dylan was uncertain, only saying, 'It might have been a voice created by Loveday House,' he said, 'in which case I must apologize. I never intended this. Or it may have been an echo from another world, which is also a possibility.'

'What the bleedin' fack are you talking about?' asked Wyvern.

'It's complicated,' said Lord Branok, raising the bar for understatement of the year, as far as Dylan was concerned.

Then Hitchcock handed Lord Branok a glass of red wine. The Lord of Loveday lifted his mask just enough to take a long drink.

Dylan glanced towards the table, and his owl eyes were sharp enough to read the place cards at two of the empty seats: *Nigel Walmsley* and *Melissa Blackwood*. The process of elimination told him that Blackwood must be Topper, the ace with the hat.

Lord Branok drained his glass, then handed it off to Hitchcock. The butler moved two steps back, and Branok took his place at the head of the table. 'I had composed myself for an apology and an explanation, but I suppose what we shall be having instead is a war council.' He sighed, gesturing to Susan and Dylan. 'Ms Strathmore, please take your seat. Mr Hardesty, please find a chair that will fit you and join us.'

Dylan took a few long strides past the table to a high-backed gothic throne up against the wall. Without any cushions, it worked, even having space for his stubby little stag tail. He brought it over and set it down where Hitchcock had already removed the chairs and set an extra plate.

'How should I begin?' asked Branok, looking to the heavens, or at least at an ornate tin ceiling and a red-glass Victorian chandelier, which Dylan recognized as a desperate attempt to stall. He was rewarded by the jiggling of a carved panel in the wall, which looked to be the door of a dumbwaiter. Branok turned to his butler, asking, 'Did you arrange for anything to be sent up, Hitchcock?'

Hitchcock shook his head, making Mash get up, exclaiming, 'Bloody hell! I've had enough of pirates!'

She tore open the dumbwaiter door, shattering the latch and revealing Nigel Walmsley, wearing a tweed jacket, and what looked like a young pirate dressed much as you might expect a pirate to be, if you had a costumer doing a gritty medieval epic.

'Mr Walmsley?'

He nodded, getting out, then looking to the assembled group while the pirate stared in terror at Wyvern and Dylan, as if he'd never seen a joker before.

Nigel turned to Jago Branok. 'Lord Branok, this is Jestin.' He indicated the terrified young pirate, who couldn't have been more than 16 years old. 'He and his mates wish to join your crew. In fact, they've already accepted advance wages for the next year.'

'What?' said Jago Branok, sounding just as confused as Dylan felt.

'My Cornish is far better than I thought,' Nigel explained, 'once I worked out their accent. Plus, the Cornish translation of *The Pirates of Penzance* that I helped Susan practise a number of years ago had surprisingly useful passages of dialogue: *Morlader Myghtern*, I am the Pirate King, yoho.' Nigel shrugged. 'It probably helped that Topper shot one and threw gold coins at the rest.' He eyed Dylan. 'Of course, I also told them you'd imprisoned the *kowrek karow*, the giant stag, since they're terrified of him, and of the mermaid, too.'

Jago told Nigel, 'Tell them that the giant stag will behave himself, or I'll shoot him personally. As for the mermaid, they are right to fear her, and we will need their help if we are all to survive the night.'

Nigel rattled something off in Cornish to the young pirate, who nodded, then descended in the dumbwaiter by himself. A minute later, the dumbwaiter disgorged Topper, a few maids, and an injured pirate, followed by about two dozen more pirates climbing up the dumbwaiter ropes like the lines of a ship's rigging.

Hitchcock defaulted to a butler's duty, getting out more plates in a fussy pattern that looked like giant seashells and setting extra places at the long table as Topper and Susan's husbands took their assigned seats. Susan filled Nigel in, with the quick whispers of a long-married couple, while some of the maids ran off and a few more ran back in, bringing more wine, charcuterie platters, and Victorian game pies moulded on the side with a satyr's head.

A chef brought one personally to Jago, who changed his mind and accepted another glass of wine from Hitchcock, then pointedly cut the satyr-head pie in two while looking straight at Dylan. 'Now, where was I? How can I easily explain our predicament?'

'By cutting the crap,' said Mash's husband, the pearly king, whose buttons identified him as *BANGER*.

'Have you heard the phrase "when worlds collide", Mr Spragg? That is what has happened.' Jago did not wait for a reply. 'There are multiple worlds, multiple universes – an infinite number of possibilities. Some are so close to identical that only an expert could tell them apart. Others are so alien as to destroy you were you to set foot in them. Most lie somewhere in between. Little differences. Big differences.'

Nigel understood. 'A world in which Meissen used different porcelain marks. A world in which you hired Queen Victoria's personal chef before he could get killed.' He pointed to Jago's chef, who gasped.

'Yes, exactly, Mr Walmsley,' Jago said, giving him a long look, 'and in that world, Victoria is still on the throne. There's another world in which Hitler never came to power, because that world's Daniel never died, sparking the Anglo-German enmity that led to the First and Second World Wars in our own reality. Worlds in which the Terror, the Black Death, or the Thirty Years War are currently occurring, where time moves more slowly than in our own. Many of my servants were rescued from such worlds.' He sighed and took another sip of wine. 'I'm sorry. This was not my intention.'

'You did this?' Wyvern hissed. 'You called them weird black flapping things?'

'No, Mr Beattie, I did not.' Jago sighed. 'My power does not work that way. My ace only allows me to sense doorways between worlds, gives me presentiment of whether I might survive the trip through, and sometimes of what or whom the key to that world might be, if any. Ms Blackwood may be able to make doorways, but only through her hat and only for what she can pull through. Still, it may have been a mistake to have her do so in such an area and especially on such a night. The etching and engraving plate were tempting fate enough, but adding Martin's painting to the mix . . .'

'So, you're saying you lit a beacon on Bonfire Night, and Topper threw on rowan wood?' asked Nigel. 'Or it's like a fairy stone – if you touch the correct number of primroses in a posy, you open the door to Faerie. Get the wrong number, you open the door to Doom.'

'A bit more literary than I'd put it, but essentially, yes,' Jago told him. 'Loveday House sits upon crossroads where a thousand, thousand worlds come together. I built it so that I might more easily access some of those doors, and also, so that I might hold others shut. There are worlds where Loveday House is only slightly different; there are others where Mad Morwen's castle still stands, and still others, like this one, where a house has appeared on the hill where one never was before, and on an island untouched by man.'

'If it's untouched by man,' asked Bushorn, 'why are there pirates? And what's with the tentacle in my toilet?'

'A good question, Mr Bushorn, which deserves a good answer. Our Loveday House is not the only Loveday cut adrift – one of the pirate fortresses of the Hounds of the Sea also broke free in the storm between worlds – but my Loveday was built to be, shall we say, reshuffleable. So rather than collapse like a house of cards like Lady Morwen's castle in 1703, the decks have been shuffled together, along with stray cards from other decks.'

'Like a passageway from Lady Morwen's castle,' said Nigel, 'or the belvedere from Marcus St Gerren's day.'

'Or even a stateroom from Captain Nemo's *Nautilus* which I kept as my Kraken Room,' Jago nodded. 'But the trouble is, the combined deck of Loveday

House and the castle of the Hounds of the Sea has ended up in a very bad place – on one of those worlds I would never willingly visit. And the only reasons we have survived is that the inhabitants here haven't seen something quite like Loveday House before and are undoubtedly wondering what they might do with it and us.' Jago sighed. 'The world we have ended in is the one the mermaid is from, and where she will undoubtedly tell them everything she knows about us if she is not stopped.'

'So, what are yeh going to do about her?' asked Banger. 'Doubt that cunt's going to be as easy to bribe as the pirates.'

Jago shook his head sadly. 'No, I doubt she will be as reasonable, especially since she came here hunted by Mr Hardesty.' He studied Dylan through the holes in his wizard mask. 'What can you tell us about your quarry?'

Dylan shrugged. 'I was Herne at the time – I mean, fully Herne.' He thought. 'She can swim like an eel and fly like a flying fish, but she's slow on land. She can make herself look like a pretty girl, can sing even more beautifully than that, and her song can hypnotize you if you're not careful.' He shook his head, but the weight of his antlers only made his brain hurt more. 'I'm sorry; that's all I can recall. I don't even know why I was after her or where I was before that . . .'

'That is scant but accurate, as far as it goes . . . but rather than continuing to call her the mermaid, I believe a better appellation might be "Monster Girl". She is of a race I call Proteans – an amphibious parasitic species that exists in many worlds. In our own world, they are as extinct as the passenger pigeon – a fortunate side-effect, I believe, of the whaling age – but in other worlds and past times, they are the source of many sea monster legends. Proteans are a sort of giant salamander or frog, depending on the subspecies, but if their tadpoles are swallowed by a mammal or even a cephalopod, they attach themselves as a parasite, growing through the creature, supplanting its soft tissues and absorbing its memories. The kraken? A Protean parasitized giant squid. Monstrous whales? Heraldic dolphins? The same. And when ingested by a land animal, well, the results are sea cows, sea boars, sea dogs, and of course mermen and mermaids.'

'Does it happen immediately?' asked Nigel.

'Yes and no,' said Jago, contemplating his wine. 'It attaches itself inoperably at the start, twining with the host's spinal column or other nervous system and spreading into the brain, but it is an infant, innocent as such, knowing nothing except what it learns from the host. Many do not even realize they are Proteans, depending on where they are in the process. But in the special places, like here upon the hill of Keun Island and the fuggy hole and the sea caves below, where the veil between worlds is thin? Well, then, the melding of the infant Protean and the adult host may hear the call of other worlds – not only hearing the sirens singing but understanding what they sing. Some have strange and terrible dreams of undersea kingdoms where they may inherit their birthright until, one day, the call is irresistible, and they feel the lure of the sea, diving in to complete the transformation and join their kind.'

'But they're a sentient species?' asked Topper.

'Very much so,' said Jago. 'Especially the ones that take octopi and dolphins as hosts – the courtiers and councillors, as it were. Protean whales are viewed as god-emperors and krakens as incarnate divinities. Parasitized humans are seen as a lesser caste – fools and mountebanks at best but prized for their singing. But compared to us, even those Proteans consider themselves a master race.'

'I've heard that phrase before,' said Bushorn.

'I have tried reasoning with adult Proteans, but . . . how should I put this? The worst are Hitler. The best? Jane Goodall, perhaps – fond of her chimp friends but still considering herself above them. Most Proteans lie somewhere between.'

'So Melusine was one of these Proteans?' asked Nigel. 'Merovech and the Merovingians? All of the mermaids of Cornwall?'

'In some worlds, yes; in others, no. There is an infinite number of worlds, Mr Walmsley.' Jago shrugged. 'But suffice it to say that we are dealing with one Protean, here and now – and one who, I fear, is more Hitler than Jane Goodall, given what happened to Colette.'

'Colette?' asked Dylan.

'The maid she murdered,' Mash told him.

Jago sighed. 'Worse, outside these walls – and even inside them, in some places, as Mr Bushorn discovered – there lies one of the home worlds of the Proteans, who view what has washed up in the storm between worlds as their rightful treasure. And the moment Monster Girl tells her folk what a prize is here, we will have to contend with more than a few curious tentacles.'

There was a long silence, nobody saying anything, except for Nigel translating for the pirates. Then they fell silent, too.

'If I still had my horn, I could finish what I started.' Dylan sighed. 'I don't call the Hunt on someone unless they bloody well deserve it. Not that it matters now, without my horn.'

'What does it look like?' asked Topper.

'Old Georgian silver hunting horn,' Dylan told her.

Topper reached into her hat, taking out a horn. 'Is this it?'

'No, that one's too new. Mine's rather dinged up.'

'Like this?' she asked, taking out a crumpled, tarnished wreck.

'No, not that bad.'

'More riders, too, from what I remember,' said Susan.

'This one?' asked Topper, pulling out a horn with a snapped strap that poured sand and seawater onto the table.

'*That's it!*' cried Dylan.

They stood in the middle of the orangery, citrus trees filling the air with perfume, the domed glass ceiling above them twinkling like the conservatory at Kew Gardens, only with fake stars lit up inside the storm shutters outside – more of Jago's technological wizardry for Loveday House. Jago had made great plans, one-part Odysseus, one-part modern science, for everyone not wishing to participate in the Hunt to stop their ears – not with wax, as Odysseus had used, but with conventional earplugs, followed by noise-cancelling headphones, and then having every sound system in the house blasting the loudest possible classical music, currently the 'Bacchanale' from *Samson and Delilah* by Camille Saint-Saëns.

To the tune of this in his unstopped ears, Nigel climbed down the frangipani tree from the Mermaid bathroom, throwing the bloody terrycloth at Dylan's hooves.

'Will this do?' he asked, almost shouting to be heard over the orchestral din of clashing cymbals, thundering drums, and clattering castanets.

The giant knave leaned down, picked it up, and sniffed it. 'If you're certain it's her blood, it should be perfect. Can't tell until I call the Hunt.' He paused. 'Why are you doing this?'

'I have my reasons,' said Nigel, not admitting it was because the shape-shifting cunt had force-fed him her parasitic newt spawn. 'I saved her life; I can take it back.'

Wyvern stared down at him. 'If you weren't a nat, you'd make a pretty good Twisted Fist.' He glanced over at Banger, Mash, and Topper. 'Not that I'd know anything about that.'

Topper glanced to Susan. 'You?'

'Not my first rodeo,' said Susan to Dylan, 'and where Nigel goes, I go. Marriage is like that.'

Bushorn had wanted no part of the Hunt, which was doubtless wise of him, electing to stay inside with Jago and most of the staff. Nigel thought about telling Susan to stay, but she was a headstrong woman, sure of what she wanted, and more than that, he took her implication that she'd ridden with the Wild Hunt before. Of everyone, she knew best what she was getting into.

'Just warning you,' Dylan stressed, 'this isn't cold, dispassionate duty; it's rage and bloodlust. It will consume you. It's called the Wild Hunt for a reason.'

'We lived through the Terror,' said the first of a dozen French maids in eighteenth century English, armed with a dozen Napoleonic era rifles, 'and that bitch beheaded our sister. She will pay.'

'*Kyjyans kapten*,' spat Jestin, which Nigel translated as *Fucker captain*. The pirate added some more Cornish, which seemed close to 'We're going to carve her up for fishbait!' Or something like that, to judge from the cheers from the more than a dozen young pirates brandishing swords.

'I'm American,' said Topper, 'and I survived both the Democratic and Republican national conventions.'

'We're Gooners,' began Banger.

'Enough said,' finished Mash.

Dylan nodded, then paused, undoing the poppers on his jersey, then pulling off his kilt for good measure.

'Ooh-la-la!' cried the French maids.

'*Kvjyans!*' swore the pirates.

'Herne doesn't like clothes,' explained Dylan, handing them to Susan, who folded them up and put them in her bag. Then he closed his eyes, lifted the old hunting horn to his lips, and blew, the blast blending with the horns of the 'Bacchanale'.

As the knave blew, the horn changed and grew, transmuting from a rather pedestrian example of Georgian silverwork to a great golden horn, reminiscent of one of the lost Gallehus horns, but made with Celtic knotwork in the shape of a dragon rather than Nordic and Roman motifs. Dylan straightened up, becoming even taller, if that were possible, and when he opened his eyes, they glowed with an uncanny green fire, while his flowing red mane streamed in an invisible breeze as he laughed and gazed down at everyone.

'Well met!' he cried, in what Nigel had to admit was a rather grand Shakespearean manner, 'oh hunters fair. Now come, my horse!' He blew his horn again – an especially echoey sound in the confines of the orangery – and then a black stallion stepped out from behind an orange tree, half there, half not, as if Magritte's painting *Le Blanc-Seing* had come to life. The stallion's eyes blazed as green as its master's.

'Come, horses for my company – mount up!'

Over two dozen black horses emerged from the trees, stepping left, one for each rider. A black charger appeared from behind the impossibly slim bole of the frangipani, bowing its head to Nigel, and Nigel found himself mounting without assistance, the horse somehow natural and comfortable, almost like a carousel horse, even though there was no saddle whatsoever.

When he looked around, Nigel realized that all the riders' eyes were glowing, even Wyvern's, who wasn't riding so much as crouching upon his stallion, his little chest claws clutching its mane as he balanced like a surfer on a surfboard.

'Come, spear!' cried Herne the Hunter, blowing a brief blast on the horn. He reached behind a tree and pulled out a huge spear with a gilded head. 'Come, hounds and smell thy rightful prey!' He stamped the butt of the spear, and huge white wolfhounds appeared, almost as large as his horse, with glowing green eyes and blood-red ears.

Using the butt of his spear, Herne tossed the blood-soaked terrycloth towards to the Gabriel Hounds. The ghost-white hounds snuffed at it and at once began to bay. Nigel felt a disquieting shift in his gut, as if some horrific parasitic newt had just heard his wife's porn-star ex set ghost hounds on its mother.

'That will serve you right, you little bastard,' Nigel whispered to it.

Then the Wild Hunt was on, the hounds running the length of the orangery, the horses cantering around Victorian ironwork benches and over a carp pond, their hooves clattering on the surface of the water like ice on a skating rink. They ran through the arch of a Japanese moon bridge and past an elegant, red antique pagoda, until they came to the grand, glass double doors at the end.

The hounds howled, their claws scratching the glass, but Jago must have reinforced it with something, for the scratches melted away almost as soon as they were made.

'Oh Loveday House, release thy doors! We ride!' cried Herne.

The orangery doors swung wide, the Gabriel Hounds flowing out like a white tide, the dark horses behind them.

Nigel was both glad and faintly disappointed that the Hunt was heading out. But as it was, Loveday House was lit up like a disco behind them, while the strains of Saint-Saëns's 'Bacchanale' concluded only to transition to Orff's 'O Fortuna'.

It was not the worst possible choice.

The Wild Hunt flowed down the bluffs as a storm brewed above them, lightning flashing and thunder clapping ominously, then they switched back, once and twice again – the long path Nigel remembered down to Keun's west beach shifting and twisting to an alien topography that reminded him of John Martin's mad vision in *The Book of the Great Sea-dragons*, with the cloud-shrouded killing moon rising over the ink-black sea. The route still familiar enough at first, then considerably less so when the Gabriel Hounds raced out onto the surface of the water, headed out into the unknown, nameless sea.

The strains of the 'Carmina Burana' receded into the distance, but the storm kept pace. Yet as the Wild Hunt raced on, Nigel heard the siren's song, singing sweetly in the mermaid's incomprehensible language. Like an echo through his nerves, he could understand the meaning of the mermaid's hymn: '*Oh great one! Oh vast one! Oh Protean god-empress! Rise up and crush my enemies, oh argonaut!*'

The realization that the tune was still 'The Maid of Amsterdam' paled in comparison to his comprehension of the alien language, which meant that the mermaid's spawn had merged with his mind . . . But even the horror of that was overshadowed as a great white shell rose from the depths – a paper nautilus large as a galleon. The mermaid rode triumphant as the gargantuan nautilus rose higher, revealed as the turbaned crown of a pelagic octopus, which looked at them with her great eyes, then appeared to smile, forming its tentacles into the approximation of an immense human visage.

Join me, the god-empress told him in his mind, in a voice like a memory of a dream. *Kill the Huntsman and take your place at my side, with your ancestors.*

Nigel glanced at Herne, the author of his pain, and beside him, Susan, driven mad by the thrill of the Hunt.

When he dies, she will drown, the god-empress told him, *as is fitting.*

'No!' Nigel cried, repulsed by the thought.

The mermaid laughed, girlishly cruel, and the god-empress's face dissolved into octopus eyes, waving tentacles, and an immense mouth with a wicked beak big as two boat hulls. It sucked in like a whirlpool, swallowing three pirates while the tentacles grabbed two maids, horses and all.

Nigel had only asked Topper for a Glock, thinking that precision with a pistol would be best against the mermaid, not thinking she'd call reinforcements, let alone her god-empress great-grandmother. But the mermaid was still there, in plain view, as was the pistol, so Nigel aimed and shot.

Bright blood blossomed on her shoulder, and she gazed at him. 'Betrayer!' she cried in the alien tongue Nigel could suddenly understand. 'Foul monkey singer! I gave you the greatest gift!'

There was probably a witty rejoinder, but Nigel was filled with rage, and bullets were always appropriate, so he fired again and again. Neither shot was as good. Susan winged her as well, nicking the other shoulder.

Then Topper pulled a Second World War bazooka out of her hat, firing a rocket at the god-empress at the same time as Herne launched his spear. Topper's missile went wide, exploding harmlessly over the sea with a loud *BOOM!*, but the spear flew fast, piercing the monster's armoured shell, then flew out the other side to skip across the ocean waves and disappear.

Pirates rode by, slashing the monstrous octopus with cutlasses, followed by maids who'd swapped their white lace caps for the red caps of the French Revolution, shooting the god-empress with their muskets, then stabbing it with bayonets. Ghostly white hounds harried it, nipping the towering shell with savage jaws, like puppies trying to eat a double-decker bus. Banger and Mash rode their horses directly over the monstrous Protean, Mash dismounting to savage it with a horseman's mace from Jago's armoury while Banger used his fists, hammering the paper nautilus shell like jackhammers. Wyvern plunged like a falcon, revealing that his feet, out of his boots, were clawed like those of a gargoyle, aiming for the monster's eyes.

The monstrous nautiloid submerged, the mermaid with it, and Wyvern flapped back up, grabbing Banger and Mash by their jacket collars and dragging them back onto their horses.

Wyvern continued upwards, dodging a lightning bolt as it arced down to Herne's hand and formed a new spear. 'She's down there!' he called, pointing with all four arms. 'I can see her.' His eyes glowed green.

The Gabriel Hounds scratched and snuffled and yelped at the surface of the water as if at prey that had gone to ground. They flew in all directions as the monstrous octopus breached, leaving the immense paper nautilus shell behind, snapping Wyvern out of the air with one enormous bite.

Herne's spear flashed out like lightning, piercing the monster once again, but then Nigel heard the *BOOM!* of Topper's bazooka, the missile flying out to strike the Protean right in one immense eye, exploding with a *KA-BOOM!!!*

as the monstrous octopus's head exploded, fountaining brains and tentacles in all directions and showering the riders with ink and gore. With an even more titanic *KER-SPLASH!*, the corpse fell back into the ocean, sending waves in all directions.

Nigel's horse cantered with sudden sea swell, and he clutched its black mane to keep from being unhorsed. Then the mermaid leaped up beside Nigel's horse, coiling herself around them both, like the tapestry of Melusine in her bath – a maiden above, a serpent below, blood leaking from her shoulders.

'Betrayer!' she hissed, her face losing its maidenly beauty as she opened her jaws . . . then losing it even more as Nigel pressed the Glock to her throat and unloaded the clip, blasting mermaid brains through her new blowhole.

'*I'll go no more a-roving with you, fair maid,*' Nigel sang as she slid into the sea, and the green light died in everyone's eyes save the horses, the Gabriel Hounds, and Herne himself.

Their prey had been killed. The Wild Hunt was at an end.

Nigel felt the roiling in his head then – the screams of ten thousand unborn Proteans, wailing bereft inside the floating giant paper nautilus shell and losing air from the holes Herne had pierced with his spear.

The Wild Hunt might be over, but this wasn't.

Nigel looked over at Herne, who was no doubt getting ready to give some suitably dramatic cod-Shakespeare speech. He had hated him for years and still did, but Susan still loved Dylan and always had; if the knave had a redeeming virtue, it was that.

But it was more than that, Nigel realized. If Dylan hadn't been stolen from Susan by the Rox War and whatever wild card weirdness had happened at its end, she would never have wandered into Nigel's life, and he would not have been there to catch her when she fell. His past thirty years of happiness, even imperfect and second-best as they'd been, would never have happened. Indeed, in one of Jago's thousand alternate worlds, they never had; the Nigel there had never even had a taste of happiness, of Susan, a star-crossed lover always fated for another man.

'I love you, Susan,' Nigel told her. 'I hope you loved me and can forgive me.' To Herne, he said, 'You don't deserve her, but take care of her anyway.'

Then Nigel put the gun to his chin as Susan screamed, 'Nigel, no!' and the Protean *thing* in his mind shrieked in sudden fear. But Nigel had made his decision. Jago had said there were an infinite number of worlds, an infinite number of possibilities. Little differences. Big differences. Maybe there was a world where Nigel lived.

But it was not going to be this one.

Nigel pulled the trigger.

♥

Dylan woke up to sunlight streaming through the windows of a bedroom with tapestries on the walls, antlers on the ceiling, and a bed shaped like a boat with a cupid on the prow. Herne had left him sometime in the night, as he always did, but Dylan still had the horn around his neck – small and silver again, but with a new strap fashioned from a long length of blue-and-gold silk ribbon ornamented with chainstitch embroidery looped multiple times. Having a strap that wouldn't break was a bonus.

As Susan came into the room, snatches of memory from the Hunt filtered back to him, including the shock of Nigel's suicide.

'Susan,' Dylan began, trying to find the words, 'I'm so—'

'No time for that now,' said Susan, unzipping her bag. 'Get dressed. We need to go.' She handed him his jersey and kilt.

'Why?' he asked.

'Lord Branok says Loveday House is now back in its original world and timeline. He would like us to join him in the drawing room for luncheon, where he will answer any questions you have.'

'I got you.' Dylan dressed quickly. 'What's the plan?'

'We slip you out the back, and you get in contact with the Twisted Fists. Wayfarer is trying to turn them respectable, as our new King Arthur is a joker – and honestly, how can they charge you with crimes from this universe when you might be the Dylan Hardesty from the next world over?' Susan grimaced. 'Not that I'll be able to fly that defence myself, so I need to get you out.'

She led the way, out of the door and down the stairs, then past the kitchens and into a huge ballroom with an inglenook fireplace to one side. There was also a portrait of a man on horseback waving a spear that looked strikingly familiar, though Dylan had no recollection of ever threatening a priest – not that he had much recollection of anything he did when he was Herne.

Susan went over to a series of gold coat hooks on the wall to the left of the painting, fancy ones shaped like sea wolves. She started yanking them in a complicated sequence Dylan couldn't quite follow, until the panel beside the painting swung inwards, revealing a spiral staircase.

Susan led the way down, and Dylan ducked in behind her.

'We're going back to the dungeons?'

'There are sea caves underneath Loveday House; they open out onto the beach. The staircase from the cliffs is damaged, and the only person who can fly got eaten by a giant octopus. My thought is that you hide until dusk, then you blow your horn and ride to the mainland, and I go back, say I was lost, and use grief to dodge any questions.'

Dylan followed her down. Every so often, the passages offered her a choice, so Susan went right or left, always opting for the deeper option or whatever door was unlocked or would yield to Hitchcock's keys.

'Are you OK, Susan?'

'Physically? I'm fine.' She glanced back at him, her eyes puffy from crying. 'Emotionally? I'm a mess – grief, shock, and fear all run together. I'm not looking forward to burying my husband or explaining what happened to the neighbours. But what I'm really not looking forward to is a murder investigation from thirty years ago.'

Dylan didn't know what to say. *Sorry* didn't quite cut it. Then any words he might have said were taken out of his mouth as Susan opened a door and, instead of finding another wine cellar, medieval dungeon, or random storage room, there was a stone staircase leading down into a cavern so vast it made Dylan feel tiny. It was not so much a cavern as an underground valley, soft phosphorescent moss on the distant ceiling illuminating the chamber as brightly as strong moonlight, which was perfect for Dylan to see by, given his owl eyes.

'Can you see?' he asked Susan.

'A little,' she said. 'Pity we don't have Topper's candles.'

She fished around in her bag and brought out what looked like a small, black rectangular mirror. When she tapped it, the glass glowed, a face appearing in it as in Snow White's stepmother's mirror: Nigel's face, happy and smiling.

'Nigel,' Susan said, her voice breaking. 'He was chuffed to get an invitation to one of Jago's parties.'

'I'm so sorry,' Dylan told her. Then, not knowing what else to say. 'You never told me you drew an ace, Susan.'

'It's not an ace,' Susan explained; 'it's just a mobile phone. You've just been gone for a while. But there's no signal at Loveday, so it's not much use except as a torch.' She tapped the screen, and suddenly a beam of light emerged from the other side. 'Wait till I show you Zoom.'

Dylan was prepared to be impressed, yet nothing could be more impressive than this cavern, which led into another and another, big enough that they had an underground river running through them. They went down, Dylan helping Susan over the dicey bits where tumbled stones had covered the path, and it took sure-footed deer hooves and giant strides to navigate them. They followed the path down until it led to a stone jetty on the underground river and there was no obvious way to go. But stepping onto the stone must have activated a mechanism, because suddenly a fanciful boat in the shape of a giant swan floated out of the cavern upstream and drifted down the river, like something from the Tunnel of Love at a funfair, stopping at the end of the jetty.

Dylan stepped down into it and helped Susan in as well.

'Where do you think it goes?' she asked.

Dylan shrugged. 'Well, water flows downhill. Must eventually get to the ocean.'

Once Susan was in, the swan boat started up again, and she said, 'I wonder if this is something else Nigel found for Jago . . .'

The swan boat floated on, around the corner, and then out into daylight. For a moment, Dylan thought they'd reached the ocean, but there was no smell of salt. Instead, there was the scent of grapes and flowers, for the river flowed on, into a cavern so huge that there was an underground sun floating in the vault of the hollow earth, and far ahead, on the banks of the river, lay a stately palace with a vast dome. Oddly antlered Chinese deer browsed the lush grass and gave Dylan curious looks as the swan boat drifted past.

Susan switched off the torch on her mobile and slipped it back into her bag. 'I don't think Jago quite got Loveday House back to the normal world.' She clutched Dylan's arm. 'We need to go back, Dylan. We're not meant to be here. It's . . . it's *forbidden* . . .'

She looked ready to jump over the side, so he grabbed her and held her tight as a wave of emotions broke over him – fear at first, replaced quickly with serene comfort and a sense of belonging, confusion resolving into certainty as memories came back in a rush. First, a terrifying wall of water, a wave threatening to crush and obliterate him, but then a flood of memories, everything that came after, everything he'd been missing.

'*Bloat*,' Dylan breathed as the block in his memories broke. 'It's just his wall, to keep strangers out. He built it to protect the Rox, but when the castle crashed down, he took us all away to the Dreamtime. It's . . . another place, another dimension. A better place, mostly. But we're home now, Susan, and you're with me.'

'What?' She looked up at the palace as the river roved closer and the walls loomed higher and more resplendent, an orientalist fantasy brought to life. 'Where are we? I'm afraid, Dylan.'

'Relax,' he told her. 'Welcome to the Pleasure Dome.'

Longing for Those Lost

by Stephen Leigh

Part VI

G ARY WOKE EARLY THE next morning. Ceallaigh was still asleep alongside him. Outside the windows, the clouds were touched with pink pre-dawn light, but remnants of the previous night's storm clouds were moving below them. Gary pushed the sheets aside and dressed. He felt uneasy and restless, as if the house's energy was pulling at him, willing him to move, to find Jago. As if he were needed.

He padded downstairs. Olympe, one of the night maids, was sweeping the floor.

'Lord Branok?' Gary asked her.

She pointed to the lawn outside. 'I saw the master and Hitchcock going down the cliff stairs fifteen minutes ago or so, sir.'

Jago was standing on the pebbles of the beach below the cliffs. Alongside him, just behind the tidal line, a body lay covered in a blanket. Hitchcock, attired as usual in his tuxedo and white gloves, was crouched down, tucking the blanket around the body. Shredded remnants of dark clouds hurried past in the wind, and the surf was high, though the sky had cleared at the horizon, sending shafts of sunlight to pierce the morning fog off the sea.

Jago, masked as always, turned to watch Gary approach. 'Dylan Hardesty's gone. So is Susan Strathmore.'

'Gone? Gone *where?*' Gary asked. The blanketed body was far too short to be Herne, and there appeared to be no antlers on the covered head. 'I was thinking that if the phone lines were up, we could call DS Truscott and tell her we had a rather large gift for her.'

'Mr Hardesty and Ms Strathmore are not anywhere in DS Truscott's jurisdiction at this point. But I do need to have her come to Loveday.' Jago pointed to the body. 'Nigel Walmsley's committed suicide, and I'm told that Mr Beattie was devoured by a giant octopus. That's something I'll have to tell the Superintendent. There's damage and injuries everywhere from the storm, and perhaps other deaths. The authorities are dealing with all that now. I suspect a suicide, a single death, and a couple of missing people that we know for certain were still alive *after* the storm are going to be low on their list of priorities. Those of the household who were injured have already been helped. I'll have Dr Quiller come up later to check on them.'

'There's also Colette, sir, but we don't have her body, and I daresay there's no record of her ever having been here,' Hitchcock added. 'Perhaps we shouldn't mention her to DS Truscott. I'll have a memorial service for her arranged with the staff later.'

'Thank you, Hitchcock. I also have staff coming to take Nigel's body to the cold store until the coroner arrives.' Jago pressed his lips together under his mask. 'I'll be having a difficult conversation with DS Truscott when she does arrive. None of our guests should leave until their statements are taken, assuming that the causeway hasn't been so damaged that no cars could cross it anyway. Hitchcock, Gary, if you'll gather our remaining guests in the drawing room so I can speak to them, I'd appreciate it. See that they're given food and whatever else they require in the meantime.'

Jago started towards the cliffside stairs - stopped, turned. Behind the mask, his eyes stared at Gary. 'I know. You're thinking I should have taken the Morwens' threats more seriously. But look—' He pointed towards the towers of Loveday House, visible beyond the cliff. 'Mad Morwen's "great and terrible storm" has passed over us, and Loveday House remains standing. The Morwens have no real power, Gary. Not any more. We both know their doors remain locked.'

The mistake was Gary's, but once said, it couldn't be unsaid.

Ceallaigh was among the staff assigned to help Hitchcock and Gary attend to the guests while they waited for DS Truscott and her people to arrive. Gary saw her across the room. 'Caitlyn!' he called out. She didn't turn, didn't look at him. Gary followed her. 'Hey, Caitlyn,' he said again. 'Good morning. Sorry I left this morning without . . .'

She set down the tray of sandwiches she was holding and turned to look at him. The heat of her gaze was stronger than the embarrassed heat that rose up in him as he realized the name with which he'd addressed her.

'I'm sorry. I called you Caitlyn. I'm so sorry, Ceallaigh. I just . . .'

'You just what?' she asked.

'It's already been a long day, and it's still morning - that's a poor excuse, but it's the only one I have. I made a stupid, stupid mistake.'

'Aye, you did.' Flatly. 'An' I have to attend to our guests here, so any apologies you intend to make will have to wait until later, though I don't know whether I'll be listening to them or not.'

She turned away, picking up the tray once more. *You idiot!* Gary cursed himself, closing his eyes momentarily. When he opened them again, Ceallaigh was across the room, talking to Topper and smiling as if nothing had happened.

DS Truscott and her entourage arrived later that morning, and Gary was once again pressed into herding the guests into interview rooms for the police. It was evening before Truscott and her people were satisfied, the coroner had taken away Nigel's body, and arrangements were made for the remaining guests to leave.

Gary went up to his room and found Ceallaigh there. He noted the closed suitcases on his bed. Her suitcases.

'Gary,' she said before he could speak, 'I feel like I'm still dealing with the emotional baggage you bring to our relationship. That's not your fault, darling, but it's not mine either. It's just there: a wall between us. You're still attached to your past and to your life on Rathlin.'

Gary started to speak, but Ceallaigh lifted an index finger.

'No, let me finish this while I still have the speech I rehearsed in me mind. Aye, I still love you. But as I've told you before, I'm *not* your Caitlyn. I won't ever *be* Caitlyn, and I refuse to be a replacement for her in your affection. I need to know yeh love *me*, not some warped reflection of Caitlyn you're seeing instead. I know yeh feel you've found Caitlyn, your step-daughter, and Duncan again here in Loveday, but those are just images that the house is pulling from inside your head. They're not *real* – but I most definitely *am* real. Unless and until you realize that and make your peace with it, I cannot be with you. So, I'll be moving back into me old apartment below stairs.'

'Ceallaigh . . .'

'No. Let me finish. My moving out hopefully isn't forever. Just give me space and time to work on things in me own head. But, Gary, love . . . You need to finally and completely let your Caitlyn go. And that *does* need to be forever.'

♠

For several months, Gary could believe that Jago was right, that the various Lady Morwens were locked away and no longer capable of causing problems. The strange visitations at night had ended – at least, there were no more than there had ever been before – and Gary never encountered 'his' Morwen when he prowled the old hallways (as he still did occasionally). Following the storm, Mad Morwen's presence seemed to have vanished from Loveday House.

Ceallaigh had yet to move back into Gary's rooms, though she had stayed with him overnight a few times recently. She was laughing and smiling again, and Gary, for his part, was very careful to never call her Caitlyn or to bring up his time in Rathlin.

'I miss having you here every night,' he told her one morning after she'd stayed the night. He poured tea into her cup and pushed the plate of Chef Daniel's scones towards her. 'These rooms feel empty without you in them.'

Ceallaigh took one of the scones. She bit into it, chewing with a look of deep appreciation on her face, before swallowing and taking a sip of the tea. 'And do you still go wandering through Loveday of a night?' she asked.

'Now and then,' he admitted, 'but I'm not looking for anyone except Lady Morwen. The others whom I've lost . . . Well, I've come to terms with my grief and put them away. I know I can't really find them here again.'

'Is that the honest truth you're telling me?' She reached out and put her hand over his.

He interlaced his finger with hers, brown flesh against pale. 'Yes. I've left the past in the past. I'll remember it fondly, but I won't dwell on it, and I won't go looking for it.'

Ceallaigh pressed her fingers against his. She lifted his hand and kissed it. 'Then I'll move back in, if you like.'

Gary grinned. 'I'd like that more than anything.'

'You have two weeks to prepare some new guise dances,' Jago told Gary a few weeks later. His mask was midnight blue, covering his face from hairline to his upper lip. Tiny LEDs were embedded in the mask like stars; Gary could even recognize a few of the constellations.

'Another party?'

When Jago nodded, the stars swayed. 'Hitchcock sent out the invitations in yesterday's post.' Jago's eyes narrowed slightly behind the mask. 'I'd have thought you'd be pleased to be working again.'

'And I am, but—'

'You worry too much. I've checked the rooms deep within the house and made certain nothing lurks there. We'll tell the guests, as always, that they're not permitted to wander the house without a staff member guiding them. Lady Morwen's storm has come and gone, and we have had no hint of her presences since. I've tested her doors again. They're still locked, and when I call for her, she doesn't answer. So set aside your worries and concerns. This will be like the gatherings I once had, Gary: a grand party and nothing more.'

There was a smile underneath the starry mask. Gary couldn't help but smile back. The memories of the last few parties still lingered, but he remembered what he'd told Ceallaigh about leaving the past in the past. This wasn't his house, and he still felt happy and comfortable here.

'Then I'll head into town tomorrow and see Richard Darke; he says he's uncovered a few guise dances that have been nearly forgotten. I'll see if I can convince him to show them to me.'

'Wonderful!' Jago said. 'I'll look forward to seeing them myself.'

In the early hours of the morning that the first guests were to arrive, there was a soft knock on Gary's door. Ceallaigh didn't wake, but Gary stirred from a dreamless sleep. When he looked, he saw that someone had slipped a small, white envelope under his door. Gary turned on the lamp on his nightstand; Ceallaigh's head faced away from the light. When he opened the packet, he found a small ruby inside. No note, no explanation, nothing written on the envelope itself.

Yet the sight of the single tiny ruby made Gary's breath stop in his throat. He glanced back at his nightstand. In the wan illumination of the lamp, he could see the pommel of Morwen's dagger in its sheath, the facets of the far larger ruby set there glittering like a bloody eye. The clock alongside the dagger proclaimed it to be five a.m.

Rubies were reputedly Lady Morwen's favourite jewel . . . Gary remembered Jago saying ages ago, when Lady Morwen had first attacked him. His chest tightened again, making breathing hard.

He dressed quickly, putting on Constance's bathrobe and placing the sheathed dagger in the pocket. Going to Ceallaigh's side of the bed, he leaned down and kissed her forehead.

'What time is it?' she asked.

'It's still early, darling. I have to go talk to Lord Branok about something. I'll be back up before you need to leave for your duties.'

With that, he left the room and went down the stairs to the ground floor. He knocked on the door of Jago's office. A minute later, Jago – still masked – came to the door, dressed as if he'd been awake for hours. 'Gary? Is there a problem?'

Gary handed Jago the envelope. 'This was placed under my door just a few minutes ago.'

Jago opened the envelope. He looked at the small jewel that dropped out into his palm. 'You're thinking this is from Lady Morwen?'

Gary nodded. 'That was my first thought.'

Jago was already shaking his head. 'Occam's razor,' he said. 'More likely that one of our staff found the ruby, assumed it had been lost by someone and put it under your door so you'd take care of it. It's a small jewel and could easily have come loose and fallen from someone's ring or necklace. Several of our guests have worn rubies.' He shook his head. 'Lady Morwen hasn't been seen in a long time. I suspect there's some other explanation for this.' Jago glanced at the wall clock. 'Regardless, there's nothing we can do about this now. Our first guests should be arriving in just a few hours.'

'You could tell them that the party's cancelled.'

Another shake of Jago's head. 'I appreciate your concern. Here's what we'll do. You and I will check those doors again immediately. If either of them is unlocked, I'll tell our guests that we've had to cancel the event. Otherwise, the party will proceed as planned, though we'll still take extra precautions. You, Hitchcock, Madame Amélie, and Elbrekt will let me know if anything else seems awry. Let me grab two torches, and you and I will go check on our Morwens.'

But they found her doors still apparently locked, and no one answered when Jago rattled and shook them.

By 5.45 a.m., Gary was back in bed with Ceallaigh.

Raw Deal

by Peadar Ó Guilín

1. Jar

MARIA PAUSED AT THE top of the steps, the crowd heaving below her like a stormy ocean with Joker Plague as the wind, whipping it into fury. Her eyes swept the edges of the dance floor: castaways clinging to seats; every surface stacked with drinks, purses, coats, and elbows, except for one island of peace in the corner: a low table and one unoccupied chair. It might have belonged to a different universe for all that anyone seemed to notice it.

Warmth blossomed inside her, because Maria knew what that meant. *I'm somebody now.*

An extravagant mocktail was waiting for her at the table. No customers approached yet, but she felt their hunger from here and could imagine their shuffling feet, their trembling limbs.

Soon, darlings. Just need to set up.

But some were less polite than others. 'You got somethin' for me?' It was Jake, shouting to be heard over the music. He had the armour of a Roman centurion instead of a torso. In Maria's book, that made him more ace than joker. He'd have a six-pack the rest of his life, and his smile, while nothing but natural, gave her flutters in places the law wanted hidden. If that wasn't a superpower, what was?

Maria grinned back at him to show she had more to offer than mere drugs.

'Hurry it up, there, love,' he shouted. 'I haven't got all night.'

Maria had been reaching into her handbag. It was full of little envelopes, each colour-coded to a particular customer – it would be a disaster to ever mix them up! – and she had already found the one with the yellow stripes she'd assigned to Jake after their first transaction.

She paused.

He waved some cash. 'I've got your money. You want it or not?' He dropped it on the table, casually, as though he were the one in charge. But it had been days since his last fix. He'd probably tried to take the edge off with weed or heroine or crack. None had worked, and now the hunger was pulsing inside him. Maria caressed it with her mind until sweat sheened his upper lip and his right eye developed a spasm.

'P-please? Please? I'm . . . I got to . . .'

She beamed. 'Of course, darling!' She stopped messing with his brain and gave him the little envelope at once. She wasn't in the business of torture, after all, but she *would* be respected. If she ever lost that, they'd rip her apart like a pack of wolves.

He ran off at once, and others shuffled over in his wake.

'Here you go, darling,' she'd say. 'Your favourite. Look after yourself.'

Their hands were eager, and why wouldn't they be? This was the best high in existence. Nothing else they experienced could bring so much pleasure, and what a bargain at a hundred pounds a pop! No wonder a dozen newbies approached so eagerly towards the end of the night. She recorded their names most carefully.

To one, she gave a mix of 30 per cent liquorice with the rest made up of dried parsley.

'What's in it?' he asked.

'Oh, my darling! However would I pay my rent if I told you? But you're going to love it.'

To another, she slipped an envelope with powdered mushroom, cardamom, cinnamon, and coffee. 'This will blow your mind!'

Her wild card insisted she tell each and every customer something of the sort; otherwise, it wouldn't affect them any more than a cup of tea would have, and why ever would they come back to her then?

By one a.m., she was turning them away. The envelopes were gone. New names were added to her little black book with code words for what she'd given them and in what proportions. Best of all, her handbag bulged with cash. Sure, she'd have to hand most of it over – best not to think about that part too closely, or about who would be getting it – but despite these 'taxes', after no more than three weeks, she'd already paid off her tuition at RADA, acquired an astonishing wardrobe, and tomorrow she'd be viewing a new flat.

Not bad for the freshest ace in London!

She caught the bouncer's eye – a huge nat called Gregor. He nodded, so she gathered her things and followed him into the storeroom behind the bar.

'All is good?'

'Better than good, darling. Cast your peepers over this!' She poured the money out onto a table, and he whistled. 'They like drugs in this country.'

He didn't know that all she was really selling were odd mixes of spice and tea, and Maria had no intention of telling him. They counted out the money, both of them terrified of getting it wrong. Finally, they had two piles of notes, one a third the size of the other.

Gregor did a final calculation on his phone. 'It is right,' he said. 'You owe the house a pound, but that does not matter, I am sure.'

Hurriedly, Maria took a tenner from her own, smaller stack and added it to the other. 'A lady is never in debt.'

'Yes.' Gregor nodded. 'That is best.'

Maria turned to go, but his hand was on her shoulder. 'Wait. Maria.' He'd never touched her before – or used her name, for that matter. 'I am sorry. You, uh, have been requested. At office.'

She froze but managed to put a smile on her face as she looked back. 'Oh?' An image flashed through her mind. It was the jar. She thought she'd never have to see it again. A deal was a deal, after all, and she was playing her part to the hilt. 'But, darling, I'm in ever such a rush. I have an appointment.'

'Yes, you do. At office. I am sorry.'

'But of course. Will you take me?' She knew the way but didn't want to go alone.

All too soon, they were outside a plain door with peeling paint. Three sharp taps, and Maria, with two years of acting lessons behind her, strode through so confidently she was practically skipping. Her smile didn't falter when she saw that the boss had company – some stranger – but she focused on Charles for now.

The gangster was a Schwarzenegger-sized statue of living marble, his face handsome, glowering. A metal chair groaned beneath him as he noted her arrival. Charles the Unkillable. That was what he called himself, although in the month since Maria had last seen him, somebody had done their best to prove him wrong. There were bullet holes across his bare chest, as well as what looked like claw marks, although what kind of beast could cut through marble like that, she had no idea.

'Well, well,' he said without preamble, his voice perfectly human. 'You're makin' hay out of your little scam, ain't ya, love? Only, see, I'm gonna need something more from you now.'

Maria opened her mouth to object, but luckily, the stranger prevented such stupidity by talking first. His utterly toneless speech was delivered by an electronic box at his throat – and no wonder, for instead of a face he had a huge, conical drill bit that extended nine inches from where his chin should be. 'WHAT SKILLS DOES THIS BEAUTY BRING TO OUR ENTERPRISE?' He stank of engine oil.

'She's an actor, innit?' Charles made no mention of her wild card talent. 'Always at it, too. Talking posh an' that. But she don't *beg* posh, right, girl?' He sniggered. 'When I caught her trying to double-cross me, she shat herself right there, Drillhead. Right where yer standin'.'

Maria's nostrils twitched as though she could still smell her moment of disgrace when Charles the Unkillable had shoved the jar in her face. In that instant, her card had turned. If it hadn't . . .

'I WOULD NEVER SHOW SUCH DISCOURTESY TO ONE OF MY WOMEN.'

'No, you wouldn't, Drillhead,' said Charles with a grin. 'You'd shut 'em up with a kiss, innit?'

The drill spun, and Maria realized it meant the man was laughing. 'ONE KISS IS ALL IT TAKES. SPLATTER SPLATTER.'

Maria straightened her back, for all the world like a woman who had no intention of throwing up. Her voice was steady, too, a little bored, even, but not dangerously so. 'And what, darlings, is it you are planning to do?'

'Simple,' said Charles. 'There's a slag who knows too much. I want her dead.'

'DO WE HAVE A NAME? A DESCRIPTION?'

'Oh, mate, I got your description right here.' Charles reached behind him, and Maria's heart began to speed up again. Mostly, the shelves were full of computer equipment of one kind or another, some of it quite old. Why he hung onto it, Maria had no idea. But there was something else he kept there, too.

He pulled out the jar, and it took every fibre of Maria's inner strength not to cry out when she saw it. It was a massive bottle of clear glass. Floating inside was the head of a young woman. The look of terror on her face, together with the uneven flaps of skin, left Maria in no doubt at all that the girl had been alive as her body was ripped to pieces.

'YOU WILL FORGIVE ME, DEAR CHARLES.' Drillhead tapped the jar with an immaculate fingernail, 'BUT THIS WOMAN APPEARS TO BE THOROUGHLY DECEASED. EVEN MR PANTOMIME WOULD NOT WANT HER NOW.'

'Sure. She looks dead. Met with an accident a while back. But she's been seen alive, innit? She was a wild card, so anything is possible. Redcoat, they called her, when she was workin' with the filth. Nah, I need to be sure this time. But it's gonna take you and Mr Pantomime and your whole crew to do it, 'cos there'll be aces where we're goin'.'

'OUR SERVICES ARE EXPENSIVE.'

'Don't worry, mate. There's plenty of loot. It's all yours whether it's that cunt down there or just a lookalike. But I *need* to know. You just get your lot together and be ready for a long drive. I'll text you the coordinates tomorrow. As for you' – he snapped his fingers at Maria – 'you're comin' with me now.'

'But,' she said. 'I wasn't expecting . . . I can't . . .'

He was already on his feet, towering over her. 'Just move it. And don't scream.'

'Why would I sc—?' But she was already turning around, and right there, an inch from her own face, was another.

It was hanging upside-down, its skin pale and paper dry, its two eyes like black marbles, its odourless breath mixing with hers. The rest of the creature clung to the lintel above the door, but by what means she couldn't have said, because an oversized trench coat covered every bit of its body.

As Maria stood there, immobile but for the trembling of one knee, a tongue emerged from the lipless mouth and rasped against her cheek.

'ALLOW ME TO PRESENT MR PANTOMIME. MY PARTNER IN CRIME.'

A trickle of urine ran down Maria's thigh.

'HE HAS YOUR SCENT NOW, IF WE NEED TO FIND YOU. I'M SURE IT WILL NEVER COME TO THAT. WE ARE ALL FRIENDS HERE.'

2. Drive

Ten minutes later, Maria was outside with Charles, still shaking. Her second visit to the office had been as awful as her first.

He led her down a series of alleyways, his marble feet bending like flesh, but clacking against the paving stones of the footpath. He wore loose trousers for decency's sake, but nothing else against the chill.

They came to a lime-green sports car with the image of a bull in a yellow shield on the front. Despite the rain, the top had been left down, for how else would Charles squeeze in there? 'In you get.'

'Of course, darling.' Maria was trying to keep up the act, but it took three tries for her hands to open the door. She shivered even more as she sank onto the soaked leather of the passenger seat.

Charles didn't immediately start the car. 'Look away,' he told her. She obeyed, but the wing mirror was angled wrong, and she saw exactly what he was doing. He produced a USB key, like the one she used to have in school for keeping her homework on. He stuck it into his arm, and even though there hadn't been a hole there it just . . . *clicked* in. Then, for two whole minutes, he gazed at the dark sky, eyelids flickering, before plucking it out again. He pressed a button and the engine roared into life.

'Beautiful noise!' He had to shout to be heard. 'It's a Lamborghini, innit?'

The car shot out of London with Charles whooping like a child, swerving outrageously on the wet roads, shouting insults as the wind pummelled Maria's shivering body.

'Where are we going?' she dared ask.

'To a party,' he said. 'In a big house in Cornwall. Wanker!' That last comment was directed at a slow lorry driver, but then, he turned to her again, paying little attention to the road, the car hurtling fast enough to make paste of them both. 'Here's what's gonna happen. I got you into the house as a nanny, yeah?'

'A what?'

'You'll look after a snotty-nosed brat – how hard can it be? Thing is, though, they always have famous people at their parties, and you know what that means, right?'

'Aces.'

'Yeah. Maybe. The owner's one for sure – Jago Branok – though what he does, I dunno. Find out who might be dangerous. Get them high. You'll have a few hours. When the party gets goin', open the door leadin' into the vegetable garden. We'll do the rest. No need for you to dirty your drug-dealin' hands.'

Maria looked down at her knees, wishing she was anywhere else in the world. *Is that what I am? A drug-dealer?* All she'd wanted was a bit of extra pocket money to see her through RADA. But one thing had led to another, and here she was, speeding towards a murder with a starring role as the accomplice. Surely that was a step too far?

As though he'd been listening to her thoughts, Charles said, 'Don't think of dobbin' me in. You do that and your parents are dead, understand? That sister of yours, too, the lawyer. Even your fuckin' cousins down in Porto. Don't think I don't do my research on them as work for me. Especially the aces. Don't worry, though.' He leered. 'I like to slip a girl a bit of carrot to go along with the whip. So, if you get us in there, use your skills to make us a few friends on the inside, I'll set you up in Mayfair after this. You'll be gettin' a thousand pounds – no, fuck it, ten thousand – a hit from now on, and that's the word of Charles the Unkillable. Ain't nobody else can offer what you got. No reason we can't both get proper rich off it.'

Something shifted under her feet. It turned out there was a blanket in the car, and it was only a little wet. He didn't object when she dragged it over herself, clipped it into place with a seatbelt, and, amazingly, fell asleep.

She woke at dawn, desperate to pee. She was still in a sports car driven by a maniac, but instead of the motorway, they were barrelling down a road barely wide enough to spit across, hemmed in by solid-looking hedgerows. 'Welcome to Cornwall,' he said. 'We're on our way to my contact—'

'Watch the fucking road!' she screamed.

He refused to obey, laughing joyously at her terror. But then the cow appeared – right there in the middle of the road. Charles had great reflexes – brilliant, in fact. He swerved around the animal, skidded, and then, at tremendous speed, the car cannoned through a hedge, bucked, and fell back, leaving Maria with a face full of airbag.

It was minutes before she could so much as move. She breathed hard, her whole right side throbbing with pain. 'Breathe,' she muttered. 'Breathe.'

Charles had gone. He hadn't even been wearing his seatbelt, and what with the roof open . . . Well, he must have been travelling at quite some speed. And where had her handbag got to?

She crawled over the crumpled bonnet and into the field beyond. Charles lay not too far away. He'd been lucky enough to have landed in some bushes but not so fortunate as to keep his back from breaking – literally; his lower half had snapped completely off.

'It serves you right,' she told him, walking over.

Incredibly, he was still alive. His neck had a crack running right through it.

'Break it . . .' he told her, breath bubbling.

'W-what?'

'Stand on . . . on my head . . .'

She stared in horror. 'I . . . I'll call an ambulance, I'll—'

'Stupid . . . slag.' He forced his own head down until the whole thing snapped off. The light left his eyes.

'Ch-Charles?'

But she didn't have so much as a heartbeat to celebrate her freedom, because, at that very moment, a wind rose, as though from nowhere. It threw her onto her back, dragged her towards the wreckage of the car. Every bush bent in the same direction, and when Maria turned, she saw a most incredible sight: the vehicle was shrinking in on itself, crumpling from the inside. Glass shattered. Metal screeched and tore as though made of paper; tyres burst. Everything twisted and spun, wrenched itself into a new shape, and that shape was . . .

Charles.

Charles the Unkillable. Naked and made this time entirely of metal. He stood there, steaming, blinking. Then, he seemed to convulse. He coughed once, and the same USB drive he'd plugged into himself before they left London landed onto the grass between them.

Charles looked down at his new body, caressed the word *Lamborghini* running across his chest.

He laughed. 'Nothin' but the best, innit? Italian design all the way.' He smiled. 'How did we crash?'

'A . . . a cow.' He didn't remember?

'A fuckin' cow! I hate the country. You got your phone? Call this number. We need a pick-up, and you'll need nanny clothes. Now, remind me of everything we talked about on the way down here.'

3. House

Both Maria's grandfathers had been fishermen, but if sea legs could be inherited, they had skipped her generation entirely. The short crossing left her a wobbling mess, for while the rain had decided to give her a break, the sight of massive cliffs rising and falling with every swell, threatened to bring up her breakfast.

Swarms of screeching gulls circled the island. Holes pocked the rock face, and above it all, as in any good horror movie, there loomed the massive, knotted fist of a house.

The perfect setting for a murder, she thought with a shudder. *Very fitting.* She didn't pray any more – people ought to look out for themselves, after all – but she couldn't help sending off a quick plea to Saint Pantaleon to keep Charles's intended victim away from the party.

'C'mon, Ivan,' somebody was saying. Even at this time of year there were tourists – all American, it seemed – and some of them had spotted her ridiculous uniform. 'Look, it's Mary Poppins! How can you be sad when Mary Poppins is here?'

A hand tapped Maria on the shoulder. 'Hey, miss? You mind taking a photograph with my buddy? He's down in the dumps, see?'

Playing nice with tourists was the last thing she wanted to do. But somewhere on the little ferry, there were bound to be guests for the party at Loveday House, and she couldn't afford to draw any negative attention, so she turned with her best smile, the one her tutors had called dazzling.

The two men towered over her, but Maria had never seen a less impressive pair. The sad one – presumably Ivan – hadn't shaved and smelled of strong drink. Once upon a time, she could have guessed the brand, but that was all behind her now, even if a dull ache in her guts still disputed the matter now and again. Black hair sprouted from his nose and ears, with further dark curls poking from beneath the neckline of his shirt.

'It's his wife,' the other whispered. This one looked vaguely familiar, although he was more blubber than man. It was a wonder the boat didn't tip over.

'No, Buford!' Ivan cried. 'Why'd you have to tell her my business?'

'Mary doesn't mind, do you, Miss Poppins?' Buford winked. 'Who wouldn't want a photo with not one, but *two* of the original American Heroes? Everybody's gonna want a piece of us at the convention.'

'Convention?' Maria asked.

'Damned straight!'

Maria remembered there'd been a show called *American Hero* when she was a kid. Something to do with Egypt, wasn't it? What she did know, though, was that every one of the contestants had to be an ace, which meant this pair was probably heading up to Loveday House, too.

'Well,' she said, 'I'm very pleased to meet—' Her breakfast chose that moment to make another bid for freedom, but she forced it back down. 'Both of you.'

She'd hidden hangovers all through her last year at school, and this was no different. She was an actress, always had been, and her new role had begun the second she'd slid this stupid uniform over her head. They wanted Mary Poppins? She could give them that; yes, she could. She was performing for her life, after all.

Ivan moved in beside her gingerly. He was swaying even more than the motion of the boat could account for. Maria kept a sneer from her face. God, drunks were contemptible, and none more so than herself – except she had beaten it, risen above it. Why couldn't this oaf do the same?

Still, best not to underestimate them too much. They were aces. If she was to survive until tomorrow morning, she'd better find out what they could do. Let's hope they were stupid enough to tell her.

'Smile!' cried Buford, raising his phone.

Maria was supposed to take the island's only taxi up to the house, but Buford insisted she come along in the limousine that had been sent down for the guests, and he chatted all the way.

'Did they tell you what room you're in, Mary?'

'Maria.'

'Oh, is that Mexican? My wife's Mexican.'

'Uh . . . no.'

'Well, anyway, good luck in finding your room. We've been here two nights already, and lemme tell ya . . .'

She nodded as he yammered on, but her attention was on the scenery. A stunning causeway gave way to a winding track that passed first a cemetery, then a small group of standing stones, before looping up towards the top of the island to end on a circular driveway before the magnificent entrance of the house itself.

She felt her breath coming fast. She must do this terrible thing. Otherwise, it would be her head in the jar. Or her mother's. Or Ana's.

'You OK, miss? Maria?'

'Never better.'

Ivan had fallen asleep, drool running over his lower lip. Despite all the hair, he looked like a little boy, at peace after big day in the park. Matryoshka was his ace name. She'd text that to Charles as soon as she got a moment to herself. The other, Buford Calhoun, had proudly declared himself to be Toad Man. 'I may give a demonstration later. You'll see.'

They weren't the only guests. A helicopter stood on a little pad in the garden, and a portly man showed his age by taking snaps of the sea with an honest-to-God camera.

Double doors swung wide as they came to a stop. To Maria, it was like the opening of the great maw in the body of a vast, grey sea monster, where every window in the facade – and they were countless! – was a merciless, hungry eye. *It knows,* she thought. *The house knows why I'm here.* A stupid notion of course, but it took courage to step out of the car beneath that malevolent gaze and smile like a starlet on her first red carpet.

A servant in a uniform every bit as antiquated as Maria's tried to take her little bag. 'No thank you, darling, I prefer to carry my own!' It held nothing illegal, but the sight of so many coloured envelopes might draw unwelcome questions.

The servant shrugged. He was a handsome chap, no getting away from it, the type who would have killed on a Bollywood poster. He liked her, too; she could always tell these things. 'Lord Branok prefers to greet staff himself,' he said. 'But today, all he could spare was the under-butler.'

'Under-butler? Is that even a thing?'

'If it is, I am he. You want I show you first to the nursery?' Even his accent was rather lovely, although she couldn't place it for the life of her. Definitely not Indian, despite his looks. 'Or, perhaps, your bedroom?' He grinned.

'Sadly, I have work to do . . .'

'Elbrekt.' He bowed. 'It is my name.'

'Maria. It is mine.' She grinned. 'Come on, Elbrekt. Show me the blessed child I'll be taking care of.'

The Americans had already passed up the steps and through magnificently carved doors thick enough to withstand a siege.

'You expecting trouble, Elbrekt?'

'Only at night, Maria.'

'I bet you cause most of it yourself!'

He didn't get to answer, because as they stepped into the hall, a great cloud of gas poured down the stairs. And then, a man wearing goggles and what looked like a pilot's jacket from the days of black-and-white movies came gliding down from the first floor on a cushion of steam. Buford guffawed in delight and even Ivan managed to look pleased.

'He's here!' cried Buford. 'I knew he wouldn't let us down!'

Maria swallowed. Another ace to add to the total. This was getting really dangerous now. Surely, *surely* Charles would have to call off this madness?

'Lead on, Elbrekt,' she told her new friend. 'Lead on.'

The steam was beginning to clear, leaving behind beads of condensation on the bannisters. Meanwhile, the guests were engaged in hearty backslapping that left the flying ace staggering under the friendly blows.

'Let us use the backstairs,' said Elbrekt.

'Because we're servants?'

'No, no! To Lord Branok, we are a family.'

Maria had worked often enough at her parents' restaurant to be sceptical of any rich man who said that, but as Elbrekt led her past a grandfather clock, through a sunny salon where a young Black woman squinted at some lethal-looking swords in a cabinet, and onto where the carpet ran out to be replaced by floorboards, he sang the praises of the house's owner. 'He took me on,' said the young man. 'Saved me from a very bad place.'

'Oh, where was that?'

'Atlantis,' he said with perfect solemnity.

'I'd have said India.'

'Well, you are clever.'

It wasn't a proper answer, of course, but his trousers were a little tighter than was good for her, and she hadn't slept more than a few hours in the car on the way from London, so she failed to pursue the matter further.

Upstairs, they squeezed past a pair of chambermaids. One of them dropped the sheets she'd been carrying and seemed to trip right at Elbrekt's feet. The under-butler helped her up, while her companion glared in undisguised jealousy, before the pair of them passed on, hissing at each other in French.

'They fall a lot when you're around?' Maria asked him.

'Sometimes.' He paused at a doorway, holding her gaze with his. 'I also can fall.'

And then, before she had a chance to make a fool of herself, he opened the door, and they were in the rich part of the house again.

4. Toys

The nursery was the first thoroughly modern room Maria had seen in the house so far. Toys of every description lay piled in baskets on the floor: plastic bricks; the guns from *Sea Trek V* – what a waste of three hours that was! – dolls and teddies and tiny vehicles of every possible description. Not a single one was on the floor. A great blackboard, as yet untouched by so much as a smidge of dust, lay waiting with a full complement of coloured chalks in the corner.

'I'm guessing my charge hasn't arrived yet?'

'Oh no,' said Elbrekt. 'The little boy passed an hour here just now. Wait, please; he is with the mother. I will find.' And with a little touch on her shoulder, he was gone.

Maria went to the window. She had an excellent sense of direction and fully expected it to look out on the sea, but the presence of a handsome young man must have been enough to throw her off, because it was the garden she saw stretching out below her.

'You're such a bimbo,' she whispered.

The old man was still wandering around, fiddling with his camera. She hoped he wasn't another bloody ace. Nearby, a gardener frowned at some roses. She was a stocky woman in overalls with padded knees. She turned to grab a trowel, and at that moment, Maria saw her full in the face and staggered back.

Charles had been right. Somebody had torn this woman's head off and stuffed it into a jar – yet here, she was alive again, working as a gardener at Loveday House. It was the second resurrection Maria had witnessed in the space of a day.

With shaking hands, she took out her phone and composed a text:

Three aces seen so far. Toad Man. A guy called Matryoshka. A flyer with goggles. All from American Hero TV. They look dangerous.

She deleted the last three words before hitting *send*. She desperately wanted Charles to cancel the mission, but he wouldn't listen if she looked like she was begging.

She heard voices in the corridor outside.

'Please, honey, don't do that.'

The phone buzzed with a message from Charles.

Is she there?

And then, a woman and a small boy were coming through the door, and it took all of Maria's self-control not to gasp.

The mum was extraordinarily pretty - a blonde woman with skin clear and creamy enough to launch any product you could think of. Except . . .

The woman smiled, her front teeth a little too prominent. 'I don't mind if you look.'

She had rabbit's ears. There was no avoiding it. They were cartoon-sized and fluffy. They moved, too, each independently of the other.

'I . . .' Maria swallowed. 'I'm so sorry. Uh . . . madam.'

'Noooo! We can't have that, can we, Fitz?'

This last was addressed to the little boy, his hand wrapped around a doll-sized soldier. He yawned, cute as a button, big eyes staring at Maria.

'I'm Julie Cotton. You must just call me Julie, like everybody else.'

'I'm Maria.'

'You're beautiful, honey, but watch out. Fitz has an eye for that. Like his dad.'

Fitz did seem to have an eye for that, all right. He smiled shyly, and Maria, easily distracted by cuteness, had no need to fake her response. This part of the job, at least, would be a pleasure.

'Is his dad here?'

'Oh, no. And please don't feel awkward about this. He passed . . . uh, some time ago.' She fondled her son's hair.

Maria's phone vibrated again. It was on silent, but Julie's ears curved at once in Maria's direction.

'You can get that if you want,' Julie said. 'I don't mind.'

'Oh no, not at all. Would it be all right if I took Fitz for a walk in the garden? I'm not sure how long the rain will keep off.'

'That would be nice. He's the only one of the three of us - you'll meet Will later - without jet lag. He was running around all morning, chasing his toys and—'

'Chasing?'

'Oh, yeah. That's right.' Julie took a quick look into the corridor and shut the door. 'Let's hope nobody else has got hearing as good as mine! Listen, Maria, there's one small thing. Fitz here is a deuce. You use that word in England?'

'Sometimes we do.' Along with unkinder terms than that.

'Well, this is supposed to be private, but you'll need to know.'

'We are utterly discreet at the agency, Miss Julie.' Not that Maria could remember the name of the agency right now.

'Fitz . . . creates his own toys, Maria. I don't know how else to put it. He seems to materialize them, somehow, but never when anybody is looking. And he won't play with anything else either.'

'Well, I can think of worse powers to have.'

'Right? You can't imagine what a relief it was for me that he was born at all. And then, well, all the worry, knowing he was latent. I didn't want an ace, anyway. All I wanted, all I prayed for every night, was that he could be a normal boy, even if his father was such an extraordinary human being. But . . . well, there's a little more to his power than that. Fitz? Show Maria how you like to play.'

'Play,' Fitz agreed solemnly. He set the soldier down. The uniform was remarkably detailed, behaving more like cloth than plastic. The soldier started striding across the room, then stopped, looking around in a perfect imitation of confusion.

'It's so real,' Maria marvelled.

'Right? Fitz must have seen a soldier do this exact thing. All these normal toys?' Julie waved her hand at the room. 'I mean, they're great, but he won't so much as look at them.'

'Maybe when he's older.'

'You think?'

The phone buzzed again, and Maria ignored it. 'Would you like to take your soldier into the garden, Fitz?' she asked. 'Then, maybe' – she looked questioningly at Julie – 'we can come back in for supper?'

Julie nodded, her long ears bobbing. 'Thank you so much,' she said. 'I desperately – and I mean *desperately* – need to lie down for an hour. I want to be fresh for the big dinner!'

She turned, and Maria couldn't help a cry of '*Meu Deus!*' because Julie Cotton boasted a perfect rabbit's tail to go along with her ears.

Julie winked over her shoulder, wiggled once to make her tail bob and, with a laugh, was gone.

After a bit of a muddle finding the stairs, Maria and Fitz made it into the garden. Both had their coats on by then, although the sun had made a welcome appearance, and a thick rhododendron hedge sheltered them from the breeze. Were it not for the seagulls and the ever-present tang of brine, a visitor mightn't know they were on an island at all.

Maria took a moment to check her phone.

Answer me, said the latest text.

Looking now, she replied, feeling the great grey facade of the house louring over her, judging her.

She hurried to catch up with Fitz. He was investigating a scrap of black fur found on a bush.

'Wow, a bit wiry, isn't it, darling? You think it's a cow? A goat? Mooo! Baaaaa!' She made horns of her fingers and chased the giggling boy around the bush for a bit to tire him out. She'd done the same with her cousins often enough on visits to Portugal. Then, although it was the last thing in the world she wanted to do, she led him off in search of the supposedly dead Redcoat, now the gardener. Best to be sure, after all.

She carried Fitz for the last part. She was glad of the warmth of his little body by then, as the sun was going down, and she was glad, too, to be able to distract both of them with the tale of *The Three Little Pigs*. 'You're lucky you got a drama student, darling,' she told him. 'Who else would do all the voices?'

But he was already asleep, nuzzled into the fake-fur lining of her coat. Just as well. The gardener was up ahead, her back to them, working on a fallen tree. And there was no mistaking the kiss of the wild card virus, either, because even as Maria watched, the woman hoisted a fallen trunk as thick as her own body and flung it away – all with one hand.

Maria cleared her throat.

The gardener turned and, at that moment, Maria found herself grinning.

'What's so funny?'

'It's . . .' This woman was old – way too old to be the same person as the unfortunate in the jar. Yes, they looked astonishingly alike, but the gardener had to be on the far side of fifty, at least. Maria felt such a sense of relief that a bubble of laughter escaped. She was not going to be a murderer after all. 'You look so familiar, that's all. I might have met your daughter.'

The blue eyes narrowed, only emphasizing the crow's feet bunching to either side. 'I got no daughters.' She turned back to her work.

'Ah, my mistake.'

It might be good to send Charles a photograph of the gardener as proof she wasn't the one he was worried about but also to show why the two might have been mistaken for each other.

'What, uh, happened to the tree?'

'Pigs.'

'Excuse me?'

'They grow 'em big round here.' There was a Liverpool lilt in her accent. 'And angry. Take my advice. You don't want to stray outdoors after dark. They'll eat anything.'

'Wow! And they can do that to a whole tree? Can I get a photo of it?'

'Be my guest.'

It was a bit of a fumble to get the phone out without waking Fitz. 'I never thought I'd see an ace working as a gardener.' Nearly had it.

'What else should I be doing? I'm happy. Or . . . well, calm.'

Maria nearly dropped her phone. 'It's just . . . Most of the aces I hear about are, you know, famous. Or working for the government.'

The woman shrugged. 'I nearly did. Believe it or not, when I was younger, they asked me to be Redcoat.'

Maria froze.

'Well, *a* Redcoat. And yes, I was flattered. That's how you are at 20. Luckily, a friend talked me out of it.'

'How? How were you talked out of it?'

The woman shrugged. 'Have you got *Sea Trek* on TV here?'

Maria had forgotten all about her phone by now. 'What do you mean *here*? But yes, I've seen the last film.'

'Good! Then you'll have noticed the lads in the red swimsuits keep getting killed before you ever even learn their names. *That's* what it's like to be a Redcoat. Five years at the most, and some foreign agent or terrorist or gangland Mussolini squashes them flat. And you know what happens then?'

'What?'

Fitz was beginning to stir against her shoulder.

'They recruit some other wide-eyed fool to take their place. I swear, they should change the name of the role to "Cannon Fodder". So, yeah, I'm glad I saw sense. And here I am, decades later, working for the very man who talked me out of it.'

Jago Branok. He seemed to rescue a lot of people.

Maria finally got her phone up and pointed at the tree, although she made sure to catch the woman's face in there, too. Click and done.

'Mommy?' mumbled Fitz.

'Let's go and find her, darling. She's had her hour's rest.' Maria's mind was reeling with the scale of the coincidence, that this gardener who looked so like Redcoat had been a hair's breadth from being a Redcoat herself. But she kept it from her face and bade farewell.

Her phone signal was poor, but as she walked back, she sent the photo straight to Charles.

Elbrekt was by the door. 'I am here to guide you,' he said with a bow. 'The house is tricky until it gets to know you.'

She didn't bother correcting his English. 'Have you met Fitz?'

'Oh yes, but he was very sleepy the first time.' He ruffled the boy's hair. 'And who could forget his lovely mother?'

'You liked the ears?'

'Yes. And the tail also!'

Fitz was getting more agitated. 'Where's Mommy?'

'Can you show us the way, Elbrekt?'

He bowed again, even more elaborately.

'Now you're showing off!'

'I was a prince, you know.'

'Oh, yes.' She grinned. 'In Atlantis, wasn't it, darling?'

This time, maybe because Fitz was with them, Elbrekt led Maria up the grand stairway. It really was rather beautiful, splitting at the centre into two smaller stairs that curved away from each other like the horns of a ram.

A stick-thin man in a black silk shirt passed them on his way down.

Elbrekt bobbed his head. 'Mr Jagger,' he said, and it was all Maria could do not to squeal in shock.

When she was growing up, her mother had bombarded herself and Ana with the music of the Rolling Stones, and for years in the restaurant kitchen, there'd been that famous photograph of him on stage in New York, halfway through his transformation into the form of a terrifying wolfman.

But she held onto her dignity, and he stalked past without a backward glance. Maybe later, she'd get an autograph. It could be a fresh start for her and Mum. Perhaps.

'His is the flying machine outside,' said Elbrekt. 'Mr Jagger, I mean.'

'The helicopter.'

'Indeed.'

At the top, Elbrekt led them down a corridor with hand-painted Victorian wallpaper and eight doors. No getting lost here, anyway. Honestly, she didn't know what all the fuss was about.

A man emerged from the third door down. It was the portly old chap who'd been taking photographs in the garden earlier.

Fitz wriggled free of her hand and ran at the stranger. 'Will!' he cried. 'Will!'

'There he is!' The man kneeled with difficulty and spread his arms wide, a sloppy grin on his face. 'Have you been behaving for the nice lady?'

'Maria,' she said, performing her best curtsey. He was naggingly familiar.

'Will Monroe,' he replied, and must have seen her eyes widening. 'Yeah, yeah, I made a few movies back in the day. I have one more in me, I reckon, and that'll be that.'

Maria made a wild guess. 'About *American Hero?*'

'Oh, she's got the brains to go with her looks – very good. Yeah, I've interviewed the more famous survivors, but with the convention, I thought I'd grab the chance to catch a few others.' He grinned. 'You know what the guests are calling you, right?'

'Mary Poppins.'

'Yeah. Gotta be the uniform. I keep expecting Dick Van Dyke to come dancing round the corner.' He struggled to his feet, Fitz happily in his arms. 'Just give us a moment,' he said, and to Fitz, 'Let's find your mom.' He knocked at the door beside his own and disappeared inside.

'Your room it is the next,' Elbrekt told Maria, meaning next door. She was surprised to be near the guests instead of with the staff. 'Lord Branok suggested it,' Elbrekt said. 'Just in case.'

'Oh, that's right! I'm a nanny.'

He opened the door and stood well back so that she would not have to squeeze by him. 'Full marks,' she said, but didn't move.

'Dinner for guests is at seven,' he said. 'Lord Branok has suggested you be ready to help at half an hour before that – if it is acceptable to you, of course. There is to be a smaller table for yourself and Fitz with food he will like.'

'Your boss has thought of everything.'

He waited, his face impassive but for a mischievous glint in his eye; the perfect servant, ready to provide absolutely anything a girl could want. She considered his square jaw, his broad shoulders, for a few beats too many.

'I'll see you later,' she said finally. Did she want him to proposition her? To ask for her number? That might be nice. Not to tumble into bed at first sight but to build things up over a few weeks or months. He'd visit her in London. The following weekend, she'd come to Cornwall, maybe meet on the mainland, and go to see the Eden Project or St Ives . . .

The problem was: Maria couldn't relax in this place. Not yet. She slipped inside and closed the door behind her. She barely even looked at the room's elaborate decorations; instead, she immediately fished out her phone, hissed at the non-existent signal, and rushed over to the window, where a single bar reluctantly flickered onto the screen. She checked her sent messages. Yes, the gardener's photo had made its way to Charles. Thank God for that! The second he saw it, he'd know for sure that the raid was pointless.

It was only now that she realized the house had got her turned around again. She expected to be at the back, parallel to the nursery and looking out over the garden. But it was the jagged cliff that lay below her, an endless drop down to the hungry sea.

In the distance, one of those replica sailing ships was struggling against the wind, and was late in the day, too, to be making for a port. But what did she know of such things? She turned back.

'Oh.'

Whoever had decorated this room had impeccable taste – and an obsession with seashells. She was no stranger to them herself, having worked a thousand shifts in her parents' fish restaurant, but she'd never seen, or imagined, such an incredible variety and profusion of them. The lampshades were mother-of-pearl. The fireplace was a veritable jigsaw puzzle of every size and shape and colour of shell. The cup by her bed was a conch. And what kind of creature made its home in the shape of a spiral? Or a Möbius strip? Amazing! Fantastic!

However, for all her wonder, the most attractive part of the room right now had to be the bed, plain though it was. She could get an hour's sleep in and still have time to shower before her next appointment with Fitz. She could—

The phone rang. It was so sudden, she dropped it on the floor and then went scrambling while her bag swung free of her shoulder.

'Hello? Hello?'

'Maria—' It cut out.

She ran back to the window. Still no signal! She opened it up so that the chilly air rushed in around her; then, she leaned outside as far as she dared. It rang again.

'Hello?'

'There you are.' It was Charles. 'Why ain't you answering my calls?'

'I am! There's no signal.' She pressed the phone as tightly to her ear as she could, struggling to hear him over the wind.

'Good work with the photo. It's definitely not her. Now, here's what I need you to do . . .'

'Do? What do you mean?'

'Shut your fucking trap and listen. It's a bad line.' But he sounded more amused than angry. 'I need you to start using that power of yours. Get a few of those aces high and open the garden door for us as planned. Eight sharp, you hear me?'

Maria stared at the phone, her mouth working. 'But . . . but surely there is a mistake, darling, no? It's the wrong woman. You—'

Charles chuckled as the wind grew stronger, threatening to drag her out and down to her death. 'They're already here, innit? The whole gang, and unless you got a hundred grand to pay 'em off - well, we're comin' in, and that's that.'

'Surely you're rich? You have a . . . uh, a hundred grand? I mean—'

'What I don't have, *darling*, is patience. You'll open the door. You'll drug some of the aces - especially that Toad Man. He's the threat. And if you don't, if the filth turns up, or if anybody's expectin' us - well, the next time you see the jar, it'll be your sister's head floating in there with your old man's cock in her mouth. You got it? Tell me you got it.'

'Yes, of course, darling,' she said, stomach churning, eyes itching and one knee knocking repeatedly against the wall beneath the window. 'I just . . . I just wanted to check you were sure. That's all.'

'Open the garden door at eight. We'll be waiting. But don't expect no more calls. The phone mast on the mainland will suffer a few technical issues. The line from the village 'n' all.'

'But what if—'

He was gone. Only the wind remained. Even the sailing ship had passed out of sight by now, though where it could have got to, she didn't know. Or care.

She slid onto her bottom, put her head in her hands and wept.

5. Billiards

Maria had never liked sports, but she liked sportsmen rather a lot. Her current favourite was an American football player with impeccable tailoring, whose slogan was: *You look good, you play good. You play good, they pay good.* That was how drugs got sold, too – at least to the class of customer who didn't need to scramble down the back of the sofa every time they got antsy.

She needed a shower to wake her up. She'd have to hide those puffy eyes and get into character again as the party girl, whose one dear wish was to make sure everybody was smiling.

She wasted no time in the thoroughly modern ensuite, but nor did she hurry. 'Calm,' she said aloud as the water washed over her. 'Professional. I am here to help, darling.'

She put the uniform back on, then made sure everything in her bag was ready: the yellow envelope; the one with red stripes; the blue one containing nothing but ground black pepper in a two to one ratio with tahini. A bit messy, that one.

She also had her book to record who got what and a discreet little can of pepper spray that she had never once had to use in anger.

The only time she'd needed it, she'd reacted too slowly. It was before her card had turned. She'd been dealing pills for a guy who worked for Charles – not that she'd even heard of Charles then. But after she was mugged and her entire stock stolen – well, that's when they took her to see the jar. Maria shuddered.

No!

She forced her body still. This was no time for panic. The lives of her family depended on her keeping her head. She had put them through enough suffering already.

So. Deep breaths. Strategy.

What if she got all of the guests high? At dinner maybe? There wouldn't even be a fight, and nobody would get hurt!

Unfortunately, her power didn't work like that. People had to accept what she offered them, and she had to warn them – or at least hint at what they were letting themselves in for.

She would protect as many lives as possible, but no matter what, she would still have to do what Charles wanted.

'Professional,' she told herself. It was less convincing this time.

Maria stepped out of her room and headed for the hall. She paused to admire the grand stairway again and to steady her heart. Servants were lighting oil lamps in the corridor – a deliberate quirk, she thought, because there'd been electric lighting in her bedroom and a thoroughly modern shower.

Come on, girl. Stop wasting time.

No sooner had she reached the bottom than she heard Buford shouting, 'You see that? Did you see it?' accompanied by the guffaws of several men. Toad Man was her main target, the one Charles considered dangerous, so she followed the laughter into a billiard room, where five guests had gathered around the table.

She'd seen three of them before, the American Heroes: Toad Man; the one with the flying jacket; and poor Ivan, AKA Matryoshka, with hair everywhere. He looked as if he hadn't found the shower yet.

The remaining two were joker twins, although the wild card seemed to have done little more than replace their hair with black feathers. Both had covered their left eyes with patches, too, however, so for all she knew they could have had feathers under there, too, or beaks, or tiny grinning skulls.

Buford had propped half his belly onto the groaning table as he lined up a shot. He glanced over as she came in. 'Well, look who it is! Mary Poppins!' He proceeded to fluff the shot and laughed. 'Why'd they have to make the goddamned pool table so big?'

She hoped he was joking.

A plate of untouched scones rested on a trolley nearby, as well as a teapot still warm beneath its cosy.

'Gentlemen.' She thrust her chin in the air, because if they wanted Mary Poppins, she could give them that. 'Are you all *Americans* here?' Good-natured nods of assent all round. 'Then, let's have some proper British tea together. I'll show you *exactly* how it's done.' She paused, as if struck by a sudden worry. 'But I'm begging you,' she said, 'do try not to throw any into the harbour this time!'

They loved it – even Ivan managed a grin – and while she couldn't stand tea herself, she made a great show of stirring the pot, while humming 'A Spoonful of Sugar' and got another laugh. They were a sweet audience, lining up in turn like schoolboys.

'I'm Howard,' said the guy in the flight jacket. He gripped a billiard cue in one hand like it might fall and crush somebody if he didn't hold it steady. 'They call me Jetman.'

'Like Jetboy?'

'Exactly! But he was taken from us too soon. Oh, it's my shot. I'll drink this after, much obliged, ma'am.'

She laughed at his quaint turn of phrase, before turning to serve the twins.

'Call me Harry,' said one.

'I'm Max,' said the other.

'What do you do?' she asked them.

'Oh, we're in security now,' said Max. He handed her a card, almost shyly. It said: HUGINN AND MUNINN. INVESTIGATIONS. DISCRETION ASSURED.

'We used to be with SCARE,' Harry said.

'Wow!' She had no idea what Scare was. She nodded slowly, though, respectfully, and they grinned back at her as though they'd never spoken to a woman before.

Ivan took his tea without a word, and finally she was face to face with the supposedly dangerous Toad Man. He held out his hand without the slightest hint of suspicion or guile on his cheerful, jowly face.

Maria hesitated. She had added a little something extra to this particular cup – just a pinch, mind! It was two parts cardamom powder to one part each of corn starch and ground chia seeds. She preferred combinations that her customers were never likely to encounter by accident. They would be addicted to it for the rest of their lives, after all. If they ever discovered the formula for themselves, why, they'd never need to pay her, would they?

'You all right, Maria?' He'd called her by her real name because she must have dropped her act long enough to allow the worry to leak out, and that only made her feel worse.

The thing was: everyone she had addicted before was somebody who had come to her explicitly in search of drugs, somebody who knew what they were getting into and did it anyway.

'You're going to love this,' she whispered. She felt the hairs stand on the back of her neck as they always did at this moment.

'Oh, I know I am!'

Everybody else was laughing at Jetman's pathetic attempts to reach the cue ball without knocking a few of the reds with the hem of his jacket, so they didn't see Buford take his first sip or pay attention to the way he set the cup on the edge of the billiard table. But they sure as hell noticed when he slid to the floor, his eyelids flickering.

'Oh my God!' cried Maria. 'I think he's having a heart attack!'

It was always best to give people something to worry about. And worry they did. He was a big man, after all. Ivan sprinted from the room. Jetman started CPR, while the twins grabbed for their phones.

Buford's right eye cracked open. 'Are you an angel?' he asked Maria. 'It's so beautiful here. My uncle always said I'd go to the other place.' He smiled, and the eye shut again.

Maria made a lot of fuss of creating a pillow out of somebody's jumper and sliding it under Buford's head. She used the billiard table's dust cover as a blanket. 'We have to keep him warm!' Then she opened a window that looked out over the darkening driveway to make sure poor Toad Man was getting enough air. She knew he was just high, of course.

Another woman came rushing in, along with a tall man in a mask and cloak. Jago Branok: it had to be.

'Buford?' cried the woman. She was dowdy and middle-aged, with a face that was more makeup than flesh, or so it seemed. Her hair was as deeply black as Maria's own. But then she produced a stethoscope from one pocket, a thermometer from another, and employed both with steady hands. Pretty soon, she was sitting back on her haunches with a sigh. 'I think he's fine,' she told Jago.

'What . . . ?' said Maria, making her lip tremble. 'What if it's my fault? I . . . I served him the tea.' She showed the cup to the doctor, then took a sip from it herself.

'Are you mad, girl?' The other woman snatched it from her hand, her face so horrified that the makeup threatened to crack.

'Oh, sorry. That was rather silly of me. But . . . but it tastes fine. He didn't try the cake, I don't think.'

But the woman had already turned away, dismissing Maria as no more significant than a stain in the carpet.

'Do not worry.' It was Jago himself, taking Maria by the elbow and guiding her out of the room. 'He's in good hands now.' Jago could have been an actor, too. It wasn't just the resonance of his voice, which she felt in her bones, but he had that elusive quality known as 'presence' – the thing you could only be born with, that she and every other young actor in the world feared they might lack.

'But . . . I still think it's my fault.'

'Ah, my dear, so many of the best people feel that way about things beyond their control.' He waved down a passing maid and asked her in French to fetch a stretcher and some of the porters. He turned back to Maria, his smile visible under the bottom of his mask. 'I know it's just a job to you, but I am glad we will have the pleasure of seeing you at dinner.'

Then, he was gone, his cloak sweeping out behind him.

6. Beast

Maria fled the scene of her crime, because a crime was what it was. She'd never thought that way before. What student didn't have a little weed or blow now and again? Apart from Maria, herself, of course! Every single copper had tried it, every judge and MP – the lords and the bishops, too.

And at least her customers never suffered side-effects. They ran no risk that a bastard like Charles would mix in rat poison to increase his margins or that the wrong dose would kill them in their sleep. Good clean kitchen ingredients were all she ever gave them.

But until this moment, she had never tricked anybody. Her customers *wanted* to get high. They knew they risked addiction – fucking idiots! Weak, weak, the whole lot of them! Choosing to destroy their own lives and, by fuck, were they lucky to have landed on Maria for a supplier . . . They had always been asking for it.

Buford, however, had not.

She wandered down one corridor and then another. She climbed a bizarre spiral staircase, where the air smelled of her father's pipe. She climbed again – a set of rickety steps made entirely of books – into a wide hallway.

Strange portraits lined the walls: solemn men and women in antique costume, every one of them wearing a mask. Her feet now trod on animal furs instead of carpets. They were fakes, though. What manner of beast sported eight limbs?

Maria paused near a window. It was fully dark outside, and she was breathing hard. Crime or not, Charles would want more of the aces addicted. She'd have to get Jago, too, if she could; she probably should have found a way to offer him something when they spoke earlier, but she'd been genuinely upset.

Below, she could see the limousine and an old Rolls-Royce, parked away for the night. Where was Charles now? Were the gang already hiding out in the garden waiting to be let in?

She checked her phone. It had no signal. Perhaps they'd already sabotaged the mast on the mainland.

She jumped when she saw a movement outside. It was just one shadow among many others beyond the light of the first-floor windows. It moved again, and at least now she could be sure it wasn't Charles or any other human, but more likely an animal. A wandering cow, probably. It was certainly large enough.

She squinted into the gloom. Whatever the creature was, it brushed up against the far side of the limo, as though scratching its hide. The car rocked, going up onto the two nearest wheels until the itch had been dealt with. Then, the . . . the *thing*, whatever it was, trundled off into the darkness.

'Fucking hell,' she breathed. No wonder you weren't supposed to leave the house at night.

Maria still had an hour until her appointment with Julie and Fitz, but she wasted it trying to find her way back to the spiral staircase – or indeed to any staircase. Eventually, she resorted to barging into rooms without knocking, hoping desperately to find a servant or a guest to help her out. All were empty of life, although several of them were furnished in ways that made the paintings in the corridor seem sane: chairs that only a giant could use or antique bathtubs with the wrought iron legs of a spider.

Was Jago completely mad? Or was this entire floor something he had inherited? It didn't matter. Time was running out.

It was ten past six before she saw another living soul. At the far end of a passage, where all the lamps had burned out, she spotted a stooped old man with a long gown that dragged on the floor behind him.

'Hello? Excuse me? Can you help me find my way down?'

The man had a lamp of his own – luckily so, because the weird furniture had begun to freak Maria out more than a bit.

'Hi, I'm, uh, the nanny. I can't—'

The lamp came up so that they could have a good look at each other. The man had no face. There was just a sickening darkness, sucking in the light. She backed away. He advanced, his empty gaze holding hers like a magnet. She retreated another step, then two, as he flowed into the space she'd just left.

And then there was nothing behind her, and Maria was tumbling down a wooden servants' staircase she must have passed in the dark. She hit a landing that knocked the wind out of her, but she was on her feet in an instant. She fled down two floors before again she saw lights and the scurrying activity of normal life, of men and women in uniforms going about their business.

A sympathetic maid got Maria back to the right corridor with barely five minutes to spare.

She ran into her own room. Had she imagined the whole thing? That strange joker without a face? The huge creature that scratched itself against the cars? This house was crazy. God, she hated it. But she had no time to worry about any of that now. She threw a bit of water on her cheeks and did a quick check to make sure the envelopes were still in her handbag.

'One minute to curtain!' she told herself and stepped out the door.

7. Isolde

The door opposite Maria's opened as she came back out. It was the doctor from the billiard room. She wanted to duck back inside, but the woman had seen her.

'I'm so sorry,' the woman said and smiled at Maria. Her makeup visibly crinkled. 'For how brusque I was earlier, I mean. I was worried for my husband. He never eats right, you know?'

'Is he, uh, Mr Buford—'

'Mr Calhoun is just fine. And thank you. He'll be down for dinner. I reckon it's the jet lag and the booze, that's all. He never does what I tell him and then tries to hide it like a sneaky little kid.' She smiled. 'I'm Margarita, by the way. Mrs Toad Man, I guess.'

'I believe Mr Calhoun said you were Mexican?'

'That's me!'

'Your English—'

'Oh, don't! I've worked in Florida my whole adult life. I—'

Julie Cotton's door opened. Fitz peered around the corner, and Maria's heart skipped a beat as he beamed at her. 'Mawia!' he cried.

'I see you're going to be busy,' said Margarita. 'Again, I just wanted to say sorry for earlier.'

'No worries,' said Maria, fighting hard to swallow back her guilt. 'No worries at all.' Everybody was so nice: the guests she'd met so far, Jago himself, Elbrekt. It took everything she had not to burst into tears.

Somehow, she kept it together for Fitz. There he was, dressed in a perfect, tiny shirt, black trousers, and super shiny shoes. He even had a red bow tie on. He was the perfect antidote to everything she was feeling. He hugged her shyly. It hurt a little, because he had stuffed one of his toys down his shirt, possibly to sneak it past Julie. As she held him, the doll moved, and Maria yelped.

Julie poked her head out of the door. Her ears were wet from the shower, but they perked right up at the sight of Maria. 'Oh, great, you're here. I'm still trying to dry my hair, and—'

'Don't worry,' Maria said. 'We'll see what's going on downstairs. Right, Fitz?'

She accepted a rucksack of spare clothing – in case of accidents – and, miraculously, they found the grand stairway straight away.

'Maybe I'm getting used to the place, darling,' she said.

Mick Jagger was in the hall along with the young Black woman who'd been looking at the swords earlier.

Mick was shaking his phone. 'There's no signal at all now. Can't you do something about this?'

Maria swallowed, feeling ill. Charles had sabotaged the mast, then. There was no stopping it now.

'I can counsel patience, sir.' The young lady wore a dark and very proper skirt. She kept her hair in a tight, little bun.

'Very funny, Moesha.'

'My phone's not working either, if you must know, Mr Jagger.'

'You only call me that when you're annoyed with me.'

'I assure you I am not.'

Fitz's grip tightened suddenly. 'You need a hug, Mawia?'

She put all the reassurance she could muster into her voice. 'No, no, my darling. I'm fine. Come on.'

The first thing she did was grab a passing servant. He was a portly white man, his uniform a smarter version of the one Elbrekt wore. His face, too, was familiar, although she couldn't quite place where she'd seen it before. There seemed to be a lot of that sort of thing at Loveday House.

'Excuse me,' she said. 'I'm trying to find the back door? The one into the garden?'

He looked horrified.

'Miss, there is to be absolutely *no* going into the garden at night.' His accent was every bit as pompous as the one she was using.

'Oh, we wouldn't dream of going out, would we, Fitz? It's just I came in that way earlier from a nice walk, and I think I may have dropped my phone there when I took off my coat.'

'Someone will have found it, if so, miss.'

'Nevertheless, if I could just have a quick look into the hallway there, I would feel so much better.'

'Very well. Isolde?'

A harried maid appeared, her arms full of logs for one of the house's many fires. 'Please take the nanny here to the garden door. Ensure she doesn't try to leave and deliver her straight back again.'

'Of course.' She smiled sweetly, opened her arms, and allowed the logs to fall onto the floor. 'I'll do it at once, since I'm not busy or nothin'. Come on!'

The butler scowled at her.

Isolde led them through the dining room, past the sitting room with its sword cabinets and displays of silverware, and down a plain white corridor where hunting and fishing trophies hung from the walls. There were large windows on the far side, but all had been shuttered and barred for the night.

Maria paused often to point things out to Fitz. Partly, this was to keep him entertained, but she was also determined to fix these landmarks in her mind so that she wouldn't get lost again. 'Look at those antlers, Fitz! Wow!' 'It's a spear! For catching pigs, I think. See those designs? You know what runes are?' Of course, he didn't know – she barely knew herself, to be honest – but the boy liked to touch everything, and more than once, he giggled at something silly she said, while Isolde rolled her eyes or tapped a foot.

'Are you from Atlantis, too?' Maria asked, remembering Elbrekt's joke.

'Not likely.'

Maria tried again. 'How do you like working at the house? It must be boring all the way out here.'

'Borin' it is not. Would that it were! But better than gettin' burned at the stake for pettin' the wrong colour cat.' She spat – literally! A great gobbet landed on one of the pristine white walls. Guiltily, she wiped it off with the sleeve of her uniform, while Fitz laughed and attempted to spit himself. 'Don't tell Hitchcock,' Isolde said, her eyes narrowing.

'We wouldn't dream of it, darling. Would we, Fitz?'

They came around the corner at that very moment to find a bit of a hallway with a crowded coatrack, a shoe scraper, and a large mat over flagstones. The door itself was like something out of a medieval film: thick oak planks with a great big metal lock.

'Wow!' said Maria. 'Look at that, Fitz! Nobody could get through that. I wonder where the key is?'

'Oh, it's safe,' said Isolde.

'I bet that nice Lord Branok keeps it on a chain around his neck!'

'An' I bet he don't. Now, you were looking for your . . .' She waved her hands. 'Your thing.'

Maria made a show of peeking under the coats and lifting up the mats. 'I don't see it here. Is there any chance we could peek outside to see if it dropped on the step?'

'You got to be jokin'!'

'They don't trust you with the key, Isolde?'

'Of course I could get the key! I been here years. But . . .'

Maria gave her very best smile. 'I'm so sorry. Listen, we'll head back; I'm sure you have lots to do. Would you like a peppermint? They're special. You'll *love* them.'

She didn't expect the maid to accept, since they weren't getting on particularly well, but perhaps Isolde really fancied a sweet just then. In any case, she and Fitz both took one, but it was only Isolde who slid down the wall, her face slack.

'No, Fitz! Don't be upset, darling. She's just having a little rest, that's all. A rest, darling. Come on; we'll go back. It's nearly time for dinner.'

She took a moment to make the other woman comfortable and hide her under a coat or two. She'd be fine in an hour. Hopefully, nobody would come across her before then . . . As for guilt, Maria found betraying Isolde easier than betraying Buford. Maybe because she could already imagine Charles's presence out there in the dark and what would happen if she disappointed him.

Carefully, she retraced their steps. There was the spot on the wall where Isolde had spat. She hadn't done such a good job of wiping it clean. And there was the spear with the runes on it. She recognized some of the shields, while Fitz called out to various animals' heads as though they were old friends. At one point, the corridor split. She turned right, but Fitz let go her hand and ran the other way.

'Wait!' she called. 'Sweetheart!'

He pushed open a door.

She followed him in, only to find they were back in the sitting room. 'Wow! Clever boy!'

Well, she wouldn't make that wrong turn again. She had it worked out now. The logs Isolde had dropped were gone, and in the short time they'd been away, the place had been given a good dusting.

Hitchcock came in from the dining room. 'Did you find it, miss?' Even his voice was uncannily familiar.

'Find – oh! Believe it or not, it was in my bag the whole time. Look!'

'Very good. Lord Branok asked that you inspect the arrangements for the young master. We have set up a table for the two of you.'

Inside, everything was ready for dinner. Thousands of pounds' worth of silverware glittered and shone, enough to make anyone working here independent for a year or two at least. But Maria had a feeling that no member of staff at Loveday House had ever stolen from their employer and that the idea would horrify each and every one of them.

A few feet away was a normal-sized kitchen table with a high chair for Fitz and a slew of colouring books, should the urge take him between one course and the next. The cutlery here was of wood rather than silver but

was beautiful nonetheless. Old stuff, worn down and softened by use. Perfect
for a child.

Fitz placed two toys on the table. The first was the bewildered looking
soldier, the second a ferocious dog. Maria tried not to look alarmed as he
used his power to set them circling each other. And then, as though it were
the most normal thing in the world, he grabbed an orange crayon and started
colouring in a bunch of grapes.

A woman wandered in, middle-aged and stocky, wearing a beautifully
tailored tuxedo, jet black with a matching bow tie and leather shoes shiny
enough to act as their own source of illumination.

Maria stood to introduce herself, only to realize they'd already met.

'You're the gardener?'

Now that she was cleaner, the woman's face bore an even closer resemblance to the one in the jar, although she was still too old.

'I scrub up well when the occasion calls for it.' She looked around at the
silverware, the polished dining table. 'Normally, of course, there's no need,
but Lord Branok does like an even number of guests, and one of our American
friends seems to have mislaid his wife.'

'Oh, Matryoshka. I heard she'd left him. Listen, I'm Maria. I don't think
I caught your name earlier.'

'Annie's good enough for me. And I know that's Fitz.' She frowned at the
toys and the unsettlingly perfect detail the wild card power had given them.
The boy didn't even glance up.

Hitchcock arrived, scowling. He made minute adjustments to one of the
table settings. Servants hurried through. 'Two minutes!' the butler called to
them, for all the world as if they were about to run onto a stage. Perhaps
they were – although in this particular theatre, the ideal was to remain
completely unnoticed.

Ivan appeared, as though he'd heard the women talking about him just
now. He stood blinking at the threshold of the dining room in a boxy,
checked suit. A bear mask dangled from his right hand. A quick glance at
the empty table and he retreated at once.

Jetman came next, still in that old flight jacket, but with a pair of silver
pistols holstered at his side. Beside him walked a woman of South-East Asian
descent in a spectacular green ballgown that left her shoulders bare. 'For
once in your life, Howie,' she was saying, 'you could have made an effort.'

'I'll never stop honouring him, honey. I can't.'

'Oh, well,' said Annie with a sigh. 'Time to start "Operation Mingle". Enjoy
your evening, Maria. Personally, I prefer to eat alone.' And off she went.

Fitz, meanwhile, was colouring in a hedgehog in purple and red. He didn't
see his mother rushing over. 'Sweetie? Honey?'

Julie Cotton looked stunning in a midnight-blue silk dress. She had chosen
a fox mask for herself, an old one with flaking red paint. She removed it as
she reached the table. 'Nobody will ever guess who I am,' she said with a

wink, her ears bouncing outrageously above her. She oohed and aahed over
Fitz's impressive artistry and kissed the top of his head.

'Ladies and gentlemen . . .' Jago Branok himself was out in the hall.
'Please find your seats. Each of you will have a nametag . . .'

'Listen,' Julie said. 'When Fitz gets like this – you know, *absorbed* – bedtime
can't be far off. I asked to get him fries, but don't be alarmed if he pushes
them around some before using them for a pillow.'

'If that happens, I'll take him straight up to bed.'

'Great! The door is unlocked. I don't mind if you go in, but if you see a
huge pile of carrots, *I* didn't steal them, and I don't know how they got
there.'

Maria laughed.

Everybody else filed in: Toad Man's wife, smiling over to the little table;
Mick Jagger, his every movement dangerous, as though he were already in
his wolf form; Moesha – far too young, surely, to be his date? Maria didn't
think they were a couple. There were no little touches, no standing close
together.

And then Toad Man came through. A *commedia dell'arte* mask covered his
face entirely, but Maria wasn't fooled. She felt him before she saw him. His
need was banked very low, having been so recently fed. But she would have
been able to find one of her customers even in complete darkness. He had
totally recovered, and he smiled broadly, waving all concerns away.

Everyone found their nametags. Couples had been split up, it seemed.

'Except for us,' Maria told Fitz.

He smiled shyly and handed her a yellow crayon. 'Fowers,' he said.

'You want me to colour in the flowers, darling?'

Jago Branok moved to the head of the table and waited there until the
chitchat and glad-handing died down enough for every buttock to meet the
right chair. The master of Loveday House had changed into a gleaming white
mask that covered only the top half of his face, his dark hair braided like a
Viking's.

'Dear friends or friends to be . . . Eat, drink, enjoy! My home and I look
forward to knowing you all better.' He smiled under the mask, and Maria
fancied she could see lines on his skin. Scarring, perhaps, like her sister had,
or some sort of joker mutation.

'Once the main course is finished, some of our lads and lasses here will
give you a demonstration of our traditional Cornish guise dancing. We have
our own instructor, too – Gary Bushorn – if any of you would care to learn
a few steps.'

Jetman's wife clapped her hands at the prospect. Ivan – Matryoshka –
stared into the spot where his food must soon appear, and everybody else
got to chatting.

One voice alone rose above the hubbub. 'Lord Branok, sir?' It was the
young American woman, Moesha. 'May I say grace for the table?'

'Ah.' Branok's head shook reluctantly. 'In this house, all prayer remains private. You never know who might be listening.'

'Isn't that rather the point, sir?'

'I assure you, Ms Brown, it is not my intention to disrespect the beliefs of any guest.'

'Of course not, sir.'

'And you must call me Jago. Please.'

She smiled, bowed her head in acknowledgement.

Waiters were already swooping in through a door at the back of the room, like a wave of bombers falling on a helpless city. Elbrekt appeared, as though summoned by a wish. 'It is coincidence,' he said, 'that it is I who serves you.'

'Of course!' said Maria.

She could tell that he was trying not to stare at the toys, but he kept his composure as he presented her with a bowl of soup and Fitz with a little basket of chips with a few squiggles of red sauce dripping over them.

'The chefs have outdone themselves!' said Maria, fluttering her eyelashes at the chips. 'And you delivered those plates with aplomb!'

'If you want a plum, miss . . .'

'No, I meant—'

He grinned, and God, he was so beautiful. She couldn't help watching him walk away either. In just a few hours, she thought, he was going to despise her. They all were. She felt utterly sick.

8. Invaders

Maria toyed with her main course. She watched everything and everyone. Servants whispering among themselves – had they found Isolde in her stupor by the garden door? The maid should be coming around soon. Would she say what had happened to her?

Snatches of conversation floated over. Mick was laughing out loud at some joke he had shared. All those around him smiled politely, but Moesha, seated several places away, frowned in disapproval.

'You're Mr Jagger's assistant?' Toad Man asked her. 'He told me about you.'

'I'm his PA, Mr Calhoun, yes.'

'So, you know, why'd they call you "Jell-O"? You some kind of ace?' That was a rude question these days, but Buford was smiling and clearly meant no ill by it.

'It's not a name I use for myself, Mr Calhoun. If the Lord has blessed me with certain gifts—'

'Oh!' called Mick. 'Yeah, don't use that name. She *really* hates it. And you'd better not be serving any jelly for dessert, Jago, or she'll throw it right back in your face!'

'No,' said Moesha. 'I would never—'

Maria had no patience for any of it. The back of her throat burned. Her palms were damp and trembling, like the first days after she'd quit the booze. The gang had to be outside the house already, sharing the darkness with whatever awful bloody animals kept people here indoors at night. Maybe one of the creatures would do her a favour and swallow Charles whole, but somehow, she doubted things would go so smoothly.

And the time to act had finally come, because Fitz's eyes were drooping. 'Hey, my darling,' she told him. He looked so very sweet, his rosy little cheeks designed for pinching. *What if he gets hurt?* She swallowed. 'Darling? I know a great story.'

'Does it have dolphins?'

'Do you like dolphins?'

'Uh-huh.'

'That's amazing, because this story is *all* about dolphins. Come on; I can only tell it in a bedroom.'

'I want to stay.'

Sure, you do, she thought. He could barely keep his head up. 'We'll come right back down after the story, I promise.'

He made no effort to resist when she swooped him up.

'Don't forget his toys!' called Julie when Maria was already halfway to the door.

'Oh! I did, thank you!' When she looked back, she found the tiny soldier and dog were both watching her – or Fitz, rather – their faces anxious now. Finally, she swept him past the dining table, with her charge earning many fond smiles along the way.

The servants liked him, too, it seemed, and a maid was waiting to guide them all the way to Julie Cotton's room.

'I know it's simple really,' Maria told her, 'but I'm not sure I'd have found my way here without you.'

The maid nodded. 'It confuses some more than others, the house. Some visitors find it simpler to walk with eyes closed.'

And with that cryptic comment, she left them to get settled.

Maria drew bedtime out for as long as she could. She made a game of brushing Fitz's teeth, timing him with her phone. That gave him a new spurt of energy, but it didn't last, and she got no more than halfway through her story before he was fast asleep. Just as well; she hadn't worked out the ending yet.

She waited to be sure he wouldn't wake again, then waited some more, shivering and feeling fragile. At last, as though he were her own child, she kissed his warm forehead and slipped out of the door.

She steadied herself against a wave of dizziness. Was it the weirdness of the house doing that to her, or was it guilt? In any case, she remembered the advice of the maid who had guided her here. She closed her eyes, keeping one hand on the wall. She turned right, to where the stairs were supposed to be, and when she opened her eyes again, that was where she found them.

Back in the dining room, everybody had finished their main course. 'Don't worry,' she told Julie. 'There's a maid with him. But he wants his colouring book back. I'm sure he'll be asleep by the time I get it up to him again.'

A lot of wine had been drunk. Matryoshka was waving his arms. Toad Man was laughing raucously, while his wife chattered with Will Monroe. Jetman's face had turned bright red, his eyes glassy, a smile fixed on his lips. 'The best comic shop in London!' he cried. 'I'll find it there; I know I will.'

The servants were busy cleaning up a mess under Mick's chair, while Hitchcock tutted at them.

Absolutely nobody paid any attention to Maria as she slipped out of the wrong side of the room and headed straight towards the garden door, hurrying along the corridor with all the hunting trophies on one side and the shuttered windows on the other. She was hyperventilating, her palms damp. All she could hear were her own breaths and the pounding of her pulse.

Oh God, what if she got lost now? Indeed, more than once, she found herself entering strange rooms by mistake. Closing her eyes didn't always help either, but she had extra help this time: whenever she got turned around, she only had to concentrate and . . . *there*! She felt it! Isolde's hunger, sated though it was, still had just enough life in it to take Maria exactly where she needed to go.

Scarcely twenty minutes after leaving the dining room, she was back before that ancient wooden door and at her feet, only waking up now with a groan, was Isolde. 'What . . . What did you give me, I . . .'

There was no more time to waste.

'I want the key,' said Maria. 'I want this door unlocked.'

And when Isolde opened her mouth to object, Maria leaned hard on that need of hers, stoking it so high that sweat broke out on the maid's skin. 'I don't . . . feel . . .'

'Fetch the key.'

'I . . . I can't . . . What if they get in? The boars, what—'

'Now!'

Maria concentrated until the woman convulsed, until foam ran over her chin and her feet drummed on the flagstones. And when it stopped, and she mewled like a blind puppy, Maria held up a peppermint. 'You'll get this, when I get the key.'

Minutes later, both women had what they wanted.

The key turned, and the door swung open as if of its own accord, to usher in a freezing blast of air.

At first, Maria saw nothing beyond a halo of light on the walls of the house itself or from some of the upper windows. Then a figure came running towards her, pounding over the lawn. It was Charles, of course – the Unkillable himself, the metal of his body glinting against the darkness. Others ran at his back. She recognized the pointed face of Drillhead, and skittering along behind, on all fours, came Mr Pantomime, the sight of his white skin turning her guts to water. There were others, too, sprinting for all they were worth, making no sound but the jangling of harnesses or the squelch of feet in the damp grass.

Maria tried to straighten her back. 'Welcome, darlings,' she said.

Charles picked her up by the neck and dragged her several feet down the hall, making room for the rest of the gang to follow. A woman slipped in, breathing hard, her face a scowl, a crossbow hanging from her shoulder. A set of stocky male triplets came next, all with serrated teeth and glowing blue eyes. The last to arrive were a crowd of assorted bruisers in combat gear. They slammed the door and turned the key as far as it would go.

It was only then Maria realized that several members of this terrifying company had blood on their clothing. One of the men at the back was bleeding from his stomach. As she watched, he slid onto his bottom beside the figure of the sleeping Isolde.

They were afraid.

'OH, THAT WAS UNPLEASANT!' said Drillhead.

'You,' said Charles. He squeezed Maria's neck until a black halo crowded the edges of her vision. 'You were supposed to open at eight.'

'It . . . it can't be much af-after—'

'THE PIGS! WE ARE DOWN THREE BRAVE ADVENTURERS, CHARLES.'

'Four,' said the woman with the crossbow. She poked the toe of her boot at the man on the floor. 'I think he injured it, though. Or made the thing angry, anyway.'

'All right,' said Charles. 'Whatever the fuck.' He had yet to release his hold on Maria, but the sight of Isolde – perhaps he thought that Maria had killed her – seemed to allay whatever suspicions of sabotage he might have been harbouring. 'They still at dinner?'

'They, uh, should be. Or having a dancing lesson.'

'That's perfect, innit? One?'

This last word wasn't a number but a name, and all three of the triplets raised their toothy heads in response to it.

'You didn't drop your gas cannisters running from the pigs?'

Each of them patted an identical rucksack at exactly the same time.

'Good,' said Charles. 'Get your masks ready.' He turned to Maria. 'What are we facing?'

She gave him another rundown of the guests. She told him about the twins, Huginn and Muninn, with the black feathers for hair. She mentioned Moesha – Jell-O. 'She might be an ace, but—'

'Ain't heard of her. She can't be much use. Nah, Toad Man's still the big risk for us. But you . . . you will help him see reason, yeah?'

'Y-yes, darling.'

'And the owner? Branok?'

All around them, members of the gang were donning gas masks. Even Drillhead had a great big hood that looked as if it had come right out of the trenches of the First World War. The only person without a mask was Maria herself. 'He, uh – Lord Branok wasn't thirsty.'

'What, you couldn't just slip it into his grub?'

'It doesn't work like that. They have to accept it from me.'

'WHAT ARE YOU TALKING ABOUT?' The hood muffled Drillhead's electronic voice.

'Nothing. This stupid cunt only did half a job for us is all. Maybe I'll leave her with half a family after we get home. That's fair, innit?'

'YOU ARE A GENEROUS AND CHARMING SOUL, CHARLES!'

'We'll see. If tonight goes well, you're gonna learn how generous I can be.' He slipped a mask over his metal head. 'Lead the way, Maria.'

She tried to – she really did – but the first two doors she looked through were for a lavatory and a root vegetable storage area of some sort.

'IS SHE PLAYING WITH US?' Drillhead whirred right at Maria's ear. 'ALLOW ME TO PLAY WITH HER.'

Her uniform was sopping with sweat, her knees practically knocking together. She wanted to beg Charles to let her go, to let her family go. And what about the guests here? Julie Cotton? Will and poor Matryoshka? What about the staff?

The drill whirred again.

Maria spun around, her chin jutting. 'Really, darling. Can't you let me do my job? Sometimes there are servants working in here, and I wanted to make sure they didn't sound the alarm.'

'YOU LOOKED LOST.'

'I could find my way out of here with my eyes closed.' She proved it then and there, leading the terrible crew unerringly towards the hunting trophies by touch alone. Here, beyond the shuttered windows, something squealed, and a shudder ran through the other members of the party. Mr Pantomime leaped six feet straight up onto one of the walls.

'That pig's not getting in,' said Charles. 'Nobody'd live in this house if it could, innit?'

Twice more, Maria had to close her eyes and concentrate to find the correct turn, but now, she had Toad Man's need to aim for, too, weak though it was. And finally, they were in the drawing room with the sounds of music and clapping hands and raucous laughter coming from next door.

The gang began to fan out, but Charles waved them towards him. He had his back to a cabinet full of silver cups and plates. When a thug in combat trousers reached for it, Charles shoved his hand away.

'Later,' he whispered. 'When we got the house to ourselves and not a second before.' Even coming from behind a gas mask, his glare did its job. 'Now, here's how it's going down. We crash through that door with as much noise as we can make. Like when you do a bank, yeah? Tell 'em all to get on the floor.'

'They're aces,' said the woman with the crossbow.

'No fucking kidding, Maven. When you fell off that building in Windsor, you must have rattled that little brain of yours, because it's obvious we just want to distract 'em a bit.'

'Why?'

'So that One' – he pointed at the triplets – 'can release the gas. You get me? Until they're all asleep, do whatever you need to counter threats, but avoid kills if you can. You saw the helicopter outside. Some of this lot could be worth a fortune.'

As the rest began preparing their weapons, Charles reached up to the top of the cabinet. What was he doing? Maria was sure he was hiding something there, but what? He caught her looking.

'You better do your part,' he told her. 'Toad Man.'

She swallowed. 'I don't have a gas mask.'

'Take 'im down quick, then. It'll send you to sleep is all. Hey! Maven!'

The woman was smearing something over the tips of her crossbow bolts.

'I said not to kill them.'

'It's slow.' She shrugged. 'And I brought the antidote.'

And then, without so much as a countdown, Charles the Unkillable strode towards the double doors to the dining room and charged through with the gang at his heels and Maria hurrying to catch up.

'Get the fuck down!' Charles screamed.

The musicians were right by the door. People in outlandish costumes, all ribbons and animal skulls, had been prancing about in the spot where the dinner table had been. Chairs were pushed back to the edges of the room. *'Get the fuck down!'*

A drill whirled in excitement. 'DOWN, DOWN, OR YOU WILL SUFFER DEATH!'

'On the floor, bitches!' A crossbow waved.

It took whole seconds for the music to die and for the last dancer – a drunken Jetman – to spin to a stop. Shock seemed to freeze everybody in their places – everybody except one.

Jago Branok leaped onto the table at the back of the room, his arm flashing forward.

Thwack! Charles staggered backwards with a silver knife lodged between his eyes. The woman called Maven reacted instantly. Even as Charles was pulling the knife from his face, her crossbow snapped, and Jago fell back off the table.

Shots rang out. A musician's head exploded.

'*Don't kill them*, you fuckers! I told you—'

And suddenly, there was a toad the size of a small car in the room, with people scattering away from it, its skin pocked and scarred and ribbed like ancient bark, steaming with God knows what poisons. Maria froze.

The creature's true power was only revealed when the tongue shot out and smashed a man in combats to a pulp.

'*Do something!*' Charles screamed.

They'll kill my parents, Maria thought. *Oh God, oh God.* She had to; she needed to—

The tongue shot out again – she didn't see where it landed. She had to concentrate, to feel the *need*. It was still there but buried deeper than it ought to have been, as though the Toad were an entirely different being from the man it had been before the transformation.

But as the room broke into chaos around her, she isolated the hunger, grabbed as firm a hold on it as she could and *squeezed*. The Toad made a horrendous rattling bellow. Its tongue smashed onto the flagstones, scattering chairs and wineglasses.

And then the monster was gone, and Buford was there in its place, shivering on all fours, puking his guts up. Maria backed out of the room.

'Gas!' somebody shouted. 'There's gas in here!'

It was powerful stuff. She saw Julie's ears droop at the first breath of it before she slid down onto her rabbit's tail. Jetman and his wife were already on the floor, with others staggering around before succumbing in their turn. Charles punched Matryoshka, except . . . now there were *two* Matryoshkas, though they appeared to have shrunk in size. Then there were four of them that only reached up to the gangster's waist, all fighting furiously. But they, too, fell as the fumes enveloped them.

A few of the servants tried to hold their breaths and fight, but Drillhead waded into them with a club while several people at the back were running for the hall.

Bodies lay everywhere: Will Monroe, bleeding from his scalp; a slack-jawed Mick Jagger lying beside him, though whether he was dead or alive, Maria couldn't tell. With uncanny coordination, the triplets known as One surrounded the wounded Jago.

Maria staggered back into the drawing room, closing the door to keep out the gas. Everything was quieter here. She leaned against the wall, hyperventilating. It was all as good as over now. She had done her part, and with the help of God, there'd be no more casualties. Except . . . off in the direction of the front doors, somebody was shooting.

'Psst!'

She looked up. The grandfather clock in the corner of the room had slid away from the wall. Behind it, was Elbrekt. She waved him away frantically, but just then, two of the triplets entered the room, still in their gas masks, and strode towards her.

'Leave her be!' shouted Elbrekt. He charged into the room armed with a hammer.

'No!' Maria cried. 'No!'

They came at him from two different sides, lightning fast for all their stockiness. He flung the hammer at one, then dived between their grasping arms, rolled towards the far wall, and jumped to his feet. He punched out the glass of one of the cabinets there with his bare hands.

Bleeding, he turned, a vicious-looking sabre in one fist. 'Stay back, Maria!' he shouted. 'Stay back!'

'They're not . . .' How could she explain that they had not come to hurt her, that she herself had let them into the house? That she had drugged one of his colleagues to do so and had put every decent person here in danger? It was too late for words to make any difference.

They swung at him with truncheons that seemed to slide off his sword with no effort on his part. They were faster than any mere nat could be, but Elbrekt seemed to know where every blow would fall, and his sabre was always waiting. And then, a quick slash broke through the guard of the triplet on his left. Both screamed; both began bleeding in the exact same spot on their shoulders, but neither stopped advancing, and soon enough, their wounds began to heal while the poor boy only grew more tired.

I have to help him.

She picked up Elbrekt's hammer and froze again. She couldn't do this. It was a death sentence for Ana, for her parents. But she couldn't leave him either. Elbrekt was exhausted by now, the sword dipping dangerously, and One was pushing him steadily backwards. Backwards towards—

Maria screamed.

It was Mr Pantomime. He was just . . . hanging on the wall, his papery tongue darting in and out of his mouth.

'Elbrekt!' Maria cried. 'He's behind you!'

Mr Pantomime dropped. The trench coat opened like a parachute and covered Elbrekt almost entirely, so that only his feet protruded. The fabric of the coat shuddered, twitched, writhed, while the chalk-white face gazed serenely in Maria's direction. Then, Mr Pantomime skittered away and up the wall again.

Elbrekt remained. There was something wrong with his skin. She pushed One aside, her entire body vibrating.

The boy had become . . . old. His flesh wrinkled and sagging. His eyes rheumy. Knuckles knotted. 'Run, Mother,' he whispered. 'The sea. The waves . . .'

She wanted so much to take him into her arms but didn't know how without hurting him. Behind her, the door opened again.

'Well, well.' Charles had come, the metal plates of his body dented, scratched, and jagged with rips. 'Look who's changed sides.'

'Run,' Elbrekt whispered again.

And Maria did, right into the passage behind the grandfather clock, weeping all the way.

Charles's laughter followed her into the darkness.

9. Gun

Maria ran. She *sprinted*. The darkness didn't stop her, nor the tripping, nor the falling flat on her cobweb-covered face, nor her clothing ripping against the rough stone that entombed her.

The only sounds were her own panting, the occasional sob.

Maria always liked to keep up a good front. That was her rule, and she tolerated no shows of weakness, not even in front of the mirror at home. *Straight back! Chin high!* That was Maria all over. Or it had been before she'd given Charles every excuse he needed to murder her family, before she'd seen Mr Pantomime at work.

The passage twisted, intersected with others. Some smelled of the sea, some of sulphur or sewage. In one place, she had to fight through a sudden urge to sleep; in another, she clamped her ears against a blood-curdling bellow loud enough to shake dust from the walls.

She had no idea how long she had been running before the floor opened suddenly beneath her. She screamed, fell, tumbled down a slope and out onto a carpeted floor.

Maria lay stunned for a moment, dazzled by gas lamps. It seemed that she had entered this small office through the fireplace, and she spat a mouthful of soot onto the dusty carpet.

'Elbrekt. Oh God, Elbrekt.'

He was dead now, or dying at least, and all because she had let those monsters into the house. And she had done this awful thing for nothing, too, because in trying to help the poor boy, she had doomed her own family anyway.

Footsteps ran past in the corridor beyond. 'Put him down here. Put him on the table. I'll need to cut open his jacket . . .' That was Toad Man's wife, Margarita.

Maria stepped outside to find a strange golden pistol already pointed at her face. Lights blinked on the barrel, and it whined slightly, as though hungry.

'Oh,' said the gardener, Annie. 'It's you.' She lowered the weapon. Blood seeped from a jagged cut on one cheek. The jacket of her tuxedo was missing, as was one sleeve of her shirt from the elbow down. 'Sorry, girl.' She didn't seem to realize that Maria was the enemy. 'Come on. We're in the library.'

Jago Branok, the master of Loveday House, lay bleeding and raving on a polished wooden table, while all over the floor were the books that had been moved to accommodate him.

Margarita leaned over him with a pair of scissors. 'I need to get his jacket off. Gary, can you sterilize a knife for me?' Gary was an elderly black man, still dressed in one of those ribbon-covered cloaks the dancers had worn. He produced a knife, as she had asked, but all he did was to grasp it tightly in one fist.

'All right, everybody, hold him!'

They tried. One of the feather-haired twins was here, as well as Mick Jagger's assistant, Moesha, and Hitchcock the butler. Each employed their entire strength on a single limb and, even so, they were barely coping. None of them bothered to ask Maria what she had done with Fitz, her one responsibility.

Branok sweated and raved. 'I know where to send them!' he shouted. '*I'll* send them! Me and mine, me and mine! They will beg and never will I open it again!'

'Can we put a sock in his mouth?' asked Annie. 'He'll lead them here.'

Hitchcock snarled at her. 'After all he did for you, you would disrespect him?'

'Of course not, but if they hear him—'

'They probably just want money,' said Maria. 'C-can't we let them have it? They might . . . might leave afterwards.'

'*No!*' cried Branok, though it appeared to be no more than a coincidence. Even so, Hitchcock, still struggling at his master's right leg, managed a vigorous nod.

'There are things in this house that no outsider - certainly none as villainous as they - should ever get hold of. Your world would not thank us for it.'

'They'll take those things anyway.' Maria hated the edge of panic in her own voice. 'We can't stop them now! Nobody can stop them.'

'The master can,' said Hitchcock. 'But only if—'

A whirring sound came from the corridor. 'HELLO, IN THE LIBRARY.'

Everyone froze.

'DO NOT FEAR. WE KNOW YOU CAN HEAR US, BUT WE HAVE KILLED ONLY SERVANTS SO FAR, AND YOUR GUESTS ARE NOW OUR GUESTS, SO WHERE IS THE HARM?' The drill spun again, and Annie readied her pistol. The feather-haired twin with the eye patch - Huginn, or maybe Muninn - had a gun of his own, too, though he had to release Lord Branok's left arm to unholster it.

'YOUR STAFF WERE VERY BRAVE. I WENT THROUGH SEVEN OF THEM' - the drill ran with excitement - 'BEFORE THEY TOLD US ABOUT THE CONTENTS OF THE SAFE.'

Hitchcock visibly shuddered. 'We can't let them have it!'

'GIVE US THE KEY, AND WE WILL GIVE YOU THE ANTIDOTE FOR MR BRANOK. WE WILL FILL OUR POCKETS, BUT NO MORE BLOOD NEED BE SPILLED.'

'What guarantees are you offering?' Annie clicked a button on the side of the golden gun and the whine it made intensified.

The man with the eye patch padded forward, handling his own gun with the utmost confidence.

'WE HEREBY GIVE THE FOLLOWING LIST OF GUARANTEES—'

The door, which hadn't even been locked, flew off its hinges. It smacked into the twin, driving him to the ground as Charles the Unkillable thrust into the room behind it.

'You!' he said, glaring at Annie. 'Dunno why you look older, but it *is* you, you filthy cunt! It must be.'

He swung for her, smashing the gun out of her hands while bullets from the twin on the floor pinged off his metal torso. Then, there was no room for any more shots. Charles and Annie were grappling. Her wild card strength was enough to rip one arm right off his body. The room filled with clangs as she began hitting him with it, while he . . . he laughed.

'Look out!' cried Margarita. Canisters rolled in over the floorboards – gas again? Charles's remaining arm landed a punch that rocked Annie back.

Then the Unkillable was backing out of the room once more. 'Do your new friends know who you are?' he shouted. 'What you done?'

Only Maria knew he was talking to her. Maybe that was why, in one smooth movement, she picked up the strange gun and fired it into his chest. The effect was more like a water pistol than anything else. A jet of blue slime shot across the room. All of it landed on Charles; not so much as a drop even touched the floor. It slipped into every crack in his metal body. Steam poured from his mouth, his eyes, from between his legs. And then, like an empty suit of armour, he dropped.

A hush fell. Even the drill had gone silent. Maria found herself grinning, her heart pounding.

Nobody else tried to enter the room, but the rest of the gang were there, all right, their shadows flickering in the hall.

Eventually, she heard Drillface ask, 'WHY ARE THEY NOT YET ASLEEP, ONE?'

Maria was wondering the very same thing herself, but she had no time to see what had become of the cannisters, because now, two of the triplets appeared at the door, wearing their gas masks, advancing behind a thick metal shield. Maria squeezed the trigger for another shot, but though her weapon whined, nothing happened this time.

'Moesha!'

'I'm trying!'

The air around the doorway shimmered, changed colour to a deep, artificial-looking red that thickened even as Maria watched. One seemed to become encased in it, like a fly in strawberry-flavoured amber. The whole room stank of sickly, fake fruit.

'The Lord knows I do hate Jell-O . . .' muttered Moesha.

Maria dared to look behind her. A pair of gas cannisters had fallen at either end of the room. Both were caught in their own coloured blocks; presumably this was Moesha's doing, too. They had already been spewing forth gas when she had trapped them, and while it continued to emerge and swirl, the whole process seemed to be happening much more slowly than was normal.

As for Moesha herself, her lips were white, her forehead wrinkled with concentration. 'If any of you good folks have a plan . . . I'd . . . I'd hurry. Can't hold three of them like this for long.'

'Sir?' Hitchcock shook Jago Branok frantically. 'Sir? We need you. We need a way out, *sir*.'

Lord Branok was still wearing his mask, but behind it, his eyes opened. 'I know where to send them,' he hissed. 'Yes.'

His uninjured arm pointed at a wall of books at the far end of the room. It slid to the right, and behind, lay a simple door.

10. Finger

They hurried through the door, with Hitchcock and Gary supporting Jago between them, while Annie and the twin with the eye patch – this one was Muninn, Maria learned – leaned against each other.

Maria was one of the last through, and she got to see Moesha's jelly-like force fields pop out of existence with a final whiff of fruit. The door shut behind them. Then it, too, was gone, as though it had never been. Maria didn't have time to worry about that, for she was too busy being cold. It was pitch dark. Damp rock surrounded them. Wind howled somewhere, and right by her ear, Moesha's teeth chattered.

A match flame appeared.

'Please look for wood.' It was Gary, his voice quiet, and, like most people she'd met here, he, too, was American. 'Or anything that can burn. We need to keep Jago warm. We're never getting back without him.'

'But,' said Maria, teeth chattering, 'he's been poisoned. Char—' She caught herself. 'The gang didn't give us the antidote.'

'The master heals quite quickly,' said Hitchcock. 'Given the chance.'

There was nothing more to be said. People scrambled around in the freezing dark for anything that might burn. Maria found some sticks, though she was shivering enough by now, she could barely keep a grip on them. She carried her load back to Gary, who had replaced the first match with a new one.

'Thank you,' he said. She was probably imagining things, but she felt warmer just from standing next to him. 'We haven't been introduced. I'm Gary.' The way he said it made him seem more Irish this time than American.

'M-Maria.'

'Well, I am sorry, Maria, but we'll need more fuel than this.'

'No problem, d-d-darling.' Reluctantly, she left the warmth of his presence, turning off into the gloom, bumping past Annie on the way.

It wasn't completely dark in here, she realized. She followed a faint light until it brightened into the entrance to a cave. This must be the side of the cliff, she thought, looking out over the sea.

But no. Her shock could not have been greater.

Beyond the cave entrance, a fierce wind screamed, and flecks of snow sped over an icy plain that extended as far as the eye could see, with not a seagull in sight.

You're not in Cornwall any more, Dorothy.

When she crept further, she heard shrieks, and there, no more than a hundred yards away, two six-legged polar bears, or polar bear-sized *things* with . . . with tusks, wrestled in the snow. She had the impression they were playing and that was nice, except she realized, *We're in their home. Holy mother of God.*

She ran back to the others. A fire was already burning there. Those weren't sticks at the centre but old bones, some as long as herself, cracked open and covered in tooth marks.

'Bears,' she said.

'No kidding,' said Annie. She didn't appear to be too worried by the fact, though. She was an ace, after all. And maybe Moesha could use her Jell-O power to slow the monsters down if they attacked.

'Will somebody tell me what the fuck is going on?' said Margarita. 'Why is it so cold?'

'Oh, just tell her,' said Annie. Nobody stepped up, so she did the job herself. 'Listen, Doctor. You're in a different world. Lord Branok travels to 'em somehow. Parallel timelines, too, which is where he recruited most of the staff, including me.'

'And . . . Hitchcock, too?' asked Margarita. 'He looks just like . . .'

'Yeah, he does. Hitchcock's movies were pretty famous where I come from, too. Especially *The Fish*.' She shuddered. 'God, when they all attack the window of that submarine!'

'I think I get it now,' said Margarita.

She wasn't the only one. Maria had seen way too much here that was strange. An under-butler who claimed to come from Atlantis and who handled a sword like an action hero. A maid who'd feared being burned at the stake. And now . . . six-legged bears. *Different worlds indeed.*

Jago groaned. 'Alfred?' His voice was faint.

'Sir!' The relief in that one syllable was profound.

'What . . . what of the guests? I remember . . . the attack. At dinner.'

Hitchcock did his best to fill him in, with Annie interrupting to supply other details. Nobody seemed to know that Maria had been involved, but her face burned with the shame of what she'd done.

'All right,' said Jago. 'Muninn?'

'Yeah?'

'My thinking is not yet clear enough to get us back to the right place. But – I hesitate to ask – does your brother still live?'

'Yes, Lord Branok. I had a quick look already.'

'That is a relief. Would it be possible to see if the others are all right?'

The twin sat back against the wall and removed his eye patch. Maria had been prepared to flinch, but in the firelight at least, the left eye seemed perfectly ordinary. He slipped the patch over to other side.

'It's to prevent confusion,' Margarita told Maria.

'Confusion?'

'Right now, he's seeing everything in his brother's line of sight – Harry, or Huginn, as he's called. Those two are linked.'

'Is *everybody* here an ace?'

'Oh, honey, I'm not. Nothing close to it.' Margarita stared intently at Muninn, wrapping her arms tightly about herself, though she stood right next to the fire, and Maria realized she was worried about what had happened to Buford. Of course she was.

Muninn grimaced. When he spoke, it was in a whisper. 'They weren't lying. Everybody's alive. Harry knows I'm watching, by the way.'

'Can you see Buford?' Margarita asked.

'Yeah. Your Toad is snoring. That old rock star, the guy with the lips, Mick—'

'*Sir* Mick,' said Moesha.

'Yeah, he's there, too. Ivan is lying beside Jetman and his wife.'

'J-Julie?' asked Maria. 'Fitz?'

'Julie's out cold. And they must have grabbed her kid from his room. They're all there together. We're lucky Harry made it to the door before they caught him, or he'd be asleep, too, and we wouldn't see a thing. We—'

He gasped, his hand flinching in front of his face, his head swinging back to smack painfully into the rock behind. 'Fuck! Fuckfuckfuckfuck! *Fuuuuuuuuuuuuuuck!*'

'What's wrong?' said Branok. 'Max?'

The twin shuddered. Sweat beaded on his feathery scalp. Eventually, he said. 'They know. The bad guys. Dunno how, but they know we're watching. There's one with a huge drill mask over his face. He . . . how did they find us out? He's holding up a, uh, a *ransom* note.'

Jago stirred himself. He still seemed weak, but at least he had his wits. 'Their demands?'

'We get back there and produce a key. Or every thirty minutes they'll kill – Aaagh!' He shot to his feet screaming. 'He! He . . .' Tears ran down his face, and he fumbled with the eye patch to put it back over his left eye. 'Oh God. I've seen some things. He . . . his face really is a drill . . . He . . .'

Margarita took him in her arms, and he wept, his whole body heaving.

'He. . . it. . . he. . . just drilled straight through H-Harry's arm. Destroyed it. Just like that, just—'

And that's when the bears attacked.

Perhaps it had been the exhaustion that made everybody forget about them, or the greater worries that awaited back at the house, or the complacency of having aces among them. It didn't matter. The creatures hadn't made so much as a rustle as they'd padded through the cave. But something – a feeling of hot breath on her neck, the alteration of the draft caused by two huge lumps of fur – *something* made Maria turn around at the last moment.

Tusks flashed in the firelight.

She flung herself back, landing on the floor, the stupid golden pistol trapped beneath her. A great six-fingered paw pinned her down, while the jaws unhinged wide enough to engulf her head.

Annie jumped onto the creature's back, trying to force its tusks away, while Moesha cried, 'You're in the way, Annie! I can't—'

But even an ace's great strength served only to slow the bear down, though the gardener strained and cursed, while someone else pumped at least two shots into the thing.

Maria was about to pay for everything she'd done: for burning the family home down when she was drunk, so that to this day, her sister Ana carried a disfigurement; for the worries she'd caused in those times; and all the terrible choices she'd made since that had left her in debt to Charles, until finally she had opened the garden door and brought horror into Loveday House.

The terrible maw strained towards her. Drool spattered her face, as though the bear could already taste her flesh. It snapped and whined, straining forward until Annie hissed, her hands slipping.

And Maria, Maria screeched at it, 'You want me, darling? You *want* me? You're going to love this! Love it!'

She didn't know what came over her, but she shoved her right index finger in between the teeth and hardly felt the pain of it when they snapped shut.

'Do you like it? Do you?'

The monster whined once more and went limp, its entire body shuddering in what only Maria knew to be ecstasy.

'What did you do to it?' asked Annie.

Luckily, Margarita had an answer. 'They might be allergic to human flesh.'

'I . . . I can't . . . breathe,' said Maria. The entire weight of the front part of the bear was crushing her. It took all of the others to pull it away.

It turned out that the second 'bear' was disabled in a jelly force field and dispatched by bullets to the head that flew so slowly the human eye could still follow them.

Moesha curled herself into a ball after that. She was muttering prayers while Margarita began asking how they were going to get back for Buford. It was only then that Maria's right hand began to really hurt, a pain both aching and hot.

'Here.' Hitchcock produced a little flask from an inside pocket. Maria could tell right away it was brandy, and an excellent one at that. 'I believe this counts as an emergency,' he said.

She shook her head. 'C-clean my wound.' She wouldn't drink a drop. What kind of weakling did he take her for?

He complied, offering her a linen handkerchief to cover the stump afterwards.

Jago was already on his feet. Truly, his powers of recovery were remarkable. 'We need to discuss our next move, decide how to drive these scoundrels out.'

'Oh, by all means.' Maria found she was shouting, and though it worsened her pain, she couldn't stop it. 'Yes, let's do that! What have we got here? A . . . a *doctor*? They'll be scared of that, all right. Or maybe Gary there can slowly warm them to death or the butler could make them a nice movie or—'

'Enough,' said Annie. 'We've got thirty minutes. Now, give me back my gun.' She snatched it herself. 'Thank you. All right, Lord Branok, we're listening.'

He nodded, and Maria tried to get a grip of herself. Annie was right. Thirty minutes was all they had. Less now, probably.

'We have other assets,' Jago said. 'For one, there is the house itself. Wherever they are now, these cockroaches, they had better stay, for they will never find their way around – that, I can promise you. But the biggest threat to the invaders are those friends of ours they have so foolishly left alive. If we can free even one of them—'

'Buford!' said Margarita.

'Exactly. Your husband is their second most powerful prisoner.'

'There's nobody stronger than Toad Man.'

'No, my lady, not stronger, but there is somebody they should fear more. Is that not so, Ms Brown?'

Moesha stirred herself. 'It is, sir. They will be sorry, but *I* will be sorry, too. He's stayed on the righteous path for seven months straight now.'

'We will do what we must, I am afraid,' Lord Branok replied. He straightened his mask. 'Our friends are still out cold, but I have a drug that should wake one or two of them. Annie, Ms Brown, you will do your best to keep the enemy from using gas against us. Ms Pais?'

Maria was shocked he knew her name but managed a nod.

'If you think your injury allows it, would you be able get Master Fitz away from the fighting?'

'Of . . . of course.'

'Now, Max, I need you to tell us what room they are in. Describe the decor for me, please.'

Muninn, still shivering, managed a nod. 'There's a squid,' he began.

11. Guts

The door in the cave wall opened again, and on the other side was not the library but a kitchen. Maria didn't so much as blink. She had long given up on trying to understand Loveday House, and she hadn't the energy to care any more. Her hand continued to throb. Why, oh, why hadn't she fed the creature her little finger instead? Or a lock of hair? Perhaps she'd been trying to punish herself, except she didn't believe in all that psychobabble bullshit. In any event, Jago hadn't allowed them to kill the surviving bear. It would awaken with an addiction to human flesh, poor thing, and no humans anywhere to be found.

Servants appeared. They came silently, from every direction. They were armed with swords and muskets, cooking implements and pokers.

'You will stand down,' Jago told them gently, although his eyes glittered behind his mask. 'We'll clear them out, don't you worry. With the help of the house.'

The last part seemed to remove some of the tension from their faces.

'The house is not really a living thing,' Jago told his guests in a whisper, 'but they will not be convinced otherwise. Come. We have at most ten more minutes.'

He seemed to have fully recovered from his wounds, and he led the group down a hallway lined with dozens upon dozens of clocks, from wooden contraptions with crude gears all the way up to more futuristic creations with unfamiliar numbering systems. Jago held up a hand to halt everyone in their tracks, then opened a door.

'Margarita, if you would be so kind as to wait here and prepare for possible wounded? Alfred will make sure you have everything you need. Now, Ms Pais?'

Maria nodded. 'The Kraken room is currently one floor above us.'

He waved impatiently. 'I'm sending you to get Fitz, but you will also have to do something important for me - for all of us. We're going to send you up in the dumbwaiter. It will open in the Kraken room at the back - right where Max said Fitz was sleeping with his mother. Take the boy into the dumbwaiter with you, but first, you will need these.' On his palm were some pills. 'We only have three, I am afraid. Military grade stimulants. Do you think you might place them in the mouths of Messrs Jagger, Calhoun, and Kazakova?'

'You want me to drug people?'

'You can't do it, Ms Pais? It's all right if—'

Laughter bubbled up inside her, despite the pain and the fear and the horror. Despite the bears. Despite – oh God! – poor Elbrekt. She couldn't keep it from her face, and in the end, she just let it come.

Finally, as everyone stared at her in concern, Maria grabbed the pills. 'Anything for you, darling,' she said.

'Very good.' He cleared his throat. 'Give us two minutes to get up there, and we others will distract the invaders with a frontal assault. We're ready for them this time. They won't find me such an easy mark.'

He opened the panel in a wall, and she crouched inside in the dark. How would she persuade Fitz to climb in here with her? Hopefully, he was still asleep. But was there even room for both of them? She counted off two minutes before pressing the second button and then, with much creaking and rattling, the dumbwaiter lurched into motion.

The door opened to what must be the Kraken room – a space with no windows whatsoever and a painting on the ceiling of the open maw of a squid with its tentacles trailing down every wall and curling up along the floor. And there, those guests who hadn't made it to the bear cave lay sleeping. Even Muninn's brother was unconscious now, his arm a bloody mess that Maria avoided looking at.

A voice called, 'Hello? Villains?'

Maria jumped, but the words were Jago's, coming from somewhere outside the room.

'We're here to negotiate. As you requested.'

'HOW KIND OF YOU. HOW TIMELY. WE WERE PREPARING A SACRIFICE FOR YOUR SEA BEAST IN THERE. PERHAPS IT WILL NOT BE NECESSARY NOW.'

Maria squeezed out of the dumbwaiter. Fitz slept beside Julie Cotton, her ears wilted. How frightened the boy must have been when those monsters had come for him. Or perhaps he had wandered downstairs all by himself after Maria had abandoned him. She swallowed. It didn't matter now.

Mr Jagger lay drooling in a corner, his body frighteningly thin. Was it the wolf inside him that had kept him so fit for so long? She had no idea. She forced open his mouth as the negotiations continued outside, wincing with the pain of her missing finger.

After Mick, she fed Toad Man. Then, in front of Matryoshka, she paused. *Wasn't he taller before?*

Drillhead was right outside the door. 'YOU FORCE US TO DO SOME-THING AWFUL! IT IS NOT AS THOUGH WE ENJOY SUCH THINGS!' The excited whirring of the drill contradicted his words and told Maria that she had run out of time.

She grabbed up the sleeping boy, feeling his warmth against her bloody clothing. 'Come on,' she whispered.

The door to the room swung open, bashing against Huginn's outstretched, ruined arm. One of the triplets was there. He – it, maybe? – would have had a completely forgettable appearance, were it not for the eyes. He smiled at the sight of her and produced a dagger. Then he paused.

'WHAT'S THAT, ONE?' said Drillhead from the corridor. 'SHE GOT IN BEHIND US? OH, BY ALL MEANS. BRING ME HER FACE.'

The triplet advanced again, stepping over Buford's belly, just as the sleeping man opened his eyes. And behind them both, another figure was awake, too, already climbing to its feet.

Maria screamed, almost dropping Fitz, who woke in her arms.

One's grin only grew wider, until Maria stopped him with a laugh that was pure hysteria. 'Oh, darling,' she said. 'You think I was screaming because of *you*?'

She covered Fitz's eyes but kept her own open as the wolf *thing* tore into One and cries of agony came from the corridor beyond.

Hurrrr . . . The wolfman licked blood from its claws, relishing the taste, before advancing on Maria and Fitz, a great red tongue lolling from its snout.

'Back!' she shouted at it. It was taller than Jagger had been – how that was possible, she had no idea – a two-legged horror that filled the room with a hot stench of rancid meat.

The eyes glittered. If the monster took its time, it did so only to build the anticipation.

'B-back, I said.'

It advanced another step, careless of the gore it trailed behind it.

'Moesha will be angry! *Moesha!*'

Amazingly, that gave it pause, and with a furious growl, it leaped out of the room.

'Mawia?' Luckily, still half asleep, Fitz had missed all of that.

'Sorry, love. I thought I was going to have to give it another finger. We'd better go now. It's going to be tight.'

Buford was looking at her from the floor, his eyes blinking furiously as he struggled back to full consciousness. 'They're out there,' she told him.

'Who?'

'Bad people.' And to a hero like Toad Man, that was all the information he needed.

Out in the corridor, somebody shouted, 'He's behind you! Look out behind you!'

Maria shuddered and ran for the dumbwaiter.

12. Charles

By the time they'd emerged from the dumbwaiter, Fitz had started acting up. He wanted his mum. He wanted something to eat. *Who didn't?* Maria thought. And if all that wasn't enough, the bloody handkerchief covering her right hand frightened him.

'It's all right, love,' she whispered. 'It's not so sore. We'll go to see Margarita, OK?'

But they weren't in the right corridor; she could see that. And probably it was her fault this time and not the bloody house, because there were a lot of buttons in the dumbwaiter, and she or Fitz must have hit the wrong one.

But she did recognize a few things. The shuttered windows told her they were on the ground floor. Dared she walk a little further? At least she knew the villains were all upstairs. She couldn't even hear the sounds of fighting from here.

'I want my soder.'

'Your soldier? You can just make another one, right, sweetheart?'

They couldn't be far from the dining room. There might be food lying about from before the attack. She hoped it would distract her little friend until the fighting stopped.

She found the front doors with remarkable ease, and moments later, they stood among the scattered chairs and musical instruments from dinner. And yes! A few petit fours remained safe and sound in one corner, alongside an intact bottle of mineral water. Mercifully, the servants seemed to have removed all the bodies.

'Thanks,' she whispered, speaking to the house. 'You don't mind me so much now, do you, darling?'

The door to the drawing room lay ajar. She bit her lip. Had they found Elbrekt's body, too? Dared she look?

'Mawia?'

'No, love. No, we're not going in *there*. We're just not.'

Instead, she set him down in front of the cakes with a glass of water. They both gobbled up the food with their fingers – 'Don't tell your mum, love!' – and by the end of it, Maria's face was just as smeared with icing and crumbs as Fitz's. It made him laugh. God, this child had the loveliest smile in the world. Who *had* his father been? She'd love to know.

'You know what we should do now, sweetie?'

Fitz never got to answer.

Their glasses shook. A great roaring sound came from the drawing room, as though there'd been a storm outside powerful enough to smash open the shutters and rush in through the house. The door swung, smashed into the wall; curtains fluttered; napkins swirled into the air. And just as quickly as it had arisen, the tempest died again.

But it wasn't the only thing that had died recently.

Charles the Unkillable stood in the doorway. This time, his body was made of silver plates, with joints of teak and glass. It steamed gently, as it had the first time she'd witnessed his resurrection, recreation, or whatever it was.

'Well, well,' he said. 'Had a bit of an accident, did I?'

Maria backed away, drawing Fitz with her.

'From what I was told, it was you who killed me last time, you filthy cunt. Shot me with a golden pistol. Still got it with you?' And seeing the look on her face, he laughed and strode forward. 'Didn't think so.'

Maria scooped up Fitz and ran for her life – for *their* lives – because she didn't trust Charles not to harm the boy. He thundered after her. Chairs shattered under his weight. The grand stairway was right in front of her now, and somewhere up there, the others were fighting the invaders. They must be winning, too, or why else would Charles have been reincarnated again in the drawing room? But what use were their victories if he could just keep coming until everybody else was dead?

She ran upstairs, staggering under her burden, doubting they'd ever reach the top. 'Stop wriggling, Fitz, please!' She was almost at the landing where the stairway split when a vase flew over her head and smashed into the wall in front of her. Fitz screeched as splinters rained on them both. She put him down, turning to face her enemy, her legs wobbling almost enough to topple her.

Charles, she had to admit, cut a truly beautiful figure at the bottom of the stairs.

He held out one massive silver hand. 'Come,' he said. 'It's not your day to die.'

'Why isn't it?' She clamped down on the shaking in her legs. She raised her chin.

'I want you to be there when I do your parents, innit? When I fuck your sister with my silver cock.'

She felt her lip curl, and when she spoke, she was amazed by how contemptuous she sounded. 'Poor darling,' she said. 'But you won't be fucking anybody after today.'

The arm wavered, then raised again, the fingers beckoning.

She didn't move but added, 'I worked it out, you see? Your secret. You back yourself up somehow on that little USB stick, and at the moment of death, you get recreated out of whatever's lying near to it. It was the car the first time I saw it. And then, I watched you place something on top of one of the silver cabinets inside.' She smiled, putting every ounce of confidence into it, becoming the part of the fearless young woman, playing it to the hilt. She wasn't trying to save her own life, because she knew that nothing would save her now, and that was only fair. But if she could make Charles the Unkillable feel even the slightest inkling of fear or doubt, it would bring her some small pleasure.

'I told him,' she said.

The arm dipped again. 'Told who?'

'Jago Branok. He knows how you do it. They're looking for your backup right now, and when they find it, he's decided he'll throw it into the ocean.

How would you like that, Charles? Mr *Unkillable*, sir? To die begging for air, only to be reborn at the bottom of the sea so you can choke to death again and again for the rest of time?'

He roared, charging up the stairs. Behind her, Fitz shrieked in terror. Charles grabbed Maria by the neck with one hand. The other, he wrapped around her skull, intent on twisting it right off her body. This must be how he had filled the jar the first time. The victim's neck had been torn off at the bottom, with sinews and bits of bone hanging free. And Maria, who had meant to be brave, thrashed and plucked uselessly at his silver hands while snot and tears covered her cheeks.

Moments later, she was face down on the stairs, shaking, weeping, more afraid than she had ever been in her life. Yet . . . yet, she was alive.

It took enormous courage to open her eyes, and when she did, Charles was gone. Just gone.

Above her, Fitz chattered away happily. *What—?*

He was playing with a new toy. Like the soldier, it was perfect in every way: a miraculous confection of silver and wood and glass, but no larger than a barbie doll. It was Charles, of course - diminished in size, but still very much alive, and she knew this because the toy's face *moved*. Its expression changed from shock to horror to fear, an endless loop of misery, of helplessness.

'New soder!' said Fitz happily.

Maria did not know how long she waited on the grand stairway while Fitz played with his new 'toy'. The soldier must have been a real person, too, she thought, once upon a time. The fierce dog had been a full-sized animal. All were things that had frightened the child in the past, and he had removed the fear in the only way he knew how.

'I'd best never get on your bad side, darling,' she told him.

'Madame?' It was one of the maids, her face white, her voice trembling. 'If you vood join with us?'

'Is . . .' Maria switched to French. 'Is the boy's mother all right?'

'Oh, yes.'

'Come on, darling. Let's go see your mom. She'll be missing you.'

The layout of the house was considerably simpler when following somebody who belonged to it. It was a crazy thought to have; Jago had denied his home was alive. Maria sided with the servants on this one, however, and she couldn't wait to get back to the relative sanity of London.

Upstairs, there were claw marks and blood all over the walls. Two servants carried past the remains of the crossbow woman, Maven, her belly a glistening red hole. Maria covered Fitz's eyes, but she herself felt nothing. All the horror had been squeezed out of her by Charles's silver hands.

In a small side room, she heard voices.

'We can start again with the exercises. I know you can do it, Mr Jagger.'

'But . . . but I enjoyed it. I . . . I had forgotten . . .'

From another direction, came Drillhead's electronic voice, 'I CANNOT RETURN TO PRISON. IS IT NOT ENOUGH I WILL NEVER WALK AGAIN? AND THAT WOLF FLUNG POOR MR PANTOMIME INTO THE SEA. HIS ONLY CRIME WAS AN EXCESS OF LONELINESS.'

Finally, they were led into the billiard room, where the surviving, uninjured guests had been brought.

'Fitz!' Julie, her eyes still sleepy from the after-effects of the gas, stumbled to her feet, arms wide, ears practically vibrating with joy and relief.

'Mommy!' The boy wriggled so hard Maria just had to put him down, and he grabbed onto Julie's leg with his free hand.

'I think . . .' Maria said, 'I think we need to talk.'

A moment of fear. 'Is Fitz OK?'

'He's fine. But his new toy . . .' She swallowed. 'You should take a look at it. You'll . . . you'll work it out.'

Most of the others were sleepy, too, but otherwise OK. Except for Matryoshka. He was shorter than he had been, no doubt about it. He was eye to eye with Maria when he stood up. He smiled; she hadn't seen him do that before. 'Mary Poppins!' he said and giggled.

'What happened to you?' she asked him.

But it was Buford who answered. Toad Man's need was stronger than it ought to be after only a single day, but she had squeezed him pretty hard during the fighting, and he would be getting desperate sooner rather than later. 'You know, Ivan can, uh, split himself into smaller parts? Well, the white-faced creature in the trench coat killed one of the Ivans. Sucked the life out of it, so when he put himself back together, he was shorter and . . .'

And more stupid, Maria realized, although Buford didn't want to say so aloud.

'They killed the sad Ivan,' said Matryoshka happily. Drool ran down the side of his mouth. 'Now I *smile* and *sing* and *dance*.' He fell down on his bum and burst out laughing.

13. Reckoning

The following morning, Maria was summoned to the library, where all signs of last night's struggle had been removed. But no sooner had she stepped through the door than it swung shut behind her, leaving her in the presence of Jago Branok and one other person: Isolde. The maid's presence came as no surprise, of course, but Maria hadn't let that slow her pace in the slightest.

She straightened her back. 'You know, then?' she said to Branok.

'You were one of them.'

'I was.'

She could see the lower half of his face, see the distaste there. Yet, he, too, kept his voice steady. 'I make a habit of learning about my guests – but a nanny? I am such a fool.' He shook his head. 'Be that as it may, I cannot let such a thing pass.'

'I was on your side at the end.'

'My people were killed!' he said, losing his composure at last. 'Do you not understand that?'

She did and better than he could know. She had watched poor Elbrekt meet his end, and that memory brought tears to the corners of her eyes and left her unable, for once, to keep up her fake accent. 'They threatened my parents,' she whispered.

'You could have come to me, child. Those scum would never have been seen again had I been expecting them. They'd have spent the rest of their lives hiding from the bears. I am minded to send you back to that place myself now, but instead, I may let you work off your debt here as a maid and—'

'No.' Maria wiped her eyes with the back of a hand. 'I'll be leaving this madhouse right now, or whenever the stupid tide allows it. Thanks for the offer, though.'

'What makes you think that—'

Isolde screeched and fell to the floor.

'What's wrong, love?' Maria asked her. 'What's that?' She cocked her head as though listening. Isolde hadn't said a word; she was being squeezed too hard to emit anything more comprehensible than a moan of desperation. 'You want something, is it, love? Something only I can give you, but not if I'm in the fucking bear cave on another planet? Is that what you're saying?'

'Whatever you're doing—' Jago warned her.

Maria ignored him, widening her eyes in mock surprise. '*Really?* You're saying one of Sir High Lord fucking Branok's precious guests is also dependent on me and that only I can free said guest? If I choose?' She looked up at the master of the house. 'Let me go,' she told him, 'and I will be kind enough to do the same for Isolde here and for Toad Man. Yeah, that's right. He's mine, too, whether he knows it or not. But if we call it quits, I'll make sure he's looked after. You never need to see me again. What do you say?'

Lord Branok was breathing fast, his hands gripping tightly to the table at his back. 'I could find other ways to convince you.'

'I don't think that's how you do things, somehow.' And then, because she couldn't stop them, the tears came again, but in a wave this time, rolling down her face, her knees knocking together. She released her hold on Isolde's mind, tamping down the flames of need as far as she could. 'I'm sorry about . . . about Elbrekt. I . . . should have come to you . . . But I was . . .' She forced the hated words out. '. . . weak and afraid. I won't stay here, though. I can't. That's . . . that's all there is to it.'

Jago shook his head in disgust. He called to somebody then, told them in French to fetch Buford. It wasn't true that she could free Toad Man or Isolde, of course. All she could do was tell them exactly what she had addicted them to, so that once a week for the rest of their lives, they could find themselves a little privacy to get high.

'Now, go,' Jago told her when she had finished speaking to a bewildered Buford. There were to be no goodbyes, not even to Julie or Fitz. 'We'll tell them you were taken ill.'

Needless to say, the limo wasn't waiting to carry her down to the village. Outside, it had started to rain, and a cold wind swept up over the cliffs to rattle the trees and set her teeth to chattering, and she hesitated in the shelter of the carved double doors.

But somebody else was leaving, too. A pair of servants ferried a set of fancy suitcases to the steps and behind them came the rock star, Mick Jagger. He seemed embarrassed to meet her there.

'Ah,' he said. 'I hear you saw me at my worst last night.'

Inside, at the top of the stairs, Moesha spoke quietly to one of the maids, and Mick watched her guiltily.

'I have to go in for treatment again,' he said sadly. Around the side of the house, the blades of a chopper began to spin.

'No, you don't,' Maria told him. She tightened her shoulders to stop them from shivering, and somehow, she dragged her very best smile out of its hiding place. 'I happen to have something that you can take any time you feel the urge. You wouldn't be the first person I've helped.' She looked meaningfully in Moesha's direction. 'No bible quotes needed!'

He didn't believe her, but he laughed anyway, and that made it easy to wrangle an invite back to London in the helicopter. No dreaded crossing of the sea. It looked rough today, the wind whipping it into a fury. She got to avoid the roads, too, skidding over the tarmac in the presence of a psycho-path, and Maria thought to herself, never again would she be in somebody else's control. She would persuade Mick to try her . . . medicine, and he, in return, would introduce her to all the wealthy, famous people of London.

This time next year, she vowed, she would be somebody. She'd live in a mansion of her own, but with no bloody bears or hidden doors or monsters walking in the moonlight outside.

Longing for Those Lost

by Stephen Leigh

Part VII

'**I NEED YOU TO COME** with me, Mr Bushorn.'

Gary could see the distress and shock in Madame Amélie's face. Her eyes shimmered with unshed moisture, and smeared mascara had left dark streaks on her cheeks. That didn't surprise Gary, given the horrors of what had happened and what she may have seen.

'I'm sorry, but I can't right now,' he answered. 'Lord Branok has asked me to help give the police those statements.'

'I understand, but . . .' Her voice choked. 'Hitchcock has taken on that task. You . . . Mr Bushorn, you need to prepare yourself.'

A horrible suspicion invaded Gary's mind. 'Have you seen Ceallaigh? I lost track of her in all the uproar. I haven't seen her since the dance. I saw her there just before those intruders burst in . . . Then everything became so confused after Lord Branok was shot . . .' Gary realized he was babbling. 'Ceallaigh's not been injured, has she? Is she OK?' Seeing Madame Amélie's expression, Gary felt a sudden, terrible weight pressing on his chest. 'No,' he said. '*No.*'

'I'm so very sorry, sir.' Tears rolled down from the corners of her eyes. 'Please, if you'll just come with me . . .'

The bodies had been laid out in the music room. The room was malodorous: a lingering mixture of smoke, gunpowder, blood, urine, and faecal matter. The dead had been covered with blankets. Too many of those blankets were stained with blood, so thickly that it looked as if someone had poured it over them in a bucket; other blankets were suspiciously truncated.

Madame Amélie stopped before one of the blankets. A woman's hand protruded from the side of the cloth covering her.

'No,' Gary said again. Sternly. Angrily. *That's not Ceallaigh's hand. I won't let it be.*

But Madame Amélie wouldn't look him in the face, mascara-coloured tears flowing freely down her sharp cheekbones.

'That's not Ceallaigh,' Gary insisted. 'It can't be.'

'I'm so terribly, terribly sorry for your loss, Mr Bushorn,' she managed to say, her voice trembling with emotion. 'We were all so pleased and happy that she found love with you.'

Gary reached down to pull the blanket away from Ceallaigh's face, but Madame Amélie grasped his hand, shaking her head.

'I need to see that it's Ceallaigh,' Gary told her. Everything inside him had gone numb. 'I need to know that it's really her.'

'Mr Bushorn, I'm telling you that it *is* Ceallaigh. But you . . . you really shouldn't look at her now; you don't want to have to remember her this way. That joker with a drill for a head . . .' Madame Amélie's head shook again, sending the tears on her face flowing into new channels. She still held desperately to the end of the stained, gory blanket. 'He . . . he was the one who killed her.'

'Show me.' Gary nearly shouted the words. 'I have to *see* her!'

Her hands trembling, Madame Amélie folded the blanket back from the head. The shock of what was revealed struck down Gary, sending him reeling to the floor on his knees, his legs unable to support him. He couldn't breathe, couldn't even cry out.

Ceallaigh's beautiful, familiar face had been ripped open, a ruin from nose to jaw. A new, obscene, and circular mouth yawned where bone, muscle, sinew, tendons, and flesh swirled together in clotted blood. But her eyes, still open and terrified, were Ceallaigh's. The red hair – matted now with blood – was hers also, as was the mask that lay near her hand.

Someone in the room was screaming, an animal roar filling the room with wordless grief and fury: a scream that Gary suddenly realized emerged from his own throat. His hands were afire, smoke rising around his fingers as he clawed at the parquet floor. The pain as blisters rose on his skin were nothing against the savage knife thrust of loss inside him.

Madame Amélie placed the blanket back over Ceallaigh's face, but he still saw it. The horrible sight remained before him until all breath left him and the wail of his grief morphed into plaintive and desperate sobs. Madame Amélie was kneeling next to him, but not touching him as smoke tendrils curled around him, his clothes smouldering on his body.

'Jago,' Gary managed to rasp. 'Where is Jago? I need Jago.'

'I'll bring him to you,' he heard Madame Amélie say distantly.

Gary felt a hand touch his shoulder. He was still in the music room, still kneeling next to Ceallaigh's body. 'Gary,' he heard Jago's voice say.

He craned his head back to look at the man. In Jago's masked face, he saw grief, compassion, empathy, and anger in nearly equal measures.

'Jago,' he managed to say, his voice hoarse and his throat sore. 'How could this have happened? You said—'

'I remember what I said. I never believed something like this could or would happen. You must believe that. This is horrifying beyond any words. Awful.' He waved his hand to encompass the room. 'Gary, so many of the staff are people I brought here in order to save them, but in the end, I failed them. Instead, they've been killed, maimed, or injured *here*, in my house, where I intended for them to finally be safe.' Gary saw Jago clench his fists, fingernails pressing red crescents into his palms. 'And your poor Ceallaigh is one of them. I can't tell you how sorry I am, Gary. I'm . . .' He seemed to be searching for a word. '. . . entirely devastated by this, and no apology can ever make it right.'

I tried to warn you and you didn't listen. But Gary had to admit that his accusation was partially a lie. *I didn't try hard enough, wasn't persistent enough. I failed Ceallaigh. It's my fault she's dead. My fault.*

'I . . . I don't think I can talk to you right now,' he told Jago.

Jago patted Gary's shoulder. 'When you're ready, I'll be in my office. Make whatever arrangements you need to for Ceallaigh. Don't worry about the cost.'

Gary went to Jago's office two days later. The door was open, and Gary could see Branok behind his desk. His mask was a black funeral veil.

'Gary, please come in,' he said. 'Hitchcock told me you'd be here today. I hope the urn I sent to the funeral home for Ceallaigh's remains was satisfactory.'

'It was perfect, and thank you,' Gary told him.

'You'll be taking her ashes back to Rathlin?'

'I've already them sent on. The current mayor will take care of them, per my instructions.' Gary took a long slow breath. 'Jago, you and I . . . Well, we need to talk about what happened and why.'

Jago folded his hands on the polished mahogany of his desk. 'Go ahead, then. Say whatever you need to say to me.'

'It's Loveday, Jago. This house is a trap. A gentle prison. It snared me – and you as well. Loveday holds out towards us a silver platter holding *too many* choices, *too many* possibilities. It makes the implicit promise that inside these hallways and rooms, if you just happen to step through the right door, you can reconnect with someone you've loved and lost. But that promise is empty. Perhaps in one of the infinite galaxies of alternate pasts Loveday holds, the V-2 that killed your wife and daughter fell elsewhere, or they reached a safe shelter in time, or the bomb was a dud that never went off. Endless possibilities. You potentially have the chance to step into a future where you never needed to grieve for your family or see their mangled bodies in the rubble.'

'I've looked for that path. I've never found the door that contains it.' Jago's finger drummed his desktop.

'But you're still searching for it, aren't you? I was lucky or perhaps cursed. I found Caitlyn and Moira here in Loveday House. Loveday's cruel that way. You know you might *still* find your family again, but you haven't. Is that why you keep opening every door you discover?' Gary lifted his hands and let them drop again. 'I know that's why I feel the temptation to do the same right now and go searching for Ceallaigh behind those closed doors. Worse, we both know that Lady Morwen still lives here. In fact, untold versions of her potentially still walk the bowels of Loveday House, and as long as that is the case, you're not safe, Jago. *None* of us are safe. Those who live here with you aren't safe, and no guest you bring here will ever be safe, either.'

Jago was silent behind his mask. Gary couldn't tell what the man might be feeling or thinking.

He exhaled, took in another slow breath. 'The only escape from this trap is to *destroy* Loveday House and all the shadows it holds. That would force us to deal with a single unique future and whatever that future alone can give us. We have to accept that.'

'What are you saying?'

'I'm suggesting we burn down Loveday to the ground and salt the earth on which it was built. Burn it down so that those other dimensions are forever closed to our world. Burn it down so that we destroy Mad Morwen's refuge in Loveday House as well. If you like, we can move out and store all the precious material you've collected, like your library. Save any or all of it, then gut Loveday and set the damn house on fire. Destroy it.

'Keep your staff: Hitchcock, Madame Amélie, Chef Daniel, and everyone else who's survived this last attack: you'll need them to help if you rebuild a new house. I'll help with that as much as I can. You can rebuild Loveday House, Jago – anywhere on Keun, maybe even on this haunted hill – but you *can't* build it on the foundations of the old castle. Mad Morwen was only a ghostly toothless legend until Marcus St Gerren built the original Loveday here.'

'Do you realize what you're asking of me?'

'Yes,' Gary said forcefully. 'And so do you. This is as difficult a decision for me as for you. It means permanently closing the portal that I used to talk with Caitlyn, Moira, and Duncan – they'll only exist for me in memories. Nor will Loveday be able to give me back poor Ceallaigh or you your wife and daughter. But it's what we *should* do. It's what you *must* do if you don't want to keep repeating what's already happened. I'll help you. So will Hitchcock and the others.' Gary held up his left hand, setting it alight so it burned like a macabre, living Hand of Glory as he waited for Jago's answer.

'No,' Jago said finally, his voice nearly a growl. 'This is *my* house, not yours. You will *not* destroy it. I can close the doors that have to remain sealed.' His fist struck the top of his desk once. 'I can do that. I can. I will. You can even help me.'

But Gary was shaking his head before Jago finished the sentence. *You thought this might be his answer. The man's as stubborn as you are. You know what has to be done.* 'No, Jago. If you're not willing to destroy Loveday and rebuild elsewhere on Keun, I won't help you. I'm sorry. If that's your decision, I'll give you my notice.'

Jago stared at Gary through the eyeholes of his mask for a long moment, as if expecting him to change his mind. Then, finally, he shrugged. 'Consider your notice accepted. You don't need to wait. You may leave whenever you're ready.'

'I'll let you know when, then. I think you're making a serious mistake, Jago. I just hope that it doesn't cost yet more lives.'

And I can't let that happen. I won't.

It took Gary two days to make his preparations, all the while saying his goodbyes to the staff and enduring their sympathies and best wishes. On the last day, he gave Hitchcock a sealed envelope, telling the butler to hand it to Jago that evening before the staff supper. 'Make sure he opens and reads it before supper,' Gary told Hitchcock, whose eyebrows raised slightly. 'It's important.'

'I'll make certain Lord Branok does so, sir.'

Not long afterwards, Gary walked away from Loveday House with his rucksack, telling Jago he was going to hire a boat to take him back to Rathlin. As soon as he was out of sight of the house, he doubled back, staying off the road and sticking to the wooded grounds. He re-entered the house by a rear entrance he'd left unlocked, where there was little likelihood he'd be noticed. Taking an electric torch and Constance's protective robe from his rucksack, he descended a cobweb-festooned stairway into the ancient foundations of Loveday, where the great chiselled beams of oak installed in the late 1800s by Marcus St Gerren loomed overhead, seated on the older stone walls of the original Loveday Castle, walls and beams supporting the mansion above.

I'm old, and I've lost everyone I cared about. Even if I die tonight, some part of me will live on in the ruins and that dim memory of my corporeal existence just might find Caitlyn, Moira, Duncan, and Ceallaigh once more.

Somewhere.

Somewhen.

Why not let Loveday House burn, with or without Jago's approval? There's nothing for me to fear, not in a universe that holds endless alternate futures.

Gary set down his rucksack on the ancient flagstones of Loveday Castle and unzipped it. He could sense the house watching, aware of him and what he was doing, uneasy and apprehensive.

'I'm sorry,' he said aloud. 'I don't know what else to do.'

There was no answer. He expected none. He glanced at Caitlyn's pocket watch. If this all went as planned, then, in this version of history at least, half an hour from now, the staff would all be seated at their long table below stairs, and Hitchcock would hand Jago the letter.

Gary pulled out several flagons of kerosene he'd taken from the garage, where they were stored for use in torches and lanterns on the grounds. He splashed the liquid onto the oak beams and onto anything wooden he could find. The acrid smell filled his nostrils and made breathing difficult, but Gary continued to spread the kerosene around, moving from one room in the underground vaults to another. When he'd emptied the last container, the air heavy with the vapours, he glanced at his pocket watch again. The staff would be sitting down for their meal; Hitchcock should have handed Jago the letter.

Ceallaigh, Caitlyn, Moira, Duncan, I hope I'll be joining you soon.

Gary tossed the torch aside; it went clattering off into the distance, throwing wild beams of light around the room. He held his hands up before him and flames emerged from his fingers. He grimaced at the pain and the rising blisters as he pressed his hands to the soaked wood. Blue flames crawled away from where his fingers touched, following the trail of kerosene.

Gary thought he heard a sound behind him, but even as he turned, his hands still alight with flame, something struck him hard on the head. As a slow darkness came over him, he had time for one thought as he drifted off: *If my attempt at arson leaves Loveday House only injured but still standing, if it was Jago or Morwen or Loveday itself that stopped me from burning everything down – well, somewhere in the infinity of possible universes Loveday holds, at least one version of me will have succeeded, must have succeeded, even if I didn't.*

What happens to me now ultimately doesn't matter.

When he woke, Gary could smell the sea and the familiar scent of distant peat fires. He was lying face-up on a grassy incline, his head throbbing with a terrific headache, his clothing damp with rain or spray. Steam rose around him like morning mist, tendrils of it swirling away from a damp robe: Constance's robe. His fingers tentatively probed the back of his skull under the tight nap of his hair; he winced as he found the swelling of a tender bruise there.

Cautiously, he lifted his head, groaning. A low, dry-stone wall blocked his view; he sat up tentatively to see beyond it, waiting until the landscape settled.

It took a few seconds before he puzzled out where he was, staring dumbfounded at what he realized were familiar sights. He was staring at the East Lighthouse of Rathlin Island off in the distance, with the sun just rising from the sea beyond and the purpled rise of Scotland's rugged coast on the horizon. He was several strides off the gravel road to the lighthouse, on a rhododendron-covered hillock maybe a mile out from the main harbour. These were paths he'd walked many times in his life, near where his home was: the cottage that had also been Caitlyn and Moira's home.

Gary blinked at the early dawn sky, at grey clouds sailing the winds above. He had no memory of being brought here, no memory beyond the moment when he'd been hit from behind. He kneeled on the grass of the knoll, and a single sheet of thick paper fell from his chest. He picked it up.

What he saw was familiar: Jago's ornate, formal handwriting, scribed in fountain pen.

> Gary – I couldn't let you do it, though I don't blame you for making the attempt. But I can no longer trust you in Loveday House. So I brought you here, one of the places I discovered not long after you became the dance master at Loveday. It's a place I'd intended to offer to show you, should it become necessary. Now, I'm not giving you the choice.
>
> This is Rathlin, yes, but not a Rathlin you ever knew. In this world, the wild card virus was never released. There are no aces, no deuces, no jokers, and Rathlin was never the dumping ground for those infected. In this world, you are the sole person infected with the xenovirus Takis-A. You need to be aware that, should you get someone pregnant, there is a 50 per cent chance that the child will be a latent carrier, with all that implies. I would suggest finding a doctor who will ensure such an accident never happens. But that now remains your decision.
>
> You'll find that Caitlyn is still alive and on Rathlin, her body untouched by the wild card. So is her daughter Moira, a young woman of seventeen who will never draw the wild card. Duncan is probably also alive somewhere in this world, though he's not on Rathlin. Perhaps he's still a Belfast policeman.
>
> None of them will know you or recognize you; in this world, none of them have met you . . . as yet. If you wish to make a relationship with any of them, you'll have to forge it anew.
>
> In your new world, Loveday House was never built. The ruins of Loveday Castle are just a tourist site on Keun Island. Nothing more. Ceallaigh, alas, was never part of this world at all.
>
> You'll never find the way back into my world, the world you came from. I have closed that door. I hope the rest of your life will be happy, Gary. Truly.
>
> But we will never see each other again.

The letter had no signature.

Gary pushed himself up, getting his legs underneath him. He walked slowly to the road, looking up and down its length; there was no one walking in the dawn. He lit a finger and burned Jago's note, dropping it to the gravel, watching as it curled and blackened. He crushed the ash into the stones.

He slipped off Constance's robe – wearing a robe over his clothing would only cause questions he wouldn't easily be able to answer, and the protection the Seamstress had woven into it would fail after a year in any case – and tossed it over the dry-stone wall into the pasture beyond. He pulled Caitlyn's pocket watch from the coin pocket of his jeans and opened it. He looked at the engraved signature from her parents, wondering if, in this world, she'd ever been given this watch.

The watch hands read twenty-two minutes past eight. With a sigh, Gary shut the watch and put it back in his pocket. His head throbbing, he turned to face west and set off down the road towards where Caitlyn's house should stand.

He wondered what he could say to them when he knocked on the door.